PRAISE FOR ZACHARY JERNIGAN'S NOVELS OF JEROUN

"To call Zachary Jernigan a fearless writer is an understatement. His universe is one of gods who make worlds only to torture the inhabitants, demigods who turn on their father, nations exterminated, wars in which the dead take sides. But what floors me is the ease with which he travels this strangest of landscapes. We pass from the mythic to the mundane and back again in the space of a paragraph. We come to know his characters with unsettling intimacy, even as their identities come under magical siege. We sense the solid ground beneath our feet and the presence of forces that could (and do) blow it back into atoms. Jernigan is part of a wave of authors breathing new life into the epic fantasy tradition we love."
—Robert V. S. Redick, author of *The Red Wolf Conspiracy*

"A science-fantasy epic that's as much a perverse hybrid as it is an homage to an earlier era when those genres weren't so strictly segregated, *No Return* is set on a world that bears wizards and astronauts equally. It also pulls no punches in its rich, visceral depictions of sexuality, martial arts, punk energy, and the philosophical quandaries of power and identity that speculative fiction uniquely exploits—and that few up-and-coming speculative writers outside Jernigan tackle with such guts."
—Jason Heller, *The A.V. Club* (*The Onion*)

"Vivid, varied, and violent. At once beautiful and terrible to behold."
—Nickolas Sharps, *SF Signal*

"*No Return* needs to be noticed. There is so much more to it than the accoutrements would imply. Populated with a fair amount of face punching, as coded by the visceral cover, it contains a tenderness and at times overt eroticism that's often ignored in science fiction and fantasy. Zachary Jernigan has something unique to say, a voice we're not hearing from anywhere else. I dearly hope more readers, and award aficionados, take an opportunity to listen to him."
—*Tor.com*

"A visionary, violent, sexually charged, mystical novel—*No Return* challenges classification. Clearly, Zachary Jernigan has no respect for genre confines. His tale of gods hanging in the sky and a "constructed man" with glowing blue coals for his eyes and a motley band of fighters navigating a harsh landscape peopled by savage creatures and religious zealots . . . Well, it's pure genius. Here's hoping it's just the first of many such works from this guy."
—David Anthony Durham, Campbell Award-winning author of the Acacia Trilogy

"[A] fascinating world, nicely-executed plot . . . and a wonderfully squishy and twisted aesthetic. *No Return* is an excellent fit for readers of Mark Charan Newton's Legend of the Red Sun series or those who enjoy the fantasies of M. John Harrison, Gene Wolfe, or Jack Vance."
—*Pornokitsch*

"Jernigan's debut is full of wonder: a smart adventure, with measures of philosophy and violence and lust. For all its strangeness and far-flung setting, *No Return* is a very human novel. Like Samuel Delany and Gene Wolfe, Jernigan can write a rousing, literary genre story that pushes boundaries and transgresses categorization."
—Brent Hayward, author of *Filaria* and *The Fecund's Melancholy Daughter*

"The greatest pleasure a reader can have is for their expectations to be confounded, to find their eye drawn word by word down a different path to the one anticipated. Genre fiction is too often comfort food, and the palate can grow complacent. *No Return* is not a complacent book and it took me somewhere unexpected and new."
—Martin Lewis, *Strange Horizons*

"Jernigan has really unleashed something unique on the world with *No Return*. It doesn't fit nicely into any boxes or cookie cutters. It's quick moving, subtle yet bold, and absolutely R-Rated and raw. . . . It's bold and vivid and it will probably make you uncomfortable, but that's not a bad thing. Jernigan takes you on a one-of-a-kind journey and he leaves you breathless, gasping, and full of new thoughts."
—Sarah Chorn, *Bookworm Blues*

"*No Return* displays the kind of prose, worldbuilding, and depth of characterization that place Zachary Jernigan securely within the top tier of fantasy authors. The prose pulls you in like a piece of art, forcing you to slow down and observe. The world-building makes you imagine maps, bar room brawls over differences in customs, kids praying to the god who lives on the moon, women making sex spells, warriors becoming one with their self-controlled, mutating body suits . . . all in a way that separates the world in *No Return* from generic fantasy—this world is alive!"
—Timothy C. Ward, *Adventures in SciFi Publishing*

"Zachary Jernigan writes with a flair for the weird and makes it endearing enough for readers to feel familiar with it. *No Return* is a magnificent debut that straddles fantasy and SF genres seamlessly and makes itself into a jewel faceting both fields."
—Mihir Wanchoo, *Fantasy Book Critic*

JEROUN

THE COLLECTED OMNIBUS

ZACHARY JERNIGAN

NIGHT SHADE BOOKS
NEW YORK

Night Shade books may be purchased in bulk at special discounts for sales promotion, corporate gifts, fund-raising, or educational purposes. Special editions can also be created to specifications. For details, contact the Special Sales Department, Night Shade Books, 307 West 36th Street, 11th Floor, New York, NY 10018 or info@skyhorsepublishing.com.

Night Shade Books® is a registered trademark of Skyhorse Publishing, Inc.®, a Delaware corporation.

Visit our website at www.nightshadebooks.com.

10 9 8 7 6 5 4 3 2 1

Library of Congress Cataloging-in-Publication Data

Names: Jernigan, Zachary, 1980-, author.
Title: Jeroun : the collected omnibus / Zachary Jernigan.
Description: New York : Night Shade Books, [2016]
Identifiers: LCCN 2016018012 | ISBN 9781597808620 (paperback)
Subjects: LCSH: Imaginary wars and battles--Fiction. | BISAC: FICTION /
 Science Fiction / General. | FICTION / Science Fiction / Adventure. |
FICTION / Fantasy / General. | FICTION / Fantasy / Epic. | GSAFD:
Science fiction
Classification: LCC PS3610.E738 J47 2016 | DDC 813/.6--dc23
LC record available at https://lccn.loc.gov/2016018012

Cover design by Lesley Worrell

Printed in the United States of America

CONTENTS

e Continent of Knoori

Nos
lom

Dareth
Hlum

Onsa

Delanjele

Casta

Delanjele

Golna

pa Mnts

Basec

Tansot

Stol

Steps of Stol

THE MONTHS OF THE YEAR

Month of Ascetics
Month of Alchemists
Month of Mages
Month of Sectarians
Month of Fishers
Month of Surgeons
Month of Sawyers
Month of Smiths
Month of Drowsers
Month of Financiers
Month of Bakers
Month of Finnakers
Month of Soldiers
Month of Clergymen
Month of Pilots
Month of Royalty

NO RETURN

PROLOGUE

The people were small, quiet, and simple. They had no name for themselves.

They lived at the top of the world of Jeroun, in a windless and barren valley with no accessible entrance, on the shore of a nameless salt lake—perhaps the most beautiful lake in the world. A deep and flawlessly clear cerulean blue under the cloudless sky, its shallow waters never froze and rarely rippled. Almost perfectly circular, it measured twelve miles across, yet the people neither fished nor set craft upon its surface. Now and then, they drank and collapsed on the shore, subject to visions induced by the ensorcelled liquid.

Their valley had once been home to a great civilization, the site of a city inhabited by the continent's extinct native people, who were called elders by common men. Mummified corpses measuring over three yards in length lay everywhere, naked to the ever-present sun. A great many lay buried in the rubble of their buildings, which had been worn nearly unrecognizable by time and sun. With few eroding forces, this process had surely taken thousands upon thousands of years. A stone could not chip the building materials.

The corpses were beautiful, black-skinned and thin-limbed like insects. Their faces were broad-nosed, mouthless and severe. Downy translucent hair covered their bodies, lengthening and darkening into bristly fur on their scalps. Many were tattooed in bright colors. Though as dry inside as the valley soil, impossibly their skin had the texture of calf's leather and tasted like sugar-preserved meat. Ground to a fine powder, their bones tasted metallic and bitter, but caused the mouth to salivate, curing thirst.

The nameless people had consumed a very small percentage of the corpses, as neither skin nor bonedust needed to be ingested in great quantities. The meat and organs were inedible and lay about in piles that would not rot. Had the larger world known what magical resource existed in the valley, empires would have waged wars, sacrificed thousands, in order to possess it. For the men and women who lived along the shores of the nameless lake, this was immaterial. To them, the elders were merely food.

While the diet provided scant nourishment for the brain, a body could survive well on nothing but elder skin and bone, guaranteeing that it need never sleep, need never worry about clothing itself. In groups of two or three the people of the valley walked the shore of the lake, all night and all day, single-mindedly stripping small pieces of skin and grinding bone ends. They walked naked even in the depths of winter and never felt the cold.

From time to time, they met others of their kind and shared a meal. They did not talk. Usually they stared at the placid surface of the lake together. On rare occasions, those who faintly recalled a friendship or long-dead romance held hands and watched the stars, but never for long.

There were good reasons not to stare too deeply into the sky.

‡

Eating elder skin and bone, a human of hardy stock could live a long time indeed. The average age of the inhabitants in the valley was over five hundred years, and the oldest individual had lived for seventeen centuries. She had in fact not been born in the valley, though her reason for coming—as well as the means of her arrival—were long since forgotten. The nameless people were her children, but this knowledge too had been lost. Time had bleached her mind of any urges other than to eat and to watch the sky.

In the valley, she alone remembered the reason men should fear the sky. She had cemented this fear in her children but was now too old or too simple to feel it herself.

Fear had become fascination.

And indeed, she could not have picked a better location from which to view the sky. The valley experienced four hundred cloudless days out of four hundred and thirty-two calendar days. The thin, cold air did not distort the constant burn of the stars or the fractured face of the world's immense, bone-pale moon.

Nor what preceded moonrise.

Every evening, the woman sat and watched as the objects rose above the horizon. The largest of the steel-colored, circular masses was nearly a third the size of the moon. The smallest could only be seen during the early morning, when sunlight reflected on its edges. Twenty-seven in all, she counted. Elsewhere, beyond the reach or understanding of the people of the valley, men called the arrow-straight arrangement the Needle, or sometimes the Spine. Unbeknownst to the woman, on the world she alone had counted all of the objects with the naked eye.

She knew on some level that they were weapons.

She had also discovered their construction. They were not flat structures, but slowly rotating spheres. They were not solid, either, but spindly, like gigantic cages.

It was as if their maker had taken thin-rimmed carriage wheels and welded them along a centerline so that the rims fanned around a vertical axis. The woman had stared long enough to note their slow rotation, the slight shift as one rim caught the light and another gave it up. This effect was most easy to see on the odd days the moon remained in the sky well into morning. The speed of the spheres changed from time to time, and sometimes even seemed to stop. Such alterations depended on factors the woman could not begin to guess.

Well into her hundredth year in the valley, the night sky had been just stars and moon. Later, one object appeared. Then two. Eventually they extended like a bead necklace nearly a fifth of the length of the sky, smallest to largest leading to the moon, twenty-nine in all. They seemed to pull the moon across the sky, led by some invisibly massive draft animal.

Over the next five hundred years they had moved slowly to form a diamond pattern, then a cross. For a while they had floated around the moon, sometimes nearer, sometimes farther from its surface, and then they trailed it across the length of the sky. For a long time, the woman thought they had disappeared completely, until she saw the edge of one peeking out from behind the moon.

In her seven hundredth year in the valley, the two smallest spheres had fallen to the earth. The woman recalled it dimly, the fiery streaks as the objects hit the atmosphere. They arrowed in opposite directions, and so she had tracked one as it sped westward over the horizon. She waited for something to happen, and when it did not she turned to the east and witnessed a great flash of light. Hours later, the ground shook. The following day a blanket of rainless clouds rolled in, almost touching the spires of the jagged summits ringing the valley.

It grew much colder for several years, which affected the people of the valley not at all. The woman felt some sadness that she could no longer watch the sky, but she had still been young enough then to take comfort in the closeness of her children. When the clouds lifted, the objects were scattered across the night sky so that not all could be viewed at once. Over the course of a decade, they moved back toward the moon, finally taking on their original, straight arrangement.

As the brains shrunk in their skulls, the people of the valley drifted apart. The woman circled the edge of the lake alone, drinking its hallucinogenic waters regularly until the greater part of her consciousness lifted free of her body. In time her children forgot that she was their mother, and she pushed them away when they approached her. A low growl lodged deep in her chest.

Now and then even the taste of skin and bone grew sour in her mouth.

She did not put a name to it, but she thought often of dying. She watched the sky and hoped to see the objects falling, their beautiful trails of fire dissecting the sky into a giant wheel. She had no religion, no memory of Adrash, the god the other men of the world worshipped, but still it was a form of prayer—a silent, inarticulate longing for change.

‡

Jeroun spun slowly at Adrash's back, thousands upon thousands of leagues distant. The moon, its gaze locked on the darkened world, loomed to his left, closer though by no means near.

Adrash floated before a motionless iron sphere, dwarfed by the wall of one immense rim. Its smooth surface extended in all directions. This close, its curvature could not be discerned. The eye tried and failed to see a furthest edge.

Welded onto its surface was a handle small enough for a large man to grasp with two hands.

Adrash gripped it tightly. He spread his legs, appeared to plant his feet on the nothingness of the void, and pulled. The heavy muscles of his chest and shoulders bunched with the effort, his sinewy torso turned, and slowly the handle moved forward. At the fullest extension of his arms he stepped to the left and repeated the process. In this way, he spun the sphere faster and faster. His body became a blur of frenzied movement.

Eventually, he stopped and drifted back from the wall, the rapidly approaching edge of which had still not come into view. A comfortable ache suffused his body. Though unnecessary, the exertion had felt good. In the past he had chosen to move the spheres with his mind, but those days were over. It was unsatisfying, somehow. Now he preferred to feel the texture of the metal, the elongation and contraction of muscle tissue.

His body was that of a man, well over two yards tall and coldly beautiful, a marble statue brought to life. But for his eyes—which glowed a harsh yellow-white, lacking iris and pupil—the seamless white material of his armor sheathed him smoothly from crown to sole, hugging the curves of his powerful frame. Broad-shouldered and narrow-waisted, he held himself like a professional soldier, spine straight, hands in loose fists. The features of his face were mere suggestions above the strong line of his jaw.

From a greater distance, he regarded the sphere. It had become recognizable as such despite its vast scope. Still farther out, the structure appeared delicate and airy due to the great distance between rims. A decorative bauble, a fragile ornament through which the stars burned. To the sphere's left, a great distance away, spun its larger brother. To the right, a slightly smaller brother. The others were not yet in sight, and the pale hulking weight of the moon suddenly seemed to loom far too near, as if it were pulling the three spheres into it.

Adrash increased the speed of his retreat. Before long the entire chain of twenty-seven spheres became visible. Positioned halfway down the line, he tried to admire the precision of their placement, their carefully calculated speeds. His last adjustment had guaranteed that once every month the sun's light would hit the spheres in a particular way, turning the Needle into a line of pale fire in Jeroun's night sky.

Of course, he would not witness it from orbit.

He considered how few of the world's inhabitants would notice the effect. Those who did would react by pressing their fists to their heads and praying, or by blotting out the Needle with one hand and cursing.

Both prospects depressed Adrash. Still, he resisted the urge to begin another series of adjustments.

For many hundreds of years, much of his time had been spent altering the positions and speeds of the spheres, an obsessive drive to find the perfect expression of his dissatisfaction. Finding this abstract expression, he believed, would calm him, heal the wounds in his soul. Ultimately, he had grown weary of the monumental effort and returned the spheres to their original alignment, stringing them in a line equidistant to each other, aligned to the moon's orbit perfectly, and thus narrowing his focus.

The only adjustment he allowed himself now was rotational speed. Once, he had spun the spheres so that each revolution matched exactly for a full year. Four hundred and thirty-two revolutions per hour. One hundred and twenty million times the rims passed before his eyes without any revelation. Then he had slowed down and sped up every other sphere in increasing increments so that the fastest two were at either end and the middle one remained still.

He felt compelled to explore every permutation. Ultimately, he wasted time, distracting himself from the decision he would soon have to make.

Return to Jeroun as mankind's redeemer, or cleanse the world of mankind forever.

‡

Unfortunately, time had only made the world's destruction more of an inevitability. Though Adrash had successfully put off the decision for seven thousand years—first by exiling himself above Jeroun, and then by creating the Needle itself—his relationship to the people of the world had not changed.

He could not love mankind, because he saw their brilliance for the thing it was: an exquisitely frail quality that could never make up for the effects of their fear. In fact, more often than not intelligence compounded mankind's negative tendencies. The aggressive wielded their intellects like weapons to subjugate the humble and the less gifted. Given free reign—and there was little reason to think they would not eventually achieve complete dominion—such men would bury what little virtue remained in the world.

No, he could not forgive men their pettiness, their squabbling, their ridiculous and violent worship. Of course, as a young god he had spent several eons encouraging this behavior, but in truth men had never needed encouraging. How could one change the nature of men? Twenty thousand years of Adrash's urging—two-thirds of his life, bent to this endeavor—had not made them more peaceful, any likelier to see reason.

Nor, obviously, did the threat of annihilation.

They could not pretend ignorance. Adrash had made his feelings known for millennia. When his words and actions had failed to inspire permanent change, he abandoned mankind for the void. As their empires had grown ever more contentious, he dredged material from the blind side of the moon and constructed the Needle. At the height of their power and hubris, he had hurled the two smallest spheres down, killing hundreds of thousands and blanketing the earth in dust for a decade. The Cataclysm, as men now called it.

These efforts to communicate his desperation had been folly, Adrash now understood. Mankind's ingenuity in the face of trial was short-lived, and Adrash did not possess the energy to continue reminding them of their priorities. He felt the constant temptation to simply complete what he had begun with the Cataclysm, and send all of his weapons to their task.

You have been too patient, he told himself. *You have waited on them long enough.*

And yet—inexplicably, in the face of all reason—hope remained. When he could stand to hear them, he listened to the thoughts rising from the world below, hoping to hear a call rise above the others and proclaim change. He wondered if his constant adjustments to the Needle of late were an attempt to signal this person, to create a sigil in the sky for a prophet to recognize.

For there had been prophets once, he felt sure: Men and women who had spoken with fearful, exquisite voices—voices that resounded into the bowels of the earth, filled the void with light, and nearly shook Adrash's heart to a halt.

They had existed, had they not?

Sometimes, Adrash wondered if he had only invented these avatars to keep from going mad.

Sometimes, he wondered if he had prevented madness at all.

Perhaps his obsession revealed the rot that had already spread throughout his soul.

‡

He turned somber eyes away from the Needle and looked upon Jeroun, a bluegreen marble rolling on a sheet of stars. A shallow ocean covered the world but for two small continents straddling opposite sides of the equator: Knoori, the home of man, and Iswee, the perpetually cloud-covered home of the slumbering elders. Everywhere else, uninhabited islands lay scattered like windblown seed.

From experience, Adrash knew the difficulties of navigating between those islands, of traveling from Knoori to Iswee. Mortal men rarely dipped foot in or sailed upon the ocean for fear of its predatory fish and reptiles, but Adrash knew those beasts numbered fairly far down on the list of dangers. Nonetheless, for eons he had preferred to live upon the ocean, where he could be alone, a man instead of a god. But for his armor, which he usually caused to retreat until it was a white helm clinging to his hairless scalp, the sun had shone on his bare black skin.

As the world turned, Knoori rose on its side, a confused mass of sharp-toothed mountains, high plains and parched barrens. Cities spotted the continent, a hundred magefire lamps revealing their shapes. Here, Tansot, a five-pointed star of purple radiance. Here, Seous, a blue snake lying along-side River Anets. The sun edged out from behind the world's swollen belly, unhurriedly extinguishing these fires. For a few seconds Lake Ten turned into a reflecting pool. The pine hills of Nos Ulom became a blanket of jadestones, the deserts of Toma molten gold.

The world was blindingly beautiful.

Adrash could not bear to look any longer. He closed his eyes against the radiance, let the tumblers fall in his mind, and unlocked his soul, allowing the world's prayers to flood in.

The first to announce itself: *A wordless cry from an imbecilic mind.*

The nameless woman called from the unmapped valley in the Aspa Mountains—a place shielded by such deep magic that even Adrash had to concentrate in order to see it from orbit.

He heard the woman's appeal with such clarity because it was old and familiar to him, but he had little sympathy for the people living along the shore of the ensorcelled lake. The majority of mankind lived in far worse conditions, though most had more variety. The old woman had stumbled onto one of the world's great secrets and used it to sire a race of idiots. While highly nourishing to bone and muscle tissue, once ingested elder skin acted on the human body like a slow poison, causing prenatal damage and retardation of the brain.

The people of the valley were useless. Adrash ignored their clumsy, aimless prayers, though they were loud. Due to the proximity of so many elders and their ancient buried magics, the valley acted as a focusing lens.

In a lukewarm way, it bothered Adrash to see so much power put to so little. There were times when he wished someone would discover the valley's secret. The resource would be hoarded and abused, of course, but it would be an interesting development. If it fell into the hands of the Stoli government, Adrash could expect a great deal more traffic in orbit. Dozens—and in time, hundreds, even thousands—of outbound mages would rise from the surface of Jeroun, high on reconstituted elder blood, eager to make names for themselves.

They would come with gifts and weapons, open hands and fingers tipped with magefire. Arcing lightning from one to another as they flew toward the moon, ready to challenge their god or simply beseech him to show compassion.

They would all die, burned to cinders by the light of Adrash's eyes, crushed to dust in his arms. His palms itched thinking about it. He tightened his fists, remembering the way a man's blood burst from his body in the void. For a brief moment he even felt the rekindled flame of his youth, a time when he had impulsively aligned himself with this or that leader, capriciously giving vent to his lust for warfare.

No, he had never been a charitable god—not a father or an easer of pain.

It would be enjoyable, punishing those who came calling at his door.

Nonetheless, he shook the vision of violence from his eyes. Useless conjecture, and ultimately an undesirable development. Best if he never had to look a man in the face again. He let his thoughts drift away from the nameless valley, searching for more encouraging, or at least interesting, voices.

Men prayed to him for rain atop the broad, slightly tilted tops of the Aroonan mesas, clasped hands permanently dyed red with the blood of sacrificed bandi roosters. They cried openly for rain, which had not come in strength for three years. Their women, who neither prayed nor begged after years of burying their children, spat at this display of weakness.

In a seedy flat above a basket shop in Jompa, a prostitute prayed for fifty cril, otherwise he would be dead by morning. He had gambling debts. Adrash knew also that the man had jaleri eggs lining his urethra and would be dead by month's end.

On the southeastern shore of Nens Abasin, a young acolyte of The Unending Luck cast her line and prayed for an old, sick fish. She had no desire to incur the soul debt for taking a new life. The order forbade her from throwing back a catch, yet her luck had been so abysmal lately that she would not hesitate to do so. Breaking the rule would undoubtedly mean more bad luck in the long run, thus reinforcing the cycle, but the girl did not care. She could not see how it mattered. Luck touched some and shunned others altogether.

Adrash felt the briefest moment of communion. He wished he could answer the girl's prayer. If he were closer to the world's surface, perhaps he would asphyxiate an old fish and let it lap upon the shore at her feet. He had once, if rarely, enjoyed this kind of intervention.

In the cold mines under the Old City of Ghys, nearly a mile below the searing sand of the Tomen Desert, a Demni mage prayed her alchemy had been correct. She could not remember if the spell was heart before liver, and what effect the wrong order would produce.

It was not heart before liver, Adrash knew. The smell of the infusion would attract diamond spiders. The mage would soon have a great deal to worry about, and for a moment Adrash was tempted to watch the ensuing battle.

Instead, he focused elsewhere. His mind touched here and there, lingering on the personal entreaties, passing over the formulaic prayers and liturgies. Prayers to other gods—those shadowy figures Adrash had once caused to live and then destroyed, and whose memory somehow managed to linger in the souls of men—he ignored. They were of the same quality as those directed to him.

Words damning him he saved for last. They were the most amusing.

He had no expectation that this time he would find what he was looking for. A singular voice might never be found. The world might be destroyed tomorrow, should he find his patience at an end. Or the world might go on forever while he spiraled into new realms of madness.

The spheres spun at his back, waiting.

PART ONE

VEDAS TEZUL

Vedas watched the square through a crack in the stockroom door.

The pulse pounded in his throat and temples, causing his vision to shudder slightly. He felt calm despite this, assured by the familiar sensation. As the street scene grew lighter, its weathered doorways and stonework angles more defined before him, he settled into the comfortable hum of readiness.

The black fabric of his suit hugged his powerful frame like a second skin. He stood in the traditional waiting stance of the lo fighter, feet shoulder-width apart, hands resting lightly atop his staff, which came to just below his chin. Back straight, knees slightly bent. A man could stand in this posture for many hours, minutely shifting his weight from foot to foot, meditating on the subtle tense and release of muscle.

Behind him, sixteen children were trying and failing to contain their nervousness. They were a quiet group. Nonetheless, Vedas heard and recognized every movement behind him. After eight hours cramped together, he had come to identify each youth's breathing and nervous habits. They scratched themselves, sniffled, sighed. They fingered the black sashes tied around their upper arms, needlessly adjusting the material that marked them as official recruits to the Thirteenth Order of Black Suits.

The acrid smell of vomit was everywhere. Someone always threw up, first time out.

15

At least, Vedas reasoned, he had not been forced to knock the weak-stomached girl, Julit Umeda, unconscious. She had covered her mouth and leaned back, causing the sick to run down her red shirtfront. The only sound had been a few drops of fluid hitting the floor. Vedas reminded himself to reward her afterward. New recruits did not typically think that quickly, especially after standing for so long.

He watched the square. The abbey master, Abse, had assured him the meeting would occur within an hour of dawn. Vedas closed his eyes for a moment and projected wellbeing to his superior, to his brothers and sisters. He imagined them walking straight-backed and proud, staff ends clicking on the paving stones, muscles shifting under the smooth black fabric of their elder-cloth suits.

It will be a good day, he told himself.

He turned from the doorway and regarded the recruits. Those who could shuffled back against their neighbors. Vedas had memorized their faces and names the night before, noting which he thought would hold up well. He was heartened to see he had been wrong about a few of them, and right about those he had appraised highly. As usual, the youngest proved the most resilient, though not always the most patient.

In the dim light of the stockroom, their faces were washed out and grim, smudged with dirt, painted to look like fierce animals or demons. Not a real whisker among them. Surely, they had spent time in front of mirrors, pumping themselves up. A few had purchased—or more likely stolen—black woolen shirts and trousers for the occasion. One boy even wore a homemade mask to complete the look.

A brief vision of Vedas's own first battle as a recruit flashed before him. He had been a little more experienced, though not much.

He reached into the fold of his hood for the sound-isolation spell, held up the vial so that the recruits knew what to expect, and broke the seal. One boy cursed softly as the pressure in the room suddenly changed. They pinched their noses and popped their eardrums.

When Vedas spoke, his voice sounded as if it came from a great distance away.

"The moment is almost upon us. You've done a good job of waiting." A brief flash of white as he smiled. His skin was only a shade lighter than the suit he wore. "I'm proud of you. It seems I've chosen well.

"Remember the signal." He held up two fingers, one finger, and then his fist alone. "At that instant I will open the door and we will charge. Follow me closely. I will lead you to the enemy's back. Locate unsuited enemies.

Double up on them if you can and don't play by the rules. Aim for the genitals and the eyes. In close quarters, remember to use your elbows and the weight of your feet. Most importantly, remember to keep focused on your target. Don't get distracted by anything else. Make me proud."

Vedas dropped the spell just before it abated. The pressure lifted. He met the eye of each recruit before stretching the hood over his shaved head. The children regarded the tall, wide-shouldered shadow before them, gazes lingering on the two small horns on his temples. Slowly, he caused the hood to crawl over his face until only his eyes were visible.

He saw momentary fear in the recruits' stares. They shuffled against one another. Most likely, few of them had seen a fully shrouded Black Suit up close, and only half-believed the claims that a man could wear cloth made from the skin of an elder and let it become a part of him, an extension of his will.

Now you know, Vedas thought. He nodded and turned back to the door. He disliked the drama the moment had required, but had grown accustomed to it. Perhaps it was even necessary, as Abse claimed, a brief spell of near-religious awe to steel the mind for what was to come. *You become a symbol*, the abbey master had once said. *More than a man—a figure worth following into battle.*

And indeed, the children had become jittery behind Vedas. The fear had not abated, but nerves would see them through.

He watched the square. Before long, from the east he heard the sound of staffs clicking on paving stones: His brothers and sisters—the Followers of Man. Softer but growing in intensity, from the west he heard the answering rat-a-tat of dueling sticks clacked together: Rivals—the Followers of Adrash, the One True God.

The recruits would not have to wait much longer.

‡

In 12472, just before Vedas's seventh birthday, his parents had relocated from Knos Min in order to assume a diplomatic post in Golna, almost two thousand miles from the only place he had ever known. At first frightened by the city, Vedas soon came to think of it as home. Knosi were well regarded in the east, and he was treated with respect. A natural athleticism endeared him to his peers.

His parents discouraged sectarianism, in fact had never subscribed to a faith, but they could not prevent their son from allying himself with the other children of Smithtown, the vast majority of whom had been raised Anadrashi. In his tenth year, Vedas was recruited by the Black Suits of the Eighth Order and began taking part in legally sanctioned street battles. His parents disapproved, but traditional Knosi culture considered a ten-year-old boy an adult, free to make his own decisions.

In Vedas's twelfth year, Knos Min raised the tariffs on Hlumi tobacco products. Relations between the countries took a sudden downturn, and the eastern nation began expelling Knosi nobles and political figures from its borders. Vedas's parents, on a brief sabbatical on the northern coast, were forced to leave without their adolescent son. For a brief time, Vedas lived in the homes of various friends, and then he lived on the street.

Word reached him of his parents' death in the Month of Royalty, 12478, almost a year after their departure. By this time, he had become messenger and errand boy to Saatreth, the abbey master of the Seventh Order of Black Suits.

Messenger, errand boy, and plaything.

The Seventh had successfully kept their history of pederasty a secret from the city's other twenty orders for over three centuries. Upon discovery of their transgression in the spring of the following year, Abse volunteered the Thirteenth to right the wrong. They removed the recruits, killed the men who had once been their faith-kin, and left the abbey a charred pile of rubble.

"I can send you back to Knos Min," Abse told Vedas. "There are a few other boys orphaned by the debacle between our two countries. But that trouble has long since abated, and the recent succession of the dictator in Nos Ulom has resulted in an oddly peaceable country. Your passage across the continent would most likely be safe."

Vedas parsed the master's language. "My parents are dead."

"Yes. I have heard." Abse offered the somber, black-skinned boy a stiff smile. "Surely you have relatives?"

"Yes," Vedas answered. Of course he did, two uncles and an aunt, but he had no interest in leaving Dareth Hlum. He only half-understood why the abbey of the Seventh had been destroyed. True, Saatreth had not been a father or a friend. He had hurt Vedas badly enough to leave scars for years to come. Nonetheless, it was the abbey that had provided shelter and given Vedas an identity.

"Relatives are often a great comfort in times of change," Abse continued. "On the other hand, I have heard that you are a talented young man." He held up a finger. "I am not obfuscating my meaning. No one in this order desires the services Saatreth desired. By talented, I mean only that word has reached me of your martial prowess."

Vedas interpreted again. *Fighting*. Here was an area in which he excelled.

"I want to keep fighting," he told Abse. An awful thought occurred to him. "I killed a boy during practice. Is this why you're making me go home? I didn't mean to do it."

Abse pursed his lips. "I am not making you go home, boy. If you choose to stay in the order, you will undoubtedly kill someone again. Sectarian battle is dangerous. That is why it is so tightly regulated in Knos Min." He paused, pale eyes fixed on Vedas, before speaking again. "If you want to continue fighting, you must stay here. You will be an acolyte for two years. If you pass martial training and your doctrine classes—no easy feat, I assure you—at that point you will be offered a suit. Understand, it is no small matter to be given such an opportunity. Suits are prohibitively costly to produce—more so every year. Most are acquired through the deaths of our brothers and sisters."

Vedas stared at the man whom he would come to know as master. The odd, fine-boned face that appeared only a few years older than Vedas's own. The small frame sheathed in black. The light in the room changed as clouds moved outside, revealing the barely noticeable designs on the man's suit. Vedas regarded the abbey master's face again, and for a moment it seemed that fractures formed upon it. A mapwork of fine lines. Paper crumpled and ironed out.

"Is this what you want?" Abse asked. "To stay here?"

Vedas agreed without a moment's hesitation.

‡

The Black Suits entered the square first. Twenty men and women, clothed head to foot in seamless black. Some had formed relief designs on the surface of their skin-tight suits. Others had thickened the malleable elder-cloth in strategic areas, creating body armor and helmets. A few had formed bone-hard striking surfaces along the forearm or shin, spikes at knee and elbow. A lone brother had grown his suit's horns into vicious prongs.

Few chose, like Vedas, to retain the smooth, unadorned texture of the cloth, and fewer still masked their features completely.

All skin tones were represented, for Vedas's order culled recruits from each of Golna's major ethnic neighborhoods. *Diversity is a strength*, Abse claimed, and so allowed the brothers and sisters a great deal of freedom. Plaited and matted hair grew from faces and sprouted from helmets. Tattoos curled around eyes. Plugs of bone pierced lips and brows.

The men and women of the Thirteenth Order of Black Suits had little in common beyond the color of their suits, the hardness of their bodies, and the horns on their hooded heads. They had become brothers and sisters through physical pain. They prayed and fought for the downfall of Adrash together, proudly displaying the color of opposition.

More than half their number preferred weapons other than the lo. These dropped their staffs upon entering the square and lifted hammers from their shoulders, unsheathed swords, twirled flails, and readied razored shields. The four who had formed weapons out of their suit material eschewed handheld weapons altogether.

The Black Suits stopped in the center of the square, eyes locked on something Vedas could not yet see. Abse, a thin, diminutive figure holding two broadswords half as long as his body, took a step forward from the group and stamped his foot, as if anchoring himself to the spot.

A howl sounded, a ragged-edged bellow that offended Vedas's ears and caused the recruits to mill uneasily at his back. He recognized the sound and cursed inwardly.

A second after announcing itself, the hellhound catapulted into the square, skidding a mere body length from Abse's feet. A crest of purple fur bristled along its broad back. Smoke rose from its drooling mouth. It stood at the shoulder taller than the abbey master.

Abse neither flinched nor gave ground. Bringing a hellhound was a serious and dangerous breach of etiquette, only technically allowed because Vedas's order had been allowed to choose the location. The abbey master would not allow this as a distraction. His eyes never left the advancing line of White Suits that followed the dog.

The Thirteenth had never fought this order, the so-called Soldiers of the Appropriate Desire, but Vedas had done his research. He had briefed every brother and sister of the Thirteenth, assuring their preparedness as best he could. Superficially, the Soldiers were a similarly outfitted, non-mage order, legally registered within the city. They had not gone south of the law for three years. Abse and Vedas had predicted a clean battle.

The hellhound said otherwise—as did the two white-suited women at point, the tops of whose staffs glowed with green magefire.

Their numbers, at least, were correct. Including the hellhound, Vedas counted twenty Soldiers, accoutered in a similar if more conservative manner than his own brothers and sisters. They had only gathered eleven new recruits, he noted in relief, and had not encouraged the children to wait in hiding before the attack. They followed at the order's back, peering through the mass of white-suited figures, trying to locate their rivals and failing.

Small blessings were never discouraged.

Best not to waste it, Vedas reasoned. A small risk might be taken to assure his recruits.

He spoke softly to them without turning his head.

"You heard it. They've brought a hellhound. Doubtless some of you've seen them at the carnival. They are dangerous, yes, but this one can't touch you. The White Suits don't have the authority to allow that."

This was technically true, of course, but it was not the whole truth. Though intelligent enough to understand instructions, hybrid dogs did not always follow the rules of the battle. Sometimes the primal urge to hunt could not be denied. The chances of an attack were slight, but it was a chance nonetheless.

There is always risk, Abse was fond of saying.

"You needn't be afraid," Vedas continued. "No one can touch you but other recruits. Keep your eyes on your enemy. Close out everything else."

No one answered. Vedas frowned within his mask. Any minute now. He focused on a White Suit, a heavily built man standing well over seven feet. A warhammer with a head that must have weighed thirty pounds rested on his shoulder. A thick chain at the end of its handle led to a viciously pronged grapple, which hung from the giant's right hand.

Vedas noted the giant's sinuous midsection, calculating how much speed it could generate. He guessed the man would create a vacuum around himself. No one would want to get in close and risk having their head torn off. Nonetheless, the man would have weaknesses. He would be slow to recover from swinging those huge weapons.

You're mine, Vedas thought. He held up his hand, two fingers raised.

Outside, Abse whistled, and as one the two groups leapt forward. Vedas caught a brief glimpse of the abbey master's small frame ducking under the hellhound's body, broadswords thrust toward its belly, and then lost sight of him amid the press of bodies. He wished Abse luck. A smart move, taking out the beast early.

Black and white mixed. The White Suits' new recruits backed away from the roiling crowd.

Vedas lowered one finger.

Magefire arced over the brawling bodies, found its target. A scream went up. Vedas recognized the voice of a sister and shut it out. He set his knuckles against the stockroom door.

The White Suits' new recruits clustered together, casting confused looks about.

Vedas made a fist, pushed the door open, and shouldered the frame aside.

Two hundred and fifty pounds of tempered muscle charged up the stairs, followed at the heels by sixteen scared children. They screamed as they flowed forth, as if the sound would drown out their fear.

‡

Three months after Vedas's twenty-second birthday, an opponent's clumsy sword stroke had disemboweled a pair of his recruits. A sister and brother, perhaps eleven and thirteen years old. Their wounds, so unexpected and gruesome, stopped the battle in its tracks.

Vedas knelt by the children. The boy was already dead, the stroke having severed his spinal cord. His sister did not so much as twitch. She lay in the street as if she had decided to take a rest. Only her eyes moved, searching the sky.

Suddenly, she shuddered and tried to lift her head.

He clamped a hand around her jaw, holding her in place.

"Hurts," she said. "What—?"

Vedas looked up, instinctually searching the crowd for Abse.

"Shh," he said without looking down. The smell struck him, and he winced. "You'll be fine."

"I want—" The girl swatted weakly at the arm holding her head immobile. "Mommy. My legs hurt. Zeb."

At once, Vedas remembered her name. Sara Jol. Zeb was her brother. Had been her brother.

He still could not meet the girl's stare. Abse was nowhere to be seen.

"Don't worry," Vedas said. "It'll just be a second."

The girl spoke no more. She inhaled three quick, shallow breaths and died.

After dinner, Abse and Vedas conferred in the library to discuss the incident. A waxpaper packet lay on the table between them. The death wage, an ounce of bonedust for the children's parents: nearly half a year's standard pay.

"They came to Golna from the badlands of southern Casta a year ago," Abse said. "They knew their children had been recruited and approved. We have no reason to expect recriminations. The man who killed them has reason to worry, of course. Perhaps his order does, as well. It was reckless, allowing the man to fight."

"We should have recognized the danger he posed."

"Ridiculous. We were at war, Vedas."

Vedas's hand closed around the waxpaper packet. "I will take it to the parents."

Abse frowned. "Very well, though it is not your responsibility."

"Whose responsibility is it?"

The abbey master opened his hands, palms up. "What are you looking for, Vedas? Let us be honest with one another. You want someone to blame other than yourself. You want someone to suffer as you suffer, and so you try to shame the order by implying that we have not taken responsibility. In your guilt you cannot see that it is not your fault when a recruit dies—not your fault, or mine. The children are warriors, just as you and I are warriors. The children are weapons for the greater glory of man, just as you and I are weapons for the same cause. You need not seek someone to blame, for there is no one to blame."

Vedas closed his eyes and breathed deep into his stomach, struggling to contain the rage the abbey master's words roused within him. Since taking over as Head of Recruits at the age of seventeen, he had heard a variation on the speech three times. He could see the reason in it, but reason did not erase guilt—a fact the abbey master did not seem to understand.

"I could have done more."

Abse rose, and still stood only a little taller than the sitting Vedas.

"How? By standing behind them, by moving their arms and legs?" A rare expression of annoyance crossed the abbey master's face. "You will not begin to think that way. A good leader readies as best he can, knowing that no amount of preparedness can assure the life of every man in his command. In time you will embrace this fact. In time, you will not cling so tightly to your pain. For now, however, you must simply move forward."

‡

The giant's grapple caught the end of Vedas's staff and ripped it from his hands. The rounded edge of one prong grazed his temple, spinning him to the ground.

He shook the stars from his eyes and rolled to the left to avoid the swiftly descending warhammer, which landed, shattering pavement less than an inch from his leg. He rose into a crouch and immediately leaned back, planting a hand on the ground to steady himself as the man swung his grapple at Vedas's face a second time. He felt the compacted air of its wake as a soft slap.

The giant grunted, obviously surprised that he had not connected. Off-balance, he twisted to bring his weapons back around. Before he could do so, Vedas shifted his weight forward, sweeping his right foot into the man's left ankle. Though it felt like striking a concrete pillar, the joint broke with a loud snap. The man did not cry out, and managed to twist so that he fell on his back. The ground shuddered.

Vedas saw the counterattack coming. Admiring the White Suit's persistence, he rolled to the right just as the warhammer fell, slamming into the street where he had just been. Momentum carried him onto his feet as the grapple arced over the man's prone body. From the ground it was a clumsy throw, and Vedas caught it easily.

The man reacted quickly, however, jerking the chain back, but Vedas was already moving in this direction. He stamped his left heel into the man's left inner elbow, deadening the arm holding the hammer and simultaneously using it as a springboard.

He calculated in the second before his right foot landed on the giant's face. He noted the thick fabric armor covering the bridge of the man's nose and reconsidered his attack, angling his foot for the neck rather than the head.

Cartilage crunched satisfyingly under his sole. The giant's roar became a gurgle and then a wheeze as Vedas landed in a crouch beside his head.

Vedas dropped the grapple and rolled clear before the giant could attack again—but he knew even before completing his turn that the man was finished, dead or in great need of medical assistance. Vaguely, Vedas hoped the battle would end soon so the man could get the help he needed. Death was an unfortunate fact of sectarian battling, best for the orders if kept to a minimum.

One must always remember, Abse often reminded the brothers and sisters, *we are tolerated only as long as we do not draw too much attention to ourselves.*

Besides, Vedas was not without compassion. He hoped the giant's faith in Adrash lessened his pain. The sentiment conflicted with the views of his order, but this troubled Vedas not at all. He had risen above such trivialities. His faith was unassailable.

Vedas stood at the center of a battle still going strong. Everyone had either paired off against an opponent or moved to assist a weaker brother or sister. Several Black Suits had fallen, but so had a handful of White Suits. Through the thick of fighters, Vedas saw Abse at the gathering's edge, engaging one of the mages. The other lay at his feet, face disfigured by burns. The staff he had taken from her spun in his hands and struck, spitting magefire.

On the opposite side of the square, Vedas spotted the recruits. He could hardly tell his own from the opponents', and started to jog in their direction.

Howling, the blurred form of the hellhound came at him as he rounded a fierce melee. Vedas had only half turned when its shoulder slammed into his right hip and lifted him into the air. He spun three times before hitting the ground face first. His limbs whipped into the ground and his suit stiffened to minimize the impacts, but he felt them all the same.

Apparently, Abse had not been successful in taking the hellhound down. The beast had not uttered a sound since the beginning of the battle, and Vedas foolishly assumed it had been incapacitated. Banishing the embarrassment from his mind, he rose.

The dog was headed straight for the recruits.

Vedas ran, knowing he would never get there in time to stop the animal if it intended violence.

What else could it be intending? he asked himself.

He was still twenty paces from the recruits when the hellhound closed its jaws around the girl's head. She disappeared under the creature's body, but not before Vedas saw the black sash tied around her left arm.

‡

Abse called Vedas to his chambers after the post-fight toilet. The two sat, separated by a small lacquered table. They ate cold dumplings and mutton and drank hot fahl tea, the reason for the meeting hanging unspoken between them as they chewed and sipped. The abbey master had never been one to rush matters, even when both parties knew the outcome.

Vedas's hood was gathered at his neck and he had made his generous, well-formed features blank. The smell of vomit and blood had not left his nose. The sequence of Julit Umeda's death replayed itself before his eyes. From experience, he knew that in time the memory would fade. It would never disappear completely.

The abbey master finally set his cup aside. "I have been mulling over a decision. Oddly, this morning's event has made it easier to make." He reached forward and gripped Vedas's shoulder. "It is not impossible that someone will hold you responsible for the girl's death. We have been lucky in the past, but we have never lost a Tomen recruit before. I do not want to see you get hurt. Therefore, you must leave the city."

Vedas nodded, unsurprised. Two months previously, Abse had been given the task of choosing Golna's representative to Danoor, the decennial tournament between the world's Black Suit and White Suit orders. For two months, he had pretended to weigh his options. All the while, Vedas had known he would be the one leaving.

Typically, the prospect filled him with anxiety. He had not left Dareth Hlum since passing its borders as a child. He did not relish the prospect of travel with others, spending nights in close quarters. The fighting itself did not worry him—he knew his own strength—but he could not imagine the moments afterward. The congratulations. The tearful thanks. Most of all, he dreaded the speech the winner would be required to give.

The fact of Julit Umeda's death had temporarily rendered these concerns meaningless.

The master's smile did not reach his eyes. "I thought I might even go to the tournament, but this works out just as well. Congratulations. You will represent the city of Golna at Danoor on the eve of the half-millennium. It is a great honor, of course."

Vedas nodded again. The honor was lost on him.

"Vedas." Abse spoke the word as if it exhausted him. "You could show some appreciation. I take the task of choosing very seriously. There are many worthwhile candidates, and my choice need not come from this abbey. In fact, I would be wise to choose from another order. For political reasons, you see."

Vedas waited. The man's chiding tone bothered him, but only slightly. Certainly, Vedas did not let it show. At thirty-four years old, having spent twenty-two years in the abbey, he had long since learned to control his emotions around the abbey master. Their interactions were routine, transparent. They were like father and son. The same waters of love and resentment flowed between them. The same fictions bound them.

"To be exactly truthful," the master said, as if his thoughts had lingered on the same ground, "I had not seriously considered going myself. Nor had

I considered another. It is a hard journey from here to Knos Min, and that is only the beginning of the trial. Golna's champion must be strong, body and soul." He gestured with his hands to encompass the whole city. Another shallow smile. "Who else would I choose?"

Vedas met the older man's eyes. "And the girl's death is a good excuse. Convenient."

Abse shook his head. "Its occurrence today makes it easier to rationalize sending you, but I would still prefer it had not happened. It is no minor thing, losing a recruit. A small fortune in bonedust will exchange hands as a consequence—a wage to the child's parents, a fee for the funeral, and more than likely, a bribe to our local magistrate. We have an excellent record, but no one is above examination.

"Making matters worse, of course, is the child's lineage. Tomorrow, someone will have to visit her family and assist with the funerary rites according to custom. Of course, there is no guarantee that this will mollify the Tomen community, but to do otherwise is to invite a riot."

Vedas raised his eyebrows. "Someone?"

"It will not be you. I will assign another person to the task—maybe two or three."

"I will go."

Abse sighed. "Do you know, I used to wish you would learn to see the world as your brothers and sisters see it. But I have stopped trying to understand your guilt. I have stopped hoping that you will be anything but what you are. Nonetheless, my acceptance extends only so far. You cannot have everything you desire."

Vedas regarded Abse, wondering how far he could push the man. He noted the fine lines at the corner of the abbey master's mouth and eyes, appearing like cracks in porcelain. At times Vedas imagined he could see the sutures of the man's skull, as if his skin was merely thin veneer over a death mask. The abbey master was an enchanted creature, it was generally agreed, but no one in the order knew just what sort.

For all the mystery, Vedas understood one thing: Abse possessed an odd mind. Even at his warmest, his emotions were never quite believable. Now and then it seemed that a construct stared out from behind his dull eyes, measuring the world in weights and figures instead of souls and personalities. Sectarian battles were mere arguments, a number of triumphs. Deaths were inconveniences, a number of setbacks.

"I represent your best chance for victory at Danoor," Vedas said. "I demand a wage."

The memory of Julit Umeda's death asserted itself again. The hellhound's jaws closed around her head. The weight of its body carried her to the ground. Vedas banished the vision from his mind, only for it to be replaced by the memory of breaking the hellhound's neck, knowing that he was too late. Picking the girl's limp body up, surprised at how heavy she was in his arms. The smell of vomit rising from her shirt.

"Please," he said.

For a moment the room was silent. Then Abse nodded.

Fate sealed, the tension in Vedas's shoulders eased fractionally. He would leave the nation of Dareth Hlum. He would travel the length of Knoori to compete in Danoor, representing Golna's Black Suits in the near-eternal dispute between the Followers of Adrash and the Followers of Man. In the land of his ancestors he would win glory for the orders and converts to the faith, or he would die.

Before leaving, he would visit the parents of Julit Umeda, offering what comfort he could.

BERUN

The city of Golna, capitol of Dareth Hlum, was an arid splinter in the easternmost flank of the continent of Knoori. Roughly arrowhead-shaped, its southern and northern shores were bordered by the split end of the river Riolsam, which the residents simply called the Sam. On both shores the privileged had built their private estates, beautiful and airy buildings of imported oilwood and glass, outfitted with private docks below broad balconies on stilts.

The clear waters of the sea some men called Jeru and others called Death-shallow lapped perpetually at the broad eastern beachfront, which the poorest residents called home. Though the shore was undeniably beautiful, beasts had a habit of hauling themselves from the water and terrorizing the citizens along the beach. As a result, the slums' makeshift defensive wall was forever being repaired.

The majority of Golna's million souls did not live near the water, however. They had spread over the rocky, dry-shrubbed hill that dominated the island, segregating themselves into ethnic communities of various sizes and economic stature. Eventually, each came to embrace and jealously guard a principal industry.

This is how Butchertown became Butchertown. Everyone trusted a Vunni with a knife, as long as it was poised over a sheep or cow carcass. Theirs was not a prosperous community, but it was safe and clean, and it comprised the northeast tip of the city. Built into the steep side of the hill, its houses leaned at crazy angles toward the sea. Blood ran in channels into the sea.

Butchertown was famous for its butchers, of course. Its pastush bakeries—the only ones of their kind outside Vunn itself—were also quite renowned. The city's most attractive prostitutes lived on the Avenue of Broken Pottery. And the Anadrashi temple in the Square of Nights, O'men As, was generally considered to be Golna's most austere.

For close to a decade, however, the community had been known for one thing above all else: the constructed man known as Berun. He had fought in and won many of the fighting tournaments the city had held in the previous eight years. Though strong men had on occasion incapacitated him with the blow of a heavy weapon, only mages and those highly skilled fighters possessing elder-cloth suits stood a likely chance against him.

He lived on the roof of a Black Suit abbey, home of the Seventeenth Order, though he himself abstained from sectarian violence. Every day from sunrise to midafternoon he rested, absorbing the sun's rays for nourishment. In order to get the most sunlight, he allowed his manlike body to relax completely, spreading into a large circular carpet of dull bronze spheres of varying sizes.

The two glowing blue coals of his eyes perched on the roof's edge, connected to the main mass of his body by a thin tendril of spheres no larger than green peas. He took pleasure in watching the early morning routines—the corral of cows and sheep, the haggling over wares in the ruins of the Shoen Adrashi temple, and the extinguishing of the red magefire lamps lining the Avenue of Broken Pottery.

The ordinary activities of men fascinated him, though it was a rare occasion when he engaged them on a social level. Too often, such streetside conversations turned into discussions of religion or money, and Berun had little use for either. This afternoon, like most afternoons, would find him in the abbey courtyard, observing the brothers and sisters at practice. Perhaps the abbey master would ask him to help with the training. It amused him to slowly choreograph an attack for the novices, and let them pummel him with their staffs.

Only large gatherings and other interesting events drew him out of the building. Fights and festivals were his favorites, but he also enjoyed taking part in the charitable works the Seventeenth organized on occasion. There were always buildings to be rebuilt, families to be comforted. The west end of Butchertown bordered Querus, a small Tomen neighborhood. Though both communities professed forms of Anadrashism, neither could agree on the particulars. Bombings, alchemical and chemical, were not uncommon.

Humans were odd, in Berun's estimation. Odd in their preoccupations. Surrounded by others of their kind, knowing their concerns were mirrored a hundred thousand times over the course of generations, they still did harm to their neighbors.

As the sole member of his species, Berun considered this odd, indeed.

‡

In the Month of Bakers he had turned twelve years old. He did not tell anyone, for the age meant nothing. In truth, he was little different from the being he had been upon waking for the first time. Experience left its mark, but his fundamental nature could not be altered.

He had not been created in Golna. The dialect in which he spoke, full of rolled R's and elongated vowels, was not common in the city. Its speakers, the people of Nos Ulom, had long been banned from Dareth Hlum. The nations were old enemies. Whereas Dareth Hlum took great pride in its religious neutrality, allowing any sect to proselytize and even battle in the street if properly registered, Nos Ulom took equal pride in its conservative Adrashism, the expression of which the government closely monitored.

Dareth Hlum considered Nos Ulom a nation of dangerous extremists.

Oddly, if this had not been the case, Berun would never have been allowed into Dareth Hlum.

Before achieving fame for fighting in the city, he had achieved notoriety in Nos Ulom for assassinating Patr Macassel, High Pontiff of Dolin. The man, arguably the most powerful religious figure on the continent, was killed in his sleep, skull crushed beyond recognition by hands twice as large as a normal man's.

Berun had not bothered to destroy the elder eyes that had been set into the rafters above Macassel's bedroom. As dictated by custom, court mages blinded a slave and implanted the elder eyes so that they could be read, after which the manhunt officially began. For twelve days, the royal mount followed the constructed man through the pinefields of southern Nos Ulom. On the morning of the thirteenth, Berun slipped across the border to Casta, leaving forty-two men dead and many more injured behind him.

The government of Nos Ulom tried its best to cover up the story, claiming Macassel had died of natural causes. They never offered an ounce of bone or skin in bounty for Berun's body.

Their clumsy efforts of obfuscation failed, and Berun became a hero to the various Anadrashi factions of the continent. Adding insult to injury, Nos Ulom's Royal Redcoats failed to stop locals from burning the home of Ortur Omali, Berun's creator and the nation's most powerful mage. Nothing of value was found in the rubble, and few believed the official story that Omali had died in the conflagration.

Of course, these events overjoyed the governors of Dareth Hlum. When word reached them that Berun was living in Casta's capitol, they sent him an invitation to a tournament in Golna, hoping the constructed man would choose to stay. The fact that Berun himself symbolized a sort of religious extremism was inconsequential. The governors wanted him for the sole purpose of aggravating Nos Ulom.

Their efforts at seduction failed. Berun proved uninterested in creature comforts and money. Fortunately for the governors, Golna had one thing that interested the construct: fighting. He had fought in Casta, where nearly everything was legal, but had not approved of the gambling houses, establishments run by men who thought nothing of pitting a man against a lion if there was a profit to be made. If a man wanted to risk his life, Berun reasoned, he should at least be given a chance.

Violence and camaraderie compelled Berun, not money. He found himself allying with the Black Suits of the Seventeenth, though he had never found reason to hate God as they did. His affection for his new brothers and sisters grew. Their passion inspired his respect. He refused to engage in their violent arguments of faith, but he would defend their abbey and fight alongside them in tournament.

The transaction was simple. He lived on the roof of a Black Suit abbey, home of the Seventeenth Order, and protected his adopted family. He gave his tournament winnings to the abbey master, Nhamed, who then filtered the funds through to the community. In return, Butchertown loved Berun.

Gradually, the White Suits moved out entirely. During the eight years Berun had called the Vunni neighborhood home, the majority of Adrashi had defected to the Black Suits due to his association with them—this, and the White Suits had never gained much of a foothold among the violently Anadrashi Vunni population anyway.

If holding a position of influence bothered Berun, he gave no outward sign, but at rare times he wondered if his convictions were not in fact his own. He wondered if he had been programmed by his creator to act this way or that, tipping the balance in the Anadrashi's favor, just as he had been forced to kill Patr Macassel. At his most paranoid, Berun worried he had been created as a weapon to strike at Adrash, precipitating the great cataclysm all Adrashi men claimed would come about if the Anadrashi triumphed.

From time to time he became lost in visions. He who did not sleep relived the murder of Patr Macassel as though it were a dream, brass fingers tight around a throat that turned to white stone, crumbling in his hands.

The episodes had become more frequent of late, repeating a message he could not comprehend.

‡

The street wavered before his eyes, signaling the beginning of yet another vision. Possessing no means to stop it, he relaxed and let the sensations overtake him.

Immediately, it was not as he had come to expect. He did not wake in the hallway before Macassel's bedroom door.

He possessed control over his limbs.

He was not alone.

A mage with hands of burnished steel walked with him through the forest named Menard, a vast pine slope north of the Aspa Mountains. He knew the location well, though the trees in his vision had grown into elder-figures: Tall, impossibly thin men of purple, lustrous wood instead of flesh—demigods cursed with a thousand arms, elongated skulls, and eyes growing like berries on their fingers. Branch-tips brushed against him like insect antennae, trying to insert themselves into the crevices between the spheres that made up his immense body.

He lumbered clumsily, as if he had not drank from the sun in weeks.

The mage talked at his side, meaning lost in riddles and bad jokes, gesturing with his hands. When he rubbed his fingers together, they sounded like singing bowls. When he clapped his hands, they tolled like bells. Though Berun recognized the mage, he could not place or name him.

It seemed they walked with a purpose, but the reason for this too escaped his grasp. He spent a great deal of time avoiding branches. He found himself grateful for the mage's constant talk. If silence descended upon them, other voices took up the slack. Quiet at first, they became louder and louder until the components of Berun's body vibrated together uncomfortably.

"Pay attention," the mage said at some point. "You are about to receive instructions." The message came with clarity in the middle of an otherwise unintelligible rant, as if the man had woken from a dream to deliver it.

Berun resolved to remember the words.

In time they came to a great manor house of blackwood and stone. They arrived without warning, without a break in the forest. He recalled entering no glade, yet the building stood in the center of a treeless expanse. Though its angular facades were dark, the structure seemed to glow under the moon.

Turning to the mage, his thousand joints creaked like a carriage's rusty leaf spring.

"Has it always been night?" he asked. His deep brass voice sounded as if it came from the other side of a wall.

His stare was met with eyes the color of wet soil.

"It will be," the mage said, and began walking toward the house.

Berun had seen the structure before. Something about it set the spheres deep inside him spinning, jerking like animals in a packed cage. He did not want to follow the mage, but a look back revealed that the elder trees had closed ranks, denying him any path of return.

‡

The manor house's immense blackwood door leaned forward in its frame, stretching above Berun's head. The stoop felt slick under his feet, as if the stone were coated in ice. He fought to keep his balance.

The mage looked up at him expectantly.

Berun struggled for a time, falling and rising and falling again. When his knees hit the stone, they rang like iron nails struck with a hammer. He tried scoring the stone itself for purchase, but the landing proved as hard as diamond. Finally, he braced himself as best he could and punched the door. His right fist and part of his forearm exploded into their composite metal spheres, showering him, falling on the stoop like marbles from a child's bag.

The door creaked open.

"It is polite to knock," the mage said, stepping into the dark foyer.

Berun concentrated, but the spheres would not return. Strangely, this did not bother him overmuch. He examined his shattered right arm in wonder, attempting to move phantom fingers. He watched the simulated lines of sinew in his forearm, marveling at the way the broken rows of tiny spheres still moved in a detailed imitation of muscular contraction.

The mage turned to the open doorway and mumbled something. His steel hands glowed softly in the darkness, beckoning. He stepped backward, and for a brief moment light flared in his face: two pinpoints of amber fire in each eye socket.

"I'm coming," Berun said. He stepped into the house, and the light failed completely. He turned to find the door closed. Or perhaps it was still open and someone had stolen the moon and stars. Gradually, he discovered that not every source of illumination had been extinguished. Not quite. A bluish glow ringed his vision. He considered this, confused.

Just as the realization struck, the mage spoke: "We see by the light of our eyes."

The double pinpoints of the mage's eyes returned, positioned before Berun, though he could not tell how close. Cautiously, he stepped forward. Solid, flat ground beneath his feet. The amber lights neither receded nor grew closer, and so he kept moving toward them. Much as he had experienced in the forest of elder trees, time lost all meaning.

Eventually radiance began to seep back into the world. He now walked down a hallway. The mage advanced several paces before him, the hem of his dark cloak brushing the purple, thickly carpeted floor. Stylized elder trees stretched from the floor, arching above them on the ceiling. As they walked, Berun thought the images became even more like elders. They took on definition until they appeared ready to step out of the walls.

The hallway was long. It did not slope upward, yet Berun found he needed to lean forward slightly in order to reach the nondescript doorway at its end.

The mage looked up at him expectantly. Berun knocked.

The door opened easily and the hallway disappeared. The sun hung in a cloudless sky. Berun and the mage stood on a vast field of short yellow grass sparsely blanketed with blooming azure flowers. Before them, the horizon was flat and somewhat close. Berun swiveled his head to look behind and found the same view. To either side, however, the horizon seemed to draw to a point a great distance away. It seemed they stood on the top of an immense wall.

He looked down. At his feet a fat man slept, dressed all in white. As with the mage, Berun recognized but could not place him.

"Kill him," the mage said. His eyes had become large, liquid pools of amber in which two doubled irises swam. Two figure eights lying on their sides.

"Why?" Berun asked. Without consciously deciding to do so, he knelt before the sleeping man and reached for his neck. He had not thought of his shattered right arm in some time, and the sight of it surprised him.

"One hand should be enough, Berun," the mage said.

Hearing his name spoken broke the spell. The artifice of the vision sloughed off like a layer of dust, and Berun became aware of his body on the rooftop in Butchertown. He knew the heat of the sun there, a very real sensation that split his worlds in two. All at once, the link between waking life and vision felt very tenuous. Berun regarded the body of Patr Macassel, then stood and turned to the mage.

"Father," he said. "Where am I?"

The mage Ortur Omali smiled. Deep within Berun's chest a sphere knocked against its neighbors.

"Wrong question," Omali said. "You should ask, 'Where am I to go?'"

Berun stared at his creator. The man had aged.

Realization struck. "You're really you," Berun said.

Omali's smile broadened. "Inconsequential. Ask me where you're supposed to go, Berun."

Confused, full of questions, Berun nonetheless obliged.

"Danoor," Omali said.

"Why?"

Omali inclined his head to the man at Berun's feet. Macassel had disappeared, replaced by a tall, strongly built man. He wore a black elder-skin suit, but its surface shifted on him like oil, revealing patches of skin that varied from light to dark. One moment, the pink paleness of an Ulomi miner. Next, the rich oilwood brown of a Knosi fisherman. He grew. He shrunk. Twice, his suit took on the hue of milk and his skin turned black.

Berun looked up. The great mage's form blinked on and off. For a moment, his entire body appeared out of focus. An intense frown of concentration scored deep lines in his face. He caught Berun's questioning look.

"I cannot quite find the focus now, but he is here somewhere. He does not invite others in. Perhaps—" His steel hand shook as it rose to his mouth and pried his lips apart. He yawned as if the muscles of his jaw were sore. "Ah. I have found him again. For all his resistance, he is nearly as open as you are, Berun. His alignment is unclear, however. I cannot yet make a decision about him. Soon, though. Soon. But that does not concern you. Your mission is simple: You will watch him, and await my command."

"Who?" Berun asked.

Omali blinked out of existence again, and reappeared after a handful of seconds. The man at Berun's feet did the same. Suddenly, the view Berun had of the street in Butchertown superimposed itself over everything. It blinked on and off. The vision started to fade around Berun.

"Who?" he asked again. "Tell me, Father."

Omali shook his head, frowned. He started to speak, stopped. For a brief moment, he had no mouth, just a smooth layer of skin below his nose. After several false starts, he finally spoke in a voice that grated like a whetstone against a rusty steel blade.

"A man who will upset the balance. He is—"

Before any more could be said, the vision ended.

‡

"My father has summoned me on an errand," Berun told the abbey master. "I must go to Danoor."

Nhamed looked up from his meal. He dipped his chopsticks in the steel cleansing cup and positioned them precisely on his napkin. The dinner items were arranged before him carefully, aligned so that each complemented its neighbor. He ran hands over thighs and stomach, as though seeking to brush invisible crumbs from him. He sighed, eyes roving around the nearly empty room, landing everywhere but on Berun.

Berun did not mind the wait. The master was an interesting man to observe. He projected an air of tense, even awkward fastidiousness inside the walls of the abbey, which clashed oddly with the wild zeal he displayed in battle.

"Explain," Nhamed eventually said.

Berun described the vision, the details of which had not faded, but cemented themselves in his mind. When he looked inward, he could recall the events as if they had occurred in the abbey the day previously.

Nhamed's eyes stared fixedly above Berun's head. "To my knowledge, your creator is dead. You think a dream enough to leave the city? There are men who will remember your name along the road." He furrowed his brow. "Men who . . . Men who will not be friendly."

"I know this," Berun said. "And yes, it's enough."

Strangely, it was. Despite his youth, Berun was not naïve. Omali had never appeared to him before, but it explained why Berun had recently experienced visions with such regularity. Surely, Omali had caused them for a reason. Perhaps this trust itself proved that his creator had programmed him for certain behavior, but Berun was not generally given to flights of speculation.

Besides, he surmised, there would be fighting in Danoor. To celebrate the new year, the city had scheduled a secular tournament to follow the contest between the Black and White orders. That alone was reason to go. For a moment, he questioned why the trip had not occurred to him before.

Nhamed's eyes finally found Berun's. "Then we will miss you. Will you . . ." The master cleared his throat delicately. "Will you return? We have grown fond of you, and the White Suits . . ."

Berun caught his meaning. "I will return," he said. "And I will bring money."

Nhamed raised his eyebrows and made a noncommittal sound. Berun assumed the man would not try to stop him, but he had misjudged people before. Men, he knew, often hid their intentions from themselves. They made decisions without knowing why.

"Well," Nhamed finally said. "If you insist upon leaving, I have just received word of another man's journey to Danoor. Golna's champion has been chosen." A sour expression crossed his face. He moved his lips, apparently searching for words. "He is, I know, a man of honor. I have never trusted his master, but I do not doubt his charge. It will be safer to travel with him. He may even protect you."

Berun refrained from laughing. "Who is he?"

‡

The abbey masters had arranged for Berun and his traveling companion to meet the following morning at the Tam Docks in Heblast, the westernmost neighborhood in Golna. Impatient to get moving, Berun arrived early and attempted to distract himself by watching the fishermen unload the night's catch from their flat-bottomed riverboats. In quick time, butcher stalls were erected. Chum buckets overflowed. Restaurant and foodstall owners filled the boardwalk, straining past their neighbors to offer money for the best cuts.

Nhamed had given Berun a description of Vedas Tezul, but he disregarded it. He would not search the crowd for a particular face. Like Ulomi men, Knosi all looked the same to him. Most likely, it would be some time before he was able to differentiate Vedas from his countrymen. It made far more sense for the man to find Berun.

Of course, resentment spurred this decision, as well. The presumption of Nhamed, thinking Berun needed protection! He wondered why he had allowed himself to be corralled to the docks, why he did not even now walk away. He always knew the direction in which he traveled, could always place himself on the map of Knoori his creator had placed inside his head. Surely, he could walk from Dareth Hlum to Danoor in three and a half months. One and a half months would have been enough time. Nhamed worried too much.

Nonetheless, Berun waited, curious despite himself. A Black Suit—perhaps the man Omali had commanded him to watch. Certainly, Berun had received no message not to accompany the man, even though his presence slowed travel considerably.

Despite having spent a day and night meditating on Omali's mystifying words, Berun had not been able to achieve peace. Indeed, his indignation only grew. He chafed at being controlled, but did not know enough to call his mission a fool's errand. What if Vedas truly did pose a threat? Berun would not revolt against his creator without a compelling reason.

Conceivably, he did not possess the means to revolt. He shifted from foot to foot, suddenly restless. Winning tournaments in Golna had bolstered his confidence, assured him of his strength. The possibility that he had underestimated his own weakness discomforted him.

The sun rose above the horizon, and the crowd began to clear from the boardwalk.

"You are Berun?"

"Yes," Berun rumbled. He turned from his view of the river and regarded the man.

As he had expected, Vedas Tezul was to most appearances a typical Knosi, broad nosed and black skinned. Unlike many of his countrymen, however, he did not wear his hair in long matted cords or as a halo around his head. Instead, he chose to shave his scalp and face bald. He had not adorned his elder-cloth suit with artistic designs or caused it to form thick armor. Overall, Berun considered the effect somewhat unimpressive, as if the man were only half-finished. Even his posture was unnaturally stiff. He looked like a man who had never become comfortable in his skin.

"Ten days." Vedas said. "Nbena is only two hundred miles. You can manage twenty miles a day?"

Berun bit back his first reply. "Yes," he said simply. Was the man an idiot? Of course he could walk twenty miles a day. He could walk miles around Vedas Tezul.

"Do you need to purchase any supplies?" the man asked.

Berun stared.

Father, he thought. *This can't be the man you want me to watch.*

CHVRLI CASTA JONS

T he old men of Basec thrust their staff-ends into the unfinished wooden stands of their small theater. They did not smile or stand in respect, and the weak sound of their applause drifted away with the dry breeze. Several of the torches had gone out during the fight, but no one had moved to relight them. Money changed hands quietly as the crowd of old men climbed the stands—white-robed figures disappearing over the hillock like undead returning to graves.

Churls lowered her tattooed arms and looked down. The boy's body lay broken on the blood-spattered dirt at her feet, a vertical dent running the length of his pulped face.

"Peace," she said, expressionless.

She patted herself down and rubbed her bare skin, checking for unnoticed injury and letting several grams of dirt float free from her leathers. Her eyes felt scratchy in their sockets. She pulled a torch from the perimeter of the fighting floor and searched the ground for thrown coins.

"Coins," she muttered. "Fucking savages."

A quick search found seven, barely worth the effort. One beer's worth, probably. She dropped the torch and retrieved her sword from the ground. Its pitted surface came clean with a little gritty dirt. Lastly, she clipped the coin belts free from her and the boy's waists, and cut each bag open. Sixty-four bona, as she had been promised. At the expected exchange rate, it

40

would get her two grams of heavily contaminated bonedust. Hardly worth the effort of conversion.

She was tired, disappointed with the fight's outcome. The boy had been trained well, and killing him had not been her intention. He never stopped attacking, though, even after she broke his left femur and kicked the flail out of his hand. Grunting through a mouthful of blood, he crawled after her. No one in the crowd called it done. Resigned, she had finally flipped him over and crushed his skull.

Fucking savages.

Still, one had to live somehow. In her own estimation, Churls possessed no other skills to speak of. Gambling had gotten her in quite a bit of trouble a year previously, so it would be some time before she could return to Onsa, where the real money was. Shame the men of the badlands had so little money. Shame they had so little talent. They took what entertainment they could from watching their boys fight, watching them die.

There were good reasons so few fighters made it out here, Churls knew. One had to be in dire straits to scrounge in the dirt for coins.

Leaving the body where it lay, she climbed the shallow steps of the theater. An odd feeling, as if she were being watched, made her pause at the top. Her heart pounded against her ribs.

"What do you want?" she asked. She tried to make her body move forward, and failed.

She turned. A pale figure stood next to the boy's corpse: A white-skinned child, dressed in a white school tunic. Her hair, her slippers, her socks—all white. Her face could not be seen from the top of the theater, but Churls did not need to see it. She would have recognized the girl's posture anywhere. Few children had ever communicated world-weariness so well, or at such a young age.

Churls had not seen her daughter for at least three months. A decade had passed since she had seen the girl alive.

"Hello, Fyra," Churls said.

The girl nodded, her gaze never leaving the body at her feet.

You killed him, she said.

"Yes." Churls sighed. "I killed him."

Fyra disappeared and reappeared next to her mother. Involuntarily, Churls flinched, just as she had done when the girl surprised her by popping out from behind a corner when she was alive. Fyra had lived with her grandmother, and as a result Churls never became accustomed to children. Not even her own daughter. The fact that the girl had become a ghost did not change matters overly much.

Fyra looked up at Churls with eyes far older than a ten-year-old's. They alone were not a shade of white, but clear and blue like her mother's.

Did you like it? Fyra asked.

Churls took a step backward just as Fyra reached for her hand. It was a coincidence, Churls reasoned to herself, yet she stared at the little hand the way one might stare at a live scorpion.

"No," she answered. "I didn't like killing him at all."

Are you sure? Fyra said. *You liked killing the last man. You told me you did.*

Churls frowned. She knew the man her daughter referred to. The last time Fyra appeared, Churls had just killed an infantryman of the Castan Third in a fair fight. He had nearly bested her, and she had enjoyed every moment.

"That's true." Churls smiled awkwardly, like a person trying on an expression for the first time. "But that was a very different situation. You do see the difference, don't you, Fyra?"

The girl looked down at her hand, and slowly let it fall back to her side.

She said, *There's no difference, Mama. This one's just as dead as the other one.*

Churls shook her head. "You're not seeing what I mean. The man I killed in Donda was a trained warrior. He and I both knew what we were getting into. The difference is clear. I know you're old enough to see it. And you can, can't you, now that I've explained it?"

Fyra disappeared and reappeared next to the boy's corpse. For a long while, she simply stared at him. Churls grew uncomfortable and tried to think of something to say. Surely, the child could tell the difference. She was not, after all, a child.

Fyra cocked her head like a dog, then cocked it the other way.

No, she finally said. *I don't see the difference at all.*

Their eyes met from across the theater. Churls formed the old words in her mind, working up the nerve to speak. *I wish you wouldn't watch me when I fight. I wish I'd been there when you died. I'm happy I wasn't. I love you. I hate you. Why don't you leave me alone? Don't leave, sweetie. Stay.* Though the words were true, none of them sounded right, and her lips would not move no matter how hard she tried. Nonetheless, a raw lump formed in her throat, as though she had been speaking for a long time indeed.

"I . . ." The word was a croak. "Fyra, you . . ."

I don't want to talk about this boy anymore, the child said. *And someone is waiting for you in your hostel.*

She disappeared, back to the land of the dead.

‡

Churls finished her fifth beer, worried that the evening might result in a bad decision. Frankly, the situation felt out of her hands. The young men in the bar, none of whom had been present at the fight but had heard of her victory—young men who were nothing like their fathers, who knew the price of killing—would not let her pay for her drinks. And as the fight and Fyra's appearance had not stopped troubling her, she decided to keep drinking.

Last but by no means least, she had no intention of returning to her hostel. *Someone is waiting for you.*

Fuck that, Churls thought. Probably trying to collect on her debt. She owed nearly sixty ounces in gambling losses. Onsa was only eight hundred miles away, and she had not been overly attentive while covering her tracks.

As if on cue, a hand fell on her shoulder. She did not tense up, but let her right fist drop into her lap like it had fallen. Closer to her sword, better position for an elbow to the groin.

"Thought I'd find you here," a familiar voice said. There was garlic on his breath. "Another drink?"

Churls closed her eyes and smiled into her empty glass. "This is a bad dream, then, isn't it? Of all the people I wanted to see, in all the world, you're the last." She turned to the speaker and winced theatrically. "You look like shit, Gorum. You know you look like shit? You woke up and told yourself, I'm going to look like shit today?"

The man grinned. "I'm one of the only friends you got left in the world. Better be nice to me."

They laughed and embraced. She held the contact longer than usual.

Over his shoulder, Churls saw scowls on a few faces. *We bought you a beer*, the expressions said. *And now you're running off with him?*

She had experienced their kind of attention many times before. In the badlands, miles from anything resembling civilization, she became something of an exotic treat. Her freckled skin and short-cropped hair, her muscles and tattoos and scars, marked her as a different species from the long-haired, slate-skinned local women. Their thin hands and feet barely peeked out from folds of draped cloth while Churls walked about in leather halter and brass-pleated skirt.

The men of the badlands thought her small breasts were cute. They thought her flat nose was cute, so too the mole centered between her eyes.

They could get possessive very quickly.

"Boys!" she yelled, disengaging from Gorum. "The round's on my friend here!"

Still no smiles, but they took their drinks while Gorum scowled and paid. He understood such things, though Churls knew his preference was to push his luck as far as it would extend, and then break some bones. He had been a fighter once, before discovering how much money could be made representing other fighters. He arranged matches for them and took a percentage of the cut.

She had been a disappointment to him of late. She had lost too much money gambling, started drinking too much, and started losing fights. As things got worse, she took to fighting easier opponents. Less money, less respect. Soon the strongarms were knocking on her door, leaving threatening messages at her haunts. She left Onsa the autumn of '98 and kept a low profile, avoiding city centers as much as possible. Gorum had not contacted her, presumably because she was no longer bringing in any real money.

They had been lovers once, what felt like a long time ago.

"How did you get here?" she asked as soon as the beer was distributed, the bill paid. They sat together at a corner table, close but not touching. His fingernails were dirtier than she had ever seen them. The tops of his forearms were sunburned. He did not like horses or camping, and never strayed far from cities. Something extraordinary had brought him to her.

"Construct horse, if you can believe it." He rubbed his thighs and grunted. She imagined the cost of such a thing and whistled. He continued. "I was actually finishing a tour of the Five Sisters, looking for talent. Not much luck. In Dunn, I received a message and knew I had to get to you. Fortunately, you were easy to find."

"Well then, that's that. What's this message all about?"

He wiped foam from his mustache. "An opportunity, Churli. Have you heard about the tournament in Danoor?"

"You can't be serious." Of course she knew about it. What else occurred at the end of every decade and attracted every madman in the world? Of course, this year's would be even madder, falling as it did halfway through the millennium. "It's a thousand miles away, through places I'd rather not go. Besides, I try not to mix religion and killing. Liable to get you killed."

"I know, but hear me out. I hadn't considered Danoor a possibility, either, but everything just fell into place." He paused to take a drink. "I looked at the bracket structure, and the odds are good—better than good, Churli. After that I concentrated on finding suitable travel companions. Of course, I can't guarantee anything."

"You never could. No one can call a fight that large. And shit, Gorum, you know I don't like being set up. No, shut up. I don't want to hear about them yet. Before I consider anything, and I'm not saying I'm going to, I need to know what's at stake. How much will this tournament win me?"

"There's two hundred and fifty pounds of pure-grade bonedust in it for you if you make it to the winners' bracket, not to mention your cuts from the preceding fights."

Churls shook her head. "Holy hell. What's the winner get?"

Gorum smiled. "One thousand—drawn on the royal reserve bank of whichever government you choose. And this is separate from the Adrashi and Anadrashi bullshit. They compete against each other for only two days, white against black. I don't even think they're fighting for dust. The real fun starts on the first day of the new year." He held up a finger. "But because the sects are hosting the whole thing, it's their rules."

"What does that mean?"

The smile broadened. "The eight fighters who make it to the winners' circle may opt out with their cuts."

Churls felt mildly insulted. "Are you saying I can't win?"

"Yes." His hand fell over hers. "The gambling houses are going mad with the news. Berun registered before leaving Golna. Even at your peak, you couldn't have taken him."

She felt more insulted, but knew he spoke the truth. "How, then," she asked, "do you know I won't be matched against him in the lower rounds?"

Gorum shrugged. "I don't, obviously. The odds, though, are in your favor. One in eight isn't bad, and they're trying to organize the groups geographically."

That kind of bracketing would not work out well, Churls reasoned, because more than a few fighters from Dareth Hlum would have dropped out when they heard Berun was fighting. Still, she could count on many people using Gorum's rationale, hoping to avoid Berun and drop out once they made it to the winners' circle. Adrashi fighters with backers, especially—men who could afford to travel across the continent in luxurious wagon trains, assured of their safe passage through Nos Ulom—would still find a way to attend.

"Still," she said. "How do I get there? Nos Ulom's not the friendliest place in the world, and I sure as shit won't go through any part of Toma."

"The people I want you to travel with aren't taking that route."

Churls looked at him, hand raised to signal another round. "What other route is there?" It dawned on her. "Lake Ten? I suppose that solves a problem, but it'll cost going through Tansot. And Bitsan isn't the friendliest city in the world, either. You stopped that fight with Hoetz just because his people had scheduled it there, remember—even though I had arranged for a . . ." She curled her upper lip. "Chaperon."

"Regardless, that's where you'll sail from. Oh, and one other thing. Neither of your companions are trackers. Somehow, you must convince or fool them into going over the Steps."

This was too much. Churls slapped the table. "That's five hundred miles out of the fucking way! What kind of fool would travel over the Steps when they could walk in a straight line through Stol?"

Gorum looked torn between wanting to grin and wanting to duck his head under the table.

"Your kind," he said. "Now let me explain."

‡

Even with all the money at stake, it took some time to convince her. The young men of the badlands waited as long as they could, eventually shuffling out with wistful glances in her direction. The bartender upended the rickety chairs and stools, and then poured himself a drink, seemingly content to sit and listen to Gorum and Churls talk.

It was after midnight when they stumbled into her hostel bedroom. They unclothed each other clumsily and made love on blankets she would not have touched sober.

For Churls, it was like walking into her apartment in West Onsa, smelling the faint mildew rot everything took on near the ocean, stretching out in her favorite chair. She missed the city, of course. She had spent most of her life away from it, fighting in some form, but she had always known in which direction home lay.

Sleep would not come. She sat in the room's only chair, flipping a throwing knife in her hand and watching Gorum sleeping. Finally, she retrieved her sword and polished the blade with spit and a pinch of bonedust.

He shook her shoulder. "I gotta go."

Her blade lay naked across her thighs. She did not remember falling asleep, yet the details of their conversation the night before had crystallized in her mind. She blinked away a map of Knoori marked with the planned route he had told her they would use.

Ridiculous. Sailing across Lake Ten. Craziness, traveling so far with strangers. She reminded herself that returning home without the money to pay off her debts was not an option. Neither, if she valued her sanity, was the prospect of remaining in the badlands. She could only kill so many untried boys before her soul withered inside her, or left of its own accord.

"Okay," she said. "You gotta go. Ten percent?"

"Yes." He pulled her out of the chair and embraced her, crushing her arms against her sides. "Ten percent. I've tried my damnedest to give you a chance at success. I wouldn't travel this far for anybody else. You know that, right?"

She pressed her cheek against his. Brief contact, a last reminder of home. He still smelled of garlic. His wife was from northern Nos Ulom, where they put garlic in everything. *To keep the dead away*, he had once told Churls.

He let go. "How much dust do you have? Do you have enough for your sword?"

She raised an eyebrow. "I always have enough for my sword."

"Good. And for money?"

"That depends. What's the interest?"

"Fuck you," he said, reaching into his pocket. He counted out waxpaper packets of dust, and handed her five of the larger ones. "There. That should be enough for travel."

She weighed them. An ounce of high grade. *Should be enough.*

"Thanks, Gorum. Any other advice?"

He stopped at the door, turned back. "As always, it's best to reign in that murderous instinct of yours. You never know when the tables will turn and you'll find yourself on the other end of the blade. A little compassion could save your life. Don't roll your eyes at me—it's true. Mostly, though, my advice is just to watch out for Berun. You've seen him fight, I take it? Back when he lived in Onsa?"

She nodded. "You took me. The fight lasted all of half a minute."

"Then you know not to expect any pity from him."

She smirked. "Contradictions, contradictions. And the Black Suit, Vedas? How reliable is this source of yours? How do you know he can be trusted?"

"I already told you: I don't. I've given you all the information I have. You'll be their guide—it's up to you to create trust."

"I'll be lying to them, Gorum, delaying them by weeks."

"You'll be saving their lives by changing their course. Listen, you can't afford not to do this. The gambling houses will send someone after you eventually. Probably several someones. Not strongarms. Dangerous people. This is the only way to dig yourself out." He opened the door. "And I went to a lot of trouble to get here."

Churls considered her response. Possibly, she would never see him again. If she died, he would eventually find out—mostly to discover the fate of his dust, maybe a little because together they had once been something.

"Thanks," she said.

‡

Churls did not leave that day. The old men of Basec had agreed to pay for two fights, and as much as she loathed the idea of killing another inexperienced boy she could not turn down the money.

Gorum had arranged a live horse for her, an extravagance he had condoned only because time was pressing. On horseback, she could expect to arrive at the designated gate into Dareth Hlum two days before her traveling companions. There, she would need lodging. She would need to bribe entry officials to inform her the moment Berun came through. With any luck, she need not touch Gorum's money until they were well underway to Danoor.

She spent the afternoon practicing in a roofless abandoned building. For the first time in days, the sun cleared above her. She thrust and parried, swinging her dull, heavy sword in tight arcs, footwork kicking up a fine cloud of dust around her. A light sheen of sweat highlighted the flow of hard muscles under the freckled skin of her shoulders and arms.

Finished, she stood, breathing easily. She retrieved the pail of water she had brought from the hostel, disrobed, and washed the grime from her body as best she could. The air and water were cold, but the sun warmed her.

She enjoyed dinner—not so much the taste but the weight in her stomach—and tried not to think of the commitment she had made. Relying on others had never been her strong suit, but facts were facts. A lone traveler was a target.

Night had already fallen when she left the hostel. She walked the treeless path to the theater alone. The boy's body had been removed. The ground had been raked and the torches lit.

Soon, the old men began to arrive. As they topped the hillock and descended into the stands, not one paused to stare at the Needle extending across the sky above their heads. Neither did they gaze at the moon, which sat massively on the razor-backed hills directly before them. The men of the badlands were not dreamers, Churls knew. They woke before sunrise to graze their goats on paperweed and thorny sage, and died defending the animals. No mystery, no mysticism in that. If Adrash chose to destroy the world, they could do nothing to stop it.

Likewise, life would go on just the same if Adrash chose to redeem it.

Though Churls did not like the people of the badlands, she felt an odd communion with them. They understood that fate could not be bargained with. It held a person like a mother holds her child, lovingly or with revulsion. One did not get to choose.

The boy Churls was meant to kill stepped into the circle of firelight. He sneered at her disdainfully, but failed to hide the underlying fear. She saw it in the set of his shoulders, the hesitation in his steps.

Looking away, she caught movement before her in the stands. It did not surprise her. She had almost expected it.

A small white figure stood on the hillock, staring into the sky.

EBN BON MARI

They commenced a light breakfast on Ebn's balcony when the sun was a finger's breadth above the horizon. Light fare, Ebn had told Pol. Nothing fancy.

A lie. In truth, she had woken two hours before dawn to oversee the preparations.

Blood warm orange and kiwi juices. Rashl eggs and sheep tripe, scrambled with dandelion greens, scallions, and bitter basil. Earling potato and pigskin fritters with hot mustard aioli for dipping. Pomegranate juice cooled with carbonated rosewater ice cubes. Rapeseed oil and mint-filled pastries. Unleavened anisebread topped with crumbled goat cheese, smoked tigerfish, and shaved horseradish. Black wine from the A'Cas Valley. Finally, lefas bean and lemon zest sorbet she herself had made the night before.

Neither spoke while eating. Pol picked at the fritters and pastries, which saddened Ebn, but his obvious enjoyment of the pomegranate juice and anisebread nearly made up for it. Being so easily swayed by his moods annoyed her, but after seven years together there were reactions she had learned to accept.

She tried not to stare at him as they sipped the wine. This, too, she had expected.

He is not so beautiful, she had tried to tell herself many times. He was not the ideal elderman, certainly: too thickly built, too coarsely featured, and all that white hair. On a darkened street, an observer might mistake him for pure human, not a halfbreed at all. In close quarters, of course, one could not fail to notice that his skin was not a shade of brown, but purple. One would not miss his double-irised eyes, which shined as though they had been plucked straight from an elder corpse—a rare trait even among hybrids.

Such distinctions meant little to him. Even on the coldest of days, he wore little clothing, clearly unembarrassed by the two closed fists raised in relief on his pectoral muscles, a mutation which made it appear as if a man were trying to push his fists through Pol's body. Of course, mutations were not rare among eldermen, but few chose to display them. Most, like Ebn, had been encouraged since childhood not to broadcast their unnatural heritage. Amongst their own, they still sought to hide who they were.

Pol had been sixteen when she first saw him. Her hearts had leapt against her sternum to see those fists on display. His pride had bewitched her.

This morning, she kept herself from staring by forcing her gaze outward, over the terracotta roofs of lesser structures. Positioned three-quarters of the way up the purple-bricked Esoteric Arts building, her apartment announced her status to the city. From the balcony one could count the brightly stained sails of His Majesty's Inland Navy, as well as measure the depths of Lake Ten by the varying hues of its bluegreen water.

The view bored and somewhat frightened her, but she pretended interest in order to busy her eyes. Eighty-seven years old, acting like a love-starved youth.

Pol sipped his wine unhurriedly, and Ebn's eyes drifted to the moon. Bone-pale, it sat in the lower quadrant of the quickly brightening sky, unwilling to set for another several hours. Nearly half of the Needle had descended below the horizon. The second largest sphere seemed to rest atop her companion's head. She squinted, trying for the fifth or sixth time that morning to determine if it spun faster than it had the day before.

It did not appear so, at least not to the naked eye. A relief. She hated the days when a change was obvious. She hated the flutter of fear in her veins as she greeted the sky every morning.

Pol set his empty wine glass on the table. "Thank you for that," he said.

She smiled. "There is one more thing." She raised her hand, summoning a servant for the sorbet.

Pol frowned after his first spoonful. "Is this lemon?"

"Yes," Ebn said, cursing mentally. The man could be so finicky.

He pushed the brass goblet forward with his index clawtip, as if it contained something poisonous.

She shrugged. "No matter." She waved the servant forward again.

Pol reclined in his chair, legs stretched out under the table. The side of his foot brushed Ebn's ankle briefly. Like a fool, she inched her calf over until their skins touched lightly. He would not notice, she knew. He was the most preoccupied person she had ever met. Also the most private. His life outside the confines of the Royal Sciences Academy was a complete mystery. Had he friends in the city? He did not seem the type. A lover? Despite their years together, he had never discussed intimacies with her.

He yawned. "I was somewhat disappointed to receive your note yesterday. I was slated for an ascension this morning. Measurements, nothing exciting, but nonetheless . . . You know the feeling, Ebn. A week without looking down upon the world feels like a week wasted."

"Yes, I know the feeling," she said. Outbound mages were loath to miss even one orbital ascension. There were only so many years in their lives, after all. "My apologies for the interruption of your schedule, but I desire your counsel on something. Recently, the changes in the Needle have caused the telescopists some consternation. We have not—"

"What is recently?" he interrupted.

"Several weeks," she lied automatically. It had in fact been over a year of increasingly erratic changes, but he need not know that. "We have not seen variations of this frequency before, both in the speed and direction of the spheres."

"Yes," he said. "I have heard rumors."

She suspected he had. In fact, he probably knew a great deal more than he let on.

"The fact will be announced to the general academy later today," she said.

He smirked and gestured to encompass the campus. "You think they will have an answer to the riddle?"

She smiled wanly but did not rise to the jibe. "We cannot keep this to ourselves."

"Of course we can. We own the telescopes. All information about the Needle is filtered through us. Everything else is myth and foreign hearsay, so easily discounted by the academy. There is no advantage in opening the discussion up. Clearly, the changes reflect a shift in Adrash himself, and finding someone who can explain the god's mind is not possible. We will have as much luck listening to seers proclaim doom in Vaces Square as we will have listening to the responses of the general academy."

She fought the temptation to concede the point. Perhaps unavoidably, he had absorbed a great deal of her cynicism. At the same time, he had not yet come to grasp the reality of academy politics: Concessions had to be made in order to achieve one's goals.

"We need funding for further research," she said. "And the best way to acquire funds is to reveal a problem that must be solved."

"If you have already decided, why am I here?"

She touched his hand lightly. "I agree with you that Adrash's will cannot be known unless he himself announces it. I also do not want to assume the changes reflect hostility, but we must assume they do. Thus, the only thing we can change is our approach to Adrash. Before the noise of the academy's panic fills my head, I want to discuss this fact. Speak freely."

A smile just touched the corners of Pol's mouth. He had always spoken freely.

"We must be more aggressive in our supplication."

She waited, but he had said all he intended to say.

"I disagree," she said.

They nodded to one another, expressions blank. It had been a year since they had last discussed their positions. She had hoped his would change over time, but it was only hope. In truth, her intention in talking with him had not been to exchange views, but to inform him of the decision she had already made. That she, Captain of the Royal Outbound Mages, needed to talk around the issue instead of dealing with it directly angered her.

Fortunately, he could read her quite well.

He sighed. "Tell me what plan you have concocted."

‡

After Pol left, Ebn squirted a solution of reconstituted elder semen and menstrual fluid into her womb. Five hours later, she had nearly reached the end of her spell-casting.

Naked, knees spread to the noon sun, she reclined on a chaise a servant had carried onto the balcony. At the juncture of her long, slender thighs, the fingers of her right hand caressed a blood-red flower. She moaned softly, in time to the waves of pleasure spreading through her body. The muscles of her stomach bunched and released. Her buttocks lifted from the cushion, fell back.

No one could see her from the apartments above, for she had erected a visibility barrier.

Her skin was the exact color and texture of eggplant, and far hotter to the touch than a human's. Veins slightly darker than her skin, nearly black, spiderwebbed and branched over the sinuous lines of her body, which was hard and angular. Like most eldermen, her mouth was small, her teeth sharp. Unlike most eldermen, her eyes were emerald rather than amber, her hair just a shade lighter than black. Her variation was not as extreme as Pol's, but it did cause the occasional second glance.

Many thought her quite beautiful.

She closed her eyes. The sunlight caught and refracted in the fine transparent down that covered her body, causing her skin to shimmer as though it were wet. She did not in fact sweat, and like a desert cat avoided touching water to her skin.

Her moans became louder as she neared orgasm, and her hand descended so that it lay flat against her clitoris. The tongue in the center of her palm lapped hungrily, and she began to gasp. Her left hand, encased as it nearly always was in a black glove, rose from the cushion. She bit a clawtip, pulled the glove off, and spat it to the floor. The tongue in this palm emerged and began licking her left nipple. The small, toothless mouth it had emerged from suckled but made no noise. The tendons of her neck stood out. A sliver of emerald flashed from behind her eyelids and disappeared. As the pleasure increased, her hips rose from the chaise completely.

A line of clear fluid dripped from underneath her right hand and fell on the cushion, where it hardened almost immediately, puckering into a clear pebble. It rolled off and onto the balcony, where a great many more were scattered.

She screamed. The sound fell somewhere between a dog's bark and a seagull's cry. No one heard it, for she had erected a sound barrier.

"Pol," she moaned as she wound down.

The arch of her body collapsed. She panted, ribs standing out on her whip-thin frame. Her breasts bobbed high and tight on her chest. Now that her hands' work was done, she balled them into fists, forcing the tongues back into their mouths and fighting a vague sense of nausea. Absently, she reached to the floor, hand still clenched, using the claws of index finger and thumb to retrieve the glove.

She pulled it on and rested a moment. Then she began to cast her spell again.

‡

She could replay the fantasy in great detail, for much of it had actually occurred. Sixty years previously, during a routine solo ascension to the moon, she had tried to seduce Adrash. Time had not made the fact of her transgression any easier to confront, yet the memory had its use. Desire of that magnitude—hunger that compelled one forward, even to the point of destruction—created a uniquely efficacious mental state for casting a spell of compulsion. Of course, she had altered the memory so that it veered from history at the right moment, ending in satisfaction rather than violence.

As she relaxed, the sounds of the city below gradually faded away, replaced by the nothingness of the void. It flooded her mind, cold beyond reason. The world of her fantasy rippled into focus, materialized into existence.

The moon's fractured surface rushed by underneath her, less than a stone's throw distant. It seemed to reach for her, drag her down. Adrash floated above her, the plain, graceful geometry of his body half in shadow. With his eyes closed, the divine armor covered him completely.

They were alone.

She shivered with fear. Though the outboud mages and their telescopists had observed the god immobile many times, Ebn did not know how she had managed to approach him unaware. Perhaps, she reasoned, he had lost himself in meditation or entered into a state of hibernation to conserve energy. Many academics believed that even someone as powerful as Adrash could not survive easily in the void.

Or perhaps, Ebn said to herself, *he has led me here on purpose.*

No, a more prudent part of her whispered. *You are here to observe, nothing more. Flee before you bring destruction upon yourself!*

She ignored the voice of reason. Knowing the act to be pure madness, she cast a spell of protection around Adrash's body, a bubble of breathable atmosphere, and joined hers to it, shuddering as the temperature dropped precipitously. Such spells never joined perfectly, always allowing a bit of the void in.

She raised the heat immediately, and cautiously floated closer to the god, drawn toward perfection beyond mortal comprehension. Here was an attraction beyond any she had felt before, beyond what she would later experience with Pol. The intensity of her compulsion felt dangerous, as though she were standing on the edge of a cliff. The tongues in her palms stirred, pushing at the fabric of her gloves.

She reached forward and stopped. She had no desire to touch Adrash with a barrier between them. The skin of her thighs and throat tingled.

Undressing was a laborious process, as the suit she wore had been designed for traveling the void, protecting its wearer in the event of a brief spell failure. All of one piece and black, sectioned like armor and tattooed with brown sigils, it came off her body like an insect's shed skin. Her eyes stayed fixed on Adrash as she pulled slowly free.

Her body was chalked in a unique bonedust blend—ground elder bone, sinew and skin, an extra precaution against the void: she had not become an expert mage due to genius, but thoroughness. Opening her fists, she allowed the mouths in her palms to open, her tongues to taste the trapped air.

Adrash had not stirred. He might as well have been a statue of white stone. He glowed in the light of the sun, brighter than the moon in the sky. She traced the outline of one heavy pectoral muscle with her left index claw before finding the nerve to lay the back of her hand against it. The surface of the divine armor was cool, only slightly colder than a man's skin but infinitely smoother. Flawless. The muscle underneath gave to pressure just as it should.

In every way he was her opposite. Thickly muscled rather than wiry, pale rather than dark, unlined rather than mapped in vein. They shared height, and that was all, she being somewhat short for an elderwoman, he somewhat tall for a man.

Her right hand went to her womanhood.

He failed to react to her tentative caress, so she moved closer, running her palm and its tongue over his smooth scalp, the contours of his body. He tasted clean, like water or snow. She avoided the prominent bulge of his genitals for a time, but eventually temptation overcame her. She ran her hand down the ridges of his belly and cupped his testicles, allowing the tongue to lick along his confined length. She closed her eyes and moaned.

Here, if she had been truly remembering rather than fantasizing, Adrash would wake. The light of his eyes would blind her and his voice would roar in her mind, flooding her, pressing against the inside of her skull until the blood ran from her ears. Then, moving faster than sight could follow, his fingers would be around her neck . . .

She turned from such thoughts with practiced ease and continued. He became hard under her caresses, but could not break free from the skin of his armor. His length stayed pressed against his testicles under the smooth barrier.

Like anyone, as a child Ebn had been educated about Adrash. *Nothing is impossible for him*, the tutors had told her. *He can split the ocean and walk around the world. He can stop the moon in the sky.* He could do all of these things, but in her fantasy he could not break free of embrace of the divine armor.

His entrapment excited her. He still had not opened his eyes, had not moved his arms or legs. Touching herself, she wrapped her legs around his, heels tight below his firm buttocks. She placed both hands on his chest and ground herself into his erection. She kissed the faint outline of his mouth, and slowly it responded—so slowly that at first she believed herself to be imagining it. His lips warmed, became hot. They parted and her tongue met his. He tasted of cinnamon and anise. His arms encircled her waist.

She opened her eyes.

Adrash had become Pol. He stared at her with two sets of pupils, and the corners of his mouth twitched. His hands fell to grip her hips. Her hearts beat off rhythm as she guided his length into her.

She screamed.

‡

For sixty years, two decades longer than most eldermen lived, Ebn had rented a closet-sized room in the southern wing of the Academy of Applied Magics library. Its single window looked out on three academy rooftops liberally covered in pigeon droppings. Beyond these, humble, single-storey buildings carpeted the broad eastern valley floor. Not a river or lake in sight.

She preferred the office to her sumptuous apartment, just as she preferred oil lamps to alchemical candelabras. Here she had built shelves that covered the walls, filling them with every important book she owned. Cracked-spined novels and pornographic picture books mingled with esoteric texts on religion and the magics. Two shelves buckled under the weight of her most prized possession: the twenty-seven volume *Historig Jerung,* Ponmargel's survey of mankind's recorded and fabled antiquity. Twenty-four millennia of history, nearly two hundred pounds of text. She had read it through only once.

From the ceiling hung her favorite models. An airship she had built as a child, struts showing through a thin sheepskin gasbag. An elephant-drawn carriage. The twelve known planets, spinning lazily around an orange sun.

Knickknacks collected during a long career lined the windowsill. Presents from associates and mementoes from travel, mostly.

Papers littered her desk and gathered dust in piles. A half circle of clear area remained, though it too was busy with ink blotches and compass scratches.

She had built a hinged bed that secured against the wall under her desk. Seven days out of nine she slept here, even though it was a mere five-minute walk to her apartment. Certainly, she loved close spaces and the smell of books, but her preference was based more upon the position of the office than its interior. The Needle crossed the upper portion of the window for a mere nine days in the Month of Sawyers. The rest of the year it sailed clear over.

Experience proved that if she saw it too often her optimism failed her. It became impossible to deny the obvious any longer: A string of steel cages large enough to affect the tides was not an ornament. It was a threat of annihilation.

Of course, the inhabitants of the world knew this as well, but they had the luxury of ignorance, of self-deception. They prayed to Adrash for redemption and fought wars of faith, believing their efforts had an effect, all the while succored into a false sense of security by the Needle's apparent immutability. Despite its fluctuations—and time had turned even the Cataclysm into a minor fluctuation, a myth—it had extended across the sky for fifty generations. It had become fact, passed down mankind's generations. For all their words of doom, few believed in the threat of actual destruction.

Ebn knew better. She had experienced Adrash's wrath firsthand, and only escaped it by a miracle. Allowed to approach him while he slept—a miracle in and of itself—she had been spared to do the work of proving the world's worth.

This responsibility weighed upon her. She considered her weaknesses, and wondered if she might not be overcome by temptation a second time. Surely, she had lived life fearful that someone would repeat her mistake. For fear of bringing ruin upon them all, she had assured that no outbound mage ventured too close to Adrash.

For decades, this cautiousness had seemed a virtue, but age had brought with it doubt. Perhaps, she reasoned, she had hobbled her mages to keep them away from the god. Perhaps she had merely been biding her time, waiting for another opportunity.

At night, she dreamt of surviving the death of the world with Adrash at her side.

‡

Ebn allowed only one person to meet her regularly in the office. Qon et Gal, her second-in-command, had been her friend since the age of six. For forty years Ebn had shared her age-nullifying treatment, a unique alteration to the standard alchemical solution developed by her predecessor, with Qon alone.

Growing old, Ebn joked, would be awful without someone to share the indignity.

Qon rolled one of the clear pebbles Ebn's spell had produced between her clawtips. She held it close to her nose and sniffed. Her eyes narrowed.

"No," she said. "I have never seen one, but I have heard of it. Apparently, sex spells require a fine touch to produce the desired effect." She eyed the full clay jar. "How long have you been working on these?"

Ebn shrugged, cheeks darkening almost imperceptibly as she blushed. "A year, approximately. I can only do it every couple of weeks, it tires me so much. Before beginning, I studied and practiced for several months."

Qon's eyebrows rose ever so slightly. "Poor you."

"Shut up," Ebn said good-naturedly. "I talked with Pol over breakfast."

"Ah." Qon's expression did not change, though she knew of her friend's attraction. She had voiced her low opinion of Pol many times, speaking honestly as a true friend should. "It was as you expected?"

"Yes."

"And these?" Qon nodded at the jar. "You intend to seduce him, then sway him to your viewpoint?"

Ebn sighed. "You think that little of me? No. I have already talked with him. He does not see our perspective, but he understands my command: Adrash must not be approached by any one mage. Making our intention clear is dependent on everyone acting in concert." A brief memory of her hands on the god's flanks flashed through her mind. "Even then we do not know what may offend him."

Qon nodded, silent. Ebn knew her lieutenant did not take the explanation at face value. She would not come out and ask if Ebn intended to seduce Pol, but undoubtedly she wondered. If Ebn did manage to seduce Pol—an act she had dreamt many times but could hardly conceive of doing—all speculation would cease. In fact, Qon would probably congratulate her.

Ebn picked up a spell, rolled it between her palms. "I have been producing these with no clear intention in mind. Talking with Pol this morning gave me an idea, however. I think we can use them to show our goodwill to Adrash."

"Are you sure this is wise?"

Spent, Ebn smiled without feeling. "No. I am not sure it is wise. But if you will sit with me I will try to explain. Maybe we can work the kinks out together."

POL TANZ ET SOM

T he taste of lemon lingered, cloying in his mouth. He prepared a heavily spiced lunch on his own and ate it over a collection of stamped forms, struggling not to let anger overtake him. Fourteen separate requisitions for alchemicals, denied in the last month.

Clipped to the final form was a note from the department bursar:

Pol Tanz et Som, M.O.: Due to the ever-rising prices of the elder corpse market, we must reject the additional alchemicals you have herein requested. Perhaps in the future, your research will warrant an expenditure of this magnitude.

You are invited, as always, to make use of recycled materials in the faculty labs.

Recycled materials! Drained, lusterless ampoules of spent magic, barely suitable for the most basic of spells! Apparently, the administration expected him to do advanced research with fingernail clippings and candle wax. Maybe they thought prayer alone could sustain him.

Pol wondered if he could bring himself to ask a senior mage for assistance.

No. He possessed little stomach for begging favors from his peers, and such eldermen were likely to report his more esoteric undertakings to Ebn. At times, he felt as if she had persuaded the entire corps to watch him. Even the most conservative of his recent proposals had been met with suspicion. Some of the junior mages expressed interest in his theories, of course, but the junior mages were powerless and thus easily manipulated. They would spy on him to advance their careers.

You are too young to be so ambitious. Wait your turn.

He brushed the forms into the trash with the gnawed ostrich anklebones. He absently popped a gingersalt candy in his mouth and considered the problem. By its very nature, the academy did not cater to new thinking, and in the ranks of outbound mages the effect was even worse. He would need to take an unconventional tack if he had any chance of acquiring what he needed to resume his research and weaken Ebn's position.

A more diplomatic approach, she had said. Ridiculous.

He left the apartment, not yet sure where he was going. The hallways were nearly empty. A quick spell, no more than a brief automatic query, gave him the time: thirty-three minutes past two. That explained it. Lunch and catnaps in the slanting sun. Eldermen were adept at many things, but afternoons were not one of them.

Pol himself felt the pull of a full stomach and sunbath, but the energy of youth sustained him. At twenty-three, his constitution was at its most agreeable. As a boy, it had seemed forever would come and go before his body would respond to his wishes. Then again, without the age-nullifying treatments that came with high rank in the academy, in ten years he would be an old man.

His thoughts, ever in movement, veered from one possibility to the next. Did he know anyone in requisitions? No. Archaeology? Geology? No. No one in the churches would help him, he felt sure—and their security was tighter than all other departments combined, their oaths the most binding. One could never underestimate their magics, either.

If Pol needed further proof of his desperation, the fact that he considered thievery sufficed.

Suddenly, a possibility presented itself to him. He did know someone in the medicines department, a young man whom he had bedded for a brief time several years previously. A human, beautiful in a thick way, not all that precocious but eager to please. A dark-haired Castan. He worked in the morgue. They had rutted on an examination table, once.

Jorrin? No. Jarres. That was the name. He had confessed to Pol that some of his mates filtered alchemical juices from the human and elderman corpses in their custody. They had made quite a bit of money this way.

Pol left the Esoteric Arts building and angled toward the White Ministry Hospital.

‡

The Avenue of Saints honored those who had died defending the name and nature of Adrash. Statues of men and women, eldermen and human, lined the avenue as it wound through the academy grounds. It was the end of summer, and the vala trees had bloomed copper and purple. Arching over the roadway, they created a perpetual twilight in which the saints took on a sinister bearing.

Evertin The Belligerent appeared ready to jump from his marble base and start hacking away with his greatsword, which scholars claimed he had called Harrowing. Domas Alastetl rested wearily on her throne, a great wound in her side, face so cunningly carved it seemed to move as one passed. And Oilo The Ghost hovered above his plinth of skulls and weapons, a fluid, ferocious form barely recognizable as human.

At the intersection of the Avenue of Saints and Villus Street, the exact center of the academy grounds, stood a statue of Adrash. Pol made a point to visit it every day, for it represented the god during wartime, in his most awful aspect—this, and it reminded Pol of home, where the iconography displayed a harsher edge than in the capitol.

Carved from a block of unveined black granite, the sublimely proportioned god stood prepared to meet an enemy. At first glance his posture seemed to convey an odd calm, but close examination revealed the tension in his neck and shoulders, the flexion of his forearms. His feet rested upon a base designed to look like a sphere of the Needle. Its rims disappeared into the ground and roadway.

The sculptor had dripped molten red gold onto Adrash's heavily muscled torso and arms: the blood of men and beasts. The god's left arm and portions of his chest and back had been carved from white marble, and the join between black and white was a sinuous line, showing that the divine armor had begun to sheath his body. Yellow gold covered his eyes. But for the armored section he was naked. The sculptor had endowed him with assets befitting a god.

Pol's eyes lingered on this detail for a few seconds. Pressing his left fist to his forehead, he bowed deeply before moving on.

He had not always believed in Adrash's benevolence. What he mirrored as a child could hardly be called faith, and what he rejected as a youth could not be called informed. He had felt as if his mother were forcing him to believe. For many years he had transferred his frustration onto Adrash, who became in his mind a bully of monumental proportions.

When he left his mother's conservative Adrashism for the academy, he carried some of these sentiments with him. A sixteen-year-old boy, elderman or human, could not be expected to recognize his own arrogance for what it was—especially when that boy had recently arrived from Pusta, the Kingdom of Stol's exclave on the coast of Knos Min, a virtual world away from the capitol. The boy's blind arrogance could be a shield against the prejudice of his peers, who thought him a backwater fool.

Quickly adapting to their fighting style, Pol learned showing mercy came back to bite more often than not. So he stopped showing mercy. By the age of eighteen, he had killed seven men in self-defense and fought eleven duels. He became known for his temper and skill, as well as his genius in the magics.

He did not defend the reactionary beliefs of his youth or the people of Pusta, both of which he had long since come to view with amused disdain. Instead, he railed against the rote pronouncements of his teachers and peers, the mindless repetition of dogma. His own faith became a thing of fire and muscle. Adrash would not look kindly upon a weak people, sitting in contemplation, asking for his favor. The god, Pol came to believe, responded to strength. He did not want followers, but leaders.

The Avenue of Saints ended. At Skintree Road, Pol waited for a gilded carriage to pass before crossing the street, though he did not bow to the nobleman or woman inside as strict decorum dictated. An outbound mage, in whose veins elder blood flowed, bowing to an earthbound human? Ludicrous.

Once out of the manicured academy grounds, one could not help notice the change in atmosphere. It stank of human and animal waste, cooking fires, and cheap alchemy. Putrid, human smells, but they bothered Pol not at all. He had become used to the fragrances during his frequent trips out.

You take too many risks, Ebn had told him on more than one occasion. Typical of the outbound mages, she rarely traveled into the city, and never alone. Attacks on eldermen, even in the clear light of day, were not uncommon. But for ascensions into orbit, several of the senior mages had not left the academy in decades.

Pol refused to restrict himself so. Urban Tansot offered a range of products and services unavailable within the confines of institutionalized academia. Inevitably, many experiences had ceased to compel him—drugs, in particular, became superfluous as he grew into his magical talent—but sex had not. Partners were for the taking if an elderman knew where to look.

He reached the hospital, a clean, austere building that contrasted sharply with its dilapidated neighbors—a common sight in Apetia, the most culturally and economically diverse neighborhood in Tansot. Technically part of the academy, White Ministry benefited from its patronage as well as the city's. Its grounds were immaculately maintained, to Pol's eyes somewhat overdone. A stereotypical Stoli statue of Adrash, farcically epic and devoid of personality, stood in the front entrance courtyard.

Pol walked past it without a glance.

‡

Jarres had grown a thick beard that did not flatter him and acquired several pounds of muscle that did. His chest strained against the white medicines tunic, and despite his serious intentions Pol found himself mildly aroused. Nothing like an old lover to tempt a man from his course, he knew.

In his estimation of himself, Pol had one major weakness.

"Tanz?" Jarres asked, eyes moving down Pol's body. "How long's it been, mate? God, what, two years? You look good."

Pol smiled. He had forgotten how raggedly the man spoke. Medicine, more than most magics, did not require a surplus of intelligence. The body was relatively simple, after all. During their affair, Pol had picked up more than a passing knowledge of medicines from Jarres—a fact that probably accounted for the relationship's dissolution. Medical mages guarded their trade secrets every bit as jealously as other disciples of magic.

Pol clasped Jarres's forearms and kissed his cheeks. "Almost three years, Eamon." Thank Adrash the other man had spoken his name first. Pol had forgotten that in public Jarres preferred to use second names: the convention in Weas, the city of Jarres's upbringing. "You look well yourself. You have certainly filled out."

Jarres laughed, squeezing Pol's forearms in return. His teeth flashed, straight and white, contrasting with the heavy darkness of his beard. Laugh lines had deepened alongside his nose, around his light blue eyes. Pol remembered why he had been so attracted to the man, and reconsidered his stance on the beard.

They disengaged somewhat awkwardly, and Jarres looked Pol up and down again, one eyebrow quirked.

"Why are you here?" he asked.

Blunt as well as ragged, Pol recalled. Yet it was oddly refreshing after his meeting with Ebn.

"I am here to ask a favor. Have you a place where we can talk? Somewhere private?"

A smile fought to reach Jarres's mouth, and won. He closed his eyes for a moment and then said, "My shift is over in eighteen minutes."

‡

Exhausted, they lay together on Jarres's bed. Pol had thrown a leg over the man's thigh, but felt otherwise content to dry alone. Unlike most eldermen, Pol enjoyed the feeling of fluid on his skin. Large bodies of water made him uncomfortable and he did not enjoy swimming, but the occasional bath was nice. Sweat was nicer. A uniquely human smell, sweat. He had come to appreciate it in the same way he had come to appreciate the smell of lake water.

Jarres blew a stream of pipe smoke at the ceiling. "Now that we're relaxed, let's have the truth. You've got a great many men to choose from in this city, which means you're here for something other than a simple fuck."

"True," Pol conceded. "I am. Do you remember when you talked about the black market with me? You had a friend."

Jarres turned his head away from Pol. "Yeah, I remember all right. They let Kolin go, Espe nearly went to jail, and I had to talk before the head surgeons—was forced to defend myself when I'd done nothing wrong. If you're looking for that sort of thing, I think you better look someplace else. Thanks for the lay, but I can't help."

"I'm not asking you to start up a business, Eamon." Pol laid a hand on Jarres's lean stomach. "I need a few things only. Me. I need them. No one else will know what we are doing and no one knows how much alchemy the corpses have in their veins until you mark it down. You could do it. You said it yourself." He inched his hand downward slowly. "Or were you just bragging?"

Jarres groaned—not in pleasure, but frustration. A bit more pushing and he would relent, Pol thought. He felt confident in his ability to reduce simple men to formulae, spells to be cast and then molded. His clawtips moved lightly through Jarres's thatch of pubic hair. The man's cock shifted, began to swell.

"I will be honest with you," Pol said. "My research is at a standstill, and I have no friends at the academy. I cannot afford to pay you much, but you will have my gratitude."

Jarres chuckled, and pushed Pol's hands the final inch.

"Just your gratitude, huh?" he asked.

Pol smiled. "This is how I show my gratitude. But you need to do this per my instructions, Jarres. I need specific things."

Jarres flexed his hips and sighed, this time with pleasure. "Yah, I can do that, I suppose. You have a list?"

"I will write it out for you afterward. I know you must be careful not to arouse suspicion, but the faster you do this for me the more grateful I will be."

"Understood," Jarres said. He yawned and stretched out under Pol's ministrations, clearly enjoying himself. "When you're finished there, how about celebrating our new arrangement? Visit the docks, see a fight like old times?"

Pol considered. It had been some time since he had seen a fight, and even longer since he had seen a good one. The docksides attracted the best. Still, there was work to be done. Planning.

Before he could answer, Jarres spoke. "You've heard of Shav? No. He's a quarterstock they've got fighting tonight. A close cousin of yours, maybe."

Pol stopped considering instantly. He would go. He had never seen an elderman's offspring, and knew no one who had. Though elder sperm fertilized any species' egg, the product of the coupling was seldom fertile. On the rare occasion that it was, its offspring suffered extreme birth defects. This quarterstock Jarres spoke of was possibly such a one. Most likely, the whole thing was a hoax, but it could not be ignored on that basis alone.

Pol wondered why he had heard nothing of it. Academy biologists estimated the world population of eldermen to be less than one hundred thousand. They were expensive and risky to gestate, but highly valued for their magical facility. Surely the living child of one would be of interest.

Or perhaps even some use.

‡

The walk from Jarres's apartment took them through two of the roughest neighborhoods in the eastern quarter of the city.

Composed of southern Ulomi and western Castan immigrants respectively, the populations of Donsiter and Torn would not brook the other's existence. Tansot's governors had on several occasions begun campaigns to turn the tide of sectarian violence, but to no avail. With the support of the city's conservative Adrashi churches, the Ulomi of Donsiter were slowly gaining the advantage over their atypically militant Castan neighbors.

This did not make Donsiter any safer. Though its denizens strutted outwardly, inwardly they feared Torn's increasingly desperate acts. More than this, perhaps, they feared being in the churches' debt. The churches would remember and extract two grams of bonedust for every gram spent in assistance. In fact, they had already begun. The church soldiers stationed in Donsiter took what they pleased.

Torn, on the other hand, had peopled itself with criminals, men and women the seniors of the community hired to help wage their war. Murderers and thieves, out-of-work and disgraced soldiers of the Tomen border, Anadrashi reformists and scrabbling gladiators, all of whom took the money offered to them and caused trouble. The streets became a place to air one's grievances with one's fist or weapon.

After dark, a man took his life in his hands if he walked the streets of either neighborhood with less than two men at his side.

Pol and Jarres armed themselves accordingly. Pol carried his hand-carved liisau, a seven-foot tall ironwood staff tipped with a foot-long dagger blade and butted with steel. He had designed the weapon to suit his unique fighting style, which blended the staff arts common to eastern Knoori and the many bladed styles of Pusta.

Jarres carried nothing so exotic. Holstered over his left shoulder was a compound crossbow, an ugly little quickdraw that had probably cost him a week's salary. Castans were famously skeptical of magic and the reliance on magic, often arming themselves with muscle-powered arms rather than the more common alchemical varieties. At his right hip swung a vazhe, a short, heavy broadsword held in contempt by nearly all Stoli swordsmen. *Better for chopping wood,* they claimed, glossing over the fact that vazhe-wielding Castans had kept Stol out of their border for nearly seven hundred years.

Pol's staff-end rang hollowly on the hard-packed earth. He refused to slink in the shadows like an animal, and had not asked the other man's opinion. Jarres did not appear overly discomfited by this.

Though he would not admit so, Pol found himself wishing for a confrontation. He had restrained his anger with Ebn. He had been patient with Jarres. He could not be otherwise, for his plans depended on Ebn's ignorance and Jarres's assistance, but the acts would never be enjoyable. Now, he wanted release.

Unfortunately, no one presented him with an opportunity. The night was quiet but for the rustling of scrawny sycamore trees lining the roadway. Before very long they arrived at Docksides Boxing, a large, low-roofed building on a floating platform at the end of two stationary docks. They stopped at the entrance to one, where a doorman waited under a single torchlight.

Pol became impatient as the sunken-eyed man held their entrance fee, a half-gram bag of dust, open under his nose. *As if the man could discern anything with such dull senses*, Pol thought. Academy studies revealed that most of the bonedust used as payment in the city tested below forty percent pure. Ground sheep bone was the most common filler. If properly trained, an elderman could smell the difference. A human? Never.

Jarres became impatient as well. "Satisfied?" he asked the doorman, whose skin looked like wrinkled parchment in the flickering light.

The doorman shrugged. "Suppose so. Smells okay. But this ain't enough."

"Not enough?" Jarres shook his head. "Put it on the scale."

Pol grinned at the doorman's expression. It was a serious insult, asking a money handler to weigh dust. The doorman spat at Jarres's feet and then dropped the waxpaper bag on the scale on the stool beside him.

"I told you," he said. "Half a gram. Not enough."

Jarres laughed, but there was a definite edge to it. "The entry has always been half a gram. What are you trying to pull?"

"Not tonight, it ain't half a gram." The doorman folded the bag and held it out so that Jarres could either take it or add to it. "Tonight's one whole, on account of the quarterstock we rustled up. Idiot's fighting that bitch Stasessun everybody loves. She's gonna kill him for sure. Biggest fight in a long time. So, one gram. Pay or leave."

Pol took out a thin leather wallet. "Here," he said, handing the doorman another bag. "Half a gram of pure, and if you insult me by smelling it I will probably murder you where you stand."

The doorman looked unimpressed and started to open the bag. Pol stepped into the cone of torchlight and leaned forward, forcing the man to look into his eyes.

"Shit," the doorman said, backing against the light pole. "Okay. Okay. I don't need to smell it. Don't touch me, please."

Pol straightened, pretending shock. "Surely, you do not think I want to?"

Jarres clapped him on the back and they entered Docksides Boxing. The tension in Pol's shoulders began to ebb away as the smells reached him. Sawdust. Blood.

Sweat.

‡

The quarterstock Shav was not a hoax. Pol had caught glimpses of him through the crowd before the main fight began. Rolling his immense scarred shoulders, loosening his bullish neck.

In most ways, he seemed the perfect compromise between human and elderman. His skin was lustrous, a rich lavender hue, and Pol could see a fine sheen of sweat on his brow. Well over six feet tall, he must have weighed close to four hundred pounds. Thick slabs of muscle hid the slight skeletal and ligamentary anomalies of his build, but he stood with a slight forward tilt like an elderman, as if he were always on the balls of his feet. Any half-competent anatomist would be able to identify the subtle differences at first glance.

His copper hair was trimmed to stubble and his features were thicker, softer than an elderman's. No sign of physical retardation marred his face.

One detail alone surprised Pol: two stubby horns sprouted high on either side of Shav's forehead.

The victor of the last fight, still swaying unsteadily, announced the main event.

"Stasessun!" many in the crowd chanted. It grew as more picked up the call.

A tall, coffee-skinned woman of ambiguous ethnicity, heavily tattooed and clad in simple gauze wrappings, stepped from the crowd. Pol could tell from her walk alone that she would be a formidable opponent. Her limbs were thin blades of muscle and bone.

The whistle sounded. She came out fast and strong, swarming around the lumbering Shav, who ducked his head into two meaty fists and took the onslaught of jabs and knee thrusts. He did not attempt to fight back, and the crowd laughed. They clearly thought the fight a washout, the quarterstock a moron. At the end of round one, he looked flushed but unhurt. Stasessun rolled her eyes, and sat facing away from him in her corner.

She started taunting him in the second round. She spat, cursed, and laughed, all the while taking carefully placed potshots at his ears and shins. Most of the crowd laughed with her, but a few held back. Late in the round, having taken her abuse without fighting back for almost three minutes, Shav launched a slow but well-timed cross that glanced off Stasessun's temple and sent her staggering. She snarled and came forward, landing a few rapid blows before the whistle sounded.

"I'm impressed," Jarres told Pol. "I've seen only a few men go past the second round with her."

Shav smiled as he walked to his corner. He bled from multiple cuts around his ears. Bruises pocked his forearms and shins. A few in the crowd crossed to his corner to offer words of encouragement. Stasessun's fans looked on in annoyance. The mood had taken a turn.

The third round began. Stasessun came forward, unsmiling. She hopped from side to side as the quarterstock watched from between his fists, the unmistakable glint of calculation in his eyes. Her first punch got through, landed square on his chin. He shook it off but did not recover in time to block the two kicks that followed, landing on either thigh. He grunted and watched her, taking hits.

By this point the crowd was subdued. They watched Shav, and waited.

The moment came. Stasessun moved in close, following a right jab with a left shovel hook to Shav's temple. He caught her fist halfway to its target and, quicker than Pol would have thought possible, caught her under the chin with an uppercut—a gracefully fluid move that lifted her off her feet.

The sound of bone breaking was clear and distinct in the silence.

She landed on the floor, neck clearly broken. Her life bubbled from her lips.

Shav tipped his head to either side, vertebrae popping loudly.

After a short pause, the crowd erupted. Pol yelled with them, cares for the moment forgotten. Men jostled against him, unconcerned that he was elderman and they human. Someone slapped his backside and he did not turn to see who had done it. He pictured Ebn there with him, back to back with the rabble, and laughed out loud. She would never understand the allure of violence, the intoxicating feeling of forcing another to submit.

"Hey!" Jarres yelled in his ear. "You want something to drink?"

"Yes," Pol answered immediately. The response surprised him. When had he last been intoxicated in public? A year? Two? No matter. Surely Adrash would approve a sacrament in his honor. In return, he would bless Pol with wine and song and violence—perhaps even a new friend in the struggle to come.

"Yes," he repeated, peering over the crowd to locate Shav. He had no intention of letting the quarterstock disappear without introducing himself. "I will definitely have a drink."

PART TWO

PART TWO

VEDAS TEZUL

The Castan Badlands lay beyond Nbena, the fifteenth gate in Dareth Hlum's five-hundred-mile-long defensive wall of Dalan Fele. Since very few had business in the badlands and no one traveled to the region for pleasure, most of the routes leading from the capitol to Nbena were ill maintained. Many could be dangerous to the unprepared traveler.

Roads that had long ago become footpaths climbed over the Turilen Mountains and crumbled into the Puzzle Sinklands. Cannibal tribes, descendants of Castan infantrymen who fought in the Third Autumnal War, preyed upon the unwary traveler in the Unes Forest. Though a few villages survived off the minimal trade closer to the gate, their people lived in fear of raiders who came from out of the scrubland. Child slaves moved through Nbena like water through loosely stacked rocks, and none of Dareth Hlum's governments had been able to put a stop to it.

Vedas and Berun took a winding, eleven-day route to the badlands gate, averaging just short of twenty miles a day. Though the pace did not tax Vedas overmuch, it took several nights to become accustomed to sleeping under open sky, and even longer to accept the reality of travel rations. His stomach grumbled constantly. He measured the fullness of his biceps and thighs, trying to gauge the extent of muscle loss day by day. Perhaps the twenty pounds he had gained in anticipation of Danoor would be insufficient.

Largely out of a feeling of obligation, for several days he attempted to engage Berun in conversation. The constructed man had little to say on the subject of fighting and war, however—little to say, period. When he did speak, he seemed sullen, as though resentful of Vedas's presence. In an odd way, Vedas sympathized. He had not wanted a traveling companion either, but Abse had insisted.

Thus it was a relief to shrug off the burden of communication, and Vedas wondered if walking in silence would soon come to feel like walking alone.

Five days out from Golna, having seen no trace of raiders or cannibals, he began thinking Abse had exaggerated the perilousness of their route across the nation. He began to hope a peaceful journey would ease the memory of Julit Umeda's death.

This proved not to be the case. Far from the centers of law, violence found them.

Two men ambushed them as they rose on the sixth morning near the lakeside town of Adres. Vedas met the first, slapping the clumsy sword-thrust aside with his palm and jamming suit-stiffened fingers into the man's temple, knocking him unconscious. Berun ignored the axe thrown by the second. It clanged harmlessly off his brass shoulder as he threw one of the stones he carried into the bandit's face, lifting the man off his feet and killing him instantly.

"That was unnecessary," Vedas said.

Berun shrugged. "They intended to kill us. They would have killed others."

The bandits wore identical silver necklaces, from which hung a golden pendant in the shape of a fist. Though valuable and by rights the victors', Vedas refused to remove them.

"They're Adrashi symbols," he explained to Berun.

"What harm would it do to take them?" the constructed man countered.

"None. But I won't dirty my hands with the task."

On the seventh day, a woman appeared on a narrow pass between the Sawback Mesas and broke a spell before them, rooting their feet in the mountain itself. Quicker than Vedas could have imagined, Berun decoupled the spheres below his ankles and jumped free. By the time he landed, his feet had fully formed. He swept the woman into the rock wall. She rebounded, and then crumpled to the ground. To free Vedas, Berun pulverized the rock around his feet. Vedas's suit stiffened under the blows, shielding him from injury but for a broken toe.

The woman bled liberally from a shallow wound above her ear, but appeared otherwise uninjured. Vedas tore a strip of cloth from her voluminous robes and wrapped it tightly around her head.

Berun lifted the leather pack from her shoulder and searched it. In addition to a pouch of dried meat and a solid ball of catgut, she had carried with her twelve spells, ranging from colorless liquids in ampoules to waterproofed firestarters. The largest was a tiny porcelain jar sealed with wax.

"I won't touch them," Vedas said. The sight of the unknown magic chilled him to the core. "We don't know what they are. Besides, I've heard stories about what happens to men who steal witches' potions."

"I'm not a man," Berun answered. "They must be useful or valuable to someone." He pressed the collection of spells to his thigh. When he took the hand away, they were gone.

Vedas did not want to kill the fourth attacker, an emaciated young man who rushed at him from a barley field deep in the heart of the Wruna Valley. Vedas disarmed him of sickle and rake easily enough, and aimed a knockout blow to his temple. But regardless of what he tried, the boy would not go under. Eventually Vedas noticed the symptoms: dilated pupils, puffy hands, and a white crust at the corners of his mouth.

Dropma Fever, spread through sweat and saliva. Given the appropriate medicines, a full recovery might have been possible, but the closest village was nearly ten miles back along the road, and the young man was in no condition to lead Vedas to a nearby homestead. Possibly, the whole region had become infected.

Fearful of contracting the disease, Vedas would have asked Berun to kill the boy, but the constructed man had run ahead to scout the hilly path before them. Not for the first time, Vedas regretted leaving his staff in Golna. Abse had forbid him to take Order property. A good ironwood staff cost almost as much as a month's provender.

No help for it, Vedas thought. He allowed his suit to mask his face and broke the boy's neck with one blow.

He still stood, fully sheathed in his suit, when Berun came pounding down the road several minutes later.

The constructed man looked from Vedas to the boy and back again. "Why did you do this? And why have you covered your face?"

"The boy was sick. Dropma Fever. I fear I might have contracted it." Vedas held his hands out from his hips, afraid to touch the rest of his body. He possessed little practical knowledge of disease. "I think my suit will protect me, but I won't be sure for a few days."

Berun shrugged, apparently unconcerned.

"I'd like to wash myself," Vedas said. "Did you see any water ahead?"

"A creek runs across the road a few miles from here."

Vedas washed himself as best he could. They began walking again.

Two day later, they crested a rise and saw the three-hundred-foot slopes of Dalan Fele.

Berun appeared unimpressed. He had seen it several times.

Vedas remembered it only dimly from childhood. He breathed shallowly from lungs that felt stuffed with cotton, tried to take in the scope of the wall rising over the tallest trees and disappearing to view on either side, and collapsed.

‡

The memory of being carried, swaying from side to side, cradled in rock-solid arms. The sun in his eyes, then shadow overtaking. A wall stretching above him. The wall falling, rising, falling again, a gigantic door. Two glowing blue orbs, hovering in the air. A cold, brassy voice repeating his name. More voices, yelling, echoing on stone. The whisper of canvas. Warm light suffusing, the world organizing itself. Tent poles. Being laid on a soft surface. Blackness. A new voice.

Focusing on the voice, rising up through layers of pain.

Vedas woke, and found that he could not scream.

"The suit should have protected him," a man told Berun. "That is, if he wore the mask the entire time." He adjusted his spectacles and stared up at the immense man of brass standing silently before him. "Did he wear the mask the entire time?"

"I wasn't there and he didn't tell me," Berun answered. "Can he see us right now?"

The man leaned over Vedas. He filled a tiny plunger on the bedside table and moistened Vedas's eyes. Once opened, they seemed unwilling to close.

"I don't know," the man—a doctor, Vedas belatedly surmised—said.

"Will he die?"

The doctor swallowed and looked down at Vedas again. "I don't know that either. He's still in the intermediate phase of the disease, which is good. Receiving the spell before the fever breaks increases his chances of recovery considerably. If the spell doesn't cure him, though, and his fever breaks, he'll only have a few days before the disease destroys his mind, turning him into an animal. Death will follow soon after."

"Is that why you've bound him?"

The doctor lifted his hand from the leather wrist strap it rested upon. "Yes. I can't predict when the fever will break, it happens so suddenly. He could be dangerous."

Struggling to focus on the conversation, Vedas's mind swam through a fog of heated torment. Every breath was agony, as if someone were holding a live coal against his ribs. The pulse throbbed in his head, a rhythmic pressure that compressed his eyeballs and sinuses. Every muscle in his head and neck ached with tension, and he could not unclench his jaw. His limbs did not pain him, but their numb unresponsiveness was troubling.

He saw the world through thick, milky glass. He could neither move nor close his eyes. When the doctor moistened them, his vision cleared only a little.

"Why haven't you unclothed him?" Berun asked. "Won't he be too hot?"

Vedas's heart threw itself against his sore ribs. He tried to move, to open his mouth or at least moan. He had not removed his suit in two decades. Only his head, anus, and the tip of his penis touched open air. He had heard of others removing their suits from time to time, but the Thirteenth taught that true connection with one's suit could only be achieved through constant contact. The thought of a stranger removing it, touching its inner surface, filled him with rage so strong it sang in his bones.

The doctor sighed. "No. Even though I live in Nbena, I'm not a fool. I used to live in Ulias, where I worked on a number of suited men. I know how elder-cloth works. Look." He laid a hand on Vedas's chest. "Do you feel that? How cold it is?"

Berun scowled. "Hot and cold mean nothing to me."

The doctor cleared his throat. "Ah. Then you'll have to trust me. Your friend has a deep connection with his suit. In a way, it knows what he needs and is trying to provide it to him. Without the suit, I suspect his fever would already have broken. Either that, or he would be dead."

Berun shifted from foot to foot, the spheres of his body whispering against each other. "You won't let him die."

"I have very little say in the matter," the doctor said. "And you haven't paid me."

An odd sound, like marbles being rubbed together in a child's hand, came from within Berun's body. A moment later, a box composed of small spheres emerged from his stomach. He plucked it free and it collapsed in his hand, revealing a collection of multicolored bags. He selected one and passed it over Vedas's body to the doctor.

The man held the bag up to the skylight. "This is good for half."

Berun selected another. "I thought I was being generous with the first."

The doctor met the constructed man's stare. "That was generous last year."

"You won't let him die," Berun said again.

The doctor shook his head wearily, slipped both bags of bonedust into his vest pocket, and turned to the bedside table. He returned with an ampoule of amber liquid, and broke it open. Vedas distantly felt the doctor's fingers as they peeled his lips back from his clenched teeth and poured the liquid down. He did not taste the spell or feel it trickling into his throat.

The smell of iron did reach his nose, and quickly overcame his senses. A shutter closed over his eyes, leaving him in complete darkness. The pain shut off suddenly. Vedas found himself alone in his mind, unable to sense his body. He drifted, untethered. No eyes, no ears, no nose—nothing. For a timeless moment, he was not a man. Maybe the spell had banished him to a far ashen corner of his mind so that it might work on the disease. Maybe the spell was not in fact working, and now he simply waited for his body to stop functioning.

Berun's last words came to him without a voice: *You won't let him die.* The phrase repeated over and over again, confounding in his current state, neither dead nor alive. *You won't let him die. You won't let him die.*

Suddenly, light burst through cracks in the shutter before his eyes and he found himself back in his body. A scorching needle bit into his mind and set his skin aflame. Every joint in his body cracked at once. He screamed, arching up from the mattress, straining at the straps that bound him. Hard, cold hands the size of shields pressed him down. Someone else pressed a wet rag to his forehead. As the sedative spell contained therein seeped into his skin, he felt the overwhelming urge to shut his eyes. His eyelids dragged closed, burning like sore muscles being stretched.

His screams became words.

"Take me home!" he yelled.

"Take me home!" he rasped.

"Take me home," he whispered before falling into unconsciousness.

‡

In the warm interior of the doctor's tent, Vedas drifted in and out of sleep. Dreams weaved around him, meshing fluidly with waking moments. A large man of gold rubble stood beside his bed, fell to the ground, rose in the body of the fever-mad young man he had killed on the road to Nbena, and then shrank to become a young girl with a black sash tied around her left arm. A candle wavered before his eyes. The flame dropped upon him, engulfing him without heat or pain. Someone spoke his name, and Vedas recognized his own voice, his father's or mother's voice, Abse's voice—droning, becoming music.

Time stretched and contracted as it does for the drugged. The passage of the moon above the ventilation hole in the tent's ceiling took hours, and the changing of the sheets under him happened in a handful of seconds. His body reacted unpredictably to touch. He neither grimaced nor groaned when someone palpated his ribs and chest, underarms and neck. He laughed instead. Tears flowed from his eyes when someone put a warm rag on his forehead.

Finally, darkness descended on his mind, complete and total immersion. He slept soundly.

"Do you hear me, Vedas?" someone said.

Vedas opened his eyes. A slow, luxurious process, letting light into his skull. It spread from there, suffusing his whole body, centering in his stomach and genitals. A warm tingling, similar to but infinitely better than blood rushing into a numb limb. Though he had experienced the effect of a spell wearing off before, this proved to be a different sensation entirely.

He smiled. The muscles of his face were sore, but it felt good nonetheless. He lifted a hand to his chest and exhaled with relief. They had not removed his suit. As reality crept back, he enjoyed the texture of smooth fabric and muscle underneath his fingers. His hand drifted over the ridges of his stomach and paused.

An erection pushed almost painfully against the fabric of his suit.

A polite cough. "Can you hear me, citizen Tezul?"

Vedas's head swiveled to regard the doctor. His hand fell to his side. "Yes, I can."

"Good." The doctor pressed fingertips against Vedas's chest, ribs, and stomach. "I think you can stand now, but not too quickly. You're still weak."

Berun walked into view. "Here," the constructed man said, offering Vedas two fingers to hold onto. Vedas gripped them and rose on rubbery legs. His bowels felt loose. Everything hurt. Running fingers over the wiry stubble on his head, he found that even his scalp was tender. Now that the novelty of the world had begun to leach away, the light in the room was too intense, the noise from outside a painful racket.

"We're still in Nbena, I assume," he said. "How long have we been here?"

"Just one night," Berun responded. He looked over Vedas's head at the doctor. "Do you have instructions? Medicines to give him?"

The doctor shrugged. "He's not dead, so the spell worked. He's cured. I'd recommend at least one night's rest before continuing your journey, plenty of water, and food. The pain is mostly muscular tension, which will fade in time. If you want to buy more sedative spells, I'll gladly sell them, but they aren't good for him."

Berun shook his head. "No. He'll deal with the pain."

‡

The town simply called itself Nbena. Its citizens on both sides of Dalan Fele wore metal badges, which allowed their free movement from one nation to the other. Apart from the Autumnal Wars, the last of which had occurred three centuries previously, Dareth Hlum and Casta enjoyed a congenial relationship. Dareth Hlum looked upon Casta as a younger, less civilized version of itself, while Casta considered Dareth Hlum amusingly tidy and idealistic.

The different personalities were reflected in Nbena's layout. On Dareth Hlum's side, the streets formed a grid. They were wide and clean, and the evenly spaced clay buildings that lined them were unpainted. Quietness and sobriety ruled. Even the stunted oaks appeared at regular intervals. On the Castan side, roads existed where foot and barrow wheel needed them to be. They were uniformly dirty. Once-brightly painted buildings leaned over alleyways and crumbled cheap bricks onto the street. Loudness and gaiety ruled.

The doctor had recommended an Anadrashi tavern on the Castan side named Brickchurch. Unlike its neighbors, it had been carved into the sheer stone facade of Dalan Fele itself. To Vedas, raised believing in the wall's impregnability, this seemed almost sacrilegious.

Standing before the tavern's doorway, he swayed as a brief spell of dizziness nearly overtook him. Black motes swam at the corners of his eyes and an odd pressure built in his ears.

Berun's fist closed around his bicep. "Steady. You have to eat. Come on." He led Vedas into the tavern's dim interior, where the air was cool and still and smelled of stone. Eyes followed the pair as they navigated the furniture and sat at a rear corner table.

Vedas leaned forward on his forearms, fighting the urge to drop his throbbing head onto them. "This isn't pleasant."

Berun grunted. "What do you want?"

"To go back to sleep," Vedas answered immediately. "I'm hungry but I don't feel like eating, which is a first." He licked chapped lips and reconsidered. "I suppose I could eat, but before that I need a pitcher of water. Plain, no lemon or mintgrass, and I'll pay the extra for ice. Then I'll eat whatever they have in the kitchen. I'm not picky."

Berun walked to the bar and ordered. Vedas watched him through half-closed lids, feeling a vague sense of unease. *You won't let him die*, the constructed man had said—but why had he said it? They were nothing more than traveling companions. Such concern made Vedas uncomfortable. He liked uncomplicated relationships, and disliked owing favors.

"Excuse me."

Vedas's eyes snapped open. Only a handful of seconds had passed, yet a woman now stood before him, short sword naked on her left hip. By the look of her corded arms and shoulders, she knew how to use it. Vedas shifted his hips slightly and inched his right hand over the table's edge for leverage. It would not be a graceful move if he were forced to defend himself. The slightest tensing of muscle in his legs and back stung sharply.

The woman's pale eyes held his. "Your name is Tezul, right? Vedas?" She spoke with a slight Onsi accent. Her voice was deep but not unfeminine.

"Yes," he said.

"And your companion? He's the construct Berun, right?"

"Yes. Who are you?"

She shifted her weight in an odd fashion, as if she had suddenly become uncomfortable. She gestured to the chair across from him. He nodded and she sat, crossing her legs to the side. For a moment he fought the temptation, and then glanced quickly down. Her calves and thighs were well formed, muscular, freckled, and hatched with scars. The tattoo of a sea serpent wound around her right ankle. She brushed short, ash-colored hair from her forehead and yawned.

Berun arrived, index finger hooked around the handle of a pitcher. The woman turned to stare up at him.

"Who are you?" he said.

"What is that?" she asked, nodding at the pitcher.

"Water. With ice."

She made a sour face. "My name is Churls. Churls Casta Jons. I have a proposition for you."

BERUN

The air grew sharper as they ascended into the badlands. Berun noticed it as a minute change in the sound of his spheres rubbing together, while Vedas experienced nosebleeds.

"You'll get used to it," Churls told him.

"Nosebleeds?" Vedas asked without a trace of humor.

She started to laugh and caught herself. "No. No, I meant the air. You'll get used to the air." She stared at her feet, opening and closing her mouth as though considering her next words carefully. None followed, however.

Eventually: "It's even drier than I thought it would be," Vedas said.

"They do call it the badlands," she answered.

He frowned. "I didn't make the connection."

She shrugged. "That's . . . understandable."

Berun watched his companions carefully. He could see the thing between them, but not as if either yet recognized it. Their conversations were infrequent and stilted, though both kept at it. Churls and Vedas reminded Berun of certain individuals in the Seventeenth—men and women who, despite forming attachments, could not succeed in forming lasting bonds. The pressures of living and fighting together overwhelmed them.

Berun had never understood human sexuality. Then again, he had not given it much thought. He watched his companions because it interested him, but he himself had no intention of assisting. If Vedas and Churls desired awkwardness, they had it. If they desired more, they would need to broach the subject themselves.

The first day wore on with Dalan Fele straddling the horizon at their backs. The nearly treeless ground, red like pitting iron, stretched before them. Some geological process had tipped the floor of the world ever so slightly, and before long Berun ceased to notice they trod an upward slope. To either side barren, saw-edged hills rose, flanking them in straight lines.

"We walk on the bed of the river Zaos," Churls explained. "It stopped flowing long before the birth of man, in the age of the elder."

She walked easily, eyes watchful. She squinted ahead and shadowed her brow to stare into the sky. Berun wondered what she was looking for. He had not spotted a ground animal since they started, and the only birds rode the air so far above them they looked like specks. Golna had scavenger birds, too. They were not dangerous as far as Berun knew.

His curiosity finally got the best of him, and he pointed these things out to Churls.

"Those aren't birds," she answered. "It's a trick of perspective. A wyrm could carry a man away in one claw, and probably tear even you apart. Fortunately, they come down only every once in a while. Adrash willing, it won't be today." She spat twice, an automatic warding gesture Berun recognized. "I'm being so watchful because there are animals that live below our feet. Earthmovers. They crest about as often as wyrms touch ground. If one does, it's best to recognize the signs early."

"They're dangerous?" Berun asked.

Churls shook her head. "Not at all. But wyrms are, and they love earthmover meat. They don't like men much, either, so I plan on being far away from one if it lands."

Berun turned to Vedas. "Have you heard of this?"

Vedas grunted. Though he had started the day in good form, hours of exertion had taken their toll. His face was flushed and his breath wheezed from him. Still, he pushed himself, maintaining a quick pace on stiff legs, only stopping to eat or drink. Even when coughing fits doubled him over, he kept moving.

Again, Berun offered to carry his pack.

"Quit asking," Vedas said. "I'll get better by walking, not resting."

Berun shrugged, by now inured to the man's stubborn pride. Vedas would walk himself to death rather than admit weakness.

Churls, on the other hand, had gladly accepted Berun's help. Instead of dividing the ungainly packs between the travelers, she let him carry the huge bundle of firewood and the eight two-gallon bladders of water. She had watched in fascination as he drew the cords of the luggage into his back, so that they appeared to grow out of his metal flesh. The extra two hundred pounds bothered him not at all.

When darkness fell, shutting off the light as though someone had blown out a candle, they simply stopped walking and set up camp. Churls dropped her pack with an audible sigh and unrolled her wool-and-down sleeping bag. Vedas lifted the firewood and water from Berun's back and then watched as Berun punched a fire pit in the ground.

"Will that attract earthmovers?" Vedas asked Churls.

She shook her head. "Back when their magics were good, the badlanders used to try and raise the animals to the surface in order to hunt wyrms, but nothing they did worked. I doubt they never tried pounding on the ground."

Berun could only sense texture and vibration, not temperature. He surmised that it must be quite cold, however, for Churls sat as close to the fire as she safely could. The muscles of her jaw jumped as she chewed her gammon. Vedas, forearms crossed loosely on his knees, stared into the fire and occasionally allowed a glance in her direction.

Berun regarded one, then the other, wondering who would break the silence.

"You aren't cold?" Churls asked Vedas. She kept her eyes on the ground and spoke quietly, obviously more ill at ease now that night had fallen—now that she and Vedas were so close. It fascinated Berun.

"No," Vedas said. "My suit keeps me warm."

"Cool, too?"

He nodded. "It keeps me comfortable. Within limits."

"It makes you stronger and faster, right?"

"A bit."

"I've seen suited men before, of course, but never up close. The White and Black orders are less common in Casta and Stol than in Dareth Hlum, and those you see are almost always fully covered." She looked up. "You can make it move, can't you?"

Though he nearly always wore the skin-tight hood, Vedas had not yet covered his face in her presence. He smiled and the edges of the hood drew in around his features. In the shifting firelight, it looked like an illusion.

Churls's eyes widened. "When I was a child, vendors sometimes displayed elder-cloth at the fabric markets in Onsa. They don't let you touch."

She leaned toward him, hand out. "Can I?"

Berun saw Vedas's right hand tighten around his left forearm. The man nodded. Churls ran her fingertips over his shoulder, and then pressed her palm flat. In the firelight his suit took on the sheen of volcanic glass, and her hand stopped moving. It lay there, rooted to him, a part of him. The moment stuck, and Berun felt a faint vibration inside himself: the nearly imperceptible shudder of a spinning sphere deep within his chest. For an instant, it seemed that a hooded figure stood behind Vedas, hand raised in the air. Poised to strike. The gleam of silver metal.

The moment broke, and Churls's hand dropped. She stood to ready her bedroll, and Vedas met Berun's gaze across the fire.

"What are you looking at?" Vedas asked.

‡

Gradually, the earth became brittle. It cracked in tiny wavelets around their feet. The slope of the ground leveled out and the wind picked up. These subtle changes trickled into Berun's mind, as did the fact that another traveler had not come upon them since leaving Nbena.

Churls took out her compass more and more often. Berun let her, though he knew they had been traveling south in a straight line for two days. According to his internal map, they were currently some twenty-five miles from Dalan Fele, roughly the same distance from the southern coast of Casta. Staying the course, they would reach the ocean in another day. The ruins of the stone bridge that had once linked Was Anul to the mainland were visible from this shore, men claimed. On a clear day, the smoldering crown of the island itself could be viewed.

While the possibility of seeing these sights enticed Berun, he could not understand why Churls had chosen this route. Even the deserts of Toma held life, but the coast between Dalan Fele and the Steps of Stol was rumored to be barren, waterless. Already, the foliage had petered out to the occasional thorny jess tree. The clouds, too high to form rain, formed an impenetrable grey roof over their heads.

Vedas gave no sign he recognized anything out of the ordinary.

Not surprising, Berun thought. The man was a city creature, and even a competent tracker could lose his sense of direction with the sun buried in the clouds.

Berun considered the situation. He would let Churls lead without comment for another day. Surely, she did not intend to continue southward toward the Steps. Undoubtedly, she had a reason for diverting them. Perhaps she meant to avoid bandits or some other danger. He trusted her, in fact enjoyed her company. Aside from her awkwardness with Vedas, she projected a confident and easygoing nature.

The same could not be said of Vedas, a man who continually aroused Berun's ire. It was not the Black Suit's arrogance, taciturn manner, or sullen moods—Berun had encountered such things before, even in the best of men. No, the source of the antipathy lay deep within, as though it had been stamped upon every sphere of Berun's being. He found himself looking for new reasons to dislike the man. He fought the urge constantly, but achieved little headway.

It was not difficult to imagine the source of this manipulation. The illusion of the hooded figure the night before had proved it. Berun regretted the fact that Omali chose coercion over communication. He could not help wondering if his father had judged Vedas inaccurately.

He feared what he might be forced to do to the man.

Father, Berun broadcast. *What danger can Vedas possibly be to you? Speak to me.*

Less than twenty miles from the coast, they set up camp as they had the previous night. The ground crackled under them as they settled around the fire. Vedas—tired but visibly healthier than the day before—watched Churls prepare a soup of dried potatoes, vegetable stock, and salted mutton. She used a travel pot with a locking lid, so as to not waste water.

"May I hold your sword?" he asked.

"Sure." She turned on the balls of her feet, drew her short, dull blade and flipped it, offering it to him hilt first.

Vedas ran his fingers over the pitted steel but did not bother testing its edge. He stood and walked a few paces away, rolling his shoulders.

Stepping through several forms, his strokes were fluid and economical. Berun knew from conversation that barehanded and staff technique comprised the majority of the man's training, but it clearly had not ignored bladed weapons altogether. While he was not a master of the short sword, Vedas was by no measure incompetent.

"Not bad," Churls said after several minutes. "But you're treating it like a sword."

Vedas looked from the blade to her face, and back again. "I won't deny that."

She stood. "You miss my meaning. Any fool can see my blade has no bite." She held her hand out. "I stole my first sword from a dead infantrymen. My brother wouldn't let me run in his gang with people who knew how to hold or care for it properly, so I had to teach myself. I imagined every tree and fence post was an enemy, and hacked away."

The weapon came to life in her hands. Each attack was a steel blur punctuated by a moment of complete stillness, the end product of her viciously quick parries and thrusts. A crushing blow to the temple. A sideswipe aimed to crack ribs. A vicious upswing into the groin. With the weight of the blade behind it, her blows would likely pulverize even the thickest bones.

She stopped as suddenly as she started, and sheathed her sword. "I called my technique The Dull Sword. Quite creative, don't you think? Not surprisingly, I'm the sole practitioner of the art. It's not the beautiful thing fencing is."

Vedas shook his head. "I've never seen anyone use a sword that way," he said, voice soft with admiration. He turned away, coughing into his fist.

Churls dropped her head. Seeing further into the spectrums of light than a man, Berun saw the flush of her cheeks and drew his own features into a smile, a demon mask above the fire.

Vedas had finally done something charming.

‡

Berun scooped handfuls of dry dirt and snuffed out the fire. He brushed the char away from the larger pieces of wood, revealing the unburnt flesh underneath, and set them near the bundle to cool. This task finished, he soon became restless. Just as he had done the first night out, he cautiously began constructing sculptures out of the firewood. He moved slowly, as quietly as a snake whispering through grass.

Vedas and Churls did not stir, and so he proceeded to the next step, mirroring each sculpture by rearranging the spheres of his body—a slow, painstaking process. The arrangements became more complex as the night wore on, until finally he achieved his goal: a break in the link, so that one group of spheres no longer touched the other. As he broke the magnetic bonds of his being, an intense feeling of pleasure passed through him. His mind blinked rapidly on and off, each instant of existence mounting upon the other until he felt on the verge of decohering completely, scattering on the ground like droplets of mercury.

Creating sculptures and mirroring their shape had been his habit from the moment he woke in his father's foundry. Quite possibly, his father had instilled the urge in him out of compassion. Berun could not sleep or obtain sexual release, and so the sculpting occupied his mind and kept his vital energies from stagnation. He was, despite his mechanical composition, a being who had inherited a man's spirit, a man's needs.

On rare occasions, instead of sensual release he experienced a hallucination, the details of which never varied. His mind drifted of its own accord and rose above the world as it shrunk slowly below him, ripping open along a seam on its far side and spreading like a blanket under his feet. He counted the multitude of islands speckling the surface of the ocean. He lost himself in contemplation of the permanently spinning storm that lay on the other side of the world, sure that if he stared long enough the clouds would part, revealing what lay beneath.

Sustaining this vision for long was an immense effort. Something always drew him away. His father, no doubt, confounding his creation for arcane reasons once more.

Berun's curiosity burned intensely, yet there was little cure for it. The world was a known quantity, and had been for millennia. Several large landmasses lay just off the coast of Knoori, many of which bore the signs of ancient inhabitation by the elders. The remains of bridges, avenues that had once linked to the mainland, lay crumbled underwater. Beyond the islands stretched the ocean, breached here and there by tiny spurs of rock never meant to support life. The outbound mages of Stol had captured this image of Jeroun from orbit—a hundred times, a thousand. Reproductions had made their way across the continent long ago.

An unending storm across the ocean? Madness.

Tonight, Berun began to feel the call of the vision early on. It lay just under the surface of his consciousness, almost frightening in its potency. He felt as if he might fall forward, crack through the thin crust of earth at his feet and never stop falling. For the first time in his life, he fought to stay grounded in waking reality. He struggled to reconnect the two halves of his being, and failed. The towering buildings he had erected to mimic the sculpture trembled as wave after wave of dizziness crashed upon him. A voice spoke from the heart of the wooden city. The ground shook with its volume, drowning out the words.

Atop a tower of bronze spheres, Berun swiveled one searing blue eye, searching for his companions.

They were gone, as were their supplies. No indentation in the ground where Churls or Vedas had lain, no sign of the fire. Instead, before him spread the complete map of Jeroun, intricately drawn in the loose dirt. Danoor glowed like a molten glass bead, and a line of fire extended from it to Berun. On the other side of the world, the perpetual storm glowed as if an island of magma were being born under its cover. The Needle blazed in the sky above, stretching from horizon to horizon, closer and more radiant than the moon itself.

Berun looked down again to see an invisible finger tracing a figure in the dirt: a man with no features except for eyes and two small horns sprouting from his forehead.

"Father!" he bellowed. "Father, what is this?"

The unintelligible rumbling voice cut off abruptly, and the wooden city drew itself off the ground. Rustling, splitting and cracking, it formed the cloaked shape of Ortur Omali.

Affection swelled inside Berun so rapidly that he immediately questioned its authenticity. Without knowingly intending to do so, he rose and took on his familiar shape. He held Churls's sword, a ridiculously small weapon in his outsized right fist. A toothpick.

The mouth under the cloak smiled, a wicked arrangement of wood slivers. "What is this! What is this!" his father echoed. "A possibility. A potentiality. The Black Suit could be a snake, could be an eagle. Could be a worm, could be a leech. One thing is sure: he is the man to watch."

"Vedas," Berun said. "He's only a fighter."

"Appearances only. Is God a man?" Ortur Omali stretched elaborately, creaking like a dead tree in the wind. His fingertips were splinters, long and stiletto thin. Two pinpoints of light flared in each eye. "There is something odd about him, child. Something troubling, or possibly even encouraging. It is tough to tell the difference, sometimes. I may need him destroyed. You must avoid attachment."

"Why? How will you decide?" Berun had so many questions, yet his mind struggled through the confused logic of dream. His brows knitted in frustration. He brought his fist up and discovered that he could not open his hand to drop the sword.

"I don't need this to kill a man," he said. They were not the words he had intended to say.

The great mage laughed: the rustle of fallen leaves. "It is not a weapon, Berun. It is a demonstration."

The air wavered before Berun. It became a curtain of shifting darkness behind which the figure of his father shuddered and fell apart. The sound of twigs snapping came to Berun distantly, and the earth shuddered beneath him. A crack formed in the map drawn on the ground. A rent opened, its crumbling edge racing toward Berun. He tried to pick up his feet, but found them rooted in place.

He tipped sideways into the black chasm.

Abruptly, the vision ended.

Berun stood over Vedas's sleeping form. Churls curled in her sleeping bag a few feet to his left. Her sword belt lay on the ground next to her, empty.

The weapon was weightless in Berun's hand.

‡

They continued south in a straight line. The air grew colder, the wind stronger. Powerful gusts kicked up fine salt crystals embedded in the thin soil and flung them against exposed skin. Vedas covered his face. During the heaviest gusts he walked half-blind, the suit material grown to cover his eyes. Churls pulled leather chaps and jacket from her pack and wrapped her head with the scarf she used as a pillow. Berun barely felt the wind or the abrading sand, but the going was slow for the other two.

They stopped just before the sun set. Instead of pounding down a fire pit, Berun concentrated to form a pick at the end of his arms and then tore a shallow depression in the hard-packed earth. He lined the windward side with excavated rocks to shield Churls and Vedas from the wind, which became even more ferocious after dark, ushered in from the ocean that lay only a handful of miles away.

It was time to broach the subject of Churls's route.

"Why aren't we headed west?" he asked after his companions had finished dinner.

Vedas looked up from the fire, turned his head to regard Churls.

She shifted, obviously uncomfortable. "I hoped I wouldn't have to talk about it." She sighed in response to Berun and Vedas's silence. "Really, I thought it was obvious. I thought maybe you'd seen the error in your plan."

"What error?" Vedas asked. "Why would we travel south?"

"Because of you," she said. Her eyebrows rose suggestively. "Don't you get it?"

"Me?" He frowned. "Are you mad?"

She sighed again. "Would you consent to travel with a cloak? Wear it at all times?"

Berun had discerned her meaning, but remained unconvinced. Before Vedas could answer, he spoke. "Casta is neutral and Stol is moderate Adrashi. There's no reason for Vedas to cover his suit."

Churls laughed. "Oh, yeah? Then I must be misinformed. I've waylaid us unnecessarily and I apologize." Her smile disappeared. "There are three tribes living in southern Casta. The Aumarveda, the Quinum, and the Lor, all three of which are devoutly Adrashi. They wouldn't hesitate to attack a heathen like Vedas. Fortunately for us, they do not venture near the ocean. Who would if they could avoid it?

"As for the moderate Adrashi of Stol, in general I've found them far less accepting to foreigners—Anadrashi foreigners in particular—than eastern lore has it. Even if Vedas is not attacked outright, he'll be a target for thieves and men eager for a fight in every hamlet. Added to this, Ulomi immigrants are common to the central valleys of Stol. Someone would undoubtedly recognize you, Berun. And unlike Casta, Stol is a land of magic users. Even you could get hurt. In all cases, a confrontation would hold us back. Our best option is to travel the Steps, where by all accounts the populous is sparse and peaceable, more concerned with living than fighting about religion."

Berun considered. The idea possessed a certain appeal. He had always wanted to see the Steps. "How far out of the way is your route?" he asked.

She licked her lips. "About five hundred miles."

"Out of the question," Vedas said. He appeared to calculate quickly. "That will put us in Danoor with less than a week to spare. It's possible we'd miss the entire tournament. We need time to settle in. There are training sessions, events in preparation for the tournament that I've promised to attend. My order must be properly represented." He looked at Berun. "Why didn't you tell me we were going the wrong way?"

Berun shrugged. "She's our guide. I trust her."

Vedas's expression did not change. "You trust her? Your master and mine gave us the route. Instead of heeding them, you're going to simply trust her?" He turned away. "I agreed to her company. I'll listen to her advice. I won't agree to this."

"Is that how you operate then, Vedas?" Churls asked, eyes fixed on the fire. "They tell you to jump and you jump? Well, their route is fucked. Neither of you have been in this area before. Nor, I doubt, have your masters, otherwise they wouldn't have told you to travel through the middle of Stol. The ground is fertile, and there are people everywhere. We couldn't avoid them. You're lucky I'm here to set you off course."

She kicked at the fire. Sparks flew and streaked away with the wind. "Listen, I want to get to Danoor as badly as you do. I have money riding there—money I need. My route is your—our—best chance to get there in one piece. So you'll miss the events leading up to the tournament. At least you'll be alive to fight!"

She shook her head. "I admit that I need you. The journey would be too dangerous for me alone. All I need you to do is trust that I know best."

The wind howled over them. Vedas grimaced and stretched out on his bedroll.

How easy it would be to leave him, Berun reasoned.

The thought lingered in his mind. As one recalls a forgotten dream, he realized he had been playing with the idea of abandoning Vedas for quite some time. With less than a gallon of water and no navigation skills, being caught in this corner of the world would have been the man's death.

In lockstep, a series of other memories came to Berun.

Yes, he had pictured Vedas Tezul's death, on many occasions. He had enjoyed it. The recognition of this fact horrified him. To have one's body bent to the task of murder was a horrible crime—to have one's mind bent to hate, yet another.

He waited for Vedas's breathing to change, signaling sleep.

"We'll do what he says," Berun rumbled softly. "He'll see that this route is best. Still, I was wrong to keep this from him."

Churls closed her eyes. "Fine."

The fire died down to coals. "Why?" she finally asked.

"I'm not sure," Berun answered. "There's something about him. I think you see it, too."

Churls scooped dirt and doused the coals. "No. I don't see anything."

CHVRLI CASTA JONS

The Steps began in the fertile southern plains of Stol, extending some seventy miles to the coast and more than four hundred along it. From a hundred miles away in southern Casta, the Steps had looked to Churls like nothing more than a smooth mountain slope. Closer, the scale was even harder to conceive. Ascending to a height of twelve thousand feet in seventeen evenly spaced, gently sloping rises, the Steps stopped abruptly at the ocean, shorn clean by a giant knife blade.

The elders had carved the Steps from the continent's longest mountain chain, it was said. For what purpose, no one knew. Along with the Dras Alas Citadel in northern Casta, the crystal dome over the island of Osa, The Inverted Bowl in the central valley of the Aspa Mountains, and the Glass Plain in northeastern Knos Min, the Steps of Stol displayed the enigmatic power of the elders. Many believed spirits and enchanted men inhabited such places. Immortal black magic practitioners and corpse miners.

As a result, the Steps were largely uninhabited. One of Gorum's friends, a scholar, had traveled southern Stol extensively. He claimed small, long-lived men lived upon the highest and most fertile steps, where unusually warm winds brought moisture in from the ocean. According to him, these men lived in a state of peace and primitive prosperity, knowing neither marriage nor jealousy. They shared their men and women, and Adrash smiled upon them. Even the rare Anadrashi who came through their lands was treated with respect.

93

Churls took the story with a grain of salt, for many of the tales she had heard differed markedly from the scholar's account. Nonetheless, she had been to the central valleys of Stol. Gorum was right: better to take her chances with tall tales and wishful thinking than violent reality. At the very least, fewer men lived on the Steps. Churls believed in odds above all else.

It was said a man could stand at the edge of the highest step and stare down at the glass-smooth face of the cliff, counting the geological layers of the world. It was also said a man must be careful at the edge, for sudden gusts could take hold of him and carry him far out over the ocean. Capricious, the demon winds sometimes returned him unharmed, but most often spun him in the sky, toying with him as a child does a rag doll. Bored, eventually the wind dropped him into the ocean or dashed his body against the wall.

Churls considered such tales bullshit. Wind was wind, and only an idiot stood up on a precipice when the gusts were strong.

Many years ago, she had shared bread with an acolyte of the Placci, a small elder-worshipping cult in Anlala. She claimed the elders had created the walls as permanent testament to their power. "They will stand immutable until the elders return to claim their kingdoms," she had told Churls.

Calves and thighs warm from walking uphill, she listened to Vedas tell a similar tale, and tried not to roll her eyes. Living in the city had filled his mind with so many ridiculous things. They walked a mere hundred feet from the edge. He could see for himself that the cliff face was not evenly cut. Shrubs took root in its crevices and huge sections had crumbled completely. Twice, they had to veer around immense rockslides. Though she never doubted some magical process had carved the Steps, she rejected the idea of their ensorcelment.

She had seen the Citadel at Dras Alas, and it too was crumbling away, eroded by wind and time.

So much for permanency, Churls thought.

‡

Each step consisted of a three-mile slope ascending seven hundred feet, topped by a two-mile stretch of grassy plain. Halfway through the first day, the clouds broke above them and warm winds blew in from the ocean, buoying their spirits and feet. By the time they stopped for the night, they had reached the base of the fifth step. Vedas, almost fully recovered from his illness, glowed with health and high spirits. For the first time in two weeks, he appeared to forget his anger over their course change.

His course change, Churls reminded herself. Berun had given Vedas the choice, after all. Thankfully, the man had seen the sense of her position. Not that being right had endeared her to him. Clearly, he was not the kind of man who forgave easily.

Churls observed him as they prepared dinner, and worried his good mood would dissolve when he woke to sore calves and thighs. Up until the Steps, they had traveled on relatively flat land. Climbing for so many miles, even at such a shallow grade, could take its toll on the fittest man.

The following morning, this proved true. Though he did not complain, Vedas looked like someone who had been run through a gauntlet. Exertion revived a slight cough, which he worked hard to conceal. The weather improved over the course of the day, blowing dry and warm, yet they still fell a mile short of the ninth step. After dinner, Churls read weariness and frustration on Vedas's features. She noted how he grunted as he stood to relieve himself.

He was a beautiful man, she admitted—but this alone did not explain her attraction. He had stubborn pride, but none of the ingrained arrogance that made so many men insufferable around women. He had little experience beyond that of fighting, but he learned quickly. Her short bow had become a formidable weapon in his hands, and he was patient enough to hunt with it. His navigation skills grew every day. On several occasions, he had noticed the signs of dangerous beasts before she did.

Certainly, she grew tired of his superstitions and his prejudices, though they did not surprise her. She had never considered Anadrashi any less prone to the irrational than their devout opponents.

What was the difference between a man who believed in God's love and a man who did not?

Nothing, as far as she could tell.

Why, then, did it feel as if there was something more to him? Why did he loom so large in her mind? She had seen beautiful men before. She had met talented, even genius men. It rankled her, being drawn as if by physical force to Vedas Tezul.

Who was he to warrant so much attention?

Berun believed in Vedas's uniqueness, surely. He had not tried to convince her that this was the case—had only mentioned it the once—but his feelings were increasingly obvious. He watched Vedas whenever the man was not looking, and Churls wondered what the constructed man saw beyond the graceful flow of muscle under the slick skin of Vedas's suit—the way the material clung to him, revealing more than it hid, emphasizing the rise and fall of his buttocks, the tensing of his broad shoulders.

She wondered what Berun saw in Vedas's restrained smile. Thick, sensuous lips framing straight white teeth made whiter against the darkness of his skin? Or merely a smile?

She had to shake off her arousal several times a day. It was pathetic and moreover worthless, feeling that way. Beyond the occasional glance at her backside or chest—a meaningless gesture, yet another male's inability to control his eyes—Vedas had never given any sign of returning her desire. Besides, she could not keep her big mouth shut. Each night, though she tried to keep the conversation neutral, she managed to offend him. He was so easily affronted, and she so easily discouraged.

If Berun were not there to interject now and then, the two would have parted ways out of frustration long ago.

Vedas returned to the fire.

"No Dull Sword tonight?" she asked. She had been teaching him the technique intermittently as they traveled. Though humorless, he was a good student. Of course he was.

He met her eyes briefly as he sat. "No."

"You'll feel better tomorrow," she said. "You're still breaking in your travel muscles."

He smiled tightly, little more than a grimace. "I had no idea there were so many muscles in the leg. I thought the hills of Golna were enough to prepare any man for simply walking uphill. And then there's my training. In the abbey, we use weighted gloves and staffs. We lift barrels of sand over our heads." He stretched his legs out and grabbed his ankles. He groaned. "I think I'd rather do that for twelve hours than repeat today."

The wind picked up. Berun shifted to the right and slowly made his torso flatter to shield the fire. "I wonder what it feels like to get tired," he said. "I notice when a task becomes more difficult, but I don't understand pain or tiredness. They're just words."

Vedas grunted and released his ankles. "You're not missing much." He angled his head to the sky. The Needle had not fully risen, and so he did not curse Adrash by touching the horns of his suit. Instead, he breathed in deeply, his taut belly inflating like a drum. "I smell pine trees."

"Me, too," Churls said. She frowned, deepening the lines around her mouth. "Wait a minute. There are no pine trees east of Anlala that I know of, certainly none in Dareth Hlum—it's too far east. How would you recognize the smell? You don't look like the kind of man who frequents perfumeries."

He grimaced. Once again, she had said the wrong thing.

"I may not look it," he said, "but I have on occasion. There are plenty of Knosi in Golna, but I wasn't born there. My parents came to the city when I was just a boy. I barely remember Grass, the city of my birth, but I do remember the smell of sagoli pines. The stunted trees lined our street like little old women in frocks. On the way across the continent, I smelled other types of pine. Slightly different smells, but mostly the same. Sometimes, I buy pine oil. I don't care what kind. Having the smell in my room reminds me of something . . . Something I might forget if I don't remind myself."

Berun shifted, but had nothing to add. He spun two rocks in his hands like Churls had seen monks do in Fali. They were nearly perfect spheres, diminishing in size every day. In a month, he had ground four pairs into marbles.

Churls simply nodded, and then retrieved her sword from beside her pack. With bonedust and spit, she started polishing, in truth to keep from confronting the silence. She could not name the emotion Vedas's words aroused in her. Sadness, certainly, but this was too general. Longing?

Yes. Longing.

Did longing make Vedas different from any other person she had known? Or was it that he chose to voice it when so many others would rather keep it buried? He did not have to say such things. He could just as easily lie, keep his secrets.

‡

Maybe he can't keep a secret, a voice said. *Maybe he's an honest man.*

Churls opened her eyes and growled softly.

She had not been sleeping soundly. Sometimes it felt as if she could predict when her daughter's ghost would appear, as though she had been drifting toward the meeting all day long. It felt disconcertingly similar to when she wandered in search of water, knowing in the back of her mind that it was close. She had always been a good tracker, a good hunter, and wondered if close communion with spirits was responsible.

Not one to indulge in such speculation by nature, Churls was forced by circumstances to consider the possibility. Five years ago, the ghost of her daughter had appeared, changing the structure of her world. The dead lingered in doorways and sat around campfires, just out of sight. The dead were real.

It was this, Churls knew, or admit she had gone insane.

She rose from her sleeping bag and walked away from camp. The moon was an iron shaving, the world shrouded. Daybreak was two or three hours away. She thought she saw the burning blue coals of Berun's eyes in the middle distance, but when she looked again they were gone, perhaps a figment of her imagination. Cool, humid wind flowed over the cliff's edge, instantly chilling her skin. Gooseflesh rose on her exposed arms and legs.

The ocean spread below her, a sky devoid of stars.

"Hello, Fyra," she said.

The girl appeared beside her. Churls fought the urge to step away.

I like him, Fyra said.

"Who?" Churls asked, though she knew full well whom her daughter meant.

Vedas. I like Vedas. You like him, too.

"I do," Churls said. "But I shouldn't. I have no reason to like him."

You think he's pretty.

Churls nodded. "He is. That's not enough, though."

Fyra walked two steps forward, to the edge. Her fine white hair lifted, became a halo around her head. Churls's fingernail bit into a scab on her forearm, puncturing it. Blood welled, and she smeared it with her fingertip until it became tacky.

"Why do you like him?" she asked.

A small shrug. *I just do. He's not like the other men you like. They say things they don't mean. They steal, they fight.*

"Vedas fights. That's all he does."

Fyra faced her mother. Churls met the stare, and it reminded her too much of looking in the mirror. Fyra had inherited so little from her father. Had someone in the afterlife told her about her half sisters, who were curly-headed and olive skinned? Had she visited them, seen her father and stepmother?

What Vedas does is different, Fyra said. *He doesn't fight for money. He doesn't kill.*

"There's no difference, sweetie." Churls straightened her arms against her sides. "And Vedas has killed before. He's killed a lot of people."

By accident, Fyra insisted. *And the girl wasn't his fault, Mama.*

Churls wondered how her daughter knew these things. Had she been watching Vedas for long, or could she simply see into his soul? Churls did not like thinking that Fyra could read minds, but somehow this paled in comparison to the thought that her child had been observing Vedas since before they met.

And then it hit her. The obvious answer: Fyra simply believed Vedas. *Maybe he's an honest man*, she had said. Vedas had been forthcoming about his recruit's death, and Churls had only half-believed him. She thought it equally likely that he had accidentally killed the child in the skirmish, and fled Golna to avoid the law. She considered this. Even while doubting his character, she had been attracted to him. Perhaps she had always believed him.

Foolishness, believing someone she did not know.

He doesn't understand you, Fyra said. *He doesn't understand people at all.*

"How do you know that? Maybe he just doesn't like people."

No, I'm right. I can see some of his memories—the strong ones, the ones that hurt. He tried to help the dead girl's parents, but he didn't know what to do. He wanted to say something, but instead he just stood there, looking uncomfortable while they cried. If you could see it, maybe then you'd understand.

Churls closed her eyes and took a step forward. The wind tousled her short hair. "He didn't say anything about that." She pictured Vedas ascending rickety stairs, knocking on a door, steeling himself to deliver the horrible news. Taking responsibility for the death of a child.

You should ask him about it, Fyra said.

Churls opened her eyes and found that her daughter had placed her tiny hand in Churls's own. She resisted the knee-jerk urge to snatch it away. But concentrating on the contact, she realized it felt like nothing. The breeze caressed Churls's hand, chilling the sweat on her palm. Holding her daughter's hand felt like air passing through her lungs.

You will, won't you, Mama, Fyra said. *You'll ask him?*

"I will," Churls said, and stood alone on the edge of the cliff.

‡

As she expected, Berun had not yet returned. Churls often woke in the hours before dawn, always to find the constructed man absent. He returned just before the sun rose. She never asked him where he had been. It was his business—productive business, sometimes. On four separate occasions, he had brought breakfast back with him. Two rodents with crushed skulls. Once, he had bagged a rodent and an owl, which Vedas refused to eat.

Each time, Berun had also returned with a new pair of rocks in his hands, ready to be ground down into marbles. Churls wanted to ask him about his nighttime activities, but could not find a way to broach the subject. Fairly certain he liked her, she did not want to run the risk of making him uncomfortable. He reminded her of Abi, the precocious child her sister had adopted. He even stood the same way, like he was waiting for instructions. Ever watchful. Sensitive.

Churls sat down, not tired in the least. Her eyes had fully adjusted to the night.

Vedas lay face down only a body-length from her, half on, half off his bedroll, posture unnaturally tense for a sleeping man. His left palm lay flat on the ground, but his fingers curled into the soil. He had pulled his right knee up until it was level with his waist, and the toes of his left foot pointed into the ground. Both calf muscles bulged with tension. He looked almost as if he were crawling, or climbing a wall.

Churls admired the twin curves of his buttocks, and wondered what would happen if she ran a fingertip between them. She indulged this fantasy while stroking her inner thigh. Her eyelids grew heavy as her fingers found their mark.

A sound behind her. A pebble shifting against another pebble.

Before she could move, Vedas pushed off the ground and leapt forward, aimed at a point just behind her. He twisted in the air as he flew, back grazing her left shoulder. She had barely begun to turn when his body, struck by something in midair, bowled over her. Pitching forward, she was unable to raise her hands before her face struck earth. Her lower lip peeled back and dirt ground against her teeth. A glancing blow, either Vedas or the thing he had caught, scraped along the right side of her head, nearly taking her ear with it. She roared into the ground.

A growl answered it.

Churls lifted her head in time to see Vedas and the cat disengage. He was a mere beat slower getting to his feet, and took a vicious swipe to the head.

The blow should have taken his head off, yet he simply twisted his neck with the impact and kept moving. He circled the cat, a darkly furred, compactly muscular beast that must have weighed nearly as much as Vedas. It spat, hind legs twitching, front paw extended, swiping with dizzying speed whenever the black-suited man tried to close in.

Vedas took another hit to the head. Churls saw the white of the cat's claws, no less than two inches long. Again, Vedas took the impact as though it were a boxer's weak cross.

Churls rose to a crouch, the taste of blood and dirt in her mouth.

"Stay back!" Vedas yelled.

She had not noticed before, but he had masked his face completely. Unbelievable, that it alone had shielded him from the cat's claws. Unmindful of his warning, she snapped her head around to locate her sword, and crab-walked backward to it. Its worn hilt felt good in her hands, but she doubted it would be of much use against the man-sized feline if it turned its attention back to her.

Snarling, the cat sprung toward Vedas. Falling under its weight, he caught its head in his hands before its canines found his throat. Slowly, he closed his fingers around its neck. Its back paws skittered along his legs, unable to hook claws into flesh. As Vedas's grip tightened, the cat thrashed ever more wildly atop his body. Its front paws slapped at his head, claws failing to sink in there as well.

Churls became aware of the sound coming from the animal's constricted throat. A low, almost human gurgle. She had heard the sound before. She had strangled men before.

She ran forward. Her blade passed through the cat's heart with expert precision, but the animal's seizures opened the gash wider, and then tore the sword from Churls's hands. Blood fountained from the wound, hitting her chest squarely, drenching her instantly.

Its heat shocked her, and she fell to her knees.

‡

The blood had created a tight film across her chest. It itched horribly, but she did not scratch at it. Her lower lip was swollen to twice its normal size, and the entire right side of her head burned as though it had been scoured with grit paper.

The sun had barely risen, and the world was beautiful. Almost six thousand feet below her and peppered with tiny islands, an expanse of bluegreen sea extended to the horizon. Sunlight passed through the shallow water as if it were glass, revealing the wrack-spotted sand below. Huge, paddle-finned reptiles drifted between the islands, their scale impossible for Churls to comprehend. Legend said the ocean was no deeper than a man could throw a stone, but this too was difficult to understand.

Men could not sail the ocean, so how could they know how deep it was?

The cat lay at Churls's feet. One leg had fallen over the edge of the cliff. Its fur was matted with blood and dirt. It had indeed been as heavy as a man. Berun had offered to carry it, but Churls preferred to do it herself. She had told the constructed man to stop apologizing. How could he have known a cat would attack?

Vedas lay recuperating. His suit had protected him from most of the damage, the fact of which still amazed Churls. She had examined his jaw and asked him to rotate his joints. Though these tests proved his injuries were not debilitating, his neck and right knee stiffened enough to worry her. Clearly, she reasoned, travel would have to wait until tomorrow. He complained, but Churls insisted he rest. She sprinkled suffun root over his breakfast, and he had fallen to sleep soon after.

It was an unexpected comfort, knowing that he lay in a deep sleep. The stress of hiding her attraction, of maintaining the fragile balance of moods between them, was so easily shrugged away. She did not have to think about answering his next question, proving to him again and again that she knew best how to lead them from one place to the next. She stood unclothed, relaxed as she always was after a fight.

She heard Berun's steps long before he reached her.

"I don't want another apology," she said without turning. "Save it for Vedas if you like, but I doubt he wants it, either."

"No apology," he rumbled. "There's a pond not far. I brought you water."

She turned. "I have . . ."

She shook her head. The constructed man dripped water from the bottom of his oddly distended belly. He had carried the water with him, but could not create a perfectly sealed container.

The spheres rolled away from the bathtub he had formed, and Churls peeked inside. She laughed.

"What?" Berun said.

"You brought a traveler with you. Look."

Berun's eyes rolled free from his face and tumbled slowly down his chest. Perched above the water, they observed the orange-scaled fish that swam in tight circles inside his makeshift stomach. He reached inside and cupped it against a wall.

"Keep it?" he asked.

"Too small," Churls said. "Feed it to the sea."

Berun nodded his great, eyeless head. "Yours, too."

Churls pushed the cat over the edge, and Berun threw the fish after it. The wind pushed both out from the cliff wall as they fell, arcing down to the distant waterline. Churls turned away when she could no longer see the cat's tumbling body, and climbed into Berun. The water was warmer than she had expected. A month's worth of grime floated free and mixed with the blood. Berun rearranged the floor of the tub, molding it under Churls's body.

She slept, and for the first time since leaving Nbena did not dream of Vedas.

EBN BON MARI

E very few years, she painted a new sigil on her voidsuit. The paint, a mixture of pigment, ground elder offal, bonedust, and reconstituted blood, soaked into the black leather, tattooing it near-instantaneously. The bond was permanent, and thus one had to be careful painting a sigil. A single misstroke and it was ruined, precious space and paint wasted. The elder skin needed to construct one voidsuit cost the academy nearly as much as a new building. Alchemical paint alone sold for forty times its weight in bonedust.

Ebn had never erred in her painting. For seven decades she had possessed one suit, the very same suit she had worn on her first jubilant ascension into orbit—a remarkable feat of preservation even among her peers, all of whom cared for their suits as if they were offspring.

Others constructed studios for their suits, directing sunlight through mirrored channels into mirrored rooms. Some kept theirs in cold storage closets, forcing a kind of stasis on the material. A few even doused their suits in alchemical light far more intense than nature provided. They hoarded their recipes, striving to reproduce the sun's spectrum of light exactly.

Ebn disapproved of these artificial means. She considered natural light more than sufficient for the nourishment of elder skin artifacts, and so kept her suit on a swiveling table enchanted to track the sun across the sky.

The demonstrable success of this technique, which seemed so crude compared to others, confounded many of her peers. Some attempted to replicate her setup, but ultimately could not rationalize leaving such a valuable possession out in the open.

It had not occurred to Ebn to worry about thievery for some fifty years. She had stitched spells of defense and detailed automation into the seams of her suit and sealed them with elder synovial fluid. The suit could defend itself physically and cast preprogrammed spells to ward off sophisticated attacks.

Like all articles of clothing composed of elder skin, the voidsuit developed a strong telepathic bond with its wearer. Ebn knew its condition at all times. With enough concentration, she could make it come to her. It lumbered like an ill-made construct, but it would power through enemies and walls in order to reach her. On an autumn afternoon in 12457, she had collapsed on the floor of the gymnasium, muscles unresponsive, the victim of a usurper's poisoning. Before the solution dragged her under completely, she summoned her suit.

It had carried her to safety, saved her life.

Though she knew it was not technically sentient, Ebn had never been able to stop herself from cooing to hers as she worked. Painting a sigil was an act of intimacy, a rare occasion to remove her gloves and let her tongues taste the air. They strained out of her palms, an oddly pleasurable sensation akin to stretching the tightness out of one's wrist, trying to lap at the paint as if they possessed minds of their own. By the time she finished painting, her hands were pleasurably sore from gripping the brush and keeping her tongues in check.

Her self-control all but spent, before capping the paint jar Ebn usually allowed her tongues to taste a tiny bit of paint. She dipped the straining tip of each organ into the thick brown fluid. The vague taste of iron and loam seemed to linger in her nose as her quivering tongues retracted into her palms. Bright motes, daylight stars, swam before her eyes. Her wrists twitched and she clenched her fists against the faint stirrings of nausea that preceded the euphoria.

She waited.

Though prepared for it, the wave always caught her by surprise. It lifted her off her feet and swept her away. Adrift in blackness, the sun nonetheless seemed to shine upon her. The same heat bathed her skin, invigorating her.

She moved her arms as if she were swimming, though she had never before swum and never desired to. She opened her mouth and the heat entered her body, tasting of lemon and rose and marrow. Time stopped and she swam.

She would wake hours later, encased in her voidsuit, arms and legs sore from the unaccustomed exercise.

Today, she painted a sigil of influence—a simple, almost elementary character designed to increase its wearer's persuasive faculty. Her tongues remained oddly quiescent during the process, only venturing forth from her palms briefly to taste the air.

Sigil completed, she sewed twelve spells of compulsion into the joints where the suit's armored plates met at underarm and groin. Hopefully, for all of their jealous watching, not one of her lieutenants would notice the slight alteration. Certainly, they would wonder why she had painted what seemed such a simple sigil on her suit, and conjecture among themselves.

Only Qon knew the full extent of her plan. The spells would increase the sigil of influence's power, allowing Ebn to draw the god's attention and amplify the mages' message of goodwill—to seduce him into looking kindly upon them, in effect. A risky maneuver, surely, yet she believed it would work. She had diagrammed and rediagrammed the spell's thaumatic output, proving its grace and subtlety.

She wondered what Pol's reaction to the plan would have been. Approval, possibly. Certainly, it was a more aggressive approach than she had ever espoused before.

She and Pol were not yet lovers as she had planned. In truth, her mind balked at the thought of using the spells of compulsion—the sex spells, as Qon had crassly labeled them—on him. But for the twelve she had incorporated into her suit, she kept them in the jar in her office, away from view. Maybe she had overthought the whole process of seduction, which should be quite simple in theory. Always in theory.

Slip them under his door, a voice urged. *Act!*

She imagined calling him with her mind, followed by his arrival at her doorstep. Undressing each other. His body under hers. Afterward, the feeling of his long torso against her back, his lips brushing her shoulders.

The spells she had created were flawless. She examined them daily. They would bend him to her will entirely.

Banishing these thoughts, she returned her suit to its table. Before capping the jar of alchemical paint, she held her right hand over it. The tongue refused to emerge from her palm. She tried the left hand, to the same result. A good thing, perhaps. The aftereffects of tasting the paint were mildly disorienting, and she needed to keep her mind sharp for the evening's ascension. Possibly, the tongues had picked up on her restive mood and responded with a rare show of empathy. Their lasciviousness had limits, she knew. They were a part of her. They understood fear easily enough.

Ebn had good reason for fear. She had failed to seduce the god once already.

‡

Of course, history proved that many before her had been equally incautious. Even those whose statues now lined the Avenue of Saints had been fools in their own right—murderers, rapists, manipulators, acting in the name of Adrash. The world celebrated men and women of violent conviction, but ultimately the actions of such individuals had driven the god from the earth. Read with a discerning eye, the story of the world was one of brutishness, impetuosity, and spite.

The creation of the Royal Outbound Mages of Stol had been no exception. A common assumption was that the corps had been created in order to commune with Adrash, to coax him back to earth, but the truth was far less noble.

Three thousand years prior to Ebn's era, the king of Stol received word that the Republic of Knos Min had begun sending eldermen into orbit. A massive espionage effort produced no evidence to support this claim, yet the king could not very well risk being shown up by Knos Min, his nation's primary rival in the elder corpse market.

In 9209 MD, several hundred years after catching wind of the original rumor, the Academy of Applied Magics sent its first elderman into orbit. This mage promptly died of exposure to the void. The academy, urged on by the queen herself, did not stop at this one death, but persisted and eventually developed magics sufficient to the task of lifting an elderman into low orbit and landing her safely thereafter.

Stol did not attempt to keep its advanced program a secret. The newly titled Royal Outbound Mages became a symbol of the kingdom's magical development, and the mages themselves became figureheads of a new class. Eldermen, hardier and more prone to magical talent, soon came from all regions of Knoori seeking employment.

At its height, the corps numbered over eight hundred individuals.

Inevitably, not all who applied were accepted into the ranks, yet Stol never failed to exploit an asset. No one knew how many eldermen perished as a result of experimental procedures tangential to the program.

Despite the kingdom's vast expenditure of resources, as time wore on the program failed to produce anything of actual or perceived value. A small but growing minority viewed the outbound mages' efforts—which at that time consisted largely of monitoring Adrash's movements—as blasphemous, asserting that no man had the right to enter the god's abode. By the opening of the ninety-fourth century, public support of the mages had eroded almost completely. Eldermen, so recently a beloved symbol of Stol, had become a suspect race, a source of anger and targets of violent reprisal.

By imperial order, the bloated program was cut to a fraction of its former size in 9365.

Oddly, this act proved foundational in energizing the corps. Reduced to a lean nucleus of fifty highly skilled eldermen, the mages reinvented themselves, purging their lore of any unnecessary ritual or tradition. With fewer resources, no longer under the eye of public scrutiny, they developed their own odd society. They restricted themselves to the academy grounds almost exclusively, fearful of a public who feared their race.

With their combined genius and magical talent, they developed and refined the voidsuit, a tool that increased each mage's magical capability fivefold. Reaching orbit in record times, they flew farther and farther away from Jeroun, even to the point of entering the moon's insubstantial atmosphere. They became fast and strong, and ultimately forced their way—through murder, deception, and magical coercion—back into ruling positions in the academy.

The majority of the mages had long since ceased to believe rumors of a competing outbound army in Knos Min, and redefined the program's mission. Convincing Adrash of the world's worth became the only goal. Over time, this became the academy's encompassing objective as well. Entire branches of magical inquiry were abandoned, faculty dismissed or executed for heterodox views.

In the span of a few generations, one question came to dominate all academic discussion: *Does Adrash love the peaceful, or does he love the strong?* Undoubtedly, the question had been asked many times, in churches and on street corners for millennia, but the development of advanced magics that allowed an outbound mage to travel to the moon—into Adrash's territory—made the issue less a matter of metaphysics than concrete reality.

How, the mages submitted, *can we approach Adrash without offending him?*

The debate went on for many years, but by the time Ebn bon Mari rose to the rank of Captain of the Royal Outbound Mages her predecessors had generally come to the same verdict: Adrash did not look kindly upon acts of aggression.

Of course, they possessed damning evidence to support this conclusion. The creation of the Needle itself seemed to have been spurred by a particularly violent display of the corps' strength in 10991. Seven hundred years later, the mage Dor wa Dol—driven mad by the sigils he had tattooed on his body with alchemical ink—had attacked Adrash, causing the god to send his two smallest weapons to earth, resulting in a decades-long winter. The Cataclysm.

These tragedies, Ebn's forebears determined, *are the result of our arrogance. We must not treat Adrash as if he were an equal met on the battlefield. Instead, we will beg his forgiveness. We will prostrate ourselves, offering gifts and tribute.*

Ebn had inherited this outlook: despite her own monstrous gaffe, she believed in it wholeheartedly.

‡

After breakfast, a knock on her door. Ebn hurried to the balcony curtains and drew them shut. The weighted hems whispered across the polished flag-stones, shutting out the sun completely.

Four of the sculptor's apprentices brought the statue into her apartment. Though each strapping human lad wore a worksuit of high-grade elder-cloth, they struggled under the weight of marble. Two strained at its head while the other two swiveled its torso, angling its massive shoulders through the doorframe.

"Could we get some light?" one asked.

"Shut up," Ebn said. "You measured everything yesterday. Your eyes will adjust."

The apprentices maneuvered the statue to the exact center of her living room and set it upright. Even in the near dark it was beautiful, but it was not yet the effect she desired. Without taking her eyes from the figure, she pointed to the curtains.

"Open them," she told no one in particular. "And when you do it, do it quickly. I want the sun to burst into the room, not crawl."

One of the apprentices shrugged and hauled on the golden rope. Light filled the room instantly, blinding Ebn for a heartbeat. The blackness fled from her eyes and the statue came into swift focus, as though the figure had materialized into her room out of nothingness.

The breath caught in her throat.

Adrash stood before her, head nearly touching the eighteen-foot ceiling. He stood relaxed, back straight and feet slightly apart. Carved from a single immense block of unveined white marble, the swells and depressions of his musculature appeared as smooth as polished glass, buffed to a high shine with several hundred grams of bonedust.

The armor had retreated from his head and neck, revealing his stylized masculine features and smooth scalp. Traditionally, sculptors used a black stone to show the true color of the god's naked skin, but Ebn preferred the purity of white alone.

His eyes were closed, his lips slightly puckered to kiss the globe cradled in his powerful hands. Though she could not see the detail from where she stood, Ebn knew the god's lips landed on Stol. She had designed it to symbolize Adrash's love for the world, but also to suggest the kingdom's centrality. For the last month she had spent far too much of her time quibbling over sketches and miniatures with the sculptor.

The chest must be just so. The genitals, just so. His thighs are too small, his head too large. She obsessed over the globe, even. The islands were too numerous or too uniformly shaped, the perpetual storm on the other side of the world spun the wrong direction. The sculptor, not to mention the entire arts faculty, must have thought her batty.

No matter. The statue was completed, and it was beautiful. Her time and the academy's funds had been well spent.

"Ebn?" Qon called from the open doorway. She stepped in. "I have been knocking for some time. I . . ." She stared up at the statue. "Good Lord Adrash. Ebn, I had no idea how beautiful it would be."

Ebn tore her gaze away. "I think I am insulted. What did you think I was doing with my time—carving a mantle-piece? Adrash needs nothing of any practical value, true, but he does deserve to be venerated properly." She could not contain her smile as she turned back to her creation. "Only now I cannot bear the thought of letting it go."

‡

Dustglass helmets cradled in the crooks of their elbows, forty-two outbound mages stood on the roof of the Esoteric Arts building. They were accoutered for a long orbital excursion, bandoliers filled with spells. Ebn noticed more than a few fresh sigils—blue and grey and red—painted on voidsuits, and approved.

A strong breeze had carried the smell of the docks, wet and rotting. Qon pulled a kerchief from her suit collar and covered her mouth, unconcerned if the younger outbound mages interpreted this as a sign of weakness. Though the smell made Ebn nauseous too, she stood stone-faced among her officers as the statue was hauled and deposited upright in their midst.

They were ready.

The moon had not yet risen, but the Needle already stretched nearly half-way across the sky. Positioned in the exact center of the roof, the marble god seemed to glow with its own inner light. Several of the older mages faced it and pressed left fist to forehead out of reverence. The younger lot stole glances at the statue, affecting airs of disdain. They could not ignore the existence of Adrash, but deference did not fit in well with the affected cynicism in vogue among the academy's young elite.

Pol stepped forward for a closer look. She could not read his expression, and refrained from asking his opinion. She admired the graceful curve of his neck above the collar of his suit. Once, not long after his arrival from Pusta, he had fallen asleep in a chair during a private tutorial. She had watched him for close to an hour, counting the doubled pulses of his jugular. Then, as now, she wanted to cradle his jaw in her hand.

She admonished herself for her preoccupation, which had only ever produced frustration.

"You know your role?" she asked him.

"Yes," he said, and patted the pack attached to his stomach. "I keep the spells at ready."

A whistle blew—a long, trilling blast that rose in pitch sharply before cutting off.

"Two minutes!" the huge tamer yelled.

Ebn and Pol retreated to the edges of the circular roof. Most of the mages had already assumed the waiting position. Helmets on, they lay on their backs, hands gripping the newly installed handles inset into the floor above their heads, feet hooked under the bar running the inner perimeter of the low roof wall. Minor magic would have secured them equally well, but Ebn thought it best not to tire anyone before the evening's major spell.

She watched the remaining officers ready themselves and then turned to the tamer, who gripped the thick shaft of the twelve-foot-tall sky-hook. A solid piece of steel, it resembled an immense shepherd's crook welded to a small, heavy platform on which the tamer stood.

"Your pet is in an agreeable mood?" she asked the heavily scarred man.

He shrugged heavy shoulders chalked with bonedust. "Seems to be. Tough to tell with Sapes, sometimes. She's temperamental, and this sort of thing's never been done before." He blew into the whistle again and bellowed the one-minute warning.

Their eyes met. The tamer smiled, and suddenly the stubby horns on his forehead seemed quite vulgar to her.

She flinched as a ragged scream tore through the night, far louder a sound than elderman or human lungs could produce.

"Better get settled, miss," the tamer said, positioning the grimy black-rimmed goggles over his eyes. "Dragon coming down."

‡

A long shape blotted out a section of stars above them. Wings the size of galleon sails forced waves of compacted air downward, pushing the voidsuited bodies into the floor. The wyrm roared again. Muffled through the outbound mages' glass helmets, the sound was nearly indistinguishable from the wind.

The beast descended and the pressure increased. Ebn craned her neck to see the tamer. He had wrapped his arms and legs around the sky-hook's shaft, but his goggled eyes were directed upward. He yelled, and whether they were incantations or encouragements, Ebn did not know. Wyrms were violently temperamental, and the elder hybrids the Tamer's Guild raised from hatchlings could only roughly be called tame.

Ebn assumed the tamer's lore would be sufficient to control the beast, for its task was simple enough. Still, she found herself mouthing a silent entreaty to Adrash for his blessing.

Apparently, he heard. The building shook as it took the wyrm's weight, and the air stilled.

Ebn opened eyes she had not realized were closed.

For a moment, the scope of the animal could not be fathomed. When she turned her head, the large black object a few feet from her head resolved itself into one of the beast's talons. She gazed up at its heaving stomach, a full thirty feet above her, and shuddered. It was so immense! She had never seen a wyrm up close. Craning her neck painfully, she located its head, which hung far out over the roof's edge. The animal seemed to be watching the city.

The tamer whooped, and Ebn shuddered again to see that vicious, wedge-shaped head swinging toward the roof. It came sailing in, and she lost scope once more: a giant black fist, a meteor tumbling out of the night sky. The visions fused, became a tooth-lined grin as long as two men, a gigantic double-pupiled eye glowing soft blue. The head lay against the stone floor, and above it floated the horned head of the tamer.

No, not floated. He stood behind the wyrm's head, and spoke in its ear.

The talons near Ebn twitched, scraping across the flagstones. The wyrm gripped the statue easily with one foot and Ebn winced, though she had strengthened the marble with reliable spells only hours ago.

The great head rose, dragging the length of its neck in an arcing line behind it. Flexing its haunches, the wyrm's stomach lowered until it seemed it would be impaled by the sky-hook. The tamer huddled under the beast, a huge man compressed into insignificance.

A cry rose in Ebn's throat as the wyrm leapt upward, sky-hook firmly gripped in its other foot. The gust of its passage pressed her flat into the roof, knocking the cry from her lips. She counted to thirty as the beast rose into the air, unhooked her feet, and slammed her gauntleted fist into the first spell on her bandolier. To her right, she saw Qon do the same.

Ebn whispered the gathering words, her own secret incantation to bind the mages' energy together and keep them safe during flight.

Immediately, she felt as if she were being pushed from either side—like a giant pair of hands squeezing her flat. Lines of red fire shot from the mages' bodies and wound together above the roof, forming a rope that shot heavenward, converging on the statue clutched in the wyrm's foot.

Any moment now, Ebn thought.

They shot into the sky.

‡

Rising swiftly under the wyrm's power, they spun slowly, a circle of suited figures at the end of a fire tether. Ebn's complex spell caused the mages' suits to repel each other, so that no one crashed into their neighbor. For all of her planning, however, she had not prepared herself for the nausea. Rising straight into orbit was one thing, spinning and being jounced around another thing entirely. She looked to the right and caught Qon's eye.

The woman was grinning.

"An odd way to enter the void," she had said when Ebn outlined the plan originally. "I see the need for the wyrm, I suppose, though I think in time we could develop a spell powerful enough to lift something as large as the statue into orbit."

"We do not have the time," Ebn said. "And I want us to be as fresh as possible when we reach orbit.'"

Qon's eyes roved over the thaumatic diagrams again. "Two questions. Will the tamer be able to handle heights of this magnitude? Thirty miles is no joke, Ebn. And will this spell"—she pointed to the projections Ebn had drawn out—"be enough to lift the statue in the event several of the less experienced mages are disoriented from the ride? Or simply afraid?"

Ebn nodded. "The tamer assures me that he can make it, and I see no reason to disbelieve him. It is his life on the line, too. From the point where he turns back to earth, it is but a short push. I have done the maths over and over. You and Pol and I could lift it into orbit by ourselves if need be."

"Would we be able to affect any spells afterward?"

"Probably not." Ebn traced the line of trajectory she had drawn, met her friend's eyes, and shrugged. "But I think it highly unlikely that thirty-nine well-trained mages will suffer fits of uselessness at the exact same time."

Qon quirked an eyebrow. "I think we crossed the line separating likely and unlikely some time ago."

POL TANZ ET SOM

From twenty miles up, Tansot was only a speck of light on the ebon blanket of earth. The stars above burned brighter every second. A vague but definite shadow above the spinning mages, the wyrm beat immense wings against air too thin for any natural creature to fly upon.

Pol pictured Shav, wrapped tight around the sky-hook, trusting in his pet's grip, shouting words of tamer lore and encouragement. As the air grew thinner, the spell the quarterstock had imbibed before calling the beast down supplied more and more oxygen to his body. He did not breathe in at all. Drawing in the cold would freeze his lungs instantly.

With greater height, sound itself began to fail. In his mind's eye, Pol saw Shav climbing the wyrm's legs and flank, shimmying up its long neck, straddling its giant head so that he might whisper directions into its ear. When his voice could no longer be heard, the violently shivering tamer crushed another spell against the wyrm's skull and pressed his ear to the wet scales, freezing the two beings together, forming a seal.

Tamer and wyrm's thoughts meshed and became one.

If the animal allowed, that is.

Even then it was a tenuous link, Pol knew, though he did not understand the process exactly. In the half-month since he had taken Shav as a lover, he had picked up more tamer lore than the guild normally allowed to outsiders. Still,

115

he was far from conversant. Strictly speaking, he had no desire to be. He knew without question that Ebn had made no study of their lore. If she had done so, her plan might not rely upon a madman and his unpredictable charge.

Pol considered the odd coincidence of Shav's appearance. Though not by nature a paranoid man, he could not avoid wondering how it was that Ebn had started looking for a tamer at nearly the exact moment of Pol's meeting one. Shav himself had expressed a similar sentiment. An odd confluence, surely, yet in Pol's experience such things often occurred without anyone's arrangement.

But coincidence or no, he could not ignore the potential in such a meeting of fates. He would turn it to his advantage by remaining vigilant, open to possibilities as they arose. The more connected he became to the world—the less like his timid peers, cloistered behind the walls of the academy—the better he would be able to mold events to suit his needs.

Fear is not an attribute of Adrash, Pol reminded himself. *It will not be one of mine.*

Ebn's spell pushed the mages farther and farther apart as gravity lost its hold, until their bodies spun nearly horizontal to the distant ground. The fiery tether binding them to the wyrm had faded to nothing in the rarified atmosphere, as Ebn had told them it would, making it difficult to see one another. The mages signed excitedly over their helmets nonetheless.

Pol did not partake in the simple conversation. Yes, he knew the plan. Yes, he knew his role. In the last month, Ebn had conducted thirteen briefings. If her officers did not yet know what must be done, they never would.

A quick and effortless spell, and Pol knew they had reached an altitude of almost twenty-three miles. Another hour, very likely.

Soon thereafter, Ebn would see the error of her conviction. Adrash had no interest in receiving supplicants, and even less interest in gifts. What need did a god have for baubles when he could cause steel monuments to rise from the moon itself? If the stories of Adrash were true—if seclusion had not turned the god into a shadow of himself—he would see their groveling as the insult it was, and react accordingly.

In Pol's estimation, the chances of the outbound mages returning to Jeroun were slim.

He sighed. Having made preparations for the worst, there was nothing left to do but wait.

He closed his eyes and considered the riddle of Shav again.

‡

The way his bulk occupied the small apartment near the docks, filling it so that it seemed he could not move without breaking something. Yet move he did. In private, Shav possessed an awareness of his outsized body that shocked Pol. Such poise could rarely be learned. Clearly, he affected clumsiness while fighting to trick his opponents.

Uncharacteristically and in opposition to the obvious hierarchy of species, Pol found himself intimidated by the quarterstock.

But it was not merely Shav's physical prowess that put Pol off balance. That the quarterstock was mad could not be denied. The sickness revealed itself primarily through his eyes, which stared through Pol more often than not, focused on images in his own mind. Sometimes his hands shook and his lips moved as though he were having a silent conversation. Slight tremors moved through him, often causing his whole body to vibrate like a tuning fork.

At times his madness bloomed into something else—something far beyond the bounds of mental imbalance, bordering on the mystical. While he slept, he spoke in different tongues.

Pol heard their cadence and rhythm and knew them to be true languages, though he recognized none of the words. His curiosity had compelled him to capture several of the monologues in acoustic jars and show them to a colleague in ancient languages. The man, obviously excited by what he heard, practically demanded to know where Pol had procured the recordings. Pol, unwilling to reveal his source, had walked away, little the wiser.

This was not all. On several trancelike occasions Shav had seemed to shift into another persona, changing tone, pitch, and vocabulary so completely that Pol wondered if the quarterstock were not in fact inhabited by other personalities. He had heard such things were possible.

Of course, he knew not to probe Shav too obviously. As their relationship developed, the quarterstock had revealed a deep, incisive intelligence, voiced in ever more sophisticated speech. Recently, he had begun to reveal troublingly precise insights into Pol's mind. He seemed to possess an instinctive clairvoyance, and as a result Pol no longer knew what to hide and what to reveal. The quarterstock seemed possessed of faculties reason could not explain.

These traits both repelled and attracted Pol. Shav was important, somehow—even if only because Pol willed it so. He had pursued Shav intuitively, unsure of his own motives, and the quarterstock seemed to be responding in kind. Like opponents in a game of yhor, they danced half-blind around one another, trying to peer at the other's pieces.

"You have a plan for me," Shav had told him the last time they met—undoubtedly, their most troubling conversation yet.

Pol finished his honey and saffron flatbread slowly, considering. A direct response seemed best. "Obviously I do, Shav. Beyond physical pleasure, I want to understand your hybrid nature. We have talked about it many times. My intentions are no mystery."

"No, Pol." The hybrid's thick fingers folded the bread around the spiced dates expertly. "That's not what I mean. I'm good at reading faces, and yours says you're hiding things from me. Things beyond pleasure and breeding. It's fine for now if you want to hide. I'll eventually figure it out, with or without your help."

Pol felt an all-too-familiar moment of paranoia, and quickly reviewed their conversation to make sure he had not revealed anything he had not meant to. He opened his mouth, sure of words to come.

"Don't," Shav said. "Denying it won't do any good. I've contacted a linealogist at your academy, and he confirmed my suspicions. A drop of blood or semen will answer all of your questions about my heritage. You have access to both. Of course, you would still need a linealogist to perform the spells, and then your study would be public. Somehow, I gather that isn't part of your plan. The linealogist was quite eager to know your name."

Pol's hearts beat harder. To be caught pursuing another guild's lore could land him in some trouble. The fact that he had no intention of casting linealogical spells would make no difference. If the administration searched deep enough, they might even discover that he had been pursuing his own unregistered research with illegally acquired alchemicals. The academy, which inherited any documents of magical innovation upon a mage's death, considered such illicit practices acts of sedition against Stol, punishable by death.

The chair creaked under Shav as he sat back. He did not need to smile to show his satisfaction. Not for the first time, Pol wondered what it would be like to fight the quarterstock—what it would be like to straddle his back and wrap fingers around his throat.

"No," Shav answered the unspoken question. "I didn't give him your name. Your secret is safe."

"Scholars and mages are jealous of their lore," Pol said, shrugging the matter away. "The linealogists are no exception. Nor am I. The tamers themselves, for that matter."

Shav shook his head. "There's more to it than that. Sometimes I think you're simply stalling, waiting for something to announce itself. I'm not . . . I'm . . ." Mouth working, he stared through Pol's chest.

The back of Pol's neck tingled as the shift occurred.

"The dragon and I," Shav finally said, voice lower than normal, words slightly slurred with the touch of an accent Pol could not name. "A halfbreed and a quarterbreed at this moment in time. The conjunction of the two is interesting, Pol. Interesting. I've seen a dragon crash into the sea, sure the animal had killed itself. Instead it surfaced, twisting its long neck and beating its wings upon the water, a great sea serpent clamped in its jaws—a sea serpent so large that it could've swallowed our tiny boat in one bite. Its skin shone like silver in the moonlight, and its thrashing frothed the sea like a child's hand slapping bathwater."

Pol did not interrupt, though he knew no mortal man had ever sailed upon the ocean.

Shav leaned forward, eyes liquid and unfocused. "The Needle had only risen halfway, and the moon showed a quarter of her face. I stared at the destruction coming swiftly: a wall of black water that blotted out the stars along the horizon. I waited and told my men to prepare themselves. Some of them prayed to Adrash, some to Orrus, and some to the devil." He dipped his head and touched his horns almost reverently. "Me, I just waited for the inevitable, almost wanting it. Most likely, I would die along with my men. An odd feeling, being that powerless."

He blinked. His amber eyes refocused. The corners of his mouth twitched, and he spoke in the voice Pol had become accustomed to.

"Someday soon, I think you'll know what that feels like."

‡

To Pol's astonishment, the statement had haunted him for days. Finally, chagrined that it should take him so long to see the light of reason, he dismissed the possibility that Shav had performed an extraordinary feat of magic. No, the quarterstock had merely read the signs of Pol's anxiety.

Though he had seen Adrash through the cloudy lens of magnification spells many times, Pol had never ventured within a thousand miles of the god. He had always run from the divine presence as he had been taught—yet if all went according to Ebn's plan, in less than two weeks he would encounter Adrash in the flesh. The thought made his hearts thunder.

Pol examined his fear, and it disgusted him.

Is this the man Adrash will see? he asked himself. *A coward?*

Shame drove him forward. A mere day after talking with Shav, he began tattooing himself with alchemical ink of his own design—a foolhardy enterprise, surely. There were precedents, but only a few, and by accounts those men had gone mad.

Gone mad? An understatement, surely. The mage Dor wa Dol, driven to such insanity by his sigils, had single-handedly caused the Cataclysm. He had been captain of the outbound mages at the time, an elderman in the prime of his ability.

Clearly, even the hardiest elderman could not handle that much alchemy coursing through his body for long.

Pol knew the risks, having researched the possibility for years. Aside from the likelihood of overloading one's body with magic, the execution of each sigil had to be exact. One misstroke, and the consequences would be dire.

Nonetheless, he proceeded.

First, his left shoulder: a rudimentary warding sigil. His hand shook so severely that the character—four simple lines—took nearly an hour to complete. When nothing untoward happened—indeed, when his voice failed to rouse the symbol to life—he painted a second, slightly more complex character on his bicep: a flight sigil. This too remained dormant despite his attempts to activate it. Emboldened and not a little frustrated, he drew a sigil on his right wrist, his left shin, his stomach.

Once started, he could not stop. In numb horror he watched his body become a canvas of inert magical symbols.

The morning sun slanted through his windows. The day progressed, and then the evening. A week passed, during which he added several new sigils. He took to wearing long-sleeved, close-fitting garments. Whatever he had imagined might happen in time, did not. The black characters lay dormant despite his every incantation. He did not grow ill or suffer visions. Disappointed that years of expectation had apparently presaged nothing, he stopped tattooing himself.

It was only on the morning of Ebn's mission, as he contemplated the prospect of his own death, that he found the exercise had produced something of value.

The act of tattooing—of risking his body for the sake of power—had silenced his fear.

‡

The world flared against Pol's eyelids. He opened them in time to see the great fireball the wyrm had belched disperse into nothingness: A lightning flash, stamping the afterimage in Pol's mind—a fluorescing cloud, amorphous and vast, dwarfing the giant serpent that had birthed it. Its long, razor-toothed jaws opening and closing.

The other mages were already moving, fingering their spell-laden bandoliers. Pol would not mirror their anxiousness. He would not fidget. When the occasion called for action, his movements would be fluid and precise.

To his right, Ebn signed with fingers that glowed blue with magefire.

One minute. On my signal.

Forty-one mages signed their understanding, and waited. For sixty seconds, Pol thought of Shav, arms and thighs tightly gripping the wyrm's skull, bonedusted skin hoary with ice crystals. Were his eyes closed behind the heavy goggles? Or was he staring down at the mages even now, thinking his inexplicable thoughts? Perhaps he watched the stars, which seemed close enough now to touch. One last look before returning to earth.

Ebn's hands screamed actinic sapphire.

Now!

Pol smashed his gauntleted fist into the second spell in his bandolier. His tether reignited as the wyrm dropped the statue. Though he did not count to be sure, it looked like all of the mages had reacted in concert. Any who had not were now untethered, and would have to rely upon their own lore to return to earth or ascend to orbit. Whether their actions resulted in death or the simple shame of failure, Pol had little sympathy.

The statue fell through the circle of mages and Pol smashed the third spell in his bandolier. His body surged upwards. He felt a powerful tug as his tether took the weight, but kept ascending. He checked his speed to make sure he did not rise too fast. Others adjusted similarly, Ebn, Qon and the senior mages among them, yet it soon became clear the action was unnecessary. Gravity pulled weakly thirty miles above Jeroun, and even the youngest mages seemed to be handling their share of the weight.

The circle drew in. Pol read excitement on most of the faces. Qon smiled and signed with quick hands, unembarrassed of her enthusiasm. The others responded in kind.

Fools, Pol thought. It would be at least another day and a half before they reached Adrash, assuming he could be located. More than enough time to poke holes in any plan—enough time to get tired and cranky and edgy. Perhaps, Pol reasoned, they needed this momentary upswell of emotion to prepare for the long haul to the moon.

Once again, he had little sympathy. The path was clear. What benefit could be garnered from deceiving oneself?

Ebn met Pol's sober look and nodded with equal sobriety.

Now the hard part, she signed.

‡

On average, an outbound mage could reach the moon in thirty-six hours. Qon could reach it in twenty-seven, Ebn in just under a day. Pol had once traveled the distance in twenty-two hours, forty minutes, a full fifty-three minutes faster than Ebn's stated record. Of course, he had publicly recorded a less impressive time. Undoubtedly, she had done the same. A smart mage would not reveal his true power unless threatened.

Of course, such threats were common at the academy and came in all varieties, as did violence. The administration did not approve of murder as a means to advancement, but they made no move to stop it. Death kept the ranks slim and mean. The mages who survived planned ahead and bided their time. Eventually, they became leaders. If they remained vigilant, they stayed in their positions for a very long time, indeed.

As he flew, Pol wondered if it might be possible to unseat Ebn without killing her. When her plan ended unsuccessfully—assuming she survived the encounter with Adrash—perhaps she could be persuaded to step down. With great care Pol might then find a way to draw her to his side. She loved him, clearly, and that could be used to his advantage.

Still, her death would be the most convenient outcome.

And if Adrash took the lives of a few of the seniormost mages as well . . .

Pol thought of the opportunities their absences would create. He fantasized, a thing he did not often allow himself to do.

Thirty-six hours passed slowly in the void. The mages had little to distract themselves. Shy two youths who had failed to activate their spells in time, each was forced to pull a bit harder at his or her tether. The alignment needed constant watching lest someone wander, and so they slept in shifts, two hours off, four hours on. They signaled constantly to one another, reminding themselves to stay alert.

The blazing stars called seductively. If one listened closely enough, the emptiness echoed with their stately, hypnotic song. Drawing energy from one's flight spells was both taxing and monotonous. Bonedust-and-honey lozenges provided nutrients, but did not fill the emptiness in one's stomach.

For the less skilled, these factors often resulted in what Ebn had termed hypnogogic drift, a state wherein the body and mind uncoupled without the mage's awareness. A drifting mage thought he was operating at full attention, when in fact he had entered a dream almost identical to reality.

When the sun came out from behind the swollen belly of Jeroun below their feet, its light created yet another problem. Though nourishing to both suit and mage, the radiation proved too severe for sensitive elderman eyes. In response, the dustglass helmets polarized, locking each mage in a dim chamber where hallucinations arose easily. Suddenly, the emptiness seemed to echo with familiar voices, strobe with color. In such conditions it was easy to become disoriented and veer off course. A single mistake could send the statue tumbling, resulting in a massive waste of energy and time as the mages scrambled to right it.

In addition, many of the younger mages had yet to develop their remote manipulation sigils. They did not fully comprehend the way a massive object moved in the void—how deadly even a spinning body could be.

But the most common danger of navigating the void was simple forgetfulness. Drawing power and keeping a steady course became routine, so easily done even experienced mages could neglect spells that preserved life on its most basic level. Heat. Air. During the outbound mages' long history, many had been lost to the void, slowly having frozen or asphyxiated to death unawares.

Thus the mages looked to each other, orienting themselves back to reality over and over again. They traveled swiftly into the never-ending night, wrapped in thin bubbles of atmosphere that distorted and magnified the stars around them. They gestured to one another, carrying on trite conversations to keep their minds busy.

Traveling slower than he otherwise would, soon even Pol forgot his pride and talked of the food in Kengsort, the weather atop Miselo Hill, the wine of the Aspa foothills.

Thirty-six hours passed slowly. Tensely.

‡

They were still eight hours from the moon when Adrash showed himself. He appeared in an instant, matching the mages' speed at the center of their spread circle. His eyes flashed like the sun itself, yellow-white and harsh, washing out the figure behind.

The light pushed against Pol. It broke upon him in wave after glacial wave, stiffening his limbs. He squinted against the glare and fought the torpor that had been imposed upon him. Slowly—agonizingly—he bent frozen fingers, formed a fist and held it before his chest, ready to shatter a spell in defense.

Shaking like palsied old men, his neighbors to the right and left began assuming similar postures. Of course, their lore would be of no use against Adrash. Holding forty skilled mages in a thrall, even one that did not bind completely, spoke of power beyond reason.

Slightly above and to Pol's right, Ebn's hands erupted in blue flame.

Sever! she signed.

The distraction proved enough to break free of Adrash's ensorcelment. Pol's mind snapped back into focus, and he dissolved his tether. In ragged order, the others did likewise. Ebn waited for the last of her lieutenants to complete the task, and then allowed the statue to float free.

For what seemed to Pol an eternity, the tableau remained static. Orbiting the radiant god, the mages appeared small and insectile in their black, segmented suits.

The intense light shut off abruptly, scoring the image on Pol's retinas.

He blinked the scene clear to find it changed.

Adrash floated before the immense statue. His sinuous forearms were crossed beneath his broad chest, his head canted forward on his thick neck. Flatfooted, he stood as if upon solid ground. He had positioned himself face to face with the marble figure, and looked down upon the world cradled in its hands. But for the cold luminosity of his eyes, he himself resembled a sculpted object, an artist's anatomical model flawlessly cast in white stone.

Nonetheless, it struck Pol that Adrash was vastly more beautiful than the statue. He committed to memory every line of the god's powerful physique. His cock stirred against the tight base layer of his suit, and a tingling radiated into his thighs.

Ebn's hands flashed again. Pol tore his eyes away from Adrash, but found that he could not read the senior mage's gestures. Arms pointed at the god, she formed circles before her chest, an arc of crimson flashing briefly between her gauntleted fingers. A spell. Pol watched in shocked fascination as the seams of her suit began to glow at underarm and groin.

Adrash did not so much as twitch in response, but Pol felt the draw of her magic. He fought a compulsion to cross the space to Ebn, to take her in his arms.

She collapsed the spell between her palms.

Adrash's head now swiveled in her direction. She beckoned to him with signs.

Come here. Come closer.

The mages watched, unmoving, as Adrash turned. He took one step in her direction, two, and started walking toward her slowly, as though he were ascending an invisible staircase. Ebn smiled and spread her hands again. The spell twisted between her fingers, now as black and viscous as clotting blood.

What madness has possessed her? Pol asked himself. The plan had been simple: *Find Adrash, present the gift, and retreat. Do not deviate from the plan.* Pol had been tasked with moving the statue forward, stabilizing it in orbit above the moon. Though he thought it foolish to approach the god in this manner, he respected the consistency of Ebn's plan. One did not prostrate with a sword in one's hand.

This is the death of us all, Pol thought.

Halfway to Ebn, Adrash stopped and shook his head, for all the world like a man trying to shake an ugly thought from his mind. He turned from her and stretched forth his left arm, pointing his closed fist at the statue. No expression could be read on his masked features.

A tremor passed through Pol's limbs. Of their own accord, the sigils tattooed on his skin came to life, blooming into twenty-two points of searing agony. The air solidified in his lungs, stopping the scream in his throat. His hearts hiccoughed in his chest and died. For a timeless instant, his bones reverberated an endless note, on the verge of shattering . . .

As quickly as it had begun, the pain ceased.

The space between his heartbeats dilated: One . . . Two . . . Three . . .

The universe rang as if struck. Pol focused on the sound, sure that if he listened long enough he would hear the words that had originally set the stars in motion, the father of all incantations, the font of all magic. Opening his mouth, he let the sound inside. A warm draught tasting of cinnamon and anise, it rushed dizzyingly to his head, his hands, the twenty-two sigils upon his body. It tingled on his lips, pulsed at the tips of his fingers, begging to be liberated. He held himself at the threshold of release, every nerve singing in ecstasy.

Four . . . Five . . . Six.

Too late, he remembered where he was, his duty to the other mages.

Too late, he started to cast the spell.

Adrash opened his hand. The statue shattered, and the light of the god's wrath eclipsed the stars.

PART THREE

VEDAS TEZUL

They traveled in relative comfort across the highest Step, averaging nearly twenty-five miles a day. The sparse pine forest suited walking, providing shade and sunlight in equal measures. Even without a trodden path, the ground remained dry and stable. No boulders rose from the earth to trip feet. Numerous small rivers provided fresh water and trout, and lakes allowed them to bathe.

Weather during the Months of Clergymen and Pilots could be unpredictable throughout Stol, yet at the top of the world it was idyllic—neither hot enough to raise a sweat, nor cold enough to chill. In the early afternoon it rained lightly and never for long, leaving the world filled with clean smells. They passed through clouds of black flies, but after a few exploratory bites the insects proved uninterested in human blood.

The tranquility of the land defied the nervousness roiling in Vedas's gut. They were making good time, but he had not forgotten the day they lost following the mountain cat's attack. Danoor would not wait for them to be waylaid again.

He was not the only one troubled. The ease of travel ill suited Churls. It made her cranky, suspicious. She held herself ready at all times. Vedas saw it in the tensing of her shoulders, the way her fingers grazed the pommel of her sword.

"Do you think the forest is enchanted?" he asked.

"Possible, I suppose." She shrugged. "This is nothing like I expected, I'll grant that. Guess one or two of the tall tales had it right. Whether it's enchanted makes no difference, though—we have no defense against sorcery, so we'd better just hope it isn't. Right now I'm less concerned about spells than I am about poison-tipped arrows and axe-wielding mountain men. I know it doesn't look like that kind of place, but I believe in being prepared."

She advised Berun and Vedas not to veer too closely to the roughshod villages they glimpsed through the trees. Vedas, having contracted her cautiousness, agreed. Undoubtedly, they were spotted and heard—Berun practically sparkled in sunlight, and he made no attempt to silence his footfalls—but the locals wisely kept their distance.

Only once did someone present himself. On the third day a young boy, short, slightly built, and nearly naked, walked across their path and froze upon sight of the travelers. He looked just as surprised as they were and, without a sound, turned and ran like a rabbit.

Vedas put a hand to Berun's arm before the constructed man could launch one of his stones. "What are you doing?" he asked. Without consciously urging it to, the edges of his hood closed in around his features.

Berun stared at Vedas's hand. "The boy may bring others."

"And so you thought to kill him?"

The constructed man took a step backward. "No." He looked at Churls and shook his head. "No. I only wanted to incapacitate the boy."

Churls's eyes darted to Vedas, and then back to Berun. "Good instinct, but we'd attract more attention knocking the boy out than we would just leaving him be. After all, his people may already know we're here. If they don't, nobody's going to believe his story. A man with black skin and horns, and another man made of metal? Preposterous."

On the following afternoon, she stopped Vedas from shooting a lone sheep. "I know we're tired of brook trout," she said, "but look at how this animal moves. It's not wild. It's probably drifted off from the flock, and I'd rather not be caught poaching or get accused of it. Herders treat poachers worse than they treat murderers."

Impressed by Churls's quick thinking and watchful air, Vedas began following the path of her gaze. He stilled his steps when she did, tipped his head to the same angle. Gradually, he started to see what she saw, hear what she heard. He learned to identify the region's ubiquitous signs of inhabitation, both recent and lost to time. A snaking stretch of bare ground became a footpath. Rounded,

moss-covered shapes—once indistinguishable to him from natural rock forma-
tions—rearranged themselves into extensive ruins that stretched for miles.

Even their route ceased to appear random. Churls nodded when he
brought it up, pointing to the paving stones embedded in the roots of the
largest trees. Suddenly, as though ordering itself from chaos, the dimensions
of the ancient highway became obvious.

It humbled him to realize how blind he had been to this fact.

Heightened awareness came with a price, however. The suspicion that they
were being watched grew as the days wore on. His skin itched under the
gaze of so many unseen eyes. He flinched at birdcalls, ducked under rays
of sunlight. He peered over his shoulder and invented figures between the
trees. He recognized similar symptoms in Churls, and knew she saw his in
turn. Neither spoke of it.

They reached the end of the highest Step without incident. Eager to put
distance between themselves and the ghosts inhabiting the top of the world,
they continued traveling by the light of the full moon for another two hours.
Churls's arms swung freely at her side. She smiled at Vedas as they set up
camp at the edge of the sixteenth Step.

He looked away, struggling to understand why the expected release had not
occurred. Certainly, he continued to obsess over their schedule. He worried
about chartering a ship across Lake Ten. And in only a few days' time, they
would be traveling in the Apusht Vales. The people of the valleys, traditionally
the stronghold of Stoli Adrashism, defended their border from the Anadrashi
people of Toma. They would not look kindly upon Vedas or Berun.

For the first time since the night the cat attacked, Vedas gave these concerns a voice, holding forth like a man confessing his sins. He regretted the
decision instantly, yet felt powerless to stop himself.

"We must catch a ship on the day we arrive . . .

"If we're not on Knosi soil by this date . . .

"We can't expect to travel as fast at night . . .

"I can't imagine what Abse would say to me if he knew . . ."

They had been over it all before, on many occasions. He had kept the
debate going long after deferring to her better judgment.

Shut your mouth, he told himself—and finally, he did.

The millstone around his neck was no lighter. In the silence that followed,
he considered what might be done to negate the words he had just spoken,
and arrived at no solution.

Berun grunted. "I've heard these things before."

Churls sighed, obviously displeased to have her good mood sullied. "I thought we were through with this argument, too, but I guess you need one more go-round. We're making the best time we can, Vedas. We'll deal with Lake Ten when Lake Ten is in front of us. As for the Apusht, you're right. It's home to some of the most dangerous men in Stol. But it's a short walk compared to what we've traveled so far. We'll move at night. The border guard are warriors, not mages. While it won't be a stroll to the butcher's, at least we know what to expect."

Vedas closed his eyes, shamed by her self-control. She had not lashed out, as was her right. Rather, she had explained matters to him as if to a child.

She would not have to do it again, he vowed. Experience had confirmed the soundness of her judgment, had it not? She had proved herself more knowledgeable than Vedas and Berun combined. If she believed they would make it through unscathed, they would.

Reason failed to alleviate the weight pressing down upon Vedas's shoulders. He massaged the tight muscles over his ribs, trying to ease the tension constricting each breath. Filled with the awareness that he had not spoken his true concern—that he could not in fact identify the source of his disquiet—he stared beyond the fire, unable to shake the conviction that something had followed him down from the highest Step.

‡

Long after Churls had fallen asleep, he lay awake, exhausted yet unable to still his thoughts. A familiar condition. As he had done every night since the cat attacked Churls, he replayed the event in his mind, imagining all the ways it could have ended badly.

All the ways he could have failed.

When sleep finally came, it offered no release. Churls perished again and again, her throat in the cat's teeth or her chest opened by its claws. Held back by invisible hands, he could do nothing to help. He watched her fall beneath the beast's weight and tumble over the edge of the world, only to rise again and succumb to another violent death.

He jolted out of the nightmare every time she turned in her slumber. Stilling his galloping heart, he listened for a sound, anything out of the ordinary.

This is pointless, he thought. *She doesn't need me worrying over her.*

Knowing this to be true—indeed, that she would consider his concern an insult—for two weeks he had hidden the signs of his distress. He remained still throughout the night so as not to alert Berun, and pushed beyond his fatigue from sunrise to sunset. He never mentioned the pain that lingered in his jaw where the cat had struck him. The joint clicked softly when he chewed his food, ached like a rotten tooth before every rain, and throbbed when he worried.

He wondered if the beast had been born of magic, if it had cursed him for taking its life.

Of course, he reminded himself, he had not been the one to deliver the killing wound. Churls's strike had been a thing of beauty, an act of stunning strength and precision.

In retrospect, he should not have expected anything less from the woman, who routinely got the best of him during their nightly Dull Sword sessions. Though unable to match his suit-assisted strength, she made up for her relative weakness with speed that outstripped his own. More than once, she disarmed him before he registered her movement—a first for an unsuited opponent, in his experience.

Unlike most combatants, she possessed only two giveaways: She pursed her lips before pressing forward, and her right shoulder twitched prior to switching her weapon to the left hand. At times she did neither, causing him to wonder if she were trying to keep him off-balance.

Their bouts were silent, humorless affairs. She breathed evenly through her nose and never showed her teeth. Afterward, she smiled tightly, as though disappointed with the outcome. He concentrated on stilling his shaking limbs.

Now and then, he caught her staring at him, as if she did not recognize his face.

Could she see through his pretense? He doubted the simple fact of his exhaustion would arouse her sympathy. But for a few brief moments of communion, following their course change he had given his resentment free reign. The gap between them continued to grow with each passing day, and he did nothing to bridge it. They could not be called friends, not by a stone's throw.

By the end of their journey they would be strangers once more.

This outcome had not always seemed inevitable. He remembered the way she had looked at him when they set out from Nbena. After two decades of celibacy, the recognition of a woman's attraction—and his own desire in response—had shocked him. For a brief while he had actually fantasized about a sexual encounter.

Now, when he caught himself staring at the curve of her clavicle, the inside of her thigh, he recoiled from his arousal.

Abse, Vedas reflected, would be proud. Though the abbey master did not stop brothers and sisters from forming physical bonds, he had made his own position clear on many occasions: *Lust clouds judgment. Remember, Vedas, we exist for one purpose above all else—to achieve victory over the enemies of man. Others have heard this calling, and felt it their duty to raise children who believe as they do, but this strikes us as too delicate a solution. Ours is the direct path. Any act that does not further us along that path is suspect.*

Vedas recognized the truth in these words, and vowed to achieve an alignment of heart and mind. Accomplishing this, reason dictated, would allow him to see his path clearly again.

And yet . . . Again? The word rang false.

Had his heart and mind been in complete agreement when Sara and Zeb Jol were slaughtered before him, or when the hellhound took Julit Umeda's life? They had certainly seemed to be, but now he found room for doubt. It seemed unreasonable that a man, knowing his cause to be just, having acted in accordance with his principles—bending his every thought toward one unselfish goal—should bear the weight of so much guilt.

Vedas considered the possibility that his heart and mind had never been in accord.

‡

Another restless night and fourteen hours of stiff-legged walking brought two facts into focus: He could not continue on his path without confronting his doubts, and one more day of traveling in strained silence would drive him mad.

The solution to both was simple, if not easy: he would have to seek counsel with Churls and Berun. The sooner he reestablished a sense of fellowship with them, no matter how fragile or slight, the better able he would be to name the problem that had so far eluded his waking mind.

Nonetheless, their arrival at the edge of the tenth Step came too soon. He prepared dinner slowly, trying to order his thoughts into a coherent pattern. An apology, a justification, or simply an explanation for himself. He suspected neither Churls nor Berun would accept an apology or fail to see through his justification.

An explanation, then. If he could make them understand the nature of his order, the specific reasons for his joining, they might help reorient him to his original purpose.

He had no intention of broaching the issue of intimacy with Churls—the thought of doing so horrified him—but he wondered if they might be able to reset their relationship, return it to its beginning. Dreaming of a physical encounter, ludicrous though the idea was, had distracted him from the memory of Julit Umeda.

Thus resolved to speak of his order, of camaraderie and shared purpose, it came as a surprise when he found himself recounting the events of the morning after the Thirteenth's battle with the Soldiers of the Appropriate Desire. His walk to Querus, Golna's only Tomen neighborhood. The smell of black pepper, cumin, and fennel. The hostile stares of dusky, redheaded men. His own stertorous breath and tightly clenched fists.

"Julit had been cremated at dawn," he said, enunciating with great care, betraying no emotion. "Her father held her skull in his hands while we talked. He pointed to the skulls above the hearth. *Julit's brother*, he told me. *Julit's uncle and grandmother and great grandmother.* He spoke softly, and his wife never made a sound. I wouldn't have known they were crying if the room wasn't so bright. They had placed lit candles on every surface, like they were trying to chase a ghost away.

"They asked me to assist in the funerary rites. According to Abse, spreading ashes is an unclean but necessary ritual in Toma, appropriate for a stranger—or even an enemy—to perform. I fit the definition of both, I suppose. Nonetheless, the request surprised me. I hadn't really expected them to ask. In Knos Ulom, a person's remains are sacred.

"They told me her favorite spot in the city was just under the Physickers' Bridge, on the Quarriton side. I used to go there as a child, too. It felt removed from the city somehow, like someone had set it aside for children. Even the homeless avoided it. The way down was tricky, dangerous for drunk feet."

Berun and Churls stared at the fire. Neither seemed inclined to speak.

Vedas let the silence stretch while he remembered. He had rolled drunks once, a lifetime ago, under the illusion of punishing Adrashi for their false piety. His gang of eleven children, not one above the age of ten, had enjoyed the implicit patronage of the city's Black Suits, who provided information: *This is how you identify an Adrashi*, and the like. The orders had armed the children and informed their rude faith, made them dangerous.

Gave them the confidence to push homeless men from bridges.

Vedas now recognized the evil of this arrangement. He counted among his blessings the fact that Abse had rescued him. Among Golna's orders, only the Thirteenth abstained from supporting the youth gangs. His brothers and sisters conformed to a code of ethics running deeper than mere doctrine. They watched over their recruits, educated and fed them, offered something better than a life on the streets. Even those who still lived at home were allowed to stay in the dormitories—a safe haven for many who would otherwise suffer abuse at the hands of their parents and siblings.

"Faith," Vedas said, angling his eyes to the sky, pressing fingertips to the horns of his hood. The Needle and the moon had risen above the Steps, illuminating the plain with cold light. "Her parents couldn't understand my faith, even though we were both Anadrashi. They had no idea their daughter had become involved with our order. It seemed to disgust them. *We're devout*, the father told me. His wife held her sickle-moon pendant before her, as though she thought it would protect her from me."

Churls cleared her throat. "You took off your suit?"

"No," he said. *No, of course not.* He considered telling her that he had not taken his suit off in over two decades, that he would not do so for something as minor as his visit to Julit Umeda's home.

But it had not been minor, had it? On the route to Nbena, he had replayed the meeting over and over again. Even with the distraction Churls provided, the event continued to haunt his sleep. On one mortifying occasion, he dreamt of Julit Umeda surviving the hellhound attack. Instead of informing her parents of her death, he went to congratulate them on her accomplishment, to welcome her into the order. He had woken from the dream, suffused with warmth, only to have the cold realization seize him again.

"Vedas," Churls said. She leaned forward, one hand raised from her knee as if she wanted to touch him but could not make herself do it. In the glow of the fire, the tattoos seemed to dance on her arm. A bear lunged, spreading its forelegs. A falcon dived, wings pressed tight against its sides. "Did you spread the girl's ashes under the bridge?"

"Yes," Berun said. "Tell us. Did you do it?"

Vedas's mouth was very dry. He moved his tongue around, but no moisture came. "I did," he finally croaked. "I took her ashes to the Physickers' Bridge. I slipped down the hill and located a spot to sit under the bridge—a place I used to go. The tide was low, so I hopped rocks out into the center of the river and smashed the urn. Her parents offered no directions, but that is the ritual among Knosi. We let water or wind carry the ashes away."

"And still you felt nothing?" Churls asked. "No release?"

Vedas breathed deeply into his stomach. He held the air for a moment, and then let it rush out. "No. I don't know what I expected to feel. I've commanded men and women not much older than Julit Umeda. Many times. A few have died. I never felt responsible. I did all that I could to insure their safety. I tried so hard to . . ."

His head dropped forward. His fingers curled into fists in his lap.

"No, that's a lie. If I tried as hard as I could to insure their safety, they would still be alive. I shouldn't try to convince myself otherwise. Millar Abo, Kelt Abbenajer, Amy Luethr, Somses Xu, Sara and Zeb Jol, Vakim Woril, Samual Honesth, Pylar Romane, Edard Hsui, Julit Umeda—I sent each of them to their deaths. I carry their memories. I can't let them go, even though wisdom says I should."

"Whose wisdom?" Churls asked.

Vedas's features twisted into a scowl. He had expected the question, but the anger it provoked took him by surprise. "Don't," he said. His lips puckered, on the verge of shaping words.

"Don't what?" she said. She held up her hand, silencing any response. "I've tried so hard not to offend you, Vedas, but that's coming to an end, right here: We match honesty with honesty. I see you trying to defend your faith when you and I both know it requires no defending. Adrash exists, and you believe he should be opposed. You believe mankind should dictate its own course. Fine. As far as convictions go, it's not a bad one. But that's not what we're talking about. We're talking about what a man does in the name of his faith."

He started to speak. Again, she stopped him with a gesture.

"Listen, the problem is that you can't separate what you've been told with what you know in your gut to be true. If you believed in your role as wholeheartedly as you want to believe in it, there would be no problem. You wouldn't have to forgive yourself for leading those kids to death because you would have been in the right all along." She chuckled without humor. "I hear you asking a question, but I don't think you're listening to yourself yet."

Berun nodded his great head.

Vedas's fists loosened, and he clasped his shaking hands together. Despite his attempts to hold onto it, the temper that had built while Churls spoke dissolved, settling within his veins, leaving him cold. His head swam as though he had been blindsided by a vicious blow. She had spoken truly: Something did indeed call from within. A question or a revelation. It whispered at the edge of comprehension, awful in its potency.

Instinctually, he fled from it, retreating to a comfortable position.

"I should have protected them," he said.

Churls sighed. From Berun came the odd rustling sound of spheres moving deep within his body. Neither moved, and Vedas admonished himself for a fool. Of course they had nothing to say. How could they put themselves in his position? Had they ever led a team of scared children, or tried to comfort a grieving parent? Certainly, Berun had never done so. And Churls—Churls was traveling to Danoor for personal gain, probably in order to satisfy a debt. Hardly a situation for a responsible person to find herself in.

I would have more luck talking with the ocean, Vedas thought, and rose wearily to his feet.

"Stop," said Churls. "Don't go. You see Berun and me sitting here, listening? If you don't want to ask yourself the question I think you should ask, fine—I'm not going to try to force you. Still, there are other questions. Why did you insist on going to the girl's house in the first place? What did you hope to accomplish? You said this had happened before, so why burden yourself before your journey? It makes no sense."

Vedas swayed where he stood, unwilling to sit back down, unable to walk away. Churls's words passed through him like an arrow through flesh, tearing a new pathway for infection, new doubts to plague his existence.

The sound of spheres moving in Berun's body increased, and then abruptly shut off. "No," he said. "It's not time to answer questions. It's time to listen. Do you know what Nhamed told me about you? He said you're a man of honor. After traveling with you for some time, I know this for a fact." He swiveled his head to stare at the sky. "You're a closed book, Vedas, and more than once I've wanted to knock your head from your shoulders, but that isn't important. You defended Churls when you didn't have to."

His eyes found Vedas again. "Quit lying to yourself. There's only one sure way you could have prevented those children's deaths, and that is by not placing them in danger. If your faith isn't strong enough to withstand the death of a child from time to time, then you will have to stop leading them into battle altogether."

Churls dipped her head in agreement. Her eyes had returned to the fire.

Vedas fought a brief spell of dizziness. His ears rang. His jaw ached.

Before words of denial or acceptance formed in his mind, a scream carried across the Step.

‡

"That's no animal," Churls said. She buckled her sword belt. "A woman or a child, the better part of a mile away. If we were upwind, I doubt we would have heard it." She nodded to Vedas. "We're taking a look, right?"

Vedas said nothing. Another scream sounded.

Berun shrugged.

Churls scowled. "I can't listen to that and just stand here. Can you?"

They ran. Berun jogged beside them, huge feet drumming on the hard ground. Whoever had screamed would certainly hear them coming, if he or she were still alive.

Vedas did not question why he had agreed to go along. He ran, and for a moment forgot his troubles. He had lost weight while traveling, and it seemed like his feet barely touched the ground. Running felt very good, in fact, like punching through an opponent's guard.

"I can see something ahead," Berun said. "Figures, three or four. Not very large, running. They look human."

"Can't be sure of that." Churls drew her sword and held it by the blade, near the hilt for better balance. "Are they moving away from us?"

"No. They're crossing our path, maybe one hundred yards ahead. There's a fourth, definitely, smaller than the others. It's running from them, not far ahead. One of the three following her runs on four legs and is continually jerked back, as if it's on a leash. Sometimes it stands on its hind legs and runs like a man. It howls like a dog."

Vedas concentrated, and caught the sound. "I hear it, too," Churls said.

"Magic or witch-lore," Vedas said. He imagined the fear the pursued child must feel, knowing what followed at his or her heels. "Leave it to me."

Berun's eyes flared. "We haven't decided which side we're on."

"I have a feeling," Vedas said. "I've been on both sides of the hunt. Good men don't draw out the pursuit like this." He pushed his legs harder, propelled forward by a visceral sense of justice. "I'll take all wagers."

Churls grunted. "For once, I'll go with the odds."

Vedas leaned forward into the night, legs as firm as iron underneath him. The hood of his suit tickled over his forehead and cheeks, slid like a lover's caress over his lips. He bared his teeth within the mask. The blood raced in his veins. The smell of his own sweat mingled with the elder-cloth, and it was the smell of home.

‡

They closed the distance. When they were a hundred feet away, the hunters released their howling creature and turned to meet them. Vedas saw that the pursuers were indeed men, squat and strongly thewed. Both carried heavy pickaxes in meaty fists, and waited in ready postures. Vedas looked beyond them as the fourth figure fell under the creature's body, and aimed in this direction. As he passed the two men, light erupted from their bodies. They glowed as if they had been turned to molten metal.

Shit, Vedas thought. He knew enough of magic to recognize it for what it was: alchemical armor. During a battle in Plastertown, a White Suit using a similar spell had fought off seven Black Suits by himself.

"Hold them if you can!" Vedas yelled to Berun and Churls. "I'll take the beast!"

He jumped. His right shoulder hit the creature's upper back and his arms whipped around its chest, carrying the body clear of the child's. He tightened his grip as they slid on the hard-packed soil, allowing the creature no opportunity to regain its feet. It howled, turning its head with blinding speed to snap at his face. The sour rot of its breath struck him like a blow, and its chomping teeth rang an odd metallic sound. It bucked and spasmed under him, but he held fast, pushing its belly into the ground, splaying its arms and legs under his bulk.

In full control now, Vedas put one hand against the back of the creature's head and savagely slammed its face into the ground. He straddled its waist, unmindful of the claws raking along his thighs and buttocks. The suit hardened in defense so that he barely felt the contact, yet the frenzied movements fueled the rage screaming in his limbs. He slid forward, positioning both kneecaps on the creature's upper arms, just below its shoulders. His hips rose into the air, shifting the full weight of his body onto his knees.

The bones gave way with satisfying snaps, and the creature howled. Vedas put both hands on its skull, twisting it back and forth, grinding the creature's face into the unyielding earth.

"Don't. Fucking. Touch her!" he spat through clenched teeth. The blood beat red waves of pressure behind his eyes.

A high-pitched whine reached his ears. He pushed harder to quiet the sound.

"*Basuz!*" a voice boomed.

"Stop!" another said almost simultaneously—a voice Vedas barely recognized in his fury. A giant hand closed around his torso and lifted him into the air. Iron-hard fingers flowed under his arms and pried them open, forcing him to drop the mewling creature. Somewhere in the back of Vedas's mind, he knew Berun held him, yet he thrashed wildly in the constructed man's grip, roaring like a man possessed.

The single, ragged note held and then fell into silence. He stopped flailing and held his body still, fists clenched, every muscle rigidly defined on his shuddering frame. After a handful of seconds, his chin dropped onto his chest and his body sagged in Berun's gigantic fingers. His jaw throbbed.

"The child?" he said. "She's okay?"

A hand slapped his face lightly, and then lifted his chin. Vedas focused on Churls's face.

"Who are you talking about?" she asked.

"The girl they attacked." Vedas located the two dwarfish men, whose bodies still radiated a warm orange light. He met one's eyes, and the look they returned shocked him. Horror. Fear etched the man's rough features, and he made a warding sign in Vedas's direction, left fist held to forehead and then thrown forward. Adrashi, obviously.

Vedas looked at Churls again. "Where is she?"

She shook her head, eyes locked on his. "Vedas, there is no girl. What we do have are two miners, their slave, and a thief."

‡

Powerful muscle shifted under the slave's hairless skin. He growled menacingly, yet somehow managed to look pathetic. The "creature" Vedas had fought was obviously a man, despite the changes sorcery had wracked upon his body. His lower jaw had been elongated so that it hooked under his nose, cheeks cut so that his mouth could open wider. Saw-edged ridges of metal lined his lipless maw. Limping upright, his broken arms hung uselessly at his sides. He turned on his leash, revealing the scars where his sex had once been.

Now that Vedas saw the man, he pondered how he could have so mistook him for a beast.

It had not been his only blunder.

Indeed, the thief was no girl. Standing a bit above Churls's waistline, the woman's face was a map of wrinkles. Clearly, she did not view Vedas as any kind of savior, for she stood behind her captors as they talked to Berun. She stared at Vedas, expressionless, but he imagined a challenge in the way she held his gaze.

Berun let Vedas down, and told him to unmask himself—to show that he was a man, not a demon. The constructed man explained that, before he and Churls had engaged in the fight, one of the miners had pointed to the fourth and yelled, "Thief!" Berun had understood the Ulomi word immediately, and surmised their identities.

"These are Baleshuuk men," he explained to Vedas. "Corpse miners."

Despite himself, Vedas breathed in sharply.

Churls nodded at his astonishment. "If I wasn't staring at them, I wouldn't have believed it either. No matter who told me." She shook her head and spoke in a softer voice. "I don't know what I was expecting, but somehow they aren't it."

Too stunned to agree or disagree, Vedas simply grunted. His mother had told him tales of the Baleshuuk, the near-mythical suppliers of elder corpses. She described them as impossibly thin like the elders themselves, yet he had heard others describe them as thick or egg-shaped, not men at all. Though few if any of the tale-tellers had ever seen one, the existence of the Baleshuuk could not be denied, as the world continued to receive a steady—though ever more expensive—supply of bonedust and other elder materials. Nos Ulom had become rich by exporting these hard, dwarfish mountain men to Stol and Knos Min, the world's most elder-rich nations.

According to legend, the Baleshuuk extracted elder corpses from solid rock as easily as midwives coaxed newborns from their mothers' wombs. It was said the miners used magic like ordinary men used forks and spoons. Vedas stared at their pickaxes and wondered.

"How can we make this right?" Berun asked.

Vedas struggled to catch the miners' response. They spoke in a thick Ulomi dialect, full of rolled R's and long vowels. Every word Vedas caught—one out of every two or three—seemed a syllable too long. Only superficially similar to Berun's dialect, the Baleshuuk's speech contained numerous alien words that confounded even the constructed man. He shook his immense head, furrowing the shelves of his brows in confusion.

Vedas did not need a translation to read the miners' expressions, however.

"They're very angry," Berun finally confirmed. "They're threatening to return with a full company of their brethren. I've tied to explain our mistake, but they don't seem to understand. *She is a thief,* they keep telling me. It's their right to punish her as they see fit."

"I agree," Churls said. "Can we pay them off?"

The taller of the two miners spoke up.

"'You ruined our slave,'" Berun translated. "'He is worth four ounces.'"

"Shit," Churls said. "We don't have that much to give. Do we have anything else of value?"

A sound came from within Berun's body, as of glass clinking. He reached down and plucked a handful of objects from his thigh. He lumbered forward and bent, presenting them to the miners. Vedas recognized them even from a distance. A collection of spells, the largest of which was a tiny porcelain jar sealed with wax.

"Where did he get those?" Churls whispered.

"A witch attacked us on a pass between the Sawbuck Mesas. I told him not to take her spells, but he did it anyway."

The shorter miner took the spells. He held them up to his ear and recited seven words slowly. Names. He handed six of the spells to his companion, who stored them in a pack hanging from his belt. The stoppered jar remained in the short one's hand. He examined it from every angle before closing his eyes and sniffing its seal.

Suddenly, he grinned. "Yesh," he said. "Yesh. Okee."

The two miners conferred briefly, and then the taller one spoke to Berun. The constructed man's hand engulfed the smiling miner's, a ritual of agreement Vedas recognized from his time at the river docks in Fishertown.

"They've agreed to part ways peacefully," Berun said.

Frowning, Churls said, "They seem happy."

Vedas watched the two miners, faces nearly split with grins. Berun had given away something extremely valuable, apparently.

A tight feeling spread outward from Vedas's chest, observing their cheer. They were still going to kill the thief, he knew. And why should they do otherwise? An old woman with no use? Surely, few would miss her around the cooking fires, the laundry buckets.

Yet he recalled how fast she had run from the howling slave. The way she stared at him even now, unafraid. She had never cursed him with a gesture. He tried to compare her to anyone he had known in his life, and came up empty. A tiny old Baleshuuk woman. Not Churls, nor a little girl with a black sash tied around her arm. Not the drunk he had helped push from the Physickers' Bridge when he was only nine years old.

"We've overpaid them," he told Berun. "Tell them to spare the thief."

BERUN

They made their way northwest toward Lake Ten under the cover of night, avoiding any sign of man. Churls, the least likely member of the party to elicit an aggressive response from the Adrashi men of the Apusht, walked point over the more exposed ground. Berun caused his eyes to revolve around his head, constantly vigilant.

They kept a lookout not only for Adrashi. Raiding parties of Tomen were not uncommon this close to the border. Fiercely independent, the people of the desert nation considered organized religion an abomination, and proselytizing to foreigners a waste of energy. Anadrashi and members of other sects had been known to buy their freedom on occasion, but Berun, Churls and Vedas possessed only enough bonedust to reach Danoor.

During the first night's travel, Vedas kept his eyes fixed westward. "It's hard for me to fully conceive," he said. "I've bought wares in Querus for years. Two of my brothers are expatriated Tomen. I know their reputation, of course. Even in Golna, they cause violence from time to time. Still, Followers of Man—people who should be my brothers- and sisters-in-arms—an entire nation living with such hatred toward its neighbors!"

Churls grunted. "I've never been to Golna, but I know many who have. You know what struck them about the city? During the day, they could walk anywhere without fear. Watchmen were posted to every street, and they

144

didn't appear to be extorting anything from anyone. Don't assume the rest of the world is like home, Vedas. In fact, I recommend you take the worst of what you've heard about other people and assume it's the truth."

"I'd prefer not to form that habit."

"Preference has nothing to do with it. You treat people like they have your best interest in mind, and nine times out of ten you get stabbed." She forced a smile. "Look, I appreciate that you don't like looking at people as suspects, but goodwill only extends so far."

He breathed deeply, visibly suppressing the urge to defend himself, to contradict her words. In the end, he simply nodded.

The act of restraint impressed Berun. Talking about Julit Umeda, the encounter with the Baleshuuk and their slave—the events had changed Vedas in a way the constructed man did not yet understand. The end result, however, was clear: Berun's automatic hostility toward Vedas had dissolved, replaced by a genuine affection for the man's unyielding awkwardness, and Churls no longer carried herself as if she expected a battle.

They pressed on through the hard, folded land. The farther they traveled from the Steps, the harsher the territory became. Winds blew westward through the valleys constantly, striking the hardscrabble earth and whistling through Berun as though he were a dried sponge. The components of his body rasped together shrilly. When he examined his innermost spheres and found them to be caked with layers of dirt, he began cycling them through his body constantly in order to keep clean. When they found water, he washed too.

Anything unrooted to the ground was carried into the dust-streaked sky. It became quite cold, far colder than Casta. Churls suffered the worst. She took a woolen jacket from her pack, removed her skirt, and pulled on tight brown leathers that hugged her hips and buttocks. Vedas took to falling behind so that he could watch her walk. The man fought to hide his attraction, but his eyes gave him away.

For her part, Churls showed no sign of noticing the attention. Doubtlessly, she did. She was, Berun knew, the subtler of the two by far.

The minor drama amused Berun.

He needed amusing. They all did. The Apusht was taking its toll, physically and emotionally.

By the third night, the wind had become more than a nuisance—it had become a frightening adversary. It hid their enemies behind sheets of dust. At times it seemed capable of carrying them into the sky. Around small, smokeless campfires, Vedas and Churls rarely spoke of their goal. They talked as if it had been abandoned. Berun marveled at the human propensity for gloom, which he suspected had infected him as well.

Increasingly, he sensed the presence of his father. Ortur Omali's spirit stalked him across the land, spying, influencing him in ways he could not yet comprehend. The memory of standing over Vedas's sleeping form with Churls's blade in his fist haunted him, causing him to wonder if he would be able to resist Omali's direct command. Though he longed to convince his father of the Black Suit's goodness, he did not desire another confrontation, another demonstration.

Best to avoid it for as long as possible, he reasoned, and muster what strength he could. Every day while his companions slept, he strived to keep his mind from drifting and becoming vulnerable to his father's will. It grew noticeably easier to focus the longer he maintained his manlike form. The more he reigned in his urge to transform, the more rooted he was to the world. As a result, he no longer built structures with his body or split himself in two.

Like a flesh and blood man, he longed for release. The temptation to give in was strong, but he resisted, found ways to distract himself.

The most effective distraction had long since become an obsession. While tracking the travelers' progress across the highest Step on the map he kept superimposed over his vision, he had made a discovery. By concentrating upon a region it would expand and focus, lending him a bird's-eye view of the landscape.

During the daylit hours, he found his attention drawn away from the local surroundings to the limits of the known world—to the ocean and its myriad islands. The continent of Knoori held many interesting sights, surely, but he longed to see places unknown to man. In an effort to comprehend the true scope of the world he had only dimly beheld in vision, he pushed at the boundaries of his map. The progress here proved slow, but the effort satisfied him, like a fight well fought but ultimately called a tie.

Beyond the satisfaction exploring the map provided him, four times now he had been able to spot groups of men whose path they would soon cross. It was difficult to locate such individuals under the cover of night, but his skills improved day by day.

Though he could not fathom why, he endeavored to keep his newfound ability a secret. He lied to his companions. *I saw a scout. I heard them approaching.*

Churls was not fooled. For four days she had listened to his explanations without comment, and then: "Tell me what you're seeing right now, Berun."

Caught off guard, he shrugged as though her question confused him.

She smirked. "I'm not an idiot, and you're an awful liar. You couldn't have seen the Tomen raiders yesterday from our position, and this wind makes hearing anything softer than an earthquake impossible. Out with it."

He glowered, searching the darkness at her back. Vedas would return from relieving himself at any moment.

"Berun," she said. "Why keep it a secret?"

"I don't know. What was I supposed to do, allow us to stumble into them?"

"It wasn't just that. I can tell when you're distracted."

His gaze shifted to her face. He examined her features, which had long since ceased to appear typical to him. No, he could not tell if they were beautiful, but such distinctions hardly concerned a constructed man. Of their own accord, the corners of his mouth turned upwards, and a new feeling arose within him, deeper than affection. He had been called out on a lie, and not because the thing had been ripped from his mind, but because another being knew him intimately enough to recognize it.

‡

He did not think overlong about why the thought of telling Vedas filled him with apprehension, for the truth spoke plainly: his father would not have the information in the Black Suit's hands.

Admitting this fact consciously only increased the agitation within Berun. For two days, he waged a silent war of wills against an invisible opponent—a master mage who contorted Berun's mind so thoroughly that it seemed he fought himself. Churls said nothing, but her concern for him was obvious. She kept close by, as though protective of a child.

They set up camp a mere fifteen miles from Bitsan, a small city on the southeastern shore of Lake Ten. He dug a shallow pit for the fire, feeling as though his entire body were close to shuddering apart. As strong as the urge was to remain silent, an equal force compelled him to assert himself. The balance could not last. The slightest tug in either direction would send him careening headlong down a new path.

Ever closer to enslavement, or toward self-determination.

"Vedas . . ." he said, and the scales tipped. The words flowed from him, accompanied by a sense of release he had not experienced since the night he had held Churls's sword above Vedas's sleeping form. He sat straighter as the great burden of secrecy lifted from his shoulders.

There, he thought when he had finished. *I've told him, Father, and the world hasn't collapsed.*

A deep frown cut furrows alongside Vedas's mouth. He kneaded the flesh of his inner thighs. "How far ahead can you see?" he asked. "Can you see Danoor?"

Aglow with his victory, Berun did not fight the temptation to brag. "I can see the Eleven Sentinels crumbling into the sea north of Grass Min. I have spent hours watching the cloth markets at Levaés. As we speak, sunlight is crossing the first of the Aroonan Mesas. I see all of Knos Min, Vedas. Of course I can see Danoor."

Churls kicked the fire's last glowing coal into sparks, and reclined under the lean-to Berun had constructed. "What does it matter?" she asked. "We won't be there for at least three weeks."

Vedas stared down at his clenched fists, and slowly opened them. "I'm expected in the first week of Royalty." He held a hand up, forestalling her response. "I'm not opening up that old argument or complaining. Still, I won't pretend I like the situation, not knowing what I'll be walking into. If there's a way to be more prepared, I want to take it."

Berun shrugged. "What do you want me to do?"

"I want you to observe the city. At the end of this month, people will start to arrive. Religiously neutral gamblers and fighters from Casta. Adrashi of every denomination and occupation from Stol and Nos Ulom. Fewer are coming from Dareth Hlum, as the trip requires travel through Nos Ulom or Toma. Because it falls on the eve of the half-millennium, Toma has prepared for this tournament for years, and will send thousands of its people northward. The largest group by far will be Knosi, and though they have pledged to keep the celebration peaceful, they will fail."

"How do you know this?" Berun asked.

Vedas sighed. "The tournament has always been followed by small-scale riots. I persisted in believing that this year would be different. I thought the celebration would overwhelm the instinct for violence, even among the Tomen. In other words, I fooled myself. I didn't want to believe the actions of my brothers and sisters could have such consequences." He nodded to Churls. "My eyes have been opened."

Churls met Berun's gaze. "Trust him," she said.

"Hopefully," Vedas continued, "the violence will be restricted to fractious Ulomi and Tomen on the outskirts of the city. If it spreads to the general populace, the whole of Danoor could be in danger. It would be very helpful to know the situation before stepping into the city. In fact, it would be good to know how things progress from the very beginning."

"Why?" Churls asked. "I don't see how that will make a difference."

Berun had been about to say something similar. He stared at Vedas, noting the way the man massaged his hands, how he avoided direct eye contact. Clearly, he would rather not divulge whatever information he possessed. For all the grace and skill Vedas displayed at fighting and hunting, he knew nothing of masking his thoughts. It was odd, Berun thought, that the man's most obvious weakness was also his most endearing quality. Few men made it so far in life without learning to lie.

"I'll win the tournament, or I'll die," Vedas said. "I expect to win. As we've traveled, I've become more confident in my skills." He caught Churls's eye briefly before looking into his lap again. "Our practices have been very helpful. And while it pleases me to think of victory, I now understand its magnitude. Winning the tournament will result in greater changes than I suspected when I left Golna. It's not a mere contest of faith. I thought it was, but it isn't."

Churls cleared her throat, but held her peace. Vedas stiffened, and then relaxed.

Berun considered his companions, the shaky ground between them, and spoke. "If Churls won't say it, then I will. There's no such thing as a mere contest of faith in this world, Vedas. You above all others should know this. To think, even for a moment, that it's possible to wage war against other men without consequence beyond the battlefield is pure idiocy. You're not a fool—don't speak as if you are."

Grimacing, Vedas ran a hand over his face. "Two months ago, I would have taken issue with those words, but you're right: I've been a willfully ignorant fool. Slowly, I'm coming to understand that men of the same order—brothers and sisters who profess the same convictions, curse the same god—can work toward opposing ends. The stated goal of the tournament is to win converts to our faith, to convince people of the power and truth of our vision. Despite my doubts, despite . . ."

He closed his eyes and exhaled. "Despite Julit Umeda, I still believe in this goal. The world is not Adrash's plaything. Men are not pawns. What I no longer believe in is my right to send an entire city into upheaval."

"How would you accomplish that?" Churls asked.

"Whoever wins the tournament will have enormous influence. Many who hear him speak will act as he commands without thinking." As if he were doing so with great reluctance, Vedas pulled a slim tube from his pack. Its wax seal had clearly been broken. "I opened this just after our encounter with the Baleshuuk. I don't know why I did. I was told not to. It contains a speech written by the master of my order. He has commanded me to read it during the New Year's celebration in the Aresaa Coliseum, which holds one hundred and fifty thousand men. Afterward, I'm to have the text copied and distributed."

He met Churls's gaze. "I don't think I can do that. Reading it alone may cause a riot. Still, I must read something. They're expecting a speech from the winner." He looked to Berun. "Will you help me? Help me monitor developments in Danoor. Read the speech and tell me I'm crazy, or tell me I'm right to worry. Please."

He held the tube out, offering it to either of his companions.

Churls took it without hesitation.

‡

They arrived in Bitsan an hour before sunrise on the twenty-first day of the month: Qon'as Du'ses, First Day of Learning.

An unexpected blessing for the travelers, it began the Month of Learning for the D'Ari A'draasis, the major Adrashi denomination of Stol's southern lakeside communities. The D'Ari measured the year with a twelve-month calendar, and ended it with thirty-six days of fasting and study. Commerce all but stopped while the sun was in the sky, and tribal hostilities ground to a halt. During the Month of Learning, violence to man or creature was forbidden, a fact all the more remarkable for the legendarily hot-blooded D'Ari.

"I've heard of this kind of luck, but never experienced it," Churls said as she and Berun walked along the city's deserted main thoroughfare. While she had established the city's peaceable nature during her dawn reconnaissance, she had nonetheless advised Vedas to stay at the campsite. "We'd better not push our luck by bringing you into town," she had told him. "It's enough of a risk bringing Berun in."

Berun did not need to ask why she wanted him along. Her look of disgust communicated more than enough. No, she did not like asking for protection, but she was not stupid. Besides warfare, the D'Ari were known for their love of foreign women. Pale-skinned wives commanded a high price from tribal leaders. Even the Month of Learning might not prevent them from laying hands on a freckled Castan.

They found an inn close to the docks. Berun and Churls stepped through the door into humid, candle-lit gloom.

"Try not to attract attention to yourself," Churls said, the hint of a smile on her lips.

For all the alarmed stares their arrival caused, Berun knew few if any of the customers recognized him. The D'Ari had fought for millennia with Nos Ulom over Lake Ten's trade routes, and by every account disdained all things Ulomi. When a tribal leader took an Ulomi woman as his wife, he removed her tongue so that she could not talk of her homeland. Conceivably, if the men in the inn knew that Berun had killed Patr Macassel, they would welcome him as a hero.

Though he would not voice it to Churls, he found himself wishing for the exact opposite. A vexing wrath blossomed within him, spreading rapidly outward from his central components, causing his body to vibrate from head to toe. He pictured himself knocking the inn's customers aside as if they were ragdolls, pulping skulls between his palms.

The spheres of his knuckles spun, and a new sensation struck him:

Pounding. Fists beating on an immense door within himself. Ortur Omali, struggling to be free, to assert his will once more—to disprove Berun's recent victory over him. The reverberations shook Berun, rattling him to the core. For several seconds he feared he might fly apart, and then two voices spoke at once:

Berun, his father said, speaking with the sound of a thousand trees being ripped from the earth, tugging his creation away from the real world. Black spots—shadow moths, flakes of ash—swam before his eyes, obscuring his vision.

"Berun," Churls said, tugging in the opposite direction. Away from madness. She spoke his name a second time.

It was enough, barely, another near-defeat. The hex dissolved inside him, and the smoky interior of the inn snapped into focus around him. His joints sagged. He gripped the back of a chair to steady himself, and the wood shattered in his fingers.

Sound ceased in the room. The man at the table before Berun showed teeth, put a hand to the hilt of the dagger strapped horizontally on his stomach. His companion's fist tightened around the handle of a heavy mug. The bartender ducked behind his counter briefly, and rose with two cocked crossbows. Instead of arrowheads, both bolts were tipped with ampoules: magic enough to hurt a constructed man, perhaps.

"Sorry," Berun said, brass voice loud in the crowded room. He straightened slowly, careful not to bump his head on the low ceiling. Talk started up again. The drummer and tambourine player resumed their soft rhythm, and the bartender put his weapons away.

Churls clapped a hand to Berun's broad back. "Congratulations on not attracting attention to yourself." She spoke loudly enough for him alone to hear. "And so much for a month of peace. What the hell happened there?"

Berun navigated the tables and chairs slowly, glad for a moment to think. He had not told Churls of his father's appearances, of course—but now that Vedas was out of earshot, he seriously considered doing so. He searched for resistance, and found none. Perhaps Omali could not rouse the energy after another failure.

What could be the harm? Churls might have something to say.

A server, clothed in a single fold of carmine cloth clasped at the neck, waited for them at a free table in the back corner. She swayed in time to the hypnotic beat, alternately exposing and covering her nakedness. Berun peered around and realized that, but for the servers, Churls was the only woman present. The men stared at her hungrily, causing the anger to flare inside him again. He clamped down on the emotion, suspecting now that his father could use it as a doorway.

He pulled a chair out and knelt on the floor. Still, he loomed over the table.

"Coffee and hash," Churls said to the server, who sashayed away.

Anticipating her question again, Berun held his hands up, palms forward. "I don't know." He reconsidered the lie. He trusted Churls. "That's not true. My father speaks to me in dreams. Sometimes, I'm fully awake. I think he wants me to kill Vedas, but I don't know if he's sure about this. He spoke to me, just a moment ago."

Her eyebrows rose fractionally. "Isn't Omali dead? No, that's not important. Are you going to kill Vedas?"

He admired the way she asked the question, as though she were asking about a cut of meat, no tiptoeing around the issue. "No," he answered. "I'm not going to kill him. I like him. Since his decision to rewrite the speech, I like him even more. The world already has enough killing in the name of Adrash. Besides, a riot would delay the real tournament."

The corners of Churls's mouth turned down. Not for the first time, Berun wondered if they would end up fighting in the same bracket. Would she drop out if this were the case? He hoped so, for he could not imagine taking her life.

"You like him, too?" he asked.

"Shit." She groaned and leaned onto her forearms. "What the hell's wrong with him? What the hell's wrong with me? I'd like to chalk it up to old age, but I don't feel that old. Sure, I like him. I have goddamn dreams about him. The kind I haven't had for two decades. And what do I get for my obsession? Next to nothing. He ignores me and I'm nervous as a fucking newborn deer around him."

The way she spoke of herself awed Berun. Despite her uneasy interactions with Vedas, he had not expected it from her. Of all the people he had ever met, she possessed the keenest, most self-assured mind.

Surely, the Black Suit was to blame for the awkwardness between them.

"He looks at you often. You don't see that?"

She grimaced. "Of course I do. So what if he looks at my ass? A man staring at your ass means nothing. He doesn't talk to me like a man talks to a woman. Outside of our sparring sessions, he flinches at the slightest touch. And even if he didn't, how would I respond? He's a religious fanatic sealed in a suit he probably hasn't removed in years. Beyond the logistical problems, that fact means something. I don't like fanatics. My parents were fanatics. My sister's a fanatic."

"And what about the speech? He wants to change it. He asked for help. This means nothing to you?"

"Orrus Dabil Alachum," she swore. "You've thought things through, haven't you, Berun? In truth, I don't know how to account for any of this. Until the night he tussled with the Baleshuuk slave, I thought he was one person. Now I think he might be another. You told me I see something in him, but the truth is I don't know what I see. Most of the time I wish I'd never met him. Then I just wish he'd—"

The server returned, and Churls made her expression blank. She tapped the server's wrist with her index fingertip, and said in a low voice, "There's a gram extra if you can give me some information. We need a boat to Ynon. Doesn't matter what size, but it has to be reputable, and it has to leave soon."

"Reputable?" the server asked slowly. Her green eyes, which had appeared glassy and unfocused a moment before, darted from Churls to Berun. "I do not know what you mean by this word."

"Flags," Churls said. "It must sail under flags. No mongrels."

The server nodded. "How soon is soon?"

"A day, two at most."

Churls's eyes followed the woman through the crowd. She stared at her mug, at the ceiling, anywhere but at Berun. She picked at her food and he kept quiet, respecting her mood, and eventually a man approached the table with an offer.

‡

They exited the inn. Churls squinted into the sun. "I don't want to go back yet."

Berun nodded, and they walked along the shore, away from the docks. He admired the way the sunlight glinted off the waves, the sound of gulls screaming. He imagined what it might be like to smell things. Men always commented upon the smell of water. He considered asking Churls if she would mind if he took a stroll under the glass clear shallows, but rejected the thought. At that moment, she possessed a fragility incomprehensible to him.

She loves Vedas, he thought. Love, too, was unfathomable.

"Even with flags, it's not always safe," she said after some time. "Pirates sail these waters. Maybe our luck will run out on the lake." She squinted into the sun. "Sometimes I think that's what Vedas wants. A big fist to come out of the sky and smash him. A confirmation that fate's aligned against him."

"Maybe." Berun sensed she had more to say, and waited for it.

"I've read the speech," she eventually said.

"I know." He found a flat stone and pitched it hard enough that it was lost to sight long before it stopped skipping. He came upon two large rocks half-submerged in the sand, and picked them up. He turned in a circle, and then laughed his brass laugh. "Look around us, Churls. In an ocean of sand and small stones, these two rocks. Rough around the edges, ready to be turned into weapons." He began spinning them in his hands, grinding them down.

They resumed walking. "What does it say?" he asked.

"It's a call to arms," she answered. "A declaration of war."

CHURLI CASTA JONS

She had resisted the temptation to masturbate for almost two months.
The last time she did so was in Casta, the night Vedas complimented
her swordsmanship. With the wind howling over them, she rose to
orgasm three times, just thinking of his body so close. She had not known
him then, not really: he had been an idealized version of himself, a dream
creature.

Now, of course, she held no such delusions. Vedas Tezul was only a man,
albeit unlike any in her experience. A confoundingly constant presence in
her thoughts, at any moment she could summon him to her mind's eye.
Hear his voice as though he stood next to her. Feel his warmth. She could
close her eyes and recall every detail of his body.

He had changed a great deal during their journey. As a result of constant
walking and lean meals, what little fat he possessed had burned away. His
waist and thighs were thinner, not so much that a casual observer would
notice, but Churls certainly did. Like a mage studying a book of alchemical
diagrams, she catalogued every sinuous line of his physique.

His face, too, had been transformed. During their first days on the Steps, he
had lost his razor. A thick, wiry black beard had come in, yet it could not hide
the leanness of his cheeks. His hair, just a black shadow clinging to his scalp
when she had first met him, grew in as a thick, helmetlike nap sparsely flecked

155

with grey. The wrinkles around his eyes had become pronounced, and the eyes themselves, a deep brown, almost black, seemed somehow more observant.

He had possessed the appearance and bearing of a young man when they left Nbena. He was beautiful then, definitely. He was gorgeous now—a singular creature that moved with the grace of a stag, unrushed and fluid. He held himself with a natural poise, as though the world fit him perfectly, conforming to his will as surely as his suit conformed to his body.

She pictured this man, an older and perhaps wiser man, as she touched herself under stained sailcloth blankets. Her hammock swayed to the violent listing of the ship, but she was determined, matching strokes of her labia with the violent movement, now and then pushing a fingertip deeper, brushing her clitoris lightly. She flexed her buttocks in time, imagining Vedas turning her sideways in the hammock, fingers prying her legs apart, an obsessive fantasy of being exposed by him again and again.

His beard rough against her inner thighs, ticklish against her anus as he lapped at her.

Probing her fingertip deeper, she pressed against her clitoris, rotating over the small, firm organ with increasing vigor. Imagining a tongue, a mouth. The occasional rasp of teeth, shocking and almost painful.

Sailors called to one another on the deck above, sounds muted by wood and rain pounding on wood. The brass bell of Berun's voice, calling encouragement. The constructed man loved being aboard the ship.

She sensed that Vedas was awake too, listening. Sailing did not agree with him. He worried about pirates and sinking, and his body had yet to acclimate to the motions of water. He fought every wave, attempting to right himself instead of moving with the motion. Time would undoubtedly prove his facility with this mode of travel, but in her fantasy he already moved with the confidence of a man born on the lake.

After finishing with his tongue, he wrapped hard arms around her lower back and pulled her from the fishnet—tightly hugging her so that she could not fall any lower, could not kiss his mouth or neck. She gripped his scalp, running nails through his short, thick hair. She tried to link her feet together behind his back, but it was too broad. His fingertips tightened into her skin, and he crushed her stomach into his face.

She breathed faster in the hammock, fingertip moving in rapid circles over her clitoris.

He held her down against the rough floor, hands tight around her wrists. They kissed roughly, tongues flicking, teeth occasionally clicking together. His mouth tasted like almonds, and she swallowed his saliva. She thrust her pelvis upward, trying for contact, but he held his body above her, hips high off the floor.

"Please," she said, and he knew what the request meant. He lowered himself slowly until his weight rested fully on her. He let go of her wrist, and both of their hands descended. She pulled her skirt high around her waist, and he formed an opening in the suit material, allowing his rigid cock to spring free.

She reached for it. He batted her hand away.

The ship rocked from side to side. The sailors' voices grew louder overhead. Churls bit her lip until it hurt, a sharp counterpoint to the waves of pleasure radiating into her stomach and legs.

He slid his length into her slowly, and she tightened immediately around him, willing him deeper. The smooth, slightly cold material of his suit slid along her thighs, an alien and unbelievably arousing sensation. As the head of his cock pressed against her cervix, she gasped. He began thrusting, not quickly or slowly, but inexorably. She wrapped her legs around his lower back and rocked into his motions, angling so that his weight fell upon her, forcing his erection to a greater depth.

He gasped. Already, he was close.

In this respect, she suspected her fantasy held truth. She had wondered many times if Vedas was an experienced lover. She thought not. He certainly did not act like one, though he possessed extraordinary control over his body. No doubt, given enough time and attention he would become a very talented lover. But the first time his rise to orgasm would be quick and ungraceful.

Sometimes, she loved quick and ungraceful.

The swells of pleasure crested and broke. Her fantasy faded to nothing as she rode her orgasm through its surges. Her back arched and collapsed in the hammock, and her legs twitched. She bit her forearm, moaning into flesh. Her fingertip twitched on and off the hypersensitive skin of her clitoris as if it were a hot coal. As the spasms wound down, she slid her hand lower and pressed the fingertip against her anus, the merest suggestion of entry.

She pushed a long breath from her lungs, and then grunted as an immense hand slapped the port side of the ship, causing it to list sharply starboard.

Screams overhead, the sound of rushing water, the snap of timber.

The ship righted, fell to port. Her hammock turned over, nearly spilling her out.

Another wave pounded into the ship, but she did not scream. She thrashed in the fabric embrace of the hammock as it spun around a second time, one part of her attention focused on getting free and the other on the deck above.

No sailors' shouts. No feet drumming on wooden planks.

The ever-present thrum of the thaumaturgical engine, a sound that had long since faded into unheard background noise, had ceased.

The ship shuddered again, tilting.

She finally managed to throw the covers from her body. As the hammock swung high, she jumped free, landed awkwardly and rolled into the wall. She shook the impact away, oriented herself, and stood, struggling for balance on the bucking floor. Vedas swung in his hammock along the far wall, apparently unaware of any cause for concern.

She took one step, and the floorboards erupted before her. A jagged ridge of black rock rose up toward the ceiling. Water rushed in through the wound and the ship pitched violently.

Her feet left the floor and the ceiling rushed to meet her.

‡

The lapping of water upon a shore. The call of birds. A dull throb in her head and chest, her heartbeat, slowly spreading to fill her body. She swam through layers of fuzzy sensation into consciousness, into the dim recognition of wrongness. She was hurt, stricken nearly immobile on a beach. Alone, apparently. Minutes passed as she gathered the tatters of her memory and wove them together.

The wind changed direction and the leaves shifted above her. Sunlight tried to force its way in through the shutters of her eyes. She kept it out. The inside of her head felt far too fragile to tamper with. She opened and closed her left fist in the cool sand. This movement alone took a great deal of effort, but she did not stop herself.

Stay awake, she told herself. *Stay here, stay now, stay . . .*

Her throat was raw and desiccated, as if it had been scoured with dry sand, and her right arm throbbed dully. When she tried to move it, pain flared so violently in her shoulder that she decided never to move it again. At best, it was dislocated. At worst, she was only imagining feelings below the joint, and the limb itself was drifting somewhere in the lake.

As she became more aware, the more her body ached.

Clearly, she was alive. This failed to lift her spirits.

Something approached from the left. She heard the *shuff* of displaced sand as it drew close.

A man.

During her fifteen years of service in the Castan Army, she had spent enough time listening to the oncoming steps of enemy soldiers. Footsteps revealed a man's weight and height, as well as a good deal about his intentions. The man approaching her now was probably over six feet in height, well over two hundred pounds. He was not trying to be quiet. The profile fit Vedas.

Images flashed in her mind: A hammock swinging wildly, the black fabric of Vedas's suit visible through the fishnet. Water sloshing below, rushing in through a tear in the ship's floor, a blade of black stone jutting. A switch of perspective, her stomach rising up into her chest and promptly dropping. Sailing through the air. Out of the corner of her eye, Vedas's hammock overturning. Blackness.

Unlikely, that both of them had made it out alive.

She took a deep breath, though her ribs ached holding it in, and simply waited. Nothing to do but wait. Were she hale, or even only partially incapacitated, she would have prepared to defend herself.

Knees dropped onto the sand beside her.

"Churls," Vedas said.

She sighed in relief. The sound wheezed and cracked out of her like air from a dry-rotted bellows, and her fingers tightened convulsively in the sand. Her heart hammered. She did not try to speak or open her eyes, but felt her lips pull into a smile. Even that hurt. Fleetingly, she considered how much the intensity of her reaction would have bothered her if she were not injured so badly. Quite a bit, she reasoned.

"Don't try to talk," he said. "You're fine. I'm going to give you something to drink."

Unable to argue with him about moving an injured neck, she let his hand go under her head. She winced as he lifted it, but the movement did not result in additional pain or the click of broken vertebrae. Something rough and hairy touched her lips, and for a moment she fought to keep her mouth closed. She lost, and a trickle of lukewarm liquid slid down her gullet. It burned as it went, but he was slow and careful pouring. She did not choke. Eventually, she realized it was not water. The sweet taste was familiar.

She must have furrowed her brow.

"It's coconut," he explained. "A fruit that grows on palms. A rare treat. I remembered it from childhood."

"Mm," she said. He laid her head down, and a bit of light peeked in through her eyelids without killing her. She decided speech might be possible. "How?" she croaked.

She heard him sit back. "We ran aground a mile or so from Tan-Ten, and fell on our port side. The storm must have knocked us off course, right into the shallows. Maybe we were running from pirates and ran into the wind to lose them. No way of knowing, because I slept through most of it. The hold was already half full of water when I disentangled myself from my hammock." She heard disgust and embarrassment in his voice. "The oil lamps had spilled, and fire ate at the back wall. The ship lurched against rock. It was clear that we were sinking, but I had no idea how fast. After I'd oriented myself, I noticed you floating near the entranceway. I got you out and swam here."

Churls smiled at his understatement. "You got me out and swam here? How?"

He grunted. "With great difficulty. I can swim, but not well. If my suit didn't provide several minutes of air, I would have drowned. I consider it a minor miracle that we made it without major injury, and I don't generally believe in miracles. Do you feel better?"

Churls concentrated. The pain had increased, yet she did indeed feel better, more in tune with her senses. Experimentally, she turned her head from side to side, wiggled her toes, and lifted her left arm. Each movement was accompanied by its own particular pain, as if she had strained every muscle in her body. She opened her eyes a crack. The blurred outlines of palm trees swayed above her. To her left knelt the black outline of Vedas.

They appeared to be alone. This troubled her, but she could not determine why. Of course, she had more pressing concerns.

"Yes," she assured him. "A little better. Not much. What's wrong with my shoulder?"

He shifted. Slowly, she was able to focus on his face. He would not meet her eyes.

"What?" she asked, and lifted her head to see. Pain flared in her ribs and she dropped her head back down. "Orrus fucking Alachum! What the hell's wrong with me?"

The weight of his hand fell on her upper chest. "Please," he said. "Your shoulder is dislocated."

"How did that happen?"

"I don't know. You must have gotten knocked around before I found you." Softly, he swore—a first, in her experience. "Never mind. I'm not being honest with you. I know why your shoulder is dislocated."

She opened her eyes and found his. He met the stare for a second only, and then looked away. Being forced to press for an explanation would normally have bothered her, if not for the obvious fact that he was so troubled.

"Why?" she asked.

He leaned forward, cupping his chin and mouth with his right hand. His words were muted as a result, and she had to strain to hear them. "I swam as far as I could, Churls, but I still couldn't make it. The waves were too high. I lost my direction and went under, hitting submerged rocks. I tried to grab onto a few that rose above the water, but I couldn't get a grip. I still had air, but I couldn't swim anymore. Too tired. The next time waves threw me against the rocks, I tried to lift your body onto them. I think it worked, because I started to sink. Alone."

He massaged his jaw as if it pained him. He nodded, an almost imperceptible movement. "I knew I was going to die, and I didn't care. I gave up, but you saved me."

For a moment, she thought she had misheard. "I did what?"

He leaned forward and slipped his arm under her shoulder blades. In one smooth movement, unmindful of her protests, he lifted her into a sitting position. She had been prepared to scream, yet it never came. The pain faded so quickly she barely registered it, and he supported her in the new position while her spasming muscles calmed and the inside of her head stopped revolving.

"You pulled me from the lake," he said softly. Warm breath on her ear. "With one arm. You grabbed my wrist and dragged me onto solid ground. You looked like you were standing on the water, but I soon realized that I had dropped you onto a flat shelf of cobbled stones. An ancient dock, worn down by the waves. I could barely see it even when I sat on it.

"My legs collapsed under me when I tried to stand, and so you dragged me behind you, all the way to shore. Your right arm flopped uselessly at your side, a result of lifting me. I kept calling to you, but I don't think you heard over the storm and the waves."

Churls lifted her head. It weighed too much, so she let it fall against his. "What happened after that?" she whispered.

She felt him shake his head. "It's insane, ridiculous, but it happened. Once we were past the waves, you dropped my wrist. When I turned to you, your eyes were closed. I spoke your name, and you wouldn't respond. Your body glowed from the inside. White, like the moon. It peeked out from under your eyelids. I touched your hand, the glow faded, and you crumpled onto the sand. I know it sounds crazy. I've tried to reason it out, but I can't."

Churls closed her eyes, listening to the swift beat of her heart. Vedas's hands pressed against her chest and back, cool and firm—and suddenly, she recalled her fantasy. With his body so close, the invention became more real in her mind than any story he could have told her. Pulling a two hundred and fifty pound man from the ocean? Glowing like the moon? She did not want to think about such things. Focusing too intensely made her head ache. Drifting felt so much nicer.

Yet something nagged at her. A piece of the puzzle was missing. She tried to stop thinking about it, but knew it would come now that she had admitted its existence.

"There is one other possibility," Vedas said before she could ask the question. "You could be a witch."

She did not dignify this with a response. Her heart was not prepared for jokes.

"Do you think you can stand?" he asked.

"I don't know." She exhaled slowly, evenly, preparing herself for movement. "Why?"

While still supporting her, he rose from his knees into a crouch. "I'd like to reduce your dislocation now, if possible. It's a common injury while training. I've done it before. It will heal faster the sooner I get to it."

"What do I have to do?"

He lifted her easily. She gasped when her arm fell, and he told her to let it hang, which hurt slightly less. Standing on her own was difficult and painful. Her legs shook and she doubted they would hold her weight. Thankfully, he supported her every movement, and finally leaned her against a tree trunk. Her eyes fluttered with the strain. She registered her surroundings as a collection of vertical shadows and harsh light.

"Something else," she whispered. "Vedas . . ."

He said nothing in response. Perhaps he had not heard.

She breathed shallowly as he lifted her arm and placed his shoulder under her armpit. She wished he had given her something to bite.

"This is going to hurt," he said.

"I know," she managed through gritted teeth. "Just get to it." She took a deep breath, and in this moment it came: the question that had been nagging at her demanded a voice.

"Berun?" she asked.

Vedas paused, and she knew the answer.

"Sorry," he said, and rose from his crouch, levering her humerus downward against his chest, forcing the ball back into its socket with a loud pop.

She screamed, and then the lights went out.

‡

He wove a sling for her shoulder out of palm leaves and a larger one to hold her body, and then set out across the island. He stopped to feed her coconut flesh, urged her to drink. She rocked in his arms like a newborn, drifting in and out of dream-troubled sleep. Each time she woke, the visions had already faded, leaving her with only a vague sense of loss.

The waking world was little more than a dream itself, a series of confusing tableaus. The sun progressed in jerks above her. The ground rose and fell so that the view upon waking was always different. A shimmering lake with Vedas's reflection in it, her own face peering over the side of the sling. Flashes of light, the sun through tree trunks. A squat, ugly animal standing before them, grunting, stamping hooves into the black earth. A wall of hieroglyphed stone.

Vedas stood upon the gnarled, red-black spine of the island, which extended northward to a distant shore. She sat up to take in the view and promptly fell back, exhausted by the minor exertion. There was a city on the western shore of Tan-Ten, she knew. Its name eluded her. *A gambler's paradise*, someone had once called it.

She licked cracked lips. "How far?" She could barely hear herself speak.

"Four miles, give or take."

"What's it called?" she managed, but fell asleep before hearing the answer. Upon waking, trees surrounded them again and the name had come to her.

"Oasena?" she asked.

"Yes. Only a couple miles to go, but the sun is going down. We'll have to stop soon."

She drifted away yet again. The next time she woke, night had fallen. She lifted her head and peered around. A fire smoldered before her, casting weak light over the small glade Vedas had chosen for camp. He slept on the bare ground at her side, sprawled as though he had collapsed there. She reclined on a bed made of palm leaves, angled so that she sat upright, cushioned so as not to roll to the side and injure her arm.

Her bladder ached. The makeshift bed rustled loudly as she struggled to rise, but Vedas did not so much as twitch. Probably exhausted, she reasoned, guilt constricting her chest with astounding force. Her mind had cleared and the weakness in her limbs was gone. She walked on stiff legs into the black forest to relieve herself.

As she stood from her crouch, a single white light appeared in the distance. Every time she blinked, the ghost of her daughter drew closer.

"Hello, Fyra," Churls said.

She allowed the girl to take her hand. Once again, she felt nothing at the contact.

The forest slowly grew in detail around her. She stared at the stars through the broad leaves, and eventually found the moon. A neat half circle, it nearly touched the black line of distant treetops. Almost morning. She had slept one whole day, and almost through the night.

All at once, she understood what had happened after the wreck. The obvious conclusion.

She had glowed white like the moon.

Vedas had saved her life, and in exchange Fyra had saved his—the girl liked him, after all. What shocked Churls most was not that the thing had happened, but that she accepted it so readily. It brought no joy to know she was safe, that Vedas was her hero, and that the dead could exert control over the living. At no point had she been offered a choice. She wondered if she had ever been in control. If she ever would be.

She removed the sling, rotated her shoulders, and held her right arm horizontal without pain.

"Did you do this?" she asked.

Yes, Fyra answered. *Do you like it?*

"I'm not sure."

The long pause made Churls look down. Fyra had screwed her face up tight, just like she had done as an infant. The expression that always preceded a fit.

"Stop it," Churls said. "You're not a little girl anymore."

Fyra frowned. *You don't like it? I can do other things. I've been practicing.*

Ice formed in Churls's chest. "What other things, Fyra? What else have you done?"

I'm not alone, Fyra said. She let go of Churls's hand and faced her mother. *There are others here. They're everywhere. Some of them teach me things, like the trick I used to save Vedas. Don't tell me I shouldn't have done it. He would have died, Mother. You would have missed him.*

The child was smart, Churls gave her that. She kneeled, and though it pained her to do so, she stared her daughter directly in the eye. "That's not what I asked, Fyra, and you know it. Don't brag about what you can do, and then tell me nothing."

Fyra reached out. Churls flinched, but resisted backing away. The child's hand passed into her chest, but all Churls felt was the steady thrum of her heart. Fyra's head cocked slightly to the side, and her eyelids fluttered closed.

I can see it, Fyra said. *Your heart. I can see through you, like you're made of ice. I met a dead man, and he showed me how to read what's inside people. He taught me to fix things that have gone wrong. There was something wrong with your heart, Mama. I fixed it. I fixed other things, too. Clogs in your veins. Scars in your womb. When Vedas pulled your shoulder into place, he damaged your nerves. He didn't mean to, just like I didn't mean to hurt you when I used your body to save him. I fixed everything, and now everything is better. Me, I did. I'm not a little girl anymore.*

Churls breathed long and deep through her mouth, pushed her fear to the side, and said the exact opposite of what she truly felt.

"I'm proud of you."

Fyra's eyes opened, flaring bright enough that Churls had to shield her own. *Really, Mama? The dead people don't tell me that. They tell me not to meddle. The world is for the living, they tell me, even when they teach me things. Don't meddle, they say. They're very angry that Vedas saw me, but I think they're wrong about everything. It's good what I'm doing, right?*

"Right," Churls said, throwing good sense to the wind. Considering how quickly her life had been hurled into disarray, how swiftly the revelations were coming, perhaps the best course of action was to embrace change. Never one for improvisation, always one for planning, she wondered how long she could sustain this philosophy before it drove her mad.

I have to go, Fyra said. *It's almost sunrise and they're yelling at me to stop, but there's one more thing I have to tell you. About the metal man with the blue eyes.*

"Berun?" Churls's heart leapt in her chest. "You saw him?"

Fyra beamed. *He saw me. At the bottom of the lake. That made the other dead people really angry, but I didn't care. I showed the metal man where to walk. I think he might have heard me, too.* She turned away, staring into the distance. She bared her teeth, flickered like a guttering candle. *Leave me alone!* she yelled, and faced Churls again. *I have to go. I hate them. Wait for the metal man. He'll be here soon, even if they don't let me show him the way. He'll find you. You'll wait for him, won't you?*

"I will," Churls promised.

‡

She encouraged Vedas to keep sleeping, but the man would not rest.

"We need to reach the city as soon as possible," he said. "Who knows how often boats leave for Knos Min? We can't afford to be delayed any longer."

Despite these words, he stopped often to listen. He looked over his shoulder, as though expecting a visitor at any moment. She read the pain on his face, and kept her mouth shut. In turn, he suppressed his curiosity about her impossibly rapid recovery.

She did not volunteer the information—did not even think about what Fyra had done. Finding a way to stay on the island long enough for Berun to reach them preoccupied her completely. She had no desire to deceive Vedas, but she would in order to allow the constructed man time to find them. A day at least.

She need not have worried.

The diffuse light of dawn revealed Oasena to be little more than a township. Nothing larger than a fishing boat floated in her shallow bay—certainly naught capable of crossing a hundred-mile stretch of open water. Vedas enquired in a bakery and discovered that a thaumatrig, a vessel most likely similar to the drowned *Atavest*, arrived from Ynon once a week. It docked for half a day and then returned.

"Tomorrow," Vedas said. "And it won't leave dock until the evening."

The muscles in his jaw twitched as they walked to the inn the baker had recommended. Churls resisted the urge to ask about the fare. He would give the details when he was ready. In the meantime, she took in the town's thatched single-floor houses, the somber flat-featured countenances of the townsfolk. The women walked bare-breasted, flat dugs hanging over short dresses woven from palm fibers. They rustled as they walked. The men looked much like the women, though their garments were of brown cloth.

Churls noted their corded arms and thick thighs, how their bodies moved and their eyes tracked, and surmised they would be formidable opponents.

An odd mood drifted through her. Not joy, no, yet it was a close cousin. Despite Vedas's dour air, she drank the sunlight as if it were an elixir. The corners of her mouth turned upward without her willing them. Somehow, she knew Berun would arrive before the ship left. They would arrive in Ynon safely. She considered the possibility that Fyra had rearranged her mind, but dismissed it. Pointless, to conjecture.

After a lifetime of useless and obsessive conjecture, this thought shocked her.

They reached the inn, and sat at one of its four small tables. A woman came from the kitchen, nodded, and went to fetch their food.

"Only the one option, apparently," Churls said.

Vedas glowered. "We won't reach Ynon until late on the first."

Calculating quickly, Churls's good mood faded. From Ynon it was perhaps seven hundred miles to Danoor. By all accounts, the trail to Danoor was well trod, but thirty miles a day for twenty-four days, during the darkest month of the year? It could be done, but she and Vedas would be exhausted by the time they reached the tournament. Undoubtedly, he had already made the calculation.

"The fare?" she asked.

"Six grams," he growled. "They can extort because so few boats come to Tan-Ten."

She smiled weakly. "But we have enough, Vedas. Barely. It can be done."

Neither of them had lost any money. Anyone smart enough to buckle her sandals carried her dust close to the body in waterproofed fabric. It was too easy to spill liquid and lose it all. Churls and Vedas had discussed their funds as they walked that morning, with one important omission. Before leaving Nbena, she had sewn a new pocket on the inside of her vest to hold the dust Gorum had given her. So far, she had not needed to touch it.

Between the three of them, there should have been enough—she should have been able to keep her stash a secret. But who knew what had happened to Berun's dust? Saying they could make it on what remained was a lie, and Vedas knew it.

Shit, she thought. *There goes my gambling fund.*

She reached inside her vest and removed the wallet. It lay on the table between them, an indictment. Proof she had kept it from him. Vedas stared at it, expressionless.

"It can be done," she said. "We'll make it to Sent in nineteen days, and rent horses for the stretch to Danoor. That's forty, maybe fifty miles a day. We'll be at the tournament by the twenty-fourth."

The innkeeper came out of the kitchen. Churls palmed the wallet, and they proceeded to eat fried trout and grilled asparagus in silence. Vedas could not sustain his glowering completely, however. Now and then he looked up, an expression she had never seen written on his face. Wonder, perhaps, or astonishment.

"What?" she eventually asked.

He jumped slightly, as though he had been far away in his mind. "Something just occurred to me," he said. "My decision has been made for me. Abse's speech went down with the *Atavest*. I now have no option but to rewrite it."

‡

In her dream, she walked down a long hall with doors on each side. Endless doors. She chose one at random, and inside sat Fyra. The child opened her mouth to speak, but another voice spoke instead. A voice from the waking world, calling her back.

She woke, and lay very still, eyes open, concentrating. It had not been just a dream. Someone had called to her. Someone had called her name, and then Vedas's name.

There! *Chuuurrllss. Veeedaas.*

She threw the covers to the side. Vedas jumped up from the floor, ready, but Churls silenced him with a gesture. She tapped her ear, and he listened.

His eyes widened.

They raced down the stairs and out the front door.

"Chuuurrllss! Veeedaas!" the voice called—closer, from out of the depths of black forest before them. A voice like a bell, deep and resounding in the pit of one's gut. Hearing it, Churls's heart pumped harder, strong and healthy and alive. She had not known how much the voice meant to her— how greatly she had come to rely upon the constructed man's presence as she walked, as she slept.

Again he called their names. Loudly enough to wake dogs and set them barking.

And then, a low rumble came to her ears. A steady drumming. Huge, heavy feet pounding the earth. Closer and closer.

Voices rose in Oasena, and the dogs began to howl.

Churls grinned, and stepped forward to meet Berun.

EBN BON MARI

For a month, the same routine before breakfast: With the assistance of a recall spell, Ebn watched the disastrous encounter with Adrash— over and over again methodically, like a composer playing an identical refrain to resolve an irksome melody. The spell made her forehead throb as it pushed against the confining walls of her skull, yet she persevered. She had missed something. Some detail that would help her to interpret the events that had transpired.

Adrash gestured at the statue.

Stop, Ebn commanded, stilling the image in her mind's eye. As always, and despite the pain of holding the memory still, Ebn lingered on the god's perfection. The graceful, sculpted proportions of his body. The lines of tension that defined the muscle and sinew of his back and extended arm. More than any other feature, she admired the flawless pearl complexion of the divine armor, an artifact she knew felt like the finest elder-cloth. Cold, infinitely smoother than skin. Her tongues stirred in her palms at the thought.

Her desire nearly overcame her every time. The memory wavered as though she viewed the scene through fire, and then lust gave way to sadness.

She would never possess such beauty. She had been a fool to think she could.

Enough, she told herself. *Enough foolishness.*

She resumed the memory at quarter-speed. Adrash shattered the statue with a gesture, sending a thousand sharp-edged fragments of marble toward the mages. His eyes blazed brighter than the sun.

Stop, right before the first impacts. At the time, Ebn had been focused on Adrash, but in her recall it became possible to examine the other mages, who extended in a glittering arc just slightly out of focus in her peripheral vision. Sunlight reflected on the polished black skins of their suits. Qon's feet were only just visible above her. Pol floated directly opposite her. Ebn focused on his face, but read nothing new in his expression.

She moved forward in time slowly, by now familiar with the grim details. She had erected a shield with plenty of time to spare, perhaps because she had subconsciously expected the attack. Silver veins flickered on the surface of Pol's suit, signaling that he too had erected a protective spell. Eighteen others, mostly talented young mages, acted quickly to defend themselves, using spells both ordinary and exotic.

Three—Qon included—cast a fraction too slowly, deflecting only some of the stone fragments.

They did not die immediately.

The remaining seventeen mages were cut to shreds near-instantaneously. Ebn watched them die. She made herself do it, though the section she suspected of holding a clue came afterward. Replaying the entirety of the disaster was her penance.

Gota fi Junnun, only sixteen years old but a promising student, face flayed as his helmet burst, torso pocked with innumerable small holes, bloomed an aura of blood that vaporized instantly around him. Hamen i Loren, Ebn's one-time lover, a man of immaculate taste and speech, was cut nearly in two by a large flake of marble. Intestines bubbled and burst from both halves of his body. Zi-Te bon Ueses, martial arts master and gambling enthusiast, was sliced from clavicle to groin but stayed conscious for several seconds, screaming a fine red mist.

Ebn watched each fatal blow, reversing the spell repeatedly so that all of her officers could be accounted for. Her stomach did not turn as it had the first few times—proof a person could grow used to anything.

In the midst of the chaos, Adrash disappeared. Ebn reversed and slowed her memory to a crawl. No fade, no wavering around the god's body, no sign at all that he would vanish. Clearly, nothing could be gleaned from this portion of memory, yet Ebn lingered on it every time. The god stood, fixed as stone. Then he did not, and it was as though he had never existed in that place. The raw power needed to enact such magic boggled her mind, horrified her in a way the deaths of the mages did not.

And here, in the vacuum Adrash had created: An anomalous event that had eluded her for the first two weeks of her search through the recalled memory. She chastened herself for taking so long to spot it, but knew how lucky she had been to notice it at all. Certainly, she could not be blamed for missing such a slight gesture during the disaster. Qon's hemorrhaging had occupied all of her attention.

The sequence lasted only four seconds. Immediately following Adrash's disappearance, Pol swiveled his head toward the moon, eyes clearly tracking a moving object. He ripped his gloves off and made a gesture, as if he were turning a globe in his hands. A heartbeat later, his eyes widened and his mouth fell open. It was this expression—so odd on Pol's typically controlled features—that had first alerted her to the moment's significance.

Stop. Ebn returned to the beginning and replayed the sequence slowly. By its nature, a recalled memory wanted to move at normal speed, and her head ached with the strain of holding it back.

There. Between these two seconds, she told herself. Something out of place.

Again. Again. Her temples pounded.

Nothing new revealed itself, yet she knew in her womb that Pol had done something highly irregular. After years of traveling in orbit, she had learned to trust her intuition. The obvious conclusion was that he had seen Adrash leaving and cast a spell in response, but Ebn could not make herself believe this. Pol's magical faculties had not progressed beyond hers. His lore was not so esoteric that she could not recognize it.

Frustrated, she moved forward to the second event of note. She watched herself fumble to hold the flaps of Qon's suit closed, willing them to mend while her friend hemorrhaged, coughing clouds of blood that frosted on Ebn's helmet. She pulled Qon to her chest and attempted to extend her spell of protection around them both. Tired from casting her own disastrous spell of influence at Adrash, the minor charm proved beyond her abilities.

In the final seconds of her life, Qon pointed in the direction of the Needle. Her expression alone had caused Ebn to turn, yet the view did not impress anything upon her. Despite repeated and painstaking examination, the spheres appeared unaltered.

Of course, she had not trusted her eyes alone. Queries over the last month had confirmed her suspicion: since the disaster, the telescopists had not observed a major change in the Needle's alignment.

Nonetheless, Qon and Pol had seen something. Had they actually followed the god's flight?

Or had they seen something else entirely?

‡

The recall spell faded. It exited through the sutures of her skull, easing the pressure within.

Why, she asked herself, *have I allowed this to happen?*

She could not pretend ignorance. She had angered Adrash by attempting to sway him with magic, an aggressive act to which he had responded in kind. Perhaps if she had stuck to her own plan and merely projected goodwill it would have worked, but she had been unable to keep her own desire from coloring the spell. Just as she had feared.

Undoubtedly, Adrash had recognized her. Sixty years was no time at all for the god.

Had she truly expected a second attempt at seduction to meet with favorable results? Certainly, she had known the risks. Perhaps she simply had not cared about risk. Qon's life, the lives of her officers? They meant nothing in the face of her overwhelming desire to possess Adrash. This had been the true reason for approaching the god, not good will.

No. Ebn rejected the idea that she had lost her moral bearing completely. True, she had let her desire cloud her judgment again, but the ultimate goal remained the same. Adrash must be convinced of the world's worth.

She sighed, massaging a kink in her neck. She rose from her couch and walked naked onto the balcony, where the air was cool and smelled strongly of leaf rot. The chill of fall had seeped into everything, but she lay on the flagstones anyway. For a few minutes she shivered, waiting for the stone to warm beneath her. The morning sun soaked into her eggplant-colored skin, feeding her nutrients essential to the functioning of her body.

Slowly, the details of the encounter with Adrash drifted from her mind. Though she would never admit it aloud, in a way the disaster had freed her. She could sink no lower. Soon, she would receive a summons from the king. He would question her judgment, and she would defend herself. Defending herself, she would finally understand the how and why of her actions. It had always been this way, testing and retesting in response to the expectations of others.

She would triumph, and renew her purpose.

Someone knocked on the door. Ebn heard the whisper of slippered feet as her servant jogged to the entry, and then the girl's high, fluting greeting. The response, however, could not be understood. The voice was too low, the rhythm of speech oddly clipped.

The short exchange over, soft feet whispered toward Ebn.

"What?" she asked. She did not open her eyes.

"There is a man here to see you, magess. Shavrim Coranid."

"I do not know a Shavrim Coranid, girl. You have a list of my acquaintances. Unless he is on official business, send him on his way."

"He is not on official business," a deep voice sounded.

Ebn's eyes snapped open and she rolled to the left. She had not yet drunk her daily alchemicals, but enough magic remained in her veins from the previous day to cast one or two spells.

Binding the intruder seemed best. She rose to her feet and thrust her hands forward in one fluid motion. The spell moved visibly along her arms, like waves cresting and breaking under her skin. Thin lips pulled back from small, sharp teeth.

She paused. The man whose bulk filled her doorway held no weapon. His hands were crossed on the immense drum of his belly.

Two stubby horns sprouted from his temples.

"I have information about one of your mages," he said. "For the right price, I will tell you interesting things about a young mage named Pol Tanz et Som."

‡

Per his suggestion, they sat on the balcony. He did not want to ruin her delicate wrought-iron furniture. "I weigh four hundred and sixty-seven pounds," he explained.

Ebn could not place the man's accent, but his lineage was clear enough. Though surgery and magic could produce a hybrid in appearance, she knew this was not the case in regard to Shavrim Coranid. Very likely, he had worn tight-fitting clothing so that his nature would be obvious to her. His every muscular twitch fascinated her, yet she fought the urge to stare.

She recognized him, of course. How had she not noticed his uniqueness the night he had called a dragon from the sky?

By surprising her, the man had gained the high ground.

He would not be allowed to keep it.

She remained naked. The man had already seen her unclothed, so there could be no advantage in dressing now. Such an action would only reveal her discomfort. Best to affect an air of amused disdain, talk as if she were accustomed to unannounced visitors and their implied threats. She would not ask how he had reached her apartment without identification, how he had convinced her servant to let him in, or how he had lived anywhere near the city without the academy discovering him.

This last proved hardest to resist. At her core, Ebn was a scholar. To her knowledge, no quarterstock of Shavrim's obviously robust mental and physical health had ever been discovered. She resolved to cast a tracking spell upon him as he left, so that she might observe him remotely before taking further action.

The servant returned with tea and poppicut pastries, and then retreated.

"How much?" Ebn eventually asked. Her expression did not change, nor did her tone. They had been discussing fall, the myriad colors of dying leaves.

The corners of Shavrim's eyes crinkled. "One pound."

Ebn smiled openly but did not laugh. "Ridiculous. I do not know what kind of information you have. I will give you an eighth of a pound, and you will tell me something of value. We will proceed from there."

"You misunderstand me." The man leaned forward slightly. "I know the worth of my information, and by all accounts you are a trustworthy woman. I do not need to see the dust right now. If you agree to pay me afterward on the condition of the information's value, it will be sufficient. You are a sorceress. I am a wyrm tamer. If you wish to detain or punish me, I cannot hope to resist. Trust, then, will bind us."

Ebn considered, then nodded agreement. "Out with it," she said, all pretense of gaiety extinguished.

Shavrim held three thick fingers up. "Pol is dissatisfied with your leadership and he intends your downfall. I do not yet know where or how he plans to do this, but he intends to do it soon. Do not underestimate his power. Despite your attempts to keep alchemical resources from him, he has acquired the materials he needs."

Two fingers. "He has somehow managed to knock one of the Needle's spheres out of alignment. Very minutely. Most likely, your scholars did not recognize it. Adrash changes their direction often enough that it probably seemed like another of his minor whims, yet if you examine your logs you will see that a slight adjustment was made on the seventh sphere from the moon at the exact moment of the god's attack."

One finger. "Prior to or just after your encounter with Adrash, Pol began to modify his body in some way. His reactions are quicker—unnaturally so. His spell-casting is improving by leaps and bounds. As I am sure you have noticed, he has taken to wearing black, close-fitting garments, designed so that only his face and hands show. He will not undress completely in my presence."

‡

Her fingernails bit into her palms. The tongues pushed back.

"You and Pol are lovers," she said.

His amber gaze did not waver. "Yes."

Her hearts shuddered in her chest, restarted off-kilter. A pressure built in her throat, as if she were being strangled. She had known it. Of course she had. The boy had always been so self-assured. He carried himself like someone who enjoyed fucking. She could see it, clearly. She was no fool, and she had her jar of sex spells to prove it.

Get off it, she told herself. *That is the least important fact you have learned.*

"Thank you," she said, and stood. She snapped her fingers and her servant appeared in the doorway. "Retrieve one pound, four ounces of dust for this man." She looked down at Shavrim. "You did not lie. That was certainly worth the money."

The quarterstock furrowed his brows. "Please sit down, Magess bon Mari."

She met his stare, shrugged, and sat. She did not doubt the man's intentions even slightly. Now that she knew the truth about Pol, the whole world felt bright and clear, her path through it obvious. Not a comforting truth, no, but knowing it was better than believing a lie.

She would crush Pol. She would force him to love her and then watch him die.

"I will take the extra dust," Shavrim said. "But you deserve something for it."

"You have more?" she asked. "He must have told you that I love him. Surely he has seen it. He has known me for too long." Her voice dropped an octave, became a warning. "I do not want to hear any more about his disdain for me. Clearly I mean nothing to him. If you have ever loved, you know this kind of pain."

He smiled without humor. "I have been betrayed before, and have no desire to increase that particular pain. Instead, I will offer you a small boon: Garrus

Eamon. He works at White Ministry, in the morgue. Recently, he was caught filtering alchemical materials from corpses. He and Pol are lovers."

She filed the name. The quarterstock had given her more than he needed to.

He stood, and offered his hand. She took it, the first time she had touched another person without her gloves on in over three decades. He did not flinch when her tongue tasted his palm.

As she walked him to the door, she marveled at the way her life had been overturned. It had happened so quickly, so cleanly, an entire limb cut from her body without pain. A few exchanged words with a stranger, and she was a new person.

She had also figured out the anomaly in her memory. When Pol removed his gloves, for a split second he revealed a small patch of lustrous black on his wrist. Ebn visualized it clearly.

A tattoo. She would not even need to use the recall spell to confirm it.

Had he really been stupid enough to use alchemical paint on his own skin?

On the other hand, if it worked . . .

At the door, she faced Shavrim. It shocked her to find that he stood a few inches shorter than her. "Why did you do this?" she asked.

"I need the money."

"Enough to betray a lover?"

He shrugged his immense shoulders. "My work as a tamer does not pay well, and Tansot is a poor place to be a fighter. Still, I am a fighter, and Danoor is fast approaching."

POL TANZ ET SOM

Pol had spent much of his adolescence along the docks of Ravos, Pusta's capitol city. There he watched the fishermen pull their catches from the teeming sea, corded arms and calloused fingers quick with the rusty latches and mechanisms of their enormous trap baskets. Naked, they scampered with odd grace over the monumental wire and steel structures suspended between the docks, dodging the man-sized pincers and jagged jaws snapping at them from below.

Their dexterity astonished and thrilled him, as did their scars and missing limbs, which rarely impeded them in their tasks. Such devotion to work had made Ravos the most successful exporter of seafood in all of Knoori. The fishermen were beautiful and dangerous and proud of their craft, and they shared their bodies as freely as they shared labor. They did not look down on an elderman boy, especially one so eager to learn.

Had Pol's mother known the way he spent his evenings, spreading his legs for men of low caste, working, drinking and carousing with laborers, she would have locked him in a cell. Had he been dimmer or less intellectually inclined, she certainly would have found him out.

Despite the time he spent with fishermen and dockhands, he did not echo their concerns or beliefs. They were a fascinating people in their own right, but hardly examples for an elderman boy. He used them, first for pleasure and then for their unique perspectives.

Few noble-born men cared to know what laborers thought of the world. Unbeknownst to the aristocracy, labor guildsmen communicated across national borders, irrespective of the restrictions placed upon them by government. They exchanged information on trade and common magical practices, and maintained extended family ties.

In Pol's opinion, these comprised the least significant percentage of exchanged information. The majority of laborers in Knos Min, Nos Ulom, Stol, and Casta practiced a highly fluid form of oral storytelling called adrasses, which recounted moments in Adrash's life upon the earth. An adrass—the events of which often began thirty millennia or more before the present age, far beyond the scope of recorded history—never referred to the god's ascension into the sky. It never referred to the Needle, or the obvious threat its existence posed to the world.

Such tales transcended the rude boundaries of Adrashi and Anadrashi, for while no sane man could deny the god's existence, he could interpret events as he saw fit—a fact that contributed to the continual development of adrasses. Even Orrust and Bashest sects, a small minority in most nations, took part in the telling, incorporating the legendary events of Adrash's life into the traditional stories of their own deities.

The fishermen of Knoori's coasts shared a particularly rich canon of adrasses, compiling the numerous tales of Adrash's life as a sailor. Of course, the people of Jeroun generally agreed the god had exiled himself to the ocean for a period of time prior to his ascension into the sky, yet only the most conservative Adrashi claimed to know his reason for doing so. Largely uninterested in his motivation, fishermen of all varieties celebrated Adrash's incredible feat of navigating the ocean with tales of superhuman strength and daring.

According to the fishermen of Ravos, the god had set sail from their very docks. They claimed he saw their bravery, their clean sweat, and was so inspired that he decided to embark upon his own adventure. He formed a ship out of steel and glass without the assistance of tools, fusing the materials together with the light from his eyes. Once finished, he pushed the vehicle out to sea alone, battling beasts along the way.

Convictions were split on the ship's name. Some swore it was *Aberrast*, others *the Oabess*. Its prow was a knife blade, fine enough that creatures learned to steer clear of it lest they be cut in two. He piloted the sixty-foot vessel alone with a crank drive and propeller of his own design. Many adrasses differed in this account, insisting that the ship was powered by sail or by thaumaturgical engine, but the fishermen of Ravos loved nothing more than a display of muscle.

They downplayed the role of the divine armor in Adrash's life. In their accounts he only grew to rely upon its power later—during the unspoken period after he left Jeroun's surface. They saw the god as a being of superhuman sinew and bone, relying upon his strength, wits, and nautical skill. Some went so far as to claim he found the armor itself while at sea, that it was a gift from the Ocean Mother, no greater than his whalebone sword Amedur, his shark-toothed club Xollet, or his narcroc-ivory spear.

Oftentimes, the armor, swords, whips, and spears came second to Adrash's most treasured possession: The sentient dagger Sroma, which he had carved from the rib of a giant elder corpse he found floating around Iswee, the floating island on the other side of the world. He carried the dagger onto the sodden land and battled the reanimated elders who defended it from man. He used it to carve the wooden skyboat *Dam Tilles*, which astronomists claim sits atop Mount Pouen, under the crystal dome that covers the island of Osa.

Adrash slept with Sroma, never let it leave his side. The Ystuhi, a religious sect of crab-catchers who inhabited the south Pustan coast, still carved blackwood statues of the god with elaborate whorls cut into his skin and the outline of the dagger between his shoulder blades. They believed Adrash had loved the weapon enough to embed it in his flesh.

A Pustan fisherman's version of Adrash would be unrecognizable, unbearably offensive, to the conservative Adrashi nobles of Stol or Nos Ulom, who revered the god as all-powerful and immutable, as distant from man as scrub grass was to sentinel oak. In this regard, Pol stood somewhere on the fringe of both groups. In the days of youthful revolt, he had been much influenced by the fishermen. In truth, he still considered Adrash a vengeful, even capricious lord. But in accordance with conservative Adrashi ideals, he believed Adrash had always possessed the armor. His other weapons were the stuff of myth.

No god would debase himself with such crude tools. Only man and elderman relied upon the strength of bone and steel.

‡

Midafternoon, Pol walked to the docks to buy a set of knives. Not any knives, either. He required a very specific design for his purpose. Garrus had recommended a bladesmith in Vanset, but Pol did not trust Ulomi and decided on a shop Shav recommended in Little Demn. He admired Tomen for their serious, frequently violent practicality. If anyone could make a knife suitable for an assassin's hand, a desert man could.

He met every stare in the street, unafraid. The unsheathed blade of his liisau caught the sun, announcing his presence from several blocks away. For someone like Pol, Little Demn was just as dangerous during the day as the night. Men could easily see him for what he was: not only an Adrashi, but one who actively sought peace with the devil.

It was an important distinction, for just as many types of Anadrashi zealot existed as Adrashi. Roughly equal in number but generally less organized than their god-worshipping brethren, one basic belief bound them: Adrash should not be worshipped. The reasons for this numbered in the thousands, but roughly boiled down to two philosophical stances—the canonical and the personal.

The Black Suit orders, for instance, taught that Adrash actively sought the destruction of the world, and could only be kept at bay by displaying one's faith in mankind, by cursing the god at every opportunity, and by physically besting those who worshipped Adrash. Though they acted in the community, they primarily expressed their faith through planned, bloody encounters with similarly outfitted Adrashi orders. Their faith was a thing of rigid order, tradition, and—though they would not admit it—a certain measure of symbiosis.

This expression contrasted sharply with that of the Rinka, a fraternal organization of former Adrashi in Northeastern Casta. Bound by the shared experience of family abuse, the members expressed their ecstatic faith in city squares and markets. Crying and screaming were encouraged as part of the proselytizing. Members often renounced drinking and gambling, and preached nonviolent opposition to Adrash through meditation and fasting.

Tomen rejected both the canonical and personal stances. They considered the existence of Adrash—whom they considered to be a demon of great power—to be a practical affront to humanity, and reacted in kind. Reasoning that Adrash drew strength from his worshippers, the men of the desert took every opportunity to take the lives of Adrashi, as well as weak-wristed Anadrashi. They valued freedom and self-sufficiency above all else, wrote no creeds, proselytized not at all, and committed no violence upon their brothers. Some claimed that within Toma existed the most peaceful society on the continent.

Along its borders, however, more men died in combat than anywhere else on the continent—a situation mirrored in their expatriate communities. But for the presence of the city watches, places like Little Demn were for all practical purposes border towns at war.

Pol interpreted the looks he received correctly. They would gladly gut him if given the opportunity.

A month ago, he might still have chosen to travel alone, but he would have seriously considered the consequences. This morning, however, he had not given it a second thought. Cool fire moved along his nerves, twitched the muscles in his fingers, urged him to move, to strike.

Do it, his stare mocked. *Attack.* He knew with every ounce of his being that an entire army could not stand against him.

He had moved the Needle.

Every day since Ebn's disastrous mission, he had awakened to the same nervous sensations, the same memory of knocking one of Adrash's spheres out of alignment. He recalled the pain of the sigils awakening upon his body—the mounting, rapturous pressure of the unknown spell straining for release—the vaguely disappointing knowledge that he had acted too late to save his brethren—and then the near-instinctive unloading of his pent magic upon the first target that came to mind. He tried to summon the exact feelings to him again, lingering on each detail as one might linger on a lover's touch.

It had been a gift from the void. A call to action, proof he could no longer sit by and let events continue unchecked. He would answer the call and make himself a leader of men, but to do so he knew he must prepare carefully.

For a brief period after the disastrous encounter with Adrash, he worried he had become too addled to continue painting sigils on his skin. But, despite all of the energy coursing through his system, his hands were sure with each stroke. He even found himself painting his back, as though his fingers had eyes of their own. Sometimes it seemed the sigils were painting themselves. The marks became more complex, esoteric, and dangerous. He became a collection of alchemical lore. A weapon.

His power would soon eclipse Ebn's. Possibly, it already had.

Odd now that I must search for knives, he thought. Such crude implements, yet he did not want to rely solely upon spells and sigils. He would not underestimate Ebn, a craftsman of magic with few equals, a mage who responded to attacks with cunning and raw power. She had even swayed Adrash, if only for a moment. Undoubtedly, she had examined her memory of the failed mission. Perhaps she had discovered what Pol had done, knew his power for the threat it was.

During the final confrontation, she would not allow sentimentality to cloud her judgment.

In this, they were bound. He prepared himself, and thought up novel ways to kill a master mage in orbit.

‡

Shav weighed the knife, flipped it a few times to test the balance. Ten heavy inches of steel, a straight handle accounted for half its length. The teardrop blade, edge ground to razor sharpness, accounted for the other half. Per Pol's request, the bladesmith had bound a fine layer of charcoal to its surface so that it would not reflect light. It was a simple, elegant weapon, a tool clearly intended for killing.

"I told you he was good," Shav said. "When will the others be ready?"

"Week's end, he said."

"You must have been robbed."

Pol smiled. "Yes, I was, and he took some convincing. He told me that if he accepted my business, he would be dead by week's end."

"Nonsense." Shav stood and threw the knife overhanded into the target Pol had fixed to the wall. His next throw hit flat and clanged to the floor. "Why is this shaped so?" he asked, running his finger over the chisel-shaped tip of the handle.

"I have designed the knife carefully," Pol said. "Once thrown, it has two tasks. First, it must shatter Ebn's helmet. Second, its weight must carry the blade forward into her skull. In many ways the handle is more important than the blade."

Pol gave this information without hesitation. He had long since ceased keeping secrets from Shav. He no longer hid his sigils. Though he had not yet discovered a use for the quarterstock, his idiosyncratic presence was oddly comforting. Furthermore, he was an excellent lover. Even his smell, which seemed to always carry the salt and rot of the sea, had an odd charm. It amused Pol to think he had once been intimidated by the quarterstock.

Shav turned his hand. The knife disappeared into his sleeve. He thrust his hand forward, and the knife appeared in it. He grunted in surprise at the blood welling up from his calloused thumb. "Why is the blade so sharp? You can practice with a dull knife, can't you?"

"No." Pol took the weapon from him. He hefted it and then flicked it underhanded into the target. "I will not chance it. The weight of the practice knives needs to be exactly the same as the killing blade itself." He pulled the knife free and repeated the throw. He moved back a pace and hit the target handle first, but got it the next time, and the next.

Shav watched, brows raised. "You've thrown knives of this design before?"

Pol shrugged. "No."

"Maybe you shouldn't get used to this, then. Handling the knife, yes, but maybe not the throwing. No doubt, it will fly differently in the void." Shav sat at the table and tore a piece of rouce bread, dipped it in green olive relish. He gestured for Pol to do likewise. "Maybe you should practice in orbit."

They sat in silence and ate. Shav's intelligence never ceased to arouse Pol's interest. Curious as to his strange companion's education, he had made subtle enquiries at the academy but discovered little. Of course, Shav claimed to have done many things. He had been all over Knoori, claimed to have fought in a dozen wars, many of which were happening simultaneously. He had sailed the ocean and planted his feet on foreign soil. For many years he had kept his identity hidden, staining his skin with a semi-permanent black ink.

Pol dismissed much of the history out of hand. The quarterstock was mad, a charming and startlingly keen liar. At times he had seemed almost prescient, but now Pol suspected he was merely a skilled observer. A man could appear to do miracles if he watched others closely enough.

"That is my intention, yes," Pol finally answered. "Unfortunately, I believe I am being observed constantly now. This morning, I breakfasted with Ebn. All scheduled solo ascensions—and thus all independent projects of study in the void—have been placed on hold. She wants the mages to maintain a constant presence above Jeroun from now on. Comprised of eighteen half-day shifts, the watch will operate as an early warning system of sorts, possibly even the first line of defense against Adrash. A ridiculous concept, of course, but Ebn is insistent.

"I have been assigned the twice-weekly task of ascending to orbit and relieving the first and fifth shifts. As you may have guessed, I will not be alone in this task. Loas, the most senior mage next to Ebn now that Qon is gone, will accompany me. He is highly skilled in the lore and unquestionably loyal to Ebn. I must find a way of silencing him so that my target practice is not revealed."

"Won't it be revealed the moment you take on another partner?"

"No. Ebn's resources are stretched too thin. It will be weeks before she can find a replacement for Loas. For a time, at least, I will be left to my own devices. Even if I am wrong, it should not be too difficult to arrange yet another accident in the void. Many of the voidsuits were damaged when Adrash attacked."

Shav shook his head. "This is far too complicated. Why not simply replace this Loas with someone you can convince to keep your secret? Someone you can buy?"

Pol had already considered this and rejected it. "Beyond the fact that Ebn would find my request for a replacement highly suspicious, I would not attempt to bribe another mage. Only someone in a weak position would accept such an offer, and sooner or later he would realize how much more there is to gain by turning me in. No, I must convince Loas to help me lift the helmets and targets into the void. I will tell him it is a last minute request from Ebn. And then, once we have reached orbit, I will kill him."

"Your plan hinges on one act of deception? What if he doesn't believe you? He will not ascend with you, but go immediately to Ebn."

Pol ground his teeth together. "I have no other options, Shav. I have so few resources at my disposal, no friends conveniently placed in positions of . . ."

He paused, struck dumb as the answer suddenly revealed itself.

He had finally found a use for the quarterstock.

"But perhaps I have been looking in the wrong places," he said. "It occurs to me that you may be of some assistance."

Shav chewed thoughtfully for a moment. "You want to use my dragon as a pack animal."

"Yes," Pol said, impressed once more with the quarterstock's acumen. "I want it to carry the helmets and targets so that Loas's curiosity is not aroused and my hands are free to attack. I can manage the weight of the helmets and targets from that point on."

"Sapes and I can only travel so high, which means you must strike your enemy well before reaching orbit. Gravity won't be on your side, so you'll have to act very fast. Are you sure it wouldn't be wiser to kill him at your convenience and allow me to transport your materials later?"

"I am sure. Time is of the essence."

"His death must look like an accident, Pol."

Pol closed his eyes, picturing the spell he would cast. His fingers twitched on the tabletop, and his tattooed skin puckered with gooseflesh. The sigils seemed to assert themselves more and more every day, whispering possibilities, temptations. "I can do it. Can I rely on you?"

Shav stood and stretched. An erection pressed against the fabric of his pants. He wrapped his fist around Pol's bicep.

"Of course you can. You . . ."

His eyes rolled up into his head and he shuddered, fingers tightening on Pol's arm. Pol waited, mildly amused by the display.

"The elderman," Shav said once the seizures had ceased. His voice was deeper than Pol had ever heard. Almost painfully hoarse, it quavered as though the quarterstock were in agony. "The elderman's name is Orrus. He is my father. He has won his first battle and will soon leave for his second. He is frightened, as he should be. He knows a wiser man would hoist sails for the outer isles, leaving the world behind. Instead, he contemplates taking from the Lord of the world his most prized possession. He is a fool."

The quarterstock knelt. His right index fingertip traced the lines of the flight sigil tattooed on Pol's shoulder. "Before he leaves, my father tells me to contemplate death. He tells me to feel my mortality in the creak of my bones and the soreness of my muscles. *With every heartbeat, you are closer to death*, he says. He forces me to smell the stench of his underarms—the smell of the body birthing and decaying life at the same moment. He tells me to know, intimately, every sign of weakness in my body, and then reject each in turn.

"He breaks my arm with one blow, kicks me as I writhe on the ground. *Remember this lesson above all others*, he says. *The body heals. It responds to trauma, to pain—not with fear, but with purpose. So must you. You need not die, my son, but in order to continue living—*"

Shav stared into Pol's eyes.

"*—you must suffer.*"

PART FOUR

VEDAS TEZUL

The Locborder Wall extended three hundred and fifty miles along the western shore of Lake Ten, from the foothills of the Aspa Mountains in Nos Ulom to the screwcrab warrens of Toma. Begun in the twenty-third century and finally completed in the thirtieth, its length documented Knos Min's former glory, before Nos Ulom and Toma applied pressure west and northwards on the larger nation's borders, reducing its area by half.

Once, an army had slept atop the wall, guarding its hundred gates and the various villages clinging like barnacles to its lakeward side, but the increasingly aggressive gestures of Nos Ulom and Toma forced Knos Min to fill many of the gates. By the midway point of the one hundred and twenty-fourth century only the three largest remained: Ioa, Ynon, and Defu. The villages had been abandoned long before and were crumbling slowly into the lake.

Adrash chose this moment to send his two smallest weapons to earth. They struck the ocean to either side of Knoori, sending tidal waves to the coasts, water vapor and dust into the sky. Thus began the Cataclysm—a tragedy of such monumental proportions that, one thousand years after it occurred, few referred to it at all. When the clouds finally parted, ending the decade-long winter, the population had been reduced by fifty percent.

189

Nothing lived along the shores of Lake Ten, which did not thaw completely for twenty years after the Cataclysm.

As the continent grew warmer, men gradually returned to the lake, and it was not long before they discovered something extraordinary. Previously unknown species of fish had survived the great freeze, breeding in vast numbers under the thick ice. Large and oily-fleshed, the animals represented not only survival, but prosperity. Generations could grow strong on food such as that. Nations whose borders had not shifted perceptibly during the famine decade now found themselves fighting to keep their waterfront property.

The race to repopulate had begun.

Without a doubt, the nation of Knos Min came out ahead. It owned two hundred and seventy miles of Locborder and its most strategic docks. A vast infrastructure for repopulating cities, fortifying armies, and communicating over vast distances still existed. The old capitol, Danoor, the new capitol, Grass Min, and the sprawling equatorial metropolis Levas sent their best engineers, fishermen and soldiers to the three cities of the lake—Ioa, Defu, and what would come to be the most important, Ynon.

Instead of waging a war of territorial conquest, however, the administrators of the three cities simply fortified the two borders abutting the shore and concentrated on hauling everything they could from the great lake. Dried and fresh fish went to all corners of Knos Min. They traded none of their catch, no matter how high the demand grew throughout the rest of the continent. All resources went to feeding, to growing. Immigrants pored in from across the continent and Knos Min welcomed them, demanding nothing but labor and loyalty of arms.

The first thing many new citizens learned about was the history of Locborder Wall, which had grown as a symbol to encompass the hopes of an entire nation.

As a child, Vedas had learned this narrative. All Knosi children did, no matter how far they had strayed from their homeland. The residents of Golna's affluent Tannerton had even erected a miniature replica wall alongside their tiny manmade lake, Tenia. Its placement confused the neighboring boroughs because it blocked the view of the water. Few understood how large Locborder loomed in the Knosi consciousness.

In Golna, Men of the Republic were considered arrogant by many of their neighbors, yet this was an unjust prejudice. Tomen were not proud of their deserts? Castans did not admire their own enterprising natures? Arrogance defined Knosi no more or less than the other peoples of Knoori. Anyone who sought to know them would come to the same conclusion.

At least, this is what Vedas had heard. He steered clear of his fellow expatriated Knosi instinctively, like a man avoiding estranged relatives. Abse had once encouraged him to spend more time in Tannerton and Foxridge, but he balked the moment his foot stepped into either neighborhood. The people were too uniform, too like Vedas. Their high cheekbones and wet soil complexions, their broad shoulders and straight backs—all of these things made them more alien than familiar.

An irrational reaction, surely, but Vedas could not control it. He had aligned himself with the Thirteenth Order of Black Suits, and by so doing had left his people behind.

‡

The entry guard looked him up and down, took his name, and waved him through.

As simple as that, Vedas returned home. Yet instead of passing into the city he stood alone under the immense, arcing gate, feeling its thousand tons of basalt pressing down upon him.

Stepping out of the shadows should not be such a challenge, he reasoned.

Surely, the air smelled no different in Ynon than it had in Bitsan. In the early morning light even the architecture looked the same: Two- and three-storey buildings of sun-bleached sycamore planks. Every fourth or fifth one had been painted, as if the owner could not stand the regularity. Locals glanced at his suit in mild curiosity as they walked by, yet their eyes passed over his features without a second glance.

He folded his arms and leaned against the wall, affecting a casual air. His companions would see through it, but he did it just the same.

A mere ten feet away on the other side of the gate, Churls tapped her foot and gave her name, place of birth, and current residence. The guard wrote the information on his form slowly, asked each question slowly. More often than not, her responses seemed to confuse him. He asked her to repeat herself several times. Finally, he stamped a square of cloth, handed it to her, and waved her through. She smirked at Vedas, rolled her eyes.

Berun stepped up, and the process began again. The guard glanced up at the towering constructed man several times—curious, but not overly so. The reaction surprised Vedas. He had expected something more elaborate for

Berun. Backup guards, a robed government mage, possibly even a hellhound or two. But his interview was identical to Churls's, down to the symbol the guard stamped on his cloth.

"Do you think that's odd?" Vedas asked.

Berun pressed the cloth to his chest, absorbing it into his body. "It is, and I'd be surprised if this was the end of it. Nos Ulom considers me a terrorist, as the Republic is no doubt aware. Someone will be watching my progress, and it will be very difficult to identify whom. It could be anyone." He shrugged. "Then again, they say more constructs exist in Knos Min than anywhere else. One more with a bad attitude might make no difference to them."

They entered the city, the streets of which were jammed tight with locals and foreigners on their way to Danoor. As the sun rose above the rooftops, ever more travelers poured from the doorways of hostels and inns and began making their way toward the western edge of the city. They waited in long lines to buy overpriced jerky and dried fruit, canteens, and sleeping packs. Vedas tried to suppress a growing sense of urgency. They would get through the city exactly as fast as everyone else.

Churls bought a change of light clothing, a new sleeping roll and blanket, and eventually located a bladesman's. She selected a corroded vazhe the owner strongly discouraged her from purchasing. He suggested a Tomen rekurv instead, a Fazees cuass, even an Ulomi dueling rapier.

"That will not even slice bread!" he called from the door as they walked away.

Churls ran her hand over the rusty blade. She popped a reddened fingertip in her mouth and smiled. "Castan steel. No substitute."

They waited in more lines. Vedas and Berun stood back a pace as Churls argued over this price, this item's quality, this vendor's attitude. Finally, finished with their shopping, they moved toward the outskirts of the city. Churls maintained a vocal presence in the crowd, striking up conversations, directing slow walkers to step aside.

Vedas watched her, amazed that anyone could be so confident in a foreign land.

He existed in a state of agitation, constantly on his guard. Curious strangers brushed their fingertips over his suit, tried again and again to strike up conversation. Men with features that mirrored his own stood in doorways and peered down from balconies, smoking joss and drinking wine. This was their city, their country. They stared at him through their long, meticulously matted locks, demanding an explanation.

Who are you? Where have you been, and why have you returned?

The answers eluded him. He struggled to feel a sense of brotherhood and failed.

No, Vedas could not call his return to Knos Min a return home.

Berun gawked at the constructs around him. Mostly small creations in the shapes of dogs and cats, there were only a few of more intricate design and obvious intelligence. A giant wrought-iron centipede with the head of a dragon. A centaur of constantly shifting gold plates. They hailed each other with waves of their appendages.

One in particular, whose form was an intricate silver and black elder, struck up a long, convoluted dialogue with Berun as they entered the ragged line of travelers striking upon Grass Trail, the eight-hundred-mile path leading from Ynon to the capitol of Grass Min. Its voice was deep but lacked resonance, grating like the magically recorded lectures Abse played to the Thirteenth's youngest students. Its tall, finely articulated body clicked metallically as it moved, jerking from position to position. An awful composition of sounds and colors, it was one of the ugliest things Vedas had ever encountered.

"Name is Tou," it finally got around to announcing. "Remember you."

"Oh, yes?" Berun rumbled, face turned away from the other construct. "I don't think we've met."

"Haven't. Heard about you." Tou craned over Berun to peer down at Vedas and Churls. Mechanisms whirred behind its thin, severe face. Four multicolored gems twitched in its eye sockets. "Haven't heard about you," it said.

Churls looked up at the hideous face. "Go away."

"Thank you," Berun said after the creature had left. "All of these constructs unnerve me. I don't know how to react."

"Any time," Churls said. "Better to not have him around anyway. Seems like the type to spread rumors, not that anyone would understand him."

Berun chuckled. "At least he's never heard of you two."

"Yeah." Churls poured a pinch of dust into her palm, spit on it, and began polishing her new sword as they walked. "First bit of good news in a long while."

‡

Grass Trail rose and fell gently on Hasde Fall, the wooded hills west of Ynon. Sugar maples and sycamores dropped their dying leaves on the stone-paved roadway, creating a multicolored blanket that rustled under the travelers' thousand feet. Sturdy wooden bridges crossed the occasional brook or small river, where fish were plentiful and easily caught. Despite the travelers' disparate backgrounds and religious perspectives, a congenial atmosphere prevailed. Were the weather not so nice, the surroundings not so beautiful, it might well have been a different story.

For all of the land's natural appeal, no one veered far off the road. The Republic owned and maintained the land, barracked its soldiers on it, and looked unkindly on those who trespassed. No signs were posted—none were required. Knos Min, for all of its legendary restraint and religious neutrality, maintained the continent's largest army and jealously guarded its supply of elder corpses. Even in the present age where men feared an end to this supply, The Republic's magical resources were legendary, as evidenced by the number of constructs owned by ordinary citizens.

Rumor spoke that a bare handful of miles from Grass Trail, Baleshuuk had not only discovered a near limitless vein of elder corpses, but were tunneling to the center of the world. Shielded under megatonnage of rock, mages of all kinds developed powerful new alchemies. Outbound mages trained in rooms where the effects of gravity had been canceled. Armies of constructs and hybrids enacted the great wars of history over and over again, in preparation for a great, continent-spanning war.

Vedas saw no reason to distrust or believe these rumors. Stol possessed outbound mages and Baleshuuk—surely Knos Min, with its obviously vast magical capability, had developed programs to maintain its position. The specifics hardly mattered to ordinary men.

Yet the second night out, such speculation dominated conversation around the campfire. Nboles, an elderman bowyer traveling to Danoor to sell his wares, sat cross-legged on his wheeled construct-trunk and spoke of the Osseterat, a hybrid ape of immense intelligence. "They live in this forest," he claimed. "The more they observe men, the more they become like men. They are stronger and faster, however. When and if the white god destroys the world, the elite of the Republic will enter the earth through tunnels only they know about. Like the Baleshuuk, they plan on surviving. The Osseterat will be their servants."

His voice became hushed and he cast glances into the forest on either side. "But what if they cannot control their new beasts? Maybe the apes won't want to be servants. Maybe they're planning, even now."

Churls laughed out loud. "A bowyer, huh? You missed your calling. But telling tall tales doesn't pay as well as selling bows, I suppose."

The elderman managed to look offended without shifting a muscle.

Vedas observed the curious interplay between journeying strangers, intimidated and bemused by their easy discourse. He thought wistfully of the day that had passed. He and his companion's swift progress had made conversation impossible.

Of course, Churls did not mind the conditions. She enjoyed the hearty exchanges, the playful insults and rumoring. Her eyes fairly glittered in the firelight. Unabashedly loud, her voice echoed into the forest. She told a joke, then told it again. Vedas kept his eyes on her more often than not, both compelled by her manner and convinced that if he only focused hard enough on her no one would feel drawn to engage him.

He knew the placement of each Knosi around the campfire. Two women, traveling together. Two men, traveling alone. He sensed their gazes upon him, and wondered what they read in his features. Did he fit the mold of their race, or had time away from Knos Min left a mark upon him? Perhaps he had ceased being a son of the Republic long ago.

And if I've relinquished my birthright, he thought, *what difference does it make? I am Vedas Tezul, of the Thirteenth Order of Black Suits. That is enough.*

He repeated these words, as if they might eventually ring true.

Now and then, he ventured a glance at Berun, whose attention could not be wrested from the three constructs closest to him. Concentration formed deep furrows between his brows. Occasionally, spheres rang together deep inside his body, startling those nearby. Vedas felt an intense communion with the constructed man. Surrounded by his own kin, he too struggled to place himself in context.

A voice interrupted Vedas's pondering: "May I sit?"

Vedas looked up at a thin, dark face. White teeth, though not really a smile. The man wore dun-colored robes and two weapons hung from his belt sash: a short, curved blade and a short horseman's pick. Rust-colored and painstakingly matted, his long hair wound around his head like a starched strip of cloth.

A Tomen, the first Vedas had seen on the road.

"Of course," Vedas said, and scooted closer to Churls to make room. The woman to his left, a Castan gladiator built like a bull, rose smoothly and walked away from the fire.

The Tomen ignored this. Slowly, so as not to cause alarm, he removed his sash and placed his weapons on the ground before sitting. The smell of fennel and mejuan, a mild hallucinogen, rose from his robes.

"*Feda Adraas,*" he said, bowing his head.

"*Adraas Esoa,*" Vedas said, surprised to find he remembered the formal greeting: *I curse Adrash—Adrash hears you.* Tomen spoke a distinctive dialect of the common tongue of Knoori as well as several ritual languages, some of the most common phrases of which Vedas had learned in the abbey.

"Thank you," the man said. "I have had bad luck, finding a place to sit. Fesuy Amendja is my name. Opas is my home."

"I am Vedas Tezul. Golna is my home."

Fesuy nodded. Something moved under the skin of his cheek, and he made a loud sucking noise. Though the Tomen only spoke to Vedas, the other travelers had lapsed into silence, watching. Of all the peoples of Knoori, Tomen very likely suffered the most intense prejudice. They were not even liked by most other Anadrashi, and for good reason. Tomen respected Tomen and no one else.

Vedas did not care about this. He merely wanted to be left alone.

"Golna, yes," Fesuy said. "I recognize it, your accent. I am well traveled. Still, it is a surprise. There are not so many far easterners in these parts. Are there Knosi in Golna?"

"Yes, two communities exist. I don't visit them often."

Fesuy spit a mejuan pod into the fire. He reached into the folds of his robes, brought forth a leather bag, and popped another pod into his mouth. He offered a second to Vedas.

Vedas stared at the proffered drug as if it were a live coal. "No, thank you."

"Not for you," Fesuy said. He tipped his head to stare at Churls.

Churls shrugged, reached across Vedas's chest, and took the gift. She bit the stem off and spit it into the fire. Fesuy followed, and they toasted before putting the pods in their mouths.

Berun's glowing eyes shifted from one to the other, obviously curious. The ritual seemed to satisfy the rest of the travelers, as wine bottles were suddenly uncorked and passed around. The elderman bowyer lit two long pipes and passed them in opposite directions. Conversation renewed.

With attention now shifted away from him, Vedas relaxed.

"I know your faith," Fesuy said. "No drugs, correct?"

"Yes," Vedas answered. "And alcohol only during celebrations. In my order, even that is discouraged."

"This is a shame. Traveling through life without release." Fesuy leaned back, and Vedas followed his gaze. They cursed Adrash together, one set of fingertips touching horns, one palm blocking out the Needle. The Tomen sighed. "I have seen only one other blackskin on the road. People say the rest came through weeks ago, from all over the continent. You are late for the revelry, yes?"

"Yes," Vedas admitted. "Though I hope to be there in time to fight."

Fesuy looked him up and down appraisingly. "Out of all Golna, you were chosen?" He smiled. "I am indeed honored to sit with you. Perhaps my worries about reaching Danoor in time are unfounded, for this is an auspicious sign—one that I will mark in the morning with an invocation. If you allow it, of course. Will you accept this small gesture in your honor?"

Berun shifted next to Churls, who raised an eyebrow when Vedas looked at her.

"Sure," Vedas told the Tomen.

‡

Pressure built in Vedas's chest, staring at the dead woman.

She was built like a bull. Her bulk lay on the paving stones, and her skirt was pulled up around her hips. Her neck had been expertly cut, deeply enough to sever the spinal cord without severing the flesh at the back of the neck. After death, her head had been tipped to the side so that the gaping wounds were exposed. Then her killer had shat on her face. Flies buzzed around the mess. A line of ants crawled through the blood to reach her.

Vedas refused to look at the horrible thing the killer had done to her womanhood, but an Ulomi man named Spofeth had no such inhibitions. He knelt at the woman's feet and stared. He claimed to have once acted as a policeman in the Pontiff of Dolin's Army, but he spoke too finely to convince Vedas of this. His wife had found the body before most of the others woke.

"Easy answer, here," Spofeth said. "We all saw her walk away when the Tomen sat down. Clearly, he didn't like that."

As much as he disliked the man's tone, Vedas could not but agree. The cut was too fine to have been done with a straight sword. And they had all seen the gladiator insult Fesuy. It was enough for the travelers to condemn the man. It was enough for Vedas. The Tomen had seemed pleasant enough in the short time they had conversed, but that was immaterial.

Will you accept this small gesture in your honor? the man had asked.

Sure, Vedas had told him, not knowing what it meant. How could he have known?

A Knosi man stepped forward. Vedas recognized him from the fireside. His white cassock marked him as an Adrashi priest, though Vedas did not know the variety. The man had seemed kind enough the previous night, had even smiled at Vedas and offered him wine which Vedas refused. A scar ran from the corner of his left eye to his jaw. It twitched as he looked at the dead woman. His mouth worked at words before they came out.

"We will bury her, and I will perform rites."

Spofeth pointed to the tattoos of serpents winding around the gladiator's heavy thighs. "She was an Usterti, Father. Witches don't believe in Adrash."

"That is irrelevant," the priest answered, iron in his voice. "Whether she believed in Adrash or not, Adrash knew of her existence. Did anyone here know her? No?" He turned to Vedas. "You knew her killer. You talked to him. Now you will carry his victim's body." He cut Vedas's reply off with a gesture. "I am not placing blame. Adrash has simply put you here now to do this thing."

Vedas thought of several responses and dismissed them all. He looked at Berun. "Will you hold her head?"

Together, they carried the woman a dozen feet off the road, careful not to tear her head from her body. Twice, Vedas nearly vomited at the smell of shit and blood. Berun quickly dug a deep grave in the soft black earth, and then he and Vedas laid the body at its bottom, positioning her as if she were sleeping. A woman Vedas did not recognize tore a length of red material from her skirts. Vedas tied it around the corpse's neck.

Churls offered her hand. Vedas took it, and climbed free. Though the aroma of freshly turned earth filled the air, he could still smell the sour stench of Fesuy's excrement, the iron of the dead woman's juices. The smell would linger, of course. It would follow him for a while until he managed to forget it.

Just as he had forgotten Julit Umeda and all the others?

He caught the priest's eye and felt the first stirrings of resentment. How dare the man tell him to carry the body? How dare the man watch him work, only so that he could spout lies over the woman? She was dead, and the god had no interest in her soul.

People were nothing to Adrash. Adrash would make the whole world a tomb.

Have I forgotten who I am? Vedas asked himself.

Before the holy man could start talking, Vedas signaled to Berun to start filling the grave.

"It is custom to leave it open," the priest began.

"Never mind your custom," Vedas said. "Speak if you must, but speak plainly. Don't insult this woman with your falsehoods. She wasn't a member of your church."

The priest regarded him for a long moment, and then put his right fist to his forehead and extended it to Vedas.

A blessing. A supplication for peace. *Adrash be with you.*

It was the wrong thing to do.

Vedas took a step forward, his fingers curling as resentment bloomed into anger—pure, righteous anger, hammering in his chest, behind his eyes, causing the world to tremble before him. Churls's hand closed around his wrist, but he pulled it away. Another step and another, until he stood before the priest. Every nervous fiber of his being ached to send his fist forward, but he could not make himself do it.

The moment held for a second. Five seconds. Ten. His muscles screamed under the tension.

Will you accept this small gesture in your honor? the man had asked.

Sure, Vedas had told him.

"Vedas," Churls said. "Vedas. What would be the point? The damage is done. She's dead, and she won't give a shit what this priest says." Her voice became gentle. "Let it go."

The tendons in Vedas's neck stood taught. A frown deformed his features.

He spat at the priest's foot and turned away.

Churls and Berun followed him to the road. They retrieved their packs and continued on. No one talked as the sun moved in a shallow arc on the horizon. The travelers they passed neither greeted nor questioned them.

Vedas's hands shook. He washed them in every stream and river. For the first time in his memory, he felt truly unclean, as if his suit were a normal garment that needed to be removed and washed. He fought the urge to scratch, to pull the constricting fabric away from his skin.

‡

Though he was hundreds of miles away, high upon a mesa, he saw it happen.

A massive woman rose from Lake Ten and stepped over Locborder Wall. Her tattooed thighs were as wide as the city of Ynon, which she crushed under her naked feet as if it were a folded paper toy. Mountains of muscle and fat jumped with each lumbering movement, shaking the water from her body. Droplets as large as lakes fell from her skirt to the earth, crushing hills and mountains, turning fields into mud flats.

Vedas ran from her across the flat top of the mesa, but not fast enough. It would never be fast enough, for she covered leagues with a single step, and his legs were heavy and slow. She would be upon him in no time at all. She roared his name, a bestial sound that threw him to the ground and threatened to rupture his eardrums. He rose and fell again. He started crawling. Over his shoulder he saw her head rise above the edge of the mesa.

So soon! She moved faster than he could ever have imagined.

Her hand reached for him, and it eclipsed the sky.

"Vedas."

The world faded. Flickered.

"Vedas."

He woke. Two glowing blue coals stared down at him from a face composed of brass spheres. A hard hand shook him gently, companionably. A low, brassy chuckle.

"Berun," Vedas said, relieved to be out of the dream. He rose on an elbow to peer past the constructed man's crouched form, and located Churls. She lay close to the smoldering campfire, which was surprisingly far away. "What am I doing over here?"

The constructed man rocked back on his heels with a whisper of metal sliding against metal. "You crawled here. One minute you were sound asleep, the next you tensed. I readied myself, thinking of another cat attack or worse, but when you started crawling I knew that something else was happening. Then you flipped over, and it looked like you were going to start throwing punches. Were you dreaming?"

Vedas lay back. The road was solid beneath him. "Yes. About the dead woman."

A rumbling sound came from Berun's chest: the sound of many spheres shifting position, rearranging themselves. "That Adrashi priest was wrong," the constructed man said. "He made a connection between you and the woman when there was no connection at all. You had nothing to do with her death." The rumbling stopped. "You're a good man, but you're not a whole man. You don't know yourself."

Too tired to protest, Vedas simply nodded.

"The Baleshuuk thief. Why did you save her?"

Vedas thought back, came up empty. "I don't know. I just didn't want her to die."

"And the woman today? Why did her death affect you so?"

The muscles of Vedas's jaw jumped as he bit down on his first response. *It was my fault. If I hadn't agreed to Fesuy's offer, she wouldn't have died.* He wondered for a moment if this was what he truly believed. Could a man be blamed for being in a certain place at a certain time? *Adrash has simply put you here now to do this thing,* the priest had told him.

"I don't know," Vedas said. "It was wrong. Evil."

Berun nodded. "True. A man who does things like that deserves no sympathy. He has become worse than an animal." The constructed man opened and closed his gigantic fists, and his eyes flared brighter. "True, I love fighting. I sometimes enjoy killing. Churls is a fighter, through and through. No doubt, we've both got our share of bloodlust. We've committed sins. But you see the difference, don't you—between us and murderers?"

"Yes," Vedas answered honestly.

"You think we should forgive ourselves our crimes, our mistakes?"

"Yes."

Berun stood, a thousand joints sighing all at once. He stared down at Vedas.

"You should take your own advice."

BERUN

Huge, sluggish fish swam in the stygian depths, their sinuous bodies only partially visible in the weak radiance cast by Berun's eyes. An arm-sized fin waving. A black eyed, blunt-nosed head, needle-toothed maw slowly opening and closing. Dwarfing the constructed man, they swam in close but never touched him. He did not smell right, did not sound right. No beating of a heart, only the steady emanation of heat. Smaller fish darted before his face, attracted by the light and warmth, but these too were merely curious.

He had been here before. During the storm that drowned the *Atavest*, the heaving deck of the ship had catapulted him into the lake, where he immediately sank—for how long, he did not know. In his despair, he forgot to count. All sensation stopped during the fall, which seemed to last forever. And then the silt floor embraced him so gently that for a moment he did not realize the bottom had finally been reached.

Immediately, he had struggled upright in the soft mud and checked his map. Nothing. Knoori did not appear before his eyes. The weight of water prevented him from summoning the map. Lake Ten sunk to a far greater depth than the sea, he had heard, so far that the sun never reached its bottom. If this were true, the likelihood of reaching land any time soon was unlikely, and the island of Tan-Ten nearly impossible. Even if he knew the general direction, how could he walk in a straight line without points of reference?

Of course, such conjecture had been pointless. Long before he reached land, his body would shut down. Like all constructs, Berun's cellular composition was largely elder, and required frequent exposure to sunlight. Unlike the physically weaker but more versatile hybrid animals, a construct possessed no digestive system, and thus could not subsist in the darkness for more than a few days. The full weight of this realization struck him, filled his being with dread so powerful that he no longer felt whole.

Unconnected to his component pieces, a mere collection of marbles, inert.

Unsurprisingly, Berun was not happy to find himself back in this place. How had he arrived here? Where had he last been? He did not know the answer to either question. He watched the sluggish behemoth fish turn around him, recalling the dread, the absolute certainty of death. To be shut off forever: this was the thing Berun most feared. Some men believed in heaven, or at least a type of continuity, and Berun could see why. The body remained warm for a time after it died. It rotted, split apart and offered its contents to the soil, spurning new growth. But a construct was not a man. It went cold, and then became exactly as it was before life touched it.

If souls existed, they resided in flesh.

Berun threw his head back and roared the tone of a great brass cymbal. Dark water muffled the wordless cry, extinguished it only inches from the ringing cavern of his mouth as if it were nothing, had never existed—yet the fish jerked and dropped to the lake bottom around him, stunned or killed by the pressure of his voice. Small and large, they littered the ground at his feet. He took no joy in this. It had not been his desire. He had not acted with intention, only feeling.

The fish lay still, and it was only a short while before others came, curious, and began feeding, turning the water cloudy with blood and scales. Blind, Berun rocked back and forth as the immense, slick-skinned bodies pushed against him. Twice, a mouth closed around his arm, scraping its needle teeth over his spheres before spitting the limb out convulsively.

The feeling of dread increased.

Spheres knocked together in his stomach. A lonely drum roll, echoing into the endless night.

He did not bother to feel hope, for he had no reason to expect salvation a second time. He tried not to conjure the memory of being saved, but it shouldered its way forward: Light blooming in the distance, shifting closer and closer, growing in definition until it became the blazing form of a small girl. White from head to toe, but for eyes the color of light passing through shallow seawater. Her soft voice speaking indiscernible words, her hands urging him forward.

What had he felt? He did not entirely recall. He remembered the slow progress, slogging through knee-deep muck, staring so long at the girl's light that it became his entire world. If he moved too quickly, a cloud of silt rose from his feet, obscuring her from him. Yes, at these moments he panicked, stumbled, fell into the muck. He learned to wait until the cloud cleared, allowing him to find her light again. Only then did he continue on. Eventually, his foot struck rock and the going became even more difficult. He fell into narrow crevices and mired his feet in loose sand, but still he followed the girl. He crawled until his head rose above the water.

It had been madness, yet it could not be rationalized away.

He had reached the island, after all.

Or had he? Doubt took root in his mind. Perhaps he had only dreamed of Tan-Ten, reunion with Churls and Vedas, Ynon and the Grass Trail. Maybe he had not stood on the shore of Uris Bay and looked through the shimmering glass dome at the island of Osa. Those traveling on the trail, even those few who possessed spyglasses and amplification spells, were not able to see that far. They asked him to describe the life that anchored itself to the clear wall. Filled with pride, he had done so. "I see huge vinetrees, crawling toward the sky. I see gigantic multicolored wyrms, perching on the tops of honeycombed nests."

Devastating, to think he had only imagined these wondrous things. Even worse, to know he had never dreamed alone, that he had always been manipulated into sleep, coerced to take part in another's vision.

Have I ever admired something for myself? he wondered. *Am I just a dim reflection of my creator?*

Berun roared again, and this time it was the word *Father*.

‡

The lake bottom shook. Dead fish slipped against one another, shuddering slowly into the muck like earthworms into soil. Berun made his feet large and flat to stay upright. Gradually the tremors subsided, and the bottom of the lake was smooth again, its dead buried.

A light bloomed in the distance before him, like it had when the girl appeared. It jumped closer and closer, moving from one position to another instantaneously. Berun felt the first faint stirring of hope, only for it to be extinguished as the source of light became obvious.

A pair of silver hands.

"Father," Berun said, words now audible. "This is your dream?"

Ortur Omali lifted a hand to his hood and removed it. Instinctively, Berun stepped back, nearly tripping on his oversized feet. The great mage no longer possessed a mouth, just a smooth patch of skin from nose to chin. His skull looked as though it had been crushed and reformed, or pulled like melted wax into the caricature of an elder. His eyes were large, liquid pools of amber in which two doubled irises swam.

This is no dream, Omali's voice resounded in the spheres of Berun's mind. *There never was a dream. This is my place. An extension of my mind. A universe unto itself, folded inside you, enveloping the world. It is both here and not here, alive and not alive.*

"That makes no sense, Father."

Omali's irises spun slowly. *Indeed. But sense is hardly a requisite of existence. Strength and strength alone dictates success. Pure will sets the stars and the planets spinning.*

Berun dismissed this claim as useless. He had no interest in cosmology or philosophy.

"Why have you brought me here?" he asked.

Omali rubbed his fingers together, producing a sound like singing bowls. *You are here because you sought release. When you pleasure yourself, you become susceptible.* He clapped his hands together and they tolled like bells. *You have been bad, Berun. Very bad. You have kept your mind from me.*

"You took control of my body."

Omali's eyes widened. *This was a surprise, that I should treat you this way, my own creation? At what point did you begin to consider yourself an autonomous creature? You are not—nor have you ever been—your own man.*

Indignation pressed Berun's hands into fists. "And yet I've managed to keep you out for some time."

Now the eyes narrowed. *Truly. You have discovered that your physical form and my influence over your mind are related. This is a small inconvenience and a greater disappointment to me. In time I will overcome your resistance, but your character is not so easily mended. When I am animate again, you will submit to some adjustment.*

Berun parsed this language. The possibility that his father existed without a body had never occurred to him, perhaps because he did not want to consider the implications. He had grown in his father's absence, had he not? He had always half-believed himself capable of overcoming his father's dream-specter, but what chance did he stand against the great mage in the flesh? Berun would be defeated, made into little more than a tool. A weapon.

It did not require a vivid imagination to picture the target. Vedas would die, and Churls would very likely die defending him.

The thought of being used to these ends caused a tightening of the spheres in Berun's shoulders and chest—a slight but distinct darkening of his vision, a wavering of the figure before him. Berun raised his right arm, opened his fist, unsure of his intent.

Stop! Omali commanded, and the world snapped back into focus, crystallized on him like ice. *You are not a man. You are my creature.*

Berun resisted the compulsion to lower his arm. It felt as if a great weight had been attached to his wrist. "You have threatened my friends," he said, though opening his mouth and forming words took a massive effort.

I have. Your black-suited friend endangers the balance. Adrash's eyes will soon be upon him. If allowed to live, he may very well throw the world into chaos. You do not see it yet, but you will. He must not fight at Danoor. He must not live.

Omali raised his silvered left hand and touched his index finger to Berun's fist. As the mage lowered his arm, Berun was forced to lower his own. Omali pointed to the lake floor, which began bubbling. A lake of black tar, boiling, from which Vedas's body surfaced.

The puppet—for it could not really be the Black Suit himself—opened its eyes and yellow light poured forth, washing out the scene around Berun.

‡

They stood on the mesa of blooming azure flowers where Berun had first recognized his father. At his feet, once again, a sleeping figure—and this time there could be no doubt as to its identity. Remembering the injury from his previous visit, Berun glanced at his right arm and found it whole.

A prediction that will not come to bear, Omali said. He stood beside Berun, face angled to the sky. *You have disobeyed and disrespected your creator, but you will redeem yourself. You cannot be my sword of justice with a chipped blade.*

"The cost of my freedom is a limb?"

Omali's laughter rang in Berun's mind. *Freedom? Why, the word means nothing to you.*

Berun regarded the body at his feet, its familiar lines. He had tried to see it as Churls did, as a thing of beauty, and failed. Vedas was no more beautiful than

Churls, the captain of the *Atavest*, or the Baleshuuk they had encountered on the Steps. Still, his features had become oddly reassuring to Berun.

"I'll resist you," the constructed man said. "I'll win this fight."

Omali turned. He floated up from the ground, orange and red robes flowing around his thin body as though he had been set aflame. Wind blew across the mesa, causing the flowers to undulate like the surface of the ocean.

You will not even try, the great mage said, fingers outstretched toward his creation.

Berun struggled to lift his arm again, and then stopped as realization hit. He would not fight in the world his father had created. He would leave. Prepare himself on his own terms, in his own reality. He allowed his anger to build, let it run through his limbs like molten lead, fusing him in place. Heavy brows came together over bluefire eyes. Brass lips curled back from brass teeth. The expression froze.

He felt the pull his father exerted on every sphere in his body, yet he knew with absolute certainty he could withstand the attack. He had buttressed himself, had become his own man through strength alone. Compressing his component pieces together, he locked himself in place against his father's influence. Deep within his chest, spheres that had always spun stopped their spinning—a fearful but exhilarating sensation.

Indeed, his father had been correct: pure will set the stars and planets in motion.

It could also stop them cold.

You will go no further with this, Berun, Omali said. He sent a second, stronger wave of force through Berun's body, trying to bend his creation to his will. *You do not want to force my hand any more than you already have. My compassion extends only so far. If you continue on this path, I will make you suffer. I will scatter you to the eight winds, Berun.*

Berun's strength wavered. He fought the urge to allow himself to expand, to mobilize himself. A voice told him that stopping his spheres would lead to death, but he knew this to be false. He possessed a body just beyond the thin shell of his father's world. He could escape through concentration, through the force of his will.

Omali laughed. *No. I have closed all the doors.*

No, you haven't, another voice countered.

Berun looked down. Instead of Vedas, at Berun's feet lay the girl in white. The girl with blue eyes. Berun's savior.

She stood, and then rose from the ground until her eyes were level with Omali's. The folds of her dress did not flutter in the wind. Unbound hair fell straight over her right shoulder, every pale strand in place. Light blazed from behind her, outlining her small form in fire. She was not a part of Omali's world, yet something of hers seemed to be leaching into his.

Beyond the fact that Berun recognized her from their previous encounter, her features were now vaguely familiar. Her face tickled his subconscious mind, but he had no time to examine it.

She extended her left hand, and the great mage shrank back.

Lavesh atross! he hissed. *So asfelz! Adramass psua!* He weaved graceful charms with his hands, locking long, thin fingers and releasing them explosively, hurling magma-red spells at her. They sizzled through the air, tearing black rents in the dream reality.

The girl smiled, and with a gesture halted the spells in flight, dissolved them. *All wrong. I know all that stuff, and I'm learning new things all the time. You're too old to learn anything new.* She held her right hand out to Berun, but her eyes stayed locked on Omali. *We're leaving. Don't try this again. I know where you live now.*

Who are you? Omali asked. His eyes had become slits of bright amber. His skin had taken on a purplish hue.

The girl shook her head, smile still in place. *Figure it out on your own. We're leaving.*

"Goodbye, Father," Berun said.

He took the girl's hand and they disappeared.

‡

Churls and Vedas woke only moments after Berun. The sun had not yet risen.

He spoke nothing of his encounter, and opted out of accompanying them into Sent to fetch the construct horses. A fellow traveler on the trail had provided the names of a few reliable stablemen, but Berun suspected the affair would take much time and haggling—a prospect he did not relish. Besides, he had much to consider. He watched his companions enter the walled city and then sat down to think.

For the first time in his existence, he noticed a difference between sitting and standing. Resisting Omali had sapped him of energy.

An hour later, the first rays of sunlight found him in a meditative posture, legs crossed, soles upturned on his knees, hands clasped behind his back. One elbow up, one down—this was now the extent of his flexibility. Just as a man understands he cannot turn his neck to look directly behind him, Berun knew his spheres would no longer rearrange per his command. They were stuck in a matrix, forming one thing only: a bronze man.

The solidification he had effected in Omali's world had crossed over to this one, and stuck. He would no longer form shovels or knives or hammers at the end of his arms. He would no longer carry items within his body. Splitting himself in two and achieving a release, *pleasuring himself* as his creator had termed it, was now impossible.

Though he had gained an advantage over Omali, strengthened his mind against the great mage's attacks, he had crippled himself physically. He could not rotate his spheres or spread himself like a blanket on the earth to take in sunlight. Without this capability, he was doomed to a life of near-starvation. His strength would be a weak thing compared to what it was.

This was not all. He tried to summon his map of the world, and failed.

Devastating losses, undoubtedly—but the suspicion that he had left a stone unturned stayed with him as the morning progressed. Suspicion became dread as certainty lodged within the spheres of his mind.

No, he had not yet discovered the worst consequence of his encounter with Omali.

When the full extent of his vulnerability became clear, it seemed he might tumble into the earth in his despair. He recalled the few times he had been impacted heavily enough that a portion of his body shattered into its component spheres. A sensation beyond pain, it was the awareness of dislocation, the opposite of the release he felt when splitting himself in two. Now that he had lost control of his malleable form, rebuilding himself after such an attack would be impossible. He could very well die. Worse, he could be dismantled as Omali vowed, scattered to the eight winds, forced to live in eternal agony.

Had he been a fool to ally himself with his companions and the wraithly girl with the tantalizingly familiar face? Had he even considered what it meant for him—a constructed man whose mind had never truly been his own—to trust his instinct?

The future was a depthless abyss, a limitless ocean.

And he had leapt into it without a map or compass.

‡

Motionless, he waited most of the morning for Churls and Vedas to return. By the time they wheeled their steel and brass mounts before him, the sun was near its zenith and he had recovered much of his energy—but could he run for four days alongside the construct horses? Forty, fifty miles a day? He did not know, but resolved to test it. Unless it became obvious, neither of his companions would know the full extent of his limitations. He would not burden them with such concerns.

Undoubtedly, they would soon discover he no longer had access to the map. He had been providing Vedas with daily updates on the movements of men in Danoor. The city itself remained peaceable, but several groups of Tomen had gathered in the foothills of Usveet Mesa, west of the city. While Berun and Churls doubted they could rouse the kind of numbers needed to threaten the city, Vedas thought otherwise.

The man would be disappointed, probably angry to discover he could no longer monitor their activity. The knowledge served as a calmative. Perhaps he believed keeping an eye on the situation kept disaster from unfolding.

Having only just won a small measure of freedom, Berun could sympathize with Vedas's frustration. His master had commissioned him with a task he no longer quite believed in. His faith bound him, as did his love for the brothers and sisters of the Thirteenth. He had not spoken of the speech in some time, though Berun had seen him scribbling notes on occasion.

Thankfully, Vedas did not ask for an update upon returning from the city. He and Churls secured their packs quietly, obviously preoccupied. She dropped her pack twice while securing it to her horse, and her angry gaze returned to Vedas again and again. In turn, he kept his back to her, far more attentive to his task than necessary.

To keep from staring at them, Berun examined the constructs, which were beautiful, sleek and seamless and overmuscled. Though not without a certain gaudy grace, the utilitarian touches incorporated into their bodies offended Berun. Saddles had been integrated into their backs, metal luggage loops into their rumps, and in Churls's construct's case, a crossbow holster into the neck. Riderless, they stood perfectly still.

"What's so fascinating?" Vedas asked. As he mounted, his horse twitched its head away from Berun, who had been staring directly into its glass bead eye.

It stamped once, twice, glaring at Berun—more of a reaction than he had expected. The construct probably possessed something of the animal from which it had been modeled: a slice of preserved horse brain or heart. Nothing so exotic as the transferred essence of its creator, of course. In this regard, Berun was unique.

He straightened. "Were they expensive?"

Vedas began turning his head toward Churls, stopped himself. "Yes."

Churls spurred her mount forward. Her face betrayed nothing. "Tell Berun how much, Vedas. Tell him how much we could've had the horses for."

Vedas looked into the sky, shook his head. "Leave it."

"No," Churls said. She nodded to Berun. "Stable owner recognized Vedas's suit. Got stares everywhere we went, in fact. Offers for sex, potions, you name it for the Black Suit. But this stable owner offered two for one. A huge discount, but Vedas here doesn't want it. It's not right, he tells me. *My faith's not for sale.*"

"It isn't right," Vedas said.

Her cheeks bloomed red. "It's my fucking money! We've traveled two thousand goddamn miles together, and your faith's been nothing but a liability. Finally, you get a chance to profit from it, to help out, and you can't do it because it's wrong. I had plans for that money."

Finally, Vedas met her eye. "Oh, yes. I saw the gleam in your eye as we passed the gambling houses."

The muscles in Churls's shoulders and thighs twitched, and Berun stepped forward.

But the woman only spat. "I make my own choices. I take responsibility for myself. I don't let my shit spill over onto others. I doubt you can say the same."

With this, she wheeled her horse around and spurred it northward.

Berun raised his brows.

Vedas sighed. "Maybe I should have done it. Taken the discount. It would have been faster."

"Maybe you should have," Berun agreed. "But I'm not one for convictions, so you can't trust me." Their eyes met. The lines around Vedas's eyes had deepened. He looked years older than when they had left Golna. "Do you have a plan?" Berun asked.

Vedas closed his eyes and nodded. Then he shook his head. "I only know what I'm not going to say. I'm no writer, no philosopher. If I'd known what I was getting into by leaving, I never would have left." He opened his eyes. "And you? Do you have a plan?"

"It hasn't changed," Berun said. "I plan on winning."

"Amen," Vedas said, and kicked his horse's brass flanks.

Berun picked two rocks from the ground and followed, metal soles ringing loudly on the packed earth. Grinding the stones in his hands, he joined the thousand-footed train of travelers following the northwesterly curve of Grass Trail to Danoor.

CHURLI CASTA JONS

They ran the construct horses from sunup to sundown—a grueling pace, devoid of joy, alleviated by only the briefest moments of rest. At night they collapsed in whatever camp they came upon, sleeping the night through as though drugged.

At noon on the fourth day, the mounts refused to go any further, their contracts at an end. Churls and Vedas immediately dismounted and removed the packs, anxious not to lose their belongings. Churls, who had lived on horseback during her three-year stint in the Castan cavalry, gritted her teeth as she pounded life into her cramped thighs. Vedas, no great horseman, moved about with enviable vigor. Yet another miracle performed by his suit.

Churls's muscles loosened during the fifteen-mile descent out of the scrub hills and into the desert. She shed clothes as the weather grew hot, stripping down to a leather skirt and halter. Before long, even these began to cling and chafe uncomfortably. She considered with some bitterness that in only a few hours it would be cold and windy again, requiring yet another change of clothes. She jealously eyed the loose cotton outfits many of the travelers wore.

From ten miles away, the city of Danoor was nearly lost amid the shifting red dunes that hemmed it on three sides. Usveet Mesa, the largest and most easterly of the Aroonan chain, loomed ridiculously large at the western edge of the city. The mountain's foothills, higher even than those ringing the valley, seemed tiny by comparison.

212

From five miles away, the mesa's scope became even more daunting. Its nearly vertical wall looked as if it were about to topple over, snuffing out the pathetic signs of civilization lying in its shadow. Churls wondered what it must be like to live in such a place. Did its people grow used to living in darkness for half the day, feeling that weight pressing down?

Perhaps it was not the mountain causing her to think such thoughts, but history itself. According to legend, Danoor had been founded upon the rubble of Hawees, an ancient elder city that had once clung to the mountainside—a city Adrash had razed in celebration of mankind's birth. Precious stones and inexplicable glass mechanisms, proof of the legend's origins, were still being unearthed from underground excavations.

As a youth, Churls had seen a few of these relics on display in Onsa. Her mind nearly buckled as she considered their age—a hundred thousand years, two hundred thousand? Academics insisted the elders had been interred in the ground long before the era of man, the modern and mythic history of which spanned a mere twenty-five millennia. Perhaps Adrash himself did not recall the age of Hawees's beautiful relics.

How, Churls had wondered as she stared at the shattered remnants of an extinct people, could men worship a god who would destroy such precious things? How could men live in a city dedicated to that destruction?

She could think of no worse place to make a home.

On the other hand, she could think of no better place to host a battle between the Followers of Adrash and the Followers of Man.

‡

As they entered the vast tent camp visitors had erected south of the city, the sun disappeared over the mesa, plunging the valley into another degree of darkness. Churls made out the many fires of the Tomen camps Berun had described in the foothills.

"You see them?" she asked Vedas. "Orrus Alachum, they've tripled in size since we last looked! There must be five thousand of them now. What do you think they're waiting for?"

He scratched at his thick, wiry black beard. For once, the weather seemed to bother him as much as it bothered her. His lips were cracked, his eyes red. "The winner, I assume. That will determine which way the riot goes, who they start killing first."

"That's a grim outlook," Berun said. "You think that's their plan—five thousand against an entire city, bloated to twice its normal size by travelers? They've done nothing so far. Maybe they've come to their senses and just decided to enjoy the tournament."

Vedas regarded the constructed man. "You can believe whatever fantasy you like, but I'm done with deceiving myself. We all saw what Fesuy did to that woman on the trail." He squinted into the distance, and then pointed to a pool of firelight below the encamped Tomen. "Another thing—what do you see at the base of the hill?"

"Another group is camped there."

"Notice anything else?"

"No. Yes. The men are wearing uniforms. They're very well organized."

Vedas nodded. "As I suspected. An army battalion, which proves I'm not the only cynical one. The Tomen intend to attack, and the Knosi government knows it."

"They couldn't stop them from entering the city?" Berun asked.

"How?" Vedas spread his arms wide. "The influx of travelers has stretched the resources in Danoor for months now. When you were last able to check your map, that army battalion wasn't here, which means they must have double-timed it from the capitol. All their general can do now is send for more troops and wait for the inevitable. Perhaps they will muster enough to stand against the threat, but I doubt it. We have riots even in civilized Golna. They have a way of spreading."

Churls chuckled at this understatement. She scanned the faces around the campfires, noted the posture of men and women as they walked from tent to tent, trading gossip. They hardly seemed concerned, but only a fool looked to the gathered masses for wisdom.

They reached the first buildings of Danoor proper, which unlike the majority of Knosi cities had never been surrounded by a wall. For millennia its relative isolation had dissuaded conquering peoples, though one could not discount its citizens' legendary fighting skill as an equal factor. Lomen, one of Churls's former lovers and gambling partners, had hailed from a neighboring region, and claimed all children of the mesas were taught to wield the ckomale, a pair of sickles linked together with wire.

Travelers thronged bone-dry streets the color of rust. Everywhere, the color of rust. Except for infrequent splashes of painted wood, the buildings were uniformly and seamlessly constructed of red clay and red sand. They rarely rose above the third floor and seldom existed in anything other than a rectangular shape. The uniformity depressed Churls, but the presence of lavish parks, where broad- and thin-leaved succulents fought for space with thorny, winter-blooming bushes and wiry jocasta trees, compensated for this.

"Not far now," Churls said to no one in particular.

"Yes," Vedas and Berun responded together. Vedas cleared his throat.

Keenly aware of how little time they had left as companions, Churls fought to keep the melancholy from her face. She had failed to determine what Vedas and Berun ultimately meant to her, though she had spent no small amount of time pondering the question.

Perhaps she and Berun could remain friends. He liked her, and might even be swayed to stay with her in the city, even accompany her home—positing, of course, that they did not kill one another in tournament.

But Vedas? She could not be Vedas's friend, even if he wanted such a thing. Her desire would always betray her.

Despite her persistent attempts to reign in her emotions.

Despite the anger this lack of self-control inspired.

The curve of his lips, the timbre of his voice, the way thoughts showed on his face several heartbeats before words ever came out: She had memorized every detail of Vedas Tezul. His presence had long ago become a dilemma, causing her every ounce as much distress as joy.

It ached in her marrow, being so close yet so far.

‡

After nearly two hours of walking, they reached the northern end of the city, which to Churls's eyes was indistinguishable from the southern. The streets were crowded this close to the White and Black Suit camps, filled with the sounds of conversation and trade. Revelers spilled from every inn and restaurant door.

Clearly, lodging near Vedas would be difficult to find. Churls wondered how long it would take for the man to comment on this fact. Undoubtedly, he wondered why his companions had remained with him for so long.

She had no answer. It was foolish to prolong the inevitable, yet she could not help herself. She stole glances at him, found excuses to slow their progress.

It took her a while to understand that such diversions were not only being allowed, but encouraged. Vedas and Berun were dragging their heels. Twice, Vedas complained of soreness in his legs and asked them to stop in a park—an awkward moment, both times, as he massaged his thighs and stretched while she examined plants that held no real interest for her. Berun was no help, standing in place as though he were a statue.

Light spilling into an alleyway marked yet another inn. Unlike the others, it appeared relatively unoccupied.

"We should stop for a drink," Churls ventured. "Say goodbye and all that. Celebrate our arrival and soon-to-be victories." She laughed, and it sounded pitifully hollow.

Berun smiled, nodded. Vedas looked northward, clearly conflicted.

"All right," he said. "Just one."

They entered the dimly lit interior, where the smell of coffee hit Churls like a friendly kiss. Contrasting sharply with the biting cold that descended with nightfall out of doors, the inn was delightfully warm and close. She whistled softly, surprised by the opulence of the room. Voluptuous Knosi women in diaphanous robes reclined on low couches, dipping folds of spongebread into various sauces, sipping from small flutes of wine. The few men, mostly soft-looking Knosi in fine silks, each had two or three women attending to their every need: peeling grapes, massaging feet and shoulders.

Reaching under waistbands.

It was all quite cozy, yet Churls understood immediately why the establishment had attracted so few customers. The influx of travelers into the city must have spurred the opening of dozens of new bordellos, each offering cheap wares. An establishment catering to the wealthy must therefore have seen a drop in business.

Churls had been to more than a few whorehouses in her day, and none of the acts performed within had ever scandalized her. Nonetheless, she could imagine few places less conducive to the kind of goodbye she had hoped for.

On second thought, perhaps it did not matter. Vedas managed to be uncomfortable in any social situation. That he had agreed to a drink at all was a minor miracle.

She sat on a couch and signaled to the bar, at the same time conducting a quick survey of the room. Several of the prostitutes were watching her. Many more had their eyes on Vedas. Churls considered how best to dissuade the women from approaching him, but shelved it as irrelevant. He would not return their attentions.

He sat opposite her. "Interesting choice," he said. "Isn't this out of your price range?"

"A little," Churls allowed. "Where's Berun?"

"He stayed outside." Vedas shrugged. "I looked back, but he just waved me in."

Churls hid a smile behind her hand.

A server arrived—a teenage girl with proportions Churls had once cursed herself for lacking. Now such women looked soft and ungainly to her. Fighting with breasts like that would be almost impossible. How did the girl know who she was without scars, tattoos to prove she had been to this place at this time? Very likely, she had never been anywhere but Danoor, traveled no farther than a nearby quarter to see her parents.

To be the daughter of this man, the wife of this man, etcetera and etcetera. Nothing more.

Churls thought of Fyra. She would be about the server's age if she were alive. What would she have said about her family, her position in the world? Would she have been a warrior, a good lover to a faithful, boring man?

"What is your desire?" the girl asked. She looked only at Vedas and cocked her hip slightly, causing the fabric of her short robe to part, offering him a view of her shaved pudendum. In most whorehouses, this view alone cost money.

The drinks would be expensive, Churls reasoned.

Of course, the girl might have revealed herself on a whim, made a flirtatious gesture for the heroic Black Suit. Vedas had received enough shy looks in the streets, suffered enough awkward greetings. Due to the lack of other suited individuals, Churls gathered brothers and sisters of the Order were not allowed to stray from camp during the tournament. A smart move. Fighters became lax if pussy and cock were free for the taking.

"Tecas," Churls answered. "Two. And glasses of water, iced if you have it."

The server ignored her and lingered for a moment, as if she expected Vedas to speak. He glanced up, eyebrows raised, and then looked away. The girl's exhalation was audible. Churls laughed out loud, breaking some of the tension constricting the muscles in her chest.

"What do you think they'll charge for the water?" she asked.

‡

She watched his hands, which were thickly muscled and large enough to envelope her own. She hated stubby or tapering fingers, but his had grown to the perfect length and thickness. Though somewhat obscured by the fabric of his suit, even the veins on the backs of his hands crossed flesh and bone in graceful arcs.

She had long ago noticed the way he touched himself constantly, compulsively, running his hands over the hard contours of his body—testing the springiness of his ridged abdomen with his fingertips, caressing the inside of his thighs—laying a palm over his heart, rubbing his heavy pectoral muscles as though reassuring himself of his own existence. He did these things, and it did not seem to matter where he was. She assumed the actions were subconscious, automatic, an expression of the sensual he did not otherwise allow himself.

She could not blame him. The things she would do with his body if she inhabited it.

In truth, there was no end to his allure. Sometimes she hated his beauty, considering its existence an affront to her desire. A gross injustice, being subjected to it every day. It had been decades since she had felt so self-conscious about her own looks. Not so much the quality of her appearance, but the differences between her and Vedas.

Walking the streets of Danoor, she had been especially aware of the disparity. Reading judgment in the dark gazes around her was easy. Knosi, after all, were famed for their flawless complexions. Her freckles, a feature she had always been proud of, suddenly seemed like so many imperfections on her sun- and wind-burnt skin.

She ordered a second round, and he did not object or bring up the time.

"A plate of bread, as well," he told the server, for which Churls was grateful. They had not eaten since noon, and the alcohol intensified her hunger.

They continued talking of inconsequential matters, lingering on details of their trip, avoiding any mention of the tournament. His gaze never drifted to the prostitutes, many of whom had situated themselves on couches closer to him. He looked at his drink, his hands. He met Churls's eyes more often as they drank. In order to eat the highly spiced food, they both had to lean toward the table. Twice, they reached for bread at the same time. Once, his hand brushed hers and did not immediately pull away.

An hour stretched to two as business picked up. It became too loud to talk softly, but she did not mind holding her tongue. Apparently, neither did he. She ordered another round, another plate of food. He leaned back and she could not stop her eyes from drifting to the bulge of his genitals outlined by the fabric of his suit.

He folded his hands on his lower belly and sighed. She heard a signal within it, dreaded hearing the words it presaged: *I have to go.*

"I've rewritten the speech."

She blinked, quickly reorganizing her thoughts and suffering a pang of guilt. She had managed to shuffle his speech to the back of her mind, had failed to make her opinion of the document more obvious. It was important. He had asked for her help. But the crash on Tan-Ten had turned her world upside-down. She had spent the last month flinching at every shadow, staying close to campfires for fear of encountering Fyra again.

And the claims the girl had made? Churls avoided thinking of these at all costs. Only the proximity of Danoor had been enough to tear her away from obsessive evasion.

"Oh, yes?" she finally said, hating the tremor in her voice. "You're happy with it?"

He sat up and rested his forearms on his knees. He offered a wan smile. "Happy's not really the word. I'm satisfied with it. I've said what I want to say, instead of what Abse wants me to say. I've . . ." He gestured vaguely. "I've come to terms with the things I've seen since leaving Golna. I'm not the same man. Abse won't like what I have to say. Many people won't like it. But it's better than the alternative, which is more of the same violence on a larger scale."

She leaned forward. "What about the Tomen?"

He grimaced. "They'll still attack. I don't see a way anyone can stop that. The longer I think about it, though, the more likely it seems that violence will erupt even without the Tomen threat. I can't explain how, but I feel it in the streets, the nervousness. I felt it on the trail, too. Hopefully my message will at least sway the fighting in a different direction, away from innocent people."

He licked his fingers clean, and then frowned. He looked toward the door, making her heart sink. "This talk reminds me, I have to get going. I have a little dust left. Not much, but I should help you pay."

"You don't have to go," she said.

"Yes, I do. The first rounds are tomorrow. You . . ." He stood, shouldering his pack. His eyes eventually met hers. "You'll be there? For the final fight on the eve?"

Her right hand twitched in her lap. Only a short reach to grab his hand. Only two words: *Don't go.*

"Tell me you will," he insisted.

"Yes," she answered, and watched him leave

‡

Two hours later, she emerged from the whorehouse, drunk and lightened of nearly eight grams of dust. Berun was nowhere to be found, so she bought a packet of sempa resin from a street vendor and smeared it on her gums. After fifteen minutes of searching, she located a normal inn crowded with reveling travelers. She ordered a lager and sat down to survey the crowd. A number of nationalities were represented, though porcelain-skinned Ulomi men comprised the majority, and Tomen were absent altogether.

At a table in the center, a group sat playing kingsmader, a Stoli tile game at which Churls possessed no skill. She knew the rules, but nothing of the nuance.

The inn's banker weighed her dust and counted out four grams in bone chips. All she had left.

She sat down, nodded to her fellow players, and selected her tiles. Across from her sat three young Ulomi men with straight backs and even straighter teeth. The youngest appeared no older than sixteen, and when he moved his arm to raise the bet his robe parted, revealing the white elder-cloth suit he wore underneath.

He caught Churls's stare and smirked. He whispered to the largest of the three, causing this man to wink at her.

She ignored them. It soon became clear that she was not the only one. The couple on Churls's right, a Stoli merchant and his wife by the look of them, frowned at the table every time one of the three men spoke. The cauliflower-eared Castan, a fighter obviously, stared right through them and did not so much as twitch at their bawdy jokes. Only the olive-skinned woman, shaven-headed and ethnically ambiguous, noted their presence with any enthusiasm. She eyed the thinnest of the three, the one with the smattering of light freckles on the bridge of his nose, as if she intended to eat him.

Churls hemorrhaged chips. Before long, she became the butt of the youngest White Suit's jibes.

"You know what they call a woman in the Castan badlands?"

"There are two types of people who can't gamble. One of them is in this room."

"Ever heard of a bluff?"

"What's the difference between an Adrashi whore and an Anadrashi whore?"

She listened and smiled when he or one of his mates announced the punchline. All the while anger stewed in her stomach. Though the boys were young and most likely had not yet mastered the use of their suits, she knew backing away from the table, getting away with a portion of her money, would be the smart thing to do.

Unfortunately, she was not in a smart frame of mind.

The scrape of her chair against the wood floor signaled a situation that would soon get out of hand. A hush fell over the room. The bald woman frowned, picked up all but two of her chips, and left the inn.

"You owe me an apology," Churls said. Her heart boomed so loud she did not hear the words.

The youth rolled his eyes. "I said a lot of things. Which one hurt your feelings?"

Churls leaned forward, knuckles on the table. "Stand up."

The largest called over his shoulder to the bar. "Get her a drink. Maybe then she'll have the courage to ask for a fuck." He looked Churls up and down. "We could fuck you."

A smile touched the corners of Churls's mouth. She switched her grip and overturned the table, sending chips and tiles to the floor. Surprised by her maneuver, the three White Suits tumbled out of their chairs and backed up close to the bar.

She rounded the table and followed with a smile so wide it hurt.

‡

The boy's cheek collapsed under her knuckle, accompanied by the satisfying crack of shattering bone. She followed her fist forward with two quick steps, shoving the boy into his companions. The three fell backward, toppling and tripping over bar stools. Someone screamed and the bartender pulled a crossbow from under the counter. The movement might as well have been in slow motion. Churls hopped forward and slapped the weapon from his hand.

"The fuck you will," she said. "Stay put and shut up."

The boy with the dented face remained down, but the other two regained their feet quickly. The smaller moved away from the counter, putting tables and chairs between himself and Churls. He was not her main concern. He had not been running his mouth. One of those who had was already down, possibly dying, and the other would soon join him.

Blood pounded in Churls's veins violently enough to make her whole body shake. She could not have anticipated how the sempa resin and alcohol would interact in her system, but discovered she liked it.

Fear could not touch her. Vedas was a distant memory.

All that remained was rage, pure and simple.

The big man, barely more than a boy himself, shrugged off his robe and pulled his elder-cloth hood over his head. He smiled and flexed his chest. Like the other two, he was beautiful, broad and sculpted and sheathed in white. His teeth were alabaster tiles, his bone-pale skin shone with health. Unlike his smaller companion, he did not look scared in the least.

"Glad you did that," he said in his thick Ulomi accent. "Been looking for a fight all night. It's too polite, this city."

As he spoke, the material of his suit thickened visibly along his shoulders and forearms. The hood covered his temples, rose over his chin and onto his cheekbones—far slower than Vedas managed with his own suit.

Churls returned his grin. "Pretty boy doesn't want to get his face ruined."

The man gave himself away too easily. The twitch of his right pectoral signaled the punch. As it flew, Churls gripped his forearm in her left hand and twisted inside his guard, pressing her back against the solid wall of his torso. Using his own forward momentum, she bent at the waist, levered down on his arm and threw him. A table split in two under his weight.

To his credit, he rolled clear and stood rapidly, guard up.

She had not moved. "Come on. Clear a way. We'll wrestle."

He kicked the rubble of the table to one side. "Castan fucking bitch. My grandparents have a row of your ancestors' heads mounted above the hearth. You know what grandpa says about them? Know what he says their mouths are good for?"

Churls pushed off from the counter. "I don't care."

The man shrugged. As his shoulders dropped, he slammed both palms into Churls's chest. The graceless, full-bodied attack took her by surprise, forcing the air from her lungs, and she stumbled backward into the bar counter. He followed with quick jabs, the first two of which grazed her temples.

Buoyed by alcohol and drugs, the light battering amused her. He was not a formidable opponent, despite the speed and strength his suit granted him.

Laughing, she batted the third punch aside, planted both hands on the counter behind her, and thrust her kneecap into his groin. He grunted, unharmed, just as Churls had expected. It was meant as a distraction.

She slammed her forehead into his nose, relishing the crunch of crushed cartilage. He reeled back and tripped on a splinter of wood, crashing to the floor.

She stepped forward and stopped, sword halfway out of its scabbard.

The man was dead.

"Shit," she said. "Shit." She set chair upright and fell into it. "Shit, shit, shit."

She felt eyes upon her and looked up. "Get the fuck out," she told the remaining White Suit. "If your other brother's still alive, take him with you. No. Don't say a fucking word. If you say anything, I'll have to kill you."

Only words. Her anger had expired the moment her backside hit the chair. She watched the man check his dent-faced brother for a pulse—another sign of inexperience. Just a glance at the boy, and she knew he was alive. Take him to a good healer, and he would be as good as new. Being young and resilient had its advantages.

The young man lifted his brother over his shoulder and walked out the door without a word. Undoubtedly, he would return with other members of his order. They would scold him for sneaking out of camp, but they would come nonetheless.

Churls sighed and dropped her chin onto her chest. Anger flared again as her thoughts touched upon Vedas.

In one evening, she had made a mess of everything.

"Barkeep," she called. "You there?"

Nothing. He had probably exited out the back. Very likely, he was now gathering a few reinforcements.

Having been in similar situations more than a few times in her life, Churls considered which would be better: leaving, or pouring herself another drink for the wait.

EBN BON MARI

Ebn breathed in the heavily magicked air, the almond-and-blood-scent of elder semen and menstrual fluid mixed with her own juices.

"You have been careless," she told Pol.

He lay on his side, tangled in his bed sheets, unconscious. Naked, she sat cross-legged before him, caressing his cheek with the back of one finger, watching the last drop of the spell of compulsion disappear into his ear canal. Her eyes lingered over his form. She outlined the fists on his chest with a clawtip. A tingling moved into her thighs. Warmth spread throughout her torso, rose into her neck and filled her head.

A far more dizzying sensation than she had imagined, being in complete control of him.

This was not the night's only surprise. She had not dared imagine overcoming him would be so easy. Picturing all the ways he might defend himself, she had planned meticulously. Never had a person walked the halls of the academy armed with so many spells. How could she have known a mere act of daring would be sufficient to the task?

Traditionally, a mage did not attack another mage in the confines of her home.

It shocked her to discover Pol had relied upon the force of tradition alone to insure his safety. History notwithstanding, a smart man would have warded his apartment against physical attacks. He would have painted alarm sigils on his bed frame. As it was, Pol's lore had been laughably easy to neutralize. She had walked into his apartment as though it were her own, and ensorcelled him while he slept.

Undoubtedly, she would replay the moment for many years afterward. Finding him asleep, as vulnerable to her as a child. Setting the vitreous sphere of her spell in the center of his perfectly formed ear. Watching it collapse into a puddle and enter him.

Though there was no formal punishment for assaulting Pol in his sanctuary, she would hardly win friends with the action. Of course, she had no intention of anyone discovering it. And even if someone did, who would believe the claim? She had lost some of her clout in the encounter with Adrash, surely, but she was not yet discredited. The foundations sunk over decades of consistent leadership could not be uprooted easily.

No one would suspect anything so disgraceful from the outbound mages' captain.

"You have been careless," she repeated, and flipped the sheet from his hips, revealing the length of his erection. The tongues, which had until now remained in her wrists, emerged from her palms slowly, almost as if the thought of what lay ahead frightened them.

"Wake up," she commanded.

His eyes snapped open, then widened as his doubled pupils focused on her. They lingered on her breasts, her lower stomach. Otherwise, he did not move. Only the muscles controlling eyes and respiration remained under his control. At the same time, her ensorcelment had heightened every sensation, forcing him to the most intense state of physical arousal.

To his credit, he did not panic or struggle against the spell. She could see this much in his gaze, in the controlled manner of his breathing. She knew him very well, indeed.

"You have destroyed your body," she said, idly tracing the sigil tattooed on his shoulder. "And for what? If you had only lingered on your plans a bit longer, you would have seen the error of your thinking. If your mind were not so clouded with arrogance, you might have recognized your inferiority and stayed in your place. Maybe in time you could have become something." She leaned forward and smiled with a mouth full of small, white teeth. "After all, I can only live so long."

She held her hands up, palms forward. The tongues strained toward him.

Now, his eyes showed panic. His breaths came fast and shallow. Prone to mutations, eldermen nonetheless possessed a near-instinctive fear of deformity among their kind. Small deviations from the norm often signaled instability of character. The most extreme mutations revealed hidden talents—the ability to cast terrible, chaotic magic.

Some claimed the proof of such beliefs lay in elderman history. *Here*, some said. *Look at this. We have never been a stable people. We have always been prone to destruction and dementia. Arrogance has always been our greatest sin.*

But Ebn had learned much of human history. She had long ago realized both species held the capacity for good, for evil. Eldermen suffered with the knowledge that they were second best in the world—a sterile, complicated race that looked upon itself as inferior, when in fact the opposite proved true time and again. Even she had all but hidden this understanding from herself. She had held herself back for too long. Mankind and its talented hybrid children needed to change, to prove themselves worthy to Adrash, or Jeroun would be destroyed.

I can bear this message, Ebn told herself. *I can be the leader of this movement. We eldermen must no longer search in the sky for redemption, but amongst ourselves. We must cleanse the world of its waste, beginning with our own household.*

She let her forearms drop leisurely, observing Pol's reaction.

"Does this feel wrong?" she asked as her tongues licked the skin of his shoulder and chest. His skin tasted of alchemical ink, copper and blood. "That I am here in your bed, touching you this way? Are you scared that I will rob you of these symbols that you have painted upon yourself? Are you scared that I will steal your power?" She shook her head. "No. No, I will not do that. They are yours. You will die with them. When your body is burning, they will erupt from your skin like fireworks, signaling to the world that a true sorcerer has died."

She pressed the claws of her right hand into his hip and dug five gouges in his flesh.

Blood flowed. A tremor passed through his lungs. His indrawn breath faltered.

She laughed, and it was an ugly sound.

‡

Her mouth rose and fell on his erection. The head of his cock touched the back of her throat and she gagged, but kept at the task. She let him feel the rasp of her teeth. The tongue of her right palm slipped in and out of his rectum, and her left hand lay under his buttocks. She lifted his hips toward her mouth, simulating the thrusts of sex.

Twice, she thought she heard him moan, but it was only the ragged sound of his breathing. His eyes twitched under their lids. She bit his inner thighs hard enough to draw blood, exciting herself with the small reactions of his body. Fluid dripped from her in viscous strings, hardening into thin crystal spells that cracked under her knees as she maneuvered around the bed, searching for unbitten skin, new angles from which to admire his body.

She longed to have him inside her, but knew doing so prematurely would result in unsatisfactory release and the failure of her plan.

No, she needed to control herself. She had inserted the most important spell, the very same that now dripped from her womanhood, just before breaking into his apartment. A modification of her own spell of compulsion, it was designed to gradually turn her desire into a tool, providing her with the anger to overcome the love she still felt for him.

For despite the damage she inflicted, as yet she could not conceive of murder. Without assistance, she would not do it. She would instead hurt him, humiliate him, possibly even ruin his beautiful body—but she would not strike a killing blow.

Her body did not have more resolve than her mind, yet it needed to.

The smell of the crushed spell rose from the sheets, warmed her lungs and loins. Her labia swelled, pulsed between her legs. She moaned and ground her wetness against his kneecap, smearing a trail of her spell over his thigh. Its surface hardened, cracked, and floated into the air, a fine cloud of diamond dust that settled upon their skins. She imagined with what horror he breathed the magical essence in, uncertain of its exact composition or effect.

It did the same for him as it did for her, filling him with fury sufficient to melt steel. Ultimately, both of their minds would swell with murderous intent—but only she would have the ability to act on it.

Despite the swelling waves of anger, her desire remained. She lifted her head and straddled his hips, positioned so that the head of his cock pressed against her anus. Slowly, carefully, she lowered herself upon his erection. It took much care, for he was larger than she had anticipated, and she did not typically allow a man this access.

"A gift," she whispered, rhythmically tightening her sphincter on the base of his shaft—a surprisingly pleasant sensation. "And a reminder of what you will never experience again." She leaned forward, one hand on his chest and one poised over his face. She pried his left eyelid open with the thumb and middle finger of her right hand, and waited until he met her gaze. "Have you always loved men? Did I mother you too much?" She positioned her index claw over his eye, nearly touching it. "Is that why you never looked at me?"

She paused, and in this moment her spell asserted itself fully, flooding her with surety and purpose. Rage, acidic and deliberate, as inexorable as the revolving of the planets, moved her finger, plunging her claw into the soft tissue of his eye.

The delicate, lashed mouth of his eyelid closed around her finger. The punctured eyeball spasmed. Tears and blood flowed from the wound, pooling in his ear and soaking the sheets under his head. His chest shuddered and heaved under her hand, and his other eyelid fluttered, revealing an amber pool, a madly vibrating hourglass.

Her finger was now buried in his eye up to the first joint. She crooked the digit and tugged, at the same time rising off his erection. After a moment of resistance, the eye came free with a loud *pop* and his penis slid free of her anus. The sharp pain made her gasp, and she inadvertently ripped the optic nerve and blood vessel free from their socket. A mild disappointment, for she had planned to prolong his pain and discomfort.

The breath wheezed from him.

The tongue in her hand flickered back and forth, in a frenzy over its prize. The iron and salt taste of blood came to her, filled her entire.

Two hearts leapt against the confining walls of her ribs as she guided his erection into her. She rocked atop him, searching for the right angle. When she found it, the temptation to begin bucking nearly overcame her.

But she resisted temptation again. Wicked magic flowed within her veins, its temper granting her control over her ferocious libido. She would drag this out, his pain, her pleasure, until she knew for certain she could strike a killing blow. As her hips slowly rose and fell, she crushed his disembodied eye against his chest and smeared the gore over his inked torso.

"Is this your first cunt?" she asked. "It is not so bad, is it? Pol, you fucking fool. If you had but submitted to me every now and then, let your pride falter now and then, you could have fooled me completely. I love you, Pol. I love you." She tightened herself around his cock, hard enough to cause a swift intake of his breath. "But you have known that for some time, have you not? And still you chose to betray me."

She thrust faster, leaned forward to press her torso to his. Turning his head so that only his good eye showed, she whispered into his ear, "Another thought occurs. You intended to betray our faith. You would see everything that I have worked for destroyed, and for what? So that you may influence

Adrash to cleanse the world? What inspired such evil thoughts? Certainly it was not me. I would have steered you away from evil."

Her thighs twitched against his hips as waves of pleasure crested and broke throughout her body, and she finally started to buck, slamming her hips into his. Her breaths came fast and shallow. She closed her eyes, moaned his name.

Of their own accord, her fingers crawled up his chest and tightened around his throat.

‡

She had kept the man Jarres in her apartment for two weeks. As the full extent of Pol's betrayal became apparent, the tortures she inflicted upon his lover grew more severe. By the eighteenth day, he was little more than a bloodless husk of flesh, kept mere seconds from death by a collection of preservation spells Ebn had extorted from the Medicines Proctor.

The progression from threats to outright torture had not been rapid, nor had it occurred as a result of the information the man provided. In truth, his account rarely varied. Instead, something within Ebn changed. She listened, and with each repeated word grew to hate the man. He came to symbolize all that had been taken from her by Pol's betrayal.

Her hope, her desire, perverted and made hollow. Her love, turned to hate.

She punished Jarres for reminding her of these facts.

She punished him when her informants revealed that Pol had not called on Jarres's home or inquired at White Ministry hospital, despite the man's nearly two-week absence. This further proof of Pol's callousness enraged her.

Jarres suffered for Pol's sins. He begged, and screamed, and Ebn erected a sound barrier to keep others from hearing.

She listened, and then she stopped listening.

Memories filled her head. Memories of Pol, the shy sixteen-year-old boy who had come into her life. Eating breakfast with him, once every month. Teaching him, watching him grow into an adult. Feeling her lust turn to devotion, knowing she could not control its headlong progression. Love's assumption of her entire life.

Pol's voice came to her on the wind, out of the mouths of strangers, woke her from a dead sleep. Hoping to hear anything new, some sign that he had not actually betrayed her, she lingered on every word and slowly killed Jarres, who only confirmed what she already knew.

The bearded man's voice became ragged. He screamed until he coughed blood. When there was no blood left to thrust up, he wheezed and he cried, and then there were no more tears, no liquid in his body. His eyes stopped tracking and shrunk within his withered face. She anointed him with alchemical salves, spells to keep his pitiful body from failing. Pressing an ear to his chest, she listened to the creak of his lungs, the parched stutter of his heart. Like so many of the sounds she had heard since Shav's visit, these too resolved into words:

You are a relic.

You are a fool.

Finally, she killed the man, silencing his horrendous, dry-rotted voice. But instead of release, the act filled her with new urges, desires that spoke with the rustle of dead leaves and old bird bones, alien cravings that whispered as softly as flakes of rust under one's feet, as quietly as hairs ripped from the scalps of corpses.

She watched the Needle rise every evening, and imagined it descending to the surface. She pictured the fiery gouges the spheres tore in the atmosphere as they fell, the new stars blooming on the horizon, the clouds of molten earth rising into the sky. She felt the world's crust crack beneath her feet. She heard the voices of millions crying to their god for salvation.

Stroking the surface of her voidsuit, she thought of ascending to the heavens—of tempting Adrash to make her vision reality.

Eventually, she found the strength to admit the truth:

Pol's betrayal had infected her soul.

His death was the only cure.

‡

And yet for several seconds she fought her own hands. "Please," she said, unable to halt their tightening on the soft flesh of his neck. Like molten iron freezing in a cast, her fingers hardened into crescent vices. "Please," she begged. "No. Do not do this."

Pol's remaining eye watched her. He breathed evenly, drawing air deep into his stomach.

The muscles of her jaw stood out as she resisted not only the spell, but her own sexual release. Slowly, she ground her hips to a halt. The saliva bubbled on her lips, stretching from her chin to his chest.

"You made me do this," she managed through clenched teeth. "If you had only . . ."

Her claws bit into the sides of his neck, entered his flesh. His breathing was not impaired, for she had still not allowed the bridge of her palms to collapse onto his windpipe. He closed his eye and a groan built in his throat. It vibrated throughout his body. The moment held—a single note.

She held herself on the verge of giving in, on the edge of climax. He waited for death.

"Wake up!" she commanded. "Wake up and stop this!"

Desperation turned to laughter and the spell thrust her forward, elbows locked so that her full weight fell upon his throat.

It was like falling upon stone. The bones of her hands and forearms rang like bells, accompanied by a pain so severe she toppled sideways from the bed. The agony spread into her shoulders, compressed her ribs and closed her throat. She writhed on the floor as a great light bloomed above her.

The sheets burst into flames, and a figure rose above the fire.

Pol grinned. Pitch smoke billowed from his empty eye socket, as though his insides had caught fire. A wide beam of golden light shot from his right eye. The black ink of his sigil tattoos arced and coiled on his skin, forming the shapes of animals and men—a dragon, soaring across his stomach—an elder, stretching its long limbs into an X. The fists had opened upon his chest, so that two open hands appeared to be pushing from within him, struggling to break free. The wounds she had inflicted upon him closed without scar.

No, she thought. *No. This cannot be.*

The cold light of his eye found her, pinned her to the floor like a specimen on an examination table. Unable to move, a scream welled up from within her but could not escape. She gagged upon it and gagged again, forcing acid into her mouth. It burned as it bubbled up through her sinuses and dripped red from her nostrils. She choked on her own sick.

Suddenly, the light passed from her, and she heaved the contents of her stomach onto the floor. Shaking from the pain, nearly blinded by tears, she managed to say one word:

"How?"

"How?" he mocked, perfectly replicating the strangled tone of her voice. "Through trial and effort. Through pain and devotion. While you plotted revenge, I made myself a conduit for power. A weapon." He descended slowly to the floor. "Commend yourself for taking me by surprise. Your spell was exquisite, and it will not die with you. No, do not try to speak. I will not hear your excuses, your plea. I do not want to hear you say that you love me again."

She regarded him, sigils snaking over his naked form. He was beautiful, and terrible. The aroma of singed meat filled the room. The sound of heavy wings beating.

"You expect anger?" he continued. "Of course you do. You have debased me, torn my eye from my skull. But now you see what I have become, yes? How could you hurt me? In a way, you have actually assisted me. I see now that suffering can be a catalyst, as can fear. Unintentionally, you have hastened a process that I would have labored upon for months, maybe even years. In the space of a heartbeat I have been transformed.

"While your hands moved to finish their task, I learned secrets beyond your wildest dreams, Ebn. In the space of a few heartbeats I saw all of Jeroun, including the land across the ocean, under the clouds, where the elders sleep. I touched the idiot minds of spiders and the labyrinthine minds of wyrms. Over all I felt the mind of Adrash, ticking like an immense thaumaturgical engine. I knew then that he was a man, different from me only in the degree of his power. I saw the worlds he has set foot upon. I saw life, and it is a mystery to me no longer. I know that we are but tourists on this world. Adrash, humankind and the elders—we are all children of the stars."

His gaze focused upon her again, fixed her where she lay, chilled her to the bone.

I have no hope against such power, she thought.

"No, you do not," he said. "Nor do you have any reason for fear. You will soon be reunited with the stars. There are so many souls to help you on your way." He spread his arms. "Many stay on this world, but never for long. So few things anchor us to earth. The void calls to us, the allure of open roads. All concern slips away, all trace of fear and responsibility. Soon you will forget the petty concerns of life. The acts of gods and men will no longer concern you. I almost envy you your journey."

She wanted to speak, and felt her jaw freed. "Is that what you are now? A god?"

"No," he said. "That will take a bit more time."

She grew colder with each step he took toward her. By the time he reached her feet, she had gone completely numb. All trace of her spell had faded, leaving her resigned. This reaction shocked her for a moment, and then faded. One should not question a blessing, and it felt so good not to worry anymore. Perhaps, she considered, this was what she had longed for all along.

To be overcome. To be bested. *The only true expression of love is submission.*

"Sleep," Pol commanded. "And never wake."

A gentle weight dragged her eyes closed, and true darkness overcame her.

POL TANZ ET SOM

He lifted the blood and the smeared remains of his eye from the mattress particle by particle, leaving the fabric spotless. He walked across the room and opened the window, allowing the globe of congealing liquid to escape. The sound of it hitting flagstones on the pathway five stories below was a muted handclap.

Yesterday, he would not have done this. He had always disposed of blood and other bodily fluids as all smart mages did: by vaporizing them. Material from one's body, most especially blood, could easily be traced back to the owner and used in spells to influence or even control him. The academy possessed no shortage of schemers and usurpers. Cleaning crews also knew how to turn a profit.

He need never worry about such trivial matters again.

"Begone," he commanded. The ash that remained of Ebn's body rose from the person-shaped smudge on the floor behind him and swirled in the air, gathering itself as if it were a spirit risen from the grave. It streamed over his shoulder, spilling into the night to be taken away with the breeze. Turning as the last of it was freed, Pol caught the final scent of her, burnt and sharp yet still possessing the trace of coriander, her favorite scent.

He would miss her, undoubtedly. At times he would be reminded of her, and think of the waste. She had been instrumental in his upbringing, and a great leader in her time. But that was long past. Age and obsession had dulled her edge.

Still, he reminded himself, what a display in her final hour! What stunning brutality and rage! If she had only turned her energy to more worthwhile pursuits. If only she were not so blinded by lust, perhaps she could have been partner to him.

At the same time, had she not defiled him and taken his eye, causing him pain beyond measure, he likely would not have undergone his transition. It might well have been years before he could challenge Adrash . . .

Challenge Adrash. His lips puckered at this new thought.

Smoke poured from his left eye socket. For a moment, light leaked from the crack of his closed right eyelid. Though one eye was closed and the other absent altogether, he saw his surroundings with perfect clarity. He leaned on the window frame, angling his face to the sky in order to see the leading point of the Needle. Through concentration, he caused the image to bloom, take on detail. His perceptions quickened. The night breeze stilled on his skin, the sounds of the city became a warbling moan, and the three spheres slowed almost to a halt.

All at once they seemed but fragile things. Rickety baskets. Toys.

This new perspective rocked him back on his heels.

Challenge Adrash, he thought again. *Is this truly what I intend?*

He examined this new goal, which had announced itself in his mind fully formed. As if he had been planning it all along. As though it were the only goal.

Searching, he found no other ambitions or enmities—a development as shocking as any he had experienced, for after years of internal dispute amongst his peers he had built up a long list of men and women whose actions had offended him.

As a scholar, he was honor-bound to punish them.

As an ascendant god, however, he felt no such obligation. He no more shared the concerns of the outbound mage than those of the average dockhand. Even Shav, whose act of betrayal Pol had lifted from Ebn's mind, was not so much forgiven as forgotten.

And when all of his earthly cares had been washed away—when all but one opponent was beneath him? What was he to do then?

He stretched, and the shadow of great wings unfolded from his arms, reaching beyond the walls of his apartment. He sensed he had become a thing of light and smoke, standing on the edge of a great precipice, waiting for the slightest breeze to carry him out over the world.

He opened his right eye and vaporized the wall underneath the open window. Only one step to carry him into the night.

He did not pause to reflect on his life, his accomplishments. He would not mourn the life of one elderman mage, but set his mind to the only appropriate task for a being of his station.

Yes. He would challenge Adrash.

‡

The night held him.

His wings grew hundreds of feet wide, and the black silhouettes of birds and dragons danced upon his naked flesh. A portion of the alchemical ink had gathered at his scalp, covering it like a helm. With a twist of his neck, a thousand fine tendrils erupted and were caught by the wind, whipping around his head before lying in a tapering point between his shoulder blades.

He freed his arms from the shadowstuff of the wings, which continued to beat of their own accord. A simple thought, almost a whim, produced a staff of frozen fire in his hands. Under his fingers its texture was solid, but it weighed nothing. The smallest desire turned it into a gracefully recurved bow, and on his thigh appeared a quiver of golden arrows. He called into being an ax, a longsword, form-fitting armor of glowing plates, each item weightless but diamond-hard.

Laughing, he returned the gleaming items to whence they had come. Mere extensions of his magical will, they would be of no use in orbit. Adrash would not be fooled by toys. Pol had spoken truly to Ebn. He had touched the mind of the god, and it was old beyond comprehension.

An intellect like that would know strength from bluster.

How ridiculous, to think only a short while ago he had plotted to bring knives and a target into orbit. The tools of children, a useless task of revenge. Truly, he had been no better than Ebn. Had Shav not betrayed him by leaving, Pol would still be embroiled in the petty task of killing her. He might never have achieved godhood at all. Surely, the quarterstock deserved as much thanks for his unintended assistance as Ebn, but it was not in the nature of gods to express gratitude to mortals.

Pol rose higher. The wind pulled smoke from his left eye, forming a long streak behind him. Like a fish caught on a line, the golden beam of light from his right pulled him ever upward. His chest inflated slower and slower, drawing increasingly thin air into his lungs. Soon, even the wind stopped.

He did not become cold, nor did he fight for breath. He burst from the bubble of Jeroun's atmosphere, shedding his wings in thin streamers of shadow.

It seemed perfectly natural to stop breathing, as he no longer felt the need to draw in air. The void sustained him, warmed him as though he were lying naked in the sun. Having been exposed to the void due to accident several times in his life, knowing the intense burn of its touch, he marveled at his lack of fear.

Could he be so sure of his own power? Might not the effects of his transformation wear off, leaving him to die in orbit?

He let such worries fall away. He would not doubt the evidence of his own senses.

As he pushed himself toward the moon, he instinctively cast a dampening spell to push all thought deep within himself. He closed his mind as if it were a safe, and then turned the key in its lock.

He had entered Adrash's abode. It was only a matter of time before the god found him, no doubt, but Pol would not make it an easy task.

‡

He flew at speeds far beyond the means of an outbound mage, yet the effort took minimal concentration. He was neither taxed nor famished by it, and soon—as though he had woken from a dream—the cratered wall of the moon was before him. A vast ocean of frozen iron, as pale as bone. Lifeless as the void itself.

Pol shuddered when a force passed through him. He shivered as though he had been doused in ice-cold water, and his vision spun. The moon pulled at his body, trying to draw him forward. She whispered to him without words how sweet it would be to give in, to open himself to the void and embrace his fate. A ridiculous proposition, yet he wavered before her immensity, caught in her charisma. How delightful to spiral out of control, let her embrace him as lover. How wonderful to give in to the goddess Noeja.

He nearly let go. He nearly fell. But just before the temptation overcame him, he wondered: *Noeja? How is it that I know this name?*

The force lessened, allowing Pol a moment to gather his wits. The moon still touched him, and for the first time he sensed her personality, frigid beyond the void itself, disdainful of all life. She breathed in and out, expanding and contracting like a glacier in its trough. Relentlessly, she sucked the marrow from Pol's soul. Instead of longing to be closer to her, he now fought the urge to run away. His fear slowly grew, doubled, tripled. He fought to find calm, and came up empty. He too would be empty, a shell, if he stayed any longer.

Fly! he told himself. *Never come back!*

But still he wondered: *Noeja? Who has given me this name?*

The act of questioning was in itself an act of defiance—proof that he would not flee, but instead challenge the force which sought to coerce him—and in response he felt a measure of heat enter his body, easing the cold weight of his fear enough that it could be weathered. He shivered like a bone-chilled man before a fire.

Tell me! he projected into the void. *Who has given me your name?*

It began as a pressure behind his eyelids. It became the drumming of hooves on a baked plain. It became the ocean pounding upon the shore. It became the subterranean rumble of the earth's plates grinding together. Finally, it resolved into words:

Me.

The voice reverberated in the cavern of Pol's skull.

I am the voice of Noeja.

Dust lifted from the moon's surface. The entire planet quavered with the volume of this announcement, as if it had truly issued from deep within the satellite's heart.

Yet it was no goddess who had spoken.

The dread that had pressed upon Pol ceased. In its wake rose the unmistakable air of amusement. Pol was filled with the sense of being humored by a wise superior, of being indulged by a patient guardian.

The voice spoke again: *You are a trespasser here, mage. Prepare to meet your god.*

Pol smiled despite the threat, despite the insult. He had passed the test. He would stand face to face with Adrash. Let the god believe he was a child. Let the god underestimate him.

Pol descended to the moon and stood, the first mage ever to do so. None had dared set foot upon its fractured surface for fear of angering Adrash. He curled his toes into the soft, powdery regolith, soil that had never been touched by air or liquid water. When he lifted his foot, a perfect imprint remained. He walked, he hopped, he leapt forty feet at a bound. He stared up at the first and largest sphere of the Needle, which hung huge in the star-dusted sky, slowly turning.

It was indeed a rickety basket. A toy.

Pol projected his joy and his challenge into the void. He waited for Adrash's arrival, wondering how the god would appear to him now that he could truly see.

‡

Light preceded Adrash's arrival, igniting the moon's edge as though it were a steel blade fresh from the forge. The stars above this curved line dimmed and flickered in response, and to his chagrin Pol found he had raised his right fist to his temple in respect. Much as the voice had nearly bent him to suicide, the light compelled him to awe.

The god rose above the horizon, a second sun. A coruscating yellow-white fire surrounded him, extending miles from his body. For a moment, the shifting corona of flame seemed nothing more than a vain display, but gradually, like snarled paint strokes resolving into an image upon a canvas, its true form became apparent.

Pol's legs quivered beneath him as he took in the bewildering scope of the massive sigil, its lines melting and flowing in a constant state of rearrangement. No, he did not recognize a single configuration—if he spent a lifetime studying the symbol, its meaning would become no clearer. Here was magic on a scale impossible to comprehend.

Fear churned his empty stomach. Lead flowed in his veins, weighing him down, sinking his feet into the sterile ground. He stood transfixed, numbed, waiting for the inevitable: a quick death, befitting a frail, presumptuous mortal . . .

The inked sigils fell like ashes down his naked form, gathering upon his calves and feet.

Slowly, his knees bent . . .

No, he told himself. *I will not allow another to do my thinking.*

With great effort, he straightened his legs, swung his frozen limbs, shook the feeling back into his hands. Terror loosened its grip on his hearts, and the blood rushed giddily to his head. Thoughts spun, and then centered. Chastened for falling pray to the god's influence yet again, he reminded himself that he possessed his own set of weapons. Awakened once more, the sigils whirled around his body like leaves in an updraft.

Another flash of amusement.

You do nothing to hide your thoughts, Adrash said. His voice was an avalanche of rocks, the rumbling of a volcano before eruption. *What you have done to yourself is impressive, but you will not last long if you cannot silence that bullhorn of a mind.*

Pol cursed himself. He had allowed himself to be distracted. He reasserted the thought-dampening spell he had let lag and widened his stance. The black forms of halfstags and diamond spiders ran across his torso. A reptilian seabeast slithered up his right leg and a horned snake wound up his left. A thousand wasps roiled in flight on his arms. With a shrug, he unfolded his wings of shadow, spreading them like night's blanket across the surface of the moon. Adrash's light did not pass through.

Better, the god said.

Magic thrummed in Pol's veins, screaming for release. He closed his eyes against the glare and saw his opponent clearly, striding forward, feet above the ground, features serene under the divine armor. He did not appear to rush, but each step brought him miles closer.

I am ready, Pol broadcast.

No, you are not, came the reply. *But you came for a fight . . .*

Adrash disappeared.

A fist slammed into Pol's stomach, rocketing him backward. His body cut a deep furrow in the regolith before his foot caught on a submerged rock and sent him tumbling. Dust puffed up around him as his limbs bent and slapped the ground. His lips pulled back from his teeth. His mouth filled with dirt.

Chalked with iron but uninjured, he rose from the ground.

Heavy arms crossed, Adrash stood at the foot of the scar Pol's flying body had created. Waiting.

Pol flung outstretched fingers forward, casting and throwing a bullet of compressed magefire at the god. With heightened awareness Pol watched it move through the void, its boiling blue surface spiderwebbed with black. As it spiraled toward its target, Pol clapped his hands together, cracking the ground at his feet. A crevice opened and shot forward at blinding speed, yet to Pol's eyes it crawled.

The bullet hit Adrash square in the chest and exploded. He did not move as the magefire curled around his torso, writhing upon him as though it were a living thing. Had Adrash been a man, it would have eaten into his skin like an earthmover diving into sand. As it was, the fire failed to adhere and dripped from him in long, liquid strings.

The crevice halted at his feet.

Adrash unfolded his arms. *These are the best of your weapons? You are a fool. Labor at your task another hundred years and maybe you will do more with your powers than nudge one of my spheres. Yes, I know you. You have ambition, but little sense. Still . . .* He cocked his head slightly. *There is something. Something more than will or talent.* He closed his eyes, and it was as if someone had snuffed out the sun.

There is something, the god said again. *Your voice. I know it. It is as if you wear another's body . . . We have been at this juncture before, have we not?* He shook his head, and for the first time an expression could be seen under the armor: a slight downturn of his lips, the faintest wrinkle between his brows.

An opportunity. Pol reacted quickly, without forethought, letting the magic speak within him. He would interpret Adrash's words later—if he lived.

The sigils writhed upon his body. They flowed up his legs and torso, gathering together on his arms, turning his skin from mid-bicep to fingertips solid black. Drawing upon the emptiness of the void, moving by sorcerous instinct, he formed an unknown spell between his hands: A dangerous, life-eating thing, a portion of nothingness crystallized, condensed, conforming to the shape of his fingers. Still, the spell was difficult to hold. It wanted to be free. He cupped his hands around it, pressed it into a small sphere. Throbbing in time to Pol's wildly galloping heartbeats, the spell's chill crept up his arms and into his chest. His teeth chattered and then abruptly stopped.

The spit had frozen in his mouth, sealing his jaw shut.

He could not hold the spell any longer. His hands flew apart and the ball of emptiness shot forward—far slower than he had hoped. It expanded in flight, wobbling like a droplet of water, contorting reality as it passed. The stars quavered through its imperfect lens and Adrash bloated into a ridiculous shape.

Pol sagged and ungracefully sat, spent by the casting. If it did not work, he would soon be dead.

Adrash's eyes snapped open just before impact. The spell hit him and instantly collapsed around his body, hungry for warmth. For several seconds the god strained against the constricting envelope, every muscle in rigid definition. He fell to his knees and bent forward at the waist, fists punching into the powdered earth. Pressed on all sides, he curled in upon himself. Just before he stopped moving altogether, the fiery sigil that surrounded him flickered, collapsed, expanded, and collapsed again.

Pol watched, struggling to make his body move. He gathered unsteady legs underneath him and stood. Cautiously, he floated toward Adrash. Though the god had stopped moving, his massive sigil continued to pulse on and off.

Pol faltered at the halfway point, struck dumb by the realization.

His magic is failing him.

Before he could form another thought, his own mysterious talent woke within him again, pounding against the interior of his skull. He threw his head back, but the scream stopped in his throat. Pain lanced through his rigid limbs, gathered in his fingers and toes. The head of his erect penis throbbed as if it were going to explode.

Through the agony, he sensed the casting of a second foreign spell.

Like iron shavings adhering to a lodestone, fragments of voidstuff stuck to his skin, covering him completely, numbing him from the outside in. Trapped, he struggled for control over his body, and lost.

The pain faded to nothing while his mind raged.

The spell moved his limbs. He strode forward, though his feet did not touch the ground. He bent, took Adrash's head in his hands, and lifted the limp body. The god's sigil flickered off every few seconds, reappearing slightly dimmer, slightly smaller each time.

Pol pulled him in close and kissed him at the exact moment the sigil fluttered off.

The moon disappeared. The universe flooded with sunlight—

—and he found himself on a field of blue flowers.

Three figures stood before him. A muscular man clothed in black from head to toe. A warrior-woman covered in freckles. A giant man composed of brass spheres. Adrash's body lay at their feet. The man in black spoke harsh, alien words, and Adrash's divine armor began to smoke, blistering and charring upon his body.

The perspective lurched, and suddenly Pol was flying at great speed over Knoori. Desert. Water. The domed island of Osa in the distance. Land. Pine forests. Finally, the Aspa range. He floated above a mountaintop valley with a lake at its center. Scattered everywhere were ruins, and among the ruins lay thousands upon thousands of elder corpses, naked to the sun. Men gathered around these, hacking them open with stone blades.

The perspective lurched again, and once more he was flying eastward over the continent. His speed increased so that he could not make out the details below. Then he was over water again: Jeru, the Great Ocean. He flew into a wall of cloud and just as quickly was out of it, descending into the alien landscape of a new continent. Glass and steel spires, entire cities of them, rose from the forests, plains and immense lake platforms. Roadways that stretched like ribbons of black silk crisscrossed the ground, and everywhere corpses lay.

No, not corpses. Living elders, glowing with life—merely sleeping. A spear of sunlight shot down upon one, and it lurched to its feet. It turned and stared at Pol with liquid eyes the color of dried blood. A sound built in the space between Pol's ears, rising steadily in volume.

The howl of a wolf.

A hundred thaumaturgical engines churning.

The crumbling of a mountain into the sea.

The elder screamed, and Pol saw no more.

‡

He woke, sprawled on the moon's iron soil. A yellow-white glow faded from his eyes. The spells were still upon his body.

Above him, the Needle was broken, its twenty-seven spheres spread across the sky. One hung stationary only a few thousand miles from the moon's surface. At the limits of unaided vision, another spun so rapidly Pol could not see its rims without quickening his perceptions.

The sight filled him with fear greater than any he had experienced since childhood—the kind of fear he had forgotten he had ever felt. For a thousand years, the Needle had stretched straight and true. Fifty generations of men had stared into Jeroun's sky, reassured or made fearful by the nearly unvarying sight of it. If they did not look too closely or were simply unobservant, they probably believed it did not change at all—that Adrash had no intention of using the spheres as weapons. Pol considered with what horror men would greet the following evening, knowing how wrong they had been.

And you will still be wrong, he thought. *This is not your god's doing.*

He turned his head. Adrash lay on the ground where he had fallen. His chest did not rise or fall. Though whole, the divine armor had taken on a dull, greyish cast.

Pol stood, swaying on unsteady legs but otherwise unharmed. Understanding that a decision must be made, he nonetheless struggled to bring his mind to bear. His thoughts swam in a thick stew, making it difficult to concentrate. He had not killed Adrash—of this he could be sure. That would not be so easily accomplished. Furthermore, why would the armor still cling to the god if no life moved within him?

The best thing would be to flee, Pol reasoned. Too exhausted to cast another spell, he stood no chance against Adrash if he were to wake. Still, Pol did not move. Already, he felt haler than he had when he woke. He resolved to wait a few moments, gather his strength.

A little time, he thought, *and I will be able to cast again.*

He did not have the luxury of rallying his reserves. Adrash twitched, and slowly began to rise. He fell twice, and rose again. Shaking with the effort, he finally lifted his head. He opened his eyes and light spilled forth, growing brighter until it pushed at Pol.

Pol braced his legs and pushed back, but to no avail. The force of the god's gaze buffeted him like a strong wind, and then began relentlessly propelling him backward.

I would go, the god said. He fell to his knees, but kept his eyes on Pol. *You have done better than I imagined, Pol Tanz, but you have not killed me.*

Pol no longer sensed amusement behind the words, which burned through his mind and constricted the hearts in his chest. He wilted under the force of Adrash's anger. He struggled against the light, all the while knowing he would be a fool to stay.

Run while you can, the god said. *You will not get the opportunity again.*

PART FIVE

VEDAS TEZUL

The dirt floor of the ring had been raked and salted, but the smell of blood and sweat lingered in the huge arena tent. Large, smokeless alchemical lamps hung from oak crossbeams and steel wire far overhead, illuminating the restive mass of attendants.

The light did not reach through the press of bodies to where Vedas sat in the east corner of the tent, however. His black suit and dark features blended with the shadows, and people left him alone. Of course, they knew he was there. They stole glances in his direction, whispered his name. Black Suits of one hundred orders, holding glasses of red wine or yellow lager, sharing joss and eating ostrich rinds from oily bags—the high and the lowborn, master and acolyte, speaking his name, pinning hope upon their champion.

He had killed seven White Suits before dusk. The day before, he had killed eight. Due to the great success of the Black Suits in the tournament, and despite the creative shuffling of the brackets, he had also been forced to kill four of his brothers and two of his sisters. The final bout, after all, could not occur between siblings of the same faith.

It had not pleased him to take any of their lives, but he had done so just the same.

And though it might have been useful to analyze their fighting styles, glean something from his successes, he shied away from these memories. He centered his thoughts, burying the past under a tonnage of mental static as

247

best he could. It was a challenge to sustain this state, despite the practice he had put into it. For two long days, he had not allowed his mind to wander or speculate uselessly. He had not followed the other fights or counseled with anyone about the standings. He had simply fought whoever stood before him.

Grey, his final opponent, was only a name, a faceless rival on the other side of the tent, just as the others had been before dying by Vedas's hand. Undoubtedly, this approach could be seen as dangerously careless.

And yet, only Vedas and one other remained.

Clearly, ignorance had not hampered him overmuch.

His body ached so thoroughly that concentration could not locate a single injury more agonizing than the rest. Lifting a knee, flexing his pectorals, or balling his toes resulted in intense pain. His right shoulder clicked every time he rolled it, and stars flared before his eyes if he tipped his head too far back. His right finger was broken. He suspected his right clavicle and several of his ribs were cracked. The stiffness of his suit alone kept his torso upright and his legs from buckling underneath him.

It had not been so bad, after the first few fights. He had won them handily enough, but this was hardly a surprise during the winnowing stage. The odds fell in a senior fighter's favor. By the eighth round, however, experienced fighters were finally being pitted against one another, and the winners became harder to predict. Men and women who had worn suits for decades traded punches powerful enough to crush elephant skulls, dodged and deflected attacks too fast for the eye to follow, and died suddenly, often before the crowd registered the killing blow.

Victors and dead men were separated by a blink of the eye.

The goal was not to teach a lesson, but to kill efficiently. Retribution or punishment required keeping one's opponent alive—a condition few smart fighters would tolerate. It was too easy to misjudge another combatant's injuries and lose the upper hand. To kill a suited man was not easy, after all. Even mortally wounded, a would-be loser could still strike.

No weapons other than the elder-cloth suits were allowed. None were needed. Sufficiently skilled in the martial arts, fused to his suit to the degree that it seemed indistinguishable from flesh, a man like Vedas became a weapon of awesome power. Only magic posed a significant threat to the brothers and sisters of Black and White orders, but magic too had been outlawed from the tournament.

Aching, struggling to remain upright, Vedas gave up on centering his thoughts and allowed himself to wonder what surprises the man Grey had in store for him. Perhaps he would fight like Ria, the thin elderwoman Vedas had fought in round six—a flurry of deceptively wild punches and knee thrusts, a confusing fusion of techniques. Or maybe he would fight like Osuns, the immense hulk of a man Vedas had fought in the tenth round—a wall of flesh taking punishment without apparent damage, only to launch an offensive so carefully timed it nearly took his opponent's head off.

Or most troubling of all, would Grey fight like Jaffe, the small brother Vedas had nearly lost to in round fourteen? Unable to land a single blow, thrown around the pit like a ragdoll, Vedas had become desperate and thrown sand in the man's eyes. Many in the crowd had booed, but an equal number had cheered when Vedas killed the man.

He carried the guilt of the act with him still. The thought of winning the tournament under similar circumstances filled him with shame, for he knew he would make the same decision again. He had rewritten the speech, and intended to read it.

But who would listen to the words of a coward?

Doubt settled upon his shoulders, weighting his bones so that he sagged even more upon his stool. He might not live to read the speech. His success had never been assured. He could be the lesser man. Had he traveled so far only to die alone? Obviously, this was the case for all but one of the fighters. Why had the thought of being defeated seemed so preposterous? Was he really such a fool as to believe himself invincible, or had he simply pushed his fears to the side for fear of confronting them?

Die alone, he thought.

The two words settled cold and solid in his gut. He clasped his hands together to stop their shaking. Deeper than the exhaustion, heavier than the doubt, the hope he had suppressed welled up within him: a terrible feeling, like standing on the edge of the Steps, waiting for the wind to either tip him back onto land or carry him out over the sea.

He fought the urge to raise his head, and failed. The whites of his eyes reflected the scant light. A brother met his gaze and took it for an invitation to approach. Vedas shook his head, and the man faded back into the crowd.

The frown deepened on Vedas's face as he tried to peer through the bodies. He shifted on his stool like a man in great discomfort. Finally, he stood, craning his neck to see into the shallow bowl of the covered arena. He searched the highest stands, the fringes and the entrances. A persistent person could get into the tent, but could not shoulder into the ranks of white- and black-suited orders, who by right sat close to the action.

He searched for Churls, and came up empty.

✝

"Tell me you will," he had said, and she told him she would.

Leaving her in the whorehouse was not an easy thing to do. He regretted it the moment he walked out the door. She wanted him to stay—this much was clear, even to someone as unused to companionship as Vedas. After months traveling together, he knew her better than he had known any woman, any person, in thirty-four years of life. Still, there was mystery to her, words left unspoken between them. She possessed urges that both scared and compelled him.

He felt crippled by his inexperience. Did she know he had never been with a woman? Likely, she had guessed as much. Did she suspect he had never kissed a woman, never held a woman's hand in romance?

Anyone would laugh at his naivety.

Yet somehow he knew that, if given the opportunity, Churls would not laugh. The woman could be coarse, but she had never been cruel. She listened well when he ventured to tell her about his past. She had not chuckled or rolled her eyes while he talked of Julit Umeda's parents, halting and awkward though his account was. Sometimes, her expression appeared to convey not only sympathy, but a deep understanding.

Of course, sharing on this level occurred with regularity for other people, yet Vedas had rarely experienced it. He wondered, if he had held her gaze in the whorehouse, lingered just a moment more in her company, might she have shown him just how much she empathized?

With every step he took away from her, the more tenuous their connection seemed. It stretched, turning their months together into nothing more than a convenience, a rational arrangement they had arrived upon to keep themselves safe.

The road was lonely, after all. They had grown closer out of boredom. Perhaps he had deceived himself in everything.

Before long, this became his conviction. If she arrived at the tournament, she would be watching out of obligation and nothing more. She would congratulate him, buy him a drink, and say she wanted to see him at her

upcoming fights. They would agree to meet up again but attach no importance to the appointment, like all mild friends did in the same situation.
Bonds extended only so far.

He reached the Black Suit camp, where his brothers and sisters welcomed
him in full companionship. They shared food and space. They introduced
themselves and exchanged histories, began songs and dancing. More than a
few offered their flesh, but Vedas felt no temptation to accept. Sharez, a lithe
northern Castan woman who had caused her suit to grow spiraling horns on
her head, made a seam split in her suit, revealing her womanhood. Briefly
stricken immobile, he watched as she took his hand and guided it to her.

"Hey," she said when he snatched it away. "Why not enjoy yourself?"

She was beautiful, and he answered honestly: "I don't know."

Though he knew abstinence was not required or even normal in most
orders, the sexual abandon of the camp shocked him. He forced himself to
interrupt an intimate discussion in order to borrow a razor, shaved his face
and head, and then went to bed alone, apparently the only one to do so.

In the White Suit camp, the situation was undoubtedly much the same.
Celebrations had a universal nature. For the first time, Vedas understood
how odd it was that he had never formed a sexual relationship, never exper-
imented beyond masturbation. Surely, he did not still carry the wounds of
youth! He had never looked upon the act of sex with revulsion. Instead, he
simply did not consider it an option. But what if he had stayed with Churls?
Would she have rented a room, shown him the error of his thinking?

Unable to sleep, he touched himself through his suit. Facing the tent wall,
separated from reveling brothers and sisters by a thin sheet of nearly translucent cloth at his back, he knew what he did was ordinary, unremarkable,
but as the erection grew under his hand he fought the irrational fear of being
observed. Peering over his shoulder, he half-expected to find her waiting
for him. Smiling. Bending over, peeling leather pants from muscular hips.
Running her hands up her backside, lifting her skirt.

Strangely, the paranoia coupled with fantasy produced the most intense
orgasm he had experienced in some time. His legs shook and he curled in
around the sensation, seeking to hold it in. He gasped unintentionally. A
moan escaped his lips.

The sadness thereafter seemed inevitable, an aftereffect of wishing too
hard. The cavity he had opened by giving vent to his longing now threatened
to consume him. The immensity of the void constricted his chest, stung his

eyes. He marveled at all the things he had never experienced, all the things he had never allowed as possibilities.

Traveling with Churls, having her close, had opened the world around him, yet he still struggled to give his desire a voice.

Yes . . . Yes. Without a doubt he wanted her.

He wanted her for more than sex—more than mere friendship or respect.

Suddenly, the thought of winning the tournament, of returning to his apartment in the abbey and reassuming his routine, seemed an awful fate.

‡

A squat White Suit came out of the crowd. The opposition's official.

"You're due," he said.

Vedas raised his arms and spread his feet for the weapons inspection. He closed his eyes as hard hands flowed over his sculpted body, uncomfortable lest he meet the stares of his brothers and sisters. They would smile, nod encouragement. One or two might spit at the official's feet or say something foul. Vedas needed none of that at the moment. Best he avoid all distraction, go into the fight feeling as little as possible.

Emotion slows reaction, Abse had always said. *Anger just as much as fear.*

Vedas thought of Churls one last time, resigning himself to the woman's absence before banishing her from his mind—a blessedly simple action now that the fight was nearly begun. Familiar sensations flooded his system, focusing his awareness. His pulse expanded to fill his body, drumming a simple beat from head to toe. His suit tightened around him. He did not feel so much as a twinge as his broken finger curled in with the others to make a fist.

The official put his hand between Vedas's legs, ran the tip of a finger along his perineum. He cupped Vedas's genitals, squeezed lightly, and then stood.

"Finished. Let's go."

The crowd parted for them. Vedas looked neither left nor right, and kept his eyes on the floor. He touched no outstretched fingers for luck. His brothers and sisters forgave such things, apparently, for they cheered as he stepped into the packed earth ring:

"Vedas!" "Vedas!" "Vedas!"

The bass throb of a drum underscored the two-syllable chant, though it could easily have been meant for the opposition, who shouted the name of their champion just as loudly. To Vedas, the words lost all clarity and became a simple rhythm.

Opposing factions, shouting with a single voice.

Vedas tipped his head from side to side, loosening his neck. Though no material boundary kept the Black Suits and the Whites from mixing, to either side an arrow-straight line separated them. Once in a while a hand shot out with a rude gesture from one side and someone from the other slapped at it, but this was the extent of their interaction.

Afterward, however—maybe then someone would push at the border.

And what about the others, the ones who stood behind the gathered orders? Onlookers, gamblers, Adrashi and Anadrashi of a hundred kinds. What would they do if he won, if he lost? And then there were the others waiting outside the tent. The entire population of Danoor, waiting for word of the outcome. The Tomen, encamped in the hills . . .

Enough, Vedas told himself. *Concentrate on the task at hand.*

He lifted his head and looked at his opponent for the first time. What he saw surprised him, but his features remained blank. Knowing how much even a glance revealed to a smart fighter, he took in details of build and stance without moving his eyes.

She did the same.

For some reason, he had not imagined a woman. Perhaps he had not thought a woman capable of making it all the way to the final bout, but this did not ring true. More likely, he had simply gone with the odds. Sisters comprised less than a quarter of the combatants.

Grey stood an inch or two taller than Vedas, and outweighed him by at least fifty pounds. Her breasts were large, but so flattened by the stiffness of her suit that they looked like immense pectoral muscles. Her gut was a tight drum, her legs barrels of smooth muscle. Her shoulders sloped like a bear's, and her hands were massive. They alone moved, alternating fists opening and closing. Vedas looked last at her face, which was large but not at all unattractive. Together with the build, her unlined olive complexion revealed her as a native of northern Dareth Hlum, a close relative of the Vunni, perhaps.

The head official of the tournament, an impartial representative from the city council, stepped between the two combatants. He reached inside his robes and produced a vial, which he dropped and then broke under the butt of his staff. Vedas's ears popped.

"Silence, please," the official said, voice amplified so that all could hear. "This will be the final bout of this tournament, the final bout of the year. Tonight marks the last day of the half-millennium, and tomorrow the city will begin hosting celebratory games. Whatever the outcome tonight, you will end it peaceably and not sully the merrymaking."

Boos sounded from both sides.

The official frowned. "Battalions are stationed in this camp, at the coliseum, and within the city itself. No leniency will be shown to rioters, regardless of race, class, place of birth, or faith."

"What of the Tomen?" someone shouted.

The official's frown deepened. "A battalion is stationed below them. Another two companies are arriving as we speak. Ample men to quash any violence the Tomen may intend." He bowed to Grey and Vedas. "Good fight."

Vedas's hood flowed to cover his face. Grey did not mask her face completely, but caused her suit to form bars that rose from her chin to the armored bridge of her nose. Shelf-like eyebrow ridges formed and the eldercloth thickened visibly over her ears.

Transformations complete, they bowed to one another.

The fight began.

‡

Vedas was the first to move.

Grey merely widened her stance, turning to follow him as he circled. He kept his distance, watching her smoothly shift weight from foot to foot. She had lowered her center of gravity without bending her back, as if she were squatting over a latrine hole. Though he could not rely upon it as fact, nine times out of ten this posture communicated an unwillingness to reach farther than arm's length for an opponent.

She would wait for him to bridge the gap between them. From there she would try to take him to the floor, counting on her bulk to overcome him. She had probably caused her suit to texture, especially along the forearms and inner thighs, creating a gripping surface to counter the smoothness of her opponent's suit. A conservative strategy, sound but ultimately limiting: Her suit and thick build granted her a great deal of protection against close-range attacks, but unless she proved faster than Vedas she would be unable to get a grip on him.

In his experience, the majority of fights ended up on the ground. He knew himself to be a capable grappler, but this time it would not be wise to end up on his back.

Neither would it be wise to rely on one strategy alone.

He limbered up as he circled, purposefully avoiding a fixed stance in order to throw her off. The ragged approach made him uncomfortable, but he thought it wise not to mirror her solid, unchanging posture. He held his fists just below his collarbones in a loose boxer's guard. He spiraled ever nearer to her. She gave nothing away.

Crouching, he swept his right foot at her left calf. She lifted her foot and stamped down, far too slowly to touch him. Otherwise, she had not changed position. Unless she was purposefully holding back, this told him something about her reaction time.

He continued circling. As he shortened the distance between them, her forearms rose. She opened both plate-sized hands and held them out from her body at the height of his biceps. He bobbed up and down and her hands followed exactly.

He shuffled in and jabbed at the right one. Her fingertips brushed the back of his hand, but could not close around his fist.

Quicker that time. Not abnormally agile, but definitely quick.

He continued moving, looking for openings. She continued biding her time, waiting for him to get overanxious and make a mistake. He darted in again and jabbed with his left. She nearly caught it. Her expression never changed.

They watched each other. This could go on for quite some time, he knew.

The crowd made dissatisfied noises. The fighters were silent.

He feinted in, pulling short a right jab. Reaching for his fist and grasping air, she threw her right shoulder forward slightly. He grasped her leading forearm with both hands and pulled diagonally across his chest, trying to throw her off balance. Her weight only shifted slightly, and he backed away before her other hand came into play.

Not fast enough.

Before he was out of range, she darted in for contact. It was a clumsy slap-strike, and the back of her left fist only glanced off his temple. He staggered but recovered his feet, shaking the stars from his eyes. She settled back into her stance. He resumed circling, noting that she now hobbled slightly on her right foot. Though her offensive movement had seemed slight, it had apparently rekindled a previous injury.

He decided to do a foolish thing. Take a calculated risk.

Hoping to catch her off guard, he repeated his last attack exactly. She was not fooled, however. Instead of reaching for his incoming fist, she lifted her right hand above it and closed her fingers in an overhand grip around his wrist.

She levered his arm down, slamming her left palm into his elbow—the exact move he had planned for her, only far, far faster than he could have imagined. His right foot came off the ground, followed by the left. His face hit the dirt.

Though his suit hardened around his arm, as she pushed his chest to the ground her weight overcame the resistance.

His elbow snapped, and she pulled his forearm back, twisting it to ruin the joint.

He bit down hard enough to crack teeth.

She ground her left knee into his back, holding a stable position. But as she let go of his useless arm to reach for his head, her weight shifted minutely—just the slightest movement of her knee to the left of his spine, the tiniest slip of fabric against fabric.

It was enough.

Vedas pushed up with his left arm, lifting his chest a few inches, and she overcorrected, trying to keep her knee in place. It slipped clear of his back and he rolled under her pelvis. The entire right side of his body bloomed in agony as his shoulder joint dislocated and his shattered elbow was crushed beneath the weight of two people.

As her hands moved to wrap around his throat, he buried his stiffened middle and index fingers in her right eye socket.

She spasmed and fell forward, dead instantly.

‡

Night had fallen while he and Grey fought, but the Needle had not yet risen.

A group of his brothers carried him from the tent toward Aresaa Coliseum. Jostled atop their shoulders and hands, right arm stiffened against his chest, he demanded to be let down. He needed his speech. He wanted to wash Grey's blood from his body. The sound of the crowd drowned out his voice. He unmasked himself and attempted without success to meet someone's eye. Eventually, nausea and lightheadedness convinced him to stop trying. He closed his eyes and surrendered himself to a rough, two-mile ride into the heart of the city.

A commotion to his left. Shouting. Vedas turned.

Head and shoulders above the tallest man, gigantic hands parting the crowd, Berun swam through a sea of black-suited humanity. He moved in a straight line toward Vedas, unmindful of the blows raining down upon him. Staffs broke upon his head. Blades broke between the spheres of his chest, back, and shoulders.

Someone called Berun's name, and another picked it up.

For a moment, the crowd was split. Brothers and sisters who knew the constructed man's reputation struggled with those who did not, trying to halt the violence.

A line of green magefire arced from a sister's staff and struck the ground at Berun's feet: a warning. The constructed man halted, pointed to Vedas, and bellowed. The noise ate his tolling words. He bellowed again, and this time Vedas heard.

"My friend!"

All at once, it seemed, the rabble cleared a path. They cheered as Berun lifted Vedas from their brothers' shoulders, overjoyed now that the constructed man had declared sides. It did not lessen their violent mania, nor did it stop Adrashi—White Suits, townspeople, and foreigners alike—from continuing to attack the flanks of the crowd. They tried to break the ranks bodily. They stood on vegetable carts and roofs, throwing rocks and refuse.

Despite the official's warning, violence had erupted the moment of Grey's death. The orders had crossed the aisle with fists and staffs raised while Vedas lay trapped under his opponent's body. It could have been no other way, of course. The Black Suits had won, but the Followers of Adrash would not let it rest there. Men would die before the evening was through.

Vedas reached up and pulled Berun's head down. "I don't have it! They wouldn't listen to me. I need to go back to my tent!"

Berun smiled. "I have it, Vedas."

"How?"

"Quick thinking." Berun's eyes burned brighter. "They wouldn't let me in, so I tore the tent down. They showed me where your cot was after that." He shrugged his right shoulder forward, displaying the strap of Vedas's pack. "I checked to make sure it's in here."

Vedas sighed and shut his eyes again. "Thank you."

The river of Black Suits surged forward. Though Berun walked with far more care than the excited brothers had, he could not keep from being knocked about by the movement of the crowd. He could not stop others from bumping into the man he carried, who winced with every jolt and collision. Vedas felt as though his bones had detached from their joints, as though his ligaments and muscles had been pulped to mush. Even with eyes closed, the world spun. He masked himself again to block out the scent of Grey's blood.

Reaching Aresaa took either a hundred years or a few minutes. Once there, a man spoke with Berun. A man who insisted upon introducing Vedas before his speech.

"No," Berun rumbled. "I'll do it. Give me the spell."

A voice amplification spell, Vedas realized.

He felt Berun climbing stairs. He heard the echo of thousands of voices shouting in a great hallway. His name. Berun's name. Then, the roar of an even greater number in open air, louder than the howl of a hellhound, louder than the wildest spring storm. Another set of stairs, much longer than the first, in a closed space that reduced the noise to a dull throb. *DUM-dum. DUM-dum.* A two-syllable word. A name.

Out into the open again. The sound of cheering was a hundred nails driven through Vedas's skull. It went on far too long. "Enough," he finally said to Berun. "Shut them up."

"Yes," Berun said.

Vedas felt the constructed man crush the glass bulb. His ears popped, and the cheering softened. It became a sustained roll of muffled thunder, far more manageable.

"Silence!" Berun roared, and the thunder stilled almost completely. He lowered his friend to the ground.

Vedas stood without aid, unmasked his face, and opened his eyes.

Tiers upon tiers of people—one hundred and fifty thousand of them—had gathered to hear him speak. Anadrashi of every stripe, from every corner of the continent. More souls than a person could take in at once. Vedas turned a complete circle, staggered by the dimensions of the coliseum. Though he and Berun stood on a four-storey wooden platform erected in the middle of the arena, they were not quite level with the lowest stand. Perhaps the stories his father had told him as a child were not so preposterous, after all. *Once, when the river Koosas flowed strong and wild, Adrash would fill Aresaa with her water and float great warships upon it . . .*

Berun's hand came into view at Vedas's shoulder. In it was a folded piece of paper.

‡

"Shit," Vedas said. *Shit.* The first unintended word of his address, echoing off the distant stone walls of the coliseum.

He unfolded the speech. The words swam on the paper for several seconds before organizing themselves in a recognizable fashion. He had written a full page in his small, tight handwriting. Four paragraphs, including an introduction wherein he thanked the city of Danoor and its representatives, everyone in the coliseum, the brothers and sisters of the Thirteenth, and Abse for sending him to the tournament.

Suddenly, the words of gratitude seemed unnecessary, even ridiculous. He skipped them and began with the second paragraph. Afraid to miss or mangle a single word, he read slowly, methodically.

"Respect for my abbey master notwithstanding, I cannot deliver the speech he instructed me to read. It encourages violence on a massive scale, violence that will result in the deaths of hundreds, if not thousands, of Adrashi and Anadrashi alike. It is the kind of message the Tomen are waiting for, but we cannot side with them any more than we can side with Nos Ulom or Stol. I do not wish to start a war, and yet I believe this is what I am being encouraged to do. I am no one's puppet."

Vedas paused his monotone reading. The stands were quiet, waiting for him to continue. He skimmed more lines, more words that only repeated his point. Unneeded clarifications. Entreaties for reason, for compassion. He skipped the entire third paragraph.

"Brothers and sisters, we are here tonight for the wrong reason. We are here because we have been told it is important to wage war upon those who disagree with us. We have been told that by winning the war Adrash is kept at bay, yet we have no proof of this. We gain the advantage over our enemies for a time and then lose it. The Adrashi do likewise. Despite the changes in fortune, Adrash still threatens us with destruction. Mankind is still held captive."

He lifted his hand, but stopped before rubbing his eyes. The smell of blood had alerted him. He became aware of a noise—the buzzing of a beehive, water cascading over rocks—and wondered if the sound arose within his own mind.

"While children are trained to kill, trained to hate, the white god waits. He waits for proof that mankind is worthy of destruction. How, I ask you, is our war supposed to convince him? How is it supposed to hurt him? I look around and it is clear that we are only hurting ourselves."

Pausing, he squinted to make out the blurred lines.

The Followers of Man need to stand . . .
Join with our Adrashi cousins . . .

He had written more—more entreaties and encouragements, words meant to ease the impact of his words. An open hand instead of a fist. Nonetheless, he let the speech fall between his fingers. He would not talk to his brothers and sisters as if they were children, or draw their conclusions for them.

The words that came next had not been written. They had been carved into the soft tissue of his brain over the course of the last three months. They had lain in wait for this moment.

"Our fellow man is not the enemy. Adrash is the enemy."

He looked up. What he had only half-heard before was the sound of one hundred and fifty thousand people in an uproar. The stands heaved like the surface of the ocean. Items arced through the air, littering the arena floor. An arrow fell just short of the platform. Magefire ignited from a thousand staffs, forming constellations in the tiers. As Vedas watched, a man fell from the lowest stand. Four stories. He did not get up. It would only be a matter of time before chaos reigned. Soon, more people would not fall from the stands. They would be pushed.

Vedas turned to Berun. "I did this?" he whispered.

"Not you alone," the constructed man said. He did not look down. Instead, he pointed to the eastern wall of the coliseum.

It took Vedas a moment to understand what he was seeing. When he did, panic gripped his throat with icy fingers.

The first two spheres of the Needle had risen into view, but they were not at all where they ought to be. They lay side by side, nearly touching. As he watched, a third came above the coliseum wall—a much larger sphere than it should have been.

Adrash had broken the Needle, and it would not take long for people to place blame.

"Time to go," Berun said.

BERUN

A dog lay in the flood gutter outside the boarded-up inn, wheezing into a puddle of its own blood. Its left forelimb was a flattened mess, as though a huge-rimmed wheel had rolled over it. Its chest was caved in and four great claw wounds had spilled the steaming contents of its bowels onto the ground.

The girl in white stooped to look at it. She reached into the animal's chest, a frown of intense concentration on her unlined face.

Sometimes they can be fixed, she said.

The dog twitched. Its chest inflated, accompanied by a high-pitched whine. Broken ribs straightened under its short-haired skin and its intestines slithered back into its belly. Slowly, even its leg started to puff up from the ground. It howled, and then abruptly stopped breathing.

The girl stood. *Sometimes they can't.*

She looked up at the small, two-storey building, which had been barricaded from within, splintered wooden boards nailed across its two broken windows. Whoever was inside had undoubtedly blocked the front and back doors with furniture.

She's in there, the girl said.

Berun saw no reason to doubt her. Not long ago, she had led him to the foot of the hills that rose from the salt flats northwest of the city. She told

261

him of the monastery that lay nestled in the valley between them, where Vedas now lay in recovery. She touched his leg, infusing him with energy as though he had lain in the sun for hours. Then she had led him back through the chaotic streets of Danoor, always a move ahead of the roving bands of rioters and Tomen, to this small inn on a side street that looked like every other side street in the city.

The owner tried to throw her out, she continued, *but she paid him more money to stay. She couldn't walk, and for a long time I couldn't find her. She can keep me away if she really wants to, but I don't think she really knows that. She just does it.*

He did not ask the girl for more—*How do you know her? Why do you care?*— for there could be no doubt any longer. She was Churls's daughter. Unable to speculate upon how she existed and what her nature might be, he nonetheless saw the bloodline clearly. How had he not noticed it before? The bone structure, the eyes, a mole centered between them, the almost invisible smattering of freckles across her nose—they were her mother's, almost exactly.

Of course, Churls had never mentioned a child, but he had seen the woman naked on the morning of the cat attack. Though she moved to hide it while she bathed, he nonetheless saw the scar on her lower belly. Undoubtedly, she had reasons for not volunteering this information.

And he would never ask. Nor would he ask her daughter to tell him the story.

This did not mean he intended to say nothing. He had suppressed his displeasure during their headlong rush to the city, but now he gave it voice. "If you can give me energy and almost heal a dying dog," he asked, "why didn't you treat Vedas?"

The girl appeared next to him. She took his hand, though he felt no pressure at her touch. *I was scared. I don't want him to know about me. Hurry!*

His craggy brows met over his nose. "He was asleep the entire time, girl. I only woke him before I left for the city." His fingers curled into fists. "You had more than enough time."

She stamped her foot, but it made no sound. *I was scared!*

"You'll do it later, then? When you've got your courage back?"

I'll think about it. She disappeared, and reappeared a moment later. *The man inside heard you talking. He's waiting with a weapon behind the bar. A big gun with two barrels. There's a table turned over in front of the door, and a lot of chairs piled behind it.*

Berun's anger did not fade. The girl spoke too flippantly about Vedas's health for his comfort. He briefly considered threatening her, telling her he would not retrieve Churls unless she agreed to make Vedas well, but could not make himself do it. Most likely, Vedas would not die from his wounds. Churls very well might come to harm if she remained in the city any longer.

He positioned himself before the door. "Where is she?" he asked.

Upstairs, third door on the left. She's asleep and probably won't wake up soon. She's recovering. The girl stared at her feet. *She made some bad choices and nearly died, but I made her better—mostly better. That was before I helped you find the monastery. I hope she likes what I did. I want her to not be angry at me anymore.*

He could not say why, but these words stilled his remaining anger. He found himself fighting the urge to praise the girl for helping Churls. He wanted to make her smile. She reminded him so much of her mother, damaged in ways beyond his comprehension. Perhaps this was not unusual. Maybe all men were fractured in the same sense, and only he had been blind to it. Still, he thought not. He liked Churls, more than he had ever liked anyone. He liked Vedas. He shared their concerns, though by all rights he should not.

The thought lingered, troubling: He should not? Who was to say what he should and should not do? His father no longer controlled him—how dare his mind act as though it were not his own? He was free to align himself with any person or philosophy he chose.

Resentment moved through him like lightning through sky.

He kicked the door, which splintered down the center but did not otherwise budge. Its edge cleared the frame as his foot struck again. Furniture crashed to the floor inside. Wooden legs snapped as the table fell over. A third kick knocked the door off of its hinges, sent it spinning into the dark interior.

In the silence that followed, he heard the distinct *click* of someone cocking a hammer. He identified the weapon from this sound alone: an alchemical cannon, a handheld weapon capable of hurling an iron ball at great speed.

"Hold it!" he bellowed into the room. "I know you have a cannon. Don't waste your shot on me, it won't do any good. I'm just here for one of your guests. Once I have her, I'll leave, and you can board up again."

A flash of light. The bullet stuck his forehead, rocking him backward. He did not even hear the discharge, so loud was the tone that reverberated throughout his body. He hummed like a struck tuning fork.

Pain. One or two of his spheres had been knocked loose by the blow.

"I've got another coming!" a voice called. "Don't come any further!"

In four heavy bounds Berun had the innkeeper by the collar. He slapped the weapon from the man's hand and lifted him from behind the bar.

The temptation to hurl him into the street nearly overcame Berun, yet he resisted. Hurting a blameless man would not ease his temper. He hungered for a fight. Once he got Churls back to the monastery, he would return to find a contender. Rioters or Tomen, Adrashi or Anadrashi—it would not matter as long as they stood a small chance against him.

"Stay put," he said, blue eyes flaring brightly enough to illuminate the room. "Don't try to stop me. Don't call for help. Don't send anyone else to do these things for you." He put the man down and turned toward the stairs.

On second thought, he turned back.

"The Castan woman is my friend. If you helped her, then you've got my thanks."

‡

On the night of their arrival in Danoor, he had left Churls and Vedas at the door to the brothel. He did not want to intrude while they said goodbye. Hopefully, they would speak plainly and honestly with one another, but he did not think this likely. It had been one way with them for too long, and Vedas could not afford to be distracted now.

After a long day of running, Berun felt on the verge of toppling over in the street. He rounded a corner and sat against a wall next to a refuse pit. He did not drift into dream or lose consciousness. Nonetheless, time progressed without him. Only when he caught himself tracking shadows along the ground did he realize morning had come. Of course, Churls was long gone, and the man who tended bar in the brothel offered no clues as to her whereabouts.

With no leads, Berun made his way to the tournament grounds. He attended the first day of fights, most of which were held in open-aired arenas, little more than shallow bowls dug out of the hard earth. Careful not to be seen, he watched Vedas from a distance. He had no desire to distract the man. Moreover, he did not want Vedas to know that Churls was not in attendance.

He need not have worried. Vedas had eyes only for his opponents. Brothers and sisters clapped him on the back as he made his way from bout to bout, and he stared straight ahead. Now and then a White Suit spat at his feet while he rested for a moment between bouts. He did not appear to notice. He did not even pause to look at the chalked bracket diagrams that had been posted at each arena.

Berun attracted attention from others, however. Men who knew his reputation conversed with him, posed for alchemical image-castings next to him. Surprisingly, as many Adrashi approached as Anadrashi. Only Ulomi avoided him altogether.

"Word has it you came here with the Black Suit, Vedas," a fat Stoli merchant said. "He won't make it through the day, I reckon. There are bigger and faster men than him."

"You've seen him fight?" Berun asked.

The merchant pulled on his mustaches. "Well, no. But I've heard others talk about him."

"Are you a betting man?"

The merchant looked like he had been asked if he breathed air. "Of course! Last year twenty percent of my income came from fight winnings. My wife has been asking for a badlander maid for years, and I was finally able to afford one."

Berun clapped the man's shoulder hard enough to make him wince. "When it comes to the final bout, if I were you I'd bet black. Your wife will thank you."

Ten rounds occurred the first day. Vedas fought eight White Suits and two of his own brethren. He won each handily except for the day's final, which occurred after nightfall in the immense covered arena. At eight feet tall, the huge Tomen from Bolas towered a foot and a half above Vedas, outweighed him by two hundred pounds. His strategy, taking punishment until an opportunity opened for an offensive, was simple but effective. Vedas worked every angle without apparent damage, and was caught twice by bone-crushing punches.

But finally, inevitably, the Tomen made a mistake. He caught Vedas with a powerful left hook and—instead of falling upon his opponent as wisdom dictated—attempted to stomp down on Vedas's head. Vedas caught the foot and toppled the man forward. From a crouch Vedas jumped six feet into the air and landed knee-first on the man's lower back, where the suit material was thinnest.

Spine pulverized, legs jerking uncontrollably, the Tomen did not beg for his life. Nor would it have been granted to him, for the rules were clear. Perhaps he appreciated falling to a brother rather than an enemy.

Vedas straddled the man's shoulders and broke his neck.

Afterward, Berun followed his friend discreetly from the arena to his tent. At its front entrance, Vedas turned to the raucous group of brothers and sisters that had followed him home.

"Get the fuck away from me," he said.

A silver-haired woman stepped forward, hip cocked playfully. "I watch you all day, Vedas Tezul. You need a relax, brother. I can give."

"Yes!" one of the men called. "Go for him!" another said.

Vedas's features twisted. He scratched at the neckline of his suit, as though the material irritated him. Berun had never seen the gesture before.

"I've had a long day," Vedas said. "Longer than yours by far. I want a meal and I want to sleep. If you interrupt either of these things I'll kill you."

Undoubtedly, this was an empty threat, but the woman did not know it. She and her friends sulked off, and Berun remained near the tent's entrance for a time, quietly turning away anyone other than tired fighters—anyone who might keep Vedas from his rest. He then returned to the city and searched unsuccessfully for Churls. When morning came he walked back to the tournament grounds and lay in the sun before the bouts began at noon.

‡

He did not enjoy the second day of fighting. Without adequate time to recover from their recent beatings, even the strongest fighters became sloppy. Men lunged gracelessly for the quick kill, taking chances no competent fighter should. They went into bouts with broken shoulders, arms, and legs. On one occasion, a woman pulled herself into the ring with a shattered pelvis. After eight years of brawling, Berun had never seen anything like it. A tournament was not supposed to be a battlefield where men were broken, but a place where skill reigned.

Pathetic, how much joy the suited spectators took in watching their most proficient fighters gutter out like candle flames. How the orders roared when two men on quivering legs eventually fell into one another, clumsily reaching for the other's throat. Few shined as brightly as Vedas, yet as exhaustion set in everyone resorted to dirty tactics.

Yes—even the best of them. Berun left the arenas when Vedas threw sand in his opponent's eyes in the fourteenth round, and did not come back until the final. He knew Vedas would make it there.

Both of the final fighters accounted well for themselves. They proved calm and deliberate in their strategies, but Berun saw the underlying weakness in the set of their shoulders and the imprecision of their footwork. So far gone with fatigue and injury, neither would have stood a chance against a healthy opponent.

When the end came, it was mercifully quick.

Subsequently, Vedas lacked even the strength to push Grey's body off him. Several brothers hoisted Vedas on their shoulders, and did not listen to him when he demanded to be put down in order to retrieve his speech. The crowd had become violent, and the Black Suits wanted to get their champion to Aresaa.

Berun wondered if they had anticipated the content of Abse's speech. Probably they had—most likely they looked forward to a violent message, an excuse to turn their newfound power against their enemies.

As Berun ran to the Black Suit camp to retrieve the speech, he considered how vastly his opinion of Vedas had shifted over time. Once, the man had seemed self-centered and haughty, shockingly ignorant of the world beyond Golna. Only on rare occasions had he shown potential. Certainly, he had saved Churls's life. As a result, Berun's affection for the man grew.

Ultimately, however, Vedas had only won Berun's respect by choosing to rewrite the speech. This decision changed everything. It proved Vedas cared more about people than faith. If he had not mentioned the speech, or worse yet believed its message wholeheartedly, Berun would have turned his back upon him with little regret upon reaching Danoor.

Aresaa affirmed Vedas's commitment once and for all. He stood before one hundred and fifty thousand people and declared war against God. He spoke nothing of faith, manipulated no myth to support his argument. Had he congratulated the gathered Anadrashi on their good works, told them to continue praying and fighting for the destruction of their enemies, they would have showered him with wealth enough to sustain him for the rest of his life.

Instead, he marked himself for death. He spoke words to spark revolution.

The spheres of Berun's body shivered with pride to hear Vedas's voice echo off the walls of the coliseum, to see the effect it had upon the assembled people. They were already rising from their seats. Some spat angry words, red-faced with indignation. This was not the message they had come to hear.

A growing minority held their fists aloft, shouting words of encouragement. They had waited for this message, even if they had never admitted it aloud.

Nonetheless, these few would not stop the majority from tearing Vedas apart.

And then the broken tip of the Needle rose above the coliseum, sending a wave of dread through the restive crowd. Soon, thousands of Tomen would flow down the hillsides and flood the city, carving its citizens from crown to sacrum with their recurved swords. For a time, even men who had been inspired by the speech would blame Vedas. Looking to the sky, counting the dead, they would say, *You have angered God!*

Berun knew then with absolute certainty that he must carry Vedas to safety. When men regained their courage, he must be alive to inspire them again.

‡

Berun crossed the northwestern border of Danoor, entering the salt flats of Neuaa at a run. At his back large portions of the city burned. Its light sent his shadow into the darkness, toward the hills and their hidden sanctuary. Before him the broken spheres of the Needle spread over the horizon in disarray. In another two hours, the sun would rise and they would be safe.

Churls shuddered in his arms. Her eyes snapped open. "Berun? What are you doing? Where . . ." She moved her shoulders, raised a hand to her face and groaned. "Make the world stop moving. Stop. Stop right now."

"No," he said, and kept running.

"Fine," she said, and threw up all over his chest and herself.

He stopped and let her down. Unable to stand on her own, she leaned against him. He helped her remove her leather halter and shook the clear fluid from it. There had been no food in her stomach. Shivering, she turned and pressed her body against his.

"You're warm," she said. "I never noticed that before."

He smiled. "You're probably the first to notice it."

"Do you have my pack?"

"Yes." He removed it and helped her get a heavier shirt on.

The edges of her wet halter gripped between two fingers, he lifted her again and resumed running. She curled in his arms and closed her eyes, though he knew she did not sleep. Every now and then she raised her head to stare forward, and he wondered what she expected to see. The salt flats extended for miles in all directions, and the hills where Vedas rested could not yet be seen. She did not comment on the Needle's new arrangement.

"How did you find me?" she asked when they were but a handful of miles from their destination.

"The map returned to me for a while," he lied. "You and Vedas both appeared on it."

She peered up at him, clearly skeptical. "Right."

As he began ascending the ancient switchbacked path up the grassy hillside, she asked, "What about Omali? I thought you lost the map when you threw him out of your head. Does this mean he has power over you again?"

He grunted. In truth, he had tried not to think of his father. "No, I don't think so."

He halted atop the rise above the small valley. He knew where to look, and still it was difficult to locate the door of the monastery or its many-slitted windows. The single-room building had been built into the hillside without disturbing the lines of the slope. As a result, it was almost completely hidden from view.

Churls peered over his arms and then slumped back against his chest. Perhaps she had been expecting a fire, or some other sign of the valley's habitation.

"Vedas did it," he said.

She did not move. Did not breathe.

"He won the tournament and gave the speech, Churls. He told his brothers and sisters not to fight the White Suits anymore. He told them to fight Adrash. This was enough to upset people. And then the Needle rose, of course. When the crowd saw it, they blamed him. They would have killed him."

She inhaled sharply. "He's alive, then?"

"Yes, Churls. He's alive. Injured, but alive. He passed out soon after the speech. I carried him from the coliseum to here. He only woke up right before I left."

He paused. He had always known he would tell her, yet he had never found the right expression.

It was too late to worry about such things now.

"Your name was the first word out of his mouth."

The breath came out of her in one long sigh, and he began the descent into the valley.

CHVRLI CASTA JONS

They stood together on the hilltop. Usveet Mesa was a black wall on their right, stretching over the horizon at their backs. The cracked-tile floor of the ancient lake Neuaa lay before them, glowing orange in the fading light of dusk. Directly across the twenty-mile expanse, the city of Danoor still smoldered. Without any breeze to speak of, a hundred thin pillars of black and grey smoke rose straight into the sky, connecting earth and heaven.

"We're stuck here, then?" Berun asked.

Churls nodded. "They're looking for Vedas, and they know you helped him escape. I didn't get wind of it, but someone's probably still looking for me, too. I didn't hole up in that hotel for nothing." She kicked a rock, sent it tumbling down the slope. Visiting the city had not put her in a good mood. "I'm sure the guard doesn't give two shits about me, but the Ulomi White Suits? I bet even in the midst of chaos they're angry about the murder of one of their champions."

Berun grunted, and she wondered what he thought of her, now that he knew what had occurred after they split up the first night. Even then, he did not know everything. She had not told him about stealing the bar's chip money, or how she found another group of White Suits the next morning and got herself in even more trouble. They broke her left femur and cracked her pelvis. They did not rape her, but that was hardly the only way to humiliate a person.

270

And of course, she had not mentioned being healed by Fyra while she slept—this, despite the fact that she suspected the girl had led Berun to the city to find her. She was not ready to discuss her daughter's ghost with anyone.

"Most of the Tomen have retreated into the hills," she said. "Some say they're waiting for Vedas to return, but I don't think that's very likely."

"Why do you say that?" he asked.

She shrugged, and wiped a strand of hair from her eye. "Why would they listen to Vedas? I can't imagine people who love fighting more than Tomen. You think they'll quit killing their enemies and start working with everyone else toward the nearly impossible goal of killing Adrash? That's ridiculous."

His thousand joints whispered as he crossed his arms. "Perhaps they've been waiting for the right message. You didn't hear him, Churls."

I didn't, she thought, and felt the familiar stab of guilt. *I let him down.*

She did not doubt Vedas's message had been powerful, yet it did not change her opinion of Tomen. The rest of the world might rally around a far-fetched dream—perhaps even Nos Ulom would one day see the threat of destruction for what it was and attack Adrash—but Toma would not. She had seen what Fesuy Amendja did to the Castan gladiator. She had made herself look.

"Will Vedas be a leader, Berun? Can you see him rallying Knosi and Stoli mages alike to battle? Sending them into orbit to die? Inspiring farmers and bartenders and fishwives to take up arms against Adrash?"

He turned to regard her. "You could ask him."

She spat. True, she could ask him. Lying within touching distance as he slept most of the previous day away in the monastery, masked and healing from injuries she could not see, she had resolved to do that very thing. She would ask him about everything once he woke.

Yet she had not done it. They had spoken less than a handful of sentences since he rose with morning's first light. Now it was as if a great gulf lay between them. They had become strangers again.

"I don't think he wants that," Berun eventually said. "He doesn't see himself as a leader."

"The good ones rarely do," she replied, surprising herself. She had not meant to say it. It sounded too much like an endorsement. At the same time, her dissatisfaction made little sense. Had she not been the one who challenged his faith in the first place? She had read the original speech, after all, and knew it for what it was.

By all rights, she had more reason than anyone to be happy with his transformation.

But obviously, she reminded herself, *I didn't help him when he asked. I kept my true opinion to myself—and why? Because I feared his reaction. I didn't want to burn a bridge.*

She exhaled loudly. "He would be a good leader, I think."

"Yes," Berun said. "You should tell him."

"He needs to tell himself," she said, thus skirting the issue. "He needs to take responsibility for his words. By leaving the city, he has left a vacuum someone will soon fill. I was in the city for less than two hours, and in that time I heard rumors of half a dozen men acting in Vedas's name. Calling men to them. Forming armies. One in particular—a quarterbreed gladiator, some are claiming—is rallying men in the Old Quarter. He has a wyrm at his command, they say."

Berun angled his face to the sky. "Perhaps this man means to help us."

She laughed. "Whether or not it's his intention, chances are he'll want to keep his power once he's got it. A man who leads others quickly gets used to calling the shots. He rarely likes it when his general comes back, quoting the regulations."

Berun looked back at the city. She chewed her lip and hoped he would say no more. Darkness was nearly upon them. Shivering as the first of night's breezes caressed her, she thought how awful it was that she did not want to be outside or inside. She did not want to be in Knos Min at all. To be home, where everything smelled of mildew and salt, where she did not have to always think of Vedas!

"Is your father still alive?" Berun asked.

"I don't know," she lied—an automatic response. Her mother had never allowed her to speak of the man, though when she was small he stopped by every now and then. He wanted to see her, but only when he drank. She had always imagined he felt remorse for leaving her, somewhere deep down where his sober mind could not find it. Yes, she knew where he lived, and a few other things about him. He probably would not recognize her if they passed one another on the street, but she would know if he died. "Why do you ask?"

"I wonder what it would be like to know for certain that Omali is dead. I fear my father will return. I fear . . ." He rocked from foot to foot, as though the ground were burning underneath him. "I fear father is the wrong word, but I'm used to it. I'm not a man."

She wrapped her arms around herself. "Is that a bad thing?"

He nodded. "It is if you want to understand yourself. You have examples everywhere. There's a person. There's a person. Where do I look? I can only look inside. There are times when I feel anger building within me, violence I don't think I can control. I wonder if it's me or that bit of my father that I'll never lose. If it's not me, then I have no purpose of my own. It would mean that I am now, and always will be, someone's puppet."

All of a sudden he stopped moving. His eyes dimmed in a way she had never seen. She reached out automatically, afraid he would fade and never reawaken.

"Are you my friend?" he asked.

"Yes," she said truthfully. "Whether or not you're a puppet."

‡

Bars of moonlight glided slowly around the interior of the monastery. For the better part of an hour, she watched one move slowly over her foot. She observed another crawl across the rough-hewn face of Adrash carved into the middle of the stone floor. No light touched Vedas where he lay on the other side of the room, but she watched two bars come within inches of his outstretched left hand.

It was perfectly comfortable in the small oval room, neither stuffy nor drafty. The temperature was just right. Shallow depressions spaced regularly along the wall fit a body well, smoothed as they had been by the backs of sleeping monks. The stone held the warmth of the day, or perhaps the memory of the generations that had rested upon it.

She could not sleep. It took all of her attention to keep the thoughts circling around the inside of her skull—and she knew they must keep moving, otherwise something out of the whirlwind might grab her, latch on, and open itself for examination.

Only, one would not be corralled. A white spark moved against the flow, shouldering its way through the other thoughts, demanding attention. Churls beat it back, sent it tumbling into the maelstrom.

But it returned, again and again.

Fyra.

Without a voice, the girl called to her mother. Churls felt it in her bones, the near-physical pull of her daughter's need. She knew the feeling well, despite years trying to forget it. She remembered returning home from whatever campaign in whichever province, picking up Fyra from her grandmother's. She remembered how she and the girl occupied Churls's small seaside house, little more than strangers. The way Fyra hid behind furniture, staring with wide eyes as though she thought her mother was some sort of monster.

All the while Churls had known, had felt as solidly as a punch to the gut, the intense ache of a child who wants something she has never known.

Because Churls had wanted it too, long ago.

Cursing Berun for putting the thought of family in her mind, she finally gave up, resigning herself to the meeting. She stood, briefly considering whether or not to buckle on her sword. It seemed pointless now. If the girl could heal a broken leg and a cracked pelvis, not to mention a hundred small bruises, she could surely take care of anything that chose to attack Churls from out of the night.

Vedas did not stir as she left. She located Berun atop the hill, keeping watch, motionless as a statue, and kept her eyes upon him as she walked quietly beside the long, thin pond that stretched like a scar down the center of the valley. The water narrowed to a point at the valley's northern end, inserting itself into a crevice, a twisted crack in the hills wide enough for a single person to walk. She felt drawn to enter here, and did not fight the urge.

A small stream of cold water flowed under her boots as she walked forward, and it occurred to her how odd this was. The verdant hills housing the valley rose from ground that saw rain less than a handful of times every year. Koosas, the only river within a hundred miles, had been redirected into Danoor many eons ago, sucking the surrounding earth of moisture.

Where did the valley's water come from?

As if in answer, she followed a turn and came to the crevice's end. She stepped out of the earthy shelter of the hills onto the baked crust of the salt flats. Suddenly, it was cold, dry enough to shrivel her lips against her teeth. She looked back and saw the juncture where the flats stopped and the hill territory began. It was a perfectly smooth line, as if the two regions had never been joined. She stepped back onto the black soil and stone, crouched, and put her hand to the earth. It was moist. She took another couple steps back and did the same. Between two rocks a small trickle of water ran. Cold, almost sweet on her tongue. Not a trace of salt.

Somehow she knew it would be as cold during the heat of summer as it was now.

Mama, Fyra called. *I can't go in there.*

Churls sighed and walked back. Fyra stood on the salt flats, the tips of her slippered toes at the dividing line. Churls leaned against the crevice wall and raised her eyebrows.

"Why is that?"

There are some places the dead can't go. Too much magic keeps us out. She lifted her heel and grimaced, as if she were pushing at the boundary with the tip of her foot. *I don't like being kept out.*

"Then how did you know about the monastery? How did you lead Berun here?"

A grin. *I knew you'd figure it out. You're so smart, Mama. I heard about this place from a dead man named Ulest, and then I told Berun how to find it. He was so tired from running, and I helped him with that, too. I made it so he won't be so tired all the time.*

Churls digested this. The act seemed markedly more impressive than healing a person, but perhaps it was just a matter of her own ignorance. Still, Fyra's knowledge was undeniably growing—and with it, presumably, her power. If the girl became angry, all the magic in the world might not be able to hold her back.

"Does he know who you are?" she asked.

Fyra shrugged. *Maybe. He's not as smart as you. He's like a little boy.* She looked up until Churls met her stare. *You don't want him to tell Vedas about me, but I don't think he will. He hasn't even told you about me, and he tells you everything. I think I'm his one secret. Everybody's got at least one—except Vedas, maybe. He can't keep a secret. You've got lots, though. Isn't it funny, how everybody shares except you?*

A muscle jumped in Churls's jaw. "Is this why you wanted to talk, to tell me I don't share?"

Yes. But there's more. I want to help. Some of the others do, too.

"Others?" Gooseflesh rose on Churls's arms and neck. "You mean the dead."

I only said some. Fyra shook her head sadly. *Some of them are angry about Vedas's speech, but most of them don't care. They say it doesn't matter what happens to the living now. They tell me to shut up. But the ones who still have people they care about don't think like that. They don't want to see the world destroyed. It's good to have a home, even if you leave someday and never come back.*

"You would fight Adrash? What can you do?"

Fyra managed to look insulted. *We can make people stronger, like I did for you and Berun. We can see inside anything and make it better. I'm good at it. I can show others.*

"Won't Adrash see? What if that's the thing that sets him off?"

That's why some people tell me to shut up. They think I'll attract too much attention and get everybody in trouble. Fyra curled her lip. *They're cowards. What can Adrash do to us? He never even noticed us. And we'll do it in secret. We'll make everybody stronger, but we won't make it a show. Still, we can't do anything if you won't let us.*

Churls almost laughed, but the horror of this statement stopped her cold. It all depended on her say-so? A war against Adrash, the awakening of an army of the dead, up to her alone? She could not make that decision now. She might never be able to make that decision.

She struggled to form an adequate response. She did not want Fyra to misinterpret her intentions. To her surprise, she also found she did not want to hurt her daughter's feelings—or close off the possibility of help entirely.

"I'm not even sure I want to fight, Fyra. I'm not sure I believe in this war. Give me some time to think."

You're lying. Fyra's expression conveyed what she thought of liars. *You'll follow Vedas wherever he goes because you love him.*

Churls did not bother to deny this. Love did not solve the problem. It never had.

"I can't tell the dead what to do, Fyra. You'll have to decide for yourselves."

You have to do it. The others aren't special like me. They won't break the rules like I do. They want a living person to tell them. They picked you. You just have to talk to Vedas first. He will help you. Promise me you'll talk to him, and don't lie to me like you did before.

Too tired to argue anymore, Churls nodded. She would not pretend there was any other way. Events had proceeded far beyond the realm of her understanding. Vedas needed to know. Not because he possessed any more intelligence or knowledge than she, but because she needed someone to share the burden with her.

"Is that all?" she asked.

One more thing. Fyra held out her hand.

Churls took it. It was no more substantial than air, of course, but she could no longer claim to feel nothing at Fyra's touch. Warmth flowed upward from her wrist, suffusing her body like smoke filling a room.

She stepped onto the flats, and the wind did not bite or suck the moisture from her skin.

I want you to look at the stars with me, Fyra said.

They lay on the parched earth, connected at the hands.

Tell me about her. The way you did when I was little.

Churls recalled with perfect clarity. She had buried the memories, but had never truly forgotten. On clear summer nights, sometimes she and Fyra had slept on the roof of Churls's house. Listening to the sound of waves crashing against the rocks below, she made up stories for her daughter's amusement—stories of gods and goddesses waging war across the void, giant ships sailing the oceans of other worlds, and kingdoms spreading their fingers toward the ends of creation.

Now and then, she told the story of a little girl who jumped from star to star, trying to find her way home. Aryf. It took Fyra years to realize the girl's name was her own spelled backward.

Do you remember, Mama? Fyra asked.

"Yes," Churls answered. "Yes, sweetie, I do."

She blinked, and the tears spilled over. She had not expected them to come, but they came nonetheless.

‡

Vedas stood in the center of the room, staring down at the graven image of Adrash. He had removed his hood, and held his left fist at the base of his neck. Slowly, he inserted a finger between suit and skin and tugged, stretching the elder-cloth ever so slightly. He did not look up when she walked in, though he could not have failed to see her.

Exhaustion loosened her tongue. "How long has it been, Vedas?"

He opened his mouth, took a deep breath and exhaled before speaking. "Twenty years. More than half my life." His eyes roved around the room, landing everywhere but on her before returning to the floor. "It's odd, but I never used to think of it as odd. I haven't felt sun or water on my skin for two decades. I haven't touched anything or anyone in that time."

This was an exaggeration, Churls thought—surely. Someone, an instructor or a friend, had run their naked fingers through his hair or patted his cheek, offering comfort. Someone had kissed him, an innocent overture between adolescents. He had not abstained from sex completely. He had taken lovers before suffering whatever wound crippled him.

She would be a fool to take his words literally, yet the images failed to resolve in her mind. She could not imagine him receiving or giving affection to anyone.

The man she had grown to love did not dissolve where he stood. He was still the same man. Rather, she realized how greatly her desire blinded her to the reality Fyra had known all along: Vedas spoke the truth. He had not touched another soul in twenty years. He had kept the world at bay with a thin fabric shield.

And yet, surely the suit was inconsequential. With or without it, he would not know how to comfort a crying child or hold the hand of a sick friend. He did not know how to kiss or make love.

Churls considered this, and her desire remained.

"I want to touch you," she said.

He did not move except to tighten his fist around the fabric at his neck.

Heart pounding at her foolishness, she took two steps toward him. The room was not large. If she took six or seven more steps, she would be standing before him.

"I want to touch you, Vedas. Will you let me?"

Slowly, he unclenched his fist and spread the open hand upon his chest. He still did not look at her, and when he spoke he did so clearly, forming each word carefully, as though he did not want her to misunderstand.

"I have pictured touching you, Churls. I have pictured taking off my suit and making love to you, but you should know that I cannot do it all at once. It won't . . ." He shook his head. "It will not be like it is in my head."

She smiled and took another two steps. "I know that, Vedas."

He swallowed, and ventured a glance at her face. She noticed for the first time how deep the wrinkles around his eyes had become, how sharp his cheekbones. His lips trembled in the pauses between sentences.

"It is not just my inexperience that makes this difficult. It is the fear of changing into someone I do not know. Perhaps I have already gone too far by disobeying Abse. Maybe I am no longer a Black Suit already. If I love someone outside the order, reason says that I cannot remain in the order. If I choose to do this now, I will be a man without a home."

His eyes found hers and finally lingered. His hand strayed near the collar of his suit again.

"Churls. You have to understand this above all else. There is no return from this decision."

"No return," she agreed, crossing the space between them. "I understand that."

EPILOGUE

The battle with the outbound mage had left Adrash physically drained, a state he had not experienced in many millennia. He needed time to recover before gathering the spheres.

Secrets had been stolen from his mind. A new god had announced himself. The corners of Adrash's mouth curved upward. He closed his eyes, but despite his exhaustion could not still his thoughts. A renewed lucidity had come upon him, as though the encounter with Pol Tanz et Som had lifted a veil from before his eyes. He floated above the surface of the moon and let his mind drift through thirty thousand years of being Jeroun's god, alighting here and there on an event, examining it for its potential. Memories that had become indistinct over the centuries now opened for him, unfolding in his mind with such dizzying, ecstatic clarity that ghosts breathed, extinct species lumbered across plains, and crumbled cities rose from the ocean.

He longed for the heat and chaos of battle, and then he longed for sensual delights. He caused his vision to become a combination of both, displacing events so that they flowed seamlessly into one another. The culminating moments of the Battle of Keyowas led to the orgy he had hosted in Knos Min to celebrate his adopted son Iha's coronation. The feast of Nwd'al'Kalah, where he had eaten his first tinpan fruit and battled his first hybrid wyrm, resulted in the destruction of The Seven Cities of Omandeias. With a memory as vast as Adrash's, the permutations were nearly endless. He added flourishes, changing faces, identities, and geographies on a whim. He acted out the parts of hero and villain, or simply observed as events transpired, powerless as any man.

Regardless of these alterations, the exercise soon became mundane, for he could not stop the cycle of history from repeating itself. The names and places changed, but the patterns stayed the same. The rekindling of his memory served only to drive this truth home.

After all, how many variations could be expressed in arrogance, deception, and greed? How many in faith and honor?

He alone could answer these questions, for he had been with mankind from its origin—had witnessed every one of its faltering steps.

In the beginning, he had found the divine armor. Assisted by its strength, he cracked men from their hundred iron eggs. He taught them the use of tools, and then watched from afar as they huddled miserably around cooking fires. Mankind was naive then, unprepared to inherit the earth. Too used to the comforts of their eggs, the reality of survival nearly destroyed them. They adapted, of course, through hardship. They became strong, became worthy of his notice. Yet with time, their concerns shifted from the preservation of their species to the deception of a business partner, the conquest of a neighbor's husband or wife. They returned, ever and ever, to the source of ease, to laziness and avarice and self-destruction. Though all traces of their true nature and history were soon lost, they could not resist becoming what they had once been.

The world was theirs. It always had been.

Men were not evil, Adrash knew. They were simply lazy and opportunistic, courageous and virtuous in very infrequent bursts.

He searched now for those moments of courage and virtue. He delved into his mind and summoned the best of humanity, reliving the moments wherein men had proved their worth. During the siege of Shantnahs, he watched Neaas Wetheron rouse her army to defend the jeweled city. Her voice carried like a bell from atop the mile-high tower she called home. He felt himself swayed by her speech, as indeed he had been twenty-two thousand years ago—but this time he switched sides to turn the battle in Wetheron's favor.

During the destruction of Grass, he watched the valiant efforts of its people to find shelter from the volcano's toxic surge of gas and rock. Not just for themselves, but for their neighbors. As he recalled, he had let the city burn, for its people had turned their backs on him. Now, he placed himself in the path of destruction, turned it away like a man brushing lint from his sleeve. No, it did not satisfy even a little to do this, for the past could not be changed. Nonetheless, he did it, as if to affirm that he would not make the same decision a second time.

Other memories he did not change. Sometimes failure was in itself a form of victory: the act of having tried. He conjured up the original city of Zanzi—a shining ornament of suspended walkways and crystal towers built by magicians only seven generations removed from their egg—and tried to save it once more. His power had just been a small thing in that primordial time, when vast herds of fire dragons still roamed the continent. While he fought one of their number, the people of the Golden City ventured from cellars into the streets, dragging bodies to safety even as the many-legged beast crushed their glass homes and dripped acid onto their bodies. Adrash watched them die. He tried to pull hope from their futile acts of charity.

It was insufficient, and his brittle hope in mankind faltered yet again.

At times his faith had failed completely, and on these occasions he had dredged material from the far side of the moon to build another sphere, another weapon. Try as he might, he could not forgive the men of Jeroun their pettiness, their squabbling, their ridiculous and violent worship.

But he could not condemn them completely. Not yet. There were signs. Still, small thoughts that needed pushing, encouraging. Selfless acts gone unnoticed by the rest of the world.

Sometimes, Adrash imagined he heard the whisper of a familiar voice.

The call of a soul that resounded even in the void. A threat and a temptation.

A catalyst.

‡

With the renewed clarity of recollection the battle with the outbound mage had gifted to him, understanding dawned upon Adrash.

He had been a fool to doubt the existence of prophets. He had imagined nothing: No seers had been conjured from the dust of his mind in order to forestall another cataclysm. True, time and isolation had dulled his ears to the sound of the singular voice in which such men and women spoke, but he should not have allowed himself to believe it never existed.

The memory of Eloue, the first to assume the voice of a prophet, bloomed within him.

He had been young, a god for a mere two thousand years. Haughty yet capricious in his hungers, he neither sought nor turned away those who would worship him. He visited Knoori and the thousand island-homes of man that rose out of the shallow sea, besting creatures and performing miracles. Reveling in his power and the thrill of physical conquest, the blood hot in his veins, he found love easily.

After spending a bracingly crisp autumn on Herouca, the lush, sugar maple-covered island that would in time become known as Little Osa, he chartered a yacht cruise around Doec Lake to celebrate the arrival of winter. He discovered the woman alone, leaning far out over the deck railing, staring into the deep luminescent waters, half of which were covered by a shelf of rock—all that remained of an immense cave system the elders had carved into the side of Mount Lepsa, king of the Coriel Range.

He admired her beauty in shadow and light. Soon thereafter he became her lover.

Her name meant "white stone" in a language only Adrash remembered. She lived in the Old Quarter of Tiama, and made her living by way of deception. While a small portion of enchanted blood moved within her, allowing her to read thoughts as easily as normal men read books, healthy minds bored her. Thus, she rarely told her customers the things they needed to hear. Instead, she used her unique skill to obtain power, make money, and amuse herself. She seduced men with her lies and charm, and then took delight in breaking them.

Her eyes were polished amethysts. She rarely smiled. Hairless skin the color of peach-flesh stretched over the muscle and fat of her body in flawless curves. It felt to his lips like orchid petals. When she became excited, a fine sheen of liquid formed on her lower stomach and thighs, and dripped from her womanhood. It tasted to him sometimes like cantaloupe, sometimes like coconut. Though her beauty was clearly a condition brought about through magic, Adrash could not stop himself from worshipping at her altar.

A most alluring pretense arose between them, eventually bound them together. She knew who he was, but treated him as she would any suitor, and he lavished upon her all the appearances of love. They traded lies, and by doing so found what they both needed. She insisted she did not enjoy sex, but he thought otherwise. She told him she coveted his power, and he knew she did not always lie.

"How did you acquire this?" she asked as they lay tangled together on the bower above the Gason-a'Loran street market. Her fingertips brushed across the line on his left wrist where the white material of his armor met black skin. Every now and then he felt her nails, as if she were trying to get under a seam, though she knew full well no seam existed. Many had tried to take the armor—which he frequently wore as a glove when not fully sheathed within it—from him, only to discover it could not be removed by any means.

He groaned, but not without pleasure. He had told her the story on many occasions. It went the same way each time, for the lie was old and worn. The enemies of which he spoke had never existed, nor had the cities and countries he named.

"That evening on Pergossas I led the men in a successful charge, halting the chimera advance line. We lost three hundred men and, weak from blood loss and starving, likely would have lost a great deal more if the enemy had not retreated to the hills outside Nusse, leaving their dead and dying for us. Chimera meat is dreadful, but it is better than dying from hunger."

Playfully, he dug his fingertips into her taut belly. She did not move an inch, and he smiled into her shoulder. Every time they moved even slightly, flowers rustled beneath them. Though winter's chill had not yet left the earth, his ebon skin absorbed the sun's heat and radiated it like a furnace, keeping her warm.

"After dinner, the healthy men went scavenging for weapons and loot. I searched further afield than the rest. I remember that our fires seemed very far away. The moon loomed above me, casting everything in ghostlight. I suppose I was afraid. Then, I saw a flash of white. It stood out because the chimera fought in dark grey armor and blackened their swords. Seeing the glove up close, it felt as if it sang to me out of the night, and I had the inexplicable urge to possess it. It came away easily and pooled in my hand like cool liquid."

"It did not scare you?" she asked on cue, voice low and serious.

"Yes, but I knew immediately that I was meant to possess the glove. I could feel it clinging to the palm of my hand, conforming to me. I took it to my tent and with great reluctance spread it on my desk to examine it. You see, I did not want to let it go. It had only three fingers, a fact I had not considered when I took it from the chimera. Nonetheless, I could not resist the urge to slip it on." He held the gloved hand before her face and split four fingers so that they looked like two. "I cannot properly describe the feeling to you. Have you ever fallen a great distance?"

She shook her head.

"Have you ever killed someone? Or felt close to death? It was very like these things combined."

She shook her head again, and he sighed contentedly. The script still amused him, and not all of it was a lie. The sensations he described were accurate.

"It is just as I thought. It will have to suffice to say that I had never felt such fear and exhilaration. Nor had I ever approached it. I blinked and the glove fit my hand perfectly. I could tell it wanted to be more than just a glove. It wanted my whole body. Some time still passed before I allowed it to cover me completely, to become armor, and this was an experience of another degree of magnitude. Only experience would prove that I could wear it without losing myself to the sensations."

"What about your men? The war with the chimera?"

"As I recall, after finding the glove I abandoned my men on Pergossas. I requisitioned a small keelboat and sailed into the Eenos Ocean."

"Why?" she asked, tearing petals from an unopened rosebud with her fingernails.

He shrugged, chest pulling against her back. "I wanted to be alone."

"What happened to your men?"

He paused. Her question should have been, *Where did you go?* She rarely deviated from the script.

He dismissed it as nothing. "I suppose they died," he answered. "Our brief victory meant little. The chimera had been expecting replacements from Belloja for some time. We had no chance. Why do you ask?"

"You had the glove. With it you could have helped the men."

"No." He disengaged his armored hand from hers and lay back on the bed of flowers. He knew she had no real interest in whether he helped or hurt men. "I did not yet know how to use it, or indeed if it could be turned to violence."

She rose and stared down over her shoulder. She did not look directly at him, instead focusing on a distant point in her mind. "But you," she said. "You know how to use the glove now. There is no limit to your power."

"Hardly," he said. "It only seems that way to you because you have so little power."

He meant the comment as a joke, but her expression showed he had failed. Her brows came together and her lips set in a straight line. Anger, a common enough emotion for her.

Her temper collapsed suddenly, and her eyes became wet.

This, he had never seen. He wanted to be somewhere else, away from a situation he had so clearly misjudged.

"Eloue. What is it?"

Her eyes found his. "Are you ever going to share it with me?"

"No," he said.

‡

On the surface, it was not an occurrence worthy of note. Many people had expected Adrash to share his power, and were disappointed when he did not. Eloue's desire for power did not disappoint him. Rather, her vulnerability did. He had not expected it, and his response shocked him. He recoiled from her and left Herouca with a feeling uncomfortably close to fear.

He had not felt fear in a long time, indeed.

Her voice lingered in his mind—her touch and smell and taste, but mostly her voice. On regular occasions he woke from deep sleep, sure he had heard her calling to him. He began to suspect more than her vulnerability had driven him away. He examined his memories of her with the perfect recollection of a young god, and in examining heard what a normal man could not hear: Layers of sound, dense and sharp, pulsating like the stars at the limit of his vision. Eloue's true voice was bliss and terror—the twitch of muscles in a man's leg before coitus and the sound of the void freezing his lungs. It both invited and repelled.

No, he had not loved her. He came to realize affection had never drawn them together. No cute lie or routine bound them. Instead, a force beyond reason had compelled Eloue to him, and he to her. After several years away from Herouca, he could not deny this fact any more than he could deny his armor's overwhelming need to be worn. Perhaps, instead of running he should have stayed and bested his fear. Had he turned his back on a great gift, an arcane magic?

More troubling still, he wondered if he had left a great weapon in the hands of an enemy.

He grew tired of thinking about it, tired of being intimidated by the unknown.

When he returned, Eloue was already dead, her home a slag-pile. Powerful magic had been brought to bear by a competitor or jealous suitor. Adrash had no interest in retribution, for her death freed him of his burden of thought. He bestowed his blessings upon the people who worshipped him and moved on. He visited the Royal Courts in Knos Min, from which his descendants, or those who pretended to be his descendants, ruled.

But the whole affair troubled him vaguely, as if something had soured in his stomach. He vowed never to set foot on Herouca again. It was only one island, and being there reminded him of his idiot fancy and miscalculation. He had squandered a possibility.

With effort, he managed to forget Eloue's voice. He traveled his realm and found lovers to replace her—women and men who had never heard of Herouca, some of whom had never heard of Adrash. Far from the epicenter of his influence, on islands unlinked to Knoori, where the men had long ago forgotten the magics needed to cross the ocean, he begat children and raised dynasties. When a place ceased to inspire him, he left.

‡

Four millennia after men spilled forth onto the world's surface, even the most advanced peoples of Jeroun had lost the ability to navigate the shallow sea and defend themselves from its creatures. The islanders disappeared due to disaster and famine, but Knoori's population continued to grow, flourishing under the stern eye of Adrash.

He made Zanzi his home. Situated at the center of what would one day be called the Aroonan Mesa, his villa overlooked the million homes of The Golden City, the largest and most beautiful metropolis in Jeroun's history. From there he traveled the continent, vanquished the last of the fire dragons, brought low the mage-kings who had installed themselves in various locales, and monitored the use and trade of elder corpses.

He reasoned his strength was not so great that another might not rival it. Though they lived in a state of suspension, the elders of the Clouded Continent were powerful enough to keep men from seeing their land, and Adrash from setting foot upon it. If the near-dead could do so much, perhaps a man might one day do more. And if the elders one day woke, who knew what powers they could bring to bear?

Of course, time would prove these fears ungrounded. Over the next two millennia he tested the limits of the divine armor, growing stronger and stronger until even the elder magic could not restrain him. He walked the Clouded Continent, grew to know its slumbering people through their beautiful artifacts. Cities that spun slowly like leaves on water. Crystal windmills half a mile high. A stadium seated for millions with a lake at its center. A field of glass war machines whose angular surfaces glittered in the sun.

Fearing the elders were the source of Eloue's true voice, he took one of their number to a secluded island and allowed the sun to revive it.

They battled like old enemies. The elder's aggression surprised Adrash, as did its expression, which so closely mimicked a man's. Perhaps the creature had sensed Adrash's intentions all along, knew it could not match him, and so spent its final energy on hate. This pride suited the creators of such breathtaking monuments.

Yet for all of its vitriol, the creature was easily overcome.

At no point did Adrash hear anything other than the sound of its breathing. It was not an enchanted being—merely a strong one. The realization was little comfort, for he had come no closer to understanding the nature of Eloue's magic.

And then, three thousand years after her death, he heard the voice again, calling from the bottom of the world.

‡

He came to the largest of the southern islands curious. He remembered cracking an iron egg on its cold, weathered rock surface, sure the men who spilled forth would perish in the harsh land. To find its people not only surviving, but thriving, after five thousand years heartened him. After all, the ocean was no friend to man, nor were its inhabitants. Oft-times, the world itself seemed inimical to man, especially those who lived on the islands. Air currents sent locusts, dry weather, and disease. Volcanoes and earthquakes returned the islands to the sea.

Eighteen-year-old Tsema had never heard of such things. If the people of his land had ever suffered, he did not care. He heard music in his dreams and on the wind, and re-created it. Not for money or fame did he play. He played because it hurt not to.

A creature born of the island's exotic magics, the smooth, long lines of his body revealed a peculiar heritage. Eyes flashed orange to match the short fur covering his whip-thin body. His fine-boned face looked more animal than man depending on the angle. His hands were large and calloused. The seven triple-jointed toes of his feet helped him adjust the innumerable gears and cogs of his musical instrument, a four-storey building of driftwood and stone, thin slabs of transparent crystal and glass. He called this machine The Element. He carried two wrenches curled in his tail, and from his belt swung a collection of lesser-used tools of odd design.

It took one hundred men to haul the creaking instrument at a snail's pace across the stepped rock surface of the island, and another fifteen men to feed them. People claimed the boy's closest attendants lived on his music alone, but any fool could have smelled the mythmaking in this. For all of the magic virtuosity the boy displayed, Tsema was no miracle worker. He had no interest in redemption, yet the people read much in his tales. He became a prophet. Even the island's king listened to his cryptic lyrics with a keen ear.

When Adrash heard the boy's voice for the first time, the world ignited and blackened in the corners of his eyes. Underneath the rich tenor and the clanging cacophony of The Element, the boy's true voice shrieked at a stone-shattering pitch. He was not as strong as Eloue had been, but in time he surely would be. Adrash had become sensitive to the voice after so much reflection.

Other things he had always seen. The auras of most men radiated tones of grey and barely rose from their bodies even when excited, but the boy's flared violet and orange, coruscating in wild arcs from his body when he sang.

Just as with Eloue, Adrash could not fight his attraction.

They lived together in the top floor of The Element, where the boy proved an excellent lover. He clearly did not live only for music, yet he sang often during their lovemaking. The otherworldly timbre of his voice aroused Adrash's libido, focusing his awareness of pleasure as it had never been focused. The boy's confident touch reminded Adrash of Eloue. His body responded as hers had. The armor—which Adrash still wore as a glove—fascinated him, though he knew nothing of its reputation.

"What does it do?" he asked.

"Does it have to do something?"

The boy spread Adrash's armored hand palm down on his thin, furred thigh. "Can't feel where it ends, where skin begins." He turned the hand palm up. "Can see no lines under it. No heart line, no love line. No age line! Man can hide that, powerful doing."

Adrash shook his head and moved his hand up the boy's thigh. The boy had not seen him covered by the armor completely, and Adrash did not intend to show him. "I acquired it in Loreacte," he lied, referring to the half-mythical land he had claimed was his home. "A clothier had it under the counter, and I saw it. He would not let me try it on, but I convinced him.

I knew immediately that I'd made a mistake, but in the end it is harmless. I have even grown to admire it."

"Love it." The boy covered Adrash's hand with his own. "Want one just like it."

The subject came up again and again. Adrash recognized the boy's desire to possess the armor and fed it, though he could not say what compelled him to do so.

He woke one night to find the boy rubbing oil on his wrist, where the armor fused with his skin. It burned slightly, but not enough to have woken him. Instead, he focused on a low sound that came from inside the boy. It reminded him vaguely of the crash of surf on rocks, wind rustling the leaves of a tree. He had never heard it before.

"What are you doing?" he asked.

The boy's head jerked upwards. His eyes were solid yellow-white. A growl began low in his throat, rumbling down through the register, into the depths of the earth below them. Before the command had been given, the armor tickled on Adrash's wrist, began rising up his forearm. He placed his palm upon the boy's chest, tried to push him down, and found that he could not. The boy gripped his forearm in steel fingers, as if trying to stop the armor's advance.

"Want it," the boy said. "Off. Now."

White rose above the boy's fingers, and Adrash felt a surge of strength flow through his limbs. Cold purpose flooded his mind. He took hold of the boy's free arm and threw him from the bed. The furred body crumpled like a stuffed toy as it hit the sharp teeth of the giant gear projecting into their room. Vertebrae snapped audibly as his head ricocheted off the metal.

Adrash stood and regarded the body. For several seconds, it seemed to him that the world was mute, that all sound had been cancelled.

He had listened to the boy's voice for so long he had ceased to hear it.

He vowed never to let this happen again.

‡

He encountered the voice of the prophet many times after Tsema. A thousand years passed between occurrences, two thousand—never more than three. Adrash heard it more clearly each time, but grew no closer to understanding its nature. For twenty millennia, the voice announced itself across the face of Jeroun, inhabiting the bodies of young and old, male and female and elderman. Its avatars were heroes and sometimes villains, but they were never ordinary.

Each attracted and repelled Adrash. As he grew ever more powerful, testing the ultimate capabilities of the divine armor, the fiercer those who spoke with the voice pursued it.

Sleum Edylnara, who wielded the crescent aszhuri blade with a dancer's grace and made love like an animal, tried to decapitate Adrash during one of their practice sessions. Adrash caught the blade in his hand, broke it, and strangled the woman. She did not beg for her life or try to tear Adrash's fingers from her neck. Instead, her eyes had slowly turned to golden fire as her true voice singed the inside of Adrash's skull.

Kengon Asperis Dafes, the Necromancer of Bridgtul, fed Adrash a potion that paralyzed him for several minutes. While Dafes's back was turned, the armor covered Adrash's body and began filtering the poison from his system. Adrash watched as the necromancer attacked with magefire, enchanted blades, and corrosive liquids. He felt nothing, cocooned safely inside the impenetrable white material. When he finally could move, he moved swiftly, crushing Dafes's skull between his palm and a marble autopsy table. The rumbling voice warbled and died, but its echoes resounded in his head for weeks thereafter.

Open Water, Full Chieftain of The Whal, Lord of Spearhandle, pushed an enchanted whalebone dagger through Adrash's left kidney during an orgy the two hosted. By this time, nearly twelve thousand years after Adrash had first heard the voice, the armor had fused with his system to such a degree that he barely felt the wound—the kidney itself healed in the blink of an eye. He twisted, pulling the dagger from Open Water's hands, and with the light from his eyes vaporized the chieftain before his closest allies and lovers. Those gathered fell to the floor and worshipped Adrash.

As time went on, the avatars of the voice ceased to be a challenge. Their acts became ever more aggressive, but depressed Adrash with their predictability. As his own power grew, he forgot his original goal, which had been to understand the voice. Like the elders, it too had proved a weak enemy.

But he wondered if the voice might one day be heard on a grand scale. What if it woke the elders and urged them to take up their glass war machines, if it persuaded mankind to gather its forces in alliance? Perhaps then he might be threatened.

Adrash discovered he desired this. Not entirely. Not yet.

Nonetheless, he could no longer bear to live in the world. With no enemies to fight and little inclination to continue policing mankind, he ascended to heaven. Weariness rooted deep in his bones. The cords linking him to mankind frayed and nearly severed.

He knew an illness had taken hold of him, but felt powerless to stop it.

He built weapons of destruction, and extracted frail promise from the minds of men.

He waited for the voice to return. Surely, it had noticed his absence. He imagined it, waiting in hibernation, gathering its power for a final confrontation. Eventually, it would announce itself. This time, he would leave it alone. Let it come to him.

He waited, and grew impatient. Impatience eventually led to weariness, weariness to forgetfulness.

‡

After three days of resting, reflecting upon the past, Adrash opened his eyes.

The light of realization spilled forth.

The cratered surface of the moon sped by beneath him, bright as sunbleached bone. Adrash smiled within the divine armor's embrace, and turned to regard Jeroun.

Four voices rose in concert from its surface with a clarity that made his bones shiver.

How he had not heard them before was a great mystery. That such souls had been hidden from him seemed nearly impossible, especially considering his first encounter with Pol. Alone, the elderman had moved one of the spheres. The act should have aroused Adrash's curiosity, yet he had written it off as an unusually powerful spell, similar to the one the elderwoman had used to bewitch him. Certainly, the outbound mages had progressed a great deal.

As, apparently, had the voice.

Voices, Adrash corrected himself. Perhaps there had always been more than one, and his ears were simply too unrefined to notice.

Regardless of the number, whatever produced the phenomenon had evolved beyond his capacity to recognize. While he waited for a sign from below—or merely for his indulgence of mankind to end—his enigmatic opponent had altered itself to fool him.

Of course, the strategy had worked. His deafness had left him vulnerable to the elderman's second attack.

Yes, the new god had stolen things from Adrash's mind, had taken them as easily as a man takes a toy from a child. Pol now knew the secret of the Clouded Continent, the location of the nameless valley that contained thousands of elder corpses, and something of the nature of Adrash himself. He knew with sufficient power any man might be a god. Perhaps he had even discovered the other voices, well before Adrash.

Adrash's cock stirred at the memory of the encounter. Such a beautiful creature, Pol Tanz et Som, composed of nothing but muscle and bone and anger. Such a vicious, self-serving mind, the fire of it leaking out of his left eye like smoke from a fumarole, the searing heat of it focusing like a spear point from his right. He would gather power to him and use it, turn good and evil to his own devices. But he was not yet ready, and so his voice roared in frustration from Jeroun's surface. Clearly, his allegiance had shifted. He meant to unseat Adrash.

What he intended beyond this, Adrash did not know.

Turning his attention elsewhere, Adrash closed his eyes again, listening.

The second voice:

Brassy thunder, the ringing of a hundred bells, the rolling of a thousand metal spheres. The sound gained strength slowly, inexorably, like a mountain shuddering into the sea. Adrash plucked memories from Berun's labyrinthine mind, marveling at the course of the creature's development. Solidification had changed the constructed man, making him frailer physically but stronger mentally. How handily he had defeated the mage Omali! Adrash could not piece together how this was accomplished, which only added to his fascination. He felt an odd kinship with Berun, whose mind could be cold and uncaring to so many, warm and sympathetic to but a few. A mass of contradictions, not unlike Adrash himself.

One thing was clear: Berun would stand behind his friends.

The third and fourth:

Churli Casta Jons. Vedas Tezul. Looking upon them now, he experienced the tug of shared pleasure, the slip and tangle of two souls entwining. He let the harmony of their voices fill him until he felt on the edge of some great precipice, as if his own personality might be overcome, and then backed away. He did not revel in the sensations of their lovemaking, though he easily could have. To do so seemed almost sacrilegious.

Despite their physical weakness in comparison to Pol and Berun, Adrash sensed these two posed the biggest threat to his existence.

For all the secrets that lay buried within her, Churls saw the world with startling clarity. She considered Adrashi and Anadrashi to be the same useless creature. Experience had shown her that worship blinded men to the truths: *Adrash is no redeemer. Adrash will destroy the world.* As she thought of the faithful, her true voice rang like steel against steel. She would not flinch from the war her lover proposed. She would look straight ahead, because only ghosts stood at her back.

Vedas, on the other hand, had only recently found his conviction. He had not yet discovered the strength of his own will. He loved Churls. Oh, yes, he loved her, as strongly as he hated the hand that had molded the world—a place where young boys were defiled and then turned into killers. Even as he and Churls embraced, he thought of killing. He rehearsed the words he would say to the people of Jeroun. Words meant to incite deicide.

The man possessed abilities he had never dreamed of. He would become a leader of men, inspiring them to take up arms against Adrash. His words would thunder across the skies, waking the elders from their slumber.

As a result, there would be a war.

Adrash considered the prospect of his own death.

He knew he could extinguish this possibility, here and now. He could send his weapons down. It was what the elders wanted, certainly. They longed to see dust covering the earth, cleansing the world of man, assured that they alone would wake from the cataclysm. Even the Baleshuuk could not survive without the sun.

The elders' entreaty was faint but never-ending, and Adrash had long ago pushed it out of his mind. He knew he could not choose the long-limbed folk over his own people—at least not yet. If he chose to blanket the world in dust, it would not be due to any outside pressure. It would not be his blessing upon the elders, but a result of mankind's choices.

How much time would it take for the war to reach him? It might be a great while before the four voices rallied enough support to truly challenge him.

Months, maybe years of anticipation.

He wondered if he could wait that long.

SHOWER

OF STONES

PROLOGUE

THE 4TH OF EVERPLAIN WATCH
SENNEN, BOWL OF HEAVEN, NATION OF ZOROL

They labored on a vast concave plain, under the bluegreen sun. Side by side, the four of them: she, her mate, and the two men they both knew but had never met before the previous day. They pulled sweetroot from the earth in silence, depositing their vegetables in the long furrows that ran poleward to poleward for nearly forty leagues. It was repetitive, backbreaking work, but they were content.

How did she know her companions were content?

She sensed it, just as she sensed the coming and going of her own thoughts.

She and her mate never looked up from their work. Now and then, she would delay for a second after picking her sweetroot, or he would finish his task a moment too quickly, and use the opportunity to touch one another's arm or leg. She would smile, and know that he too smiled.

Newly arrived and unused to the plain, the newly arrived men would occasionally rise, stretch the kinks from their backs, and turn in slow circles, peering with shaded eyes at the world around them—for no practical reason, surely. The sun arced overhead so slowly as to be still in the sky. The breeze came consistently out of the bottom pole, bending the sea of golden grass with nary a ripple.

The only objects surrounding the plain were the tall, thin wind-gatherers clustered to the right-up-poleward, a series of low purple hills to the left-bottom-poleward, and next to the hills the bleached skeleton of the abandoned tensii warren.

The wind-gatherers were simply wind-gatherers. Mindless, immobile beasts stretched to the task of collecting energy, they could be found anywhere. The hills, too, were not special. They folded upon themselves without so much as a rocky outcrop, only subtly changing color as the sunlight crawled in glacial inches over them.

The warren, she supposed, was a unique thing, looming over the near horizon like a massive wooden cage, like the trap for some immense crustacean. The world possessed only five such structures, monuments to an unknown race. People had once devoted their lives to its study.

But it too never changed. It never had in anyone's memory.

In her younger days, she had done as all local adolescents did, and climbed the warren's latticed interior, ascending broad bone avenues to its three-thousand-foot height. Like everyone else who completed the trip, she was disappointed to find the structure just as it appeared to be—a massive skeleton, picked clean of any sign of its ancient inhabitants. It was beautiful in its way, but no more beautiful than any natural feature. She had seen the ocean from its summit, and this had occupied her attention far more fixedly.

Still, she could not begrudge her new companions their interest. Prior to moving back home in her thirtieth month, many places had compelled her. The world had much appeal. As one grew older, however, one's focus shifted. She had become content to harvest and recall the violence of her youths—to listen to the breeze, take joy in the touch of her mate, and anticipate the arrival of two strangers she had known in a thousand lands, a hundred bodies.

‡

The day grew no hotter or colder, the shadows of their bodies no shorter or longer. The protracted cycle of the day aroused no urges (here, women and men ate and slept whenever they felt the need), yet hunger hit the four of them at the same moment. This was no coincidence. She and her mate stood as one, their new companions following a heartbeat later. They stretched, eliciting a few pops from their spines, and once more shaded their eyes to peer around the circumference of the shallow depression.

She winked at her mate and spoke his name, the fondness clear in her voice. He grinned, pulled her off her feet as though she weighed nothing, squeezing her tightly to his massive chest as she wrapped her pale, corded arms around his thick neck and breathed in his brassy scent. Over his shoulder, she grinned at the two new men, whose faces she had known for generations upon generations.

A slight smile pulled at the corners of the lighter-skinned one's mouth, but he said nothing.

The darker one simply stared.

They sat in the dirt and grass. From their packs came salted beef, vinegared seaweed, and raw slices of the ever-present sweetroot. It was delicious, as was nearly all food after working in the outdoors, under the sun. Under *any* sun, really.

Finished but still hungry, the darker of the two strangers lifted one of the sweetroots he had picked. He fished a knife from the pocket of his rough cotton pants and deftly sliced the vegetable into four sections. They shared it in companionable silence.

She examined the men she knew but had not yet spoken with. Both looked much like she remembered, much as they had for uncounted ages.

The shorter and heavier of the two, the quicker to smile and laugh, had skin the color of creamed chicory broth. He stood like a man forever bent forward into the wind, with meaty shoulders hunched and chin tucked into his collar. She had never known him as a child—no, not in all the lives they had shared—but she imagined him muddling through, fighting and winning battles he had never intended to fight, simply wanting peace, a place to belong.

The second man . . . she could not help thinking of him as father to the first, though she knew this was wrong. Tall, black skinned and muscular, he held himself with a straight spine, broad shoulders thrown back, chin high. A position of habit, not true disposition. As with the other, she had only known him as a grown man. Regardless, she knew that as a child he had lorded over his peers, only with the onset of adulthood learning how not to be a tyrant, to be strong without recourse to coercion.

She liked the first immediately. In time, she knew she would grow to love the second. Just as she always had. She regretted that they chose to be alone for so much of their existence. She and her mate could stand to be apart for such a short period: they found one another readily, falling into one another as fate dictated. Even through the occasionally cloudy haze of her memory, during moments when she could not seem to differentiate one life from the next, their longing for each other was clear.

But these two?

They only came together where the need presented itself, typically in an engagement of war, of revolution. When the violence exhausted itself, when death became too much to bear, they came to her, to where she and her mate had built a small life. They carried their pain with them, bearing it on their own, remaining silent until there was something to say.

‡

What the dark one said first never varied.

"Do you recall the conditions of my death?" he asked, white eyebrows nearly meeting over his nose. He furrowed his brow. His lips quivered as he sought words for the idea he knew to be true.

"My *first* death," he clarified.

She tipped her head back and smiled into the sun.

"You're asking me to remember ancient history. But yes. I could never forget. I'd only just died, myself." She laid her hand upon her mate's knee. "You still lived, dear—remember? And yet you'd already lived such a short, eventful life."

Her mate nodded his massive head, heavy features serene.

She returned her gaze to the black-skinned man. She nodded to him, and then to the man she could not help but think of as his son. Her smile waned slightly.

"And you? Well, you'd both been alive for far too long. You were dangerous to yourselves and a greater danger to our world, threatening the existence of an entire continent of people." She clucked her tongue and shook her head. "These are simple things to say, of course, as if the millennia had turned you from men into monsters. This is nowhere near the truth."

The black-skinned man frowned. "What is the truth, then?"

She sighed. The wrinkles at the corners of her eyes deepened.

"Normal men can indeed be turned into monsters—ordinary, unimaginative monsters. Even with their lives preserved for eons, they are of one design. But you, you were never normal men. There was something of the monster in you from the beginning, an awful potential. And your children, your siblings, they too . . ."

She shrugged. Her gaze centered on an indefinite space between the two men. For a span of seconds or hours, she was not among her companions. Her name changed, and changed again. She grew taller, shorter, but no broader, no darker.

She was another time, another place. Another woman.

Telling a story, again and again.

‡

Eventually, from a great distance away, the lighter-skinned man said, "You spoke of our world, a place of origin. What was this place called?"

She blinked, struggling to hold onto the question. She had not completely returned to them, but existed in a liminal space, in the interstices between a hundred lives.

Her mate gripped her knee, causing her to sigh.

Her anchor hit soft earth again, connecting her to this time, this place. "Jeroun," she said. She repeated the word, her smile once more radiant.

SHAVRIM THRALL CORANID

C ertain facts were indisputable, even to him, and the most basic was
this:

Not long after the birth of men on Jeroun, less than a thousand
years following their emergence from slumber, the god Adrash had engineered a gift for the world.

A son.

A lavender-skinned, devil-horned boy named Shavrim Thrall Coranid.

He was not born, but tipped from a jar. Nonetheless, he grew as if he
were a child.

The people of Jeroun thought of him as a human boy, knowing he was
not—knowing he was a unique creature only in the approximate shape of
a child, composed of man, elder, and god in equal proportions, possessed
of an immortal body and a vast unfilled intellect. They understood he
had neither birth mother nor true father, that he had been conditioned
from conception to think of Adrash as his creator, yet they persisted in
thinking of him as the god's proper son.

This sentimental illusion faded as Shavrim grew into adulthood and
assumed his formidable stature, and disappeared completely when Adrash
took him as lover. Though the god had not announced his intention to
take Shavrim into his bed, the shift from child and son, to demigod and

lover, happened fluidly, as though it were the only possible outcome. As though it were fated.

Men had no reason to doubt that fate and the will of Adrash were one and the same.

Shavrim had no reason yet to doubt, either.

‡

"You are mine, but I am not yours."

He had heard these words many times, always in moments of intimacy. It did not hurt to hear them. He appreciated that Adrash spoke plainly, refusing to call what they shared love. Resentment would indeed come—it could not be avoided entirely, even in one created for the role of companion—but for decades Shavrim considered the words appropriate, even comforting, a frank assurance that all continued according to a plan set out for him.

A plan he neither understood nor cared to understand.

A plan that simply *was*.

Of course, he had little enough reason to complain over his lot. The world offered him many delights beyond communion with Adrash. With the god's blessing, he took thousands of lovers. He ate countless varieties of food, drank every drink. He experienced each diversion concocted by the vibrant cultures of man, and became himself a source of fascination and joy.

Though Jeroun bore the scars of a long life, having already outlasted its first race of people, the birth of mankind had made everything new, full of light.

‡

Or rather, this was how Shavrim recalled it now, eons after Adrash abandoned the world to madness. He knew it to be comfortable fiction, a lie, a bandage over old and unhealing wounds. For certain, he misremembered the world as more beautiful, more alive than it had ever been, just as he misremembered Adrash as more cruel, more inhuman.

Sometimes, this fact made him uncomfortable.

Other times, he did not care. The events of thousands of years, stored in the branching neural tissue of his spine and limbs, collected over the course of his long, slow adolescence, could be changed if he concentrated—or simply ignored—hard enough, and as he grew older he found little reason to recall with perfect clarity events that had ceased to matter.

All pasts were versions of pasts. Thus, he interpreted whatever version he liked.

The most important of what he interpreted, however, the most impactful—these were facts.

Of this he felt sure, or at least fairly confident.

‡

And so the world had seemed new, full of light, and then it had stopped. Not all at once, true, but being that Shavrim's existence would be measured in glacial ages rather than decades, compacting normal lives into insignificance, the process could feel no way other than sudden.

It was the first morning of his four-hundredth year. He and Adrash sat on a red-tiled terrace overlooking the ocean (what island he could not now recall, and it did not matter), enjoying breakfast, talking inconsequentialities, when, as though they had been having another conversation entirely—a deeper, more cutting conversation—the god spoke eight words.

"Do you really think you are enough, Shavrim?"

Shavrim set his cup of tea, small in his outsized hands, on the table between them. Not yet worried, merely confused. "I—" He searched for the proper expression, and arrived at a smile. Despite his labyrinthine knowledge of the world and its peoples, his vast collection of experiences, his face was rather blank. Not a man's at all, but that of a child. Just as the world saw him.

"I . . . I don't know what you're asking me, Adrash."

The god smiled, beautifully. Every movement he made was beautiful, a display of perfect grace. He sat, legs crossed at the knee, naked and at ease, every muscle relaxed yet defined. Warmth radiated from his jet skin: this close, he was a source of heat as sure as the sun itself. He wore the divine armor as a skintight cap in the shape of a helm, its filigreed edges giving the odd impression of white hair on his forehead, white hair curled around his ears.

"I do not mean this to hurt you," he said, ignoring Shavrim's guffaw of contempt. "Nonetheless, it *will* hurt you. At times I feel dissatisfied with this world, with you—with me. Boredom is as good a word as any, Shavrim." He waved his right hand vaguely. "But this is not your fault. I will not blame you for being predictable as I designed."

Shavrim blinked. The skin of his face felt tight, suddenly hot.

"You are a symptom of my thinking," Adrash continued. "And my thinking on the matter of mankind has been incorrect. For five centuries I have given them too much what they want, and they are becoming complacent, unwilling to grow. I am annoyed by their lackluster art, their spineless leisurely expressions. As exhausting as mankind's displays of aggression can be, I am saddened to see the fight gone out of them." He broke Shavrims's gaze, and stared out to sea.

"I am tired of being the world's nanny, of shielding everyone from harm. Furthermore, I need other sources of companionship lest I go mad. I made a minor miscalculation with you, stretching your development unduly. That mistake must be addressed. You must stop being a child."

"Adrash," Shavrim said. "Adrash, I . . ."

The god shook his head, silencing his creation with a gesture. "I am sorry, but you have no words of relevance to this. I have decided, already, on a course of action, for you and for the people of Jeroun. I have waited to enact my plan for too long already. My evasion of the topic, I fully believe, is part of the problem." He sighed. "But enough navel gazing. Soon, within the year, you will have brothers and sisters—five companions. You six will act as mankind's inspiration, but also as its aggressors. You will spur them to grow. *You will grow up with them.*"

He stood, and walked down the steps to the beach.

Shavrim followed, massive shoulders bowed, arms hanging limp at his sides.

‡

The feeling of discontent persisted. It grew, and only rarely retreated to a comfortable distance. Surely, Shavrim had experienced moments of unhappiness before—on rare occasions, his desires had gone unfulfilled—but these were as nothing compared to this new malaise. He absented himself from Adrash for weeks at a time, visiting the places he thought he loved and then quickly leaving, unsatiated. He found himself in new beds, but experienced nothing new.

The world had not changed, not yet.

And then, within a year, as Adrash promised, the first of five siblings was tipped from the jar: a girl, gray haired and thin-limbed, clawed at hand and foot and as pale as sun-bleached sand. Adrash passed the child-like creature to Shavrim, and Shavrim stared into her bluegreen eyes as she stared back. She did not cry, which made him resentful. He felt sure he had cried upon breathing his first breath.

"Bash Ateff," Adrash named her.

A month later, the second arrived: an unnaturally ruddy, stubby-winged boy Adrash named Orrus Dabulakm. Shavrim took to him immediately, liking the sound of his hoarse cries better than the sullen silence of the sister who had come before him.

The next month, the third—a thing of indeterminate gender, a neuter or a new sex entirely—tumbled forth and stood unaided, but did not open its eyes for twelve days. When it did, two slowly spinning wooden orbs were revealed. Adrash called this blind anomaly Sradir Ung Kim, and seemed especially fond of it.

The fourth and fifth were engineered together, a matching pair. They spilled from the jar locked together, small and hairless and pearlescent, nearly metallic, and refused to untangle from their embrace for a full day. Afterward, they became uncomfortable if separated for longer than a few minutes. Ustert and Evurt Youl, Adrash named them.

"These," Adrash said when all five were situated in their nursery high in Adrash's main keep overlooking the arid Aroonan plains, "are the bringers of a new age, Shavrim. A minor pantheon. As their elder sibling, it is your job to guarantee they keep to the path I have cut for them."

Shavrim nodded, and did not ask just what path this was. He would learn in time.

‡

"I've killed men before," Shavrim said a decade later.

He and Adrash stood on the foredeck of the *Atavest*, watching the five young demigods cavort unafraid in the shallow, glass-clear water. The sea was no place for earthbound creatures, but today the god had created a hundred-foot sphere of will around his ship, halting the dozens of streamlined serpents and fish—which had quickly been attracted by the smell of flesh—from coming any closer. The siblings dared each other to swim up to the barrier of huge, circling predators. Soon they pushed their courage even further, reaching out their hands to brush the scaled flanks, risking the loss of limbs to giant, toothy mouths.

Adrash smiled. "Adorable," he said.

Shavrim ground his teeth together. "Are you listening to me?"

"Yes, I am, Shavrim. A moment, though." Adrash opened his right hand, revealing five coins. He threw them in an arc, causing each to hit the water and fall to the sand a body's length outside his protective barrier. "We do not leave until each of you has retrieved your coin!" he called, and then turned away from the siblings' whoops and cries in response.

"I know you have killed men, Shavrim. It is a joy to watch you fight." His left hand, which he had caused to be sheathed in the featureless white of the divine armor, fell on Shavrim's right shoulder. "What I am talking about now is different. You have never killed a man for any reason other than sport—a sport whose rules both parties understood and accepted. A sacrifice. This will not be the same. You will kill for a purpose. You will kill in response to a threat."

Shavrim laughed, though it had an edge to it: it was a sound he did not enjoy hearing come from himself, a sound he would not have made a decade previously. "A threat? How many men constitute a threat against me? A hundred? Two hundred? A battalion, either way. You're joking with me, Adrash."

"I am not. Men will soon be a great deal more formidable than they are now."

"How?"

Adrash turned and leaned his forearms on the railing. Shavrim sighed and followed suit, surveying his siblings at their dangerous play. There was no real risk, he supposed: though not as sturdy as their eldest brother, each was possessed of an immensely durable body. They would never bleed out or have their heads severed from their bodies. Should they lose a limb, it would regrow. Orrus had recently lost one of his growing wings to a weapon master's blade, and already its replacement reached half the size of the original.

Sradir and Orrus, Shavrim's favorite and least favorite, had already retrieved their coins. Orrus, forever dissatisfied, plagued by voices he could not name, frowned at his accomplishment and dived under the hull—to sulk, for reasons no one but Shavrim understood. Sradir bled from a shallow wound in its side, but it stopped as Shavrim watched. It looked up at Adrash (not blind, they had discovered, yet not seeing as men saw, either), a small smile on its oddly angular, androgynous face.

It did not even glance at Shavrim.

"You said men will become stronger than they are now, Adrash. How?"

Adrash clapped as the diminutive twins shot forward and retrieved their coins, Ustert landing a stiff-fingered jab into the snout of an advancing bonefish. He laughed as Bash, who could never resist showing off, swam slowly but gracefully toward her coin, rolling away from snapping jaws effortlessly, and picked up the final coin with her mouth. Shavrim wondered if he and Adrash's conversations had always been so broken, if the god had always been so distracted. He also questioned his own moods. Had he not been happy, being Adrash's lover but not the center of his world? Had he not been content, even overjoyed, to be part of a greater plan?

Yes, he had. And no, Adrash had not always been as he was now.

"Men will discover a secret," Adrash finally said. "Something right under their nose. Tell me, have you ever wondered why I included elder material in your makeup? Elder corpses are rare, but besides not rotting like a man's body does they are virtually useless. Correct? Was I merely being sentimental for the people this world has lost?"

Shavrim flexed his fists alternately, in time with the doubled beating of his hearts.

"I was not," Adrash said, needlessly. "There is more to elder physiology than anyone knows, a fact I have hidden from the world but will hide no longer."

"What is *more*?"

Adrash chuckled. "You are becoming irritable in your middle age, Shavrim. Good, I suppose: anger will be useful, though I would not have you unhappy every moment of the day." He smiled, white against black. When Shavrim only grunted in response, the god's smile grew. "Power is what we are discussing. Immense power, outshining even the oldest technologies that existed before your birth and only remain in memory."

"And the rarity of elder corpses?" Shavrim asked. "There's a solution for that, as well?"

"Yes. There is a graveyard—a graveyard for an entire species. You will reveal it to the world."

‡

He did so, exactly as commanded. At the foot of The Steps, the elder's greatest monument, a mountain turned mausoleum, he helped excavate the first perfectly preserved corpse.

And immediately set it aflame.

The gathered people marveled at how it burned but was not consumed. Shavrim then reconstituted its ancient blood and allowed ten men to take sips of it. They battled each other for a day, sustaining wounds that would kill normal men. Lastly, he fed every individual a small measure of the corpse's ground bone. A week later, having eaten and drunk nothing, having not slept an hour, the people stood hale.

They celebrated, and began mining their new, nearly inexhaustible resource.

Thereby, men grew into maturity—or rather, into the wielding of power. Within two generations, the world had split and its peoples had become fractious threats to each other. Their arts turned violent, viciously inventive, seasoned with elder-corpse fire and blood. They relied less and less upon what remained of their old technologies, and then proceeded to forget this inheritance completely. Manipulating their acquired magic consumed them completely. Old cities were abandoned and new cities built, spanning chasms and straddling mountaintops, each lit by the glow of thousands upon thousands of magelamps.

Adrash rejoiced in mankind's rekindled passion. He orchestrated their development, wielding Shavrim and his siblings like blades, cutting nations in two, separating culture from culture, beginning wars and stopping wars. He spoke of symbols, of the importance of identity, and using arcane means fashioned weapons unique to each of his creations:

Sroma, a long silverblack knife for Shavrim: a malevolent item, possessed of its own ill personality. It did not speak in words, but made its desires known easily enough. Shavrim cherished and despised it by turns. He tasted blood when it bit into flesh.

Jhy, a razored throwing circle for Bash, which passed through steel and rock as easily as it passed through flesh. Bash kept it close to her at all times, but always sheathed. She used it rarely, and only against the strongest mages, as if only to prove a point.

Deserest, a glass spear for Orrus—a weapon he refused to use.

Weither, an oilwood and leather sambok for Sradir. In its owner's hands, the diminutive whip became a blur, a devastating shadow that severed even the most armored men in half. Sradir never used its proper name, instead referring to it as Little Sister.

Ruin and Rust, a pair of short swords for Ustert and Evurt: blades that never grew dull and would not be tarnished. Oddly, Ustert, who seemed always on the verge of an outburst, who lived with abandon, wielded Ruin with a cold detachment, while Evurt, the quiet one, carved with Rust in wild arcs, almost as though he were trying to throw the weapon away.

Thus equipped, no army on the face of Jeroun could stand against them.

This fact ate at Shavrim. He had been warned of threats. Initially, when he spoke of his concerns to Adrash, he received smiles and hints of further developments ("Have faith in me, Shavrim. I don't labor to provide you with tools for your defense simply to watch you wave them about."), but as time passed the god's enthusiasm took on a dark, solipsist edge. Adrash spoke rarely, his moods unpredictable. He spent time away, always just out of reach, leaving the increasingly complicated task of governance to his eldest creation, often for years at a time.

Each time, coming back crueler, more inscrutable.

The thin persona of a man sloughed away, revealing the madness of divinity.

‡

Simplifying the first millennia after the introduction of elder magic, turning such a vast length of time into one color, one feeling, proved appallingly easy for one who had never been human and could only approximate the concerns of one. Surely, the change in Adrash had occurred gradually: Shavrim had known it then and certainly knew it now, yet in retrospect it was shockingly abrupt, as rapid as a droplet of ink clouding into a pail of water.

One day, he had known his creator intimately, felt the god's moods as if they were his own—or thought he did, though the distinction makes little difference. And the next, he struggled to understand the capricious demands of a stranger, an incomprehensibly powerful being who forced his creations to betray the very people they had been engineered to assist.

One day, Shavrim had been a child, trusting, and the next . . .

‡

"The world would be better without him," he said, the obvious conclusion to a hundred years of long and evasive arguments. Finally, he said it.

And then, he said even more: "He must be destroyed."

Ustert grinned, revealing her sharp teeth. She threw one shapely silver leg over her twin's and laughed. "Grief, Shavrim, that's a nice thought. But there's no chance of it happening. I don't like him any more than you do—haven't liked him since I was small enough to be mistaken for a corpse miner—but we're six against a god. Besides, he's not really *here* any longer, is he? Off on his little ship, father is, doing who knows what."

"Don't call him that," Evurt said. He sat as rigid as his twin was relaxed, a thin bronze statue of a man. "I don't like it when you call him that. He's not our father."

Ustert rubbed his cheek with the back of her hand, causing Evurt to grimace.

"So, you're not in love anymore," Bash said. She flicked at an imaginary piece of lint on her coat. "So, you've been abandoned, forced into a role you never wanted and aren't suited for." Her seawater eyes met his, and her features softened. "You used to hate me, eldest brother. I know you did. But I'd hate to think you wanted me gone from the world. Give it time. Maybe you'll feel differently. Maybe he'll feel differently."

"This isn't about love," Shavrim said.

Sradir nodded, expressionless as only it could be. "Of course it is not, Shavrim. Bash is speaking in her metaphors again."

Ustert grinned.

Shavrim looked to Orrus, who shrugged with both shoulders and wings. "I'm in," the winged demigod said in his rasp of a voice. He tapped his head and then gestured to encompass each of them. "All of us are in. We can pretend otherwise, but it's the fact."

Bash opened her mouth and then closed it.

"Yes," Evurt said, just as his twin said, "Fuck."

Sradir gazed woodenly at Shavrim. "Many will die. Even we may die. Are you that in love with mankind?" The corners of its mouth rose fractionally. "Love being a metaphor, mind."

"We aren't men, so love is not the word," Shavrim answered. "Love is never the word for us. But I won't see mankind pushed and pulled by his whims any longer, given the tools of war and domination and then crushed for their arrogance when they use them. I won't be one of those tools any longer." He stood and paced before them. "So, he's gone for a decade, two, even three. He'll be back, and who knows what he'll do then? Even absent, he exerts his influence. You can't tell me you don't all feel it. It limns our every word, our every gesture."

Silence—as close to assent as they would give. Shavrim pressed.

"We're a reflection of Adrash, and we're slowly going mad with him. We all know the result of madness on our scale, which is terrible enough, but on his? The world will be burned to a cinder, should he continue down this path. We'll be carried with him. We'll be responsible."

Bash shook her head. "But what if we're what's causing him—"

"No." Evurt stood abruptly, dislodging his twin. He made a cutting motion with his left hand. "No. We have heard this before, sister, heard it and dismissed it. The question is irrelevant because it has no answer. We may be the source of Adrash's disease—or we may not be. It does not matter. We are the cure, either way. The *only* cure."

The room grew quiet, ever the result of Evurt choosing to voice more than a brief complaint. Ustert reached forward and drew her twin back down onto the couch, wrapping her arms around him. Sradir closed its eyes, blank-faced. Bash raised her eyebrows at Orrus, and Orrus turned his intense gray gaze to Shavrim.

"We look to you," Orrus said. "Perhaps we shouldn't, but we do."

Shavrim nodded. He knew this, had relied upon it. There were advantages to the way his mind functioned, how it forced thoughts to branch out along pathways throughout his body, causing him to arrive at conclusions only after long and repetitious thought. One day he would come to feel overwhelmed by the lifetimes he had accreted in his stretched neurons, but it had not happened yet. He still possessed wisdom unique to him.

He crouched and pressed a huge palm against the sun-warmed marble floor, a floor he had slapped his bare feet upon as a child. He remembered being scolded by a tutor for running. He had scolded his siblings for doing the same when they were young.

"I won't pretend we're a family," he said. "I won't pretend we even enjoy sitting here with each other, especially not in this place. We're not saintly, by any metric, but we're not part of the disease spreading in Adrash's soul. Of this I'm sure. I think it more probable he engineered us too well to our task, and that our task was more complex than he let on. He couldn't predict what would happen to himself in time, but he knew the risk. He knew, and created us to keep himself from the void." His fingers stroked the leather sheath covering Sroma. "He even engineered us weapons for the task."

He heard an intake of breath—Bash—and held up his hand, forestalling her words of denial.

"I'm not saying he made plans for his own defeat. He will not concede to us, like a man taking medicine. He has let himself forget our full purpose, and we let him."

Sradir opened its eyes and locked stares with Shavrim.

"*We let him*," she said. The words were neither challenge nor agreement. "Well. No more of that."

‡

In the Month of Soldiers, Adrash ended his self-imposed exile of two hundred and seven years by landing the *Atavest* on the southwestern coast of Doma. Announcements, which would in time become slow and expensive, dependent upon massive reserves of elder-corpse materials, traveled quickly from Adrash's hand. Mankind—not one member of which had known their god in the flesh—rejoiced with a month-long celebration.

Despite the passage of two centuries, Shavrim's siblings required no reminding or spurring to their purpose. Indeed, time had only increased their violent resolve. They allowed the celebrations to come to an end, and then met Adrash in the scrub desert of central Gnos Min, just beyond the eastern wall of Curathe.

The god read their intention immediately. Undoubtedly, no great act of premonition: all six had been conspicuously absent from the festivities.

The battle began without a word exchanged.

‡

Thirteen hours later, four of the six siblings remained. What had been the city of Curathe ticked as it cooled before them, a vast shallow bowl of fused ceramic.

Shaky on his feet, nearing a point of exhaustion where reality blurred around the edges, Shavrim experienced a vision of what the place would become in only a few months' time. Rain, falling in the Month of Mages (not a monsoon—nothing so monumental as that—merely a few tantrums, brief reminders of a wetter time), creating a temporary lake, a waystation for migrating birds and orr-bison, a place fleetingly filled with the low-throated burp of desert toads.

One day, too soon, men would stop and wonder at it, ignorant of its origin.

"Well done," Bash said, voice heavy with sarcasm. She wiped at the blood under her nose, and spit a tooth onto the ground. "We've got him on the run."

"Shut up," Orrus said, fist tight around Deserest, the weapon he had always declined to use.

Ustert remained silent. She held her right hand out to her side, as though expecting her twin to take it.

Shavrim closed his eyes, allowing himself to be buffeted by the wind.

Adrash had taken Sradir first. A wise move, Shavrim thought: he had always suspected it was the most powerful of his siblings. Then he had chosen Evurt. Another wise move. Without her twin, who knew what Ustert would be?

One battle, and already they had lost two of their number.

Had he anticipated anything else?

"I hadn't expected it to hurt so much," he said, so softly he thought no one would notice, but he heard the rustle of Orrus's wings and knew his brother had heard. Of course. He and Orrus had always been close. They understood one another, how deeply, Shavrim would only know in the millennia to come—alone, searching for meaning as the world spun slowly toward destruction. Searching, while he gradually succumbed to his own madness, the compounding of a thousand voices.

And yet it was Ustert who spoke in response.

"Yes, it hurts. Of course it hurts." Her voice was flat, characterless. "You always lie to yourself, eldest. You practice the worst sort of deception, hiding from what is plainly true, what is obvious to everyone but you. We were a family, or as close to family that the phrasing becomes unimportant. Whether we liked one another had no bearing on this fact. If you'd stopped, for one moment, and looked up from your worship of Adrash, your sadness over losing him, you'd have realized this sooner. Now it comes, and you think you feel pain. You feel nothing compared to me."

They waited one night to recover, sleeping on the open ground within an arm's reach of each other. Closer than they had ever been.

‡

The four moved on to Danoor, which already lay smoldering in the shadow of the Aroonan mesas. They passed through the rubbled grave of Lantern Light, turning away from the bodies that littered the brick-paved streets. Death—this they understood. An individual man's life held little importance, after all, but a city's worth? That many innocent souls possessed a weight, demanding acknowledgement even from demigods.

Adrash taunted them by being just a step ahead.

They were fast, but still crawling in comparison.

In Grass, where tradition said the first men had awakened from their ancient slumber, the god waited, hanging in the sky above the city, his aura shuddering around him in radiant golden waves. He was a man-shaped shadow at the center of a new sun, motionless. Taunting, still.

Ustert spat onto the dry earth. "Listen to me. He won't take one or two or three of us. He takes all four of us, or we kill him. This ends now."

No one responded, but all were agreed.

Shavrim peered through waves of heat into the city. From as close as a mile away, it appeared as though it had been left untouched, but as they entered its gates Shavrim saw that everyone—those visible in the streets, but the effect surely extended to those indoors—stood or sat frozen in place, either held in temporary thrall or, more likely, halted forever in the state of death. Such a thing was not beyond Adrash's power, though Shavrim imagined the act drained him considerably. A small, grisly boon to his attackers.

By unspoken agreement, a simple acknowledgement that events would unfold exactly as quickly as Adrash willed, they walked into the city. As they neared the central square, lesser buildings seemed to shuffle aside to reveal the full glory of Adrash's temple: this, the most ancient of structures, famed as the site of mankind's birth on Jeroun. Shavrim had always considered its warm sandstone edifices and encircling gardens beautiful. They remained so.

Upon their stepping into the square, Adrash commenced his descent from the sky. Slowly, maddeningly so.

Shavrim unsheathed Sroma, gooseflesh raising upon his arm at the touch of its hilt. He stretched his arms wide, muscles bunching massively in his back. He tipped his head to either side, cracking vertebrae. He touched the two small horns on his forehead.

Orrus stood, glass spear gripped in two hands before him, wings pulled in close to his back. He had never flown before the age of twenty, and then only under pressure from Shavrim. He would not fly now: it would do no good against Adrash.

Bash spun Jhy around the upraised index and middle fingers of her left hand. She also spun Weither, Sradir's recovered whip, by its lanyard. She had always been the showoff, and Shavrim admired her athleticism. He had never told her this, but surely she knew.

Ustert likewise held two weapons—her own sword, Ruin, and her twin's sword, Rust—and stood, rooted to the ground by two wide-set feet. Of the five siblings, only she had beaten Shavrim in armed combat. She had never let him forget it.

Adrash reduced the blaze of his aura as he descended. Nonetheless, by the time he landed on the steps of his temple the light from his eyes alone proved sufficient to throw acute shadows from every standing object. His four living creations squinted against the radiation, unfazed, while the people gathered in the square, struck immobile in the seconds after death, blistered from the heat.

The god stood, unmoving, encased head to toe in the flawlessly white embrace of his armor. Despite himself, as always, Shavrim admired the graceful lines of his creator's physique, its contours accentuated rather than hidden by the divine material, and felt the accompanying rush of desire. He risked a glance at Bash and confirmed the flush in her pale cheeks. She, too, could not hide her attraction, a fact which had always angered her.

It had been tens of decades since she or Shavrim had shared Adrash's bed, yet their bodies would not allow them to forget.

Orrus had not moved a muscle, revealing to Shavrim an altogether different type of strain. He had been, since birth, the least favored of

Adrash—a hurt he would not allow shown on his features but still felt keenly. Ustert, conversely, had forever been a focus of the god's praise. But now, having witnessed the almost casual dismemberment of her twin, she shook with rage so thinly controlled that Shavrim feared for her. She would be a danger, very likely to herself.

Thus arrayed, they waited for the inevitable.

Hello, children, Adrash said, directly into the interiors of their skulls.

‡

The moment held, and in Shavrim's memory would forever hold— the moment separating being one of four whose souls rang in union, discordant though it was, and the next . . .

‡

It was two hours after dusk in the ransacked city of Danoor. He reclined naked on a flat clay roof, savoring the last of the day's trapped heat before it seeped out from underneath him. There was a distinct sharpness to the desert air, and he felt it—less than a man would, true, but enough to make him slightly uncomfortable. In truth, he enjoyed this unique sensation of discomfort. No matter how long-lived, one never forgot the feeling of home.

Though the city's fires had been doused, the smell of burnt timber and clay lingered.

Far off in the unlit night, beyond the border of Shavrim's orderly terri- tory, someone screamed.

And above Shavrim—far, far above him, leagues and leagues beyond the envelope of air that surrounded the world—the heavens were shat- tered. What had been Adrash's greatest weapon, the ultimate symbol of his madness, a constant feature of the night sky generations of men had known as The Needle, now extended in broken orbit around the moon, each of its twenty-seven massive iron spheres spinning through the void on unplanned trajectories.

No longer in the god's control. No longer kept from falling.

Shavrim smiled, unashamed of the conflicting emotions the sight evoked. He admitted to himself that he was not quite happy, no, that in fact the sight of the world's approaching doom filled him with remorse— but also that he felt a sense of satisfaction, of appropriateness, of *You've really done it now.* He considered with what emotion his lost siblings would have greeted the sight, and his smile widened. He said each of their names, names left unspoken for longer than he chose to remember. He spoke to them in a language the world forgot twenty-five thousand years ago.

His words were not, despite the evidence of his own eyes and hands, for the dead. He concentrated and projected them in a simple but taxing extension of will, broadcasting on a wavelength he alone had discovered, a wavelength unheard by anyone except the five ones caught in between, those unique souls who lingered in the spaces between life and death.

Souls who, for many millennia, he had believed were constructs of his own madness.

"Sisters. Brothers," he said. "This is the thing I would not admit aloud until now, but with the world on the brink of death, it seems a good time to unburden myself—of delusion, perhaps, though if I'm to be honest (and why shouldn't I be?), I know there is no perhaps, no maybe. There is no delusion, only truth. Or rather, I should say *madness* and truth. In each of the lives I live, in each of the voices of the past I let overtake me, your voices are clear. You are a constant, even in the madness I've allowed root. Your voices grow weak. They fade in and out, but they're always here."

He laid his left palm flat upon his chest. His right fist closed, and slowly his smile faded.

"You might wonder, why is it that brother has never spoken to us before—why has he not sought to make contact with us? It's a good question, for which I have no proper answer other than cowardice. I died with you, and then woke to bury you. Some contact wounds, and never heals. You may as well ask why I've avoided Adrash. Fear. Fear of what you've each become in the absence of your bodies. I know myself, even when I'm not myself, for that person is only myself in a different guise, living another life. I do this so that I avoid absolute madness.

"And yet I do not—*cannot*—know you. Not any longer. I am a body, and you are . . . I don't know what you are. Besides, it's been too long. I've forgotten too much. I've chosen to be alone, and grown used to it. Being alone is easier than having a family. When you have a family, you are responsible to each other. It's easier to navigate the world without that burden. Why should I be the one to live with it? Why must I be the eldest?"

He sighed, shook his head. That last note of petulance, he wished he could take it back, reword it. It was too late in his long life to express such things, even to the wind. Every word—he should not have spoken any of it. There was too much to say, and he was failing to communicate any of it.

A northerly wind flowed over the rooftop, and he shivered.

"Listen to me," he said, disliking the weak sound of his voice. The act of projecting, of summoning ancient words and buried sentiment, had exhausted him. And he still had not voiced the most important of what must be voiced. He disliked entreaties.

"Listen to me," he repeated, nearing a whisper now. "Look at the sky tonight, and know there is need for us yet. Yes, even as we are, mad and lost and even half rejoicing in what has occurred. We stood together once. We can do so again."

He closed his eyes, breathing deeply for the space of twenty doubled heartbeats.

"Please. Help me keep the world alive."

‡

He listened, growing colder and more convinced of his foolishness as the moon and shattered sky passed slowly overhead. Less than an hour went by, yet it felt like three. When he finally admitted defeat and stood, his joints creaked. A new weight had settled into his bones. He suffered a moment of lightheadedness and wondered—were he a normal man, if the moment would have inspired suicide. Perhaps it was the perfect time to pitch himself from the roof.

If he were a normal man, release would have been just that easy.

Not for the first time, he considered the curses placed upon him.

The first:

To be so unreasonably loyal to mankind, knowing what he knew of its members. Their pettiness and greed, their pretensions of greatness. He had suffered more of their failures and fought in more of their wars than Adrash had, yet he was the one who could not fail to sympathize with them, to want more *for* them. Oh, he had killed many of their number (just as often in joy as anger, truthfully), but this was no contradiction. Humanity existed as a mass, and only exceptionally as individuals.

And individuality? This was his second curse:

To be alone. To think on the scale of a god, and have no other gods except the ones that had abandoned you. To have known how it feels not to be alone, and to have squandered it.

He considered aloneness as he descended from the rooftop and entered the games hall from which he ran his new territory. The air was warm inside, but not uncomfortably so. Despite the number of men and women gathered in friendly competition, it was not loud. People greeted him, though not warmly. They tried—they always tried—but he was simply too intimidating, too alien, looking nearly like a man without at all being a man. Furthermore, he was their leader. He moved among them like a predator, with odd grace for such a large person.

"Shav," said Laures, his first lieutenant, a woman chosen for her intelligence, but also for the fact that she rarely spoke more than his name. It amused him slightly, the fact of her faith: she worshipped the goddess Ustert. If only she knew what kind of creature his sister had been, how dependent she had been upon her twin, perhaps she would not be so warmly inclined. Usterti believed all the wrong things about their goddess. They had robbed her of her love, made her into a solitary creature.

He nodded to her on his way out the front door.

Into the street, peaceful again. He looked either direction and set off south, intending to inspect the barricades . . .

‡

And fell to his knees.

Out in the night, closer than he could have imagined, a voice spoke— a voice he recognized instantly—a coincidence too extraordinary given where his mind had only just passed.

Vedas Tezul, it said.

Shavrim toppled onto his side and shook violently upon the ground, struggling against the shock to his body and mind. He fought to order his thoughts, to respond before the connection was severed, but before any true headway could be made a second coincidence announced itself, its voice fainter than the first but equally distinct after so many thousands of years.

Churls Casta Jons, it said.

"I . . . I . . ." Shavrim stuttered, jaws cramping and jumping. "I . . . will . . . will . . ." He bit down hard, speaking through gritted teeth. "Find . . . you."

‡

He received no confirmation that either had heard. He lay immobilized in the street until early morning, when his lieutenant Laures found him and dragged him inside. She said nothing. He stared up at her as she struggled with his awkward weight. He would not thank her, yet a portion of his mind felt gratitude, though not for her current efforts: perhaps thinking of her faith had allowed his mind to open just enough to let his sibling's voices in.

I am coming, brother, he thought. *I am coming, sister. We will be together soon. We will seal our fate, as a family.*

CHVRLI CASTA JONS

After the sun set, Churls shaved her head with his razor. She considered why she did it and arrived at no answer. She had never been one for symbols. Her hair had been short enough for the purpose, already.

Afterward, she cut a long rectangle of fabric from a sheet and wound it around her sinuous torso, flattening her breasts before fastening on a tight, stiff leather vest and back scabbard.

Another almost unnecessary act: her breasts were small enough, as they were.

She sneered at her face in the monastery's one mirror, a vanity item she had been surprised to find in the building's cellar, and wiped at a bead of blood on her scalp.

Her reflection unnerved her. Nearly a week spent in bed recovering from her injuries, followed by two weeks of waiting for her daughter to bring back good news from the city, had resulted in a visible change in her appearance. Her arms and thighs were thinner than she preferred. The freckles on her cheeks and shoulders, typically a near-solid mass of brownish red, had faded to a speckling.

She pulled on the pair of the rough woolen pants she had found in an alcove. They were looser than she preferred, binding in odd places. Why could men not fashion pants that fit properly?

The back of her neck began tingling.

"You can come in now, Fyra," she said.

Her daughter sharpened into existence at Churls's side, colored all in shades of white but for the pale blue of her eyes. She stood to within a few inches of her mother's shoulder, and had not been alive for well over a decade.

She screwed her features into a grimace. "It looks . . . bad. And it's bleeding in the back."

"Forgive my clumsiness," Churls said. "I had a beard when I was your age, but it fell out when I had you. As a result, I'm a bit rusty at all this." She met the girl's unimpressed gaze and fought to keep the hope from showing on her own features. "You're sure you've got a fix on them? You're sure—about all three of them?"

Fyra nodded. "For the third time, Mama, yes. I'll lead you right to them. If you want, I can . . ."

Churls buckled her belt. "I don't want. To quote you: *for the third time*, no. Also, to repeat myself, we have no idea what will happen to you if you're attacked by whatever sort of mage Fesuy's hired to shield Vedas and Berun from sight." *Not to mention keeping you at a long arm's length,* she did not add. "It's enough that I let you scout. I won't risk putting you in the midst of a fight with someone that strong."

She caught the slight upturning at the corners of the girl's mouth. "And yes, that means I just admitted you're very strong. Still, you're not as strong as your mother. Not in the same way. And you're definitely not as mean. I won't hear any more about it."

Her daughter said no more. A surprise. Churls had expected a rebuttal.

She felt grateful, but also slightly awkward about the exchange. Their banter, a thing that had only started in the absence of Vedas and Berun, seemed to proceed naturally enough between them—as it should have for a mother and daughter alone, surely—yet Churls could not escape the fact of its novelty. She and Fyra had never talked that way while the girl lived. She doubted its authenticity. Furthermore, to speak so casually inspired a sense of disloyalty. She could not sustain a constant state of worry over her missing companions, but suspected she should at least make the attempt.

Fyra cleared her throat. Made a throat-clearing sound, anyway.

"You're crying, Mama."

Churls wiped her eyes with a tattooed forearm. "Shit," she whispered. She breathed deeply into her stomach. "Fyra. You will not accompany me. I do this alone. Do what you like for me now, but you don't set foot beyond these walls. I need you to say you understand me."

To her credit, the child did not immediately agree. Churls approved.

"I understand, Mama," Fyra said, "and I mean it this time. I won't leave. But first, you need to promise *me* something. Something big."

"What?"

"You need to keep your promise. You need to tell him about me. About *us*."

Churls tipped her head back to stare at the bare rock ceiling. The room suddenly seemed too close, crowded, as if the dead had gathered at her daughter's word. To hear Churls's answer.

"You don't know what you're asking," she said. "There's no war against Adrash. Vedas failed to rouse anything but ire and violence. His speech threw the world into discord."

She pointed heavenward, gesturing beyond the tonnage of stone separating them from the wrecked night sky. "He damned us all, and you know what, girl? I don't care, because in the end he was right. We've been living under threat for too long, cowed and in denial. If we all die in flames, we all die in flames, and there's nothing to be done. Not by you, not by me. I just want him back, and I'm going to get him back. Him *and* Berun. Beyond that? You can't make me care beyond that—not right now."

Fyra's hands tightened into fists at her hips.

"You lied to me."

Churls's head dropped. A growl built low in her throat. Suddenly, the seven-hour hike to the city seemed like an interminable delay. She wanted everything over and done. She would see everything over and done, and then she would think.

She spoke slowly, carefully. "I'm not saying I won't tell him, Fyra. I'm just saying it'll make no difference if I do." She looked up, offered the girl a weak smile neither of them believed. "Now, please, do what you're going to do to help your mother save the day, alone, and then do nothing else."

For a moment, Churls thought her daughter would refuse, but the girl merely rolled her eyes and stepped forward into Churls, filling her with warmth and light.

✝

The Nehuaa Salt Falts comprised nearly half of the area of northwestern Knos Min. The flat, featureless landscape had once been the bed of an inland sea scholars called Littleshallow, and now provided salt for an entire continent. A rainless, lifeless, maddeningly uninteresting terrain, it seemed the whole of the world when one traveled upon it. Any destination rose out of the cracked white floor as though floating, mountains and cities alike standing still in the vague distance, never growing any closer until one gratefully stumbled into them.

Twenty miles of this landscape lay between the monastery and Danoor.

Churls barely registered the distance or the time it took to cross it. She did not look behind her once to see the hills ringing the monastery fade into the night. She barely looked at the city before her. She ran, legs solid yet spring-light beneath her, losing herself easily in the rhythm of feet hitting earth. The quietly rational part of her mind worried what Fyra had done in order to allow her access to such an immense reservoir of energy—worried what the wage would be when it inevitably ran out, and whether or not she should have saved it for later—but she easily silenced it.

Too easily, she reasoned, and dismissed this too with a smile.

Her fear, a thing she had barely allowed a voice. Erased entirely.

Her annoyance at being forced into a concession, posing as a man. Gone.

Point in fact, she had not felt this good in a long time, certainly not since Vedas and Berun's abduction. In her current state, she found it surpassingly simple to absolve herself of the guilt she had given free rein for the last month.

It had not been her fault, the ambush. She could not have prevented it, given her knowledge at the time.

Her anger had fled, as well. Berun had been right to swat her across the room—an action that knocked her unconscious while simultaneously depositing her behind a row of crates. She had not appreciated how quickly the constructed man came to his conclusion and acted to keep her from being taken as well.

Of course, no one liked waking up alone, abandoned in a dangerous city with a shattered clavicle and a row of broken ribs. A twenty-mile walk back to safe shelter would not help, either.

No wonder Fyra did not like being ordered to stay away. She had sobbed (rather, made the ghost motions of sobbing) when Churls collapsed at the top of the hill overlooking the monastery. Churls had nearly killed herself by walking so far with such injuries.

"You should've called to me, Mama," the girl had said. "I would've heard. You make me so angry."

Churls grinned at the memory. Damn, but she was enjoying herself.

The euphoria lasted until the moment she entered the city's outskirts and forced herself to a walk: an act that was like stopping a massive grinding wheel with bare hands, or swimming against a swiftly-flowing river. A sense of sadness overcame her, as of an opportunity lost. She could have kept going, cutting around the city, running until exhaustion overcame her. There she would have collapsed, succumbing to sleep without worry . . .

"Stupid useless fucking . . ." she whispered, feeling like a fool.

The moon and scattered spheres of The Needle loomed full in the west, casting ample light into the deserted streets. When she had last passed through this part of the city, there were still people about, but now the buildings at the outskirts of Danoor stood abandoned—that, or the people who lived in the low, red clay residences were keeping quiet, lights out.

She kept to the shadowed side of the street, moving deeper into the city, drawn without pause toward the target Fyra had planted in her mind. She unsheathed her short, dull sword and gripped the blade near the hilt for balance.

It felt good in her hand, warming to her touch quickly, as though coming to life.

She found herself grinning again, and realized she had been humming.

"Kill Rhythm," Battle March of the Third Castan Infantry.

‡

The guard tried to scream. His tongue flicked through his teeth, pressing wet and warm against her palm. She clamped her hand tighter to his mouth as his life flowed down the front of his shirt. His struggles slowed, stopped, and she lowered him gently to the ground.

She admired the small ceramic knife in her hand—it had been the guard's only a few seconds ago, before she slipped it from his hip sheath and used it to slit his throat—and decided to keep it. She would finish Fesuy with her own sword, but the thought of using a Tomen weapon to strike the first blow struck her as poetically sound, appropriately disrespectful.

A quick circuit around the house revealed no further guards, a fact which confirmed her impression of Fesuy Amendja. The man was arrogant, stupidly so. After the risky maneuver of leaping over the heavily-sentried barricade (an act that seemed to have cost her the last of Fyra's imparted vitality), she had encountered few men and even fewer women, all but three of whom she had been able to avoid. Those three had died easily.

Though the sun still sat a half hour below the horizon, to have so few people about in a contested area seemed appallingly neglectful.

She picked the front door lock and entered the darkened two-storey building, dragging the dead guard with her.

Immediately, she felt it. The muscles of her jaw suddenly tingled, as though she had bitten into a lemon. The sensation built until it was an ache, which quickly spread throughout the bones of her skull into a steady, pounding throb. Her knees nearly gave out, but she leaned her back against the door and rode out the worst of it. Surely, whatever Fyra had done to her caused an increased sensitivity to whatever magics were in the building.

Surely, whatever Fyra had done to her would compensate to minimize the effects.

Any moment now . . . she thought. *Please* . . . But the pain persisted.

The light warned her, a second too late. An elderly Tomen woman rounded the corner, stepping down from the stairs at the end of the hallway. She jumped when she saw Churls, dropping her lantern with a glass clatter.

Churls flipped the ceramic knife. Underhanded, it was an awkward throw. The pommel glanced harmlessly off the woman's shoulder and struck the plaster behind her, but by that point Churls had already taken two steps in a run toward her target.

The woman got out one syllable of a warning or curse before Churls's forearm crushed her windpipe. Churls pinned her enemy against the wall and watched as the light fled from her eyes. For several seconds afterward, she held the woman there, heart pounding heavily enough to shake her entire body, breaths labored and painful as she struggled to keep them quiet.

Listening, over the roar of her pain.

A footstep on the landing above. The strike of a phosphor match.

Bright spots swam before Churls's eyes as she hauled the dead woman out of this new person's line of sight. The muscles of her chest and stomach had tightened with the pain, constricting her. She could not breathe in enough air, and tore at the buttons of her vest, alleviating the pressure slightly.

Above her, voices. Two men. She recognized one of their words.

Shira.

Her eyes shot to the ceramic knife, which lay on the floor at the foot of the stairs.

She did not think. Thinking would do no good in her current situation.

She rounded the corner and charged up the steps, sword in hand. Both men stood, stunned into statues by her appearance. She ran the first through his left lung and slammed into the second, carrying them both to the floor. They rolled twice before she got the upper position, and then struck him twice, open-palmed and in quick succession, forcing shards of cartilage into his brain, killing him instantly. She stood and pulled her sword free of the first, hastening his death by drowning.

The house woke up around her. From the sound of it, there were far more than a handful of men. Perhaps Fesuy had not been so incautious, after all.

She ran down the hallway, where she knew Vedas and Berun would be found.

‡

The two girls Fesuy had slept alongside—she would not think of them as women—sobbed in the corner. The man himself lay unconscious on the bed, naked, wrists and ankles tied and linked behind his back, bleeding into the sheets from a shallow cut on his temple. A heavy chair, propped against the doorknob, kept anyone from easily entering the room from the outside.

Of course, every member of the household knew Fesuy would die if they tried to enter, and this kept them out. For now. It was only a brief matter of time before they stopped caring and came in, regardless of the threat to their leader.

Churls finished her second search of the room, which every instinct told her *must* contain Vedas and Berun, and limped over to the bed. Fesuy groaned as she flipped him over. When she wound his long red hair around her hand and pulled him onto the floor, he woke and began cursing her, first in Tomen and then, when she let his head drop onto the rough wood floor, in Common.

". . . dick I'll rip out, your asshole I'll fill—with blades I'll . . ."

She knelt and slapped him, hard. "Shut the fuck up. Where are they?"

He started to speak, paused. She met his stare. When his eyes registered their recognition, she smiled. She pulled the knife he had kept in his bedside table from her boot and waved it. The pain in her jaw and temples had only increased, but she would not allow this to show on her face.

"So, you dress to look like a man," he said with a sneer. "You should not worry about that. You looked enough like one, already. In this camp, no one would have touched you. I have fifteen men in this house, all unmarried, and not one could I have convinced to lay with you."

"Thirteen," she said. "Your men are easy to kill."

She drew a shallow, straight cut on his lower stomach, and crossed it with another. He snarled and spit in her face.

"Where are they?" she asked again, pointing the tip at the X's junction.

He spit again, and she pushed the knife into him.

He screamed. Fists pounded on the door.

"Where are they?" she asked a third time, twisting the man's own blade in his guts. Not a fatal wound, not yet. He screamed again, louder, and the door jumped in its frame as his men hurled themselves against it. She stilled the knife and repeated her question, watching his face.

He tried to spit at her yet again, and got it no farther than his own chin.

She took his face in her hands, leaving the knife sticking out of his belly. "Where, Fesuy? You have them here. Tell me where they are, and I'll leave you to your men. A good healer will have you up and about in a couple weeks."

He began cursing in Tomen again, but his eyes gave him away.

Her head whipped about to stare at the ceiling in the northwestern corner of the room. A ladder leaned against the wall underneath. It was an item she had mistaken as decoration, for which purpose they were sold throughout Danoor. She again hauled Fesuy by the hair, trailing blood behind. When the door burst open, she wanted him close at hand, but knew it would only stall the inevitable.

She needed to find Vedas and Berun. Now.

The ceiling was not high—only seven feet or so. This fact had not struck her before, but now it seemed noteworthy. Even the hallways had been a greater height, maybe nine feet. She examined the corner Fesuy had focused on, and nearly cried out in her delight. A square had been cut out of the plaster. It lay nearly flush with the rest of the ceiling, rendering it nearly invisible.

Her discovery had not been missed by Fesuy, who now began yelling instructions to his men. The door bucked harder in response.

Churls knelt, pulled the knife from Fesuy's belly, and plunged it into his chest, straight through his sternum. She screamed, pulled it out and hammered it home again—too hard: she felt something pop, something tear. She wished, for a handful of seconds while she stared at the hilt of the weapon protruding from him—gritting her teeth as agony bloomed in her right shoulder—that she had been able to draw out his pain.

She recalled the earnest smile on his face, several months ago, a lifetime ago, when he handed her a mejuan pod and they toasted it together. She recalled the smell of shit that rose from the body of the woman he killed the following morning.

The door burst open, sending the heavy chair crashing against the bed. Fesuy's men roared, and the girls in the corner screamed. Churls climbed the ladder and slammed her palm into the ceiling panel, shoulder screaming in protest.

She heard rather than felt the snap of bones in her hand. Uncaring, she hit the panel again. It levered up, and she pulled herself into the dark space beyond.

Every bone in her skull pulsed in redoubled white-hot agony. She shrugged it off as so much noise, slapped the ceiling door closed, and jammed the point of her sword into its unhinged edge. It would not hold against a concerted effort to open the panel, of course, but she hoped to have another solution soon.

She turned in a half-crouch, rapidly cataloguing the contents of the low room.

No windows. In the center, a single magelamp, set very low. A woman sitting behind it, eyes closed, legs crossed, apparently unaware of any cause for alarm. The mage.

A mountainous, man-shaped heaping of brass spheres, dimly seen in the far corner.

Beside it, a low camp bed. Upon it, a dark-clothed body.

‡

She limped over to the mage and kicked her in the stomach.

Immediately, the pain in her head ceased. She nearly fainted in relief.

The mage yelped as Churls pulled her head up by the hair. Her eyes slowly focused.

"Hello," Churls said through gritted teeth. "I'm your new boss. You do what I fucking say, immediately. Show you understand me."

The mage nodded, fear in her eyes.

Churls did not smile. "Good. There are people trying to get in here, so you have only seconds to secure this room. Fail, and I kill you."

‡

Ten seconds. Twenty. The pounding on the ceiling door continued. Thirty.

"Bitch," Churls said, tightening her grip on the mage's greasy hair. "I'd take me *very* seriously. Make this happen, *right n—*"

The pounding stopped.

"They're asleep," the mage said. "All of them."

‡

"And me?" Churls asked. "Why am I not asleep?" She needed to know what threat the mage was to her.

The woman swallowed, her eyes searching Churls's face. She was clearly Knosi, not Tomen. Potentially, a good sign: perhaps she had no loyalty to Fesuy.

"I'm not sure," she said. "Something's standing in the way. I can't touch you." Panic crossed her features. She had admitted to trying it. "Please . . . I wouldn't . . ."

Churls clapped the mage on the shoulder with her good hand. "Yes, you would. Keep them asleep, and we all live for a bit longer."

She crossed the room to her companions, bent partially over to keep from brushing the ceiling. Vedas lay immobile, sheathed completely by his black elder-cloth suit—worrying, as she had only seen him do so while conscious—but his pulse and breathing were strong. Her eyes avoided the hollow of his belly, the prominence of his ribs. His arms and shoulders were noticeably smaller. Slowly, with one good hand and a barely functional second, she untied his wrists, which had been tightly bound with steel cord to the bed.

As for Berun, she had no way of checking on his status or removing his immense shackles, and so ignored him for now.

"Vedas," she said. She put her hand to his chest and shook him slightly. "Vedas."

No response. Churls limped back to the mage and crouched before her. The woman flinched away.

"What's wrong with them?"

The mage's confusion was obvious. "Asleep. I told you, everyone is asleep."

Churls kept herself from slapping the woman, barely. "Not them. Everyone sleeps but the people in this room. Wake them, now."

She did not wait for a reply, but went and knelt by Vedas's bedside again. She repeated his name, and waited as long as she could—perhaps thirty seconds—before turning back to the mage and gesturing her impatience. The mage, still obviously frightened, shook her head and protested ignorance.

"I don't know when they'll wake," she insisted when pressed. "They make me keep them out for most of the day. I allow the Black Suit to wake for feeding and voiding himself, but they still make me keep him in a daze. It always takes him a while to come to, longer each time. I can't force it or I risk hurting him. The construct I've only allowed to wake twice so the Titled Amendja could speak with him. He was weak, nearly insensate, both times." She pointed toward the roof, only five feet overhead. "The sun. He needs it, and I can only give him so much. Enough to keep him alive, no more."

Churls stood to examine the roof. "Increase the light," she ordered.

The magelamp brightened to a small sun, illuminating the bare room and revealing yet another ceiling panel above Vedas and Berun. Churls reached to unlatch it and paused.

"*Everyone* is asleep?" she asked.

"Yes," the mage said. "And no one is on the roof."

Churls opened the panel, letting it fall back onto the roof. She looked quickly around to confirm what the mage had said, and also to determine if her assault on Fesuy's home had alerted any of the locals.

No one ran wild through the streets. She noticed a few more people about, though none seemed in any hurry. She relaxed slightly, thanking fate for thick, insulating clay walls.

The horizon glowed faintly, only forty or fifty minutes away from showing the sun. She wondered how long it would be before someone noticed the blood below the front door, noticed the missing guard, or failing either simply tried to enter the building for business. She doubted the mage could defend the entire structure from attack. Mages were specialists, after all: to become skilled in manipulating a man's consciousness took time and effort.

She checked on Vedas again, saw no change, and crossed the room again.

"Can you keep people from wanting to enter this building?" she asked the mage. "Or, better yet, can you make them disinterested in entering the building?"

"Yes. I can turn individuals and maybe small groups away from this building." The mage met Churls's stare and held it. The woman's eyes were dull and half-lidded. She had been overexerting herself or—more likely, Churls imagined—had been forced to overexert herself. Nonetheless, there was now a note of defiance in her expression. She had realized her value to Churls.

"But I can't do it and keep everyone asleep," the mage said. "It's just too much."

Churls sat back, and for a moment refused to think.

The moment passed, and her shoulders slumped.

"Fuck," she said. "Fuck, fuck, fuck."

‡

Churls could not trust the mage not to wake everyone in the home once she was otherwise occupied. As a result, Churls brought the woman along.

Blindfolded, as she could not conceive of forcing anyone to watch her at her task.

Nonetheless, the mage understood what was occurring immediately. Even an unconscious body made noise in the process of dying. Inside the house, it was very quiet.

Thankfully, killing the two girls Fesuy had bedded proved unnecessary. They would not be able to escape the bonds and gags Churls used to restrain them. The rest, however, were clearly warriors, capable of a great deal more. She could not risk one getting loose, and so did what needed to be done. It remained a far, far from pleasant task—she had never killed an unconscious person, even an enemy—but at least, she reasoned, they were not the sort of men the world needed in greater quantities.

She breathed a sigh of relief: it seemed the only innocent death on her hands would be that of the woman she had killed upon entering the building. Then, in a small, nearly overlooked room on the first floor, she discovered two small children.

She removed the mage's blindfold and forced the woman to look.

"Dear Adrash," the mage whispered. Her eyes were wet, but her disgust with Churls was clear. "Why are you showing me this?"

Churls laughed without humor. "I'm showing you because something needs to be done. I won't kill them or tie them up, and I have no way to get them somewhere beyond these walls. There's too great a chance of our being discovered, even if I could get them to a place of relative safety. Tell me you can push yourself a bit harder."

They regarded one another. Churls anticipated the woman's refusal, and her resentment flared. The woman had allowed Fesuy to capture Vedas and Berun, an extraordinary feat considering their combined abilities. She had kept Fyra from finding them for an extended period of time. And now, now she would make an argument as to why a simple task could not be done?

Churls curled the fingers of her left hand into a fist.

"Please," she forced herself to say, voice flat.

Slowly, as if to draw out her slight success, the mage nodded. "I'll need them closer to me, however. That will make it easier."

Churls took one child in her arms, the mage took the other, and they returned to the attic.

‡

The day began, entering the room from its sharp angle to crawl slowly down the western wall. Neither Vedas nor Berun woke. Instead of watching time pass, Churls occupied herself by fetching bedding for the unconscious children and dragging bodies one-handed to the cellar. She made a good sweep of the floors, as the thought of tracking blood around the house sickened her.

When she could not rationalize avoiding it any longer, she explained the situation to the two frightened girls trussed on Fesuy's bed. They stared at her, comprehending only with repetition. Clearly, each had been sheltered and understood little of the language used beyond their country's border. Both looked horrified by the suggestion that Churls would assist them in using the toilet. They did not want her to touch them for any reason.

Churls sighed. "Fine. Piss and shit yourselves all you want. When you need water, you'll let me know in your own way."

She checked with the mage, who assured her that all was well, that she had deterred three people from approaching the house. The morning became afternoon. Her companions continued to resist waking, and so Churls took another camp bed from one of the lower rooms and placed it alongside Vedas's. She held his limp hand and did not sleep. She could not sleep, in fact—for fear of the mage trying something odd in her absence, but also, simply, because she had run out of tasks to keep her mind distracted. Even her worry over the fate of Vedas and Berun, the constant factor that had kept her from taking the broader view, was now at an end.

Whatever happened, would happen together.

This realization brought her comfort, but also consternation. She could no longer ignore the world around her—a world going mad.

A world that her lover had brought into existence.

This fact bothered her less than she would have imagined. Truthfully, it distressed her more that she could not summon the expected outrage, that she had not lied to her daughter. Vedas had been right to deliver his speech, exhorting men to stand with each other against Adrash. She approved of it, still, despite the chaos it had created. Staring at the night sky, denying or openly accepting the reality of what The Needle represented for generation after generation: neither spoke well of mankind. Both perspectives had warped the world into a place where no progress could occur.

Why labor to change anything when it might soon come to naught? *Better to stir the pot slowly, or not at all. Keep shuffling into tomorrow.*

She could no longer countenance a world like that, but berated herself for being so brutal in her assessment. How could she look at the falling sky and prefer it to an uncertain, but certainly longer, future? (A preference, she reminded herself, even Vedas did not share. He persisted in punishing himself for what he had done.) Surely, men could do nothing to stop Adrash from exerting his will.

In this light, mankind standing up for itself made no difference. Was it not a sign of their immaturity that anyone would rail against the inevitable, fighting the unstoppable?

No, she insisted, against all logic.

No more bowing, she thought. *No more accepting our fate calmly.*

‡

At the end of the world, she had begun to believe in something.

She found herself half-hoping to stop.

‡

"Madam?"

Churls jumped. She had not been asleep, but she had not been properly awake, either. "Yes?" she asked, blinking away the brightness of the sky through the open ceiling panel.

"The big one—Berun. He is waking."

She rolled onto her feet and knelt near the constructed man's head, staring into the coal-black spheres of his eyes, which gradually began to glow reassuringly blue. She laid her hand on one massive, rubbled shoulder. Cold marbles under her palm.

"Berun," she said. "I'm here. It's Churls."

The mage cleared her throat. "I might not stand so close to him."

Churls grinned, and only flinched slightly when Berun shuddered and then heaved himself up from the floor, straining against the massive iron manacles bolted into the floor at his wrists and ankles, mouth opening and closing in silence. She kept her hand on his shoulder, and continued to repeat his name and tell him hers.

Just as suddenly as he had woken, he went still, falling back to the floor with a thump Churls felt through her feet. She leaned forward and shielded his brow as the glow began to fade from his eyes.

"No," she said. "No, Berun. Come back, right now."

A low sound, barely audible, came from his open mouth—the call of a bass horn from two battlefields away. Churls bent her ear to catch it.

". . . you. Safe. Vedas. Safe?"

"Yes," she said. "We're both safe, though Vedas hasn't woken yet and we're stuck in the middle of Fesuy's territory." She squinted above her head. "There's a skylight. I have as much sun coming in as possible, but I worry it's not enough. You have to be able to move, and soon. We don't have all the time in the world."

"I feel it, Churls. Thank you."

For several moments he remained silent, and Churls assumed he had said all he would.

And then:

"Two days."

‡

At midnight, the mage called from above. Churls stopped her restless pacing along the second-floor hallway and climbed the ladder to the attic.

"He's waking, but slowly," the mage said. "Don't force it."

Churls turned toward Vedas, but the mage called her back. In the magelight, the woman's reddened eyes were entirely without white. They reflected no light, as though completely dry. Blood-colored sleep granules had gathered in their corners. Her lips were cracked, around them a layer of white crust: dried spit, of course, but also a fair bit of the bonedust she had been surviving on for several days.

"I can't keep this up," she said. "I need a rest."

It was easy to believe her, yet . . . "How did you cope when Fesuy was running things?"

The mage's smile was ugly. "You killed my replacement, Shouz. He wasn't very good—he'd never been trained properly—but he serviced for a few hours every night."

"I can't think about this right now." Churls looked across the room to Vedas, bathed in moonlight, and her left foot stepped in his direction of its own accord. She paused just before reaching him, however, and cursed. Without the mage, they would be ruined. "No. Never mind. I do need you. I'll arrange something after he wakes. *After.* One more hour, you understand? Then you can rest. I promise I'll find a way."

Vedas's chest rose under her palm. He moaned. She brushed her hand along his arm, noting its thinness with sorrow, and intertwined her fingers with his. Her heart shuddered against her ribs, caused her throat to constrict with its feverish beating. She flushed, feeling the stare of the mage at her back, and nearly let go of his hand. Instead, she gripped it tighter.

"I'm right here, Vedas. Wake up. Let me know you're alive."

The black elder-cloth peeled back from his eyelids, and he turned his head toward her. His eyes vibrated visibly in their sockets as he tried to focus on her. Slowly, as if struggling to control it, he caused the elder-cloth to retreat further, revealing the gauntness of his bearded face. She kept the worry from clouding her features, or hoped she did.

"It looks good," he croaked. His hand tightened around hers. "I like it."

She smiled and shook her head. "Fuck if it does. I look like a melon."

He chuckled, which began him coughing. He let go of her hand and levered himself into a sitting position with obvious difficulty, protesting her assistance. For a moment, his entire body shook. She gave him water. He drank it slowly, displaying his rare and sometimes rather maddening capacity for self-control.

No throwing up water for Vedas Tezul. Regardless of how thirsty.

"Berun?" he asked.

"Don't answer," she answered before the constructed man had an opportunity to speak for himself. "Conserve your energy." She turned back to Vedas. "I'll sum everything up for you: It's the twelfth of Sectarians. That makes it almost three weeks that you've been kept here. It took me that much time to recover and then locate you, longer than I'd hoped. Berun tells me it'll be two days before he's ready to leave. We'll need him at full capacity."

Her voice dropped. "I don't know if we can rely on Fesuy's mage to shield us from view completely."

Vedas looked over her right shoulder, expression unreadable. "She's keeping people out? Impressive. What about Fesuy—the others? Everything's cloudy in my mind, but I seem to recall quite a few of them."

"Sixteen soldiers, including Fesuy. Plus one woman—a maid, maybe. All dead." She held his gaze until it became clear he would add nothing to this pronouncement, and pointed to the southeastern corner of the room. "I found two children on the bottom floor. The mage agreed to keep them asleep. And in Fesuy's bedroom are two girls trussed up like calves, probably shitting themselves as we speak. I think they think I'm some sort of sexless monster."

He raised his eyebrows, thoughts left unsaid.

"You're tired," he eventually said. He stared at her puffy right hand. "You're hurt."

She nodded. "My shoulder's not feeling so great, either."

He lifted his left hand and looked at it, clearly concentrating. It took several dozen heartbeats, but eventually, crawlingly, the elder-cloth retreated from the tips of his fingers, up to the second joint of each digit. The skin revealed was a markedly lighter shade of brown than that of his face and neck, the color of diluted coffee.

She closed her eyes as he ran his fingertips over her bristly scalp. He traced the seams of her skull. Gently, she pulled him toward her.

They kissed, both tasting horrible, neither caring.

‡

Vedas offered to accompany her on the roof while the mage slept, but she declined. Considering his condition, she thought it best that he raid Fesuy's icebox and fall asleep with a full stomach, which, despite his protestations to wakefulness, he did promptly upon finishing his meal.

She paced alone, a mindless circuit: around the roof in one direction until she reached the skylight. Turn back. Around again in the opposite direction. Her mind wandered aimlessly, snapping back to task at the slightest sound or movement in the streets. Near dawn, just as she began to ask herself whether or not it was wise to be sleepwalking so close to a twenty-five-foot fall, it happened.

A shadow passed across the moon.

She crouched, peering up to see a line briefly bisecting the bone-white circle.

A tail—she knew it instantly. She had heard the rumors of the man who had once been a tamer and now controlled a significant portion of the city. They said he had brought his pet with him, though as far as she knew no one had actually seen it.

Her eyes tracked the animal's flight. Its form was difficult to determine against the night sky: gliding rapidly over the rooftops, blotting out stars as it went, the details pieced together only gradually to form an image. The gull-like wings, which appeared overlarge when compared to the thin, streamlined body at their juncture. The long, arrow-shaft-straight neck led by a smallish tapering head. Lastly, the tail, which stretched behind to nearly twice the length of the neck.

When she had turned three complete circles to follow its flight, realization struck.

It was becoming larger.

She turned toward the skylight just as the mage screamed.

Vedas had reached her by the time Churls dropped into the attic. He straddled the woman's chest as her body spasmed beneath him. Elbows locked, he pressed her head to the floor, palms tight over her eyes. Churls came to his side and immediately surmised that his efforts would fail. Blood poured from beneath his hands, pooling quickly under the mage's head. Already, her spasming was dying down.

"Leave her," Churls said. "She's dead already."

His posture did not relax. "What's happening?" he yelled.

Before she could reply, a crash sounded behind them. Berun had ripped his manacles free of the floor. He rose, each of his thousand joints creaking shrilly, standing with half of his broad torso above the skylight. Churls watched him turn a slow circle, tracking the beast on its flight.

Vedas stood beside her, bloody hands on his knees. She waited until his coughs subsided.

"Do you remember a rumor about a man with a dragon?" she asked. "A man they call the tamer?"

‡

After several revolutions and one aborted attempt to lift himself onto the roof, Berun sagged, propping himself up against the skylight.

"It's coming down," he said, voice disconcertingly faint. "Go."

His companions refused. Vedas readied the two children as Churls climbed down to untie the girls on Fesuy's bed. She slapped them into wakefulness and led them around the room to get the blood back into their limbs. They stumbled and righted themselves, terrified of her, not wanting to be touched. Vedas pushed a screaming child into each of their chests and yelled.

"Fao! Fao!" Go! Go!

The girls hardly needed to be told. Both were gone without a word or backward glance. The front door slammed as they exited the house, and

Churls let out a deep breath she had not realized she had been holding. She gripped Vedas's hand, tugged him weakly toward the attic.

He resisted. "Why here? Why now?"

"I don't know." She ran a shaking hand over her face. "No, I suppose I do. It makes sense. He runs part of the city. Fesuy was a rival. When I killed him and forced the mage to focus on keeping people out, the secret became plain to any mage hired to listen to the right voices. This man—the tamer—he's come to claim Fesuy's land before someone else does."

They stared at one another. He opened his mouth, but she held up her hand. She closed her eyes tightly against the world while she worked out things she suspected would appear simple in any other state of mind.

"No, you're right," she said. "He could've attacked Fesuy any time he liked." She nodded upward. "There's a dead woman there to prove it. Not only that. He has a wyrm. Why hasn't he used it before now?"

She did not wait for his answer. It would not have mattered, she supposed: they were not leaving Berun alone, frozen into place where he stood, an easy target for the wyrm's grasping claws. She climbed to the attic, Vedas at her heels. They squeezed around the inert form of the constructed man and stood on the rooftop, searching the sky.

Vedas gasped. Churls followed his gaze and only just kept from following suit. She had been looking high, hardly expecting the animal to have banked so sharply into a descent—to be so near. Instead of measuring its body against the stars, she now tracked its movement relative to the vertical wall of Usveet Mesa. Moonlight played along metallic purple-black scales, shifting focus from one wing to the other as the animal altered course to keep its lower wingtip from brushing the occasional three- or four-storey building.

"Orrus Dabil Alachum," he swore. "It's huge. I heard the stories, but I never imagined . . . It's going to collapse the entire building when it lands."

Churls smiled grimly in agreement and sat. She patted the rooftop next to her. "Nothing we can do then, is there? Besides, it's better to be on top of a falling house than inside it. Sit with me, Vedas."

He stared down at her, clearly at a loss. She sympathized.

"Is that you, Churls?" he asked. "Churli Casta Jons does not—"

"Churli Casta Jons is injured and exhausted," she said. She patted the rooftop again.

He sat, and together they waited.

‡

The pressure of the wyrm's downbeating wings pressed them flat, driving the air out of their lungs. The gale ripped tears from Churls's eyes, but she refused to look away as the sky above her was eclipsed, becoming a massive, heaving reptilian belly. The beast fell and seemed to continue falling until surely she must be crushed. Vedas gripped her hand tightly enough to grind her knucklebones together, but she barely felt it. Her mind had become a howling cacophony. She anticipated nothing, patient while her lungs burned for air, lost in wonderment and terror.

Huge, carriage-sized talons spread to grip either side of the rooftop, causing the entire clay structure to groan like a living thing and crack like falling timber. Even when the wyrm settled itself and the pressure in her ears finally let up, noise enveloped her. A massive sound, as though a thousand bellows were being compressed simultaneously, came from above.

Breathing. The expansion and contraction of lungs larger than herself.

The spell broke, and she remembered her own body's need. She inhaled, far too fast. Pain stabbed through her chest and she rolled onto her side, shaking as her lungs seized inside her. She thought with a clarity that surprised her . . .

Hypnotized by a bloody big lizard. What an idiot thing to happen.

She finally regained control of herself and pushed up into a crouch, holding out a steadying hand to Vedas as he got shakily to his feet beside her.

The wyrm's belly heaved above them, a smoothly muscular wall of alien flesh. When the animal breathed in, its scales lowered near enough to touch. The house continued to groan under Churls and Vedas, quaking alarmingly with every shift of the wyrm's wings—wings that extended over several nearby buildings, shielding the sky from view entirely. It was said by men who made their livings along the deeper shorelines of Knoori that oceanic creatures could reach an enormous span, but without water to support a body, how could it possibly . . . much less fly . . .

Churls and Vedas exchanged a wide-eyed look, and she surprised herself by recalling a moment when, as a child, she and a neighbor boy had nearly been trampled by a draft horse that reared before them. They had shared the same stunned expression of horror and amazement.

"The head," Berun said, voice almost unheard over the sound of the wyrm's breathing. His next words were lost, merely a fading brassy undertone.

The head. Churls and Vedas turned to watch it swing in toward them upon its long neck, its perpetually grinning visage growing and taking on definition. It was a great, predatory wedge, bony and sinewy and blunt, filled with recurved teeth that hung down from its upper jaw even with its mouth closed tight. Its eyes burned with a visible amethyst light and smoke poured from its nostrils. Long past the point where Churls thought it would stop growing, it grew, until it was before her—massive, an entire creature of its own. Able, should it choose to, swallow her whole without pausing to chew.

A man sat upon it. He slid down its side and dropped onto the roof.

It took several seconds for Churls to see him as anything other than a small thing standing next to the wyrm's gigantic head. She blinked, and the image reoriented itself.

He was not a small creature, except by comparison to his pet. Though not unusually tall (she marked him at a little over six feet in height), he was immensely broad through the shoulders, chest, and thighs. In loose-fitting garments, he might fool someone into believing him fat, but his tight, sleeveless vest clearly strained against slabs of muscle. She knew his belly, ample though it was, would be a solid drum if collided with it. It would be ridged with muscle, a steel washboard.

This was a man not easily knocked down, or even swayed from side to side.

He wore a leather cap and a pair of smokeglass goggles. She could not yet tell the color of his skin or determine a likely nationality.

"You are Churls and Vedas," he said. He spoke softly in a baritone rumble, yet it carried easily over the sound of the wyrm's bellows-breathing. He looked down at the constructed man near Churls's feet, torso half-in, half-out of the skylight. "And this, I assume, is Berun."

"Well done," Churls said. "You know our names and you ride a dragon, and I bet they call you the tamer for fairly obvious reasons. What do you want?"

To her annoyance, he chuckled. He took a step forward, and she tensed. Vedas did not move perceptibly, but the elder-cloth closed around his features. She wondered why he had not done this earlier—it would have helped him breathe as the wyrm came down—and realized he had likely decided not to on account of her. She could not be shielded from it, and so neither could he.

She clenched her teeth and put her hand on the pommel of her sword. She was not as good with her left arm, and the weight of her gimp right shoulder would throw her off. Still, her opponent stood unarmed.

Next to a dragon, she reminded herself.

The tamer stopped after two steps, smile in place. He held up a broad, placating hand.

"To talk to you," he said. "That's what I want, and all I expect. If, afterward, you decide to accompany me, so much the better."

"Accompany you?" Vedas asked. He exchanged a glance with Churls. "That won't be happening."

"So certain," the tamer said. He lifted his goggles, turned on his heel, and walked to the edge of the roof. "I'd not speak so hastily." He waved them forward over one shoulder, not looking to see if they came. "Fesuy had a sizable population of dangerous men under his control—warriors with considerable martial skill, Tomen mages with less, and even a few rented mages of other nationality. A few of these last possess considerable talent, enough to do damage to anyone left on this roof. They're waking up along with the rest."

He turned back, seemingly unsurprised that neither Churls nor Vedas had moved. He patted the side of the wyrm's head. The animal did not react: it was a stone fallen from the sky, still smoldering.

"Try as she might, Sapes can never keep from causing a stir when she lands. This time, we even lost the element of surprise. I went out of my way to alert you to our arrival. I assumed you wouldn't run, and I was right." His smile returned. Despite herself, Churls noted that while he was not attractive, he had a distinct charisma. "I mean it as a gesture of trust between us. I'm dealing with you openly, making my intentions obvious."

Churls heard shouts from the streets below. "Make them more obvious," she said.

The tamer nodded. "I'm no friend to Adrash. Neither are the three of you." His eyes locked on Vedas. "I believe your words were, *Our fellow man is not the enemy. Adrash is the enemy.* They're words I agree with exactly, words that seem to have sparked a reaction in the heavens. You've been blamed for beginning the end of the world. You no doubt believe yourself responsible."

Vedas remained silent. He could have denied it, Churls reasoned, but anyone would have pegged it as a lie. He had delivered his speech, whereupon the whole of Danoor had witnessed the rise of the fractured Needle. There was no one else to blame.

She expressed as much.

"Attaching blame doesn't solve every mystery," the tamer said. "There are times when events coincide in such a way that the answer seems obvious, but is in fact a greater mystery. This is such a time. I know the only man who could be responsible. He is an elderman by the name of Pol Tanz et Som—a mortal creature like you, now likely dead."

Vedas made a sound halfway between sigh and groan. "And? Get to the point."

The tamer quirked an eyebrow. "I thought the news would be welcome. You are absolved of guilt."

"A name is all you've given us, and a name is useless. The situation is unchanged. Offer us something, or leave."

A shout sounded from the street. Very close. Fear of the wyrm would keep Fesuy's people away for a few minutes yet, Churls guessed, but it was only a matter of time before the line broke. She did not want to go with the tamer, but he had forced their hands by killing the mage. He held every advantage. They were treed prey, and he knew it. Whether or not he minded drawing the moment out, however, resulting in the injury or death of one of them—this remained to be seen.

Her gaze fell upon Berun, inert and vulnerable.

"The tamer won't leave us here," she said to Vedas. "One way or the other, we're going. It might as well be now."

Vedas shook his head in disagreement.

Churls resisted the urge to swear. "Quickly, then, both of you. Come to some kind of terms."

The tamer removed his goggles and leather cap, revealing two tiny horns that sprouted from his forehead, mirror-images of the ones Black Suits such as Vedas wore on the hoods of their elder-cloth suits. He dipped his head at Vedas, as if to acknowledge this fact.

"I offer this: an opportunity to change the world. To free men of tyranny." He lifted both hands to the sky. "The proof is above us, Vedas

Tezul. Adrash's will is not total. Tell me this displeases you. Tell me, and I'll go away."

Vedas said nothing.

The tamer did not press his advantage by raising his voice in encouragement. He did not proselytize obviously. Instead, his voice dropped nearly to a whisper.

"Come with me," he said, "and I'll show you how to make good on your word. I'll show you a way to stop hating yourself for what you *think* you've done."

‡

It was this last statement, Churls knew, that decided him. Without a path to redemption, a man would watch the world burn. With a measure of hope, the same man . . .

Well. He would not be the same man, would he?

CHVRLI CASTA JONS

After they arrived in the tamer's quarter of the city, she waited long enough to confirm that Berun remained undamaged from the flight (a handful of minutes exposed to the slanted morning sunlight allowed him enough energy to utter three words: "Go, Churls. Rest.") before she collapsed onto the bed in the room provided for her and Vedas.

Exhaustion should have taken her immediately. When it did not, she lay perfectly still, pretending at sleep. She listened to Vedas as he paced, sat for minutes in heavy silence, and got up again. He held his breath and let it out explosively. Finally, at the point where words seemed ready to erupt from him—at the point where she nearly gave up, herself, and admitted to being awake—he exited the room.

She sighed in relief, and rearranged herself into a more comfortable position.

No, she did not want to talk yet about what had happened. She felt, in fact, that the issue need not be confronted at all. Vedas could feel betrayed by her insistence that he come to a resolution with the tamer for as long as he needed: eventually, he would admit the situation atop Fesuy's roof had been unworkable. To take the stand that he had in delaying an inevitable decision, letting pride cloud fact for even a moment, had revealed more about himself than she considered wise.

347

They had already given up something by trusting the tamer. Vedas need not volunteer more by making his fears so apparent.

He had not needed more information atop the roof. He had needed to be convinced to step off the roof.

Sleep came halfway. She lay awake but dreaming, reliving the flight from Fesuy's territory: the exhilarating drop of her gut as the wyrm rose in mammoth surges, its wings snapping like ship sails—the spaceless, agreeably nauseating moment of freefall during each upthrust—the wind warm but cutting over her scalp, in her eyes, pushing her first one way in the saddle and then the other, now and then slamming into her as though trying to toss her out into space—and over it all, the sound of breathing, titanic and utterly inhuman. No shift from inhalation to exhalation, just one long sustained howl of air sucked into the creature's cavernous lungs, a roar that filled every open space in Churls's body, forcing the awareness of her own fragility.

She had loved every horrifying second, and loved every second again, momentarily safe and warm, bathed in sunlight from the open window. The waking dream hardly needed improving the third and fourth time around, yet she managed it: instead of gripping the handles of the saddle, Vedas wrapped his arms around her stomach, pressing his chest against her back, his rough cheek against hers. She gripped the hard cords of his forearms, laughing at his childlike fear, careless in a way the world never seemed to allow. When the wyrm suddenly dropped toward an open area of ground at the northern tip of the city, he squeezed the air from her lungs.

They landed, and entered a bedroom filled with morning light. She took him on the floor, roughly, and then let herself be taken on the bed.

She woke fully and masturbated while her arousal remained, before Vedas returned. Using her left hand, it took longer than usual.

The act left her with the vague feeling of guilt, a feeling she expected and dismissed with a small measure of difficulty. She would not be celibate with herself, not in her fourth decade and certainly not with the world in the state it was, yet she also comprehended how little experience Vedas had with intimacy. Unjust though he undoubtedly knew it was, he would be hurt to discover her pleasuring herself. He understood the baser needs of a person only in theory.

Denial had long since become his way of life.

While she could respect this measure of discipline in a man, she regretted the ways in which it made him inflexible, unwilling to give himself over to joy. Vedas had taken to physical intimacy with an intensity, single-mindedness, and talent she had anticipated, enjoyed, and lamented. She wanted him to stop thinking for one damn minute of his life, yet knew he would not. Not now, having had a hand in plunging the world into madness.

She growled into her pillow. It tired her to think of him any longer, to consider her prize, and how it was not perfect. He had given more of himself than she had ever believed he could.

Her own selfishness gnawed at her, and eventually carried her into dreamless sleep.

‡

Someone called her name. She came out of sleep with the back of her neck tingling.

Instinctively, she knew it was well past midnight, into yet another day, and that she was alone. Vedas had chosen a bed in another room. She thought it likely he had not done it out of spite, but kindness—to allow her uninterrupted rest. It was exactly the kind of decision he would make.

"When are you going to learn?" she mumbled, then: "You can come in, Fyra."

Her daughter materialized at the foot of the bed. Churls resented the smirk, but said nothing.

"You're hurt," the shade of a girl said.

Churls held up her puffy right hand. "I am."

"Your shoulder too, and your left ankle. I can fix them."

"I know."

"But I'm not going to, am I?"

Churls let the question hang between them. The girl sought only to help, and it cost Churls nothing to accept. It would make them both happier. Churls tried to remember what her own mother had denied her. Less than she had shared, surely. The woman had allowed far too much, making it easy for Churls to disappear into the ranks of the infantry, ducking her responsibility to Fyra.

Mother and daughter stared at one another, the bed an ocean separating them. Churls considered how maddening it was, having a child. It had always seemed to consist of such awkward moments, where an errant word could tear everything apart.

"Fyra," she said. "I'd like to stop having the same conversations. How about you?"

The girl squinted, skeptical. "Sure," she said.

"Good. Then we'll start right here." Churls patted the bed before her, and forced an approving smile when the girl sat. She held out her broken hand, wincing at the twinge in her shoulder. "Encourage it on its way, Fyra. Don't fix it completely—just do enough to make it heal faster. No, I don't want to go over why. You know why, because I've said it over and over again. When I'm ready to reveal you to Vedas, I will. Nothing you can say will make it go faster, so just leave off it. Either that, or do it yourself. I can't stop you talking to him."

"No," the girl said. "I'm not going to do that, even though he should know about me. He already guesses something. He saw you *glowing*, Mama."

She had a point, one Churls had been studiously avoiding thinking about for months now. On their journey to Danoor, their ship had breached in the shallows of Tan-Ten, and only Fyra's assumption of Churls's body had saved them. It was madness to deny this event, yet Vedas seemed equally intent on letting it pass out of memory, or at least conversation.

Though grateful for this unexpected pass, their willingness to hide from one another saddened her. He had seen her naked many times—had seen her womb-birth scar, as obvious as a tattoo.

Instead of arguing the point, Churls simply nodded. "Then why not tell him? It should be easy for you. You're not bound by all of these—" She waved her good hand around. "—rules, are you? You don't have to pay attention to me. You can do whatever you want."

Fyra shrugged. "What I want to do is keep my promises." She poked her index finger into the flesh of her mother's palm.

Warmth radiated into Churls, ceasing her aches. She closed her eyes and sighed in pleasure. If she had access to Fyra's abilities, she would never have to worry about money again. No drug had ever worked so quickly. It loosened her tongue.

"You were always too serious, daughter. Promises are for adults to try to keep. When you're young, you lie, and you get away with it because you're young. Be young—you might like it." She opened one eye to look at the girl. "Besides, you never told me you wouldn't tell him."

Fyra shrugged. "I can make a promise to myself."

Churls chuckled. "Thank you."

"You're welcome."

The oddly companionable silence stretched. Churls enjoyed it, keenly aware of how imperfect the world was. How imperfect it had always been. Men deluded themselves when they believed in *better days*, some bygone era when the sun shone brighter. Better days had never existed. Joy had always been stolen, and sweeter because of that fact.

It ended when Fyra removed her finger from Churls's palm, forcing unclouded awareness once again.

"How did you know it was safe to come?" Churls asked.

"It wasn't easy," Fyra said. "You told me I couldn't leave to look for you, so I had to get someone else to do it. Her name was Elya. She died in the city a few months ago, when the riots started. She didn't want to do anything for me at first, but I was nice to her. I showed her how to do some things, and so she found you."

Churls was tempted to ask Fyra to clarify further, but resisted. She had no clear idea how the dead communicated or what their existence looked like, only that her daughter was unique among them, better at interacting with the material world. There were factions, some of which had aligned themselves with Fyra—and, by extension, Churls and Vedas. They wanted to be of some assistance in the war they imagined Vedas had begun.

"And now that you're here," Churls said, "I imagine you have an opinion on the tamer?"

The girl's features twisted in annoyance. The light she radiated grew into a small blaze before dying down again. "You know how upset I get when I can't figure things out, Mama."

Churls waited for more. She grew impatient and gestured for Fyra to continue.

"There's nothing else," the girl finally answered. "He's like looking at a black rock. I know there's something inside him, but I can't see it. He shouldn't be able to do that. Even the mage who hid Vedas and Berun, I could see her, just not what she was doing. It was like she put a big blanket over what I wanted to see. But the tamer? I don't think he's a mage. I don't think he's human. I think he's something nobody's ever seen."

‡

He cooked breakfast himself, a thing that struck Churls as odd. It was not that he was a man, or even that he was the man who had a day ago stolen them from atop Fesuy's stronghold—no, it was simply that he seemed so at ease, as though acting out a morning ritual with family. He radiated good will, putting her in an agreeable mood despite her sizable reservations.

Vedas worked at glowering, and more than once opened his mouth to speak, but she recognized how forced the performance was: he, too, could not resist being swayed by their host's inexplicable mood.

It did not hurt when the meal turned out to be delicious. Churls had been eating dried stocks for well over two months. She had nearly forgotten about food, and took to eating like a person starved. For once, Vedas was not shy in his expression of enjoyment, and ate three full plates. The tamer, not to be outdone, matched both of them.

Churls watched their host without trying to shield the fact. He seemed not to mind, meeting her eyes now and then with a frank smile before returning to his food.

Without doubt, the tamer was one of the most compelling men she had ever seen. Though his skin was a lighter shade of eggplant and his broad build was the polar opposite of a true hybrid's, much about him reminded her of the eldermen she had known. (A quarterbreed, she had heard him called, a mythical creature that could not, should not, exist, an impossible mating of elderman and human.) He possessed the same amber-colored eyes, the same black pelt over his scalp. A similar sort of sinuousness defined his face, as if every muscle were larger and closer to his skin than a man's.

Muscle, in fact, would quickly become an overused word if she were forced to describe him. A fighter by trade, she had surrounded herself with soldiers and athletes for most of her adult life, and even among their number the tamer's physical development was a spectacular oddity. Lions and draft horses were adequate comparisons, not men.

More remarkably, she knew, unreasonably yet with certainty, that what she saw was no product of training: he emanated good health in a way she had never before encountered, more like a fixture of existence than a fleeting portion of it.

Vedas, while far more attractive to her, nonetheless appeared somewhat brittle in comparison. It was as if, all at once, her eyes had been forced to recognize what lay inside him, waiting and always growing—a feature obvious but until now overlooked.

Death. Now acknowledged, it could not be unseen.

She looked at her own freckled forearms and saw it in herself. It struck her, how little it mattered, to suddenly discover something one had always known. She squeezed Vedas's hand under the table.

"What a strange mood this is," she said. "It's not what I'd expected upon waking. I'm not angry or nervous. In fact, I'm not even suspicious, and that makes me very suspicious." She met the tamer's open gaze again. "Let's start at the beginning. You're not what you appear to be, are you?"

He nodded. "Likely not. What do I appear to be, Churls?"

"A man, more or less." She paused, considering her words. "Though I doubt it's less."

The tamer laughed and slapped the table, causing their plates and silver to jump.

"Clever. And right to the point." He folded his napkin expertly and placed it beside his empty plate. He touched two thick fingertips to his stubby horns, both of which were slightly darker than his skin, appearing in texture like a fingernail. "I'm not less than a man. In truth, I'm further from a man than your friend Berun is from a stone sculpture. I won't demure in that regard. I—" His head tilted to the side, eyes staring over Churls's shoulder. "Speak of the creature itself, and it arrives."

A creak made her turn. Berun slowly made his way down the stairs leading into the kitchen. For a moment, she fought the urge to offer him assistance, and then gave up. She stood and went to him, wrapping her good arm around his massive right one. His craggy, outsized features drew into a smile as he looked down at her.

"Berun," Vedas said. "Vedas," the constructed man returned. The words were spoken with little obvious feeling, but Churls recognized their hard-won affection.

"Welcome again, Berun," the tamer said. "You need no food I can provide, clearly, but if there's something else I can do, please ask."

Berun stared at their host in silence, and then rumbled, "I've been left alone to recover for one day and an evening, and now part of the next morning. My ears have been open the entire time. You could have visited with me and explained yourself. Vedas woke from his rest briefly to lay upon the roof with me. He said that we're being encouraged by your men on the lower floor to stay here, to continue resting, that all will be explained. And so . . ." He made fists and rested them upon the table. Not quite, but almost, a threat. "I need nothing but for you to explain yourself."

The tamer's smile disappeared. He nodded, stood, and took their plates.

When he turned around, a fractured expression had altered his features markedly. A new man stood before them, one who appeared neither friendly nor particularly sane. His left eye rolled up into his head, and the other twitched madly as it settled briefly on each of them.

Churls fought the nearly overwhelming urge to send her chair skittering across the floor behind her, to place distance between herself and him. Vedas slowly lifted his hands to the table's edge, likely to prepare himself for upending it. Berun's eyes flared briefly, two magnesium-blue flares.

The tamer made a series of gutteral utterances while his lips moved, neither sound nor movement appearing in concert. Slowly, however, his throat managed to catch up with his mouth, and an alien vocabulary emerged, veering between utterly indecipherable and disturbingly familiar, putting Churls in mind of every time she had heard spats through thin tenement walls or from across a collection of tents. The odd word caught and guessed at.

She spared a glance at Vedas. His brow furrowed as he sought to comprehend something that clearly continued to slip away.

‡

Finally, the tamer's alien words ground to a halt. His left eye rolled back into place and his features evened out, solidifying into a glare he shared with each of them in turn.

"Shavrim Coranid," he said in a strained whisper.

Churls raised her eyebrows.

"Shavrim Coranid," the tamer repeated. He repeated them a second time, and slapped the table. Color bloomed in his cheeks. He closed his eyes and bowed his head, breathing audibly through his nose, struggling, obviously, to contain his anger. When he spoke again, it was with a voice shaking in rage, struggling to not become a shout.

"I am Shavrim Coranid." He looked from Churls to Vedas, brows raised. "Shavrim Coranid. *Shavrim. Coranid.* This . . . This name means . . . This name means *nothing to you?*"

His gaze settled fixedly upon Vedas. Churls looked from the tamer to her lover—the former, shaking from head to toe, and the latter, unnaturally still—and imagined that if she passed a hand between them it would encounter resistance. She opened her mouth to speak, and found, quizzically, that any question would be unnecessary.

She anticipated Vedas's nod a heartbeat before it came. When it did, she shadowed it. Berun stood immobile, a question creasing his features.

Vedas nodded. Churls nodded.

And then they both, at the same moment, said yes. Yes, the name meant something to them.

‡

"A name, once heard, cannot be forgotten," she had once overheard a Bashest priestess tell a practitioner. The words possessed a ring of truth to them, though Churls's mind had never been particularly suited to remembering. Faces, names, dates, she could not recall them beyond their moments of relevance, yet she knew with a peculiar certainty that she had never forgotten a single thing. Once acquainted with a place or person, even the most dim memories could be summoned again to help navigate oddly familiar streets, to understand a near-stranger.

As a small child she had taken ill with bone featherings, forcing her mother to visit a sawmage: not even someone who worked on livestock, no, but a local man who healed pit-dogs and other fighting animals. (They could not have afforded someone who worked on livestock.) When her mother mentioned his name a decade later, Churls did not associate it with the event she remembered only fuzzily.

She did, however, experience a surge of discomfort upon hearing it. The sawmage's name, which, of course, she could not now recall, was *ugly*, even offensive. It seemed wrong that it had come from her mother's mouth.

Had hearing it actually caused her to rub the long, jagged scar the man had left upon her right thigh? She recalled doing so, but it hardly mattered. The rush of emotion that had accompanied two small words—a name, surely, she had only heard a smattering of times as a sick-unto-delirious child—had not been an imagined thing. She had not created it out of nothing. It existed, a permanent connection to a place and time.

Likewise, she could not dismiss her reaction upon hearing the tamer's true name. It had not been immediate, no: it had built slowly within her, an increasingly undeniable pressure between her ears each time the man spoke.

Shavrim Coranid, SHAVrim Coranid, SHAVrim CORanid.

When it finally registered, when she could not discount her reaction as an ordinary response to the man's anger, it was as though it had always been a part of her, this name, and attendant to this name a weight, a collection of impressions beyond the scope of recollection, pressing upon her without discomfort, welcomed without conscious volition—as if a door had been opened into a previously undiscovered room, admitting a stream of vaguely familiar people who spoke in nearly-recognizable languages, who told tales of places she could almost picture.

All of this, at once. In a flash of awareness, her skull had become pregnant with associations she could not yet contextualize. She admitted the possibility of it being the product of enchantment, but it hardly mattered. If Shavrim Coranid were powerful enough to place such a complex sense of recognition within her mind, then all things in his presence were suspect.

‡

He collapsed after hearing their affirmations. Berun lifted him easily and took him upstairs. In Shavrim's room, the three of them stood silently around his bed for several minutes, staring at his motionless body as though it were a fascinating vista, a landscape they had seen a lifetime ago, perhaps, or had heard described by a relative. Churls spared a look at her companions, just in time to see them doing the same. They avoided meeting each other's eyes.

Without a word, Berun turned and ascended to the rooftop.

Similarly content not to speak, Churls and Vedas returned to their room, where, after a long period of examining the floor between them (she, feeling not the slightest trace of awkwardness, but instead a mounting sense of purpose, of waiting for the exact moment to move), they embraced. Slowly, they undressed one another—she completely, he as far as he would allow her to peel back his suit. She pressed her fingernails into the elder-cloth and carefully expanded holes that he allowed to form in the material, slowly revealing his chest, belly, upper and lower back, and buttocks.

She stopped before going lower, her hands playing over his rawboned torso. Inexplicably, sadness no longer gnawed at her to see how wasted he had become. For a fleeting moment, his frailty seemed appropriate, even beautiful. Its impermanence appealed to her, as did his atypically casual reaction to it. He had always been so worried over his body, touching it as though he thought it would suddenly fail him. As if, having lost something, it could never be regained.

It was a preoccupation born of privilege. He had always had enough to eat, enough spare time to train. A man like him had no reason to worry, and so he did.

"You just needed to lack for something," she whispered to herself, slipping her hands around his ribs and squeezing him to her, possessively, protectively. His fingertips ran lightly up her back. Gripping her head in his hands, he kissed her, tongue flicking over her teeth. When he pulled away, his arms fell around her shoulders and he buried his face in her neck. She shuddered at the scrape of his beard. Gooseflesh rose, covering her from head to toe.

They pulled each other onto the bed.

Immediately, she knew it would not be as it had been before. Unclothed, Vedas had always possessed a hint of nervousness about him, a feature now entirely absent. He moved as he had always done in his element: she thought of the sparring they had done, the times she had seen him confront an opponent, reacting fluidly, refusing to be rushed yet without an ounce of hesitation. At times, he became animated in a manner she had not yet seen, eyes wide or eyes shut, grimacing and smiling, abandoning himself to his sensations. He did not hide himself from her, or worse, try to impress her by taking control, but instead responded to her naturally, like it had always been a familiar thing between them.

"You're *here*," she breathed when they surfaced for air.

"I am," he said, and surprised her by returning a knowing smile.

She buried her fingertips in the thick nap of his hair and pushed him downward.

Afterward, they lay together, spent, touching only at the hands and crossed ankles, comfortable on a level she had rarely felt in the previous year of traveling and fighting and worrying. Of course, now that she acknowledged it, it began to fade. She fought to keep it from going away, and failed.

She frowned, her suspicions finally demanding full attention.

Somehow, he precipitated her words. She felt it in the air a moment before he let go of her hand.

"Vedas," she said. "We need to question this. All of it. Even if we don't want to."

Out of the corner of her eye, she saw him turn away from her. "I know," he said.

"It feels this good to you, too, doesn't it, what we just did, how we are now? It feels right, but you and I aren't . . . I mean, we haven't . . ."

"I know."

She squeezed his hand, grateful he had filled in the blanks. "It's not just that. There's also this feeling of . . . knowing? Shavrim, that name, it . . ." Again, she searched for words. "It means something to us. I could feel the moment when we realized it, together—both of us. Just like here, now, it feels real, *full*, like something obvious I'd forgotten."

"Like a dream," he said, "one you only recall later, because of a smell or a series of words. It didn't exist, and then—" he snapped his fingers "—it does."

She nodded. "Yes. Exactly. But we don't wake up from life, Vedas. We're not dreaming."

"You know there's more to the world than we see," he said. "I may be opposed to Adrash, Churls, but I'm not blind to the way forces other than he have bent creation. Miracles occur, beyond our reckoning. I'm not saying I'm convinced, but who's to say Shavrim Coranid isn't revealing something to us that we should know, something greater than ourselves?"

"Something greater, Vedas? No. The world has been shaped by many hands, but what of it? The events that appear as miracles, then and now, are exercises in power vastly greater than we can summon. They're impressive, no doubt, but they're also normal, completely of this world. Inexplicable things don't happen." She closed her eyes. "Nothing I've experienced would lead me to believe there's anything more than this, right here, this moment with you—"

Her last word ended in a croak.

The quality of the air had changed. Concentrating against the hammering of her heart, she realized that Vedas's breathing was no longer audible. His thumb, which had been rubbing at the back of her hand, had stilled.

She had been about to lie. Not to keep silent about Fyra, but to actively mislead.

Vedas released her hand and sat up. His suit slowly began to mend, circles closing to cover the areas of his back and upper buttocks he had allowed her to unveil. She pinched the bridge of her nose, grimacing, then swung her legs over the side of the bed and quickly pulled her clothes on. She allowed one glance to confirm that his nakedness had been covered completely.

"Fyra," she said. "Fyra, it's time."

‡

They stared at one another. The girl defiantly, chin up. The man expressionlessly.

"Fyra," Vedas said, voice flat. "You're the daughter."

The girl looked to Churls, who shrugged.

Fyra nodded. "Yes."

Vedas gestured for more. When neither mother nor daughter spoke, he sighed. He met Churls's gaze levelly, eyebrows raised.

"*Nothing you've experienced would lead you to think there's anything more than this, here?*" He pointed at Fyra, a clear indictment. He smiled, utterly humorless. "A bit of an untruth, isn't it, Churls?" The smile vanished, replaced again with a blank expression. He turned back to Fyra. "Please. Explain to me what your mother couldn't, or wouldn't."

Fyra surprised Churls by sneering at him. "Don't act like that," the girl said. "Mama made some mistakes. I wanted her to tell you, and that made me angry. But you . . ." She pointed at him, returning his earlier gesture. "You could have asked her after Tan-Ten. You didn't, so don't blame her for just now getting around to it."

After a brief pause, Vedas dipped his head in acknowledgement of her point.

They waited, Churls resolved not to speak. Finally, the girl caved.

"Ten years," she said. "I've been dead for ten years. Almost eleven. I wasn't always around. For a while, I don't think I thought anything at all. I was sleeping, I guess."

Vedas appeared to accept this without difficulty. "And now you're present—all the time? Hiding? Watching?"

The girl blushed a warm pink. Churls had never seen it happen before, not in life and certainly not after death. She had thought the girl's ethereal form incapable of generating color other than the blue of her eyes. Seeing it affected Churls in a way she could not have imagined.

It hurt, seeing it. Color in her daughter's cheeks.

She turned toward the window to hide the expression on her face.

"No," Fyra said. "Not always. I can't be here all the time. Even when I really want to be, it can be hard. The dead call me back. Not everyone wants me here."

Vedas shifted on the bed. Churls sensed his eyes on her, but did not turn back. She had invited Fyra into the room: the two of them could do the rest. She would not influence what information they did or did not share with each other.

"Why?" he eventually asked.

"I saved you and Mama on Tan-Ten, and then I fixed her shoulder after you hurt it. Don't say it. I know you didn't mean to, but you did. There are ways for the dead to be part of the world, to help the living, but most of them are afraid of doing it. They don't want to attract anyone's attention, especially Adrash's. That, or they're not good at crossing over."

"But you are?"

"Yes. Yes, I am. Better than anybody, ever."

Churls heard the smile in her daughter's voice, and grinned in response. The expression fled upon hearing what Vedas said next.

"And Berun—does he know about you?"

The question hung in the air. Churls fidgeted with her belt buckle, and made herself stop. Now that the issue had been broached, it seemed pure, embarrassing foolishness that she had avoided it. And yet, so much had been successfully avoided for so long, what did one more avoidance matter?

Just after rescuing Churls and Vedas in the shallows of Tan-Ten, Fyra had indeed appeared to Berun, leading him to shore, saving him from a slow death of light-suffocation under Lake Ten. Days after Vedas's speech, she had almost certainly helped Berun find Churls in Danoor, though neither the constructed man nor Fyra admitted to it. What Churls had never ascertained was whether or not Fyra had revealed her identity to Berun.

"I think so. I helped him," the girl said. She glanced at Churls. "Twice. But I can't be sure if he knows exactly who I am."

"Well, then," Vedas said. He swung his legs over the side of the bed and stood. "There's an easy way to be sure."

He opened the door and left without a glance back.

"That went well," Fyra said.

Churls sighed. "You have an interesting definition of *well*, daughter." She gestured Fyra toward the door.

"Not yet," the girl said. "They can wait. Give me your hand. There's no reason not to fix it now, right, Mama?"

Churls thought of arguing, but saw little point. Berun was patient, and Vedas could stand to pace through a minor delay.

As radiance flooded her body, touching every nerve and rendering it liquid, Churls reflected not on the violence or the tension of the last several days, but on all the talk. There had been too much. She could not fight the sinking feeling that like Vedas she had given too much away, that she had been careless in her words and revealed something she would regret. Of course, filled with Fyra's soft healing fire, she could not put her finger on just what she had lost—or if, indeed, anything had been lost. Perhaps it was mere paranoia, the result of having talked herself into a corner. She had never liked ceding control.

"Fyra," she said. "Why didn't you tell him? About . . . about . . ."

The girl smiled. "Yes, Mama? Tell him about what?"

Churls's head swam. Her tongue was thick, heavy in her mouth, and then it seemed as if it had fled her body entirely. She blew air out between her lips, causing them to flap. She laughed, though she saw no humor in the situation.

Her lips worked at the words before they came out:

"The . . . dead. How they want to . . . help us. A war. *The war.* Why not?"

"Be calm, Mama," Fyra said. "I'm trying to do something. You're more than hurt. There's something else, something I couldn't see before, when you wouldn't let me in. Let me figure it out." She flickered, growing in brilliance and then subsiding. One moment, she seemed of normal size, and the next she was a toy in Churls's outstretched hand.

"Fyra," Churls said. "I'm more than . . . hurt? Fyra?"

She fell back onto the bed. Her eyelids fluttered, vision losing focus. She labored to roll her eyes downward, to locate her daughter. Her limbs shook, no longer under her command. Gradually, the room grew dark, fading into black around the corners of her eyes. Closing in upon her.

Sleep, Fyra said.

‡

She woke, and immediately sat upright. The room possessed a startling clarity around her, a sharpness that cut through her disorientation. The blanket under her hand, the reflection of the mirror . . . every object she saw seemed suffused of its own light. Less than a handful of minutes had passed, she knew immediately, yet a longer span of time had passed inside the confines of her skull.

Fyra materialized before her, unusually faint.

"Mama," she said in a voice that sounded as though it came from another room. Worry made her look decades older. "Mama?" she repeated, squinting as though she were having trouble making out the woman sitting before her.

"Yes, Fyra?" Churls asked. Her voice, richer than she remembered, fuller in her throat and ears. She reached out with a steady hand, marveling at the texture of her skin, its smoothness and inexplicable, almost metallic sheen. Her fingertips stopped a mere hairsbreadth from her daughter's cheek. "Fyra, what is it? What's wrong?"

The girl's eyes widened, and she shrunk back. Her form wavered like a guttering candle.

"Mama? You're not alone," she said, and disappeared.

‡

Churls's brow furrowed in confusion.

"Fyra?" she asked. "Where did you . . . ? What did you . . . ?"

She blinked, and the world turned gray.

No, it did not turn gray. It grew dim. It was as if a shadow suddenly passed over the building. She stood and crossed to the window, leaning out to squint at the sun.

The sky stretched overhead, a clear bowl of blue, yet to her eyes it seemed drained of its vibrancy, filmed over with a layer of grit. As her gaze descended, the world darkened until the street below appeared shrouded in fog. She looked at her hands, and there it was again, clear in the calloused, labor-worn flesh of her palm.

Death. Once acknowledged, it could not be unseen.

Alone, without someone equally fragile with which to share her realization, it pained her to see. It was like an unhealing wound, a cancer. The vision of her mother, laid out in her aunt's threadbare bedroom, came to her. It had only been three years ago, but she still dreamt often of the wake. A fully-grown adult, inured to death—an experienced soldier, no less—her heart had nonetheless pounded as she took her mother's hand, finding it cold, its skin a parchment stretched over bird-thin bones.

She retreated from the window, hugging herself against a coldness rooted deep in her marrow.

"Fyra?" she asked. "What's happening, girl? Come back."

A painful knot formed in her throat. She had never seen her daughter's remains. She had been away, avoiding home and every responsibility home meant. Her mother had buried Fyra a month before Churls returned. Churls had not been there when her mother died, either—had missed it by days.

The world operated in cycles: one got what they deserved, in the end.

Churls would die—alone, she knew.

She retreated further until her backside hit the bed. She flinched, and reached back with shaking fingers to uncover the mattress. Her eyes never left the open window, as though she expected the arrival of death itself. The sheets still smelled of Vedas, yet another kind of longing.

"Fyra?" she repeated, knowing the girl had gone back to the dead and would not return for some time. Her daughter had discovered something, and taxed herself in the process.

Churls cursed. The world never stopped moving underneath her.

Though the temptation existed, she did not give in to irrational self-pity. She did not say her mother's name, or Vedas's. There would be no use, she reasoned, of wishing for comfort from either of them. Her mother had surely passed out of existence upon death. She had known her own strength, had come to terms with her place in the world in a way Churls could barely conceive. Inys Casta Jons had accumulated no soul-debt, no unfinished business, and would not have stuck around to watch over anyone. She had been ready for death.

And Vedas?

Churls shook her head. She did not close her eyes, did not sleep. She stared at the window until the sun passed directly overhead, until its direct rays no longer entered the room, and then she went downstairs to get drunk.

‡

She saw Vedas leave. He met her eye briefly as he passed through the games hall that made up the first floor of Shavrim's headquarters, but his expression gave nothing away. She watched the flow of muscle under his suit as he walked out the door, aware of her sad desire but unable to do anything about it. She sniffed at her fingertips, which still bore a trace of them both.

"Another," she told the bartender.

Five ales in, she ordered a sixth and then a seventh. An eighth and a ninth. She reached the point where she not so much thought about anything as let thoughts revolve around her, touching her awareness only briefly. Muddy-headed, she came to two swift, resigned conclusions she would not have been able to arrive at sober:

Vedas's anger—there was nothing she could do about it. There never had been anything she could do. They were, the two of them, too wounded to be anything other than a mess, moving from one feeling to the next without any means of control. Had she the ability to do it all over, she likely would make the same mistakes. Different words, same foolish sentiments.

What Fyra had said—it made no sense, and would make no sense until the girl returned, so why consider it any more than she had to? Fyra would not allow harm to come to her mother, if it were within her power to prevent it. And if she could not prevent it?

Churls ordered her tenth ale, scowling at the bartender when the woman raised her eyebrows.

There was, of course, a third issue that could not be completely ignored. She raised her eyes to the ceiling and winced.

Berun.

Berun, with whom she had shared so much—with whom she, in some ways, felt a deeper sense of connection than Vedas. He had listened without judgment, an immediate sympathy between them from the beginning. He had never asked anything of her, had expected only . . .

"Shit," she said to herself. What had he expected?

Trust. To be treated like any friend should be treated.

She ordered her eleventh ale.

"Fuck," she muttered after three sips, and rose unsteadily from her stool.

She ascended to the roof of Shavrim's base of operations, pausing before taking the final step onto the still-warm clay surface, peering around until she located the mountain of rubble that was Berun's cross-legged form. His gaze, she could see, was directed away from her, toward the sporadically lit city. She felt the chilly mass of Usveet Mesa, looming behind her.

She shivered, and opened her mouth to speak. She closed it again when words, even his name alone, failed to come.

Her fingers curled into fists. Her cheeks flushed. Impotent, she pivoted clumsily to leave.

"Churls," the constructed man rumbled, drawing the sound of her name out.

"Yes," she whispered, and took the final step onto the roof. She crossed to where he sat and stared down at him for a moment, unsure of her next move. He turned his craggy head up to her, the glow of his eyes intensely blue, a searing radiance in the darkness that made her blink. She swayed in place, and his massive hand came up to the small of her back, steadying her. She reached back, her own hand covering only a portion of his.

It struck her for only the second time since they had known one another: he radiated heat. Far less than a man, but it was something. It made him more human, though he might take offense with that summary.

What had he said when she noticed it, that first time? She could not recall. She wondered if it would come to her later. She hoped it would.

"I'm sorry," she said.

He laughed, a deep metallic tolling from within his great chest. "Sorry?" he asked. "Sorry for what, Churls?"

She broke his gaze. "Fyra. I should have told you."

A slight pressure upon her back. "Sit," he said.

She sat. His arm remained behind her, close but not touching. A minute passed, and then two. She finally rolled her eyes at her own foolishness (what would a constructed man care?), and leaned over onto his shoulder. His arm moved to support her back. She felt subtle shifts in the way he held himself as he accommodated to make her more comfortable against him—a thing, she imagined, he would not have known to do before meeting her.

"I need no apology, Churls," he said. "I *want* no apology. I told you, when we came into the city for you, I recognized her. I wasn't mad at you then. I'm not mad now. You have your secrets. From Vedas, you've kept secrets. Apologize to him, if you must apologize to someone."

She smiled grimly. "He and I may be past the point where apologies mean anything." She gestured out across the city. "He's out there now, and not here. I think I may have broken everything."

He shook his head. She saw it in her peripheral vision, and felt it through his body, the slide of his component spheres over each other.

"No. You've broken nothing. You give Vedas too little credit. Once, he wouldn't have thought about his anger. Not long ago, he couldn't see out from under his guilt, the hate he directed at himself. But now? Now, he's a different man. You're the first thing in his mind. If you can't see that, you're a fool. A friend, but still a fool."

He smiled down at her. "I almost think we've discussed these things before."

She remained silent.

"You'll see," he said. "The world is on the edge of death. Even as I am, not a man, I can see how wrong it would be to witness everything die without knowing who truly cares for you. You care for me. We share a bond." He tipped his head, touching his forehead to hers. "Again, even as I am, I can see this."

She nodded, not trusting herself to speak.

"And Fyra?" he asked. "She's still away, among the dead?"

She wiped at her eyes, though they were dry. "She's gone. Off to wherever she goes. Beyond where the world can touch her, beyond even Adrash."

She looked to the sky, where the broken Needle spanned. Drunk, it no longer filled her with the same fear. She was, however, suddenly aware of her anger. How dare the world be kept on a tether, threatened so? Who gave Adrash the right to hold the world in a thrall?

It was an idiot question, of course. Strength gave him the right.

And now—who but the dead could oppose him? She thought, for the thousandth time, of what it could mean to accept Fyra at her word. To accept her and her companions' help, to wage a war upon Jeroun's one true god.

As though his thoughts had strayed to a similar place, Berun spoke.

"And what of our captor's claims, Churls? Do you really believe our captor has a way to make good on Vedas's speech, to wage war upon Adrash? I saw what passed between you and Vedas. You recognized Shavrim. His words mean something to you."

She nodded, her eyes riveted on the chaotic view overhead. "I did recognize him. As did Vedas. I assumed you did, too." When he said nothing, she knew her assumption had been wrong. "But beyond the sense that I remember him? There's a void. No context, no specific memory. It's like it's been removed from my mind." Her voice dropped to a whisper. "Or maybe we're being manipulated. Of course we are. How could both Vedas and I both remember him? How could I know anything about the man's claims?"

"You're asking me?" Berun asked, amusement clear in his voice. "You, who are haunted by the spirit of your daughter, are asking me, a constructed man who has been assisted by that same spirit, what is possible? You're asking a half-broken creature, only recently freed from the bonds of his creator, for advice on the workings of gods and men?"

"I am," she said, finally lowering her eyes from the sky, meeting his bright gaze, holding the connection.

Searching.

"Fate help both of us, Berun, but I am."

VEDAS TEZUL

For the third night in a row, Vedas dreamt of the silver woman, cold and desirous of his warmth, a perfect complement to him: a needle of cold light, a finely focused lance of pain in the center of his being. They made love, quickly to suit her and then slowly to suit him, trading aggressions and tendernesses, moving as one mind. Knowing one another, as intimately as siblings. They referred to each other so, in fact—*sister, brother*—yet the words were puzzlingly alien, familiar and unfamiliar at once, altered to suit minds approaching but ultimately eclipsing human.

For the third time, the experience confounded him. He had never dreamt, aware of the dream. He had only ever been an unwilling participant, a mere inhabitant of his own body, forced to act and to believe wholeheartedly in the reality of his mind's illusion. Now, however, he knew himself as Vedas, the Vedas of the waking world, *here*, aware, alone, of one mind . . .

Yet not alone. Of two minds. Himself, and another.

Another, whose body and thoughts were as intimately recognizable as his own.

In his first and second dream, this had been the extent of it: the deep awareness of himself as someone else, less an occupation than a transformation.

368

In this, his third dream, however, he became aware of a new aspect, a pressure within his body, a looming awareness in both minds. As of an oncoming storm, or the tingling sensation of knowing someone is about to enter one's room.

Within the dream, dawn came to an end. The sun peeked above the belly of the world, instantly igniting the interior of the vast golden room in which the two made love, piercing through the amber lenses of his eyes, causing him to pause, mid-thrust.

He—the one who was and was not Vedas—quirked his head to one side, listening. His companion lifted her silver head and peered over her shoulder at him.

"Brother," she said. "We're not done."

"I know, sister," he responded. "A moment. First, say my name. I need you to say it."

She smiled, showing two rows of sharp white teeth. "Say please."

"Please," he said.

She spoke his name. He sighed in realization, and spoke hers.

‡

His eyes snapped open. He was alone, he knew instantly. Nonetheless, he rose and searched the room thoroughly. The crawling sensation of being watched persisted, just as it had on the previous two evenings after he woke from the dream. If anything, it had increased.

Sleep was a shore too far, and a new question had arisen.

He would seek answers, once more.

He descended to the first floor, into the games hall. Walking the room counterclockwise, he made himself meet the frank stares of Shavrim Coranid's men. Most were Knosi, openly curious about one of their cousins in a way he was only slowly becoming accustomed to. The assumption that, as countrymen, they had something in common, appealed and repelled in equal measure.

A few black-suited individuals smiled, offering him spots at their tables. He declined each with a polite wave of his hands, a gesture he had acquired from observation.

Undoubtedly, everyone in the hall knew who he was. What he had done.

They were allies, presumably, yet some among them—the paler-skinned Castans and Stoli, in particular—appeared discomfited by his arrival, shuffling their seats closer to their tables, shutting him out. He smiled at this, sadly amused without really understanding why.

Upon sight of his target, he became self-conscious. He straightened his already rigid spine, painfully aware of the thinness of his arms and legs, the hollows in his torso.

Laures, Shavrim's first lieutenant, stood where she had the two nights before, leaning against the wall with her arms crossed beneath her breasts. Unlike any Black Suit he had ever seen, her hands and forearms were bare, unprotected by the elder-cloth. Oddly again, though not entirely unknown in his experience, she wore clothes over her suit: a thin hempen vest and loose pants of the same material. Both were dyed the red-black color of dried blood.

"It's for the Mother," she had told him during their first conversation. "It symbolizes what she left after birthing the world."

He stared, uncomprehending.

"I'm Usterti," she said, as if that were sufficient explanation.

The name had communicated nothing singular to him, then. He pretended to understand what she had said, knowing it would not fool her. He knew what an Usterti was, of course. In theory, he knew a great deal about the religion, but theory carried him only so far. People did not act as books had led him to believe they would. They did not talk in straight, easily-comprehended narratives. Appallingly often, they did not even slightly resemble the pictures he had painted of them. He had heard all Mother-worshippers were witches or pornographers, ugly inside and out.

Laures was beautiful, long-limbed and athletically proportioned, clear-skinned, darker even than he. She wore her hair short, woven in tight, ordered rows upon her scalp. He thought it strange, how attractive he could acknowledge her to be, yet how little her form appealed to him. It seemed wrong that he should view her as more of an object, an abstraction worthy of admiration but not lust. Reason argued that if he had spent his life among his own people they would not appear so coldly uniform, like a series of glazed statues.

"Vedas," she said, the trace of a smile on her lips.

"Laures," he said, leaning against the wall at her side, affecting her casualness.

"Here again," she said. "You shouldn't be. The morning will come sooner than you think, and Osa's no small trip." Her eyes traveled up and down his body appraisingly. "You're not the Vedas Tezul I heard described as the winner of the tournament. You have no fat, and precious little muscle, to burn up. Go to sleep. Recover as much as your body will allow."

He only just kept from wincing, and shook his head. "I can't sleep. I have another question."

She laughed. "I already told you all I know about Shav last night. What little there is to know, you know. Trust me."

"No. It's not him I want to talk about." He made himself meet her stare, fighting the impulse to keep what secrets he had. If she had any loyalty to Shavrim (and he had no reason to believe she did not), she would tell him everything Vedas said. Perhaps, to Shavrim, the words would mean something. Perhaps he would be able to fill in the holes before Vedas could, using it to his advantage, manipulating them even further. With truth or with lies: it made no difference.

Vedas saw no other option, however. Without an answer to this newest question, sleep would continue to elude him.

"The Mother you spoke of," he said. "Ustert. There are things I seem to recall about her."

Her eyebrows rose fractionally, half her mouth moving with them. Regardless, he noted the way her posture stiffened. The fingers of her right hand twitched on her left bicep.

"You knew her then, did you?"

He kept his expression sober. "I remember reading a series of stories about her—stories from before the world was born."

She dropped all pretense of joviality. "Stories? Lies, you mean."

"They were not written by your sisters, obviously. They were written by men, trying to understand." He ignored her chuckle of contempt. "I don't mean to offend you by talking about them. I'm not insulting you, nor am I trying to get at secrets you don't want to reveal. All I'm asking for is confirmation that such tales exist."

She shrugged. "Ask."

Men are not a thing one talks about with an Usterti, he had been informed. "I could be wrong, but in one of them . . ."

Out with it, he told himself.

"In one of them, Ustert had a twin. A man, or maybe a boy."

After a moment, she nodded.

"Do you know his name?" he asked. "Will you tell me?"

‡

She had an answer for him. It showed on her face, yet for the space of many heartbeats she visibly fought with herself over whether to voice what she knew. Perhaps it would be a breach of her faith to utter the name.

Just as he was about to tell her not to worry, to absent himself and make another attempt at sleep, she spoke.

"Evurt," she said. "His name was Evurt."

He shuddered as something within him stirred.

‡

He turned to look back at the city. Only eight miles out, and already it had become a vague spread of dirty, jumbled earth. Behind it, the vertical wall of Usveet Mesa stood, shutting out half the day, cutting off any view to the west. Distance had only served to make it larger: as the mountain's true scope became apparent, it began to loom even more, to oppress.

He wondered what kind of people would settle at the base of such a monolith. Had his ancestors longed to be humbled, every day—to be reminded how meager their efforts were? They could not hope to outlast the mountain. It would continue to stand, inviolate, exerting no effort while they struggled, generation after generation, to etch their names in shifting sand.

It had outlasted one species, already.

Human beings are fools, he thought. *And the ones who came before them were fools.*

This thought sat cold within him.

Shielding his eyes, he surveyed the cloudless sky until he located the winged shape of the creature guarding their exit from the city: Shavrim's pet Sapes, itself a hybrid of wyrm and elder, a living link to that superseded species. He lifted his right hand, spreading his fingers wide, sliding his palm smoothly over the atrophied muscle of his chest. Not even true contact, but feeling transmitted through two layers of cloth composed in part of elder skin.

"And what if you die within it?" Churls had once asked. He recalled the feeling of her fingertips, brushing over the edge of a hole he had caused to open in his suit. Back and forth over his right hipbone, from bare skin to covered skin. It surprised him to realize he could not tell where one ended and the other began.

"I'll rot," he replied. "Someone else will use my suit."

"And if you die alone, at the bottom of a crevice?"

"I'll rot," he had repeated, suddenly and profoundly uncomfortable.

Sapes' form disappeared against the sheer black wall of Usveet Mesa. Vedas dropped his hand and turned back to his companions. Churls had stopped to watch him, concern written on her features. He met her stare for a moment, expressionless, allowing nothing to pass between them, and then shifted his gaze to Berun, Shavrim, and Laures.

To his annoyance, they too now stopped to regard him.

"I'm fine," he said. "Keep walking."

He waited for them to move before resuming his own progress. He stared at their backs, lingering on the broad form of Shavrim for several heartbeats, struggling to understand how he had ever allowed the man to convince them to abandon the city. How, despite the madness of the man's words—the very idea that a means to defeat Adrash existed, that anything other than the entire mass of humanity could stand against Jeroun's only god!—traveling to Osa had come to seem the right choice. The only choice.

He struggled against this increasing sense of surety, if for no other reason than one among them needed to. Churls and Berun, the two voices who had long argued against Vedas's own certainty, had agreed to Shavrim's goal surprisingly quickly. Perhaps they had not required as much time to come to terms with the situation (a situation, he reminded himself, that amounted to sitting and waiting for the world to collapse) and simply accepted Shavrim at his unlikely word, yet this sounded an unpleasant chord within him.

A thing was either true, or it was not. One did not arrive at truth by wishing it were so. From the moment they met Shavrim, they had been pressed against the wall by circumstance. This was not a position from which a wise choice could be made.

Feeling helpless was its own form of tyranny. He knew this. He knew it better than most. He had lived most of his life oppressed by a false truth.

✝

They stopped out of the way of the wind, in a dry stream-bed where the skeletons of cottonwoods arced overhead. He did not attempt to conceal his exhaustion, but waved away their protests when he offered to gather firewood, just as he had when they told him he need not carry any of their supplies. He climbed the sandy bluff and returned with armloads of fuel—first kindling, which he found scattered at the feet of the dead trees, and then larger branches, which snapped like bones in his shaking hands, covering him in dust, making him sneeze.

On his fourth trip, he walked a handful of paces away from the trees and stood motionless in the spare, cold light of the desert, breathing heavily, savoring the brief moment of solitude. Looking into the sky, he counted the scattered spheres of the Needle: seven, eight, nine . . . and then a tenth rising above the horizon. He resisted the urge to touch his fingertips to the horns of his suit, cursing Adrash with a gesture. A small gesture of defiance, fighting reflex.

His lips moved. Again and again, he formed the name—*Evurt*—but did not say it aloud. A simple act, giving voice to thought, yet it struck him as more than a mere word. A name was a summons to its owner. He wondered if Churls had felt the same when she realized her daughter had returned from the dead, as if every moment alone were pregnant, existing always on the verge of saying it. *Fyra. Fyra. Fyra.* Drawing the girl into reality.

He wondered if Churls knew yet another name, now.

Ustert.

He shook his head, seeking and failing to clear it. There was no reason to assume Churls had experienced anything like his dream. He had never taken a lover before her, and suspected his inexperience was leading him to false conclusions.

As always, logic failed to alleviate his worry.

Upon returning to the camp for the seventh time, he realized he had gathered far more fuel than necessary. He stared at the pile of wood he had created, brow creased. Waiting. Berun, Laures, and Shavrim had left for a perimeter check, leaving Churls alone to set up the tent. He felt her gaze at his back, or he thought he did: when he finally turned, her attention was fixed on her task.

He pretended to concentrate on building the fire, longing to bridge the silence between them but suspecting he should preserve it for as long as possible. She was stronger than him, more practical and persuasive. A lifetime outside an abbey's walls, making due alone, had made her capable of discerning judgment, while he, he was no judge at all.

If he opened himself up to her, she would sway him away from doubt. For two days, he had restricted himself with her, engaging in only the briefest of exchanges.

He knew himself to be a fool, or perhaps he was a coward: it made no difference. A part of him remained in Danoor, struggling to make sense of what had occurred there. An even greater part of him remained in Golna—would always remain in Golna, unchanging.

His fist tightened around a wrist-thick branch until it cracked. Behind him, Churls paused in her work. She had heard something, in that sound alone.

"It's how often I wasn't in control," he said. He swallowed, cleared his throat. He opened his mouth and then closed it. The quiet stretched.

"What did you say?" she eventually asked.

He shook his head and returned his attention to the fire.

Berun, Shavrim, and Laures returned. The constructed man settled down, his dusty spheres squeaking like damp cloth to brass fixtures. His eyes were dimmer than Vedas recalled seeing in some time. Clearly, he was tired, or as close to tired as his body could become. Vedas had never determined what, if anything, Berun felt. Surely, he was not as mighty as he had once been: an injury suffered during their journey to Danoor (an injury Vedas still did not understand) had resulted in him being unable to alter his form or rotate the spheres that made up his body, severely restricting the amount of sunlight he could receive as nourishment.

They nodded to one another.

Shavrim spoke quietly to Churls. She shook her head and he laughed, clapped her on the back, and put a hand on her shoulder to steer her over to the fire. He met Vedas's stare with no trace of animosity: in fact, he smiled openly as he sat, as though they had shared a joke.

Vedas felt no anger. This *did* anger him.

Churls spared no glance at him as she crouched to warm her hands. He stared at her bare head, his desire undeniable and frustrating.

Laures, observant, looked from her to Vedas, and gave him a small, sad smile.

Shavrim cleared his throat.

"Weapons, Vedas. We should talk about weapons. When you lived in the abbey of the Thirteenth Order, I assume you trained with many different kinds?"

The question took him by surprise. It should not have. They had left the city for a reason. A mad reason, of course, but Shavrim had at least been forthcoming about just *how mad*. They were to retrieve weapons Adrash had left on the domed island of Osa—weapons the white god had hidden for fear their existence would threaten his own.

"Ah," Vedas said. "Weapons. I'd forgotten for a moment." He stopped himself, just in time, from allowing sarcasm to creep into his voice. He had agreed to their course of action. No one had put a knife to his throat.

He opened his hands, as if to accept a gift. "Yes, I am familiar with most weapons."

"Familiar? How familiar?"

"Familiar enough," Vedas repeated.

Shavrim laughed. "Modesty doesn't suit you. Would you show me?"

Vedas stood, swaying slightly. His suit hardened subtly along the back of his legs, assisting him without his consciously willing it so.

"I don't think . . ." Churls began.

He looked down at her, daring her to finish the thought.

She opened her mouth, and then promptly shut it.

This too made him angry.

‡

Shavrim selected a pair of short swords for the two of them, both similar to Churls's vazhe yet certainly sharper. Before giving his even an exploratory swing, Vedas weighed it in both hands, examining the scrollwork on the pommel, identifying a northern Tomen hand. He possessed extensive knowledge of blades, though they had never been his favorite sort of tool. He preferred striking surfaces, concussive edges.

He walked a few paces from the fire and turned. Shavrim lifted his shirt over his head, threw it to the dirt, and followed. The sword appeared comically small in his massive fist.

Not for the first time, Vedas appraised the man as an opponent.

Thickly built, he mused, *would be an understatement.*

Had Vedas been at peak condition, Shavrim would still have out-massed him by a factor of two. They stood at roughly the same height, both rather taller than average, but only one needed to turn sideways to make it through doorways. Typically, this would not have caused Vedas more than a few moments of calculation. He had faced much larger combatants, both suited and unsuited, and knew best how to use their size against them.

But Shavrim did not move like a man weighed down by muscle. Though he hid it rather well by moving slowly, Vedas recognized the grace in his movements for what it was: a deeply ingrained sense of *place* within the world—a proprioception far beyond what training could produce. It was as if he were a fixture, a center upon which everyone around him spun. With a slight twitch of muscle, he would send an opponent flying. Vedas excelled in fighting because he possessed such a center. He recognized this in Shavrim, and felt sure his was recognized in turn.

As Vedas pulled the hood of his suit over his head, his gaze lingered on the two small horns on Shavrim's broad forehead. They sprouted seamlessly from his flesh several inches directly above his eyes, darkening slightly as they neared a point.

No casual observer would fail to notice the similarity between the hood of the elder-cloth suit Vedas wore and the head of Shavrim Coranid.

Like all things about the man they had once called the tamer, this made Vedas suspicious. It seemed too great a coincidence. Beyond this, it caused a small, superstitious part of Vedas to wonder if the man were possessed of some arcane fighting ability. He feared it, and he feared very little when it came to violence.

He had known only one other man who roused the same emotion. Abse, the abbey master of The Thirteenth Order of Black suits—the man who had identified in Vedas the potential to become a great fighter . . .

Abse would not flinch away from a man because of a coincidence, a vague feeling of unease.

Vedas took a ready stance, arms loose, legs set wide, the tip of his blade wavering slightly, purposefully, the head of a snake. The elder-cloth flowed to cover his face. It constricted around him, wonderfully alive and responsive, hardening to cup his genitals, becoming shields over his kidneys and vulnerable clusters of nerves. All traces of fatigue fled his system. He stood, sheathed completely. By comparison to his opponent, he was only a thin black shade.

From the corner of his eye, he saw Churls and Laures stand.

Shavrim moved, just as quickly as Vedas suspected he would. Sword low, rigid. Vedas waited until the last moment, anticipating the other's move correctly: as Shavrim's blade came up toward his wrist, Vedas flicked it aside and turned, stepping laterally, allowing the larger man to step past him. Having confirmed his opponent's speed, working on instinct, he immediately ducked. Shavrim's blade severed air as it passed inches above Vedas's head, creating a sound like tearing paper.

Vedas cut diagonally, aiming for the other's midsection.

. . . and stopped at the merest contact.

Shavrim froze. Vedas pressed his blade to the flesh just below the man's ribs. His right arm was a rod of steel, welded to the weapon in his hand.

"Familiar enough," he said.

After several heartbeats of silence, Berun burst out laughing, a huge joyous bell of a sound.

The tension fled from Vedas. His arm fell, and he started shaking. To his surprise, he did not have to force a smile at Shavrim, who clapped him on the back hard enough to rattle his teeth. A spell had been broken, he sensed—not a great thing, no, but it was a relief to feel an easing of his animosity. He and Shavrim returned to the others, where he expected to be received with the same lightheartedness.

Churls stared into the fire, unwilling to meet his gaze.

Laures simply looked from one to another, and offered him another sad smile.

"What?" he asked. He waited until Churls peered up. When she did, he could read nothing in her expression. "What?" he asked again, raising his voice. He looked around at his companions. The mood had turned, clearly, in the space of seconds.

"Is there something I don't know?"

"No," Churls said. "They're responding to me. My mother always said no one could be happy when I'm in a bad mood."

She stood. "Now would be a good time to talk."

‡

They stood just out of earshot of the others, awkwardly distant from each other. For Vedas, who had made a habit of not touching others beyond training and fighting, the realization of their physical separation came as a shock. To not touch Churls, even simply to take her hand, took a physical effort—an effort he had been making for some time, in truth before their failed attempt to capture Fesuy and hold him accountable for the murder of a stranger.

During his captivity, Vedas had never dreamt. Fesuy's mage kept him deep, deep below the level of recall. A blackness, a void, was all that remained. Even when they woke him, to allow him to eat and relieve himself, his mind was a smoked lens. And yet, in those blurred moments, he thought of her, regretting his inability to connect, chastising himself for being intimidated by urges that (for all other men, he imagined) came naturally. He had anticipated his own death, knowing he had not lived a single moment of truly forgetting himself, of *letting go*.

He took a step forward. The muscles in his shoulder jumped as he began to reach for her.

"Vedas," she said. "I'm worried. I'm worried, and I'm angry." She held up a hand to stop him from speaking. "We'll start with the worry."

He nodded, feeling like a child.

"What you just did with Shavrim . . ." She jerked her chin in the direction of the fire. "I've trained with you for months now, and you've never shown me anything like that. Either you've been lying to me about your skill, which I think is unlikely, or there's something happening here we need to acknowledge and try to understand."

He opened his mouth to deny it, and thought otherwise. "Are you sure?"

"You're not?" she said, squinting at him as though trying to determine if he were serious. Her features softened. "Vedas, I *know* you. Even at your peak level, you couldn't have deflected that first strike, dodged the second, or much less finished with your own. The first technique is simply too precise a technique for you, and the rest, well . . ." She shook her head. "He moved faster than I've ever seen you move, which means you moved faster than you should be able to move. In your condition, this is obviously—"

"Understood," he said, fighting the nonsensical urge to defend himself. He tipped his head back to look at the chaotic sky, fixing his gaze on the closest madly-spinning sphere. "You do realize, of course, this is one among many strange occurrences, Churls? I gave a speech, and on that very night the world proceeded to fly apart. The world blames me, and then Shavrim tells me it's not my fault—and furthermore, that something can be done about it. By *us*. And now look where we are."

He leveled his gaze at her. "Oh, and then the other interesting bit. I've recently learned something new about you, haven't I? A daughter—and not any ordinary daughter. In light of all this, it hardly seems the time to start questioning something as benign as my sword-arm suddenly becoming quicker."

She closed her eyes and breathed deeply. Vedas stared at her freckled face, thinner than he had ever seen it. Not beautiful, no: she would not be described as beautiful by most. She had told him that, as a child, she had often been mistaken for a boy.

He took her hand. "I'm sorry," he said.

Without opening her eyes, she smiled, lips parted slightly. "It wasn't right of me, but I didn't know how, Vedas. I was never . . . good . . . at being a mother. I don't know how to talk about Fyra, or *to* Fyra, much less deal with the questions I have about her existence. She wants to help us, she and other dead who feel as she does. And now . . ." She opened her eyes. "As you said, *look where we are*. What are we doing?"

He squeezed her hand, and she squeezed back, lightly at first, and then harder, until they were both gripping with fierce intensity. He eased up, and eventually she followed.

"Will you sleep next to me tonight?" she said. "Or do you want to be alone for whatever's coming our way? I don't want to be alone."

"I will. I don't want to be alone, either."

She kissed him, lightly. She smelled strongly of the road, of dust and sweat. Like him. He dropped his head so that it rested against her sandpaper scalp.

"And the risk? The reason you've been keeping me at arm's length, Vedas?" She shook her head slightly, scratching against his forehead. "Don't deny it. I know there's more to your avoidance than just being upset at me for keeping secrets. You think I'll convince you what we're doing is right. You don't see that I have every bit as much doubt as you."

"Then why? Why are we here? I want an answer for this."

She slid her hands under his arms and embraced him. He returned it, no longer reluctant.

He felt, rather than heard, her chuckle.

"Haven't you learned yet?" she said. "Living life with the expectation that you'll always have an answer when you want it—that is the surest recipe for unhappiness. Answers come only in time. And right now, with the world on the verge of death, time is the one thing we don't have."

"So, it really is just that, following a madman or nothing?"

"I think so, Vedas. We've reached the end of the road. That, and that alone, is why we're here."

‡

He went to bed with her beside him and did not dream. He slept as if dead, like he had under the mage's spell. He woke and, though not whole, felt a great deal better.

The same could not be said of her, he saw immediately. Her eyes were red-rimmed and watery, and she flinched at his first touch. They worked in silence with the others, taking down the camp.

"Dreams kept you awake?' he finally said, as casually as he could.

Her fingers worked at a knot in the tent lines, and then stilled. She did not answer, pretending, perhaps, that she had not heard. Slight though the movement was, he caught the small, quick turn of her head in Laures' direction.

‡

Three thousand years previously, the Summer Wars had cut a vicious swath through eastern Knos Min, resulting in the destruction of seven cities. Marept, the most northerly and least populous, was burnt nearly to cinders by the invading Tomen—a bedraggled contingent of several hundred men and women, all of whom had smelled defeat on the wind and chose to imbibe the fire spells their leaders created for just such an occasion, creating a miniature organic sun in the city center.

Alone of the seven cities, Marept had never been rebuilt. The wind would not even deign to bury it, and so its bones were left to bleach. Of course, legend told that it had begun to die well before the Summer Wars, that the River Sullen had spurned the city for dumping tannery toxins in its once-clean waters. Certainly, some event had caused the waterway to change course, for it ran now nearly two miles west of the city it had once run through.

The people of northern Knosi felt deeply about their rivers, having so few of them. They attributed personalities to each, talking as though about distant relatives. A river like Sullen, though rarely navigated, was known to every schoolchild. Even Vedas, who had spent the vast majority of his life away from the country of his birth, who had avoided his people whenever he could—even he remembered his mother's tale of Sullen's anger toward the people of Marept.

Staring at the river's surface now, he felt his mother had spoken truer than she could have known. Surely, she had never stood where he stood, thirty miles south of the only bridge to even bother crossing the river, nearly a stone's throw from a once-great city the world had been content to let slowly crumble into the desert.

"Sullen," Churls said at his left. "That's a good name for it. I hardly even want to fill our bags with it."

He grunted, tipping his head back to stare into the chalky, overcast sky. He reached and let his fingers graze hers. She took his hand, and all at once he wanted to be far away, ignorant of the world. In a place where no one dreamt of dead gods.

No, he did not want to ask her what had kept her awake.

Laures walked to the water's edge and spit. "My mother said any river east of Danoor was haunted."

"That would make nearly every river on the continent haunted," Churls said.

Laures turned to her with a smile. "My mother was a fool."

Berun shrugged with a shrill sound and waded into the river, trawling two huge water bags in his left fist, holding their comestible supplies high in the other. Most of his body disappeared, invisible below the surface, until only the top of his head showed at the halfway mark. Here he stopped, lifted the hand bearing the water bags and crooked a finger, urging them forward.

Shavrim followed first, chuckling. Vedas and Churls entered the piss-warm, sluggish current together.

Just before his feet left the sandy bottom and he began his first stroke, Vedas looked back to see Laures still standing on the bank, head turned as though she were listening for something. She bit her lip—an expression of anxiety on her face so out of character that he stopped for a moment to stare.

He nearly called to her.

And then a dark line bisected her forehead, accompanied by the sound of a honeydew being rapped sharply with a knuckle. A smattering of dark spots bloomed in a circle at the center of her face.

Vedas tipped his head to the side for perspective, and felt his testicles rise.

An arrow bolt protruded between her eyes.

Laures took one unsteady step toward the river and collapsed into it.

A cloud of dust rose in the distance beyond where she had stood.

‡

Shoulder to shoulder, they raced toward the dead city. The earth shuddered under their feet, out of time with their steps: Berun kept close at their heels, arms wide as he ran, offering as much cover as his massive body could provide. Now and then, an arrow clattered against his brass spheres or hit the ground to either side, yet the bowmen were clearly only harrying their quarry, conserving their missiles until a clearer shot presented itself.

Vedas sprinted ahead of the others and reached the first fallen column of Marept, taking a defensive position and surveying their pursuers. An arrow shattered on the stone before him, but he paid it no mind. It would hurt to be struck, undoubtedly, and might even break bone, but his suit had tightened around him. It would minimize any impact while preventing the point from entering his flesh.

He counted. *Ten . . . No . . . Twelve.*

All mounted on horseback. Stiff red-haired, clearly Tomen.

Six of the men held staffs that glowed with greenish magefire at their tips. Vedas had been surrounded by such mages on one or two occasions when Fesuy woke him enough to fully comprehend his surroundings. They were immensely dangerous—he had sensed this before, and knew it in his gut now. Even under the watch of Shavrim's wyrm, they had found a way out of the city.

"Fesuy's men," Vedas said when Churls and Shavrim were safely beside him, blocked once again by Berun, who stood, facing the approaching men, undoubtedly aware of the threat they posed even to one such as he.

"How do you know?" Churls said, squinting around the constructed man. "And besides, how could they have left Dan—"

"He's right," Shavrim interrupted. "And how it was done hardly matters. Sapes can only do so much to suppress magic, and her eyes can be blinded by someone with enough skill and alchemicals." Frowning, he looked from side to side. "We can do nothing from this position except die. We should get deeper into the city."

They moved rapidly, Berun clearing a path before them, lifting and heaving huge blocks of masonry out of the fractured roadway and throwing them behind his companions to block their pursuers. Though Vedas had seen Berun perform extraordinary acts of strength before, the display of force shocked him. Several days of receiving direct sunlight had clearly invigorated the constructed man, but the wage for doing so would be monstrous.

Once they reached a defensible position, Vedas predicted, there would only be three to stand against the coming storm.

No conversation would be heard over the sound of crashing masonry and Berun's thunderous steps, yet a quick glance confirmed to Vedas that both of his companions had come to similar conclusions. He met Churls's grim expression, and wondered how much of his own concern could be read under the mask of his suit.

"There!" he only just heard Shavrim shout.

A stone building lay directly ahead, alone amid the rubble. Standing, more or less, open to the sky but with all four walls intact. Vedas scanned it and thanked fate that Shavrim was no fool. It would be fairly defensible. Having stood for ages, it likely would not collapse upon them.

Berun lifted a massive fallen pillar that blocked the entrance, and roared as it slipped from his hands to fracture at his feet. He backed up and then took two steps toward the wide doorway, dropping his shoulders and ramming a broken section of the pillar, skidding with it into the interior of the building. His foot hit the left side of the doorframe, causing fragments of stone to rain down.

Vedas winced, but the walls failed to even shudder with the impact.

Berun remained inert as Shavrim leapt over him. Vedas pushed Churls forward, and then offered cover as best he could as she knelt to check on the constructed man.

"—am . . . fine," Berun said, his voice a faint brass rumble. "Defend . . . selves."

Churls nodded, tight-lipped, and moved into the shadowed security of the walls.

Outside, it was utterly silent. Undoubtedly, Fesuy's men had ditched their mounts to navigate the rubble Berun had left in their path, and were now advancing on silent feet toward their holed-in targets. They would be unafraid, utterly sure of themselves. They had little reason not to be. Perhaps this would play to Vedas and his companions' benefit.

Vedas immediately quashed this brief optimism. Any advantage would be fleeting, ultimately meaningless. He smiled cheerlessly at Churls.

She read the expression, even under the elder-cloth, and rolled her eyes. "The fun never ends, does it? It won't be long now."

He nodded. "No, it won't."

Turning full circle, he examined the large, open space of the ancient building, knowing without a doubt that they stood within one of the more important buildings of Marept. A temple, perhaps, or a civic structure. The walls extended nearly thirty feet overhead: they were thick, ably hewn without mortar, simple stones cut and fit precisely into place. It was no surprise that it still stood. For a moment, he wondered about the people who had labored to build it, and felt keenly the injustice of it all.

To have built such a place, so cunningly, and have it abandoned to this appallingly slow decay. It must aggravate the dead, he reasoned.

"Better it were destroyed," he muttered.

"What?" Churls said.

He rubbed at his eyes. "Nothing." He peered over his shoulder at Shavrim, who stood stock-still at the door, surveying the scene outside. He lowered his voice to a whisper. "This will go very badly, likely very quickly. What of Fyra? She could help us."

Churls crossed her arms, features carefully composed. "She'd be here, Vedas, if she could. I don't want her badly hurt—if she *can* be badly hurt, that is—but I'm no idiot. I realize the straits we're in. I've been calling to her as best I can since we left the river."

"What could be keeping her away? Has something taxed her unduly?"

"Does it matter? She's not here."

The muscles of his jaw jumped. He considered challenging her, demanding an answer to the question she had clearly avoided. Instead, he turned away to join Shavrim across the body-length span of the door-way. Rubble crunched softly under Churls's feet as she came up behind Vedas and crouched. She placed her hand on his back, and it surprised him, how welcome she felt touching him, and what effect it had. His annoyance was not so much forgotten as immediately put into context.

She had secrets, and they hardly mattered now.

Outside, all was still. And then a crow cawed just to the left of the entranceway.

Vedas caught Shavrim's wry glance, and raised an eyebrow in return. It had been an extremely clumsy signal from the Tomen's point man.

Six lights briefly flared, several hundred feet directly before them. The two men turned away from each other, ducking inside the shelter of the doorframe.

Vedas wrapped his arms around Churls just before a beam of sizzling radiance shot through the entrance, punching a hole through the build-ing's rear wall. Even with his eyes tightly closed, the magefire's brilliance shone through bone to light up the interior of his skull. He felt the heat of it even through his suit, bathing his back in flames. His pain increased, doubling and then tripling. Rather than fighting it, he focused upon it until it suffused him, smoldering everywhere within him without ever igniting.

Churls, however, had not even the protection of a suit. She screamed, and it was the sound of an animal being torn limb from limb. As though in response to her agony, the elder-cloth tightened and jerked spasmodi-cally upon Vedas's frame, threatening to tear his arms free from her, yet he only tightened his hold, shielding her as best he could.

She continued screaming, one long, raw, sustained note of torture. It went on and on, until it was a finely focused lance of pain in the center of his being.

‡

Once again, something within him stirred. It more than stirred. It opened its mouth within him and roared to match her pain.

The roar became a word. A *name*. Its utterance was a declaration of out-rage and conquest. Vedas was overwhelmed in an instant, shoved to the side of his own consciousness, a mere watcher. A tamed beast, ridden.

‡

He stood up and walked into the magefire coursing through the door.

He walked into brilliance, glancing down only briefly at the prone silver figure of his lover.

His *lover* and *sister* . . . but these two words were insufficient.

He smiled. Words used to describe what they were had only ever been the tools of men. Like men, words soon faded into nothing.

But a name? *Her* name?

Ustert.

This name would not fade.

This name meant more than all the souls of mankind combined.

‡

Evurt walked out of the temple and extended his right arm. The fallen column of flame his enemies had summoned flowed around his taut bronze form, quickly thinning behind him into a river, a stream, before withering altogether. His palm now pressed against a solid wall of shifting light, he began walking forward, pushing the magefire back toward its source—back toward the men who had the gall to attack him and Ustert.

A man came at him from the left, leaping over a low wall. Evurt turned his head only slightly, taking in the form of his attacker calculatingly: tall, ruddy, robed, a stiff crown of hair wound around his scalp. A curved sword held in both hands, close to his ribs.

Evurt waited until the man was nearly upon him, anticipating exactly how the cut would arc up from the hip, before casually slapping the blade, breaking the steel in two and shattering every bone in the man's hands.

Evurt heard this last fact, in perfect detail, as the snapping of twigs under one's foot.

He reached out toward the man and snapped his neck.

Two more men came in swift succession, from the right and the left. Instead of encountering either physically, Evurt took two swift steps backward at the last possible moment, spreading his palms as though parting a double swinging door, causing the tunnel of magefire to bulge, engulfing both off-balance attackers. They opened their mouths in silent screams, their skin crackling and blackening instantly. In seconds, they were ash under his feet as he continued forward.

Abruptly, the magefire died.

Evurt did not stumble or blink in surprise. The expression on his angular, hairless face remained neutral until six men rose from kneeling positions behind their upraised staffs, three archers with drawn bows at either side. At this point, he smiled across the hundred-foot span separating him from them, revealing small, sharp, even teeth.

"Hello, corpses," he said in a long-extinct language.

Three arrows shattered into splinters upon his chest without rocking him back an inch. The fourth and fifth he caught and threw back faster than human eyes could register, with such force that they nearly disintegrated on their flight back to their targets. Regardless, both mages were killed instantly from the force, thrown off their feet to land some distance behind their startled companions.

He walked toward them slowly, smile unwavering. He opened his arms and let their arrows die upon him, their spells sizzle and fade into nothingness over his sculpted body. He felt no more than a slight tickle, occasionally, only at the fringes of an attack displaying true talent.

But what was the talent of a man? Nothing, compared to him.

As he neared them, he switched between languages, all dead, repeating the same phrase:

"These are the wages of arrogance," he said as he turned back an arrow—as he redirected the flow of two spells and with them bore holes through the chests of the ones who had sent them—as he reversed the charge of another and turned its caster to ice . . .

As he, with a twitch of his fingers, fused the feet of the remaining four men to the ground.

They tried to pull free, but quickly realized their struggles were useless. The bowmen dropped their bows and reached for their swords. The remaining mage stopped his efforts entirely and raised his chin in defiance. Evurt crossed the remaining distance to them, swatted two of the warriors' blades away, and took the third. Decapitating all three with such skill that each toppled gracefully sideways, he caused the mage to be drenched in blood.

He reached out and slowly, inexorably, pried the staff from the mage's hands. He broke the weapon over his knee, causing a brief flare of sparks to erupt from its lit end.

The mage spit upon Evurt's chest.

Evurt recognized the curse the man spoke next, and knew something of his parentage.

"This is the wage of arrogance," Evurt said in archaically-accented Tomen.

He thrust the jagged ends of the mage's own staff into the meat below the man's clavicles, carrying him to the ground to the sound of both ankles snapping, impaling his shuddering body upon the sun-baked dirt. The mage screamed until his voice ran out, and then screamed some more.

Evurt cocked his head almost curiously, and then tore the man's lower jaw off, silencing the cries to a bubbling exhalation.

‡

Behind him, a voice called his name. It was not his sister's. Nonetheless, he recognized it, let it resound within him.

He turned, slowly, unafraid but not without a measure of caution.

Shavrim stood in the temple's open doorway, hands open at his hips.

Evurt's brow creased in confusion. The temple . . . he knew it from the frieze above its door, had been received by its priests on several occasions—Ustert, standing at his side in the courtyard, impatient as he was with their lengthy prostrations and rituals . . .

Better it were destroyed, he had whispered. *Then we'd never have to be this bored again . . .*

The smell of orange blossoms . . .

Agolet was its name. *Agolet, Twin Temple of Marept.*

But it was not at all as he remembered. He looked from side to side, his consternation growing.

This was a graveyard, forgotten, its tombstones toppled.

Marept—what had become of the city?

"Evurt," Shavrim repeated. "Brother, it's been too long."

"Don't use that word," Evurt said, but quietly. Shavrim would still hear it, he felt sure. It would hurt him, possibly. He had always liked the idea of family. He was often more like a child than man, as a result always on the verge of offense. Evurt had no small affection for the horned fool, and certainly respected his power, but he could rarely resist taking advantage of his brother's lamentable sensitivity.

When had they last spoken? What of the others? What of . . . what of Adrash?

Evurt shook his head, grimacing, suddenly frightened of his own dim-wittedness. He had never liked asking for clarification, always preferring the answers he found for himself.

"What is this?" he said through clenched teeth.

Shavrim began walking toward him, steps measured, open hands lifted to either side, presenting no threat.

"You called to me, Evurt. Look at yourself."

"Called?" Evurt echoed. "When?" He looked down at his torso, run-ning his hands over the muscular ridges of his belly, noting their odd softness and texture. His hands—he lifted them, turning them over, wondering at their appearance. They were . . . thicker? Yes. Thicker. He stared, and they seemed to shift in color, becoming a darker bronze, nearly black, losing their metallic sheen.

For a moment, he even saw the suggestion of veins on their backs, an imperfection, a marring upon his flawless skin. He turned his head to stare at his shoulders, which, again, seemed broader than he remem-bered. He lifted a leg, horrified to find this outsized, as well, a pillar of animal gristle.

All at once, his vision shifted. The world darkened, losing focus and vibrancy. He blinked, trying to clear away the film before his eyes, but the effect remained. The strength fled from his limbs and he slumped, as though lead had flooded his veins. He took two faltering steps backward, uncomfortably aware of wanting to run, to flee.

His foot caught on a rock, and he stumbled.

He did not fall, however. He was caught. Shavrim stood before him, gripping him tightly below the underarms, holding him easily at arm's length.

"Brother," Shavrim said. He pulled Evurt into a crushing embrace. "You are not you. You cannot sustain this kind of activity. Rest, and then we'll see each other again."

To his horror, Evurt discovered that he was nodding—that he had lifted his arms to embrace Shavrim.

Clearly, he was not himself.

The world shuddered around him, in time with the jagged hammering of his heart. Blackness encroached at the edges of his existence.

He closed his eyes, allowing darkness to overtake him.

VEDAS TEZUL

THE 20TH TO 25TH OF THE MONTH OF SECTARIANS MAREPT, THE REPUBLIC OF KNOS MIN, TO VAL

Someone held his right hand in a firm grip. It took him several minutes of concentrating on his fingers and palm (disturbingly, they were naked) to realize this fact, yet upon confirming it he did not move or alter his position in the slightest for fear of revealing that he had woken. Instinctually, he remained motionless, and the rationale for this too took him several minutes to work out.

He knew no one with so small a hand.

"I know you're awake," the girl said. He knew the voice instantly.

"I am," he said, suddenly, intensely present within his body, as if her voice had made him aware of every sensation. His palm started sweating. Wanting to pull his hand away from hers, he nonetheless resisted, maintaining his meditative stillness—for reasons that, even upon examination, became no clearer. In the space of a few breaths, the urge itself faded.

"Your mother," he said. "She's . . . ?"

She squeezed his hand even tighter, flooding him with warmth. "She's fine. Angry and confused, but fine. You, though, you're still not right inside. I'm working on it."

Working on it. "How long have I been asleep?"

"Three days. You'll need two more before you can travel. Are you in any pain?"

Again, he felt an urge—to shake his head—and did not act on it. He had not opened his eyes. Oddly, he felt no desire to. He wanted to know if they were still in Marept, if Shavrim and Berun had been injured. He wanted to know what he had done, but could summon neither the memories nor the curiosity.

He felt *good. Protected.* As though it were all in someone else's hands.

"No," he said. "No pain, Fyra. Whatever it is you're doing, keep doing it." His brow furrowed. "How are you holding my hand? How can I feel it?"

She laughed, and he smiled, feeling lightheaded, carefree.

"Oh, I'm doing so much more than making you feel like I'm holding your hand, Vedas. What I'm doing right now is mostly keeping you from making stupid decisions, like getting up before you're ready. Influencing you is hard because you're so stubborn about being upset all the time. I probably should have just kept you asleep, but there's something I need to tell you. *Before* everyone else knows you're awake. I want you to take this with you, back into sleep. When you wake up, it will be important. Do you understand?"

"Yes." Yes, he did. How could he forget this feeling?

"Good," she said. Her grip lessened, and it was like being doused in cold water. A great portion of his serenity immediately fled, allowing worries a voice. When he truly woke, what would he recall from before his injuries? Would he hate himself for not forcing Fyra to let him speak to the others?

The girl sighed loudly. She said his name in a tone mothers used toward their children. "Stay focused on right here, right now. I told you, my mother's safe. So are Berun and Shavrim. The world hasn't ended. But you *do need to pay attention.* Promise me you won't forget what I say next. Tell me you can keep a promise."

He frowned, worrying at her intensity. "I won't. I can. I promise."

He did not hear her moving. Perhaps she made no sound. He sensed, however, that she had leaned toward him, placing her mouth close to his ear.

"Someone's trying to keep me away," she whispered, "and that someone is *inside you.* I don't know what he is or what he wants. He's too powerful. I'm scared of him." She made a sound, a soft, distressed cry. "It gets worse. You're not alone in this: there's also someone—a soul, a personality—inside my mother. I knew it the other day, after we first talked. I saw her there, seeing out from behind my mother's eyes. Maybe the same has happened to Berun, too, but it's harder to tell with him."

The words resounded in his head. *Someone. Inside you. Inside my mother.*

The muscles of his belly twitched as he thought to sit up, to do anything but allow the situation Fyra described from continuing. His neck flexed twice, convulsively, lifting his head a few inches before it smacked back against the pillow. Each movement, accompanied by sharp flashes of pain referring throughout his body.

"Stop!" Fyra hissed. She gripped his hand tighter once more, saturating him in bliss so rapidly that he giggled. "Don't try to move. You can't do anything about this in your condition. Besides, he's not with you now. All of this will make more sense when you're recovered. For now, you just need to know about it, and know who's behind it."

Through the haze of contentment, his terror was an abstract thing.

Incurious, he asked, "Who?"

"Shavrim," she answered.

He thought, unconcernedly, *Of course.*

His eyes shot open, through no effort of his own. Fyra's coldly radiant head was poised above his, her pale hair hanging down around both of their faces, linking them, enclosing them in their own private space. He stared at the off-white freckles patterning her nose and cheeks, the mole centered between her eyes, struck by how like her mother she was.

"I know you're a good man, Vedas Tezul," she said. "Keep your promise. Remember—"

"I'm not," he interrupted. "I'm not . . . good." He chuckled, not caring what he said. It struck him, suddenly—it was *wonderful* to not care. He had always felt guilty unburdening himself of anything, as though he were tying stones around his listener's neck, so he had rarely done it. "I've watched children die, Fyra. I've trained them, knowing they might die. I lived with this awareness, that it could happen, and still did it. I was punished for this long before it ever happened. Some people are cursed. When I was a child, like you, there was a man—"

"Shut up," she interrupted in turn, squeezing his hand again to fill him with her warmth. She shushed him. "Quiet, Vedas. I've seen what happened to you. Don't make that face. I'm not a child, and no one is cursed. Now, you have to listen to me. You have to keep your promise: remember what I've said. Carry it with you into your dreams. And when you wake, healed and back to your normal, angry self, do something useful with it. Don't let me down."

He smiled, shuffling his awkward admissions of guilt to the side as easily as he had voiced them.

He promised he would not let her down.

‡

An hour before sunset, Shavrim returned from hunting, three large desert hares dangling from his meaty fist. Vedas rose and began preparing the fire. Churls looked up from cleaning the first of the hares, exchanged a quick glance with Shavrim, but said nothing.

"I'm fine," Vedas said. "Stop worrying over me."

A private smile tugged at the corners of his mouth. He had said such words to her on far too many occasions. In truth, he felt more than fine—incredible, as though he had woken from the soundest sleep of his life. Constraining the energy in his limbs, hiding the effects of what Fyra had done from Shavrim, was far more a danger than overexerting himself.

Of course, it was not only Shavrim he kept the secret from. He doubted Churls knew what her daughter had done, though her quizzical glances revealed a good measure of suspicion.

She would know soon enough, of course.

Thinking on this, he came to a decision. All at once, there seemed no reason to wait.

He winked at Berun across the fire. The constructed man's features broke into a frown, followed quickly by a smile. His eyes flared briefly.

"Vedas," he said. "You are in unusual spirits."

"I am, Berun," Vedas said, voice low, not bothering to broadcast his words. They would hear him just fine. "I'm refreshed and full of new thoughts. There are things I need to consider. Did you know, for instance, that Usterti believe in more than their goddess?"

"I did not," Berun said.

Shavrim raised his eyebrows, expression open. Vedas admired his acting.

Churls did not so much as pause in her preparations. She angled her face, which still bore the tight redness of what appeared to be (but he knew was not) a sunburn, down toward her task. She, too, knew how to hide, though not as well.

Vedas nodded, and spit upon the firestarter in his hands. It flared to life as he reached forward to place it amid the kindling. He grinned. Unusual spirits, indeed. He felt incautious, even mischievous, as if Fyra had infected him with a portion of childhood.

Or, he reasoned, he might be feeling the influence of the one Fyra had warned him about. This did not strike him as likely, though: the dreams he had experienced, both before and after he had spoken with the girl, did not lead him to see Evurt as the frivolous sort.

Regardless, his smile vanished. Even thinking of the name was enough to constrict his throat.

Nothing for it, he thought. He would make himself speak it. He would make it real.

"Oh, it's true," he said. "In the abbey, I studied the witches' sect. They're not fond of talking about anything other than the Goddess, I gather. I asked Laures about it before we left, and I thought she might attack me for having the gall. She did confirm what I'd been taught, however." He blew into the kindling, watching it catch, and then sat back. "A few of their stories tell of Ustert's brother—her twin—a figure who died or merely passed into oblivion."

"Fuck!" Churls yelled, dropping her knife to grip her left hand. "Cut myself." She stood, glaring at Vedas. "What in the hell are you talking about?"

"Ustert," he said. He swallowed, took two quick breaths. "Evurt."

She flinched.

Berun's head swiveled from one companion to another, one shelf-like brow raised questioningly. "These names," he rumbled, "they mean nothing to me."

Shavrim chuckled. "It's a miracle they survived unscathed, those names. There's something to them, I suppose, an indelible quality. Even the pronunciation—it's been much the same throughout Knoori for, oh . . . well, it's been millennia." He spread his heavy arms. "You want to hear what happened, Vedas? You want to know what it means?"

Vedas nodded.

Shavrim returned the gesture, and then looked up at Churls. "We'll wait while you clean and bandage the hand, though I doubt you'll need to. Ustert Youl would hardly let you die from such a minor scratch. Even

in your body, in her doubtlessly confused state, she'd not suffer that kind
of indignity."

‡

As Shavrim talked, the memory roused itself from the back of Vedas's
mind. He easily recalled the heat of the magefire, and wrapping himself
around Churls in an attempt to protect her.

The . . . *assumption*, he began to think of it—this came to him in
fragments, like a puzzle being assembled before his eyes, accompanied by
sensations that pricked at the nerves embedded in his muscle, skin, and
bone. He clenched his fists and released them, twitched his shoulders and
fought the urge to stand and act out what he knew his body had done.
Impossible things.

Thoughts and emotions flooded his mind, disturbing in their alien
intensity. Arrogance beyond human reason. Anger, cold and fathomless.
Confusion upon the discovery that he, Evurt, stood in another's skin. And
attendant to the confusion, disgust. Vedas's body, even the way the world
appeared dim through his feeble human eyes, had repulsed Evurt.

This, most of all, chilled Vedas to the marrow.

He knew, now, how a god looked at humankind. The disdain, he had
expected. Even the humblest merchant, risen to enough influence, soon
became a master of contempt. Power begat this perspective, Vedas knew,
and men could not entirely resist thinking of their neighbors as less than
human: at various points in the history of the world, peoples had been
enslaved and even made extinct. The cousin of such violence existed in
every man. He could know that hate more intimately if he allowed himself to blame others for his ills.

It was appallingly easy to create divisions, to build walls instead of
bridges.

The scorn of Evurt served to render all of his thoughts on the subject
irrelevant, as if all of history had been as meaningless as children arguing
over the rules of a game.

As if failure were an inescapable taint, written into the very flesh and
soul of mankind.

‡

Vedas wanted nothing to do with gods. He never had, even when he believed all but one to be mere fictions, remnants of a long and deluded past.

And now, sitting before him, yet a third god made real.

That is, if Shavrim were to be believed. Vedas wanted to disbelieve him, but could not.

"Why us?" was his first question.

"I don't have that answer, Vedas," Shavrim said. "It's not as if I can ask my brother now, is it? He has retreated, or you've pushed him to the back of your mind. But, at a guess? You're strong, and you were in the right place at the right time, openly opposing Adrash on the world's largest stage."

He dipped his head to Churls. "You were equally strong, if not in many ways stronger, and you'd fallen in love with him. You must have been a tempting pair, a lodestone for Evurt and Ustert."

Vedas neither accepted nor rejected this, though he allowed himself a measure of relief. How might he have reacted, had Shavrim claimed a god had inhabited him since birth—directing his every move, placing him strategically at this exact point and time?

"Why are they here at all?" was his second question.

Shavrim gripped his crossed ankles and rocked back, angling his face toward the open sky framed by the four walls of the ancient temple. Vedas followed his gaze, letting the pause stretch for several minutes before impatience compelled him to break the silence.

He opened his mouth—and promptly shut it.

The spheres of The Needle had been rearranged slightly. The two that had appeared closest to Jeroun were noticeably smaller. Both spun at a much-reduced rate. In addition, four of the smallest had been clustered together near the moon.

Surely, he reasoned, an encouraging sign, yet he could not feel hope.

"Consider your past," Shavrim finally said. "Three score years and some, correct? The Needle has appeared the same, throughout. It has been a fixed thing. But three scores and some is no time at all. Still, it feels like something, no? You feel older, seasoned. Consider how alien former versions of yourself are to the man you have become. How few choices he made that you would make. How much of a fool he was, Vedas. Hold that awareness in your mind. Truly feel it, the regret and anger at your own stupidity, your cowardice and impotence.

"Now, consider what you would do if you had even more time, perhaps millennia, to meditate on the actions or inactions of that fool. Would you not grow to hate yourself as no man has hated himself? Would you not wish to die, knowing you could never right your mistakes? Tell me that would not be the inevitable outcome of a life that long."

Vedas fixed him with a cold stare. "You wish to die? Somehow, I think you're not trying hard enough."

Berun looked from Vedas to Shavrim. "Agreed. You tell us of your relationship to these—" he grunted "—gods. You tell us you are one of their number. Now you want death, perhaps the easiest thing for a man to achieve. No wonder you talk of fools."

Shavrim smiled, unwilling to take offense. "Wishing to die and dying are two separate things. I continue breathing not for lack of trying to quit. On occasion, that is: I've come to embrace my immortality. But this is not my point."

"Get to it, then," Churls said. Without glancing up from her work—which she had continued, despite her wound—she gestured at Vedas with her skinning knife. "He asked a question, Shavrim."

"Which I was attempting to answer. Forgive me. I've spent many lifetimes *not* revealing what I am. I've had no practice at it, yet I'd prefer for you not to fly into a rage when I tell you this is all my doing. But that is not within my control, is it?"

When no one answered, Shavrim's smile dipped but did not disappear. He pointed to the moon, sighting along his thick forearm with a squint. "For most of my life, I've had Adrash over my head and five siblings buried under me. Humanity is the bridge between those two worlds. Though your expressions, and those of your creations—" he nodded at Berun "—are not my own, I'm fairly fond of you. My family and I once fought on your behalf, when we first identified the madness in our creator. Twenty thousand years later, when I felt the presence of Evurt and Ustert again in the world, I decided I must persuade them to help me."

Vedas stood, restless with questions yet unable to decide upon the most pressing. He massaged his temples and cracked his neck, trying to ease the tension that suddenly seemed bent on crippling him. Since Churls had rescued him, he had swung from one reaction to the next, one extreme giving way to another with no time to adjust. The earth was unstable beneath his feet.

Fortunately, Berun had not been similarly affected.

In addition, the constructed man had learned the art of sarcasm: "You *felt* the presence of Evurt and Ustert? And this simply *happened* to coincide with Adrash destroying The Needle?"

"No. It wasn't a coincidence. I told you the name of the elderman responsible. Pol Tanz et Som incited this. There is no other explanation."

"And how did he do that?" Churls said. "You're telling us Adrash couldn't simply swat him away? Who is this elderman, that he should inspire such world-shattering rage?" She stood, circled the fire and crouched, one bloody hand on Shavrim's shoulder, face only inches from his. She spoke through a tight jaw. Spittle flew from her mouth. "Is he another god, then, or is he merely . . . *ridden*, like me? Or Vedas? Will we wake up tomorrow and find Berun taken, too?"

She slapped him, her right arm a silver blur.

The sound of the impact, the crack of timber.

Shavrim's head whipped to one side and he threw out an arm to steady himself.

‡

Vedas tensed. It took him several heartbeats to realize just why he had done so, beyond the clear threat of Shavrim reacting to the blow.

He stared at Churls's bare arm, upraised and rigid, every muscle limned with tension.

Sun-red, freckled skin. The faded markings of tattoos. Nothing more.

And yet, his eyes had not deceived him.

She had struck with the arm of the Goddess.

‡

Shavrim chuckled.

A handprint of hare blood was now emblazoned across his left cheek. His own blood welled at the left corner of his mouth. He licked his bruising lips and nodded.

"Well delivered," he said. "When you are as I am, Churls, you learn to appreciate anger that cuts to the point. At the same time, you avoid what is necessary to speed the process up. Don't let my age fool you—there are things that frighten me. I have abilities beyond merely remaining alive, but they are a threat if allowed too deeply. I've not lived so long without . . . sequestering my existence, without forming identities that were thereafter abandoned. Within me are all the lives I've lived, a smattering of which possessed unusual insight. A few of these former Shavrims are anxious to return."

He stood and retrieved one of his packs. He removed a bundle of thin steel chain and threw it to Churls.

"Wrists and ankles, as tight as you're able," he said, presenting his back to her and kneeling.

"A chain?" Berun said. He got to his feet, his thousand ball joints sighing. "I can hold you tighter than any chain."

"You cannot," Shavrim countered. "This is no ordinary chain, and I'm no ordinary man. No disrespect intended, Berun, but the one I'm summoning would have no problem proving just how greatly your strength is outclassed."

Berun crossed his immense arms. "You are bleeding. From a slap."

"Indeed," Shavrim said. "But it wasn't Churls who slapped me, not entirely—just as it won't be me before you in a few moments. It'll be a wilder, more brutal creature, kept in check only through the will of the man I am now, a small voice of reason attempting to quiet a storm."

Berun grunted, and turned away.

Churls stared at the chains in her hands. For a mad moment, Vedas imagined she would strangle Shavrim with them.

She began binding his wrists. "Who is this former self, this wild creature?"

"A seven-thousand-year-old relic," Shavrim replied. "A fool and a mass murderer. On occasion, I've given in to self-pity, allowing my hatred for Adrash to cloud my mind. During one such period, I traveled to the southern Tomen coast. I persuaded the locals there to accept my presence by telling their fortunes and fighting in their border skirmishes. I've always been good at the latter, but the former? Somehow, possibly by way of the madness I'd allowed to creep into my soul, I tapped into a potential I'd never known I had. I listened, and for the first time truly heard the dead."

Churls paused in her task. She could not avoid a quick glance in Vedas's direction.

"The dead?" she said. "What do you mean?"

"I mean those souls still lingering near the living, unable or unwilling to leave the material world behind. They have much to say. Some are able to read the future—or predict it well enough to appear to read it. They have access to every moment of their lives. They observe us without our knowing. Because of the threat inherent in rousing my former self, I'd hoped to wait until proof presented itself concerning Pol Tanz et Som, who I believe to be dead. He was powerful, yes, and uniquely tempting for me: he inspired me, on many occasions, to bring my own former selves to the fore. Certainly, he was fated to madness because of what he'd done to himself, yet I don't believe he was inhabited by one of my siblings.

"As for Berun, I feel quite sure that he . . . I think I would have recognized . . ."

He shook his head and lowered himself onto his side, allowing Churls to bind his ankles to his wrists.

"No," he said. "Enough waiting. This is wiser. It's better to know for certain, now."

Vedas caught the man's expression. It could not be mistaken for anything but fear.

Shavrim met Vedas's stare and lifted his chin, gesturing to their packs. "Hold a blade to my neck and remain ready. If I appear about to break my bonds, or if my state persists past the point where I've confirmed or denied our suspicions, slit my throat. I'll bleed, but I won't die, and it will weaken my body enough for me to reassert control of myself. In that case, leave me here and continue on. I'll meet you in Ual, eventually."

Without waiting to see if his order was followed, he closed his eyes and took four immense breaths, the last of which he held still within him long enough to make Vedas concerned.

He took a step toward Shavrim just as a great shudder ran through the horned man's trussed body. Shavrim groaned, varying in pitch as the air—more air than lungs should hold, surely—passed out of him, finally winding down to a grating wheeze. The skin of his face, neck, and upper chest darkened, exactly as though he were choking. With a mighty gasp, he breathed in again. In, fully, and out, fully, the process resumed. Each time the cycle completed, the shuddering became more violent.

Churls backed away. Vedas put the point of his sword to Shavrim's throat, maintaining pressure upon it throughout the paroxysms. Berun continued to stand silent, arms crossed, glowering at the scene.

‡

The shuddering stopped. Shavrim's left eye opened, revealing a madly vibrating pupil. Gradually, it stilled and focused on Vedas, who pressed the tip of his blade more firmly to the man's throat.

A smile slowly pulled at the corners of Shavrim's mouth. The right eye slowly opened.

The huge, bunched muscles of his shoulders swelled as he tested his bonds.

He grunted, and his smile grew wider.

When he spoke, his voice was an octave lower—so low and accented that several seconds passed before Vedas realized the words were intelligible.

"—that limp-pricked fool," he said. "Friend to ghosts, fucker of men."

"Are you talking to me?" Vedas said.

Shavrim regarded him silently. To a casual observer, he may have appeared still, yet Vedas noticed the subtle muscular contractions in his thighs, belly, and upper arms that gave him away. Shavrim was testing the chains, methodically, searching for a weakness, determining where best to apply his strength in order to escape.

"No," he finally answered. "I'm not speaking to you. I'm speaking to the faggot I've turned out to be." He raised his head and inclined it quizzically, as though listening. He sniffed and sneered. "Or perhaps I'm wrong. You've the stink of one who's been buggered, and also of the dead. Of course, you *are* going to die. All humans smell of the dead. I may be getting confused."

"I have questions for you."

A nearly sub-audible laugh. "Of course you do. It's not as if I don't know why I'm here. The world is at its end, and all of you . . ." He lifted his head and winked at Churls. He whistled at Berun. Vedas kept his blade steady. ". . . believe you can do something about it. Pissing idiot idea. Adrash was more than a match for the six of us gods, and now you . . ."

All at once, his body went rigid. Vedas readied himself, but the man did not attempt to break free. In fact, after only a moment Shavrim dropped his head onto the ground and let it roll back, causing Vedas's blade to etch a fine line of blood on the man's throat.

"Ah," Shavrim said. "Ah-ha, ah-ha. Now I see. It took me a moment, but there it is. Hello, brother! Hello, sister! Can you hear me?" He looked up at Vedas, one eyebrow raised. "Are you in there, Evurt? Come out, come out!"

Vedas allowed himself several heartbeats of reflection, shining a torch around the interior of his skull, searching for the interloper he knew to be hiding there, before answering. He increased the pressure on Shavrim's neck, forcing the man to rest his head upon the ground or have his throat slit.

"It's only me," Vedas said. "And I have questions that need answering."

Shavrim's amused expression did not fade. "Oh, ask, Vedas Tezul. Ask away."

"You know of the elderman Pol Tanz et Som?"

A slow nod. "Yes. Another buggering, presumptuous little shit." Shavrim raised his chin to the night sky. "Still, he did accomplish this, more than most of you mortals ever will."

"Is he alive?"

No hesitation. "Yes."

"Where is he?"

"Don't know. Don't care." He flexed at his bonds, no longer attempting to hide the fact.

"Is he like us?" Vedas gestured to Churls. "*Inhabited?*"

The chain rustled as it shifted on Shavrim's wrist. "Like you two, you mean . . ." His eyes widened, and his voice lowered to a whisper. "Oh, good. Oh, very good." He smiled, and his voice rose. "Pol, I have no idea. He has talent, and not a tiny bit of madness. But the bloody big man made of balls, there, behind me?"

Berun uncrossed his arms.

"Yes! You!" Shavrim called over his shoulder. "The fool I've become didn't see it, right before his eyes, but I do. Hello, neither brother nor sister! Come out and play with us!"

The constructed man took two steps toward Shavrim and halted, stock-still, as though both feet had become rooted to the ground. A whisper-soft sound of metal rubbing metal cut through the air: the closing and opening of his great fists.

"The name, then," he said. "Speak it."

"Sradir Ung Kim," Shavrim said.

Berun's head swiveled from Vedas to Churls. "The names he spoke to you meant something. They stirred you. But there is nothing in this name, Sradir Ung Kim. I feel nothing. He is wrong."

"I'm not," Shavrim said. "You're merely thick. Sradir is within you, and it will come out. Soon, if I am any judge. It was always an odd one, choosing its odd moments." He grinned at Vedas. "You'll enjoy when it when it shows itself. Sradir was—*is*, I suppose—an unusual creature. It never seemed to get humans, the way the rest of us did. A wooden heart, that one."

He flexed at the chains once more, swelling his chest and heaving with every muscle. The chain groaned, and Vedas prepared to do what was necessary.

Fortunately, the links held. Shavrim simply grunted and rested his head upon the ground.

"Shavrim?" Churls said. Her voice made it clear which iteration of the man she had spoken to. "Shavrim? We have our answers, or as good as we're going to get. Come back now."

Shavrim laughed. "Oh, he'll not be coming back. And you haven't all your answers. I have more to say about the dead. There's another that hovers around Berun, and he means the world no good. He'd see a blanket of ash covering everything. Why? Who knows?" He shrugged, flexing once more at the creaking chains before subsiding with a contented smile. "And then there's the little thing my weak heir hasn't quite worked out. I'd particularly like to talk about her, as she seems to have a legion at her command."

"The little one?" Churls said.

"Yes. The one standing behind you."

Churls turned, and Vedas looked up.

But Fyra had already disappeared. A second later, she reappeared at Shavrim's back. After a brief pause, she closed her eyes tightly and thrust her ghostly hands into his shoulder.

Shavrim gasped and the girl cried out. Screams ripped from both of their chests, creating a disharmony that grated awfully upon the ears.

‡

They struggled: he, away from her, and she, away from him. Her arm seemed stuck inside the man's flesh, though such a thing was clearly impossible in her insubstantial state. The screaming continued, unabated—Fyra continuously, a siren screech unhindered by lungs, Shavrim pausing only for harsh gasps of air—while both sought to undo what had occurred.

Vedas kept his blade pressed to the flesh of Shavrim's quivering throat, not in the least dismayed by the cut he created there. He had never slit a throat, but he knew the difference between a shallow wound and a killing wound. He knew it by feel.

"What's happening?" he shouted to Churls. Berun closed around Shavrim and held him down, avoiding contact with where he and Fyra were fused.

"No idea!" she answered, taking one step in his direction, only to take one step back. "Fyra! What are you doing? How can I help you?"

The girl brought her teeth together, altering the pitch of her agony without lowering the volume. Her voice resounded inside Vedas, settling in the pit of his gut, in his bones. His temples throbbed. It took a will to stand: he fought the temptation to simply let his knees fail beneath him.

Shavrim's voice grew hoarse. He coughed between breaths, flecking the ground with blood.

Churls's indecision had come to an end. She ran forward and knelt at her daughter's back, thrusting her hands through the immaterial body, placing her palms flat upon Shavrim's shoulder, just where the girl's wrists entered. She leaned her head forward—*into* Fyra's own, creating the illusion that they shared a skull. Churls shook as she pushed, clenching her jaw against the vicious rattling of her teeth. Her breathing came in quick, shallow bursts.

She closed her eyes, and the girl's opened. White smoke poured out, evaporating above Fyra's head. The girl's lips came together, shutting off her scream so suddenly that Vedas flinched. Still, a humming issued from within her: the sound of her pain continuing behind her sealed lips, building up within her small form. She rocked back and forth in time with Churls, and gradually, hairsbreadth by hairsbreadth, more and more of her wrists came free.

Shavrim's screaming intensified with each pull, raw like a wound ground in glass.

Berun kept his broad hands on the man's upper arm and thigh, holding him down. Vedas thanked fate for it, too: without the constructed man's help, Shavrim's seizures would surely have prevented Churls from assisting Fyra. The girl would have been thrown around like a rag doll.

Vedas kept the blade to Shavrim's neck while circling around his head, coming to Churls's side. He reached for her, intent on helping in any way he could. By pulling with her or merely laying a hand on her shoulder. If power could be transmitted through Churls to Fyra, then surely . . .

"No!" mother and daughter yelled in unison, halting their movements. Fyra's radiance doubled, tripled. A metallic sheen fell over Churls, as though she were reflected in a silvered mirror.

Vedas reached forward again, only to be stopped as Churls's head snapped up. Her face had taken on a harsh angularity. Her eyes were two golden slivers of light.

"No, brother," she said. "Let us do this work. Afterward, you do yours."

She turned back to her task, the appearance of the Goddess fading.

Fyra and Churls began moving once more, a moan escaping their lips, increasing in volume until it was an oddly-pitched chorus, as of a hundred voices howling—

—and, for a moment, appearing at their backs, disappearing through the temple's back wall, rank upon increasing rank—

—kneeling, hands upon each other's shoulders—

—rocking back and forth, in time with Churls and Fyra, adding weight to their struggle—

The dead, coming to aid one of their own.

Vedas blinked and they disappeared, leaving the afterimage tattooed upon his eyelids.

Below him, Shavrim cried out again and again, a series of hoarse, surely agonizing coughs. Fyra had managed to pull nearly half of her hand free.

"Hold steady, Vedas," Berun cautioned.

Vedas looked down to see the tip of his sword in the dirt. He pressed it home once more.

Churls's movements became increasingly jerky. Now, her elbows were locked. Only her neck and shoulders moved back and forth.

Nonetheless, it was enough. Finally, it was enough.

With a gasp from both parties, they fell back—Churls onto the ground, Fyra partway submerged in the ground at her side, half-in, half-out as though she were floating on her back on the surface of a salt lake.

Shavrim gave one last gasp and went slack, head lolling on the ground.

Vedas dropped his sword and knelt at Churls's side. Her pulse was strong but irregular. Her breathing came in jerky inhalations and shuddering exhalations, in through the nose and out through barely parted lips. Under her eyelids, her eyes swam in twitchy patterns. He watched her for the space of a dozen breaths and then willed his suit to unmask his face. Mind struck unfathomably blank, a sound in his skull like the hiss of calm waves, he bent to kiss her.

"Vedas." Berun's voice seemed to arrive from a great distance away, his methodical, accented speech tinny in Vedas's ears. "What are you doing?"

"This," Vedas answered. He pressed his lips to hers, and the world dissolved.

‡

The sun hung directly before him, though he did not shield his eyes. He stared at it directly for an indeterminate time, several heartbeats or the better part of an hour, wondering at its appearance. He had never before noticed, but it was not a stable, unvarying thing. The sun pulsed, expanding and contracting slightly. It breathed, varying its light in intensity from one moment to the next.

Someone squeezed his hand.

He shook his head, and finally registered his surroundings

He stood on a vast, red-soiled plain carpeted in white and yellow flowers that swayed in the breeze, moving like the surface of the sea. The horizon was close, a knife's edge or a table-end. It smelled as it always did on the outskirts of Danoor, away from cooking fires, inefficient plumbing, and the press of bodies.

He breathed in the ancient, baked dust smell of the desert, and knew.

The plains of the Aroonan mesas were a holy place. None but the Aroya people and their closest descendents were allowed to walk on the heights. This restriction was one of the oldest and most binding rules of the Knosi people.

He could not bring himself to care about trespassing. His mind moved glacially, catching up to his curiosity slowly.

Someone squeezed his hand, and he turned.

Churls stood at his side, the fingers of her left hand entwined in his right. His *naked* right hand, he noted by feel.

He looked down. His suit had retreated far up his arms and legs. The borderline between skin and suit was chaotic, appearing almost like the torn edges of multiple strips of fabric. Centered upon his chest was a perfect circle of flesh. Small holes in the elder-cloth peppered out from it, forming a five-limbed swirling pattern that extended onto his shoulders and arms. He had never chosen to make such designs upon his suit. Point in fact, he doubted he possessed the skill necessary to make such a thing occur.

Examining the design, he registered a second shock.

Where exposed, his skin reflected the slanting sunlight as though it had been flecked in metallic dust—as though he had been at work at a grinding wheel, honing the edge of a tool. He scratched at the portion of his exposed chest, and then stared at his upraised hand. He made a fist, and the skin of his knuckles did not pale slightly as it stretched over the bone underneath: instead, each knuckle warmed in color, glowing bronze under his nearly black skin.

He looked at Churls again. Her skin had once again taken on a metallic aspect to match his own. Silver to his bronze. Vaguely, muzzy-headed, he recognized the significance of this.

She smiled at him oddly. The lines of her face were subtly wrong. No, even its structure was wrong, marked by higher cheekbones and a thinner jaw. The skin of her face seemed too tight, stretched taut and glistening over the bones of her skull.

His lips formed two names, but he spoke neither.

Churls. Ustert.

Her smile widened, revealing two rows of small, perfectly straight teeth. His cock stirred, and he grimaced, tightening his suit around his genitals, clamping down physically on his arousal. Without taking his eyes off Churls, he rubbed at his jawline, finding it smooth, as hairless as that of a child's. His scalp, too, was without a hint of budding hair. His hands felt oddly outsized, palms too broad over his mouth, fingers extending too far around his cranium.

He searched for words to express his concern. He wondered if it would even be wise to do so. He did not want to reveal more of his own ignorance, having revealed enough ignorance to account for several lifetimes.

"Quit worrying," a voice said. "You're safe here."

Fyra stood before them, her expression calm. Unlike when they had met, she was now painted in the shades of life. Her pale, freckled skin shone with an inner light. Her eyes were liquid, the color of seawater. When she grinned at him, he returned the expression automatically, unself-consciously. He had once, as a child, smiled that way. He drew strength from the solidity of her presence.

"You're not completely you, Vedas," she said. "Neither is Mama. I couldn't prevent bringing something of them here with you. They wanted to see this, I think."

"What?" he asked. "Wanted what?"

"Vedas," Churls said. "Do you know where we are?"

He shook his head.

"We're in the land of the dead. A vision, sustained by those who have passed."

He tore his eyes away from Fyra, though breaking the contact between them took a physical effort.

"How do you know this?" he asked. "This is all your doing, the two of you?"

Churls nodded to Fyra with an expression of unclouded affection Vedas had never before seen. "A lot can be passed between a mother and daughter, in the moments where they struggle together. We know each other better now—far, far better than in life, undoubtedly. And it's not our vision completely, Vedas. We're not alone."

Between heartbeats, an army of thousands grew behind Fyra, silent and arrayed in every style of dress the world knew. Vedas's gaze passed over those closest to him. The sun shone through a few of their bodies as though they were formed from glass. Most did not visibly breathe, for why should they? Some were stiff and gray, granite statues rather than men. Many were strangely flat, an image on a canvas. Not one appeared as substantial, as concrete, as Fyra.

He recalled her claiming to be *better than anybody, ever*, and he no longer doubted it.

The girl stepped forward, taking his left hand. Together, they faced the dead.

‡

For a time, nothing moved, and Vedas became aware of a sound.

A low thrum.

The first hint of the ocean lapping upon the shore.

Thunder, so faint that it could have been imagined.

It was all of these sounds, but it was also a symphony of voices. He knew this, and did not know how he knew it.

The dead could not hide their thoughts, not completely. They wanted to be heard.

"Magess Um," Fyra said. "Tell him what you told me."

One among the assembled ranks stepped forward. Skeletally thin and nearly translucent, she was a mere whisper of a person, wrinkled and wrapped in dun robes. Despite her worn and watered appearance, she held her chin up, holding Vedas's stare. She did not stoop, and stood only an inch or two shorter than him. She could have been his grandmother, such was the similar hue of her skin, the nap of her hair, and the straight breadth of her shoulders.

"This is Jojore Um, former Magess of the Knosi Kingdom under Queen Medn," Fyra whispered. Vedas looked down at her, surprised by the note of respect in her voice. "She is the oldest of us, much older than I knew any of us were. She has experience no one else has, by thousands of years. It is an honor to talk to her. Listen."

Jojore did not smile. She did not even open her mouth.

Vedas Tezul, weak-blooded cousin, she said directly into his mind. Hers was a flat, haughty rasp of a voice, heavily accented though comprehensible. *I am not pleased to meet you. Nor am I impressed by what I see. Regardless, you are standing here before me. You are at a crossroads, with the fate of all life drifting in the wind. Wish that it were otherwise, it matters not at all. You will have to do.*

Vedas frowned, but not at her words, insulting though they were. A series of nearly colorless slowly-moving images of himself accompanied her speech, forming in his mind and quickly collapsing, as though she were shuffling through a bystander's memories of him.

. . . ten or eleven years old, running along an avenue in Golna, carefree . . . older, into his early twenties, thinner and likely stronger than he was now, lifting an opponent amid the chaos of a street battle . . . holding the body of Sara Jol . . . and only days past, atop Fesuy Amendja's stronghold, facing the man he had then known as the tamer.

Yes. Him, Jojore said. *You are not to doubt this man, Shavrim Coranid. And yet you are not to trust him. He is legion inside himself, and there are worse than the one the girl just saved you from. There are worse than even the being Shavrim is now suspects. He has forgotten much that is a danger to you, to himself.*

"How do you know this?" he asked. "Why should we trust you?"

Fyra dropped her head and groaned.

Jojore's expression hardened. *You will address me by my title. You will call me Magess Um. I am doing you a favor, never forget it nor doubt me. I know these truths because I know the relic Shavrim claims to have been.*

She sneered, and an image came to Vedas of Shavrim, naked, painted in swirling patterns from head to toe. He stood on a battlefield, alone, breathing heavily and surrounded by corpses. *I was one among the dead who helped him see likely paths to the future. I would not discuss with him the fates of goat herders or fishermen. I would only speak to him matters of importance, of life and death. I grew to know him. I heard him when he came back into the world, just as I hear whenever he takes that aspect.*

"You know who he really is—who he claims to be?" he asked. She scowled, and he forced himself to add her title.

I do. And he more than claims. He is what he says he is. I am not blind, as you clearly are. I know his nature just as I know your own, beyond the thin shield of your mind, your fragile skin and bone. She turned her head to Churls. *As I know who you are. You are both ridden, hosts to souls older and more powerful than any in the history of the world excepting Adrash and Shavrim. They should not be here, but it is beyond our will to keep them out entirely.*

Vedas winced as two blinding images of Ustert and Evurt seared into his mind's eye.

. . . the two of them, svelte and severe as knifeblades, silver and bronze, locked in a violently passionate embrace on a massive bed, in the very room he recognized from his own dreams . . . and then, both standing, hand in hand, alongside four others, Shavrim among them.

The image passed too quickly to gather much detail beyond this, but Vedas imagined that one among them possessed wings.

Jojore nodded. *The pretty one. His name was Orrus Dabulakm. He was Shavrim's favorite. And this one . . .*

The image returned, held. It shifted suddenly, and he stared directly at the tallest of the six figures. She—or he: Vedas could not tell—seemed to stare directly at him with dull, featureless eyes. Thorns grew from her shoulders, elbows, and knees. She held in her hand a short whip.

. . . is Sradir Ung Kim.

Her sneer returned. *Yes, the . . . artificial man . . . he too is ridden, as the relic Shavrim claims. He is not his own creature.* She looked pointedly at Fyra, then at Churls. *But he has never been his own creature, has he?*

Churls shifted her weight from one foot to the other, clearly uncomfortable. "That's not my secret to tell," she said. She opened her mouth to speak again, and then closed it. She angled her head forward to peer at Fyra. "Why did she look at you?"

Jojore made a cutting motion with her left hand before Fyra could respond. *Enough, you foolish people. Enough secrets. Time is not infinite.* She met Vedas's gaze again. *There will be a reckoning for the one called Berun. It will come from two directions: from Sradir Ung Kim, and from his creator Ortur Omali. Sradir will act as it will—no, I cannot read its intention—but Omali is known to us, to many of the dead. He cast an immense shadow in life and is still felt here from his place in limbo. He is wounded, but still the most powerful agent of those who would see the Needle fall and rupture the crust of Jeroun, extinguishing life's fire.*

"Churls," Vedas said quietly. "You knew of this . . . possession?"

"Yes," she said. "It wasn't my secret to t—"

"Shut up," he said. He shook his head, marveling at everything that had been kept from him, all that would continue to be kept from him if he did not insist on being enlightened fully. Keenly aware of his anger, he nonetheless understood it as an unproductive emotion, a petty thing that could not be allowed to last: Churls had had her reasons for keeping him in the dark, as had Berun. He would not blame them, no, yet he would not remain in ignorance.

Their hesitation could not be allowed to shape events.

He released Churls's and Fyra's hands. The world dimmed perceptibly—perhaps, he reasoned, because he could not exist alone in the world of the dead. He likely did not possess the understanding or will sufficient to sustain the link.

As if to confirm his suspicion, Churls reached for his hand.

He stepped forward, out of her reach, and gripped Jojore Um's upper arm.

The texture of her skin, like volcanic glass. The widening and narrowing of her dark eyes. During several long seconds, he seemed to stare at her through a darkening tunnel, the bright dream of the dead fading around him in increasingly constricting waves.

"I am not your weak-blooded cousin," he said, hearing his words through a wool sheet, a thin wall. He did not yell, but increased the volume of his voice with each sentence. "I am full-blooded Knosi, son to full-blooded Knosi. I am Vedas Tezul, the man who declared war on Adrash. I am ridden by a god, and still live and speak in my own voice. I will not be talked to as if I were a child. I will not be told what to do, kept in the dark, or moved about like a game piece—by you, by Evurt, by anyone." He smiled tightly. "You will acknowledge this."

For a moment, she looked as though she would reject his assertion. Slowly, however, one corner of her mouth turned up. She nodded, and the daylit mesa snapped back into focus.

Finally, she said. *A reason to hope in you. No cousin of mine comes crawling.*

He leaned into their embrace, and whispered in her ear.

"Don't tell me anything more. Show me. Show me everything."

‡

Shavrim lagged behind them for the two days it took to reach the docktown of Ual. He waved them forward when any member of the party slowed to accommodate his pace. He kept his features carefully composed, though now and then he huffed in annoyance.

Vedas could not resist making the comparison to himself. On the trip to Danoor, he too had been injured and labored to keep up with Churls and Berun. He too had refused to accept any concession to his condition. Watching Shavrim struggle, Vedas fought to reconcile his distrust with a newfound sympathy. When night came, he stared across the fire at his clearly exhausted companion, trying to piece together what Jojore had revealed to him about the man.

(No, despite what he had learned, he could not bring himself to think of Shavrim as a *god*. The world already possessed one too many deities. Vedas denied the label, as though denying it would do a damn thing.)

The weight of time: this, Vedas could not easily comprehend. How could a being exist in a body so clogged with lives, the identities and recollections of millennia? Thanks to Jojore, he now understood Shavrim had been made, in much the same way Berun had been made—that the man had been designed from the outset to withstand the physical and intellectual rigors of immortality. Whereas Vedas possessed one mind housed in the fragile confines of his skull, Shavrim's mind branched and divided throughout his body, compartmentalizing his ponderous existence, allowing him to close and open doors to all but forgotten memories.

And yet, even with this knowledge, Vedas could not conceive of the pressure upon the man's shoulders. Though aware of the limitations of his own knowledge, as well as the impossibility of any true comparison to mortal men, he could not prevent himself from reading much in Shavrim's defeated expression.

What occurred in Marept had broken him in some fundamental way.

To his surprise, Vedas found himself warming to the man. Shavrim had never acted on Vedas or his companions' behalf, but he had also never lied. He would see his family returned to him, and this stirred buried recollections within Vedas. Had he not wanted a family, a place to belong? Had he not tried, for most of his life, to achieve some sense of peace and justice?

He did not hate understanding how he and Shavrim Coranid were alike.

In truth, since communing with Jojore, he had discovered an untapped reserve of compassion for both Churls and Berun. He felt warmly inclined toward Fyra, protective, affectionate in a way he had never before allowed himself around children. The urge to chastise himself emerged, for it was as though he had forgotten a thing so obvious he should never have been able to forget it.

Churls. She had lived with a burden far heavier than his own—far heavier than anyone could be expected to endure. As the trainer of recruits for the Thirteenth Order of Black Suits, he had seen children die, knowing himself to be responsible, or at the very least complicit. But Churls? His knees grew weak every time he contemplated the bleak weight, the overwhelming guilt, of losing a child rarely seen and never truly comprehended. Churls had willfully neglected her daughter, choosing wrongly each and every day she spent far from home.

She had not deceived herself in anything. She had known she was running.

Not for the first time since leaving Golna, Vedas appreciated the power of experiencing unclouded vision. He had once considered himself a man of insight, aware of what moved those whose lives intersected briefly with his own, but to truly comprehend what another felt, the total acknowledgement of their mistakes, their joys and failures and boredoms . . .

Oh, yes, he loved her.

He would use this word, *love*. He would mean it for the first time since childhood, when love was an automatic function of living, of being dependent upon someone. Committing to it, as they traveled through the desert toward a seemingly impossible goal, ridden by forces they could not as mortals grasp, struck him as appropriate.

The mortal mind could be illuminated. Even someone as crippled by doubt, as awkward from self-imposed isolation as he could experience a communion with others. There was considerable risk, but he now understood the risk must be taken if one were to make it to death a complete man.

Of course, *man* could mean so many things. Berun, too, suffered in ways Vedas could sympathize with. Vedas recalled all the ways in which he himself had been manipulated since the death of his parents, first by one and then another abbey master. They continued to exert their pull, even from death and across the continent, telling him that he had lost his way, that he had betrayed his order and the oaths taken there.

Of course, as with Churls, what he knew of suffering in this regard paled in comparison to Berun, who had never had room enough to call himself his own creature—who had at every step been under another's thumb.

Haunted, the three of them. He, Churls, and Berun shared this bond. His friends had known this intuitively and supported him, well before he knew himself.

Friends. Yes. In addition to love, he would use that word. It brought a smile to his face.

And Fyra?

Fyra. To whom they owed their lives. For which she continued to exhaust herself, asking nothing in return. She possessed an unquestionable loyalty to her mother, and, for reasons Vedas could not fathom, a growing sense of attachment to her lover and Berun. She had become invested in their combined fate, to the point of acting as emissary, rousing the dead from their fear, convincing them to risk their own existence to oppose Adrash.

Ostensibly to oppose Adrash, he reminded himself. Everything beyond helping her mother was secondary. She was still a child, for all her power—a child who did not know the wage of her offer.

Jojore knew, however.

We could help you, and stand a chance of surviving, the dead magess had said as they stood and surveyed a blasted, permanently twilit plain—an outcome, one of many, in which Adrash let the Needle fall to earth. *The girl, however? She will die a death beyond death. She will pass out of existence. I am not always able to read the wind, but this much is clear. Know the wage of choosing to accept our help.* Her expression grew hard. *It is a small wage, cousin. She is just one girl. Powerful, yes, but still just one girl.*

He had nodded, but only in confirmation of the conclusion he had already reached. Churls would not lose her daughter a second time.

‡

The nations of Knoori could not easily be linked, one with another. The magic needed to communicate over vast distances existed, but the expenditure was too great for the commoner. As a result, news traveled glacially.

Having no family to speak of, Vedas had never given this fact of existence much thought, yet traveling to Danoor had altered his perspective slightly: he had often longed to communicate with Abse, seeking counsel over the long journey.

Of course, had he received such counsel, he might well have delivered the speech the abbey master had written—a document that sought only to cement the power of the Black Suits, altering the dynamic not at all, keeping warring parties in their old positions. Had he listened to Abse, he would never have allowed his doubt to take such firm root, or his desire for Churls to bloom. He would not have become something other than Vedas Tezul of Golna, a child in a man's body, a mind bound by the cords of dogma. He would not have a hundred new doubts, or a sense of purpose despite the doubts.

Certainly, he would not be staring at a statue of himself, at a crossroads far from Danoor.

He looked away, horrified. The smell of saltwater filled his head, though the ocean could not yet be seen. Over the flat northeastern horizon, he could make out a gleaming arc of reflected light, an incomprehensibly huge bubble stretched over a vast portion of the earth's belly: Osa, or at least the top of the immense crystal dome that covered their eventual destination.

He concentrated on it intensely, as if by doing so he could convince the others to turn their gazes away from the embarrassing object before them.

"Well, this is odd," Churls said.

Shavrim grunted. After a moment, Berun began laughing. Heat rose in Vedas's cheeks.

The statue stood, propped in the sand two miles west of Ual. It was a crude, half-sized thing with exaggerated musculature and even more exaggerated genitalia, painted black from head to toe. In one hand it held a roll of paper. His victory speech.

A sign hung from its neck.

UAL IS LOYAL TO THE PROPHET VEDAS TEZUL
IF YOUR ALLEGIANCE LIES ELSEWHERE
LEAVE OR BE DROWNED IN OUR SEA

Churls resisted laughing, but could not hide the amusement in her voice. "It's really quite flattering, Vedas. You're a hero."

She frowned exaggeratedly at his expression, and squeezed his hand.

"Come now. We'll be welcomed like royals. After Danoor, shouldn't we thank fate for anyone kindly disposed toward us? We could have walked into a town overrun by Adrashi."

He met her stare and she sighed.

"Fine," she said, and pressed her palm flat against the statue's forehead. She walked forward, toppling it easily to the ground. Over her shoulder, she smiled at him. "What? They're about to meet the real thing, anyway, so what's the harm in a little sacrilege?"

He tried to see the humor in it. He did. She raised her eyebrows. He admitted defeat, and smiled at her. It was a forced reaction, but to his astonishment it helped: as he passed the downed statue, the situation suddenly struck him as comical. He experienced the increasingly familiar suspicion that, should he choose to view the world differently, the world would indeed appear differently. Was it necessary to view events through such an uncharitable lens? What, he asked, did it profit him to greet each day with a wary eye? He had always been dying. The world had always been dying. It would all end one day, and what would be left of Vedas Tezul?

He stopped in his tracks, turned back, and stooped to shoulder his wooden likeness. Shavrim watched him. He nodded, expression unreadable, when Vedas stood.

Berun looked from one to the other. "What are you doing?" he asked.

Vedas shook his head, not entirely sure, but suspecting he would know in time.

‡

The residents of Ual had little to spare, but they spared all of it to accommodate their prophet. He balked at their generosity, but in the end relented.

They slaughtered a ewe within a half hour of his arrival, prepared and set dinner for twelve men between the three of them, and made up his and Churls's room in the town's one inn as if hosting (just as she had predicted) a king and queen. Joyful and embarrassed at all the attention, full to the point of bellyache and more than a little drunk, they fell asleep before the thought of making love occurred to either of them.

At two hours past midnight, he rose and left her. His movements were silent, even to his own ears. He had felt sluggish upon entering the room, but he felt light and strong upon leaving it, filled with a purpose he did not need to question. Following the compulsion, he smiled tightly in anticipation, his jaw clenched and his fingers balled into fists.

He would go, but he would not be corralled.

His brother waited for him in the town square, arms crossed, under the broken sky. This word—*brother*—formed on Vedas's lips, but he suppressed the urge to speak it. He clamped down upon the sense of familiarity that threatened to dictate the conversation before it had even begun. A door closed in his mind: he locked Evurt as best he could behind it.

"Shavrim," he said.

The man canted his head forward, causing the moonlight to catch oddly on the stubby horns sprouting from his forehead. For a handful of seconds, they appeared larger than they had before, sharpened into vicious points. Stretching, reaching . . .

Vedas kept himself, barely, from taking a step back.

Shavrim's left eyebrow lifted and he raised his chin, breaking the illusion. He smiled—a touch sadly, Vedas estimated. Vedas had seen the same expression on Abse's face many times. When the abbey master's most gifted disciple had not reached the correct conclusion. When events did not turn out as the abbey master planned.

Abse had been able to recognize immediately, the moment when Vedas's sympathy shifted away from him.

"Vedas," Shavrim said. There was no question in it.

"Yes. That is my name."

Shavrim nodded, eyes bright, intent. "It is. It is. And yet you're here, where I expected Evurt to be." He sat, cross-legged on the ground. He gestured that his visitor sit. "I won't pretend this pleases me, Vedas, but there's little I can do. You're surprised that I tell you this? Let me ask—do you think I've been honest with you? Have I been forthright?"

"You have," Vedas said immediately, and then discovered room to doubt his surety. He considered several responses, and then shrugged before sitting across from Shavrim.

An odd decisiveness had settled upon him: he would allow the man to lead, to either tell the truth or implicate himself. He would trust himself to tell the difference between the two.

Behind the closed door in his mind, he felt a force push back against this resolution. Evurt did not want to wait, yet Vedas found it easy to dismiss his impatience. Each inhalation seemed to anchor him more firmly to the earth. Even his newfound affection for Shavrim did not fade. In fact, it was if they stood upon equal ground for the first time.

They stared at one another, silent.

Shavrim broke first. He laughed suddenly, as though Vedas had told an amusing joke.

"You're an interesting man, Vedas Tezul. When we met upon Fesuy Amendja's roof, I told you I could show you a way to stop hating yourself, never imagining you might come to terms with yourself alone. Every rumor I'd heard had led me to imagine you as the most inflexible sort."

Vedas said nothing.

"To be clear, mine was a genuine offer. Adrash is not invincible. He can be wounded. He might even die. What I did not share then, but shared soon after, was the way in which you'd be able to make good on your word—not through your own efforts, but through my brother's."

He sighed, and his sad smile returned. "Yes. I had hoped to see Evurt again, to fight alongside him, despite what damage it might do to you. I thought he and Ustert were the world's best chance. I still worry that they are, that we have missed an opportunity at an entire world's expense. Their assumption of you and Churls may still happen, of course. I won't lie and say it wouldn't please me. Regardless, there's substantial doubt in my mind. Perhaps they chose vessels less wisely than they could have. Perhaps you are too strong to be taken and used in the manner they intend."

Vedas said nothing. He closed his eyes as the pressure behind the closed door intensified.

After a long pause, Shavrim said, "Perhaps this is a good thing, however."

The pressure doubled, tripled. Vedas considered clamping down upon it entirely, grinding Evurt's influence to a halt before it became overwhelming, but did not. Shavrim would not stop attempting to rouse his brother. He would test Vedas, again and again.

Might as well have it out now, Vedas thought.

Evurt did not deign to respond.

"Perhaps you are what the world needs," Shavrim said. "Two mortals. After all, if Evurt's strength is insufficient to overcome you, what use could he be against our father?"

The pressure increased until Vedas's skull creaked with it, bathing him from crown to chin in pain so intense he struggled to loosen his jaw to scream, yet loosen his jaw to scream he did. He opened his eyes, and a golden light poured forth from them, fractionally easing the weight pressed against both temples. The colors of the night bloomed around him suddenly and Evurt's consciousness, menacingly alien and disdainful, flooded his own. He rocked from side to side dizzyingly, as though his body, his mind and soul, were being pulled from either direction.

As though he were scales, measuring shifting weights.

"Shavrim," he said in one croak of a voice while another, steadier voice spoke simultaneously, saying the word he had not wanted to say.

"Brother," Evurt said.

In this one word, Vedas heard the god's satisfaction, the arrogant presumption, and his anger flared in response.

Losing to Evurt was not an option.

Thus, he would not lose: it was this simple. His teeth snapped closed and he growled, like a mutt cornered in an alley. His eyes closed, like shutters on the invading sun. His hands rose to his head, and gradually he stopped rocking. Then, after an infinity of fearing his skull would collapse upon itself, of holding back the raging divine tide within him, he found control once more.

The light slowly faded from his eyes. Evurt howled from behind the closed door.

"Shavrim" Vedas said. In one voice. His own voice. "You can stop trying." He shrugged. "Or don't. I can't summon the interest to care, either way. I know what you're doing, and Evurt won't be coaxed that easily from where I've put him." He stood, pain a forgotten memory, smiling down at Shavrim without an ounce of anger. It was easy to simply choose a mood. He wondered why he had decided, on so many occasions, to be angry or fearful. He questioned why he had let himself be pushed from one period of uncertainty to another for so long.

"Try again and again, but I know you better than you know me. Knowing you, I know something of your sibling. He has immense power, but he's caged where I can see him. I will instruct Churls and Berun how to feel their presence, and how to stop them. If they want to assist our efforts, we will allow them. We. Mortal men and women."

Shavrim's brow furrowed. Vedas imagined he saw a measure of fear in the man's expression.

"Know me? Know me *how*?"

Vedas bent down to Shavrim's ear and said Jojore Um's name. Then he turned on his heel and walked away.

‡

Halfway between the square and the inn, the girl appeared at his side and took his hand. He smiled down at her, not sure if she had assisted him and not particularly caring. His mood would change, undoubtedly, to a familiar, long-worn state of worry and fear, as soon as he woke from the charitable disposition that had taken hold.

The glow of victory did not last forever: there would come a time when, for Fyra's own safety, he would have to tell her to go—to leave them to their fate, in Shavrim's hands . . .

But it would not be now.

He gripped her hand and stopped. In silence, together, they watched the slowly and swiftly spinning spheres of the Needle, the threat of the world's destruction, pass overhead. He did not see them with Evurt's eyes, but with the limited vision his mother and father had birthed to him. The components looked as they in fact were farther away than all the steps he had walked on the face of Jeroun. The scattered entirety of the Needle could be nothing more than it always had been to a mortal, earthbound man.

Indistinct and unknowable. A blight upon the order of the heavens.

Nonetheless, at that moment, it was beautiful beyond measure. It was a decision to view it so. It was a denial of reality.

He accepted this now, understanding he would not make the same choice again.

‡

In the morning, he rose with Churls, awkwardly accepted the provisions Ual's mayor publicly insisted on gifting to him, and made his way to the docks with his three companions.

Townsfolk stopped him along the way and asked for his blessing, which he gave reluctantly. "You have it," he said again and again, grimacing more than smiling at the small, black-skinned men and women, wrinkled into early grandmothers and grandfathers by the strong, salty wind and ocean sun.

Churls failed to keep the amusement from touching her features. The people knew her by reputation, as well, and smiled warmly in response to her expression, as though she too had blessed them. Berun, also known by his association to Vedas, accepted the company of the town's few children with good grace, holding his massive arms out low so they could swing from him.

Shavrim walked several body lengths behind Vedas and company. The townspeople gave him a wide berth, likely because they had caught some news of further events in Danoor. Even as isolated as they were, it was clear someone had passed through recently. The mayor appeared uncomfortable next to the broad, horned man, but he listened intently to what Shavrim had to say. They had been talking since leaving the inn.

Vedas wished he could listen in on their conversation, for he did not know how Shavrim had, without violence, convinced the mayor to allow them to lower a sea-gate that had been closed for millennia. Perhaps it had simply been an exchange of bonedust, yet Vedas did not think so. He supposed he would never know, for the townspeople crowded around him, clamoring for his attention, his touch, hungry for a person he could only pretend to be.

Eventually, they reached the docks. Or, rather, the two stone jetties and Ual's sad collection of fishing vessels, not one of which looked large enough to accommodate the four of them, especially considering Berun's mass. Certainly, they would capsize the moment anything large enough to survive on the open ocean poked its snout against their hull.

Admittedly, Vedas knew little of seacraft. He had lived two miles inland of the ocean for most of his life, and learned next to nothing about it beyond the danger it presented. Golna possessed the resources of a metropolis to defend itself from seagoing creatures of Jeroun, many of which happily hurled themselves out of the water and against the city's walls. The city also sat near one of many fishable rivers stocked heavily with smaller, adolescent versions of the oceangoing monsters that gave birth to them.

Ual, however, had no such resources. It had an altogether more novel way of drawing sustenance from the sea.

Vedas shielded his eyes against the early morning glare upon the mirror-flat water (a highly unusual occurrence, numerous villagers had told him, to have such a calm day this early in the year—a good omen, many of them said, with forced expressions that belied their words) and the top of the distant inverted bowl over Osa, searching for the fifteen-foot-high stone pillars of Ual's only claim to fame: its coastal wall, which extended out from the town's shore nearly ten miles and arced to either side for nearly thirty miles, creating a relatively safe haven for fishing.

Now that Vedas considered it, it struck him as odd that so few visited or even spoke of Ual, for its people were surely extraordinary. It was common to say no one set craft upon the surface of the sea, yet the people of Ual did so daily. As they had done for millennia.

Men needed to speak in definitives, Vedas knew. They needed to reduce the world to comprehensible portions. And thus, the people of Ual and their incredible, ancient construction allowing them to do the impossible, were ignored.

Men did not sail upon the sea.

The woman next to him—small, sunworn, to his eyes identical to the woman next to her—laid her left hand upon his arm and pointed with her right.

"It's not easy to see. There is a blurred line, just below the waterline." Her eyes were wide as she stared up at him. "You're really going there, to the gate? Only the wall walkers"—those townsmen and townswomen who maintained the wall's integrity, Vedas had learned—"go anywhere close to it."

"No," Vedas said, squinting to see what she claimed was visible. "We're not going to it. We're going beyond it."

She spit into the tiny waves lapping at the rocks below them. Her neighbor did likewise.

Shavrim stepped up behind Vedas, causing both women to move to the side, allowing him space to stand. The horned man lifted his shirt over his head, inflating his massive chest with salty air. He clapped Vedas on the back, beaming as though they were old friends.

"Time to go," he said.

Vedas nodded, relieved. Without looking, he reached and found Churls's hand. They moved through the crowd more easily now with Shavrim at their side.

Berun rose from the pile of children he had let play upon his sitting form, the great bell of his laugh booming loudly on the still morning air.

But for the mayor, they left the townspeople behind. As they stepped onto the second, slightly larger jetty, Churls stopped him.

"Turn around and wave. It's the least they deserve for the hospitality."

He followed her order, awkwardly.

The people of Ual waved back and cheered, though he doubted their hearts were in it. Men did not really sail upon the sea, even in Ual. Beyond the coastal wall was the haven of animals beyond the scale of man, a shallow, glass-clear expanse of certain death. And should Vedas somehow manage to defy the inevitable and reach the shore of Osa, an impenetrable wall of crystal lay between him and his mad destination.

The people of Ual waved goodbye to their prophet.

‡

He kept his eyes forward as they set off. The boat's small thaumaturgical engine chuffed and barked at his back, with Shavrim at the tiller. Berun lay between Vedas and Shavrim, evening out the weight of their cargo at the boat's head. A strong breeze kicked in as one of the few clouds in the sky obscured the sun, and then died as the sun peeked out again.

Churls squeezed his hand. She rose into a crouch, leaned over their piled supplies amidship, and made her way toward the bow. She leaned over it for a moment, and then laughed.

"Come here!" she called. "You have to see this."

"What?" he asked, not wanting to move. He had no good memories of his last time upon the water, on their way to Tan-Ten, and the boat he sat in now felt far less stable than the *Atavest* had. Of course, it was one-tenth the size.

"Just come here," she responded.

He made his way forward, far slower and more painstakingly than she had. Pausing at the port gunwale for a moment, he peered down into the depths, surprised to find the bottom of the sea so close—no more than ten or fifteen feet below him through startlingly clear water, dappled with crisscrossing lines of light. Fish and aquatic reptiles, the cousins and spawn of larger creatures, the mainstay of Ual's diet and scant industry, darted from rock to rock.

An odd sadness crept into him at the realization that he had never before stared into the sea, that this one opportunity to do so would be so fleeting. He considered what it must have been like, growing up in Ual, knowing their manmade corner of the sea so intimately that any incursion into it—be it a creature that had grown too large, too dangerous, or a breach within the coastal wall, allowing the outside ocean in—felt like a wound in one's own flesh.

To know a thing outside of oneself, so intimately . . .

His left hand went to the neckline of his suit. He slipped the tip of his index finger between the elder-cloth and the skin at the nape of his neck, encountering resistance as the material peeled back from its tight embrace of his body. It was a disturbingly invasive sensation, but he had grown used to it, like one worrying at a torn cuticle.

"Vedas?" Churls said.

He shook his head and peered back toward the shoreline, finding it had retreated further than he had imagined possible in such a short amount of time. A crowd still stood above the tide, though already it had thinned. He imagined many of them had returned home, to stare at their hands and consider an uncertain future. The mayor had looked on the verge of crying as they pulled away from the dock.

He must surely be scared, Vedas thought. *We're opening his sea-gate. We might leave it open, destroying his and his ancestors' long and meticulously held balance.*

He reached Churls on wobbly legs. She offered him a sympathetic smile but no hand in support.

The fingers of his right hand closed around what he thought to be the tip of the boat's bow. He leaned forward cautiously and looked down into the parting water. For a moment, he saw nothing, and then his perspective shifted as his eyes registered what Churls had seen. A black, cartoonishly muscular torso. Outsized genitals. Below that, water-stained legs. He turned his head and stared into one large, white-painted eye of the statue he had carried into Ual. His hand rested on its head.

It had been bolted onto the boat's prow, making of it a figurehead.

He rose into a crouch and turned, muscles taut on his frame, all trace of physical awkwardness aboard-ship forgotten.

Shavrim did not need to turn his head. His eyes were already fixed on Vedas. He stared intently, with no trace of an expression.

"What is the meaning of this?" Vedas asked.

Shavrim's eyebrows rose, but otherwise his features remained neutral. "You claim to know me," he said. "And this makes me rather curious. Did you know I would do that?" Without breaking eye contact, he reached behind him and shut the thaumaturgical engine off. "Did you know I would do that?" He stood as the boat rocked violently back and forth in the absence of forward momentum.

Berun began to rise.

Shavrim bent forward to lay a hand on the constructed man's massive shoulder.

"This is not violence, Berun. This is us coming to terms."

Vedas forced himself to stand at the head of the pitching boat. His suit stiffened around him instantly in response to his nervousness. He forced it to unclench, and found his balance. Easily.

Churls's hand pressed to his back as she rose. In support, not to steady him.

"I've been thinking since you left me in the square last night," Shavrim said.

"And?" Vedas said.

Shavrim gestured expansively. "I'm left wondering what you really think, Vedas. Do you think I want my family back badly enough to risk the entire world? Do you think I'll keep trying to summon Evurt and Ustert, to the detriment of our plans? No. Don't answer. I'll tell you. I will not. I don't know that you alone are sufficient to oppose Adrash, and I doubt my siblings are willing to share their power. Nonetheless, we won't be deterred. I'll do what is necessary to preserve this world, even to the point of opposing those for whom . . ."

He broke eye contact to stare at Churls, and then at Berun. "Do you hear me? Do you know what I'm saying?" He pointed to the bow and his voice boomed. "Do you know what that means? It is a betrayal."

He frowned, letting emotion alter the set of his features until he resembled a different man. His hands fell straight to his sides, dragging his shoulders down with them.

"Perhaps . . ." he said. "Perhaps we're all fools. We could be wrong in everything."

He sat heavily, rocking the boat. He started the engine and Vedas looked away. Churls wrapped her arms around his shoulders and pulled him close, leaning back against the hull. Berun lay immobile, staring at the sky with eyes that could not close.

The whole day open before them, windless and bright, their journey resumed.

POL TANZ ET SOM

THE 25TH OF THE MONTH OF SECTARIANS TO THE 1ST
OF THE MONTH OF FISHERS
ASPA MOUNTAINS, THE KINGDOM OF STOL, TO DANOOR,
THE REPUBLIC OF KNOS MIN

For one hundred days, Pol slept. For four months, he dreamt of plummeting out of the sky.

He fell, exhausted nearly to death by his headlong flight from Adrash. His skin scorched, crusted over, and peeled away as he entered Jeroun's atmosphere. His arms and legs whipped about violently enough to dislocate his joints, causing him to be pummeled by his own fists and feet as they flailed, drawing blood from his sensitive new flesh and sending it in arcs around his spinning body.

The sigils he had tattooed upon himself with alchemical ink—the spells that had been brought to life, granting him the might to stand against a god—were gathered as solid black masses at his hands and feet, as a coil rope of black hair wrapped around his throat, choking him. All were inert, useless.

His eyelids had been burned away. Heat and wind had fused his one remaining amber eye motionless in his skull, and turned the empty socket of the other into an aching pit. He fell blind, his never-ending state of agony preventing him from sinking into unconsciousness.

He lived, just barely, unable to think beyond the pain.

The ground rose up beneath him, a granite fist.

When he smashed into it, blackness enveloped him.

There was a timeless instant where he felt nothing. A breath before . . .

‡

The dream began again.

And again.

And again.

‡

He woke, screaming. Not a full-throated sound, but a piteous, rattling wheeze that caught in his throat the moment it emerged. He inhaled convulsively and then coughed dry, blood-flecked sputum into the cold, thin air, curling around the aching hollow of his gut before screaming again—more fully this time, a bellow of ignorant rage that lasted until he could do it no more. He breathed in and out, deeper each time, calming himself.

It took the space of several heartbeats to believe he had stopped falling, to make his right eye organize the colors before him as images.

Gravel. Fractured planes of rock underneath.

Lifting his head took a monumental effort. The muscles of his neck screamed in palsied protest. Gritting his teeth against the pain, he looked about.

Rock faces before him, rock below and to the right.

To the left and above, sky cloudless and unbroken, painfully blue.

He examined the rock floor and walls more closely. To his eye, they appeared recently fractured, white along their angles. Many bore long gashes, five-rowed and straight. Without willing it to do so, his hand reached out, spreading fingertips to fit into the gouges. He raked his nails along the channels he had created without remembering, and then laid his palm against the cold stone, exploring the concavity beneath him.

He shivered as the realization struck him.

Here is where I came to earth.

Even with the abilities the sigils had granted him, it was a miracle he had survived.

And yet . . . *where* had he come to rest?

He rolled over, slowly, and crawled to the edge of his jagged platform. Below him extended a nearly vertical wall of bare gray rock, weathered by wind and time. Below that, dizzyingly far, the angle of the rock grew less severe, becoming a surface upon which snow could cling. And further, so much further down, the world spread out in white folds, broken here and there by thrusting spires of granite.

He had seen this vista from above the world, many times. It had once seemed just another place, high and isolated, the home of goat-milkers and idiot hermits.

It had *once* seemed . . .

His head whipped around, causing black spots to swarm before his eyes. The rock face above him shielded the view, but he felt the pull of the secret he had stolen from Adrash's mind.

He tried to stand, but his legs would not support him. He fell back, lightheaded, gritting his teeth in impatience. The second attempt was no better. The third, and his legs held beneath him. He stretched his long, angular body up the wall of rock before him, peering over its lip.

The heady perspective nearly sent him tumbling backward, but his thin fingers found purchase in the stone. He blinked the sense of disorientation away, letting his gaze steady upon the mountain's summit—or rather, a broad portion of it.

He grinned, revealing small, even teeth. His legs were suddenly firmer beneath him. He knew now, for certain, where he was.

When his strength returned, he would ascend to the mountain's hollowed-out peak. He would walk into the valley of the nameless people. He would dip his hands into the clear blue lake at its center, and run his hands over the worn remains of the forgotten city of the elders, older than recorded time.

And everywhere, he would find corpses. A storehouse of power the likes of which the world had never seen. With the talents the sigils had bestowed upon him, it would be an easy thing to gather the corpses together and transport them to wherever he liked.

His grin grew wider. Dry laughter erupted from his chest as he lowered himself into a sitting position.

Lacking even the energy to access a simple spell to be sure, he nonetheless sensed a disappointing amount of time had passed since he fled from Adrash. Weeks. Months, perhaps. Regardless, his spirits were not dimmed. Without consciously making the decision to do so, he had guided himself where he most needed to be.

‡

He lay in the sun throughout the day and, after taking in one contemplative look at the broken sky as it rose above the world, slept when the sun died. The wind, carrying air cold enough to freeze water to steel, failed to even stir him in his slumber. In the morning, he felt full, though he had eaten nothing. He stood on solid legs and walked to the edge of his eyrie, staring down the wall of his prison with one corner of his mouth upraised.

Yet his hands shook. He examined them, stained black with latent magic, and backed away from the open height. A searching thought (timid enough at the beginning to embarrass him, even alone) caused the boundaries at his wrists to quiver. He looked down at his ankles and saw that there, too, the alchemical ink had become agitated, the amorphous sigils eager to rise up his legs and arms, forming shapes, covering him in the symbols of his magical will. Those spells that had gathered on his scalp, mimicking long hair, lifted from his back and shoulders as fine filaments wavering in the wind, a hundred thousand snakes woken from hibernation.

Gooseflesh rose on every inch of his naked, eggplant skin, and the open hands raised in relief on either pectoral muscle grew in definition, as though someone sought to push out from the inside. His testicles lifted as his cock stiffened painfully. His right eyelid slowly opened, allowing smoke to seep in a thin stream from the black cavity of his eye socket.

The world bloomed into dizzying color. For the space of several breaths, his hearts pounded hard enough to shudder his vision. A wave of nausea bent him at the waste. He retched, yet had nothing to summon from his stomach.

He had been afraid, yes. He had not known if the sigils would respond to his commands after such time and grievous injury.

As good as their rousing felt, he forced them to still upon his hands and feet. He would not be arrogant now, giving in to temptation before his body had fully recovered. Not when he was so close to his goal. He lay upon the cold stone, allowing the sun to soak into the roots of his body, his thoughts drifting to the knowledge he had gleaned from the dead following Ebn's assault and then stolen from Adrash's weakened mind during their battle.

He recalled the elder he had seen and encountered on the Clouded Continent, and it was an epiphany too reality-altering to do him much good—as was the revelation of Jeroun being only one planet among many: scholars had already posited this.

And the existence of an afterlife? What did this matter? The dead were insignificant, a concern only among themselves.

What he had learned about Adrash's nature, too—his existence as a man before assuming the mantle of godhood, how blind he had become to the world he once actively ruled—enticed him while remaining altogether too abstract to be of any use. Adrash was a force nearly beyond measure, answerable only to an equal force: understanding his past or madness would add little of value.

But those frustratingly blank identities, those mortals without names who had stood on a baked plain before Adrash? He worried at these like a loose tooth, trying to dredge something useful from his memory, a detail he had not seen in the moment of revelation.

The Black Suit, a Knosi, beautiful in a boring way.

The freckled woman, whose face he had disliked immediately, viscerally.

The constructed man of brass spheres, eyes glowing actinic blue.

Pol had not the slightest clue about the first two. Not even an itch of recognition. The third, however, he sensed he should know. Holding the image of the artificial creature in his mind created a disconcertingly slippery effect, as of trying to keep water from dripping through one's hands. He had heard a story about a constructed man, had he not? He had studied the creation of constructs, and there had been one particular example . . .

He tried to picture the classrooms of the Academy of Applied Magics, places he had always known. His brow furrowed in concentration. He placed himself in his own apartment, and could not remember where his bookcases had been, or whether his bed faced the east or the west.

The name of his first instructor.

The identity of the man who had deflowered him.

His mother's stern face . . .

Summoning *any* memory from before his transformation in Ebn's bedroom proved difficult. In fact, even the details of that night were blurred around the edges. She had raped him, he recalled. He winced, recalling pain and shame greater than any he had ever experienced.

But what had she *done*, exactly?

Suddenly, it struck him as very important that he remember—as though, by doing so, it would unlock the other memories eluding him. As if a door would be opened inside him.

‡

Another day passed while he waited to be strong enough.

Another day, during which his memory became no clearer. Impatience pressed upon him, as though someone were staring over his shoulder, urging him to act. It built until he shook with it, impotent in the face of it.

And then, just as the sun dropped below the jagged skyline and the scattered spheres of the Needle began rising in the east, a face rose out of the mist clouding his recollection.

A broad, lavender-skinned, horned face. The face of a quarterstock. Pol had come to know it in the months before his cathartic encounter with Ebn.

Shav. His name had been Shav.

A madman, given to spells of dementia . . . of appearing to be one man and then another . . .

All at once, Pol remembered every word.

‡

The dragon and I. A halfbreed and a quarterbreed at this moment in time. The conjunction of the two is interesting, Pol. Interesting. I've seen a dragon crash into the sea, sure the animal had killed itself. Instead it surfaced, twisting its long neck and beating its wings upon the water, a great sea serpent clamped in its jaws—a sea serpent so large that it could've swallowed our tiny boat in one bite. Its skin shone like silver in the moonlight, and its thrashing frothed the sea like a child's hand slapping bathwater.

The Needle had only risen halfway, and the moon showed a quarter of her face. I stared at the destruction coming swiftly: a wall of black water that blotted out the stars along the horizon. I waited and told my men to prepare themselves. Some of them prayed to Adrash, some to Orrus, and some to the devil. Me, I just waited for the inevitable, almost wanting it. Most likely, I would die along with my men. An odd feeling, being that powerless.

Someday soon, I think you'll know what that feels like.

The moment snapped into clarity within the dim confines his skull, creating a scene so vivid it was as though he were seated again in his apartment on an atypically hot day in the Month of Clergymen, the year previous. He stared at the quarterstock named Shav and thought it odd, what he now knew without doubt. What he should have known then:

Shav was no madman. Disturbed, but not mad.

Perhaps not even disturbed, but very clever.

Or even inspired.

In his mind's eye, Pol reappraised the broad, horned wyrm tamer, doubting every assumption he had made about the quarterstock: indeed, he now found himself wondering if the term quarterstock even applied. It had been the easiest determination to make, for Shav had never denied it. Moreover, what else existed that appeared as he did? Not a man and not an elderman, but a thing in between, a manlike creature singular in creation.

Yet the quarterstock itself was a near-legend. No one alive in Tansot—in fact, anyone in the recorded history of the city, the place where eldermen had always been most numerous—had verifiably documented the healthy offspring of an elderwoman. To assume one had suddenly appeared in Pol's life, just as he desired an asset worthy of note . . .

An asset who spoke such odd, portentous words.

At the time, Pol had dismissed Shav's rambling monologues. Surely, he had reasoned, they were merely the digressions of a precocious individual, the fictions of a talented mind severely maladjusted by the vagaries of unusual parentage. Beyond material assistance as a tamer, Shav could have no insight applicable to Pol's situation.

Now, however, he was forced to admit he had been wrong. The account of the dragon—it could only have been an allusion to events to come. Soon after the words were spoken, Pol and eighteen other outbound mages had ascended into the sky, bearing Ebn's gift to the god, a massive statue in his likeness. Before they reached the moon, Adrash appeared and with a thought shattered the statue, sending its pieces in a wave of mutilation toward the mages, killing all but the most skilled. Pol could do nothing to prevent their deaths.

Helpless.

Someday soon, I think you'll know what that feels like.

Pol lingered on these words. He had been horrified, true, but had he felt helpless?

No. No, he had not. Perhaps, at the beginning, for the briefest hesitation, he had not known what to do, but within heartbeats of seeing the statue turned into a bomb he had been filled with purpose, first to defend himself, and second to . . . to . . .

He gasped as the sigils spun to life on his whip-thin body, rising into a whirlwind of countless long-tailed sperm on his forearms and legs, whipping around his shoulders and neck and lower belly as they recalled with near-sentience their awakening upon him. He collapsed onto the cold rock, smoke pouring from his left eye, fingers twitching one motion over and over again—the same motion he had used to release a spell upon the Needle, altering one of its massive spheres slightly, announcing his challenge to Adrash before he had even thought the wages of this action through.

Coils of concussive force leapt from his outspread fingertips.

The rock face before him fractured like a broken mirror before crumbling onto his legs. He pulled his feet free before more of the wall fell upon him, and nearly tumbled off his perch. Teetering toward death, the upper half of his back over the void. Arms outstretched, rigidly under the control of the sigils. The spell bore into the mountainside, pushing him inch by inch backward in the process.

He could find no purchase. He would fall.

"No!" he roared, tightening the spasming muscles of his stomach, attempting to sit.

As he fought to regain his balance, one of the sigils on his arm formed itself into a black circle and rose upward from his flesh as a tendril, wavering in the wind as though it were a charmed snake. Pol focused on it as its tip ballooned, stunned into immobility despite the danger.

The sigil formed a face, black on black, horned.

"Waste no more time," it said. "Learn to fly."

Pol screamed as he tipped over the edge of his perch. The wind ripped the voice from his mouth as he fell. There was no time for thought, no time even for fear. Certainly, there was no time to recall the second portent Shav had spoken to him . . .

‡

Before he leaves, my father tells me to contemplate death. He tells me to feel my mortality in the creak of my bones and the soreness of my muscles. With every heartbeat, you are closer to death, he says. He forces me to smell the stench of his underarms—the smell of the body birthing and decaying life at the same moment. He tells me to know, intimately, every sign of weakness in my body, and then reject each in turn.

He breaks my arm with one blow, kicks me as I writhe on the ground. Remember this lesson above all others, he says. The body heals. It responds to trauma, to pain—not with fear, but with purpose. So must you. You need not die, my son, but in order to continue living—

—you must suffer.

‡

Pol dropped, head first, as fast as a body must drop, yet his perceptions were reduced to a crawl, drawn out into one long howl of wind—an avalanche in his ears, a needle in his eyes. Rigid-limbed, he spun as the spell continued to pass from his fingers, warping the air before him like heat radiating above a fire, strafing the mountainside in cracks as he rotated to face its solid wall again and again.

The mountainside. It loomed closer each time he regarded it.

Spiraling, caught and stretched in a sluggish current of time, horrified and fascinated at once (at his predicament, at his foolishness for not being more attentive when events had been playing out), he found space within himself to consider Shav's words.

He placed himself, once again, in his apartment. He held a knife in his hand.

It had been near the end of the Month of Pilots, three weeks after Ebn's disastrous goodwill mission. Confident the display of power he had recently shown was only the beginning, the birthing of greater magic within him, Pol nonetheless forced himself to caution. He would not underestimate Ebn. She had swayed a god, after all, if in the brief moment before his rage returned to him. Pol would not rely upon the dimly understood nature of his sigils, but attack his superior using brute force.

A knife, cunningly crafted, intended for her skull.

Shav had offered the support he could—first the knife, second the assistance of his wyrm, Sapes—before succumbing to yet another of his spells.

You need not die, but in order to continue living, you must suffer.

Pol cursed himself for not drawing the obvious conclusion sooner.

Shav had known, or at least predicted.

A month after he and Shav's meeting in his apartment, his plan of attack frustrated, Pol had committed an act of supreme foolishness, relying upon tradition to protect him. Ebn, the more opportunistic of the two, broke into his apartment, breaching the oldest of etiquettes dictating how eldermen treated one another, and humiliated him. After ensorceling him into a state of immobile arousal, she raped him. Despite the aggression of the act, she still could not summon the rage to kill him and so resorted to greater violence.

Finally, she had torn out his left eye.

He recalled the agony, the humiliation. He recalled a pressure. Voices, calling him to transformation . . .

You need not die, but in order to continue living, you must suffer.

A sudden gust of wind pushed against him like a cold slab of glass, tipping him lengthwise in glacial motion, sending his feet into the mountainside. He braced for the pain of contact, of his skin being flayed against the rough wall.

When it came, however, it was more intense than he could have imagined, drawn out into one torturous moment. Reactions slowed, he watched in paralyzed horror as his bloodied feet rebounded from the wall and rocked his upper body toward it. The closer his hands came, the more damage his spell did to the rock, boring into it in doubled lightning lines.

When his hands finally passed into the mountainside, he screamed. The mineral, heated to its vaporization point, blackened and bubbled the skin of his fingers. His wrists. His forearms.

He fought helplessness through the red haze of his torment. Soon, his face would hit the wall and he would be dead. There would be no fractured rock beneath him when he woke. He would not wake.

Learn to fly, his sigil had said.

Learn to fly.

‡

A timeless moment before his forehead touched the mountainside, he did just that. A voice—or several voices: he would never be sure—whispered wordless directions, spoke a command Pol felt more than understood, and he remembered.

He had once possessed wings. They had carried him into the night sky from Ebn's bedroom. They had borne him to orbit.

He tipped his head to the side in slow motion, cracking vertebrae. He then tipped it to the other side. Fully inhabiting his pain now, taking succor from it, he flexed burnt hands now under his own control. He increased the power of his spell, pushing himself back from the mountainside before closing his fists and entering into a full dive.

He was an arrow, suspended in amber. *Enough*, he subvocalized.

The wind tore at him as time reasserted its normal pace. He bared teeth into the gale, grinning at the swiftly approaching ground. With a few muscular twitches, he corrected his spin.

As he spread his arms out to either side, stretching the kinking muscles of his shoulders, wings unfurled from his back. Blacker than a moonless night they grew, doubling and then tripling in width, becoming assets befitting a creature of legend, a god.

He arched, letting his wings cup the wind. His bones creaked as his body took the weight of gravity only feet from the snowy mountainside. His dive flattened into an unsteady soar over the frozen landscape. Quickly, he righted his shuddering wings and flapped down once, twice, three times, his confidence growing as memory took hold.

He flew. It was as though he had been born with wings.

‡

Before him, an invisible wall shielded the valley. He knew of its existence from his contact with Adrash, but understood little of its nature beyond the scope of its power. It had served to hide the valley from all but the most powerful gaze for all of human and elderman history.

Until Pol, that is. He saw through it easily, first through the phantom organ of his left eye and then through his unaided right, gazing down upon the lifeless plain. Cradled at the valley's exact center, bluer than any memory of blue, was the lake. Upon seeing it, his mouth began watering. He had not drunk since before the turn of the half-millennium.

A smile rose to his lips as he recalled the taste of cold water. Water he alone would drink. Glory he would never be forced to share.

Regardless of his excitement, he forced himself to caution, angling his charcoal wings to slow his approach. The alien ache in his bones grew more severe, the closer he came to the barrier. The remainder of his self-congratulations came to a grinding halt as the fractaling sigils fled from his leading fists, en masse, flowing like ink over his sinuous torso to gather as static, as jittering ants on his legs. The sigils flowing from his scalp flattened on the ridges of his back, tapering into a point above his buttocks.

All at once, the coldness of the air registered. He shivered.

Pressure built, centering into a tight knot of resentment behind his eyes. He stopped his chattering teeth by clenching his jaw until it rang, and stretched his fists out before him.

Anger became determination. With a twitch of his wings, he dove forward.

The wall did not physically restrain him. There was no pain. Nonetheless, he cried out as he crossed the threshold, for the error—the wage of his impetuousness—was immediately clear. Ebn had been a master of dampening spells, but even she could not have accomplished so thorough an effect.

At once, the sigils were thrown into chaos on Pol's body, spreading and contracting like tides, pooling and bursting without pattern. The vision in his phantom eye faltered, flickering to him an image of the valley below and then failing utterly. His wings began to diminish. They rippled, no longer rigid along their length.

Struggling for any measure of control, using his legs as crude rudders, Pol managed to turn toward the lake.

Despite his rapid descent, by the time the water stretched beneath him he still flew too high. Soon, he would be beyond it. Possessing neither the strength nor the alchemical faculties to turn around for another pass, without considering the injuries he might sustain, he curled his wings around himself and fell.

Below, the surface of the lake was a mirror, reflecting the noon sun as a perfect circle. He kept his right eye open and focused upon it, letting its light sear into his skull, seeing his shadow become a black hole at its center just before his body hit the water.

It came to him, fully, a complete memory in the breath before impact:

He had been laid out by an attacker before. Once, years previously, a fellow mage—Pol's senior by a decade, resentful of the younger elderman's quick advancement—had nearly killed him with a simple, outsized concussion spell that blasted him thirty feet into an iron cauldron. He recalled the feeling of its impact, being slapped by a giant hand, and then the near immediate rebound of his body against an immobile surface far harder than his own body.

Then darkness.

Then, all in an instant upon waking, the awareness of the fragility of one's physical being. The sudden rush of memories . . . of bones breaking, of flesh collapsing.

He did not have the benefit of losing consciousness, this time. He remained aware as his body crumpled against the unyielding surface of the lake. His joints flexed and strained, threatening to snap. His bones, from the smallest to largest, creaked and rang. His neck bent at a sharp angle, driving his skull to the side and crushing it against his left shoulder, forcing his teeth down upon the tip of his tongue and severing it clean.

The surface yielded, as though he were a pebble dropped into molten sand. The lake drew him under. Lungs flattened, arms and legs immobilized by his wings, he could do nothing but sink through the glass-clear water, watching as the world grew dimmer. It seemed to him it took far longer to reach the sandy bottom than it should have, and when he came to rest it was as though a soft hand cupped him.

His mouth opened and closed, releasing a cloud of blood that turned his vision red. The sun, dim through the water, wavering in the turbulence of his passage, became a baleful eye.

Life flitted before his eyes, tiny and nearly translucent. His eye flicked from one creature to another as they moved back and forth through the bloodied water, and finally formed an image. Shrimp. Smaller than their cousins fishermen netted in Lake Ten.

Eldermen hated water. They wanted nothing to do with anything that came from water.

A smile formed on his lips.

He opened his mouth again, and took the lake into his lungs.

‡

Swim while you can, Adrash said, eyes flaring in darkness. *You will not get the opportunity to do so again.*

Pol stared at the stricken god, whose armor appeared slightly gray under the weight of water. Having exhausted himself, he weighed his options. There were none. The god would recover before him. And so he turned and swam, as fast as his weary body would swim, through an openness of sea that was not open at all, but which pressed upon him from all sides. Black and cold and swarming with life, he felt the weight of sinuous bodies, monstrously-jawed and behemoth, eager for any morsel of flesh.

He escaped through the most shameful of realities: only because of his own smallness, his own insignificance in comparison, did he survive. Nonetheless, smallness notwithstanding, he could not rest. There was nowhere to rest. He had to continue pushing himself, beyond the point of collapse, breathing in the sea itself, lest one of the beasts finally notice him.

All the while, at his back, Adrash fumed in the shattered remnants of his abyssal palace, injured but not yet dead.

Pol had failed in his task. Before long, the god would repay him for his presumption.

And so Pol swam. He reached land and flopped onto it, choking on air.

But even here, above ground, he had not truly escaped.

‡

How long his eye had been open, he did not know. Someone stood over him, swaying from side to side, undulating like a flag in the breeze, like kelp rooted to the sandy lake bottom. He wondered how it was a person could be where he currently lay and survive.

He yawned, jaw popping, and gasped: the air entered him as a knife.

Water bubbled in his chest and then burst forth, searing his throat: the knife left him.

He fell onto his side and curled inward, coughing and gagging upon water, mucus, and blood. He shook violently on the cold ground, breathing raggedly until he could breathe evenly. The pain remained—in truth, it inhabited him from head to toe, occasionally flaring into prominence in one area and subsiding to allow another agony to bloom—but it no longer obliterated thought.

Air.

Concentrating on the shifting ground before him, on the fingers of his clenched left hand—a hand which seemed also to shift, growing larger and then smaller—he suffered a moment of doubt. What if he had never landed on the mountainside? What if Adrash had killed him and he was now but one of the dead, waking in one of the many hells he had never quite been able to convince himself did not exist? His mother had been fond of discussing the various hells a man might inhabit once he died.

Some among the Usterti sect believed in a place between life and death, where a person would be forced to relive an awful fate (drowning, typically: the Usterti were fond of tales of drowning)—that is, until the Goddess smiled upon that individual, lifting her free of torment.

The corners of his mouth turned down. He spit blood and mucus past the throbbing, shorn tip of his tongue. It steamed for only a moment before freezing.

I'll not start believing such nonsense now, he thought.

He rolled over and regarded the person standing over him. He blinked, and slowly the figure took on definition.

A human male. Small, naked, gray skin a hairless mapwork of fine lines. Eyes bulging out from his skull, his lips pulled back in a perpetual grimace. Shrunken-cocked, testicles nearly nonexistent. He should have been shivering with cold, moving to keep hypothermia at bay. Instead, he seemed content to simply stand and stare. The longer Pol regarded him, the less the man's body undulated from side to side, leading Pol to believe he had been drugged or concussed. Concussed, likely, oxygen deprived from his near drowning.

"You—" He cleared his throat. "Who are you?"

The man did not respond, did not appear to have heard. His eyes remained focused on Pol's, but behind his gaze Pol sensed nothing.

Pol looked from side to side, finding his wings a crumpled mess spread around him. Two wet sheets, pathetic, lacking any structural integrity. With shaking hands he gathered them, shook the water and ice from them, and draped them across his body. He shook until he was no longer frozen, and then sat up, immediately burying his head between his knees.

"What are you looking at?" he asked, expecting no response from the man.

There was none. Pol chuckled without humor and wondered if he had been wrong to dismiss the idea of hell. To spend eternity with the mindless, he surmised, would be a very effective hell indeed.

‡

Eventually, he raised his head.

He blinked.

Before him lay an elder corpse.

Beyond it, a trail of roughed earth stretched. It had been moved.

All thoughts of hell fled his mind. He peered up at the man standing over him. He could not recall if Adrash's memory of the valley had included inhabitants. Surely, it had not.

"Did you drag this here?" Predictably, the man did not answer. Pol pointed to the corpse. "You, you brought this here." He stood, looming over the man. He lowered his face until it was level with the other's. "*Is. This. For. Me?*"

The man's eyes shifted to the corpse. Pol nodded, though his companion failed to notice. The man took a step and bent, crouching toward the corpse. He extended a hand, and for the first time Pol noticed a flint, little more than a crude edge, clutched in his fingers. Grasping one of the corpse's forearms—which ended as a ragged, bloodless stump just below the wrist—the man used his primitive knife to cut a small strip of skin free. He placed it in his mouth and began chewing contentedly, then repeated the process.

He pivoted and held the flesh up to Pol.

Pol nearly slapped it from the man's hands. It was not that the thought of eating elder disgusted him. After all, he had used alchemical solutions made from the bodies of elders for much of his adult life, externally and internally. He had survived for days in the void of space on nothing but bonedust, as had all outbound mages.

No, it was the *sacrilege* of seeing an elder corpse so abused. The corpse trade had produced a variety of associated guilds, each of whom possessed their own secrets and unique paranoias, guaranteeing that few whole corpses made it out of Stol or Knos Min. The Academy of Applied Magics contained only one whole elder corpse on display in its central library—an entire city's worth of riches, a storehouse of alchemical power beyond the ability of any single man in existence to possess. Pol had spent many hours studying it, lingering on and memorizing every physical detail of the three-yard-long body as though it were that of a lover. Or a parent.

To see it treated so casually, solely as a food source . . .

He watched the man chew. His stomach gurgled and growled, and a cramp bent him double. He took the strip of skin and placed it in his mouth, surprised to find the taste immediately sweet, its texture like soft leather. Chewing on it, his mouth became wet, as if he just taken a drink of water. A coppery taste, similar to sagoli berry, replaced that of his own blood. The severed tip of his tongue tingled, became warm and then quickly numb.

He shivered in pleasure as the warmth spread quickly from his mouth, suffusing him in the space of twelve indrawn breaths. A moan escaped his lips.

The man watched Pol with no trace of understanding. He returned his attention to the corpse, now using the flat side of his rock as a rasp, sanding away at the protruding end of bone at the elder's wrist. After he had created a small pile of dust in the hollow of the corpse's belly, he wetted his middle finger and dipped it in. He offered the whitened fingertip to Pol.

Pol ignored it, and instead took his own measure of bonedust—far more than he had ever consumed at once. The familiar sensation of wellness, of focus intensified, further bolstered the steel in his legs.

He concentrated on rousing the sigils from their slumber, but found them dampened still, gathered once more on his forearms and calves, immobile. Unless he found the source of the shield's effect and put an end to it, he would not soon be taking advantage of the alchemical resources he had found. Given the singular nature of the effect, he figured it to be an artifact of elder magic. The possibility of him halting it after incalculable millennia seemed unlikely.

He turned a complete circle, examining the jagged peaks that ringed the rubble-strewn valley. On his own, it would be a challenge to climb beyond the dampening wall, but while dragging a corpse? Two corpses or three? Even with his strength returned to him, the task would be considerable.

He stretched, vertebrae popping. An itch under his skin—the feeling of walking from a cold building into the full heat of a summer's day: the awareness of a fever building in the body: the sensation of being too large for one's hide—made him shiver.

"You," he said to the man who still crouched with his finger proffered. "Do you have anything to say of value? No, clearly not. Do you have a leader, someone I can speak with?"

The man simply stared.

Pol shrugged free of his ruined wings and slapped the man, who stumbled backward but did not fall, did not cry out or grunt. His eyes widened only fractionally.

Fingers curled into fists, claw tips biting into the flesh of his palms, Pol advanced and threw his weight into a right cross that broke the man's cheekbone. Pol felt and heard it shattering, savoring the perceptions. He savored also the sound of the man's shout of surprise, his choking sob thereafter, and followed his first attack with a sharp kick to the ribs.

Four. Four snapped ribs. Pol grinned.

He took the crude knife from the man's shaking fingers and severed his wings, letting them fall uselessly to the ground. They were the stuff of intense alchemy, a product of the sigils. Once he resumed his power, he would grow a new pair more glorious, more substantial than the last.

He plunged the knife into the man's thigh.

Behind him, someone cried out. He turned to see another man—no, it was a woman, though they appeared so similar the distinction hardly seemed pressing—running toward him.

Pol's grin widened.

Pain had been a transformative factor for him. Perhaps it would inspire these fools to speak something worthwhile.

‡

In truth, he had no plan. He did not believe the inhabitants of the valley would prove able to communicate anything of value. They were clearly ancient, their meager lives extended by a steady diet of alchemicals that nourished the body extraordinarily while atrophying the mind. They had sat on the world's most valuable treasure without using it.

No. He had no plan. He merely wanted to cause pain.

As he circled the lake, he found others like the first two, and left them crippled behind him. Not one fought back, though in a similar way to the second, a few expressed concern for their neighbors without understanding what was occurring. Or, indeed, how to help. These he enjoyed hurting the most: their confused impotence amused him as much as it fueled his anger.

"Fight back," he said, repeatedly through his laughter. "Do *something*."

And so he made them scream.

Eventually, night came and he stopped. The bare ground failed to chill his naked flesh appreciably. Nonetheless, he found himself longing for a fire, a thing more alive than the creatures he had broken over the course of the day. He avoided looking into the sky for a time, and then relented to the inevitable. He had seen it before, but always at dusk.

Now, with its twenty-seven broken components stretched across the bowl of heaven . . . closer than they ever were.

Massive. Somehow, more massive than they appeared when viewed from orbit.

I did this, he mouthed.

He slept, and in the morning she appeared to him.

‡

Just like the others, though more weathered around the eyes. Wrinkles of expression, perhaps, as opposed to exposure to the elements.

He met her gray-eyed stare and recognized a depth behind it, a measure of awareness he knew did not exist in the others. Even the manner in which she crouched before him, resting her elbows upon her knees and letting her hands fall casually—it spoke of a distinct personality, something he had not yet seen among them.

She nodded, as if she had followed his train of thought, and stood. It was only a dozen steps to the lake. She walked into it up to her knees and turned.

"*Wwwwwwaa*," she said in a croak of a voice, a voice which never spoke. She lifted her left hand and stared at it, examining both sides before meeting his gaze again. Slowly, like a child doing so for the first time, she crooked her index finger for him to follow.

"Are you the leader here?" he asked.

She cocked her head to the side, doglike.

Curious, clear of the aggression that had informed the previous day, he rose.

They stood in the lake, she staring up at him, he staring down at her. Distantly, he recalled his mother. She had been a small woman, far from beautiful. Oh, how he had wished for her to be as silent as the woman he now regarded. Knowing so little of anything, she nonetheless had had an opinion on everything.

"What are we doing?" he asked.

The corners of the woman's mouth quivered, trying to arrive at an expression. She shook her head and bent at the waste, cupping her right hand to gather water. She mimed lifting it to her mouth and drinking.

"Why?"

She shook her head again, repeated the drinking gesture.

He shrugged. Obviously, the water would have some effect, either ritually for her or physically for him. Perhaps his consumption of the water had been responsible for his confused, perceptually altered state upon waking the day before. Drinking it again might leave him vulnerable. At the same time, none of the valley's inhabitants had expressed the slightest aggression toward him.

Gazing into the woman's eyes, he found no animosity, only an intensity he could not contextualize.

He crouched and dipped his hand into the lake.

"You first," he said, gesturing with his chin.

She looked down at her reflection in the water and smiled, slowly, apparently making sure of her expression before meeting his eyes again. He winced at the sight of her toothless gums, black with untold age.

She drank, filled her hand a second time, and drank again.

He followed suit without smiling.

Remaining in a crouch, he waited, watching the still lake surface for any sign of a change in his perception. When none came and he grew impatient, he decided to stand.

Several minutes passed. He decided to stand again.

Instead, he fell backward into the water. The woman tumbled sideways, following him under. She wrapped her arms around him, pressing his arms to his sides. He did not fight her. Why would he fight her? She was beautiful, like his mother had been. He barely felt the pressure of the blood-warm lake around him. He breathed it like air.

When she kissed him, he breathed her.

‡

"Death doesn't exist here. Time is an illusion."

He stood along the shore. He turned full circle. Around the lake rose the forms of gray stone towers, tall and blank-faced, creating a skyline as severe as the peaks ringing the valley, a cityscape utterly unlike the cities of glass he had seen in Adrash's vision of the Clouded Continent—different enough, in fact, that he immediately doubted its fidelity. An elder, dependent on the sun for its sustenance, would never lock itself behind windowless walls.

This was no true city of the elders: this was the product of a stunted imagination, a recreation of a thing that had never existed.

Nonetheless, he took in with interest the groups of elders he spotted. The creatures, their naked bodies tattooed brilliantly, their large double-irised eyes liquid in the sunlight, paid him not a moment's attention as they walked from place to place. Their locomotion, stately and deliberate, struck him as awkward, wary of their surroundings.

"No," he said under his breath. "That isn't right, either."

He paused. Someone had said something to him, had they not?

With great difficulty, he tore his gaze from the oddly moving elders. Even in their wrongness, they were compelling.

He nearly took a step back at the woman's altered appearance. A lustrous, emerald-scaled gown clothed her from just below her breasts to mid-calf. Her figure, athletic and almost prototypically feminine in its proportions, bore no resemblance to that of the person he had met in the valley. They shared a similar bone structure, no more. Her eyes, also, had changed, brightening to reveal an increased awareness, a vitality she had lost.

Drinking of the lake had been transformative for her. Unlike the city extending dull and oppressive around them, she was a genuine artifact of the past.

Looking down at himself, he discovered she had changed nothing about his appearance. The sigils remained still on his arms and legs. His cock appeared pitifully small to him, as though it too had been affected by the dampening spell.

He sighed. "What did you say?"

She gestured to encompass the valley. "Death doesn't exist here. Time has stopped."

He grunted and looked away, back to the city. Her beauty unnerved him. He had never liked women, much less human women. Licking his lips, he recalled how she had brought him here.

"I'd rather not spend eternity with you and yours," he said. "And I won't. I'll be leaving soon, with something of value. Tell me, why have you brought me here?"

"You don't want to know who I am?" she asked.

"No," he said. He rethought this answer. "Unless it has value, I don't want to know."

"Fine," she said. "I had hoped the bringer of my death would be interested in me, somehow—even impressed with my vision, here, where I've kept my true self from the white god for hundreds upon hundreds of years—but maybe that's too much to ask at the end of my long, pointless life."

Out of the corner of his eye, he saw her gesture toward the city. The elders dropped where they stood. Their buildings each fractured vertically with a crack of thunder, and then crumbled to the earth. The corpses deflated, mummifying in the ever-present sun. The rubble of the city slowly wore at the edges. Soon, the valley had returned to its present form.

Turning to the woman, he found she had aged. Her gown had lost its sheen.

She snapped her fingers, and it was night.

Above them, the Needle spread in its shattered beauty.

"You want me to tell you something of value," she said. She tipped her head back to view the heavens. "You did this. I know this fact in my bones. The souls of the elders proclaimed it the moment you dropped from the sky. I've waited ever since, these hundred and six days."

He huffed in annoyance. "This is of no value. I *know* what I did, woman. Quit guessing, speaking nonsense of elders."

"Guesses?" she whispered. "Nonsense." She crossed her arms below her withered breasts and closed her eyes, letting her head fall slowly to one side. Listening. "Pol Tanz et Som: that is your name. You confronted the white god and injured him gravely before fleeing. And where did you flee? You fled here, hardly aware of doing so. Now, you desire two things: the resources you've found here, the bodies of the elders. And, second, the knowledge to apply the powers you covet."

She lowered her arms and met his stare. "Am I close?"

"You are," he conceded. "But how?"

She grimaced. "You don't listen, do you? Or perhaps you still doubt. The elders speak to me. They've grown to trust me with their secrets. We share a similar vision."

"I see only corpses."

"You see wrong."

He considered disagreeing with her—he had seen elders, hibernating yet well and truly alive—but another concern came to the fore. "Vision? What vision is this?"

She laughed and regarded the sky again.

"This conversation goes nothing like I thought it would. You wait nearly two millennia, and you have certain expectations. I thought, when you came, you would know more. I suppose it doesn't matter. I've gotten what I wanted, what I deserve for being so patient. When the world is poised so . . ." A look of rapture painted her features. " . . . so beautifully, you don't ask for more."

He slapped her. She fell to her knees, causing the vision she sustained to flicker out. For a handful of seconds, he was underwater, staring into her gray eyes, breathing her in. He fought nausea at the thought of their intimacy, the fact that he had allowed it to occur.

"Make sense," he said to her. "I don't care about your expectations. Tell me of this vision you share with corpses."

She wiped blood from the corner of her mouth. "My vision is of devastation. It is of fire erupting from the crust of the world, of dust blanketing its face for eons."

She pointed skyward.

"It is *this*, Pol Tanz et Som."

‡

They started to move, so slowly at first that he thought he imagined their motion, then perceptibly quicker as the world's anchors set in and pulled. Increasing their spin as they drifted further and further from their positions, growing visibly in size as they closed in upon the world, the spheres became objects of menacing beauty, perfectly balanced on a scale beyond human reason. As large as moons, as deliberate as death, their leading rims began glowing with the friction of entry, of pushing aside the first protective layers of the world.

Against the dictates of logic, as though possessed of their own poetic will, the larger spheres paused before initiating their plummet, allowing their smaller companions to enter the atmosphere first, dissecting the night with lines of fire.

The Needle fell, and Pol did not keep from himself a sense of satisfaction. This fate—surely, he reasoned, anyone who had lived under the

Needle would welcome it. Perhaps they would not admit it to themselves, but somewhere, in untouched corners of their minds, death held more attraction than continuing to live under threat. Men desired certainty above all else.

The ground shook underneath them as the world was impaled upon the Needle. The sky roiled with red and black lightning-shot clouds.

The woman stood at his side, smiling as her vision played out.

Eventually, she pointed into the ruins.

From among them, a figure emerged: tall, over three yards from sole to crown, walking in an assured manner unlike those ill-drawn elders to which the woman had given brief life. In the flickering light of the end of the world, the elder's feature seemed to shift, the length and set of its bones fluid.

Watching it, Pol was seized by recollection. As a child, he had seen a reptile drag a fisherman into the water. The man did not scream: he did not have the time. His mates had cried out, but even at his young age Pol had known their efforts would prove useless. The man was dead—not because he was unfit, destined for death, but simply because nothing of his world could stand against a creature of the sea when it chose its proper moment.

Pol resisted the temptation to ready himself with a spell. It would not have worked, even had he not been trapped under a dampening spell. Not here. Here, now, he would be powerless. He had walked, of his own volition, into another world. He had seen that world in Adrash's mind, perpetually covered in cloud. Slumbering.

The broad-shouldered elder stopped a body length from Pol. Even halted, it never entirely stilled. Though it did not breathe, under its vein-mapped skin a colony of insects crawled.

Head tipped slightly to one side, double irises spinning, it appraised him.

An offer, it said into the interior of his skull. Its voice, like a wasp's nest fallen at one's feet, or a bass string struck violently next to one's ear.

When it did not speak again, he cleared his throat. "Who are you to offer me any—"

The elder squinted, pulling its head back on its long neck. *Do not speak to me this way. It is an insult. It is ugly.*

Pol lifted his chin. "I'll speak to you as I see fit."

The elder took two steps forward, closing the distance between them. Pol inhaled the scent of it, cumin and longras leaf, seawater and the dust of libraries—and under these aromas, a tide so closely under the creature's dark, finely-furred skin that it leaked out through its pores . . . its blood, similar enough to his own though infinitely stronger.

His sigils stirred on his forearms and calves, tickling.

Impudent child, the elder said. Instead of anger, however, Pol's mind was filled with an air of amusement. *I will not punish you for your physical limitations. Speak with your vulgar food parts. We've not slept so long that we've not grown accustomed to the sound of your speech, horrifying though it is. We need not belabor this communication.*

Pol shrugged, having accepted his role as a child. "You spoke of an offer."

Yes. An offer. It gestured to the agitated sky. *We would see the world of man end.*

Despite himself, Pol laughed. "You've likely overestimated my power."

No. We know of you, and your encounter with the white god. You yourself would be a god. Already, you are close to achieving your goal. Not one among your people, or certainly among men, could have broken the Needle as you did.

Still, you could have more. We can help you be greater than you ever dreamed.

"The god of a dead world? Thank you, but I'd pictured a fair bit more than that."

The woman at his side cackled at this. Almost quicker than his eyes registered, the elder stepped to the side and backhanded her, sending her body spinning high into the black mirror of the lake. The vision she had created did not fade or flicker. In fact, it only solidified.

The elder returned its amber gaze to Pol. *Your picture is pitiful. Imagine a world where you are not a leader of men and eldermen, but a leader of elders.*

Pol opened his mouth to speak, and found he could not utter a sound.

Enough. We do not demand an answer now. We know your mind, and it seeks dominance. You will grow tired of being a god among men. When you grow tired, you will erase this era and usher in the new.

How? Pol thought.

How is this not clear, child? The elder stepped back and held its arms aloft. *Bring down the sky. The pact among ourselves—to not reveal ourselves*

or wake until the world is again clean of the interloper, man—is universal,
but the method of man's extinction is not generally agreed upon. Some wish
to wait. Some have tried to rouse other individuals to our cause, charlatans
and magicians. But I and my families are not . . . patient. And so . . .

It gestured vaguely, in an oddly human fashion.

The muscles in Pol's jaw jumped as he ground his teeth together. "Intriguing. But this is of no value to me in my battle. Give me something I can use, or I'll not even consider your offer. Sleep forever, if it pleases you."

A horizontal line appeared below the elder's cavernous nostrils. It grew in definition and then split, revealing human teeth. Its corners turned up. As Pol fought to keep from taking a step backward (he would admit to being frightened, yes), the elder's body shed height and width. Its rawboned body thickened, taking on the proportions of an athletic man. Its skin color, already near enough to black, darkened further. It grew the pendulous genitals of a man, but these were quickly sheathed by the new skin it had grown.

No. Not skin. A suit.

Pol stared into the face of the Knosi featured so prominently in Adrash's mind.

Vedas Tezul, the elder said, its newly formed body mouthing the words.

Its body shifted again, reducing in size as its shoulders narrowed and its hips widened. In seconds, before him stood the freckled woman whose features offended him so.

Churls Casta Jons.

Now the elders body ballooned, taking on mass outward and upward. Its skin turned from flesh to spheres of brass. From under its shelf of a brow, two blue coals glowed.

Berun.

The names meant nothing to Pol.

These three stand in our way—in your way. Each possesses power untapped,
though the avenues of their power are lost to us. Like the white god, they defy
our abilities to read. At times, they can be seen, but never can they be heard.
For days now, they have been absent entirely from our minds.

The elder returned to its original form and leaned forward, nostrils widening as it sniffed at Pol. *Like you, elderman, they are disappointingly opaque, a dangerous instability. Only their intentions are clear. They would halt the spheres in the sky or send them into the void. They would see the age of man never end.*

Pol kneaded his temples. This had gone on long enough. The sigils, restive, divided and subdivided on his forearms, forming faces that leered at the elder.

"Where?" he said. He held up a hand to halt the creature from speaking more. On his palm, a horned man grinned and winked. "Mind, I've agreed to nothing. Reason says I should enjoy my time as a god before I decide to have done with the world. However, if these individuals are as powerful as you claim, they are a threat to me. Tell me, now, where I can find them."

The elder pulled back from him. Its long finger pointed to the sigils.

Impossible. Silence these . . . abominations.

Pol smiled at its discomfort. "I think time will prove how much power I can summon. Tell me. Now."

‡

Danoor, the elder said.

BERUN

S *radir is within you, and it will come out. Soon, if I am any judge.*

These words remained. They stuck. They angered Berun in their refusal to be forgotten.

Sradir—the name meant nothing to him. Surely, this fact disproved Shavrim's claim.

Surely, it did. *Surely.*

Attempting to reason the words away simply fixed them more securely within his mind. By the morning of his third day under the dome of Osa, he found himself distracted constantly by thoughts of harm. He played out the scenarios of his own assumption by an alien god—as if by imagining the worst outcomes they might suddenly strike him as ridiculous, impossible.

But it was not impossible. He knew this better than anyone.

Being taken forcibly by the will of another, pushed out of his own mind, woken to find people injured or dead at his own hand . . . it had occurred, and the nation of Nos Ulom considered him a murderer for it. Any reassurance he had taken from the death of the one responsible proved short-lived, however, for his creator would not be bound by the laws of death: on the journey to Danoor, Ortur Omali had nearly reassumed control over his creation.

Berun had been forged as a tool. To think he could redesign himself according to his own whims now was the purest presumption. He had not overcome Omali alone in their final battle, after all. Fyra had been there, landing the final blow for him.

What did it matter if he did not know the name Sradir Ung Kim? Had he known Omali could call him from his place among the dead?

‡

From dawn to just before nightfall, they traveled northward and upward, over a sparsely-treed landscape of folded rocks and algae-covered lakes, finally reaching the foot of their destination—the monolith Shavrim called Adrashhut. Surrounded by rubble at its base, it rose, straight-edged and severe, giving the impression of a sudden, violent upthrust through the mantle of the earth.

It looked to Berun like the tip of a sword coming out from between a man's shoulder blades.

"There," Shavrim said, pointing a third of the way up the sheer face of the mountain to a sharp overhang. "That is where he deposited the weapons." He breathed in deeply, inflating the muscular drum of his belly. His eyes widened and an unself-conscious grin lit up his features. "It smells the same here. Exactly the same. My nose, after millennia . . ."

"I'm happy for you and your nose," Churls said. "How do we reach the cliff?"

Shavrim instructed them to cover one eye and then the other before regarding the cliff face a second time. Stairs appeared, zigzagging upward, but with each shift of the eye they disappeared again, melding back into the slate-colored stone.

Vedas looked away first, and began setting camp. He remained subdued throughout their supper, just as he had done since their arrival on the island. Churls kept his hand in hers, often leaning toward him to cast glances at the darkness over his shoulder. Despite Shavrim's assurance—"Nothing here will hurt you. Osa is a sanctuary."—she could not keep herself from caution.

Berun looked from her to Vedas, affection battling the uncomfortable awareness that he had been left out of an important discussion. He did not resent Churls for keeping Fyra a secret, yet she and Vedas and the girl had clearly interacted with Shavrim on some arcane level during their encounter in Marept. Even had no time passed after Vedas kissed Churls, their eyes would have given them away: they had come out of their trances haunted.

Apparently, they felt Berun did not need to know what had transpired.

He avoided anger in response. Anger had been a pathway for Ortur Omali to influence him in the past, and could be so for another. Nonetheless, he found his fists clenching of their own accord as he stared at Vedas and Churls.

They were his friends. They cared about him.

Surely, they did.

‡

After his companions fell asleep, Berun left them. He could not stand the thought of a whole night spent staring at their sleeping bodies, listening to their breathing.

And so he climbed.

The stairs were hardly worn by the millennia of exposure to the elements: each appeared cut to the exact same dimensions, sharp edged and straight. At every turn in the switchback, Adrash had created an alcove where one could turn and ascend the next series of steps.

In each alcove, rising from the floor, a part of the mountain, sat an altar—and upon each altar a statue. Berun paused in the alcoves before resuming his climb, again and again, examining the figures the god had carved. Predictably, the majority were warriors, men and women in assorted modes of dress, wielding swords and axes and spears. Few bore alchemical arms.

To Berun's surprise, there were eldermen and constructs among them. For obvious reasons, the constructs held his attention. He had never seen such variety, had never known such sinuously elegant creatures existed. A few were nearly identical to men, identifiable as artificial only by the thin lines of their mechanical sutures.

The final five alcoves stretched nearly double the size of the others, with proportionally larger altars and statues. The first contained a tall, thin woman with claws bared at the end of each arm. The second featured a winged man, arching his back with his open mouth to the sky. In the third and fourth, he found twins, angularly built and naked. Though their posture mirrored one another, one appeared rigid, the other relaxed.

He recognized them by Shavrim's description. He mouthed their names.

Evurt. Ustert.

The last space held the depiction of a unique creature, neither clearly man nor woman, human or elderman. Thorns grew from its shoulders, elbows, and knees. A series of knoblike growths extended down the lengths of its oddly jointed arms.

He stared at its harsh face, lingering on the wood-textured eyes, and knew its identity.

Still, he felt nothing.

He ascended a final time, the broken sky unobscured by another set of stairs above him. The spheres of the Needle spun in their orbits, and he imagined what would occur to Osa if they fell. Would the crystal covering the island shatter? Would it hold, showing the death of the outer world through its perfect lens, holding the decay within itself?

Berun reached the summit. Open to the elements and significantly worn by time, an altar sat, unmoored to the mountain. It had drifted over time, in fact, due to wind or rain or tremors: a third of its base hung over the edge of the cliff.

Upon the altar was a carving of Shavrim.

He knelt before Adrash, hands open in supplication, eyes desperate. Pleading.

Berun took it in his arms and moved it back from the precipice. He did not understand why he had been inspired to do so, but he did it, regardless, wondering if this were the moment when he ceded control to Sradir.

Shrugging the concern off, he knelt at the edge of the cliff and tried to find a measure of the calm he had once thought so easy to achieve.

He did not find it. In truth, he found only more doubt.

Yet the night passed overhead, and the sky did not fall. He resisted asking himself how many more such nights the world would be allowed.

‡

In the hour before the sun rose, he halted his meditation and watched the largest inhabitants of the island wake from their slumber.

Methodically, beginning with the westernmost individual and spreading to either side, as though they had timed it for the most dramatic effect, blunt reptilian heads rose on sinuous lengths of neck from each of the massive honeycombed nests anchored to the lower heights of the crystal dome. As many as six individuals, variously colored and sized, inhabited the largest structures.

Generations of wyrms, greeting the new day.

When the sun rose fully over the back of Jeroun and reflected in the heights of the dome downward, bathing the enclosed world of Osa in bewitched light, the creatures emerged fully. They faced the morning and stretched, their long finger bones showing through the thin membranes of their wings.

Hearing their harsh calls to one another, his features drew into a frown.

He leaned over his crossed legs and peered over the edge of the cliff. The camp his companions had set the night before remained shrouded in shadow, but his eyes were adequate to the task. He watched Vedas emerge from the tent, left hand rubbing the leanness of his belly, right hand lingering at the neckline of his suit.

The man could not accept the reality of himself, Berun knew. He refused to be at ease in his own body. Nor would he return to the time when wearing a suit felt right, for it represented a way of life he no longer lived, convictions he no longer held.

Berun shifted his brass bulk, not in pain, no (unless a component of his body became unmoored, he would never experience true pain), but certainly discomfort. He would never grow used to being confined to one form, stuck in a man-like shape, never to fully touch the sun again. In this, he felt communion with Vedas. Both had been betrayed by men they were expected to trust—Vedas's abbey master Abse, on the one hand, Ortur Omali on the other—and paid a physical toll as a result.

Vedas turned, his hands falling to his sides.

Churls emerged from the tent, shrugging her shoulders and swinging her arms. She peered into the sky before slipping her arms around Vedas's waist, laying her head against his chest.

The spheres of Berun's teeth ground together. He stepped back from the cliff's edge, surprised by the intensity of emotion he felt at the sight of her.

I never liked the bitch much, a voice said. *Evurt took all the good material, leaving none for his sister.*

Berun spun around, but he was alone on the cliff top.

Calm yourself, Berun.

Reedy and measured, the voice held a trace of amusement. It sounded utterly unlike he had imagined it would. He had assumed something colder, more estranging.

You assumed wrong, Sradir said.

"I don't like this," he said. He turned back to the thousand-foot drop. "I don't like anything that is happening."

I know. Imagine how it must be for me, though, constructed man.

"No. No, I don't have to imagine any such thing." He folded his massive arms. "This is different than what happened with Churls and Vedas. I'm awake, aware of your presence, like you're sitting across from me. How is there room within my mind? What happens now?"

A chuckle. *So many words. You believe I must do something?*

"I do. Why else would you be here, if not to act?"

Perhaps for the view. I've been waiting for the proper time, listening only, but I see I should have done this sooner. You have wonderful eyes—in many ways, better than my own. It's a pleasure to view the world from my current vantage point. Please, look down the mountain again. I wish to see my brother Shavrim as you see him.

Berun considered denying it the request, but relented.

Shavrim emerged from the tent.

His eyes focused directly on Berun.

Oh, hello, Sradir said. *That was fast. Raise your hand, Berun. Raise it. He's seen us.*

‡

They stood together on the cliff, the four of them.

"Hello, Sradir," Shavrim said. He bowed.

Embarrassed, Berun bowed back.

Tell him hello, Sradir said. *No. Just say anything. I'll correct you if it's wrong.*

Berun paused, and then said hello.

Good, Sradir said. *I like someone who can improvise.*

Shavrim stared into Berun's eyes, clearly searching. For what, Berun did not know—a sign, perhaps, that he had found a proper ally, one possessed of sufficient strength to take his or her host by force. Ustert and Evurt had been a disappointment in this regard.

It would be easier to force you, yes. But I think not.

Churls stepped forward and laid a hand on Berun's arm. He fought the urge to pull it away as Sradir recoiled within him. Quickly, he was becoming used to how Sradir would react, how it would feel when it did.

"Berun," Churls said. She too searched his eyes. "Are you . . . are you *you?*"

He forced a smile down at her, and Sradir relented a bit.

I don't hate this one, it said. *When I can see beyond the aura Ustert has placed over her, she's actually quite likable. Not beautiful, but cute in a rough way. A dull sword is an appropriate tool for her.*

"I'm fine, Churls," Berun said. "I'm me. This is not as it is for you and Vedas. Sradir is . . ."

If you call me nice, I'll kill you.

" . . . more agreeable."

Churls smiled and embraced him, her arms extending only halfway around his torso. He patted her gently on the back, meeting Vedas's gaze over her head. After a moment, the Black Suit nodded, though his expression remained sober.

Shavrim opened his mouth and closed it. He opened it again.

"Agreeable," he said. He repeated the word, as if hearing it for the first time.

‡

I've learned something, Berun, and I've made a decision. We do this, and then we leave.

His foot slipped. He formed a question in his mind.

No, don't ask why. I'm not forcing you to do anything. I'll explain, and you'll agree—for your own good. Now, concentrate upon your task.

Curious but unwilling to push the matter, he planted his foot more solidly and flexed, causing the hundreds of joined spheres in his knees and shoulders to shriek with strain. Next to him, Shavrim roared, thick slabs of muscle shaking. Gradually, the panel of stone upon which they pushed began to move, revealing the outline of a massive door into the mountain Shavrim had assured them existed. It ground shrilly in its frame, inch by inch, extending further and further into the rock face.

Berun's foot slipped a second time . . . a third time. Shavrim paused to catch his breath, repositioned himself with his back to the slab, and began pushing once more.

The door cleared its frame. Berun shot out a hand to prevent Shavrim from falling as the door tipped forward and slammed soundly home into a recess in the floor, melding again with the mountain.

Enter, Berun, Sradir said, avid. *Beat him to it. You did most of the work, anyway.*

Amused by Sradir's pettiness, Berun kept his arm out, palm pressed to Shavrim's chest, preventing the man from advancing.

"Leave it," Berun said. "I'll check."

He entered the chamber alone. Once his trailing foot cleared the doorway, six torches bloomed into life, revealing a circular room perhaps six yards across, its wall covered in relief carvings of faceless bodies locked in embraces both violent and erotic. They appeared to shift in the firelight. The longer Berun stared, the more they seemed to move, undulating in a circle around him, first in one direction and then the other. He imagined a flesh-and-blood man would become dizzy.

An impressive effect, he noted, yet it was as nothing compared to what sat under each torch. Statues, so cunningly carved that they nearly breathed in the flickering light, lifelike enough that he expected them to rise from their cross-legged posture, held weapons in outstretched hands. Somehow, Adrash (for it could only have been a god who possessed the skill to create such life in stone) had managed to convey the reluctance of the offering: the figures appeared ready to snatch back their weapons if the taker proved unworthy to wield it.

Shavrim, the first on the left, held a long, dark, silverish knife.

The winged man—*Orrus*, Sradir whispered—held a glass spear.

Ustert and Evurt held a pair of short swords, silver and bronze. *Ruin* and *Rust*.

The thin, clawed woman—*Bash, my dear departed Bash*, Sradir said—held a razored circle.

And Sradir, first on the right . . .

Before he had registered the desire to do so, Berun bent and took the short whip in his left hand. Though tiny in his outsized fist, he could not deny an immediate sense of appropriateness, of *utility*. His mouth drew into a sneer even as a part of him relished the feeling. He had always eschewed weapons.

Prior to his last encounter with Omali and the freezing of his form, it had never been an issue. He had been any weapon he wanted.

I'm sorry for what you've lost, Berun.

He grunted. Behind him, Shavrim cleared his throat and entered the room, with Churls and Vedas following. Shavrim picked up his knife, flipped it end over end into his left hand, and then slipped it into the sheath he wore at his hip. It was a casual gesture, but Berun had been watching carefully.

A tremor had passed through Shavrim when his hands left his weapon's hilt.

Yes, Sradir said. *Well observed. He's not immune to its touch, just as I'm not to mine. And Sroma is a great deal more powerful than Weither. It's possessed of its own mind, and he's cautious of its influence. As he should be.*

Features blank, Shavrim glanced at Berun as he picked up Orrus's spear and Bash's circle.

"You have something to say?" the horned man asked.

Berun did not answer. His attention was suddenly elsewhere.

Churls and Vedas stood separated by several feet, staring down at the statues of Ustert and Evurt. Their hands stretched toward one another in the exact position of a clasp, as though they believed themselves to be holding hands.

Berun looked away and then back, trying to convince himself that their bodies were not thinning while he watched, that their skin had not taken on a metallic luster.

Your eyes aren't deceiving you, Sradir said. *They're nearly here. The bitch, especially. She's close. Can't you smell her? Like curdled milk.*

Berun took one step toward Churls.

Slowly, like an egret following its prey, she swiveled her head toward him without moving another muscle. Vedas mirrored her. Their eyes were blanks, silver and bronze.

"Sister," Churls said. "Brother," Vedas said.

Never could wrap your minds around me, could you, fools? Don't move, Berun. Don't speak a word.

Disinterested, Churls and Vedas turned back toward the statues. As one, without moving the position of the hands that still seemed to be linked, they moved forward to grip the hilts of their swords.

Shavrim paused at the doorway and turned back. His hand strayed to the knife at his hip.

Sradir sighed. *You wanted them here, brother, and now . . . what? You want to stop them at their point of entr—*

Its last word died in a fading hiss.

A light, harsh enough to briefly overload even Berun's eyes, flared in the center of the room.

It died as suddenly as it had appeared.

In its place stood Fyra, clothed in a jointed suit of blindingly white armor. In her right hand she held a sword—also blindingly white, a proper match for Ustert and Evurt's weapons, though sized for her small stature. She took four quick steps to a point equidistant between her mother and Vedas and swung her blade up, as though attempting to slice an imaginary opponent from pelvis to chest.

It was a clumsy maneuver, directed at nothing, yet it produced an immediate effect.

Churls and Vedas gasped and pulled their arms in, cradling their hands against their bellies. Shuddering, they turned toward Fyra, their movements no longer synced, their skin and eyes losing the godly hue. Vedas bared his teeth and growled, but it quickly became a wheeze. Churls did even less, merely opening her mouth to emit a constricted breath.

Without another sound, they fell sideways toward each other.

Sradir made a whistling sound that reverberated through Berun's head.

Fyra turned and leveled her sword at Shavrim. Her arm shook slightly. *You want to be separated from your soul, ugly man? I've never done it, but I'd like to try. We'll see who wins.* She flipped the faceplate of her helm down, staring through the eye slits of a mask that resembled her mother exactly. *This is a place of power. You knew being here would make your sister and brother stronger.*

Shavrim nodded. "I did. And I was wrong to allow them to enter. Ustert and Evurt are too strong, too unpredictable, to allow full control. I see that now."

Fyra laughed, and sounded nothing like a child. *Good for you. You should have seen it sooner. Take the weapons out yourself, and then carry my mother and Vedas outside.*

She turned to Berun without waiting to see if her order was followed. She was tired, clearly, her sword arm dipping only to be righted with a jerk. He stared at the wavering tip of her ghostly sword, wondering how much damage she could do with it.

Good question, Sradir said, its voice near reverential. *I'd seen her in your mind, but I'd never imagined . . . how wonderful . . . How is it she's even here? The crystal should have shielded her from entering. The strain of maintaining control—*

I can't hear you, the girl said, her voice barely a whisper, *but I know you're talking.* She took two faltering steps toward Berun, lifting her sword to keep its point between his eyes. *He's my friend. I helped him when no one else could. What are you going to do with him?*

Sradir paused, a pressure building. When it spoke again, its voice held a new quality, a resonance he imagined radiating outward from the spheres of his mind.

Girl, I'm going to finish what you started.

‡

After two days of travel, Berun stood before the barrier of crystal separating him from the sea.

The sea, and his creator.

"You're sure?" he asked.

For the hundredth time, I'm sure.

He spoke the words Shavrim had taught him and waited. After Shavrim had spoken them five days earlier, the reaction had been near instantaneous, but Berun did not worry, for both Shavrim and Sradir had anticipated a delay or even a failure. The spells keeping the island closed were ancient beyond human knowledge. Only Adrash had discerned their nature, and only his children could gain entry by uttering the phrase to unwind the arcane lock.

Though inhabited by Sradir, Berun could not properly be called Adrash's child.

In truth, he did not mind the wait. He did not relish encountering Ortur Omali again.

He pressed a hand to the clear wall. The thickness of the crystal—were it a liquid, he could have reached only a quarter of the way through—distorted the view of the rocky shoreline at the foot of the dome. A long, reptilian creature had crawled out of the sea to sun itself, its back bowed unnaturally by the warping effect.

Your mind, Sradir said. *It's like this creature as you see it now. You've been distorted by the spectre of your fear. You've been warped, set up to be broken. We're about to change that, Berun. Speak the words again.*

He let his hand drop. "Do you swear? This is your true intent, to help me?"

I promise you. I won't lie to you.

"Then tell me this. Why are you the way you are now? I see Shavrim. I watch him. He clearly didn't expect you to be as you are. How can I be assured this is not an act? How can I be sure you aren't lying to me, leading me to my doom?"

That's an easy answer. You can't. You can be sure of nothing. But time passes, and we're all changed, even gods. I didn't expect to be as I am now. For the span of my life, I expected to succeed Adrash, rule with an ironwood fist. I did not expect to one day ride a constructed man through forgotten forests and help him fight his dead father.

He felt her shrug, though how such a thing could be communicated was beyond him.

But here I am. And you have to trust your instincts about me.

He nodded and said the words.

Again, Sradir said. *Together.*

"Uperut amends," he said, Sradir harmony to him. "Ii wallej frect. Xio."

A dimple appeared in the crystal and pushed toward the outside world, creating a visible tunnel through the enchanted material. It widened quickly, creating a passage large enough for a domesticated cat, a dog, a child standing upright. Berun stooped slightly and entered it.

You've never smelled the sea, Sradir said. *I just now realized. Sad.*

He paused before leaving the shelter of the passageway and gazed out at the calm water. "What should I expect?"

Sradir laughed. *A battle, Berun. Expect a battle.*

‡

Immediately, he sensed something had changed. His own awareness of himself—of his body, the relation of each component sphere to its neighbor—intensified until the world itself seemed to fade around him. He expanded as everything else in existence contracted. His chest ballooned, creating a dark space within which his two innermost spheres knocked together. A lonely, hollow sound. He had heard it before, but not since he froze himself into the shape of a man.

"Father . . ." he said.

Berun, Sradir said. *Stay with me. Focus on me.*

He fell to his knees on the cragged shoreline, his vision flickering in and out, replaced by stretches of blackness, blackness beyond which there could be no return.

If souls existed, they resided in flesh. He did not want to die, and be nothing.

You will not die, Sradir said. *But he* is *coming. Prepare yourself.*

Concentrating upon Sradir's voice, the world slowly swam back into clarity. The sea seemed to call to him, neither in the voice of Sradir nor the voice of his father, and so he stood, creaking from each of his thousand joints, and stumbled to the waterline. Seized and emboldened by an idea he would not, could not give words to, he walked. More surely with each step, into the water. Not so much confident as resigned to his fate.

"Let him follow us," he said just before his head fell below the sea. Glass-clear shallows rose above him, twenty and then thirty feet. Sand gradually covered the stones of the shore.

He walked, and did not look back.

Sradir remained silent. It had been in his mind long enough to know he had been crushed under deeper water than that of the sea.

At first, he believed himself to be imagining the darkness brewing before him, but soon the reality of it proved impossible to deny. It became a heavy weight upon the surface of the water, appearing like the growth of distant clouds on a clear day. It spread, a droplet of ink, its fine tendrils reaching toward him.

You may have gotten this backward, Berun, Sradir said. *He did not follow us. We've come to him.*

Berun, his father called, drawing the name out into the long creak of ships' masts bending in the storm. It reverberated as the crack of thunder.

Berun stumbled, righted himself sluggishly, and kept walking.

"Father . . ." he said. Water muffled his voiced into incomprehensibility. Nonetheless, he knew he would be heard. "How—why—are you here? Why do you plague me?"

No, Sradir said. *Don't think of him as father. He is a sorcerer, a back-alley mage. Think of him as a thing, a thing with no power over you.*

He laughed. Existence was not so simple as deciding upon ways to think.

Much of existence is exactly that simple, Berun.

Omali repeated his name, loudly enough that the world rumbled under Berun's feet.

Creatures fled from the encroaching darkness. Sleek, torsional fish snapped at each other in panic while evading the claws and teeth of equally frenzied reptiles. Their massive bodies whipped past Berun, flattening him to the sea bottom, lifting him from his feet and sending him spinning. But for a few reflexive bites, the animals ignored him.

After they had passed, he dropped to the sand unscathed and rose. Overhead, the sun shone through thirty feet of inky saltwater, appearing more foreboding than the moon through storm clouds.

When his innermost spheres tolled together in his deep chest, they created an achingly lonely sound. A familiar sound. He and Omali had once visited Corol, a northern Ulomi city caught in the thrall of plague. There they watched infected men and women walk the streets, dull chimes locked around their throats. It had been Berun's first exposure to death.

Bring out your dead, Omali called, echoing throughout Berun's body. *Bring out your dead . . .*

Berun's vision darkened. His joints loosened, sagged.

"Help me," he said to Sradir. "I'll fall apart."

I will. And no, you won't.

They concentrated together, and the spheres within his chest slowly ground to a halt. His ankles, knees, and hips solidified under him. The darkness, however, intensified around him, forming itself into a nearly solid thing against which he struggled to make headway.

Yes, he still walked. Without a glance behind, he pushed himself forward, into the darkness his creator had made. The ink swirled around him, forming and reforming half-recognizable images. It eddied around his feet and tugged his shoulders from side to side. He swayed, nearly tipping again and again, but he persisted.

Fear had not been removed from him: he felt it ever more keenly. Sradir kept itself in the forefront of his mind, but otherwise maintained silence.

It, too, he imagined, could not predict the outcome of this encounter.

‡

An orange light bloomed in the ebon distance, as of an alchemical torch being lit in the gloom of night. It did not grow brighter or larger, yet he knew it to be advancing toward him. He sensed it in the same way a ship captain sensed an oncoming storm or the wind about to die upon his sails—as a fact of living, undeniable in its potency.

When the darkness surrounded him completely, the light split in two.

He stopped. Before him stood Omali. Two brilliant amber lenses, liquid and glowing like glass fresh from the kiln, had replaced his eyes.

Bubbles of light poured constantly from their surface, rising into the blackened water as two thin streams of light. His body had changed from their last encounter, as well: skeletally thin and pale, his hairless nudity revealed no trace of his sex. He possessed no mouth, no ears, and only two closed slits for nostrils. To Berun, his creator had come to resemble a creature born to inhabit caves, far from the light.

An eater of worms, Sradir said. *Say that. Now. Call him an eater of worms.*

Berun shook his head, transfixed by his creator's stare.

Your days of pretending are over, Omali said. He lifted his right hand and opened it, revealing the webbing between each finger. His open hand became a fist. *You will now submit to me.*

Sradir's voice grew louder. *Do it, Berun. Say he's an eater of worms.*

"Eater . . ." he said. "Eater of . . ."

Omali tipped his head to one side and turned it slightly, revealing an earhole Berun had not seen. The bubbles streamed more quickly from the sorcerer's eyes as he stepped back. A pair of long, thin swords grew in his hands.

(No, Berun noted. They grew *from* his hands, drawing material from his own body. His arms, already thin, became twigs as the blades lengthened.)

What is this? Omali asked. *Your mind is corrupted. Tell me, who is this interloper? It is different from the girl.*

Well apprehended, magician, Sradir said. *Attack him, Berun. Don't answer or delay. My strength is yours. Do it, now.*

Berun's eyes flared as Sradir unfolded itself and stood inside him, wearing him as though he were a suit of armor. For the space of several seconds, he basked in the sensation of wellness—a sensation he had not experienced since the days when he could bend and mold himself to any form. Each component of his body tickled against its neighbor in readiness, sliding into new configurations, moving from his interior to his surface. Dirt, gathered from months without washing in the desert, rose around him in a red cloud.

He closed his massive hands into tight fists, savoring the piercing sound of brass rubbing against brass. The simulated muscle of his frame bunched and writhed. The corners of his mouth curved upward into a grin.

He was an alchemical engine once more, primed and rumbling.

Allowing himself no time to doubt his actions, he stepped forward unencumbered by the water and wrapped his arms around Omali's shoulders, crushing the small man to his chest. His forearms and hands flowed into a fluid mass of spheres, cohering into two constricting snakes seeking to crush the life out of their prey.

But Omali would not be crushed. His frame, while frail in appearance, was harder than stone. It possessed strength to match its opponent's. Omali flexed against the bonds Berun had constructed, inexorably lifting his creation's arms. As he did so, he tapped the edges of his swords along Berun's flank. Where it touched, Berun became numb.

Candles, one by one, snuffed out.

For the first time in his existence, Berun lost contact with elements of his body.

He had heard men describe pain before, of course. This seemed far worse, however, an absence where there should have been only connection. It was worse, in fact, than the rare occasion he had been struck hard enough to remove a sphere entirely.

Worse, even, than being stuck as a man-shaped thing.

No, it's not, Sradir said. *You're being manipulated to fear, Berun. You must not—No! Hold your ground.*

Berun had dropped Omali and backed away.

You are a mistake to be rectified, Omali said, arms spread wide, the points of his swords leveled at Berun. *Clearly, I was too liberal in the freedoms I allowed you. This is immaterial now. Now, I will have you and the thing inhabiting you evicted. I have much to do, and it cannot be accomplished in this wisp of a body. It is strong, but I need something more . . . permanent.*

He strode forward.

Berun backed up a step before Sradir halted him.

I'm sorry, it said. *I'd rather see you fight this battle, but we don't have the option of losing. I need your body as badly as Omali does.*

The sorcerer's swords came down. Through no order of his own, quicker than he would have thought possible, Berun's hands came up and caught them. Immediate numbness in his palms resulted, but Sradir did not so much as flinch. The god caused Berun's wrists to rotate until, with a muted crack of bone, the blades broke.

Omali screeched as blood pumped from the wounds. Bubbles streamed from his eyes and burst incandescently. He tried to back away, but Berun's fists were locked in position. His feet were rooted to the sea floor.

Sradir opened Berun's mouth and spoke with his voice, with a clarity that the constructed man could not have achieved underwater. "You want to know who I am, magician? I am Sradir Ung Kim, Wood Heart—heir to Adrash."

Omali shook his head. *No*, he said in a strained whisper. *There is no one by this name. There is no heir to Adrash.*

Sradir laughed through Berun's mouth and pushed Omali backward with his right hand, leaving his left clenched around Omali's broken sword arm.

The spheres of Berun's chest erupted outward, ejecting something quickly to the surface.

His right hand—Sradir's right hand—rose from his side and closed around a handle.

Weither, Sradir had called it. Berun had not known himself to be hiding the whip.

The god brought the thin weapon low, arcing it near the constructed man's hip and flipping it fluidly into a backhanded, slanting cut across Omali's torso, severing the sorcerer from rib to shoulder.

No expression crossed Omali's face. He uttered no sound as the seam split and the top half of his body toppled backward.

Sradir stepped forward through thick clouds of blood, pushing Omali's lower half to the side. It crouched near the wounded man as the trail of radiant bubbles stopped flowing from his eyes.

"Now," it said. "Now, you die. It will be . . ." It smiled. "Permanent."

It reached forward, covered Omali's face with Berun's broad hand, and slowly crushed the sorcerer's skull.

No stranger to violence, Berun nonetheless quailed at the sight. Blood, bone, and a liquid radiance erupted from between his fingers, the last of which bent like smoke toward his face. It wavered before his eyes, a living, vital thing. His instinct was to pull away from it before contact, but Sradir kept him from doing so: it caused his mouth to open and drink the golden essence.

He fell back as the inky darkness dissolved above him. He stared at the sun through thirty feet of suddenly clear water, the vision faltering in each eye, off-time, a stuttering rhythm.

Holding himself together became impossible against the will of Sradir, and so he decohered. After each component sphere loosened its grip in the matrix he had created, his body spread out as a mat of brass upon the sea floor. Under his own control, this would not have bothered him. He had once done exactly this to gather sunlight.

Under another's control, it was agony.

You'll likely not believe me, Sradir said, *but I'm sorry.*

Apologies meant nothing. He had been betrayed.

True. But I'll apologize, nonetheless. I'll apologize also for what hasn't yet occurred, what you can't prepare for. Hold steady, Berun. You have eaten your maker. Digesting him will not be pleasant.

‡

Sradir did not lie. It was as far from pleasant as Berun could have imagined.

In life, his creator had not carried within him an ounce of compassion. No sentimentality or allegiance. No quarter given to anyone. Possessed of a vision of brutal clarity, he coerced others to his own ends without a trace of regret, trading in lives as though they were coins. Near the end of his first mortal existence, a madness had taken root in his mind, focusing the dark lens of his intellect on the deficits he identified in humanity itself.

Berun flinched from the reality, the immensity, of Omali's narcissism.

The pact he had made guaranteed the end of an entire world, the creation of a wasteland that would exist for millennia—simply to usher in an age where his hands would not be tied, where his words would be as law. He had been bound too long by the will of kings, ground under the heel of lesser men only because they possessed the resources to do so.

But the elders—the elders, hibernating away under permanent cloud cover, shielded in a state of suspension, guaranteed him a place at their table, a king among kings. A god. They seduced him with the only object of his desire, and so he planned. Alone among men, he discovered a pathway to life after death. A true life, among the resurrected heirs of Jeroun.

He had designed Berun as his vehicle.

First, to enact his will against those who would prevent the fall of the Needle.

Second, as a body in which to weather the death of the world. A place to hibernate away the long afternoon that followed.

‡

The sun set and the creatures of the sea returned to their hunting. They circled around Berun, clearly curious but unwilling to touch him. He kept his eyes to the sky as the moon rose, dragging the disjointed halo of the Needle with it. Through the rippling surface of the sea, each sphere appeared dangerously mobile, shuddering in its orbit as though eager to fall.

He imagined them falling, and wondered why he would do so.

Human curiosity? Sradir said.

He considered pointing the obvious fact out to Sradir.

It snorted dismissively. *You're more human than not. And no, before you ask: there's no part of you that desires the same ends as your maker. You're your own man. In your desires, you always have been.* It paused before continuing. Perhaps it wanted an answer he would not give, a sign he had forgiven it for its deception.

There had never been a question about the outcome. It had defeated Omali handily, and this fact angered Berun more than its assumption of his body.

You thought we were in this together, Sradir said. *Tell me, Berun—have I ruined everything?*

He grunted. "Answer it yourself. My mind is yours to read."

Not true. There are aspects hidden even from me. I'm a good guesser, and that's all.

"No," he said. "You're a good liar. And I'm bad at discerning truth."

Outcroppings of rock began appearing under his feet. On the moon-light-dappled sea floor, they appeared like the backs of burrowing creatures. He trod heavily upon them, causing his body to ring like a bell, and tried to still his thoughts.

Sradir said nothing, for which he felt gratitude, which in turn inspired annoyance.

The island of Osa proper began. He ascended the jumbled, twilit steps of stone ten, twenty, thirty feet, and rose above the surface of the sea.

Standing on the shore, a thousand rivulets of saltwater sluiced from his body. Above him stretched a wall of crystal, reflecting the night behind him perfectly.

The sky. The sea, reflecting the sky.

He said the words without Sradir. "Uperut amends. Ii wallej frect. Xio."

The passageway opened immediately. He spared the sea no backward glance.

‡

He traveled a night and a full day before Sradir spoke to him again.

Wait. Stop, Berun. Please stop.

"Stop me yourself," he responded.

His pace slowed as Sradir ground him to a halt gently. He saw no point in resisting.

I'm not doing this to show you I can. You know I can. Look up. Look around you.

He lifted his head and did so, finding himself at the foot of a low wooded hill.

"Yes? What of it?"

You haven't looked up from the ground for an entire day. Take a moment and see with these brilliant eyes of yours. This is the world we wish to preserve.

He considered refusing, but once more, what would be the point in it? Each of Sradir's displays of power served only to dispirit him.

Turning a full three hundred and sixty degrees, he took in what he had noticed only as obstacles to be overcome. Behind him lay gently sloping plains, fold upon fold of golden grass and sparse forest. Miles and miles of geography, trampled under his feet in his haste to reach his companions. In the distance before him, blue mountains rose in the center of the island, his ultimate destination.

Closer at hand, a creek wound down the slope of the wooded hill. It met another creek at the hill's foot, and together they formed a narrow, swiftly-moving river that disappeared into the forest to the south. He imagined how a man would have viewed it—as unthreatening, idyllic, a place to rest a body after a long walk—and decided on a proper response.

He shrugged. "It's beautiful."

Sradir kept him from lifting his foot and moving on.

It is, yes, but that's hardly all. You're being willfully dense, ignoring the fullness of what's before you. Curiosity is not something you've ever had to force yourself to feel, so don't start pretending disinterest now. How do I know you're pretending? I haven't been in here, wasting time. I've observed you. Fact is, I'm the closest you'll come to a lover, a true friend, or a parent.

"You could equally well be an enemy. A very good enemy, I'd add."

Sradir sighed. *What occurred between us, I regret. If there had been another way, then I would have chosen it, but there wasn't another way. To assume I mean you harm is ridiculous. I don't ask for your thanks, but I expect you to realize the threat Omali posed to you. Ask yourself, would I have done what I did if I meant you harm? I'm here to help us toward a shared goal. That's the entirety of it, Berun. That's all I want you to see.*

"You said you needed my body."

I did. I do. I need your physical form to enter this world. Otherwise, I'm little more than a shade of my former self, content to wither away as time counts down to a close. When the threat to the world became clear even through the haze of that half-life, I focused upon the one soul attuned to my own.

You, Berun.

I fought the inertia of death and immortality both, because there's something about you. I wanted to return, yes—the world still holds its sway—but if not for you I wouldn't have found the strength to do so.

He shook his head and tried to raise his foot again. This time, Sradir relented. He climbed the hill, descended its other side, and continued. His gaze remained fixed on the mountaintops rising over each successive summit. Overhead, wyrms corkscrewed through the sky, calling to one another with nearly human voices.

As the waning sun sent tall shadows before him, he finally relented to his desire.

He stopped and tipped his head back.

"It's beautiful," he said.

Yes, Sradir answered. *It is.*

‡

As promised, the land led him to it. A mile due south of the weapon repository, Adrash had carved a roadway into an ancient lava flow. It descended ten miles into a verdant thorn bush and cactus-studded plain, ultimately depositing him at the entrance to his destination.

He passed a hand over the finely pitted surface of one massive basalt pillar that helped form the entryway. It and its neighbor rose fifty feet over his head, the crossbar at its height extending nearly twice that length. An army could have passed through, thirty men across. A family of wyrms could have roosted upon it. He wondered what Adrash's intentions had been, creating such a massive monument. Had he been so bored with existence?

Yes, Sradir said. *That's it, exactly.*

He climbed a broad stairway of black stone, gazed down into the partially cloud-covered valley, and found his sense of scale confounded a second time.

Though he had known a valley to be his destination, a ridge of stone had shielded it from view during his descent along the lava road. Nothing from Sradir or Shavrim had led him to expect anything other than a natural feature of the land.

Surprise, Sradir said. *Welcome to Shavrieem, useless monument to my brother.*

Berun rocked back with a shrill creak.

An entire nation could have attended games in the coliseum Adrash had carved into the immense, almost perfectly circular depression. Danoor's Aresaa Coliseum, itself the most massive stadium on the continent, could have fit inside the terraced space alongside a hundred of its reproductions. Row upon row of stands, divided by staircases that plummeted the better part of a mile, circled the walls of the valley.

Even the lowest seats possessed a spectacular view, rising nearly three hundred feet above the earthen floor. Gated entryways, each large enough to sail a galleon through, were spaced at regular intervals in the walls below them, leading Berun to believe that more construction existed beneath the valley itself—immense tunnels, holding cells, and training areas.

He sensed amusement, but also a measure of annoyance, from Sradir. *Adrash never was one for half measures. Boredom drives even a god to extraordinary measures. This pleased him for a time before it too became something of a sore subject. We once shared this place as a sanctuary together, a place removed from humanity, but after the creation of Shavrieem . . .*

It waved Berun's arm in a vague gesture, almost as though it had briefly forgotten itself.

Silent, he wondered at the odd intimacy of the moment.

One of the low-hanging clouds shifted to show a greater stretch of the coliseum floor. He immediately focused upon the temple revealed at its center. Roughly hewn from red stone and open to the elements on all sides, it stood out from the clean, complete lines Adrash had crafted.

Shavrim's answer, Sradir said. *Not that Adrash ever noted its existence.*

"They were not happy with each other?"

Frequently.

He started down the nearest staircase, the spheres of his feet automatically conforming to the steps. More and more sure of his balance, he moved ever faster while keeping his eyes focused on the temple. Shavrim had been no more specific than to say they were to meet in the valley, but Berun felt confidant that he meant the temple.

As if in answer to his assumption, Shavrim walked out of the temple's shadow. Shirtless, newly scarred over the length and breadth of his torso. Carrying the black knife Sroma in his left hand.

From miles away, their stares locked. Berun kept his features carefully composed.

Hello, brother, Sradir projected. *We return in triumph.*

Shavrim closed his eyes, as though weighing these words. He nodded slowly, stone-faced, then turned away and re-entered the temple.

Sradir made a clucking sound. When it spoke, Berun knew it was only for the two of them.

Oh, Shavrim. You always knew how to ruin a good thing.

‡

The dynamic between the three had changed: Berun recognized this the moment Churls and Vedas stepped from the temple's interior to greet him. Though both had thinned further in his brief time away, they appeared well rested, far from frail. Indeed, they appeared harder, knife-like, every muscular twitch more defined on their frames.

Shavrim followed several paces behind, breathing heavily, three long wounds raked across his chest. There were lines on his face that had not been present only days ago. His red-rimmed eyes scanned the heights of the valley as if he expected an attack.

Churls ran to Berun, light-footed in a way he had never seen her, ready to leave the ground. She wore calfskin leggings and a thin, tight vest, revealing the hairline cuts on her arms and shoulders, most of which had already scarred over. Her skin tone struck him as subtly wrong, too even, without the warm redness she had always possessed after days under the sun. The freckles had faded to nothing on her shoulders, upper arms, and bare scalp. They remained on her face only as a spattering over the bridge of her nose.

He had always admired her freckles. So few humans possessed them.

"Berun," she said, wrapping her arms as far around him as she could. "You're free now." She released him and laid her palms flat upon his chest, her eyes bright and clear. "And you're warmer than when you left, like a fire's inside you."

Yes, you silly bitch, Sradir said coldly. *He's got me now. I'm the fire inside him.* The god stretched partway into his limbs, and—for all the good it would do—Berun braced himself against another assumption of his body. Sradir relaxed, however.

She's closer to the surface, Berun. Ustert. You can feel her just behind your friend's smile, can't you?

He could, and it pained him to recognize it. He forced himself to rest his hand upon her head, fighting the revulsion Sradir made no attempt to hide.

"It's the sun here, under the glass," he said. "It seems to have an unusual effect over time."

Vedas did not quicken his pace like Churls had, but he smiled warmly. Barring the severe angularity of his face and body, he appeared much the same as he always had to Berun.

That is, until the man stood within touching distance.

Close up, Berun could see the fine lines raised in relief upon Vedas's suit. Repeating vortices, geometrical patterns upon patterns. They shifted subtly as Berun watched, growing and reducing, birthing and dying. Vedas could not have created such intricate work on his own. No man could have done so.

Berun made sure to keep his stare from becoming obvious. He composed his features into a pleasant expression and gestured to encompass the valley.

"This is our training grounds? Is it not rather overlarge, Shavrim?"

The horned man's smile did not reach his eyes. "Likely. But I know of no better way to attract Adrash's attention than to return to this place."

Berun looked from Shavrim to Churls, Churls to Vedas. "This is the extent of your plan?"

Shavrim nodded. "You expected more, constructed man? Some elaborate plan to lift us from the earth and hurl us into the void? No." He stamped his foot, causing the heavy muscles of his thighs to jump. "He comes to us. We force him to fight us on the earth we've claimed for ourselves."

He flipped his heavy black knife twice, and then threw it at Berun.

Berun lifted his right hand to slap the weapon from the air. Upon contact, a great blast washed out the vision in his eyes and threw his body backward thirty feet. Senses scrambled, he tumbled end over end, throwing up great clods of grass and dirt. He came to rest, and though the thought of getting to his feet occurred, he could not make himself do it. All at once, he had forgotten where he was, how he had come to be on the ground.

Footsteps. Berun levered himself up and stood, swaying as he sought to reorganize his thoughts.

A threat. There was a threat. Footsteps.

He fell over, tried to rise, and eventually managed to sit.

Someone slapped his head, righting it. It had turned completely around on his shoulders.

Shavrim swam before him.

"Yes, Berun," he said. "Light and sound and violence. We'll need more of that. After thousands of years, I no longer remember how *not* to shield myself from Adrash. Thus, it's up to us to shout our challenge as loudly as we can." He crouched, a not unkind expression on his face. "And you—you'll need to learn to defend yourself a bit better. Death will come wielding more than knives."

‡

When his companions' breathing changed, signalling the depth of their slumber, he rose and walked a mile west from camp. He sat, cross-legged in the grass, and slowly let his spheres uncouple and spread out. The glowing blue coals of his eyes focused on the temple as his body undulated and then began forming itself into a replica of the building. It proved taxing work, for it had been some time since his form had been fluid enough to do so.

Sradir remained silent, undoubtedly aware of his intent.

It took numerous attempts, but finally, on the seventh, he toppled one of the pillars and allowed it to detach completely from its neighbors, achieving the separation of his being into two distinct parts.

Sradir gasped as the wave of pleasure crashed over them.

Berun fought to hold himself apart, as two entities, sustaining the sensations. The thousand spheres of his body rang a wild harmonic tone, repeating and intensifying in waves to match his wildly stuttering senses. His eyes flared on and off in the darkness, pulsing from brief star to cold stone over and over again. He became aware of Sradir, sharing the moment, lending him the strength to draw it out longer.

Time stretched from the two poles of his reality.

When both of his and Sradir's efforts could maintain the division no longer, the sculpture he had created of himself dissolved into a pool of brass once more. The components he had separated were reabsorbed into the greater whole, and the sensations wound down.

He rested in companionable silence, vision rotated to the sky. Much like the wyrms he had seen on his way to the valley, the beauty of the Needle could not be denied.

Yet it took him several minutes to notice the change in it.

One of the largest of the spheres, which had for months been positioned over the constellation Indusc, had been moved further back and closer to the moon. He stared at it, dumbfounded by this change—by the change, but also by his own willful ignorance. A god moved the heavens according to his own whim, and until that point he had not bothered to consider how odd a thing this was.

He had always observed men, noting the ways in which Adrash's existence altered the course of their lives.

But the very fact of Adrash? This, he had not considered.

He formed a mouth. "Has it always been this way, Sradir? Is it this way elsewhere?"

Elsewhere, Sradir said. *Where, elsewhere?*

He focused his eyes on prominent individual stars, on the wispy backbone of the sky (each miniscule speck of which, Omali had claimed, was itself a star), and finally on the bright smudges and whorls scholars claimed to be the immeasurably distant homes of other stars.

Entire collections of stars, millions upon millions, each with its own collection of worlds.

Sradir chuckled. *What do you think death is? There's a world of the dead, as you well know, lying under and above this world. There's a way to other places, as well, but no one returns once they've left, and thus no one can say what lies beyond.*

It's a place of theory, Berun. Perhaps Adrash knows, but he's never told.

"You didn't answer my first question. Has it always been this way?"

Sradir let him feel a portion of its discomfort. Or, possibly, it could no longer easily hide itself from him.

I wasn't born. I was created. I held the jar that housed my body before its decanting. It was a small clay container, no higher than a man's knee, no heavier than a water barrel. After my creation, my education—he could hear the sneer in the word—*began in earnest. Adrash, no more a father than Omali was to you, dictated the terms. I learned what he'd have me learn. Even after millennia, I still doubted . . .*

My point, Berun, is that I am . . . I am . . .

"You don't need to finish, Sradir. I understand what you—"

I do, and you don't. You persist in believing we're quite different, but there's a reason your mind resounded with mine. We are much the same. Despite having spent so much time with my creator, having witnessed his moods over the span of many human lives, having inherited so much from him, I look at the sky now and I wonder what passes through his mind. I pretend to know, but in reality?

I know nothing. I'm here with you, wondering. Has the world always been this way? Does each world possess a god it must overcome to achieve adulthood? There are no answers to these questions. We fight, you and I, against what we can see.

‡

"Drivel," a flinty voice spoke. "Answers are for the taking, Sradir. You merely need to know which screws to put to which thumbs."

Berun's eyes swiveled to the source. In the moonlight stood a tall, pale-skinned man, naked from crown to sole. Creatures crawled upon his sinuously muscled torso, and an odd darkness flowed from his back, obscuring the land behind him.

No. Berun reappraised what he saw.

This was no man. At least, not fully. Before him stood an elderman, though unlike any elderman he had previously seen. What had first appeared to be creatures crawling over him were in fact black shapes, one-dimensional images of wyrms and wolves and tentacled creatures. They shifted from form to form, chasing one another around the angular length of his body, avoiding only a hands-print deformity on his pectoral muscles and a massive scar raked across his abdomen.

The darkness at his back revealed itself to be broad wings, deep and without mark or feature.

One double-pupilled, amber eye appraised Berun. The other was a smoking pit.

Unnoticed at first glance, a gray-skinned, naked woman lay crumpled at his feet. Her chest rose and fell in fits. Blood leaked from her left ear.

The elderman stretched his arms lazily, like a man recently woken.

"Get up," he said.

Hello, Orrus, Sradir responded.

‡

Berun did not question if Orrus was an enemy. He did not need to.

Without a word exchanged, they began circling one another. Berun expected Sradir to take control, but it seemed content to let him lead. He remained aware of the god within him, of course. He felt the strength of it at his fingertips, a potential violence he knew had only been hinted at with Omali. The spheres of his left forearm shifted, sprouting outward from his palm, pushing Weither into his hand.

Orrus's right eye widened at the sight of the whip. Smoke poured in gouts from his left. With a muscular twitch of his shoulders, his wings snapped wide, lifting his feet briefly from the ground. The black images spun faster upon him, ripping themselves to shreds only to re-form in other shapes. He bared small, sharp teeth.

Berun refused to be put on the defensive. He coiled his legs and jumped forward, closing the distance between them by half. Lengthening his right arm into a hook, he swiped at Orrus's chest, making minimal contact but still managing to spin the elderman to the side.

He ducked as the elderman's wing hissed toward his head and continued moving toward his opponent. Just as Orrus turned fully to face him, Berun's right shoulder plowed into Orrus's lower belly.

His arms wrapped around Orrus's hips, trapping the elderman's left hand in the process. Causing the spheres of his feet to flatten and broaden, he prevented himself from tumbling to the ground and arched backward, lifting the flailing elderman into the air before slamming him into the earth.

A second time. A third. Orrus snarled and struggled to break free.

Watch his hand! Sradir shouted. *If he gets it loo—*

Orrus pulled his hand free as he rebounded against the ground a fourth time. More rapidly than Berun could properly register, the elderman gestured with both hands.

A violet light erupted and Berun was struck, thrown forty feet into the air. He spun end over end, spraying uncoupled spheres from the gaping hole in his left shoulder, roaring in the only sensation analogous to pain he had ever known.

Hold on, Sradir said just before he hit ground. He felt the god enter his limbs, forcing him to deform slightly to absorb the impact. Nonetheless, more components shot from his wound.

He growled into the soil and levered himself up, spheres flowing from his chest and back to mend the hole in his shoulder.

Orrus stood before him, ink-covered arms crossed.

"Should have had your puppet use the whip," he said. "He's quicker than I thought. He could have had me with that first blow."

Berun sensed Sradir's question before it was spoken, and relaxed his jaw.

"He's no puppet," it said. "Can't say the same about yours. Who are you, brother?"

Orrus—or the elderman Berun thought of as Orrus—grinned. "*Who are you, brother?* What a wonderful thing it is to be asked such a question. Two days ago, I was a rather charmingly awful young mage named Pol Tanz et Som. Now, after a tangle with a rather temperamental dragon, not to mention the burning of a city, I'm still him." He shrugged. "Him, and not him. I've taken the best of what I found in his mind and incorporated it."

Berun's mouth drew into a sneer. "You've become a talker in your old age. Oh, and a fool. We were not enemies. We need not be enemies."

"Much has occurred since the death of my original body. This is an understatement. Had you returned to existence before now, like Evurt or Ustert, perhaps you'd have become something more interesting than the sorry, sentimental thing I see cowering in this . . ." Orrus chuckled. "Pile of rubble. Adrash favored you above us all. To see you now, like this—well, it's satisfying, is what it is. Almost as satisfying as replaying Bash's death. She, like you, had no true resolve."

Berun's brows drew together. "What of Bash?"

Orrus waved his hand dismissively. "As I said. Dead, at Pol's hand. Her puppet had her way with him. Instead of taking the opportunity in two hands, Bash simply watched. She always was too seduced by pleasure. You need an appreciation of pain to truly make something of yourself."

Sradir pointed to the woman, who still lay crumpled on the ground. "And her?"

"A key to this place, no more." He shook his head, an expression Berun could not name altering his features. "I've never had the benefit of being one of Adrash's pets, privy to all the secret words."

Sradir stared at the woman, intensely curious but unwilling to say more.

Instead of speaking again, she chose surprise. She caused Berun to lunge forward, arm raised to slash downward with Weither.

Just before the weapon made contact, Berun's body collided with a spell neither he nor Sradir had seen, a piece of the night distilled and propelled so slowly that all Orrus had required was a target unobservant enough to walk into it. He had found that target, and once struck by the spell Berun's body ceased to move. He struggled against it, but it was as though he had been encased in concrete. Only his eyes remained under his control.

Fuck, Sradir said.

At his back, a shout. He recognized the voice as Churls's immediately. He concentrated and heard the pounding of three sets of feet.

Orrus took a step to the right to look past Berun. "Too late, fools," he said, and reached up. Taking Weither in his right hand, he snapped his wings open to their full width. The muscles in his legs jumped as he crouched to leap.

Oh, no, Sradir said. *He doesn't have the strength. He's not about to try—*

Orrus left the ground, dragging Berun into the air with him.

‡

I feel I've underestimated him.

It was expressed with a trace of sad amusement, but Berun could not bring himself to see any humor in his situation. Orrus had lifted him far above the earth—so far, he could not conceive of a way in which he might survive the fall. He watched the moonlit ground below, looking for a last sign of Churls, Vedas, or Shavrim, but they had risen to too great a height. He imagined they would near the surface of the dome itself soon.

I'm sorry, Sradir said. *Again. It seems I've let you down.*

He could not bring himself to be angry with the god. It had allowed him to attack on his own.

It had been he who failed, ultimately.

No. I won't hear anything about failure. Sometimes, you're simply not strong enough. There's no shame in fighting and losing. Everyone must experience it at some point.

Sradir spoke quickly, aware of the time. How little time.

I remember the moment of my death. I struck Adrash only once, merely scratching his armor. He laughed at me and then, as easily as a man swats a fly, killed me. I was no failure in death. The moments where I failed had all been in life. I didn't even recognize them as failures. That took many thousands of years to see.

He took little comfort in this. No second life awaited him beyond the veil.

Sradir, now fully inhabiting him, made yet another attempt to break free of Orrus's spell, flexing her own phantom limbs in time with Berun's efforts. Nothing gave, and they both collapsed inward upon the other, their consciousnesses co-mingling. Together, he felt an immense weight lift from him.

Will you let me say something to you, Berun?

He would, but before anything could be said Orrus cursed.

A white light bloomed above them, and the elderman swerved suddenly, rocking Berun from side to side beneath him. For a moment, he imagined he would be dropped, but Orrus held firm. As Berun swung, he lifted his eyes to the light.

Sword in hand, she hovered above Orrus in full armor, flapping wings to match her opponent's, blindingly white to his depthless black. He could not see her face, but he assumed it held the same expression of grim determination he had often seen grace her mother's.

Behind her, he saw her reflection in the dome. They had nearly reached it.

Before Orrus could move, Fyra dove downward, her blade arcing into his left wing where it joined his back.

He shrieked and dropped Berun.

Sradir, sensing the failing of his spell, lengthened Berun's left arm, reaching.

She wrapped his fingers around Orrus's ankle and dragged him down.

‡

Wrapped in Orrus's wings, they fell. Stunned by Fyra's attack, Orrus quickly lost any advantage he might have gained.

Berun bound his hands. He flowed into the form of an iron manacle and enveloped the winged god's body, crushing it until he and Sradir felt the give of his spine.

It snapped.

Orrus screamed and they formed an arm with Weither gripped at its end, drawing the weapon savagely across his throat, severing skin and cartilage, setting his blood free to the wind.

Next, they ripped his wings from his body and let them flutter away.

Orrus's mouth gaped open. His one eye rotated backward into his skull. Still, they would see him not mortally wounded—they would see him dead, never to return.

Small spheres flowed from Berun's body, swarming over Orrus's face. They entered the elderman's empty eye socket and made jelly of the interior of his skull. Neither Berun nor Sradir relished the task (he keenly sensed Sradir's regret: it and Orrus were not true family, no, but they had not hated one another in life), yet they would not be dissuaded.

Blackness emerged from Orrus's nostrils and reached toward Berun's face. Understanding Sradir's intention—the nature of its grisly talent—he did not object when his mouth opened to drink the essence of Orrus and his puppet, Pol Tanz et Som.

Neither would live on, but their memory would exist in whatever remained of Sradir after Berun's death.

Berun envied them all their legacy.

Finished, he and Sradir pushed Orrus's corpse away and aimed toward the earth. Berun's body became a teardrop shape, his two eyes at its leading point, watching the darkness approach.

How long could they fall?

Soon, now, Sradir said. *Goodbye, Berun.*

"Goodbye," he said. He could not hear his own voice, yet it hardly mattered. Sradir had always heard him, regardless of whether or not he spoke.

‡

A breath before impact, she appeared below him.

Unarmored, smiling, arms reaching out to him for an embrace.

Not goodbye, she said.

He hit the floor of the world and shattered into a thousand pieces. Housed in each component sphere of his body, his consciousness was thrown upward and outward.

Thoughts skittering into dissolution—

—he felt himself coming down as a shower of stones—

—and then felt nothing more.

ADRASH

Adrash drifted in a slowly decaying orbit above the surface of the moon.

Every muscle stood out in tension upon his tall, broad-shouldered frame. Twisted by grief and anger, the features of his face were made ugly even under the flawlessly smooth exterior of the divine armor. The light spilled from his eyes as his passion crested and broke, again and again. Now and then, he reached up to press his right palm flat against his chest.

To count his heartbeats, as though seeking to confirm his own existence. As though fearful of losing the one link tying him to reality.

Orrus died.

Sradir died.

He forced himself to relive the moment of their deaths, saddened by the loss but more stunned by his ignorance. Only in their final seconds had their identities been revealed to him, had the full implication been apparent. The fact of his children's existence—how could such a thing have been hidden from him for so long? How could he have heard their voices, killed their hungry avatars on so many occasions and still failed to recognize them? Pol Tanz et Som had come to him, fresh from the murder of his mentor—an elderwoman who must surely have housed the soul of Bash.

Adrash had stared the ascendant god in the eyes, yet had not truly seen.

Clearly, his mind had blunted over the course of his long life. Perhaps he had never possessed an intellect equal to his godly pretensions.

His right hand returned to his chest. He pressed fingertips against the heavy muscle of his left pectoral, testing its firmness. He prodded the ridges of his belly as a coldness settled in his gut. His fingers slipped over his genitals. He squeezed, grimacing at the thought of his impotence and only releasing his grip when the pain became too much.

Turning away from the moon, he let his gaze fall frustrated upon Jeroun.

Just before Vedas Tezul's party left Danoor, a void had opened. Once as easily read as words printed on a page, Vedas's mind and those of his companions had become all but impenetrable. Adrash could still observe their actions while under the open sky—just as he could for all men, no matter how talented at masking themselves.

He could do this, but no more. Not any longer.

The near perfect recollection of their minds remained, however, and it pained him to realize how obvious their inhabitation should have been to him. Mere mortals did not think such thoughts, or come to know one another so thoroughly despite their insecurities and moral divisions. Regardless of the arcane magic he had assumed existed at their disposal, they could not have developed advanced martial skills so easily.

Most tellingly, they could not have found themselves under the dome of Osa, holding the marvelous weapons he himself had crafted for his children.

As he watched Vedas and Churls mourn for their fallen comrade on the floor of Shavrieem, he was shocked to discover they had come to resemble Evurt and Ustert. Both were considerably thinner, hardened to familiar blades. The woman had even begun shaving her scalp.

Had he really been so blind as to ignore bodies . . . faces?

It spoke of more than a faltering mind. It spoke of a willful disregard.

And yet, surely, he had needed a period to recover after Pol's attack. He had expended much of his strength keeping the spheres of the Needle from spinning out of control. Was it not conceivable that exhaustion had kept him from the revelations that now struck him as plain?

No, he thought. *No excuses.*

Another concern nipped at him. For the first time, he found his interest aroused by the third remaining member of Vedas's party—the wyrm tamer whose name had never been spoken, who confounded analysis by appearing as a blank in Adrash's mind, defying curiosity with his frank lack of distinguishing features. Individuals such as this had been known to exist. They cropped up now and then, though rarely in positions of influence.

But this one? He had ruled over a portion of Danoor. He had sought out Vedas and Churls, and thereafter held his ground during their encounters on the way to Osa. At times, he appeared to lead. What had seemed to Adrash the simple effect of an opportunistic individual, one seeking to take advantage of Vedas's fame after the tournament in Danoor, suddenly seemed noteworthy.

He focused on the broad, ugly tamer, and discovered he could see no further than the first layer of the man's swarthy, sun-reddened skin. The harder he concentrated, the more the man's mind slipped from his grasp.

Even the man's appearance was an assumption: it too could not be focused upon. The second his attention was elsewhere, he fought to remember the man.

Adrash's brows knit together as he poured his strength into the effort of seeing.

‡

The tamer helped Vedas and Churls gather what spheres they could from Berun's dismembered body, but did not otherwise interact with them. When they stood around the pile they had created, he said nothing in remembrance. After several minutes, he left them to their sorrow, returning to the temple Shavrim had built in adolescent protest so many thousands of years previously.

Passing near the entryway, he retrieved a dark, indistinct object he had set against one of the temple's columns. A moment later, he returned from the building's interior and sat on its front steps, running his right hand along the length of the object positioned across his knees.

No. He was not running his *hand* along the object's length. He held two objects, one applied to the other. Ignoring the man, Adrash concentrated upon the longer object.

When it suddenly swam into sharp relief, he nearly gasped.

The man held a blade as black as night, whetting its constantly renewing edge as gently as one stroked a lover's thigh.

Sroma.

Less a fabricated thing than a creature in its own right, an elder-artifact outdating humankind's habitation of Jeroun, it was the one weapon Adrash had not created for his children. In the earliest days, when he alone had stood upon the surface of Jeroun, recovering from the long navigation between a home he had never known and a place he had been created to rule, it had called to him.

It had called, and so had another—a four-fingered glove, whiter than snow.

He had weighed both in his hands and chosen the divine armor, thus eschewing the knife. Each would not inhabit the same space as the other. No, not even to be held. Eventually, Adrash had bequeathed the knife to Shavrim, creating a name and lying about its provenance. His first child had never known the value of the thing he held, had never known he alone had been created to wield it.

Adrash returned his attention to the man, imagining his gaze as the searing tip of a poker, fresh from the fire. He slammed his focus into the shield protecting the man, willing it to fail.

‡

The man paused in his task and looked up, expression unreadable, head cocked as if listening. He then stood and shrugged the illusion away.

Adrash's heart stuttered. It quaked, painful in its intensity.

The man could be no other than Shavrim.

The seconds lengthened as Adrash realized the depth of his first child's deception. How it had been accomplished did not matter. All that mattered were the millennia that had passed.

Alone. They had both been alone.

Neither had needed to be alone. Together, time could have been a cure.

Instead, it had only rotted the framework of Adrash's mind.

The white god ground his teeth together and turned back to the moon. A furnace was stoked between the walls of his skull, was released from his eyes as twin columns of fire. Below him, a half-mile circle of regolith turned into a boiling lake. Vapor shot upward and immediately cooled in the airless void, rebounding against him as an iron rain.

When his rage finally exhausted itself, he closed his eyes.

The lake settled, fused into a shallow bowl. He descended and lay upon its swiftly-cooling surface.

‡

With the full acknowledgement of his foolishness, came resolution.

All three would die. He would not particularly enjoy it, just as he had not enjoyed ending their lives nearly thirty thousand years prior, but this was immaterial. He would see their bones bleaching in the sun, and realize his work done.

He dug his fingertips into the iron floor beneath him and arched upward, attempting to ease the pressure lodged in every muscle. His nostrils twitched as the divine armor filtered the merest particles from the void, tailoring it to his mood, his unspoken needs.

Death was not his sole concern. Duties yet remained.

The smell of blood filled his head, and he opened his eyes again to take in the nearest sphere of the Needle. The seventh largest, it spun only a few hundred miles from him, looming massively in the star-shot darkness. Had it been placed before him, it would have obscured his view of Jeroun entirely.

If he neglected it any longer, it would soon begin a rapid descent into the moon.

He gestured toward it with his open left hand, drawing further from the well of power within himself, but also from the armor sheathing him in its cold embrace. The muscles of his arm flexed and shuddered with the strain.

The sphere quaked in its spin, and slowly backed away.

One, five, twenty, a hundred miles. It appeared to him as if it were waiting, impatient.

He sympathized, but it would have to wait a bit longer. He would briefly rest, and then he would kill what remained of his children. Only with that assuredly behind him would he allow himself to return to the question that had plagued him for so long:

Had the world proved itself worthy, or had the spheres of the Needle waited long enough for their promised day of destruction?

‡

He allowed himself to move at a leisurely pace—the very pace at which an outbound mage such as Pol Tanz et Som had once traveled to and from Jeroun. Hurrying would afford Adrash no advantages, and moreover, by not taxing himself he took full advantage of the divine armor's unique capabilities. It warmed itself in the sun as did a freezing man before a fire, replenishing itself and stoking the flames that existed deep in the crafted core of Adrash's heart.

For perhaps the hundred-thousandth time of his existence, it struck him as odd that his body worked in such perfect concert with the armor, that together they had crafted a god. He could conceive of no way for his creators to have anticipated such a fusion.

Of course, he had never known his creators. By the time he woke, alone and soulbound to the iron egg *Jeroun* as it sailed the void, carrying the descendents of humanity, his creators were little more than shades of living men, a collection of ghosts wandering the long rust-pitted halls, muttering to themselves, standing forlorn watch over the rows upon rows of unborn men.

Nonetheless, their intent in his creation was clear. It could not be denied, for purpose drove him in those unimaginably early years. Slaved directly to his mind, the caravan of vessels stretched one hundred miles and occupied every bit of his attention. Its navigation, while largely intuitive, ensured his constant preoccupation: he learned to care for it as intensely as a father cared for his children.

This obsession nearly proved disastrous, however. Once deposited upon the surface of Jeroun (no, he knew nothing of the world his people had left, and so christened the new world with the first name to mind), he procrastinated on his next mission. He knew it must be done—indeed, a part of him ached for it to be done—but nonetheless he kept those he had transported closed within their caskets and bottles.

For a decade, he walked the face of the world he had named, longing to return to the cold spaces between worlds where he alone had been master.

Despite the distance separating them across the face of Jeroun, the eggs would open as one. Once opened, they would not be closed.

His creators had not been stingy in his makeup: though in appearance and spirit a man, his body could withstand considerable damage. It would live for eons, storing its memories within the split courses of his marrow. He possessed an inborn desire to lead, an instinctive awareness of how to coerce. With violence, if necessary.

And it would be necessary, he knew. During his journeys over the continent of Knoori (the second vessel that had followed *Jeroun*), he had seen the modified men outfitted for war in the various holds, arrayed like blades fresh from the forge. He had seen their beasts of war, their machines of destruction. There existed factions he had never anticipated, and they would challenge him as readily as they fought amongst themselves.

He delayed the inevitable.

Yes, because he was a coward.

Only when he found the armor had he roused himself to do what must be done.

‡

Now, as he moved between the moon and the world he had guided and then abandoned, thinking upon events he had not let his mind fall upon for millennia, he came to several inescapable conclusions—conclusions, he could not avoid admitting, he should have reached long ago.

For all his strength, he was a coward still. The armor had been his crutch.

It should have hurt. He did not like this word, coward.

Yet it did not hurt. It hardly mattered, for death awaited him.

He saw this, without avoidance. Whatever decision he reached after the murder of his children, he could not allow a coward to continue living in his body.

The world would die, or it would continue living. Free. With no god to dictate its course.

‡

He entered the atmosphere directly above Osa, slamming himself against air compressed into steel by his swift passage. His body neither flexed nor snapped in two. Flames hotter than those of the sun cocooned him but did not obscure his sight, which remained focused on his destination.

Once within breathable sky, trailing smoke, he outraced sound to the accompaniment of a massive clap that shook the earth below, flattening trees and causing rockslides.

Osa lay fixed before him, a circle of jade in an aquamarine setting. It expanded in his view rapidly, taking on detail. He smiled grimly, recalling its beauty from within the dome, regretting his next action while fully committing to it.

He would not walk into the island as he once had—not now, after so many eons away. He would arrive as an agent of destruction. Pitiless, without remorse.

A fraction of a second before impact, he finished projecting the words.
Uperut amends. Ii wallej frect. Xio.

It was a finely calculated move, potentially dangerous even to one such as he. The dome, he had discovered over the course of several centuries after arriving upon Jeroun, was neither a solid nor a liquid but a state between, granting it permeability and immense structural integrity—tensile strength enough to withstand even a direct blow from Adrash.

Whenever a passageway into it opened, however, the surrounding area became brittle.

Arms crossed before his face, he flew into the dimple marking where the tunnel had begun to form, slamming through the elder-forged material as though it were a thin pane of glass. A halo of crystal scattered around him as he slowed fractionally and turned in the air to view what occurred in his wake.

Cracks branched out from the hole he had created. They were thin and regular at first, each extending no more than a few hundred feet before stopping.

For the briefest of moments, he thought the dome would be able to repair itself.

But no. The cracks thickened, spreading, spider-webbing to the sound of thunder.

In the space of one second, the dome went from glass clear to opaque with innumerable fractures.

Halfway through the following second, the entire structure liquified and fell.

He turned back to earth and outraced the crystal rain, coming to a stop and righting himself a mere foot above Shavrieem's killing floor. Relaxed, arms crossed over his chest, feet slightly pointed toward the ground, eyes dimmed to a low radiance. He remained in this position a moment, utterly still, staring at the temple Shavrim had built.

He gestured, toppling it over.

At his back, a familiar soul spoke his name, and it began to rain.

‡

"Shavrim," he said, speaking aloud. His own voice was much as he remembered it. He did not turn away from the ruined temple.

"Do me the favor of showing your face before we begin," Shavrim said.

Adrash smiled within the divine armor, turned, and obliged his first child. The enchanted material opened as a pin-sized hole at his scalp and grew, flowing over his features like oil over ice. He turned his black-skinned face toward the sky and let the rain—already diminishing to a light misting—enter his mouth. He tasted Osa, his smile growing wider.

He breathed. The air smelled, felt on his skin, much as he remembered it.

"Have I changed?" he asked, lowering his gaze to lock eyes with Shavrim. "It has been a good while, after all."

"No," Shavrim said quietly, stare fixed on his creator. "Some things never change."

Adrash bowed his head and set his feet upon the earth. "As with you, though it looks as if you've recently taken some beatings. It's a consolation, is it not? There are few constants in life."

Shavrim shrugged his heavy shoulders, expression blank.

To either side of him stood Vedas and Churls. Adrash looked from one to the other, left eyebrow raised. At once, he determined that Evurt and Ustert had not assumed control, merely influence. Though both humans bore the signs of their inhabitation, from this distance neither could be confused for truly ascendant gods. They stood stiffly, shoulders thrown back, chins up, Ruin and Rust clenched tightly in firm fists, yet to Adrash their fear was obvious. He could see it, smell it.

Regardless, they did not flinch from his gaze.

In another era, discovering two individuals able to defy the will of his creations would have overjoyed him. Simply to relieve the tedium of observing the cycle of human existence, he would have studied them, turned them to his advantage or set them up against his own interests.

Now, it was an insult. He had come to ground to greet his children before their deaths. To look at them through clouded glass, through . . .

"You're beautiful," he told Churls. It was no lie. Few, if any, would call her pretty, but there was a coarse allure to her. He nodded to Vedas, amused to note something of his own appearance in the man. "You, as well. Welcome, both of you."

"Your welcome's a bit late," Churls said. "We've been here a while."

Adrash's smile did not diminish. "I welcome guests, even when they trespass."

Vedas lifted his horned hood over his scalp. The elder-cloth flowed to cover his face. His suit was a lovely thing, Adrash noted, filigreed with slowly-altering designs the man could not have produced on his own: surely, an external sign of Evurt exerting what control he was able.

"I think you've confused which of us is trespassing," the man said.

Adrash laughed.

Shavrim made a cutting motion with his open left hand. "Enough. I wanted to see your face one last time, and I have. Cover it and let us begin."

"No," Adrash answered. "I want to feel my naked fingers around your throat, Shavrim."

Holes opened in the divine armor, at all twenty fingertips and toe-tips, retreating up his forearms and calves, thighs and biceps. It slipped to uncover his genitals, his sinuous torso. Before long, the only white that remained was an egg shape upon his chest.

He was more beautiful than any man had ever been. His features were generous, almost prototypically masculine. No hair marred his sculpted perfection—no scar, no blemish. He appeared as though he had risen whole from a lake of cooling obsidian.

He stretched languidly, feeling their eyes upon him, and then planted his feet.

"Now. First one, then the other. Or all together. It makes no difference."

‡

They surrounded him. He faced Shavrim, but his awareness extended well beyond himself—far enough, in truth, to render sight unnecessary. Even without his armor actively covering his body, the three presented little actual threat. During the earliest years of mankind's history on Jeroun, even with his own enhanced makeup, he had been appallingly vulnerable when unarmored, but experience had only made his bond with the artifact stronger, more efficacious.

A small part of him lamented this fact.

Vedas broke line first, coming in low with Rust in his right hand. Assisted by Evurt, he covered the twenty feet separating them quickly. His thrust, while graceful enough to catch most opponents unawares, was nonetheless pitifully inadequate against an opponent such as Adrash. He watched it coming in, no more rapid to his perceptions than dripping sap.

He let Vedas in close, then spun and slapped the blade away. He softened his blow to the man's temple, but it still sent him twenty feet in the air to land in a heap near his lover's feet.

She helped him up.

Adrash returned his attention to Shavrim. "This is what you've been training them to do, boy? Hurling themselves against a wall might have serviced your cause equally well."

Tight-lipped, Shavrim raised Sroma and advanced. Adrash strode forward to meet him, arching backward to avoid Shavrim's first downward strike at the last possible moment, savoring the cool wind of it on his chest and belly. Gooseflesh rose on his forearms and inner thighs, a nearly erotic sensation.

Shavrim shuffled his right foot forward to pivot before Adrash and levered his blade upward, aiming its edge between the god's legs. Adrash bent at the waist, head-butting Shavrim while thrusting his arms forward to catch the blade between his palms.

The enchanted metal rang in his hands. As expected, loathing radiated from the weapon at his touch, suffusing his body with its cold fury.

Yet it was not quite what he had anticipated. The force of Sroma's hatred, so much greater than he recalled, nearly brought a gasp to his lips. It seemed it had found more reason, during its long entombment, to rage. Perhaps the armor had changed, as well, so gradually that he had failed to notice. The thought troubled him mildly.

His grip faltered and Shavrim pulled Sroma free. Adrash turned in time to slap the blade to the side as Shavrim tried to disembowel him, and stepped into his opponent's guard, laying his left palm flat upon Shavrim's chest.

He straightened his arm, snapping Shavrim's sternum, sending him flying backward.

Adrash ducked. Churls's sword, aimed to take his head from his shoulders, passed less than an inch from his scalp. Before her swing had completed its flat arc, his hand shot up and gripped the blade. It sliced into his palm to the bone, yet he hardly noticed the pain (indeed, before he registered it, his body had begun to heal, pushing the blade out from his flesh) and wrenched the sword forward.

The woman held on, allowing herself to be hurled over his shoulder. He threw her sword to the side.

She rolled cleanly and popped to her feet, fists up. He was there before she stood, however, standing at her back. He wrapped his right arm around her neck and lifted her from her feet. Burying his nose in the space behind her ear, he breathed in the aroma of her stale, ordinary human sweat. His cock moved against her bare leg, but it was only a stirring.

Vedas ran at him. Adrash backhanded him to the ground with his remaining hand, almost as an afterthought. The man's right arm lay across his chest at an odd angle. He did not rise.

He frowned, spoke directly into Churls's ear. "You'll be the first to die. Goodbye, Churls. Goodbye, Ustert, for what you've been worth."

He tightened his grip. Her fingertips dug into his forearm. Her heels slammed into his thighs. He leaned his head forward as though he would kiss her cheek, peering at her eyes as her life fled, hoping to see something more—a sign that either she or Ustert had more fight in them.

She pursed her lips and tried to spit, but could not summon the breath to do so. Drool ran down her chin, onto his arm.

"This is all too fast," he whispered. "I'd hoped . . ."

Her body stiffened, and he grunted in surprise.

Her nails had bitten into the flesh of his forearm, drawing blood. He watched in shock as the cartilage of her windpipe pushed against his flesh and forced his wrist out. She sucked air into her lungs, arching against him. White light poured from her eyes and her grip intensified convulsively, the tips of her fingers slipping like sharp teeth between the corded muscles of his forearm, nails scraping over bone.

Pain. Shocking in its novelty. Fury in its wake.

He roared and flung her from him. She flew, carrying a pound of his bloody flesh in her hands.

Cradling his arm, he witnessed with wide eyes as her body failed to impact the earth: it came to rest like a feather stopped in midair, horizontally, four feet above the ground. She sat up and swung her legs to the side, as if she were getting out of bed. When she stood, her feet did not quite touch the ground. Her eyes lost some of their radiance yet still glowed, as if a light had been struck in her skull.

He assumed, momentarily, that Ustert had finally achieved greater influence over the woman, but the assumption quickly proved false. No child of his had ever possessed such a bearing. Or such a light. He fought the ridiculous temptation to shield his eyes from it.

He glanced at his mangled forearm, horrified to find it had not yet begun to heal. A substance, blacker than the night, blacker than the void itself, mixed with his own blood deep in the wound.

As he watched, it disappeared. Into his body.

A memory tugged at him upon seeing it.

Pol. During their battle, the elderman had hit him with a spell composed of a similar substance.

With a thought, the armor flowed from Adrash's chest to cover the injury.

"Who are you?" he asked. He gestured to her with his unarmored hand as though he were choking her. To his puzzlement, no strength came to his aid. Though he had so recently moved the spheres within the void, he could not lift her from where she stood.

"Answer me," he said through gritted teeth.

The woman only spread her arms.

Lights bloomed to either side of her, and rapidly coalesced into forms. Into figures, shades of white upon white. An old Knosi woman, unbowed by her age, a defiant cast to her jaw. A second Knosi woman, perhaps in her midtwenties, alluring, as hard as a knot of oak. After a shamefully long pause, Adrash recognized her. She had died, just before Vedas and his companions' arrival in Marept.

Both women stood weaponless, with arms crossed, no trace of nervousness about them.

The younger one spat. The fluid fluoresced into nothingness before hitting the ground.

"I told you to answer me," Adrash said. "Who are you?"

"Me, plus a couple trespassers," Churls said with the faint trace of a smile. "You'll never know their names. But these two? Say hello to Jojore Um and Laures Kasoert." She looked at one, then the other. "Go. Get them up."

Quicker than their steps would suggest, the ghostly women moved to Shavrim and Vedas's sides. They reached down to both, *into* both, their arms cut off at the wrists in each man's chest, and then lay down, disappearing completely into the men's bodies.

Shavrim and Vedas shuddered. Screams tore from their throats as they bridged up from the grass. Their eyes opened as spotlights. Adrash watched, fascinated despite the clear threat, as they regained their feet. Shavrim winced as his sternum snapped audibly back into shape. Vedas gasped as his arm straightened with a resounding pop.

Churls cracked her knuckles and grinned.

‡

One came after the other, closing him in, reigning blows upon him at speed, as quickly as he could deflect them. He returned the violence, landing hits through their lesser defenses while admitting the tide had taken an inconceivable yet undeniable turn.

How such a thing could be done—he did not bother asking. He did not allow himself the room to wonder who could have such power. There would be time to determine what had occurred once the threat had been neutralized.

With a thought, the divine armor covered him completely. He batted his opponents' hands and feet away, and with three open-palmed strikes pushed them back. Turning in a circle as they stumbled, he allowed the blast furnace within him to crack its seals and overflow. From his eyes it came: a fountain of flame, engulfing his opponents.

No. Not engulfing. Flowing around. The shields they had formed flickered against his fiery onslaught, limning their bodies in shifting, actinic blue as their spells counteracted his attack. Regardless, their defense was not entirely effective. The heat demonstrably wore at Vedas and Shavrim, causing them to fall back under the blaze.

Churls, however, kept her smile in place and lunged forward, landing a viciously quick punch to Adrash's gut. He grunted, and the fire from within faltered. She blocked his clumsily upthrust knee with her left forearm and jabbed stiffened fingers into his throat.

The fire died as he choked for breath.

She followed with a flurry of punches to his jaw and cheeks. Shavrim and Vedas returned, battering him from side to side. He slipped on the wet grass, falling beneath their fists and heels. The white light of their eyes bathed him.

Pain, so odd that it quickly became an abstraction, a wave, a feeling to lose oneself within, became his reality.

His children pummeled him into the ground. Into a grave.

‡

He did not make the decision—that is, he did not consciously resolve to move.

Yet move he did. He shifted from one place to another, a near-instantaneous maneuver he had never used anywhere but within the void, where no atmosphere impeded his progress. (Moving so quickly, even against something as insubstantial as air, had never seemed an advisable course of action.)

He stood for only a moment, in the position his unspoken desire had deposited him, before his legs collapsed and he crumpled upon the ground.

Further agony.

It felt as though a massive hand had slapped him from the sky, pulping every bone in the right side of his body. He groaned into the night, and then screamed when he rolled onto his back. Broken bone-ends ground together, clicking in his hip, his shoulder. Breathing in and out produced pain so sharp that his vision blurred.

A figure obscured a portion of stars above him, staring down with radiant eyes. Churls. A second figure came up beside her, placed his hand in hers.

They were a good pair, he noted, equally broken, beautiful in the same frail, human way, neither bending to what fate appeared to have in store.

They had retrieved their weapons. Churls put the edge of Ruin to his throat.

Vedas caused the elder-cloth to unmask his features. He flipped back the hood of his suit.

"It all seems to be happening so quickly now, doesn't it?" the man said.

Adrash did not answer. It did indeed seem that way. A life could be so long, yet it still failed to teach one about death. That moment, he had always known, would not be meditative. Time would not wait, but hasten the end. It would come too fast, rendering all the periods of one's life into a fleeting memory, no more substantial than any other life.

He had lied to himself. He would have let a coward continue to live in his body, as long as it could. He would not have chosen death.

For the world, yes, but not for himself.

Vedas crouched at his side. "Not the wisest move. You've crippled yourself, and for what? A hundred yards? You've gotten nowhere, for no reason. Should have let us kill you. Now, you're going to die here, in this undignified position, throat slit like a hog." He frowned. "For all that you've done to shape the world, no one is here to remember you, to mourn for you."

Adrash ignored these words. They were meant to offend, and he could be offended no more. He willed the divine armor to retreat from his head, and spoke through a broken jaw.

"How?"

"How, what?" Vedas asked. "How are you beaten?" Grim-faced, he tapped the flat of his sword against Adrash's ribs, sending twinges through the god's torso. "Through superior forces. With the help of others who wouldn't see the world made a grave."

"That's not . . ." He paused, embarrassed by the slurring of his words, the trail of drool that ran from his mouth. "That's not what I meant. These others . . . You're not Evurt. You've pushed my child out completely."

"Evicted, without remorse," Churls said. She shrugged. "We couldn't have done it on our own. As Vedas said, we had help. It almost seems like there's a lesson in that."

Vedas gazed up at her with an unreadable expression.

"Let him see the victors in this battle," he said.

She nodded, and the light fled from her eyes as two radiant, phantom figures stepped from within her. One did not have to stoop as she emerged, stepping to the side. The other very much did, unfolding his broad form from within her and stretching to his full height.

The girl bore an unmistakable resemblance to her mother.

The constructed man—the constructed man resembled no one but himself.

‡

He admitted to himself: he was afraid to die. If there was a life beyond death . . .

"What are you?" he asked.

The girl smirked. "I'm a dead girl." She pointed to Berun. "He's a dead person."

Adrash tried to shake his head, and gasped. The relief he had been counting on, the immediate easing of pain his unique physiology had always provided, appeared never to come. The body he had known as his own, a constant over the long course of millennia, was now infected. His awareness of the divine armor dimmed, too, until the artifact no longer felt a part of him. It was as if he had been swaddled in wet sheets, encased in plaster.

"That's no answer," he said.

"I'm fairly sure it is," the girl countered.

Shavrim appeared above him and crouched opposite Vedas. He gripped Sroma in his right hand, tapping its flat against his left palm. His expression held a measure of regret.

Adrash's first child had never been as callous as his siblings. He had tried. He had rebelled. But he never was the leader he desired to be. He had been an odd choice to lead a revolt against his maker. Love, the desire to be a family in more than just words, clouded his vision.

"Some mysteries go unsolved," Shavrim said. "Even you, observing from on high, privy to so many secrets, don't get everything you want."

Adrash moved his uninjured arm carefully, arousing as little new hurt as possible. He gestured to the sky, the scattered components of the Needle.

"What will you do with this? Left alone—"

"They'll fall," the girl said. "We know. We're not fools."

Adrash allowed himself a chuckle. It turned into a cough, which speckled the white of his armor with red. The cough turned into a scream as something shifted within his chest cavity, pressing down upon his heart. The organ pumped against the intrusion. With each rhythmic shudder, agony erupted, coursed throughout his body.

The girl looked to her mother. Churls nodded.

The torment stopped when the girl reached into his chest. Warmth suffused him, blissfully.

Leaning in close to his face, the girl whispered. "I know what you think is so funny. How will we, weak little things, get up there? Even if we did, what would we do?" She smiled. "You have no idea what I'm now capable of. I've stolen skills from your children, and from one hateful elderman. They knew things—things you never suspected they knew—some things *they* didn't know they knew."

Her smile widened even further. The light pulsed from within her.

"I've learned better than you what it means to be a god."

She stood, removing her hands from his chest. He gritted his teeth against the pain that abruptly resumed, breathing shallowly against the scraping of bone in his right lung. The world dimmed perceptibly, vibrating to the rhythm of his spasming muscles.

"You," he choked out. "You misunderstand me. Left alone . . ." He grimaced, struggling to form words from thoughts. "This task can't be left to you. It can't. It's too much—you're not—only I . . ."

"No," Fyra said. "There is no more you."

"Do it," Berun said, nodding to Shavrim.

Shavrim rose, Sroma in hand. He regarded the knife for several seconds, turned it over to grip its blade, and passed it to Vedas.

"I can't," Shavrim said. "Or I won't. It makes no difference."

Vedas stared at the weapon. "You lived for thousands upon thousands—"

"No," Shavrim said. He shuddered. His eyes closed, and when he spoke it was with an altogether different inflection—an accent Adrash recalled intimately.

Speaking modern words, Shavrim nonetheless spoke in the manner of the ancients.

"It will be you," he said. "It will be now." He stretched his arm toward the Black Suit.

Though doing so caused new hurts to bloom, Adrash held his breath. No human had ever touched Sroma. He doubted anyone gathered suspected what it meant to wield it. Adrash himself did not know what end the elders had sought in crafting the knife.

Vedas did not move. He paused.

In that pause, another stole his fate.

‡

She dropped her own sword and stood, taking the knife from Shavrim. She weighed it in her hands.

"Balance," she murmured. "It has a nice balance."

Her knees bent. The blade flipped vertical in her calloused grip.

Falling upon Adrash, Churls plunged the blade into his chest.

EPILOGUE

THE 2ND OF NIGHTTIDE WATCH
SENNEN, BOWL OF HEAVEN, NATION OF ZAROLIES

They labored on a vast concave plain, under the pale rose moon and her five smaller children. Side by side, the four of them: she, her mate, and the two men who had become like brothers to her. They pulled sweetroot, depositing their vegetables in the long furrows that ran poleward to poleward for nearly forty leagues. It was repetitive, backbreaking work, but they were content.

Particularly content, for they were tipsy. The sweetroot in the far up-poleward rows had fermented over the course of the immensely long night, and they sampled it liberally. As per usual, they did not talk in their work, yet still they managed to communicate, stepping jokingly upon one another's toes, jostling one another with their hips as they moved down the line.

Seasoned by three days and nights on the plain, the two men did not look up from their work. The black-skinned man no longer stared fixedly at the moons. The lighter-skinned man did not steal glances at the black-skinned man.

They were focused on their task—yes, even drunk, or even when a gulling croaked and lifted from the ground only a few feet away from them, redepositing its long, land-awkward reptilian body a bit further away. The first night, both had been fascinated by the creatures. She understood, of course: in their southern climes, people did not train

507

animals to fertilize the sweetroot fields during the night. They woke to shit on their own soil.

She smiled, thinking of the joke she had told about southerners. It amused her to see how a world modified its inhabitants, to make light of the variations between people. Some would foment hate over such things, but having known a thousand types of person, not all of them human, guaranteed she could not summon an ounce of indignation over their divisions.

This did not mean she loved mortals easily, however. Time had made love for anyone but her mate and the two whose arrival she always antici-pated difficult. She no longer sympathized with their limited awareness. She could be brutal, unfeeling, and so left the easy tenderness to her mate, who had retained through his lifetimes a sense of commitment to charitable work.

She alone bore the burden of remembering. Though her mate would quickly locate her in whatever place they found themselves, he needed to be reminded of who he had been. It came as a great relief to him when she told him. The story fit. He had been a hero, after all.

But the two men?

They came to her and her mate in peace, but also in need, knowing only two things—two things they had struggled to put to words their entire lives. They had lived before. She had been there when they died.

Beyond this, they held their suspicions.

They had not been good men, had they? For all their trying, they were missing something—had always missed something.

Could she help them find it?

‡

They became hungry at the same moment, and sat in the dirt and grass. From their packs came roasted corn, honey-cured boar, and cakes formed of the ever-present sweetroot. Somehow, the food became more delicious with each passing meal. Now that their gathering was complete.

(Of course, drunkenness might have had something to do with it, as well.)

They ate quickly, each of them grinning through their packed mouths, each eager to have the story at its end. Picking up where she had left off at the end of the previous meal, she nodded to the lighter skinned of the two men and finished the tale in two sentences, without fanfare.

"And so I killed you, because you asked me. You wanted to come with us."

He nodded, rough features settling into contentment. He had spoken only a handful of words since arriving, and never asked a question. Of the two, he never required further clarification.

His companion, on the other hand . . .

"Is it still there?" he had asked the previous night, head tipped back to stare at the moons. "Is the Needle yet in place?"

"What of the elders?" he had asked. "Surely, they tried again."

"Why would you save me?" he had asked. "I deserved no compassion."

Now, he said, "But your mother—you loved her enough to do what none of the dead had done before you. What became of her? What of Vedas, and all the others?"

She answered these questions the same way she had answered the others.

"Not everything has an answer."

He shook his head, smiling through his frustration. "You're not curious? What if there's a way to know, an arcane science or magic to determine . . ." He gestured broadly, to encompass the world. "There are only so many places for a soul to go. You might see her again!"

She cut a sliver of fermented sweetroot free and placed it in her mouth, relishing the tart fizz of its juice. A second, third, and fourth slices went to her companions. She sensed each person's mood as her own. Her mate, satisfied after a long period of work. The lighter-skinned man, appeased to know what he now knew.

The black-skinned man, frustrated but unable to rouse the rage that defined every life he lived.

Her hand, sticky with fermented sweetroot, pressed against his warm cheek. She called him by his old name, and he shuddered slightly at the sound of it.

"I'm going to tell you what your friend—" she nodded to the second man "—told you, just before your first death. He said, *Some mysteries go unsolved.* This doesn't mean there's no truth to be found. Courageous acts aren't erased simply because you don't know what their ultimate effect was. Most importantly, perhaps, the existence of a mystery negates no love anyone has ever felt."

"But don't you want to know?" he asked. "Don't you want to see her again?"

"I suppose," she responded. "Eventually. But for now, I think I chose my fellow travelers wisely. We can be a family, even if just for this moment. A hundred, a thousand years hence, I bet we'll be sharing the same moment, or one just like it. This is enough."

"Is it?" the lighter-skinned man said. "Is it enough?" His hand moved toward the black-skinned man's knee, as of its own accord, but stopped short of contact. He drew it back to his own lap.

She willed him to move it again, crossing the border between the two.

She willed them to be a family, if only for now.

A GLOSSARY OF TERMS

Academy of Applied Magics—The Kingdom of Stol's most well-respected academy for the study of magic, and also the only known center for the study of outbound magics.

Adrash—The god of Jeroun, wearer of the divine armor. Thirty thousand years ago, beyond the memory of man, he cracked mankind from iron eggs and helped them populate Jeroun. He is rumored by some to have once been a man. The divine armor—an artifact of unknown origin, superficially similar in some ways to elder skin/elder-cloth artifacts—affords him powers beyond any man or elderman, to the point that he can survive in the void and create the planetoid-sized spheres of the Needle from the raw substance of the moon. He is rumored by some to have once been a man able to father children, demigods whose roles have long since been forgotten or altered into sectarian myths.

Adrashi—One who believes in Adrash's benevolence and his intention to redeem the people of Jeroun. In general, Adrashi are more organized than Anadrashi. In Nos Ulom and the Kingdom of Stol, Adrashism is the state religion.

Alchemical (Solution)—A broad term for all solutions composed of materials harvested from elder corpses. Alchemical solutions are the base for every spell. Alchemical ink is a particularly regulated—and highly expensive—form, as it is quite dangerous to the uninitiated mage.

Anadrashi—One who believes in Adrash's malevolence and his intention to destroy Jeroun. Anadrashi also believe in mankind's fitness to rule Jeroun on its own. In general, Anadrashi are less organized than Adrashi. In Toma, Anadrashism is the state religion.

Baleshuuk—The highly secretive corpse miners of Nos Ulom. A dwarfish race of men, Baleshuuk have for thousands of years used their magics to extract elder corpses from the ground. Primarily stationed in Knos Min and Stol, where the largest mines exist, their existence even in these places is largely unknown to the general populace.

Bash Ateff—The second demigod created by Adrash, and the wielder of the razored circle Jhy. She is worshipped by a very small minority in Dareth Hlum, Casta, Stol, and Knos Min. Bashest sects worship her as the mother of Adrash, and believe that she will ultimately convince Adrash not to destroy Jeroun.

Black Suits—A martial order of Anadrashi found in all nations of Knoori except Nos Ulom. Marked by their black elder-cloth suits and the distinctive horns they cause to form on the hoods of these suits, their primary goal as an institution is to fight White Suits and win converts to the Anadrashi faith. By doing so, Black Suits believe they strike a blow against Adrash, keeping him from attacking Jeroun. Black Suits orders are relatively uncommon and secretive outside Dareth Hlum and Knos Min.

Bonedust / "Dust"—Pulverized elder bone used for various purposes, including currency. Rubbed on almost any surface, it acts as a protective, shielding the material from damage as well as extremes of temperature. It is also a base material for many alchemical solutions. When ingested, it hydrates the body. In many areas, bonedust is contaminated—sometimes purposefully cut—with other substances. Like every other elder artifact, bonedust is subject to periodic inflation due to supply issues.

Casta—Newest of Knoori's nations, a democracy having no official state religion. The capital of Onsa, located on the northern coast, is its second largest city after Denn. Unless locally enacted, in Casta there are no laws prohibiting gambling, prostitution, or drug usage, but there are strict laws prohibiting sectarian violence. Castans of the north are generally light skinned, often freckled, while those of the interior and south are generally darker, shading into slate colors in the badlands. Geographically, Casta is split between the fertile rolling hills of the north and the semi-desert and desert badlands of the south.

The Cataclysm—The decade-long winter caused by Adrash sending the two smallest spheres of the Needle into the ocean to the east and west of Knoori approximately one thousand years ago.

Construct—A magically created intelligence, housed in a variety of different body types. The body and mind are typically composed of bonedust, metal, and a collection of more esoteric materials, the exact "formula" of which is the construct-maker's closely guarded secret. Casta and Toma are the sole nations that do not regulate the creation of constructs. They are most common in Knos Min.

Dalan Fele—Dareth Hlum's five-hundred-mile-long defensive wall, which forms the nation's western border with Casta. Seventeen gates allow access to and from the interior of Dareth Hlum.

Danoor—The oldest inhabited city on Jeroun, and the third largest by population in Knos Min. It is situated on the plains just east of the Usveet Mesa, and has for hundreds of generations hosted the Tournament of Danoor.

Dareth Hlum—One of Knoori's nations, a democracy having no official state religion. The capital of Golna, located on the eastern coast, is its largest city. Generally, Dareth Hlum allows public, organized fights between Adrashi and Anadrashi sects as long as no onlookers are harmed. Citizens vary widely in appearance, but skin hues are generally darker than the people of northern Casta, Nos Ulom, or Stol. The most geographically diverse region of Knoori, the various mountain chains that cross the nation contribute to many different types of climate and terrain.

Elders—The extinct race that preceded man's birth on Jeroun, whose artifacts and landworks are of a scale beyond the means of mankind's magic to reproduce. Little is known of their culture, but many uses have been found for their buried corpses. Primarily, they are used to create alchemical substances. Their eggs and sperm—next to skin the most prized of all elder substances—can be used to inseminate any living animal and produce a hybrid creature. Extrapolating from the nature of hybrids and manufactured elder artifacts, scholars note that elders must have been extremely long-lived and hardy, as well as photosynthetic. Due to their continual harvesting for thousands of years and the increasing depth which miners are forced to go to acquire them, elder corpses are ever more expensive. Some fear the supply will soon run out.

Elder-cloth—Any material containing thread made from the skin of an elder. Far stronger than normal fabrics, over time elder-cloth binds itself to the wearer, assisting in limited biological functions. If close-fitting and of a high grade, elder-cloth makes the wearer stronger, faster, and less subject to physical harm. Like all elder artifacts, cloth of this kind must be exposed to sunlight often in order to continue functioning. Elder-cloth can be dyed any color.

Elder Skin—Skin harvested from elder corpses. The second most prized and thus expensive of all elder materials, elder skin is used almost exclusively for the production of clothing, being used as thread to make elder-cloth and as a leather item itself. When worn as leather, it grants its wearer increased strength, speed, and protection from injury. Though not as malleable in nature as elder-cloth, leather of this kind forms a bond with its wearer to such a degree that it can be commanded to move remotely. Because of the damage it causes to the brain, ingestion of elder skin is illegal throughout Knoori.

Elderman / Elderwoman—A hybrid of man and elder. Exhibiting great intelligence, physical stamina, and speed, without age-nullifying spells their average lifespan is somewhat less than forty years. On average, their magical talent far outstrips that of humans.

Evurt Youl—The fifth demigod created by Adrash, twin to Ustert Youl and the wielder of the short sword Rust. He is no longer worshipped on Jeroun, but among the Usterti he exists as a small figure in her mythology—a forgotten or deceased twin.

Hasde Fall—The wooded hills west of Ynon in Knos Min. Rumors say that the Knosi government possesses magical facilities and training grounds underneath the earth in these hills.

High Pontiff of Dolin—A man or woman elected by his or her peers to head the Orthodox Church of Nos Ulom. In many ways the most powerful of Knoori's religious heads, his or her position is neither hereditary nor guaranteed for any length of time; he or she may be elected out of office at any moment. Due to the nature of conservative Adrashism and its role as the official state religion, the Pontiff exerts a great deal of secular control in Nos Ulom.

Hybrid—The product of an insemination of elder sperm or egg and another animal's sperm or egg through artificial means. The resulting creature generally exhibits greater intelligence and physical stamina than its non-elder parent, but also diminished lifespan and deformities. A large percentage are stillborn.

Iswee—Home of the hibernating elders, located on the other side of Jeroun. Hypothesized about by the outbound mages of Stol who have seen the constant cloud cover, its existence is unknown to others.

Jeroun—The home of man and elder, a highly habitable planet with one moon.

Knoori—The largest continent of Jeroun and the sole home of man, composed of the nations of Dareth Hlum, Casta, Nos Ulom, the Kingdom of Stol, the Kingdom of Toma, and the Republic of Knos Ulom. Though several large islands lie off of its coast, none are currently inhabited.

Knos Min—Knoori's oldest nation, a republic having no official state religion. The capital of Grass Min, located on the northern coast, is the third largest city next to Levas. A haven for intellectuals and expatriate professionals, Knos Min is the most magically advanced nation of Knoori, possessing roughly half the continent's elder corpse reserves. Long rumored to have a corps of outbound mages and other martial mages, the strength of the nation's military is rivaled only by the Kingdom of Stol's. Knosi are only marginally less uniform in appearance than the Ulomi, displaying dark brown skin tones and wiry black hair. Generally flat and arid, the nation nonetheless possesses several great mesa ranges, atop which the ground is quite fertile. Old-growth forests grow in the southeastern lake region.

Lake Ten—Knoori's largest lake, from whose fresh waters Knos Min, Toma, Stol, and Nos Ulom take a great deal of their sustenance. Officially, its waters are not the property of any one nation. Its shorelines are, however. Its sources are the Thril Rivers, which begin in the Aspa Mountains in Nos Ulom. Its sole outlet is the Unnamed River of Toma.

Locborder Wall—A defensive wall that extends three hundred and fifty miles along the western shore of Lake Ten, from the foothills of the Aspa Mountains in Nos Ulom to the screwcrab warrens of Toma. Its length defines the greatest border along Lake Ten that Knos Min ever achieved. The vast majority of its length still belongs to Knos Min.

Lore—The combined skills, practices, and traditions of a particular mage or mage group.

Mage—A human or elderman whose education grants them a great deal of knowledge about spell creation and casting. Mages are both self-taught and formally trained, though certain nations and regions discourage the independent practice of magic. The most specialized of all mages—the outbound mages—can perform feats of almost incalculable power, lifting themselves from the surface of Jeroun and surviving in the void of space.

Magics—The creation and casting of spells. The word is nearly synonymous with Lore.

Medicines—The branch of magics that deals with the physical form of the body. Often considered the least demanding of all magics due to the great efficacy of elder alchemicals on the body, medicines is one of the most common and necessary of all magical disciplines.

The Needle—Twenty-seven iron spheres Adrash created from the material of the moon, held in orbit as a visible threat to the people on Jeroun. Though they have maintained a stable arrangement for a thousand years, for the first five hundred years of their existence the spheres were arranged in a number of ways.

Nos Ulom—One of Knoori's nations, an oligarchy having Adrashism as its official state religion. The capital of Dolin, located in the central valleys just north of the Aspa Mountain chain, is a relatively small city of less than fifty thousand souls. Of all the nations of Knoori, Nos Ulom is the most repressive, its government the most autocratic. Ulomi are the continent's most uniform people in appearance, displaying unblemished, cream-colored skin and generally curly, straw-colored hair. Geographically, the nation is mountainous in the south and composed of high, fertile tableland and pine forest in the north.

The Ocean—Variously known as the Sea, Jeru, or Deathshallow, the ocean is shallow and laps upon the shores of many islands. It harbors a startling variety of marine life, much of which is quite dangerous to man. Due to this danger, it has not been navigated by man for many thousands of years.

Orrus Dabulakm—The third demigod created by Adrash, and the wielder of the glass spear Deserest. He is worshipped within a few rural, isolated communities in Dareth Hlum and Casta. Their myths tell that he is the son of Adrash. Orrust people believe that it is not Adrash moving the spheres of the Needle, but Orrus—and that by destroying Jeroun, he will give birth to a new paradise.

Osseterat—Hybrid apes of near-human intelligence that are rumored to live in Hasde Fall.

Outbound Mage—A mage trained specifically to achieve orbit and travel in the void. Stol alone openly uses this type of mage, though rumors suggest that Knos Min also possesses outbound mages. Though a few outbound mages have been human, the overwhelming majority of them are eldermen, who exhibit a greater potential for magic and greater stamina. Each mage wears a vacuum suit—composed of leather made from elder skin—on which he or she paints sigils. The mage also wears a dustglass (bonedust-reinforced glass) helmet. The suit and helmet protect the mage from vacuum for a brief period of time should his or her spells fail. The purpose of the outbound mages is to monitor Adrash, though much knowledge of Jeroun has been gained by the activities of the corps as well.

Osa—A large, circular island in Uris Bay. It is covered by an artifact of high elder magic, an immense glass-like dome upon which a variety of life clings. Wyrms and other large creatures, most not seen on the mainland, live near the dome walls. With intense magnification, abandoned cities can be seen on the slopes of Mount Pouen, the island's largest peak. No openings appear to exist in the dome.

Pusta—An exclave of Stol. The capital is Ravos, located on the northern coast. Differing from Stol in many respects, the culture of Pusta inherits much from its multiethnic fisheries, which are the most technologically advanced in Knoori and extend along the entire coastline.

Quarterstock—The extremely rare offspring of a hybrid. The majority of hybrids are sterile, and the vast majority of their offspring never come to term. Even if they do, a very small percentage live. Of those that live, an even smaller percentage are unaffected by mental or physical retardation. No comprehensive study of a healthy individual—human or animal in origin—has yet been conducted.

Shavrim Thrall Coranid—The first demigod created by Adrash, ostensibly the leader of his siblings, and the wielder of the sentient silverblack knife Sroma. Though a pivotal part of the early history of Jeroun, nearly all vestiges of Shavrim's identity have disappeared from the minds of mankind. Among the Tomen people, however, a legend is told of an immense, immortal man with remarkable skills—particularly, the ability to tame animals or keep them at bay, allowing him to take to the air on the back of a wyrm and even navigate the sea.

Sigil—A particular type of spell that is painted on a surface using alchemical ink. It is usually "activated" by the recitation—verbally or, if the mage is sufficiently powerful, mentally—of a specific set of words.

Sorcerer—A mage.

Spell—An alchemical solution that—when activated by thought, incantation, or physical action—produces a magical effect. Hundreds of thousands of such spells, each varying according to the particular mixture of elder components, are produced and cast every day for a variety of tasks. The easiest spells to produce and cast affect inorganic materials: moving the elements, creating a current, etc. The most difficult spells to produce and cast affect living substances: changing one's structure, extending one's life, creating constructs, etc. The efficacy of a spell decreases the farther away the mage is, a fact which makes influencing an object over long distances—as in the sending of a message—difficult.

Sradir Ung Kim—The fourth demigod created by Adrash, and the wielder of the oilwood and leather sambok Weither. All vestiges of Sradir's identity have disappeared from the minds of mankind.

Sroma—A large, silverblack knife found by Adrash before the birth of mankind on Jeroun. A sentient elder artifact similar to the divine armor, its existence appears to stand as a counterpoint to the armor, acting as opposing forces. Shavrim is the only being to ever hold it other than Adrash.

The Steps of Stol—An earthwork monument created by high elder magic. It begins in the fertile southern plains of Stol, extending some eighty miles to the coast and more than four hundred along it. Ascending to a height of twelve thousand feet in seventeen evenly spaced, gently sloping rises, the Steps stop abruptly at the ocean. Most of Stol's elder corpse reserves are buried within it.

Stol—One of Knoori's nations, a kingdom having Adrashism as its official state religion. The capital of Tansot, located on the eastern shore of Lake Ten, is its largest city. Moderate Adrashism is the general rule and all Anadrashi sects are allowed to live peaceably within the kingdom's borders, though they suffer persecution in the central valleys. After Knos Min, Stol is the most magically advanced nation of

Knoori, possessing roughly forty percent of the continent's elder corpse reserves. The only state with a known outbound mage program, the strength of the military relies much upon magical developments from the Academy of Applied Magics. Stoli people vary widely in appearance, but are generally light skinned. Geographically, Stol is generally hilly in the north, descending into fertile valleys in the central region, and rising to great heights on the Steps of Stol in the south.

Tamer—A mage who specializes in taming and controlling large, exotic, and hybrid animals. Their lore is far more esoteric and difficult to master than the many readily available spells used to help control draft animals, entertainment animals, and pets. In rare cases, the tamer achieves a type of telepathic bond with his or her animal. In Casta and Stol, the most daring and specialized type of tamer exists: the hybrid wyrm tamer.

Tan-Ten—The island at the center of Lake Ten. Oasena is its only city. The people of Tan-Ten have never shown interest in power or political maneuvering, but have on many occasions successfully defended their island from invaders.

Thaumaturgical Engine—A construct used to create kinetic force. Unlike constructs that mimic biological creatures, an engine is rarely imbued with more than the most basic intelligence needed to follow simple directions. Due to the expense of creating and maintaining engines, those produced are most often used in barges or other large transport vehicles.

Toma—One of Knoori's nations, a kingdom having Anadrashism as its official state religion. The capital of Demn, located on the southern coast, is its largest city. Possibly the most religiously militant of all the people of Knoori, Tomen nonetheless value the personal, nondogmatic expression of Anadrashism more than any other. The people vary considerably in build, but are generally dusky skinned and rust-haired. Toma is the most arid nation of Knoori and, but for the Wie Desert in the southwest, the hilliest.

The Tournament of Danoor—The decennial tournament between Knoori's White Suit and Black Suit orders, which occurs on the last day of every decade. A fighter is chosen from every town numbering more than two thousand souls. He or she then travels to Danoor and is allowed to fight in the tournament. In the end, one Black and one White remain. Accordingly, along the way fighters will inevitably have to fight brothers and sisters of their own faith. The New Year celebration starts after the tournament champion's speech, wherein he or she typically extols listeners to convert to the winning faith. Usually, secular fighting tournaments begin the next day.

Ual—A small town in eastern Knos Min, positioned on Uris Bay. An otherwise unnoteworthy locale, it is remarkable only for the singularity of its coastal wall, which creates an enclosed pool of seawater thirty miles long and ten miles wide. Though it is common to say no men set craft upon the ocean for fear of what resides in it, the men and women of Ual have kept their sea-gates shut for millennia in order to hunt juvenile fish and reptiles before they grow to dangerous proportions.

Ustert Youl—The sixth and final demigod created by Adrash, twin to Evurt Youl and the wielder of the short sword Ruin. She is worshipped by a relatively large minority in Casta and Knos Min. A loosely organized sororal community of mages and apothecaries (often referred to as witches, though this term is widely used even in Adrashi and Anadrashi contexts), Usterti profess a variety of beliefs, bound only by the understanding that the Goddess governs all existence. Due to this ambiguity, a great deal of mystery surrounds the community.

The Void—Near-Jeroun orbit and outer space.

White Suits—A martial order of Adrashi prevalent in all nations of Knoori except Toma. Marked by their white elder-cloth suits, their primary goal as an institution is to fight Black Suits and win converts to the Adrashi faith. By doing so, White Suits believe they encourage Adrash to redeem Jeroun sooner. Orders are relatively uncommon and secretive outside southern Nos Ulom, Dareth Hlum, and Knos Min.

Wyrm—A dragon of immense size. Highly intelligent and extremely temperamental, they do not come into contact with men often. This is due mostly to the fact that most food is taken from the open ocean. Only a small minority of dragons hunt large prey on the continent. Hybrid wyrms are not common, but do exist in Stol and Casta.

ACKNOWLEDGEMENTS

First and foremost, thanks to my talented and gorgeous wife, my precocious and adorable son, and both sides of my awesomely supportive family.

Thanks to all the friends—readers, authors, professors, former coworkers, childhood pals I haven't seen since I was ten years old—for being so enthusiastic about my writing.

Thanks to the editors at Night Shade Books who helped make my Jeroun books a reality: Ross E. Lockhart, Jeremy Lassen, and Cory Allyn. Allyn, in particular, deserves huge credit for making this classy omnibus edition a reality. It's rare in publishing that you get a second chance to make a first impression, and I appreciate it.

ABOUT THE AUTHOR

Zachary Jernigan is a critically acclaimed author of science fiction and fantasy. His novels include *No Return* and the Nebula Award–nominated *Shower of Stones*. His short fiction has appeared in *Asimov's Science Fiction*, *Crossed Genres*, and *Escape Pod*. Jernigan lives in Northern Arizona.